Willa Anderson (1890–1970) st          at the University of St Andrews where she         rst class honours degree in 1910. She studied Educational Psychology and moved to London to become a lecturer and Vice-Principal of Gipsy Hill Training College for teachers. She met Edwin Muir during a visit to Glasgow in September 1918 and they were married within a year. Working as a costing clerk for a Renfew shipbuilding firm at the time, Muir was making a reputation by writing criticism for *The New Age*, but was deeply unhappy with his life and the Glasgow environment. Spurred by his wife's confidence (he later said that meeting her was 'the most fortunate event in my life'), Muir moved south in 1919 to begin his career as a full-time writer, and later, again with Willa's unfailing encouragement, as a poet. The couple travelled about Europe in the early twenties, living in Prague, Germany, Italy, and Austria. They collaborated in the translation of modern writers, most notably plays and novels by Lion Feuchtwanger, Kafka's *The Castle*, and Hermann Broch's *Sleepwalkers* trilogy.

Willa Muir's only two novels were *Imagined Corners* (1931) followed by *Mrs Ritchie* in 1933. *Mrs Grundy in Scotland* (1936) is a cultural essay, while *Living with Ballads* (1965) offers an extended study of oral poetry from children's singing games to the great Scottish ballads. *Belonging* (1968) is a memoir of her years with Edwin Muir from their first encounter until his death in 1959.

# Willa Muir

# IMAGINED SELVES

Imagined Corners
Mrs Ritchie
Mrs Grundy in Scotland
Women: An Inquiry
'Women in Scotland'

EDITED AND INTRODUCED BY
KIRSTY ALLEN

CANONGATE
CLASSICS
69

This edition first published as a Canongate Classic in 1996
by Canongate Books Limited
14 High Street
Edinburgh EH1 1TE

*Imagined Corners* first published in 1935 by Martin Secker.
*Mrs Ritchie* first published in 1933 by Martin Secker.
*Mrs Grundy in Scotland* first published in 1936 by
George Routledge and sons.
*Women: An Inquiry* first published in 1925 by The Hogarth Press.
'Women in Scotland' first published in 1936 in *Left Review*.

The publishers gratefully acknowledge
general subsidy from the Scottish Arts Council
towards the Canongate Classics series
and a specific grant towards the
publication of this title.

*British Library Cataloguing in Publication Data*
A Catalogue record is available on request

ISBN 0–86241- 6051

Set in 10 pt Plantin
by Alan Sutton Publishing Ltd,
and Hewer Text Composition Services, Edinburgh
Printed by in Denmark by Norhaven Rotation

# Introduction

This volume gathers together, for the first time, some of the real and the imagined lives of Willa Muir, one of the finest female intellectuals that Scotland has produced this century. Many of her works have been out of print for more than fifty years; others have never yet been published. Here, at last, is another major missing piece from the jigsaw of Scottish women's writing.

Willa Muir is an enigmatic character. She prided herself upon her forthright honesty and conversational bluntness; yet behind the façade of robust simplicity lurked a muddle of conflicting ideologies and multiple selves. Her life embodies the contradictions and paradoxes which suffuse her writing, lending it a sense of rich and troubled tension. She was a Scot who resented Scotland, although her writing is obsessively Scottish in its themes and attitudes. She was an enthusiastic, evangelising champion of gender equality; yet she voluntarily sacrificed her own identity to that of 'the poet's wife'. She was a committed reformer who never aligned herself with any political or ideological movement. She was a catalyst for the minds of philosophers and artists. She presided over cultural coteries in the Scotland of MacDiarmid's Renaissance, and the 1930s London of Eliot, Spender and Pound. She won universal admiration for her conversational brilliance and energy as well as for the power of her mind. And yet, in spite of all this, her own publications were greeted with a surprising and resounding indifference. This volume proves that they were, in fact, often ground-breaking and progressive insights into central issues of culture and gender.

Muir's commitment to the feminist cause exerts a particularly profound influence upon her writing. She was an early supporter of suffrage and a very vocal advocate of women's rights. As a student at St Andrews University in the years immediately before the First World War, she was a founder member of the controversial Women Students Suffrage Society and a leading proponent of the equal rights of women to an academic education. The brilliance of her mind never gave her any cause to doubt her intellectual parity with anyone—male or female.

*Women: An Inquiry* (1925) explores some of her earliest theorising about gender and the necessity of completely integrating women into every echelon of an enlightened society. As a thesis, it is as entertaining as it is intellectually unconvincing. To the late twentieth-century reader, and in the light of modern feminist thinking, it seems sadly dated and misguided; but in its own historical context and as a work contemporary with Virginia Woolf's *A Room of One's Own* it is a fascinating document which offers a remarkable analysis of the nature of femaleness.

Its most fatal flaw is its postulation of the absolute symbiosis and complementarity of mutually exclusive male and female characteristics; and its conclusion that both men and women have a pre-ordained societal rôle. The work is an unconscious endorsement of the patriarchal system which had kept women in the home—and in the submissive position against which Muir constantly rebelled. A beautifully ironic postscript is added to the thesis in a comment which Muir—in all seriousness and as an illustrative instance of her schizophrenic feminism—made in a letter to Violet Schiff shortly before the work was published:

> I hope you like the essay. It is not good enough to make me feel confident; as a matter of fact, I am a little twittery about it. If I had been a man I could have done it with less effort.[1]

Her thoughts about gender developed with the years and

1. Willa Muir in a letter to Violet Schiff. Dated from Montrose, 25 November 1924. From the collection of Muir/Schiff correspondence in the British Library, London.

with the societal changes of an ageing century; but she never relinquished her vision of absolute equality.

While her husband, Edwin, favoured the 'myth' at the expense of the 'story', she emphatically and exuberantly inhabited the world and 'belong[ed] to the Universe'.[2] She was an ironically meticulous witness to the foibles and foolishness of humanity, often unnervingly astute in her ability to caricature or capture the essence of a personality or a society. *Mrs Grundy in Scotland* (1936) adroitly creates a complex socio-cultural indictment of a national psyche from a stock of minute observations. It is an undiscovered gem of Scottish historical thinking and an explicit illustration of Muir's quirky brilliance as a social commentator.

Her professional expertise was in the psychological field. As a postgraduate student in experimental child psychology at Bedford College during the First World War, she constructed an 'analysis of the problems raised by sex in education',[3] and developed an enduring interest in the workings of the conscious and the unconscious intellect. It was a fascination which invariably and incessantly insinuated itself into the fabric of her fiction and informed the minds and motivations of her characters.

This psychologised fiction is perhaps most successfully and persuasively realised in the sections of *Imagined Corners* which explore the painfully emergent self-knowledge of Elizabeth Shand and Elise Mütze. These two Elizabeths embody the qualities of quiet endurance and undemonstrative resilience which are common to all of the women in Muir's fiction. Elise is an instinctive feminist with the intelligence and the courage to recognise and release herself from the shackles of the patriarchal Presbyterian culture of her Calderwick childhood. She has sacrificed neither her femaleness nor her freedom to the emotional and physical hardships which have been the product of her convictions,

2. Willa Muir, *Belonging* (p. 14). London: The Hogarth Press, 1968.
3. Appendix E, Annual Report 1916. The Carnegie Trust for the Universities of Scotland.

and has consequently developed an indomitable and exquisite awareness of herself and her world.

Elizabeth Shand, in comparison, appears initially to be a victim of the culture in which she has been reared. An underdeveloped sense of self has caused her to confuse lust for love in her relationship with Hector; her vision of marriage is entirely shaped by the time-worn expectations and stereotypes of a patriarchal society. She, like Hector, has always:

> . . . accepted unthinkingly the suggestion that women were the guardians of decorum—good women, that is to say, women who could not be referred to as 'skirts'. Good women existed to keep in check men's sensual passions. A man, driven by physical desire . . . is mad and reckless, and his sole protection from himself is the decorum of women.

It is only when Elizabeth is finally freed from Hector (and his unreasonable and inbred expectations) that she can begin to explore the emotional and intellectual aspects of herself which extend beyond the bounds of Hector's all-consuming physicality.

> She saw with immediate clearness that it was only inside a room, in the world of talk, of articulate expression, that Hector was trivial. Out of doors, with no roof but the sky, he was like an impersonal force. In loving Hector she had loved something transcending both of them.
>
> The life which had streamed out through her feet, as if into a sea out of which all creatures rose like waves, returned upon itself as she lay rigid and flowed up—up, like sap rising, until she felt as if her head were branching. This was the other end of her vision, and she knew what it represented. It was the world that Elise had recalled to her, the world of thought, of ideas, spreading into the vast impersonal abstractions which made another infinity.

There is, without a doubt, a certain latent and inherent strength in Elizabeth's character which will carry her beyond the pain of the novel's closing pages and onwards into a new world of independence, self-knowledge and self-reliance. Self and sisters are, as both Elizabeth Shand and Sarah Murray learn, the only real sources of strength and support upon which a woman can rely: 'If it wasn't for the women the world would be in a gey queer state. And the women got little credit for it.'

The radically feminist assertiveness of the fiction is curiously incompatible with *Women: An Inquiry*'s conservative exploration of the symbiosis and complementarity of the sexes. The cautious traditionalism of the theory is infinitely removed from the explosive and unconventional extremes by which Muir's fictional characters assert their individuality and independence. Elise in *Imagined Corners* consciously sacrifices her 'respectability' on the altar of freedom and, consequently, lives a life of banishment and exile; Elizabeth Shand's rejection of Scotland and of men is a somewhat revolutionary renunciation of her roots and her marriage; and Annie Ritchie's pursuit of a meaningful identity in *Mrs Ritchie* drives her to practise the most horrifying and domineering tyranny.

The institution of marriage is rendered virtually meaningless and moribund by the force of this necessarily strident and assertive individualism; Muir paints an overwhelmingly pessimistic picture of the relationship between men and women. Hector and Elizabeth's relationship, for example, is the product of a purely primitive and physical attraction and is utterly devoid of any emotional or intellectual communion. Each of them is in love with an ideal partner and a model marriage; and not with a realistic sense of self and other. Their entire relationship is apparently built upon a rôle-play of social constructs.

Johnny and Annie's marriage in *Mrs Ritchie* is also born out of deceit and disguise. The young Annie Rattray's mask of gently wooing womanhood utterly blinds Johnny to the terrifying harridan within—and ultimately traps him into the baleful hell of a loveless and soul-destroying marriage.

> [T]he warmth, the answering, absolving tenderness that he was entreating remained locked away and inaccessible, locked up like the prim, clean house and to the door that guarded it Johnny Ritchie could not find the key.

The only apparently positive and mutually fulfilling

union within these two novels is Elise and Karl's undoubted love match—but this relationship has, significantly, been consigned to a mythical past before *Imagined Corners* actually begins. And the reader gradually learns that even the liberated and independent Elise has been a reluctant muse and mother to her beloved Karl.

> Her vitality, he had said, was all he needed to provide him with vegetative material on which to feed . . . Women were like grass, he said; they were the fundamental nourishment . . . Anonymous nourishment, thought Madame Mütze, remembering how she had objected to the description.

Muir was only too aware of the painful and frustrating invisibility which was implicit in 'nourishing' a poet.

Muir's own artistic creativity and the trail of her narrative occasionally become submerged beneath a tide of professional psychologising. *Mrs Ritchie* was justifiably criticised by various contemporary reviewers for its spate of abstract theorising and its disconcerting resemblance, in places, to a psychological 'case study'.

> Dislike untouched by the humour that turns it to satire or by the humanity that gives the miscreant at least the semblance of a sporting chance, is a dangerous emotion for the artist; and the acrimony shown here towards the subject is not of the kind that vivifies creation. In spite of the careful photography of the details, the lingering thoroughness of the dissection, the result is nearer to science than to art, and not to the more vital form of science.[4]

And yet this justifiable criticism ought not to blind the reader to the powerful and profound story which lurks behind the almost overly academic analysis. The alienatingly unsympathetic portrayal of Annie Ritchie in the novel's later pages is amply counterbalanced by the earthily attractive figure of Bet Reid and the sensitively delineated character of Sarah Annie. The novel also offers an uncompromisingly and uncomfortably explicit

4. Anonymous reviewer in *The Times Literary Supplement*, 13 July 1933.

indictment of the rationale and the horrifying reality of the Great War. Muir always described the 1914 war as 'the great shock in my adult life . . . which knocked me to pieces for a while';[5] and *Mrs Ritchie* embodies her abhorrence of the false incitements by which men and nations are driven into conflict.

> What made it ghastly was the systematic organization of warfare under the banner of Bunk, making chaps fight for Bunk called patriotism or Bunk called God. A man could fight and be reconciled to his enemy and quit fighting; but Bunk could go on fighting for ever and ever, Amen . . . A man could use his fists, or even a bayonet, a bomb, or a rifle, but Bunk used big guns and tanks and poison-gas. A man could kill his enemy and be quit of him, but Bunk preached immortality and kept alive a mob of vengeful ghosts.

Muir's own voice and vision are never far beneath the surface psychologising, politicising and philosophising of her fiction. She was utterly incapable of dissociating herself from her critique of the actions and the actors in her fiction. By the same token, versions of herself and of her life populate each of her novels to such an extent that autobiography and fiction become inseparable; we are brought face-to-face with the author through her writings. *Imagined Corners* is a virtual retelling of Muir's Montrose childhood and portrays the author in the combined Elizabeths; a later and unpublished novel entitled *Mrs Muttoe and the Top Storey* is an undiluted record of the three happy years which the Muirs spent in Hampstead in the early 1930s; and *The Usurpers*, a 1950s novel about her post-war experiences with the British Council in Prague, is almost libellously factual.

There might even be a certain desperation in this relentless mirroring and expression of her own life and personality. Willa Muir's adult life was haunted by a fear of the anonymity of the 'poet's wife'; of being merely the willing catalyst to Edwin's creativity; of being silenced by his greatness. It was a fear without resentment; she loved him

5. Willa Muir. *Belonging*, (p. 20). London: The Hogarth Press, 1968.

passionately, completely and enduringly. But occasionally, and especially in her later years, she was wistfully regretful about the conscious sacrifice of her own claims to literary eminence.

> I am a better translator than he is. The whole current of patriarchal society is set against this fact, however and sweeps it into oblivion, simply because I did not insist on shouting aloud: 'Most of this translation, especially Kafka, has been done by ME. Edwin only helped.' And every time Edwin was referred to as THE translator, I was too proud to say anything; and Edwin himself felt it would be undignified to speak up, I suppose. So that now, especially since my break-down in the middle of the war, I am left without a shred of literary reputation. And I am ashamed of the fact that I feel it as a grievance. It shouldn't bother me. Reputation is a passing value, after all. Yet it is now that I feel it, now when I am trying to build up my life again and overcome my disabilities: my dicky back-bone for instance. Because I seem to have nothing to build on, except that I am Edwin's wife and he still loves me. That is much. It is more in a sense than I deserve. And I know, too, how destructive ambition is, and how it deforms what one might create. And yet, and yet, I want to be acknowledged.[6]

It is a tragically modest request, and one which her lifetime never granted. The publication of this collection of her writings is the first real recognition of her qualities as a writer and as an intellectual. We can at last re-evaluate her work and assure her of her deserved place within the Scottish canon.

And yet we must beware the natural and proprietorial urge to nationalise her. Paradoxical personalities are resistant to simple classifications. Her Scottish pedigree and her alliance with the writers of the Scottish Renaissance should not blind us to her internationalist qualifications. Nor should we glibly slot her into the 'feminist' category, simply because she was a woman writer with a female agenda. She was, throughout her lifetime, denied her

6. Willa Muir. *Journal* 1951–53 (20 August 1953)
   Box 6. Willa Muir archive in the University of
   St Andrews Library.

literary independence and individuality; now her reputation deserves its autonomy.

This volume is a celebration of the life and work of Willa Muir.

Kirsty A. Allen

# IMAGINED CORNERS

# Contents

CALDERWICK 1912

# ONE

## I

That obliquity of the earth with reference to the sun which makes twilight linger both at dawn and dusk in northern latitudes prolongs summer and winter with the same uncertainty in a dawdling autumn and a tardy spring. Indeed, the arguable uncertainty of the sun's gradual approach and withdrawal in these regions may have first sharpened the discrimination of the natives to that acuteness for which they are renowned, so that it would be a keen-minded Scot who could, without fear of contradiction, say to his fellows: 'the day has now fully dawned,' or 'the summer has now definitely departed.' Early one September there was a day in Calderwick on which the hardiest Scot would not have ventured so positive a statement, for it could still have passed for what the inhabitants of Calderwick take to be summer. Over the links and sandy dunes stretching between the town and the sea larks were rising from every tussock of grass, twitching up into the air as if depending from invisible strings, followed more slowly by the heavy, oily fragrance of gorse blossom and the occasional sharpness of thyme bruised by a golfer's heel. The warmth of the sea-water was well over sixty degrees and the half-dozen bathing coaches had not yet been drawn creaking into retirement by a municipal cart-horse.

All this late summer peace and fragrance belonged to the municipality. The burgh of Calderwick owned its golf and its bathing, its sand and its gorse. The larks nested in municipal grass, the crows waddled on municipal turf. But few of the citizens of Calderwick followed their example. The season for summer visitors was over, although summer still lingered, and the burgh of Calderwick was busy about its jute

mills, its grain mills, its shipping, schools, shops, offices and
dwelling-houses. The larks, the crows and the gulls, after all,
were not ratepayers. It is doubtful whether they even knew
that they were domiciled in Scotland.

The town of Calderwick turned its back on the sea and the
links, clinging, with that instinct for the highest which
distinguishes so many ancient burghs, to a ridge well above
sea-level along the back of which the High Street lay like a
spine, with ribs running down on either side. It was not a
large enough town to have trams, and at this time, the Motor
Age being comparatively infantile, there was not even a bus
connecting it with outlying villages: but the main railway
line from Edinburgh to Aberdeen ran through it, and it had
an extra branch line of its own. In short, Calderwick was an
important, self-respecting trading community, with a fair
harbour and fertile agricultural land behind it.

On this clear, sunny day in early September – a good day
on which to become acquainted with Calderwick – a bride
and a bridegroom were due to arrive in the town, the
bridgroom a native, born and brought up in Calderwick, the
bride a stranger. Human life is so intricate in its relationships
that newcomers, whether native or not, cannot be dropped
into a town like glass balls into plain water; there are too
many elements already suspended in the liquid, and newcomers are at least partly soluble. What they may precipitate
remains to be seen.

## II

Of the various people who were to be affected by the
precipitation, Sarah Murray was one of the most unconscious. She had her own problems, but these did not include
any reference to the newly married couple. At half-past six
she was still asleep, but the alarm clock beside her bed was
set for a quarter to seven.

She woke up five minutes before the alarm clock was due
to go off, and stretched out her hand to put on the silencer, as
she did every morning. By a quarter past seven she was on
her way downstairs to the kitchen, stepping softly to avoid
disturbing the minister, whose door she had to pass. If a
celestial journalist, notebook in hand, had asked her what

kind of a woman she was she would have replied, with some surprise, that she was a minister's sister. Throughout the week she was mistress of his house, and on Sundays, sitting in the manse pew, she was haunted by a sense of being mistress of the House of God as well.

She found Teenie, the maid, watching a tiny kettle set on the newly lit kitchen range.

'Put that damper in a bit, Teenie,' she said, 'you'll have us burnt out of coal.'

Teenie turned round and burst into tears.

'I canna thole it, Miss Murray,' she sobbed, smudging her face with a black-leaded hand. 'I'll have to give notice. Tramp, tramp, tramp half the night, up and down, up and down, and him roaring and speaking to himself; I havena sleepit a wink. I canna thole it.'

Sarah lit the gas-ring and transferred the kettle to it.

'You're needing a cup of tea, and so am I. Whisht now, Teenie; whisht, lassie. You must have slept a wee bit, for he was quiet by half-past three.'

'It's no' just the sleeping, Miss Murray, it's the feel of it. I canna thole it any longer; I just canna thole it.'

Teenie's voice wavered and the sobs rose again in her throat. Her eyes had deep black rings under them.

'The kettle's boiling. Get down the cups, Teenie.'

Sarah's voice was firm. They sat down on either side of the table and drank the tea in silence. Together they lifted their cups and set them down, and whether it was the sympathy arising from common action that brought Teenie more into line with her mistress, or whether the strong warm tea comforted her, she was much calmer when the teapot was empty.

'Don't give me notice this morning, Teenie,' said Sarah abruptly. 'It's not easy, I know, but if we can hold out a bit longer. . . . And I don't want a strange lassie in the house while he's like that. He knows you, Teenie, and you get on well enough with him, don't you?'

'Oh ay,' said Teenie. 'When he's himsel'. But whenever it begins to grow dark, Miss Murray, I canna explain it, but it just comes over me, and I'm feared to go upstairs when he's in his room. And his feet go ding-ding-dinging right through me. And it's the whole night through, every night the same, and I canna sleep a wink, not even after he's quiet.'

'You'll go to your bed this very afternoon. . . . I'll see to that. . . . I'll get the minister to take him out. And, shall we say, try it for another week and see what you think? I don't want to lose you, Teenie, after two years.'

Teenie flushed.

'I ken you have it worse than me. But I canna thole it for much longer.'

'Another week?'

'We'll try it,' said Teenie, getting up.

'We'll try it,' echoed in Sarah's mind. She had never yet admitted that there was anything she could not stand up to; she believed that persistent attention, hard work and method could disentangle the most complicated problem, and she despised people who did not apply themselves. Her brother the minister, the Reverend William, she could not despise, for he was unremitting in his duty, although his duty seemed to her at times a queerly unpractical business. Still, all men were queer and unaccountable. But even the worst and wildest of them were not so unaccountable as her younger brother Ned, whose conduct was driving Teenie into hysterics and forcing Sarah herself to realize that human energy is not inexhaustible. She was tired, her head ached, and the mere thought of Ned exasperated her. Besides the way he carried on during the day he was wasting the gas every night in a sinful manner, and even after he was in bed she could not go to sleep until she had peeped through the crack of his door to see that the gas was turned off. William's salary could not stand it. It was all so unreasonable. What made him do it? What on earth made him do it?

But from this question, against which she had battered herself in vain for months, her mind now turned resolutely away. If there was any meaning at all in life Ned was bound to come to his senses again. Of course.

'We'll give it another week, then, Teenie. Mr Ned's bound to get better. I must say I don't see how he could get any worse.'

Sarah smiled wryly, and even the effort of smiling strengthened her returning faith in the reasonableness of life.

She gave herself a shake and set about the business of the day.

On the first floor the Reverend William Murray, awakening slowly as he always did, was also strengthened by faith, but not by faith in the reasonableness of life. His faith grew out of the peace which surrounded him in that half-suspended state between sleeping and waking wherein his spirit lingered every morning, freed from the blankness of sleep and not yet limited by the checks and obstacles of perception. His eyes were shut, and his vision was not prejudiced by the straight lines of roof and walls; his ears were shut, and in their convulsions there reverberated only the vibrations of that remote sea on which he had been cradled, unstirred by desire or regret, at one with his God. Slowly, almost reluctantly, his spirit returned to inform his body, ebbing and shrinking into the confines of consciousness. He lay still, scarcely breathing, trying to prolong the transitory sense of communion with the infinite; but his awareness spread out in concentric rings around him, and he knew himself as William Murray, lying in bed in the manse of St James's United Free Church, Calderwick. Even then he did not open his eyes. His thoughts would presently follow him and rise into their place, the first thoughts of the morning which were sent to him as a guidance for the day.

During the past fortnight his first thoughts had been more and more conditioned by the existence of his brother Ned, and on this morning too it was with an indefinite but pervading sense of reference to Ned that the thought came to him: yonder there is no forgiveness, for there is no sin. It was an immediate crystallization of experience, and he felt its truth. In that other world forgiveness was superfluous, for there was no sin. There was neither good nor evil. . . . That startled his newly awakened consciousness. He opened his eyes and got up.

The thought persisted, however, as he shaved. No sin; that was the state he was striving to attain, a life wholly within the peace of God. But neither good nor evil? That meant the suspension of all judgment as well as of all passion. Yet he was uplifted by the mere idea that the peace of God was neither good nor evil. . . . To know all is to forgive all, someone had said. He stared at his own reflection in the mirror. How much better simply to accept without for-giveness! Could he meet Ned on that plane perhaps he could cure the boy's sick spirit. . . .

'Ned's still asleep,' said Sarah, as she poured out tea, this time China tea from the silver teapot. 'I'm going to leave him till he wakens. It was half-past three when he put out the gas.'

William said nothing. He looked so absent and so pleased that Sarah could not resist giving him a tug.

'Teenie's threatened to go, William, if this lasts much longer. It's got on her nerves.'

'Teenie? Oh, surely not. Tell her to keep her heart up; I don't think it'll last much longer. I think . . . '

He paused. It was difficult to explain to Sarah.

'I have an idea,' he went on, 'but I haven't quite thought it out. Still, I believe . . .'

Sarah felt so irritated by the way his spoon was wandering round and round in his teacup that she knew her nerves were sorely stretched as well as Teenie's.

'William, it mustn't go on!' she said. 'In the first place, we'll be ruined. What with the gas, and a fire on all day in his room – we can't do it much longer. If he doesn't come to his senses soon we'll have to – to send him away.'

Her words were indefinite, but as she and William looked at each other neither doubted what was meant. William stopped stirring his tea. With unexpected force he said in a loud tone: 'No! That would be inhuman. That would be unchristian. What can you be thinking of, Sarah?'

Sarah covered her eyes with her hands.

'I'm so tired! You don't hear him at night, but he's just over my head, and the tramping up and down, up and down' (unconsciously she echoed Teenie's words) 'drives through and through me.'

William rose from the table to bend awkwardly over her.

'My poor Sarah, my poor lassie. Of course you're tired. but bear up just a little longer; we'll do it yet. He's our own brother; he's bound to be all right.'

God never forsakes his people, he was thinking to himself.

Sarah dropped a tear on his hand and looked up.

'Could you take him for a walk this afternoon? I've promised Teenie an afternoon in bed, and I think I could do with a rest myself.'

'I'll take him out this afternoon,' William's voice was confident. 'It's only Friday, I can finish my sermon to-morrow. But can't you take a rest now?'

'No; I have to get flannelette and stuff for the Ladies' Work Party, from Mary Watson's.'

Teenie could give Ned his breakfast when he came down, she was thinking. He was nicer to Teenie than to his own sister. . . .

Before letting herself out Sarah mentally rehearsed her various errands and the number of yards of flannelette she needed. She never simply went out on impulse, nor did she expect to be surprised by anything in the streets. She could have predicted what was to be seen at any hour of the day. It was now ten o'clock, and as if noting the answer to a sum she observed that the baker's van was precisely at the head of the street and that the buckets of house-refuse were still waiting by twos and threes at the kerb for the dust-cart. She would have been disturbed had things been otherwise. It was a satisfaction to her that everything had its time and place; that streets were paved and gardens contained within iron railings, that children were in school, infants in their peram-bulators, and hundreds of shopkeepers waiting behind clean counters for the thousands of housewives who like herself were shopping. The orderly life of Calderwick was keeping pace with the ordered march of the sun. She could hear the prolonged whistle of the express from King's Cross as it pulled out of the station. Punctual to the minute.

## III

At about the same time, in the same town of Calderwick, and only round the corner from the manse, young Mrs John Shand was buttoning her gloves and tilting her head to study, in the long mirror, the hang of her new coat. It had a perfect line, she decided; most women, of course, wouldn't have the shoulders for it. Whatever Hector's wife had on, bride or no bride, she would be put in the shade by such elegance.

Mabel Shand smiled to her own reflection, an approving smile. Her teeth were strong, white and even; her skin was naturally fresh and finely textured. She bent her knee slightly and admired the fall of her garments; most women's thighs were too short, but she had a long and graceful curve from the hip to the knee. She felt that she was marked out for superiority, unlike the majority of the Calderwick women, botched and clumsy creatures who should be thankful for anything they could get.

Her gloves were buttoned. While she was still at school she had read in a magazine that no lady ever left the buttoning of her gloves to be done on the stairs or in the hall or, horror of horrors, outside the front door. Mabel had never forgotten that, and in her marriage she had her reward. From a farm in the village of Invercalder she had, two years ago, hooked the biggest fish in the town of Calderwick, John Shand, the head of an old-established firm of grain merchants and flour millers.

Sarah Murray, too, had been born in Invercalder, where her father was the village schoolmaster, and like Mabel had been promoted to Calderwick, so that, geographically at least, their worlds were the same. But either because the grey stone schoolhouse stood bleakly on a hill at the west end of the village and the farm lay snug in a hollow at the east end, or because a schoolmaster's time-table is ruled by will while a farmer's is governed by capricious seasons, life in the schoolhouse was hard, angular and rigid, whereas in the farm it was kindly and easy-going. Mabel accordingly was left to form herself, but Sarah was rigorously formed by her father, and the process had been so thorough that she had no inkling of it. From the kindling of the first fire in the morning to the blotting out of the last light before going to bed she found the whole justification of life in the fulfilment of daily routine. That routine Mabel Shand ignored, in so far as a Calderwick woman could ignore it. In the same way she ignored the orderly activities of the municipality; it gave her no thrill of satisfaction to know that her bread was regularly delivered and her dustbins emptied daily. Sarah, if she had pictured a web of the world, might have regarded herself as one of many flies caught in it by God, her sole consolation being the presence of the other flies and the impartial symmetry of the web, but Mabel lived at the heart of her own spider's web, and every thread from the outside world led directly to herself.

Mrs John Shand came down the steps of number seven Balfour Terrace just as Sarah Murray rounded the corner. She might as well walk up with Sarah, she thought. Poor old thing, what a frump!

Sarah paused and looked round. 'Are you going up my way, Mabel, to the High Street?'

'Yes; to the new house, you know. Hector and his wife are coming home this morning.'

'Oh, I'd forgotten they were coming to-day. They've been up Deeside, haven't they? I've never seen Mrs Hector; what's she like?'

Mabel nearly shrugged her shoulders.

'You'll see her in church on Sunday, I suppose. She's considered clever.'

You won't like that, thought Sarah, but checked the thought immediately. Even though she had known Mabel from childhood she tried to be charitable towards the wife of her brother's leading elder.

Mabel's face twinkled for a moment as she recalled the first occasion on which she had seen the present Mrs Hector Shand. Hector had whirled her up to the University to meet the girl, and Elizabeth had turned up for tea in a cheap, striped cotton frock and sand-shoes. Sand-shoes!

'That's a nice coat, Mabel.' Sarah was trying to atone for her uncharitable thoughts. 'New, isn't it?'

'First time on to-day. Latest fashion, my dear. John likes it immensely.'

'No doubt.'

In spite of herself Sarah's tone was blighting. It was long since she had had a new coat, and what with one thing and another, Ned's gas and coal and keep, it would be a long time before she got one.

She always dries up when I mention John, said Mabel to herself. And John would never have looked at her in any case.

'How's Ned?' she asked.

'Not any better, I'm afraid.' Sarah's voice lost its edge. 'Mabel, I simply don't know what to do. What *can* we do?'

Mabel felt a vague discomfort.

'Ned's always very nice to *me* whenever I see him.' It sounded almost like self-defence.

'That's just it,' burst out Sarah. 'He's nice to everybody except to me and William. It doesn't matter what we do. Yesterday it was a newspaper he said I'd deliberately hidden from him because there was a job in it he meant to apply for. He said I was always interfering with his happiness. It's so unjust, Mabel; it's so unreasonable: the more I think of it the more desperate I feel. I've tried everything; I've coaxed him and scolded him and ignored him, and he just gets worse and worse. I told William this morning that if—'

She stopped herself. When Ned came again to his senses it would never do for Mabel to be in a position to tell him that Sarah had even thought of sending him away.

'You've known Ned all his life,' she went on. 'Was he ever like this when he was going to school?'

'He was always shy.' Mabel's discomfort was increasing. 'It wasn't easy to know what he was thinking.'

'But you used to bicycle in to school with him every day, Mabel. Surely you would have noticed if there was anything? I've racked my brains and racked my brains and I can't think of an explanation. He was so brilliant at school and at the University, and he was always as quiet as a mouse when he came home. Even when he had that breakdown in his finals he wasn't like this.'

Mable's uneasiness was now tinged with excitement. It seemed natural to her that she should be the centre of the world to others as well as to herself, and she had always suspected that what had unsettled Ned in the beginning was her marriage to John Shand. It wasn't her fault, was it? She had flirted a little with the boy, but then she had flirted with so many boys. A kiss or two meant nothing when one was sixteen. It wasn't her fault. But it must have left an impression on Ned. She could wager that no other girl had ever kissed him. Half rueful and half pleased she glanced sideways at Sarah. Of course Sarah wouldn't understand.

'He'll get over it,' she announced confidently. Then on a sudden impulse she added: 'I'll help him to get over it if you like. Let him come out to golf with me this afternoon.'

Sarah's excessive surprise and gratitude might have betrayed her to a less indifferent observer.

'Oh, that's nothing,' said Mabel. 'Tell him to come round for me at two o'clock.'

Sarah hesitated.

'It's so good of you that I don't like to suggest – but do you think you could possibly come round for him? It's so difficult to get him to do anything.'

Mabel raised her eyebrows. However, the occasion was an extraordinary one.

'Very well,' she said.

Even though her relief was tempered by self-reproach Sarah turned down the High Street with a lighter heart after parting from Mabel. She felt confusedly that William's Christian charity towards all the world was on a higher level than her own suspicious judgments, but she found it difficult to believe in Divine grace without concrete instances. This morning, however, she had had a lesson. Let that be a lesson to you, she told herself sharply, emerging from her depression into the imperative mood which she mistook for God.

That was a common mistake in and around Calderwick, and Sarah's father, who had passed it on to her, was not its originator. Even her brother William could not eliminate the imperative mood from his speculations, although his use of it was quite opposed to Sarah's. 'God's in His heaven, therefore all must be well with the world,' was his version, while Sarah's, as she made her way towards Mary Watson's shop, could have been expressed as: 'All's well with the world – or nearly so – therefore God must be in His heaven.'

Mary Watson's shop was another stronghold of the imperative mood. Miss Watson felt it her duty to see that all was well with the world around her, in case God should be jeopardized in His heaven by aberrant humanity. Her father had been an elder in St James's United Free Church, and although she had inherited his business as a draper she had not been allowed to inherit his eldership, which was perhaps the reason why her moral vigilance, unremitting in general, was especially relentless towards the minister and elders of that church. It was the boast of the town that Mary Watson had driven three ministers away from St James's in as many

years. Even William Murray's mildness had not disarmed the
doughty woman; she dubbed him 'Milk-and-water Willie,'
and told him to his face that he would never win grown folk
from their sins.

Usually, on entering Mary's shop in the High Street, Sarah
felt that she had interrupted a tirade against her brother. The
over-loud tones of a customer saying hastily, 'Aweel, I'll just
take these, Miss Watson,' never failed to make her bristle.
On this occasion, however, she found the shop empty, and,
still remembering her lesson, even smiled pleasantly in
Mary's face, saying: 'Lovely weather for September, isn't
it?'

'No' sae bad,' admitted Mary, 'But a'thing's very dry.'

Things were not drier than her tone. Her attitude said
plainly: 'I don't take it as a favour that you come into my
shop: it's only your duty to support a member of your own
congregation.'

As the bales of material were unrolled with a thump and
measured off on a yardstick Mary's tongue was as active as
her hands.

'I suppose you've heard that the Town Council has granted
a licence to the braw new Golf Club? That's a fine state o'
things, Miss Murray. There's mair pubs than kirks in the
town already. I hope the minister is to do something about it?
The Town Council should be weel rappit ower the knuckles.'

Sarah was well aware that Mary regarded the minister as
incapable of rapping anyone over the knuckles. His failure to
rap the Town Council would only become another grievance.

'You should stand for the Town Council and do it yourself,
Miss Watson.' This was a hastily improvised defence, but its
effect was unexpected. Mary bridled.

'Me, Miss Murray! What would put that into your head
now?'

'I'm sure the minister would agree with me.'

'Aweel, I'm no' saying. If you and he think it's my *duty*—'
Mary's face was impassive again.

'Of course it's your duty.'

'Ay, now, I never thought o' that.'

Mary slowly folded up the stuff and made it into a neat
parcel.

'I'll see what my sister says till't.'

Then, as if conscious of weakness, she added in her sharpest voice:

'And you might tell the minister that he hasna darkened our door for mair than twa months. My sister's a poor bedridden woman, and even if he wasna the minister it wad only be decent of him to give her a look-in in the by-going.'

## IV

Number twenty-six High Street, which was being prepared for its new master and mistress, was approved by Mabel. Like every house in the old High Street, of course, it had to be entered from a 'close', but once the narrow close entrance was left behind a fair-sized paved courtyard opened out, framed by two respectable Georgian houses, pillared and porticoed, with clipped box-trees set in green tubs before the doors. Dr Scrymgeour's name shone resplendently on one door, and on the other a smaller and more modest brass plate read 'H. Shand'. Mabel's eye fell on that as usual with a slight sense of shock; she could never think of Hector as H. Shand, a householder. She became very much Mrs John Shand as she looked at it; she stiffened a little and examined the big brass bell-knob on its square plate and the whitened doorstep. Both were speckless. That maid wasn't going to be so bad.

The said maid was breathless when she opened the door, and her eyes were shining.

'Miss Shand's here,' she said. 'An' everything's like a new pin.'

'You must never answer the door in a kitchen apron. You must always change into a clean one to open the door, Mary Ann!'

'But that would keep folk waiting.'

'Better to let them wait. Better still to keep a clean apron under the dirty one, and then all you have to do is to slip it off. Try to remember that.'

Mrs John Shand sailed into the hall.

'Are you there, Aunt Janet?' she called in a clear voice.

'Here, my dear,' came the answer in a deeper more muffled tone. 'Up here in their bedroom.'

Mabel mounted the stairs, still armoured in dignity. It was her sole defence against the thought of her husband's young half-brother, who annoyed her by making her feel like a schoolgirl. He was the only young man who had ever kissed her with indifference. But she was Mrs John Shand now.

Aunt Janet appeared in the doorway.

'How are you, my dear?' She pecked Mabel's cheek and went on without a pause: 'I think everything's all right now; the sheets are airing and the kitchen's in apple-pie order.'

'I had to check Mary Ann for coming to the door in a dirty apron,' said Mrs John Shand. 'Do you think she'll be all right?'

'Oh, she's strong and willing, and, you know, my dear, we can give Elizabeth a few hints, perhaps, now and then, you know.'

Between them there vibrated a mutual though unspoken opinion that Elizabeth would need those hints.

Aunt Janet drew Mabel into the bedroom and lowered her voice.

'It's a good thing I came up here. Do you know, that girl had set out the chambers *under the beds*.'

Mabel could not resist the reflection that Hector had survived more shameless facts than unconcealed chamber-pots. Nor was Elizabeth likely to be a stickler for propriety.

The flicker of mirth in her face did not escape Aunt Janet, who became almost voluminous as she enfolded young Mrs John in benevolence.

'I know you'll do your very best for Elizabeth, my dear. She hasn't as much social experience as you, but she's a dear girl – a dear girl. And she's so clever you know; she has done very well at the University.'

'Clever she must be,' admitted Mabel, trying to shake off her aunt-in-law, 'or she would never have got Hector to marry her. She's the only woman who has ever managed that.'

If there was any personal feeling in these words Aunt Janet did not notice it; she observed only an aspersion on her beloved nephew.

'Hector may be thoughtless, but he's not so bad as you and John think. I assure you he's not. And he's so conscious of

Elizabeth's goodness in marrying him. "She'll keep me straight, Aunt Janet," he said. "I promise you I'll go straight." Poor boy, he has so much against him.'

She absentmindedly patted the eiderdown on the nearest of the twin beds.

'Oh, Elizabeth will keep him in order,' said Mabel, walking to the window and staring out of the garden. Aunt Janet was too irritating.

'A dear girl. A dear girl.' Aunt Janet furtively wiped her eyes. 'I'm sure they'll be happy.'

In the kitchen Mary Ann was singing to herself. 'Isn't it fine,' she was thinking, 'a bride comin' hame to her ain hoose? My certy! they'll be here in half-an-'oor. Where's that clean apron?'

William Murray stood looking out of the window, his hands clasped behind his back, while Sarah piled the dirty dinner-dishes on a tray. Now that Ned was actually out of the house she felt exhausted; the exertion of lifting the tray was almost too much for her. She would be thankful when she got into bed. So precisely regulated was her scheme of life, however, that she thought it rather a disgraceful weakness to lie down during the day, and for the same reason it did not occur to her that William, being stronger and less tired, might carry the tray into the kitchen.

Nor did it occur to William. He had not quite escaped the influence of his father, who had ruled his house, as he had ruled his school, on the assumption that the female sex was devised by God for the lower grades of work and knowledge, and that it was beneath the dignity of a man to stoop to female tasks. But although this assumption lay at the back of William's mind it appeared so natural that he had never recognized it; if Sarah had asked him to carry the tray he would have taken it willingly; the assumption merely hindered him from thinking of such an action. So he gazed out of the window, meditating on his sermon and on Ned.

'Judge not, and ye shall not be judged: condemn not, and ye shall not be condemned: forgive, and ye shall be forgiven.' That was his text. The thought which had arisen in his mind that morning had given it a new aspect; he was looking at it from a longer perspective. Instead of being an absolute virtue forgiveness was merely a second-best, a concession to ordinary flesh and blood which was too imperfect to enter at once into the full peace of God. That blessed state, he thought, could not be conveyed in words alone to those who had never experienced it; but perhaps it could be transmitted by contagion. . . . It was a state of fearless trust in the love of God, a fearless acceptance of the universe, acceptance without criticism, without fear of criticism, without self-consciousness. But most of us, he thought, live on the defensive; we live as if under a jealous and critical eye. 'Thou God seest me.' For such timid creatures the leap into the infinite space of God's love is too great; small fears must first be cast out, small encouragements given. That was the purport of his text: to cast out people's fear of each other, as a step on the way to boundless trust in God.

Ned was clearly an extreme instance of human mistrust. He filled the world with the shapes of his fear. Every act, every word, every inflection of other people's voices he construed as hostile; kind words appeared as hypocrisy, kindly services as specious intrigue. His fears were so monstrous that mere persuasion could not dispel them; he must be cured by the greater force, the more absolute revelation. The text was not enough for Ned.

'Did you notice,' said Sarah, 'how Ned flared up at me when I told him Mabel wanted him to golf with her? And the things he said about her! But when she came he went off as meekly as a lamb. . . . I don't understand it. It seems as if we brought out the very worst in him.'

Ned's tirade was still rankling in Sarah's heart.

'You think I don't see through you!' he had shouted when she mentioned the proposed golf match. 'Low, sneaking cunning,' he had reiterated. Women were snakes in the grass. All alike. Not one better than another. . . . On the whole, it was a comfort to Sarah that he had abused Mabel too. But when Mabel appeared, gay and pretty, asking him if he cared to golf, he had become even excessively complaisant. It tortured Sarah to think that Mabel could succeed where she had failed.

'No, no,' said William, turning round. 'We don't bring out the worst in him. He fears us less than other people, that's all. Other people impose a constraint on him. Don't let such ideas discourage you. Go to bed now and sleep a little.'

'What are you going to do?' Sarah still lingered as if there were something left unsaid. She did not herself know what it was.

'I shall visit Ann Watson,' said the minister. 'Go to bed now.'

Reluctantly Sarah withdrew, reminding herself again that she ought to feel grateful to Mabel.

William walked slowly by unfrequented by-roads towards the house where Ann Watson lay in bed. The sand-scoured, windswept little streets were filled with clear light; everything was sharply focussed as if seen through a reducing lens; above the plain grey-stone houses the sky was pale and remote. Clear and thin and sharp as the air were the voices of the passers-by, for the Calderwick dialect is born in the teeth of an east wind that keeps mouths from opening wide enough to give resonance to speech. The shrill almost falsetto tones pierced the minister's medit-ations; he ceased to think about the peace of God, and remembered the querulous voice of Ann Watson. In spite of himself, his heart sank a little at the thought of the close-lipped, tight-fisted old woman. He turned a corner into a cobbled lane, at the end of which the Watsons' house stood at right angles to the others, enclosed by a fence and presenting a blank wall to the street. Here Ann and Mary Watson had been born, and here they would die. Here as children they had played among the cobbles, like the children playing there that day. The minister paused to watch half-a-dozen little girls who were rushing, with screams of simulated terror, towards another girl standing by herself in the middle of the lane.

'Mither! Mither!' they shrieked. 'I'm feared!'

'Tits!' said the 'mother', 'it's just yer faither's breeks. Away ye go!'

Back they all rushed pell-mell to the Watsons' gateway.

'What are you playing at?' inquired William, laughing.

The girls crowded together shyly and looked at him.

'Bogey in the press,' one of them suddenly spoke up.

'And is this the press?' he pointed to the gate.

They nodded, giggling.

'Oh, well,' said William, 'I don't mind the bogey. I'm going right into the press; look at this.'

He opened the gate and went into the garden, followed by an outburst of disconcerting childish laughter.

My bogey is just as much of a fabrication as theirs, thought William, walking along the narrow paved path to the front door. Why did children like to frighten themselves?

He lifted the big knocker and rapped it firmly before he noticed that the door was ajar. A shrill scream sounded within the house, and he took it as a command to come in. He pushed the door open and saw across the kitchen another open door leading into Ann's bedroom. She was half sitting up in bed, so that she had a clear view of the kitchen.

'Oh, it's you, minister! Come away in. Have you seen that lassie o' mine?'

The minister looked round the kitchen as if the lassie might be hiding somewhere.

'She's awa' oot half-an-hour syne to go to the baker's; set her up with her gallivanting,' said Ann, still stretching her neck towards the kitchen. 'I'll give her a flea in her lug – Oh, there you are, you good-for-nothing jaud!'

A sulky-looking girl bounced in past the minister, and set two loaves of bread on the dresser.

'Dinna leave the bread there!' screamed Ann. 'Put it in the bread crock. And see that you put the lid on right.'

The minister advanced and sat down on a horse-hair chair beside the bed.

'You wouldna believe it,' went on Ann in the same high scream, 'what I have to suffer. Folk just take a pleasure in spiting me. I canna trust that lassie to do a thing right.'

A loud rattling from the kitchen fireplace answered her.

'What are you doing there?' cried Ann.

The minister got up and shut the bedroom door.

'I don't like to see you worried, Miss Watson,' he said. 'Never mind the lassie. It's you I've come to see.'

'It's all very well to say never mind the lassie,' grumbled Ann; 'if I didna keep an eye on her she would have everything going to rack and ruin. And she puts things where I canna bear them to be, just to spite me. And my sister Mary's every bit as bad. You wouldna believe it, but yestreen she changed every stick o' furniture in the kitchen, till I was nearly blue in the face. I kept that kitchen for years, and I kept father's auld chair in its right place beside the dresser, but last night nothing wad please her but to have it out at the cheek o' the fire for her to sit in. I tell you, I've made Teenie put it back beside the dresser, and there it'll bide. We'll see what my lady has to say till't when she comes hame.'

'But if Miss Mary wants to sit in it—'

'She'll no' sit in it! Na, she'll no' sit in it! The shop's hers, but the house is mine, and I'll no' put up with interference. Day in, day out, I've had to mind the house while she was fleein' all over the town enjoying herself; she needna think she's to have everything her own way here as well as outside. I may be bedridden, but I'm no' done for yet.'

Ann nodded her head vehemently, and drew down her upper lip. She had forgotten the minister and was carrying on an inaudible quarrel with an invisible opponent. William Murray found himself looking at her as if for the first time. Her long, hard face must have been handsome once. And once she must have been a little girl playing outside on the cobbles. He felt a sudden sympathy for her; it was touching to see a human soul journeying from one infinity to another in such a narrow cage.

She was still nodding her head, but her lips had ceased to move. So he addressed her again:

'How did you come to stay at home while Miss Mary took over the shop?'

Ann, without knowing it, might have been affected by the sympathy in his voice; at any rate she now answered him simply and directly:

'Because I aye had to keep the house, you see. Mother was like me, helpless wi' rheumatism for years an' years, and I was the handiest in the house. She couldna bear to see Mary flinging the things aboot, so I bude to bide, and Mary gaed to help father in the shop. And she just stayed on there. I never got a chance to do anything else. I've just been buried alive here – buried alive.'

Her high voice quavered.

'I dare say,' said the minister, 'you didn't feel like that while your father was at home? He must have liked you to keep house for him?'

'I aye got on fine wi' father,' said Ann. 'I aye got on fine wi' father. . . . But Mary wadna let me in the shop. An' I'll no' let her in father's chair. Na, I'll no'.'

'And yet,' said the minister, 'she and you are all that's left on this earth of your father.' He put his hand on hers. 'You were bairns together,' he said.

Ann's mouth opened in amazement. But what she was going to say remained unspoken as her eye met the minister's.

'We're all bairns together,' he went on: 'bairns frightened to believe in the love that's behind everything, the love of our Heavenly Father. There's a lot of love in you, Miss Ann, that has never had a chance.'

The Reverend William Murray walked down the lane much more briskly than he had come. Ann had suffered him to read 'a chapter', and had even asked him to put up 'a bit prayer'. Instinctively his eye sought the pale sky, now veiled with insubstantial clouds through which the light of the declining sun was softly diffused. The firmament, he said to himself, with a new realization of the word. A firm basis. An enduring reality. It did not even enter his mind that there were people in the world who might regard his firmament as a mere illusion of beauty woven of light and air. The Reverend William Murray did not doubt the universal validity of his personal experiences.

## THREE

I

Mr and Mrs John Shand, as was fitting, gave a dinner in the
evening to welcome the bride and bridegroom, a family
function, the only other guest being Miss Janet Shand.

The dinner itself was a success. Mabel had studied even
more intensively than usual her stock of ladies' magazines,
and the table decorations, the glass, the silver, the modish
little mats recommended instead of an enveloping tablecloth
by Lady Fanny of *The Ladies' Fashionmonger*, had all
attained the high standard set by that arbiter of refinement.
And had knocked Elizabeth flat, decided Mabel.

Such a satisfactory conclusion ought to have made her
happy. But a hostess, a figure who carries the main burden of
civilization, whose difficult task it is to invent a progressive
notation for mankind's faith in the ability of the human spirit
to surpass itself, cannot ignore the more rarefied ingredients
of a dinner-party, the blending of temperaments, the flavour
of conversation, the pleasant aroma of expanding minds. A
dinner-party that provokes quarrels is like a bouquet
containing nettles, and it was undeniable that all three of
them now remaining by the fireside, Mabel, John and Aunt
Janet, were nettled.

John was standing with his back to the fire. He was a tall,
bulky man with reddish fair hair; his features were large but
harmonious, and the beard he wore dignified his appearance.
In spite of the beard, however, there was something simple
and childlike in his face; perhaps it was the candid expression of his blue eyes which had no eyebrows to give them
depth.

'She's much too good for him,' he said.

Aunt Janet laid down her knitting again. It was a custom

that she should spend the night with John and Mabel after dining there.

'You have always misjudged Hector,' she objected.

'I think his wife has misjudged him. A quiet, sensible girl like that: what induced her to marry him I can't think.'

Great lump that she is, said Mabel to herself, with irritation.

A hostess is only human, and Mabel had had a trying afternoon before her dinner-party began. Ned Murray had not proved amenable. She did not mind so much his absent answers to her questions – although it is annoying to have someone answer 'Yes, yes,' to everything one says – but she could not stand his behaviour to the other people on the links. She would never been seen in public with him again. A man who scowls at people and mutters and turns round to glare at them is a compromising partner. And on top of that Hector had been almost rude to her.

'Hector has a most affectionate and loving nature, and nobody is more unhappy than he is when he does wrong, poor boy,' said Aunt Janet.

John tut-tutted. 'He has no moral sense. And his loving nature is too promiscuous for my taste.'

'He's too sensitive, John, that's all. Girls simply throw themselves at his head. He can't help being so attractive to women.'

'Tut!' said John again; 'he uses women to feed his vanity. You're not going to tell me that that poor girl he ruined – Duncan, wasn't she called? – threw herself at his head whenever he bought a cigarette from her? Much he cared for her! His sensitive heart didn't keep him from clearing out to Canada when he was given the chance.'

'But he confessed the whole story to me, John, with tears in his eyes.'

'That was just another way of getting rid of it. A few tears are an easy price to pay. You're too soft with him.'

Janet Shand's short-sighted eyes filled with tears.

'I know him, John, as well as if I were his mother.'

'Well, well.' John stroked his beard. 'Let us hope his wife will take a stronger line with him.'

Aunt Janet picked up her knitting with a sigh.

'Elizabeth is very young, of course.'

Elizabeth, she felt, was not quite the right kind of wife. There was something about Elizabeth that made one uncertain. . . .

'Four years younger than Hector, isn't she?'

'Yes, John; only twenty-two.'

'Well,' said John, 'Mabel's only twenty-three, and she has sense enough.'

'Too much sense to marry Hector,' said Mabel, preparing to go upstairs.

'I think Hector's insufferable,' she burst out as she was brushing her hair. 'I wish he'd go and live somewhere else. Must you take him into the mill, John?'

'I can't very well keep him out. He's a Shand, after all.'

'He's a bad Shand.'

'I didn't know you disliked him so much.'

'I *detest* him,' said Mabel, brushing her long hair furiously.

'I haven't much use for him myself. . . . But I passed my word that if he settled down I'd take him on. . . . You needn't see much of him, you know; and Elizabeth's a sensible girl, don't you think?'

'I think,' said Mabel, and bit the words short.

'I'm sorry for *her*,' she added. But she deserves what she'll get, her thoughts ran on, as she brushed and brushed the long strands of her bright brown hair.

After he turned out the lights and got into bed John made one more reference to Elizabeth:

'It's funny to think that there's another Elizabeth Shand now, isn't it?'

'Why – of course,' said Mabel. 'They're not like each other, are they?'

John chuckled.

'About as like each other as fire and water. I'd give anything to see Lizzie dealing with Hector.'

'What would she do?'

'If she's still what she used to be she'd have him deflated within ten minutes. There wouldn't be much left of him.'

'I wish she'd come and do it,' murmured Mabel.

All through the evening the phantom of the other Elizabeth Shand, his sister, had haunted John, and now that he was safely under the bedclothes he allowed himself the indulgence of thinking about her. He had tried for so many years to forget her that even now, when anger had died away, he felt his persistent affection for her as a weakness to be indulged only when his head was under the blankets, when the respectable citizen of the daytime had merged into the boy of five-and-twenty years ago. He was startled by the painful leap his heart gave when Mabel murmured: 'I wish she'd come and do it.' He had not known how greatly he desired to see Lizzie again. Twenty years it was since he saw her last. She must be thirty-nine now, three years younger than himself. But that was absurd; he could not picture Lizzie as a mature woman. A wild thing she had been, always in hot water. What a day that was when their father had married again! She was three miles down the coast when he found her, hatless and coatless; she made him miss the wedding too, and she must have been at least twelve then; yes, Hector was born a year later, thirteen years' difference between them. . . . What an extraordinary thing affection is, John reflected. Aunt Janet was always down on Lizzie; she couldn't stand Lizzie; and yet, there she was, sticking up for Hector who wasn't fit to black Lizzie's boots. Lizzie was a wild creature, but not a selfish one. On the other hand, his own affection for Lizzie was just as unreasonable as Aunt Janet's for Hector. Lizzie had behaved scandalously; she had outraged everything he stood for; he had been ill with rage when she ran off with that foreign fellow. Yet that was in keeping with Lizzie's character; she was always dashing into adventures. It had been she who had discovered the disused pottery miles from home where they set up house for so many weeks one summer. He could remember the tumbledown shed, with a low bench covered with dust and fragments of baked clay, fluted moulds broken and crumbling, whorls and handles lying in careless heaps. With closed eyes John re-traversed the road that led there through a hot summer's afternoon, with Lizzie, like an elf, darting from one hedgerow to the other, until she discovered the overgrown side-path, and set off down it at a run. She would never keep on the main road, not Lizzie. Nobody knew what it meant to him when she ran off with that German. He nearly threw up

everything to go after her. But even if he had tracked her
down, how could he have brought her back to be a perpetual
reminder of disgrace? A drunken father was bad enough
without a dishonoured sister; no family could have lived them
both down. Yet though he could justify his anger and his
estrangement from her the long companionship of their
childhood was still alive and seeking fulfilment. Twenty years.
She was nineteen then. But when he dreamed of her, as he did
now and then, she was always a slip of girl. . . . He drifted
into sleep with the vague idea that he was stumbling through a
dark forest of lofty trees, pursuing a brilliant butterfly that
would dart off at a tangent and would not keep to the path.

Mabel Shand had never seen her sister-in-law, and, like
everybody else, was unaware of John's passionate regret for
her. Like everybody else, too, she knew the facts of the
scandal; Elizabeth Shand had run away with a married man,
a foreigner, the head of the modern languages department
in the Calderwick Academy. Mabel also had the benefit of
Aunt Janet's comments, including the information that
John could not bear to have his sister's name mentioned;
but she had been surprised shortly after their marriage to
hear John say lightly: 'You remind me of my sister Lizzie;
she was a gay young thing something like you.' He had
added hastily, 'But you have more sense,' and Mabel
realized that the comparison was intended as a compliment.
Of course she had more sense; she knew too well the value
of social prestige. Her position as John Shand's wife was
more worth while than any fly-by-night nonsense of true
love. Mabel had no intention of falling in love. She preferred to see others in love with her. She had fancied
Hector, but that was when she was a mere child, and now,
lying in bed beside John, she was convinced that she hated
Hector. The thought flashed through her mind with savage
suddenness: 'I wish I had him here; I'd *smack* him!'

Her body quivered with the intensity of her feeling.
Smack him, good and hard, she would.

## II

About the same time Sarah Murray was sitting in her
bedroom with a rug over her knees and a shawl round her

shoulders darning stockings, as she listened to the irregular tramp of Ned's feet overhead. He would stand for a long time on one part of the floor and then stride up and down speaking to himself with increasing vehemence in high tones of exasperation, only to fall silent again, standing motionless on some other spot. He had come in from his golf match taciturn and sullen, but at tea he had brightened up when William asked him how many he had gone round in; his one nasty remark had been made quite jokingly, that the links were all right if it weren't for the people on them who infested the grass; they should be combed out like fleas. After that he had opened the piano, which he hadn't done for months, and played beautifully for a long time until she asked him for something out of the *Messiah* and then he brought his hands down with a crash and stamped out of the room, saying: 'O God!'

He had refused to come in to supper until she and William were finished; since then he had been walking up and down in his own room at the top of the house. Sarah looked at her watch; it was now midnight. Three hours he had been going at it, and might go on for three hours more. What could it be that was troubling him? What could it be that kept him turning and turning round it like an insect on a pin? He had crumpled up the local weekly and thrown it across the room; she had smoothed it out later and looked it over to find what cause for offence he had discovered in it. But there was nothing. Nothing in particular. The usual records of sudden deaths and police cases; local appointments, farmers' dinners, auction sales, and the movements of prominent citizens. She had noticed, for instance, the arrival of Mr and Mrs Hector Shand at their house in the High Street. But how could any of it conceivably enrage a sane person? Insanity? Sarah's hand shook as she darned. The footsteps upstairs seemed also, with furious persistence, to be darning an invisible hole across the room.

'I can't stand it,' said Sarah aloud. 'I must do someting or I'll go crazy.'

She stuck her needle into the stocking and got up. She tiptoed upstairs, although she feared that Teenie was not asleep, and listened at Ned's door.

'Security!' she heard him cry, half sobbing. 'Surely that's not much to ask for? Security's all I want.' His voice died away into mutterings; then it rose again. 'Good God! They have to do it at somebody's expense, but why me, me? Couldn't they work it off on somebody else? It's incredible, logically and mathematically incredible—' He came to a dead stop on the floor, continuing the argument with his voice rising hysterically at the end of every statement. 'With hundreds of millions in the world to practise on they make a dead set at me. All I ask is peace and security and they all climb by kicking me down. Are all the low, sneaking, cunning imbeciles to enjoy a home and a job at my expense? Just because I'm not so low and cunning as they are? Good God!'

He was silent again as well as motionless. Sarah's heart was pounding wildly against her ribs. This was sheer raving. It was no use merely to listen; she must go in and bring him back to a sense of proportion. She opened the door. Ned started. 'Get out!' he screamed. 'Can't I have peace even here?' Sarah spoke mildly, to her own astonishment, for she was shaking. 'I've only come in to see that you haven't let your fire out, Ned. You always forget to put coal on.' The fire was actually half dead. Sarah went firmly towards it and made it up in silence. She could feel Ned's eyes burning into her back.

'That's all right now,' she said, rising from her knees and dusting her hands. 'You won't catch cold now. Are you working on your mathematics?'

'Why? What sneaking cunning is at the back of your mind now?'

'I though you were swotting for your examinations?'

'That's it! That's the conspiracy again! Nobody would believe what I have to put up with!'

'I don't see why an examination is a conspiracy.'

In spite of her fears Sarah said this in the voice of one who is convinced of being reasonable and a little coldly superior to the unreasonableness of the other party.

Ned advanced upon her as if we would strike her. She stood her ground.

'Everybody has to pass examinations. You're not the only one,' she said.

'Oh, I'm not, am I not?' he sneered. 'Does everybody have to sit an examination twice, tell me that? Is everybody compelled to do things over and over again – and *why* I should be persecuted, God knows! What good does it do you? Anybody would think you'd be glad to see me in a job instead of sneaking behind my back —'

'Nonsense! I didn't make you fail in your examination —'

'I didn't fail in my examination!' screamed Ned. 'It's a lie. It's a lie. Liars and hypocrites! Am I to be downed because you are liars and hypocrites?'

'Calling me a liar won't change the facts,' said Sarah. 'You failed because you were ill; that's no disgrace.'

'Ill, was I? What are you going to saddle me with next?'

Ned's voice was less bellicose, and Sarah pressed her advantage.

'No disgrace at all to be ill. But it will be a disgrace if you deliberately leave yourself unprepared for the next time. And you can't pass examinations if you don't go to bed. You know very well what Dr Scrymgeour said.'

'To hell with Dr Scrymgeour! To hell with you, too! Get out of my room!'

Sarah got steadily enough to the door, and turned round for a parting shot before shutting it:

'And if you don't believe you were ill, just go and ask him. Good-night.'

She managed to get downstairs to her room without stumbling. She was shaken, but in some queer way triumphant.

The footsteps above did not worry her so much. She lay in bed listening.

'I wonder if he's forgotten all about it,' she said to herself, 'and can't account for it?'

For the first time since Ned's unreason had bewildered her she saw a glimmering of reasonableness in it.

Ned was apparently walking more aimlessly; there was not so much hammering of his feet on the floor-boards and he stopped more frequently.

Finally she heard him fling himself on the bed, and dragged herself upstairs again to make sure that the gas was turned out.

All was quiet and in darkness.

*The Glass is Shaken*

## I

The sentiment of family reunion that rises in flood over Britain towards the end of every year had always carried John Shand with it, but this year, to his own astonishment, he found himself deliberately surrendering to it long before Christmas. Even in his office he caught himself daydreaming that Lizzie was in Calderwick for Christmas and the New Year. Instead of attending to the papers before him he was conducting Lizzie all over the mill, and she complimented and teased him about the success he had\made of it. She stayed with him in the house at Balfour Terrace; they laughed together at breakfast and were still laughing in the evening. They reminded each other, for instance, how they had climbed over their own garden wall and plundered a pear-tree, leading a band of young brigands into their own territory. And finally had to bury half the pears beneath a mound of ivy leaves, after all, although the six of them had eaten and eaten, throwing away larger and larger cores as their appetites began to fail. Not one of the six was left in Calderwick but himself. . . . On another autumn day they had gathered all the red and yellow leaves they could find because Lizzie swore that she could brew a magic potion out of them. They had brewed it in a silver coffee-pot in the wash-house. She was a little monkey.

He went up one evening to an attic merely to look at an old rocking-chair on which they had once played waves and mermaids, with their legs buttoned into coats and tied up with shawls to resemble fish-tails. The old rocking-chair could still rock valiantly. But Lizzie was – where was she?

Twenty years ago he had torn up her letter and thrown it in the fire. He had sent her a communication through his

33

solicitor, assuring her that an allowance of one hundred and fifty pounds would be paid to her yearly but that her brother wished never to see her again. That allowance had been paid scrupulously, even when he could ill afford it; nobody knew anything about it, not even Mabel. He had insisted on letting Lizzie understand that the money was hers by right, her patrimony, for if she had guessed it was a gift she might have refused it. But she had accepted it. Tom Mitchell sent it to her every quarter. Tom Mitchell must have her address, of course.

He rose from his desk almost in agitation. There was nothing to prevent his writing and inviting Lizzie to come home for Christmas. Nothing, except his own bitter words of twenty years ago, which were vanishing like grains of dust, blown away by the wind of Lizzie's presence in his imagination.

For an irritable moment or two he caught himself regretting that he had a wife and other responsibilities. How could he explain to Mabel and Aunt Janet that he was going to invite Lizzie? It would set tongues wagging in the town, he knew; and for the first time in his life he wished that he was a vagabond. Could he not shake himself free and set off alone? His imagination, however, which was definite and clear when it played around the familiar scenes of Calderwick, faltered in confusion before the uncertainty of such a journey and the faint suggestion of dishonesty surrounding it. For he would have to pretend that he was going away on business.

His conflicting selves tormented him. But the anguish which contracted his heart when the idea occurrred to him that Lizzie might refuse to see him, or refuse to come, overwhelmed his hesitations. He must see her again; that was all. And he must see her in the most honourable manner, without subterfuge. He would invite her home to Calderwick, let gossip say what it liked, and he would write to her in such a way that if she still cared for him she would not refuse.

He shut himself up in his study for several evenings writing and rewriting the letter: *My dear Lizzie. Twenty years ago we were both fools.* . . . That would make her smile; that would make her feel indulgent. But was it not possible that it would only infuriate her? If she had bitterly resented his silence a light and easy attempt to resume their relationship would undoubtedly infuriate her. She might have suffered during these years; she must have suffered; one cannot do wrong with impunity. *My dear, dear Lizzie. Will you ever forgive me?* But that wouldn't do; he had been quite right in his attitude; she must have recognized that. Even now he was braving public opinion in asking her home; and his position in Calderwick was now unimpeachable. How impossible it would have been to bring her back twenty years ago! After all, it was she who had been in the wrong, flagrantly in the wrong.

He wished that he knew at least what kind of woman she had become. A hundred and fifty a year must have kept her from sinking into the very gutter, he thought grimly. That, indeed, was why he had settled it upon her. Still, human nature being what it was, as she had taken one wrong step she might have taken many. A woman of ungoverned passions, nearly forty, a coarse licentious figure, his common sense told him, the female counterpart of their father, and, being a woman, ten times worse than their father, that was what he might reasonably expect to find.

He leaned his head on his hands, shutting his eyes. And once again the delight of Lizzie's presence enveloped him; he could have sworn that she was somewhere in the house, and that they were going to have a vivacious evening together. While his eyes were shut he felt it impossible that Lizzie should have become anything but just Lizzie.

He suddenly realized that her address would be some kind of a clue to her circumstances, and decided to ask Tom Mitchell for the address before writing the letter. This decision somewhat restored his cheerfulness and carried him to the lawyer's office early next day.

Tom Mitchell had never seen the big man so embarrassed. The childlike look in his eyes was more evident than ever. He stood behind the chair offered to him, refusing to sit down, as if he feared to be drawn into explanations. The lawyer, a small rosy-cheeked old man who was a walking graveyard of family secrets, pulled out a drawer.

'Ay, weel,' he said, in an affectedly broad accent, 'it just happens that Miss Lizzie sent me a letter for you some months syne, with positive instructions that it was not to be given to you unless you speired after her. Man, she must have jaloused that you were going to do it. Or else you must have jaloused that the letter was here. There's queerer things happens than that.'

John Shand made a step forward.

'Bide a wee, bide a wee; I'll find it in a minute. Here we are. To John Shand, Esquire.'

He held out a thin bluish envelope, larger than those usually seen in Calderwick. The same handwriting, said John to himself, as he eagerly snatched the letter. Lizzie always printed her capitals instead of writing them.

'When did this come, Tom?' he asked in a casual voice.

'Nineteenth of July.'

'And where is she now?'

'South of France. The address will be inside. Sit down, man, and read it.'

John put the letter in his pocket. As jealous as if it were from his lass, Tom Mitchell remarked to himself. He could feel it there all the way down the street. Dear, dear Lizzie. He had been an unconscionably long time in jalousing the message. Nineteenth of July. And this was the twenty-eighth of November. She might have been in great trouble; it might even be too late now.

He stopped on the pavement, his heart in his mouth, plucked the letter out of the envelope, and read it, standing on the kerb.

'My dear John, – This is to let you know that I am now made an honest woman of – much against my will, but the man is dying and wouldn't take no. It's not Fritz, by the way; I shed Fritz long ago; but it's another German, a friend of mine for years. I am now Frau Doktor Mütze, which is to say Mrs Doctor Bonnet, so you see although I threw my bonnet over the mill it has come back like a boomerang. I don't think he can live for more than a month or so. We did it last week. I can't explain it all now, but I feel that I ought at least to tell you, for I know how much importance you attach to getting married and things like that. But I don't want you to think I'm proud of it. I don't want to tell you either, unless

you are feeling friendly towards me, so I'll instruct Tom
Mitchell accordingly. Anyhow, there it is. Love from Lizzie.
Villa Soleil, Menton.'

John laughed as he crammed the letter back into his
pocket without folding it. Mrs Doctor Bonnet. Love from
Lizzie. The same old sixpence, he said to himself in glee; the
same old sixpence!

In his first exuberance he wrote her the letter of invitation
and gummed down the flap of the envelope before he
rememberd that her new-made husband might be dead by
this time. He checked himself. It was indecent to be so
overjoyed if Lizzie were a widow. Yet he could not feel
grief-stricken; her being a widow was the best thing that
could happen; it would set her free to come home. He tore
up that letter, however, and wrote another. When that was in
its envelope he took it out at the last minute and added as a
postscript: 'Do come.' Then he went out to post it himself.
Before he slid it into the letterbox he looked again at the
superscription, 'Frau Doktor Mütze', and grinned like a
boy.

Now that the letter was posted he realized how much of
himself had gone into it. His heart had not stirred in such
secret delight since Lizzie's disappearance – not even on his
wedding-day. Something hidden very deep seemed to have
come alive again. He felt like whistling, and he had not
whistled for fifteen years, he dared say, yes, fifteen years at
least.

I must have been growing old, thought John. That was
what growing old meant, saving up one's energy, no
whistling or running or jumping. There was a flight of stone
steps leading up to his own front door; he took them in two
strides and paused at the top to reflect that Lizzie would
certainly push him down again if she were there. What were
steps for!

## II

Mabel was feeling pettish. For days John had been mooning
about as if bewitched, shutting himself up all evening and
either looking at her as if she were not there or evading her
irritably whenever he came out of the study. One might as

well be married to a log. It was a pity John was so old.

Their marital relationship had been well regulated during the two years of their marriage. After John's first ardours were over she had escaped his embraces except on Sunday mornings when they lay longer in bed. These Sunday-morning embraces now had the sanction of tradition, and Mabel sometimes wondered if John kept them up because they were a tradition. It was a pity John was so old. A woman so well made as she was should have a husband to match her.

She looked up resentfully from her magazine as John came in.

'Are you going to change?' she asked.

'Won't take me a minute,' said John, balancing himself on his toes before the fire.

He would break it to her after dinner, he was thinking.

'You're growing fat, John. Must do something to take down your tummy.'

'Am I?' John looked down at his waistcoat and fingered his beard. Mabel noted with satisfaction that he seemed dashed.

'Do I look very old, Mabel?' he asked in a surprisingly humble tone. Mabel's possessiveness reasserted itself.

'No, you don't, darling; you look very dignified, but not old. A little less on the tummy would be an improvement, though.'

'I'll do exercises every morning,' decided John. He still lingered, however, and then brought out the question which had been troubling him.

'Should I shave my beard off, Mabel, do you think?'

Mabel was astounded. She had never seen him without a beard.

'I don't know what you'd look like without it!' she cried. 'Oh *no*, darling. It gives you such a distinguished look.'

John went upstairs to change and as he looked in the glass he could hear Lizzie saying: 'Saves you washing your neck, doesn't it?'

He laughed out loud.

If he took off his beard, Mabel was thinking downstairs, I might as well be married to anybody.

She gazed idly at an illustration to the story she was

reading. The hero and heroine were standing clasped in each other's arms, a typical magazine embrace, with the woman swaying backwards and the man masterfully overtopping her. She had a hand on each of his shoulders, pushing him away; when the inevitable kiss came she would enjoy it with a good conscience because of this show of resistance. Mabel's eye lingered on the picture. It came into her mind that the hero's shoulders were like Hector's, and although startled, even shocked, she felt for an infinitesimal space of time that it would be thrilling to stem her hands against Hector's broad shoulders and push him away with all her strength.

During dinner and afterwards John and Mabel were more talkative than usual. Perhaps they were each trying to atone to the other for a secret feeling of guilt. John found it easy, at any rate, to confess all, or nearly all, of what was in his heart. Mabel, apparently, had nothing to confess.

## TWO

On looking at them one could never have told that Hector
and John Shand were half-brothers. John resembled his
Highland mother; with his big frame and his reddish fair
beard he might have been a viking from the Western Isles.
Hector was like the Shands; his wrists and ankles were small
and sinewy, his hands and feet small and beautifully shaped;
he had a swarthy skin, black hair and dark hazel eyes, so
quick in movement and expression that he seemed to be
always on the watch. For his size he had uncommonly broad
shoulders, and whether it was the shoulders or the nervous
hands or the quick, ready eye that endeared him to women
he was, at any rate, extremely attractive to them.

His mother, a delicate, submissive woman, had died
shortly after he was born, and he was brought up by Janet
Shand, who expended upon him in double measure the
affection she felt for his father, sharpened at times to a keen
edge of anxiety lest he should grow up to resemble his father
morally as well as physically. Janet could never rid herself of
the knowledge that the Shand men were sexually unbridled;
even her own brother had given her a queer feeling; she
could not look at him without remembering how often he
was reported to lie with women in the town. It was indeed
difficult to think of anything but bodily appetites when one
met Charlie Shand.

Thus the atmosphere in which Hector Shand grew up was,
one might say, heavily charged with sex between the two
poles of Janet's anxious abhorrence of the subject and
Charlie Shand's open devotion to it. Before the boy was
twelve his father had become so dissolute that he was a
byword in the town. Shamed to the soul, young Hector
found little comfort in the thought of his mother, for his

Aunt Janet always spoke of her with contemptuous pity as of a poor spiritless thing, who was no wife for Charlie. Hector became convinced that his heredity was tainted; he became fatalistic about it; he persuaded himself that John had escaped the curse only because he had a different kind of mother, and he resented his half-brother's robust superiority.

Nor did school help him to escape from his fatalistic preoccupation. Examinations made his stomach queasy with nervousness. Everything that he knew ebbed out of his mind when he was ordered to set it down, and his increasing nervous tension in the ordeal invariably discharged itself in a way which made him miserable and strengthened his sense of inborn guilt. In every bodily activity, in every game he played, he had a lightning correspondence between his body and his brain, but the mere sight of ink and paper was enough to paralyse it. A problem in arithmetic, which, given real bricks, he would have solved, became a torturing muddle of cubic feet; rules of grammar, which unconsciously in speaking he adhered to, changed into malignant mnemonics which he could never retain; and the simple recording of facts, even facts that he knew well, such as how best to guddle for trout, was subject to a mysterious standard of appraisal called 'style' which was never defined, and for which, apparently, he had no natural gift. He took it for granted that books and all that they stood for were beyond his capacity, and sustained himself against humiliation by his prowess in games, and, in later years, by his success with women. He had found nothing else in life.

Every morning on entering the office of John Shand & Sons he felt a faint recurrence of the old nausea. He would add a column of figures five, six or even seven times before assuming that his answer was correct, and even then he convinced himself only by totting the whole up on his fingers.

'Is that how you count, man?' said John, one day. 'That's how they used to do it in the Stone Age.'

'Is there nothing else you can give me to do?' burst out Hector in a rage. 'I can't stick at these damned figures all the time.'

John wheeled round. His manner was curt; he had been

irritable for some days past, for he had not yet solved his own problem with Lizzie.

'I want to see whether you can stick to anything at all once you've begun it,' he said, and went away without waiting for an answer, being in a hurry to get to Tom Mitchell's.

Hector turned white. John always roused him to defiance. John was always expecting him to make a mistake of some kind, and not only expecting it but waiting for a chance to say: 'I thought as much.' By setting his teeth Hector could only just cope with that; here, however, was a new obstacle to overcome, the deadly suggestion that even if he could master anything he lacked steadiness enough to stick to it. It was a deadly suggestion, because in his own experience of himself Hector found nothing to rebut it.

He gritted his teeth, but the figures swam before his gaze. The office window looked into the deep well of the yard, where horses were backing and carts unloading. In spite of the sick distaste he had for the office Hector liked the rest of the mill; even the men who worked in it were better than the clerks, he thought, who were all elderly dried-up machines like John himself.

'Hell and damnation!' He clapped the ledger to. In the outer office he paused and said to the head clerk who peered at him enviously over steel-rimmed spectacles: 'If Mr John asks where I am, Mason, you can tell him I'm taking a turn through the mill.'

He had a child's delight in watching belts whiz and wheels go round. The impalpable flour that floated in the air sifted over his head and shoulders as he lounged from one corner to another, edging his way between piles of full sacks. He liked the smell of the mill, a compound of machine grease and the fragrance of grain; he liked the regular thud thud of the big dynamo which shook the whole building as if a giant were trying to kick the walls out. He watched the fat golden grains of wheat go sliding down the chute in a lazy mass, and turned up his sleeve to plunge his arm among them.

'That's good wheat,' he yelled to the man in charge.

'Mains of Invercalder,' the man yelled back. 'Best wheat in the haill countryside.'

That was Mabel's father's wheat. I should know good wheat when I see it, thought Hector, bitterness overcoming him again. A whole year and a half on that damned Alberta farm. What he didn't know about wheat wasn't worth knowing. Horse-feed, too, he knew something about that.

'Damnation!' he swore again, emerging into the yard. John's last remark was still active. He hadn't been able to stick to farming anyhow. Could he stick to anything?

He nodded to the carters tramping over the mud of the yard with bits of dirty sacking laid over their shoulders. Probably that was the kind of job John thought him fit for. 'Wouldn't that jar you?' he found himself sneering; the Canadian phrase had not occurred to him for a long time. Hell, what a life it had been!

He leaned against a doorway and watched the horses; their haunches were wrinkling, and their great bearded feet were braced against the cobbles. On his farm he had felt something like that, like a brute in blinkers between two shafts. He rememberd his disgust and forlornness at the plough-tail; he had even kicked at the ploughshare with his heavy boots in a senseless frenzy of rage, and sent long imploring letters to Aunt Janet. What maddened him most was the feeling that he had been turned down by the whole lot of them, even by Aunt Janet. And then Aunt Janet had assured him that all was forgotten and forgiven, and on that assurance he had sold up his farm and come home to make good.

It was more than a year since he had come back, but he was still angry when he remembered how John had so high-and-mightily washed his hands of him. It was the affair with Bell Duncan that did it; everybody turned against him when that came out. And what was there in that? The girl was asking for it. Fellows had done much worse than that. His own father had been a damned sight worse. And he was only a boy when the affair began; he was heartily sick of the girl by the time she started slandering him right and left. Glad enough he had been to clear out when they offered him the chance. But in any decent family the whole history of the affair would have been different. As it was, they merely clapped blinkers on him and stuck him between two shafts, the shafts of a plough.

It was a raw afternoon, and to the dull rage he felt was added the discomfort of cold. With an abrupt jerk he turned and marched up to the office again, hurled a ledger on the floor and put on his coat, hat and muffler. Without thinking he then went out through the main gateway facing the dock. It was high tide; the dock-gates were open, and a dirty-looking steamer was warping her way in. A rope came curling on the quay beside him, and was knotted in a trice round an iron post rooted among the worn granite setts that surrounded the little square of deep water. Foreign-looking chaps, thought Hector, as he glanced at the crew leaning over the side, and he strolled away to see where they had come from. *Elsa*. Kjobenhavn. Copenhagen. Strange, clipped syllables were tossed along the deck, and he listened to them with a vague pleasure in the strangeness. Calderwick wasn't the only place on God's earth after all.

He wandered round the dock, peering into the water. One corner, the corner nearest to Dock Street, which led into the heart of the town, always used to be foul with straw and floating rubbish, he remembered, a nasty, stagnant corner which would be damned unpleasant to fall into. It was still as dirty and foul as ever. On a dark night, he reflected, it would be easy to come down to Dock Street and walk right over the edge into that scum. When he was a child that corner had always given him the creeps. He gazed into the murky water. Better to drown in the open sea than in that stagnant muck.

He shivered and turned up his coat collar. Damn it all, he would get even with John yet. There was Elizabeth to back him up. Elizabeth swore that it took a higher kind of courage to come back from Canada than to stick on out there. So he hadn't been a quitter when he left the farm. He had come back with more money than he started with. Nobody could say he was a quitter. Damn it all, if he was an out-and-out rotter Elizabeth would never have married him, and there was precious little about himself he hadn't told her.

Elizabeth made a fellow feel he had some guts in him. He would go home and shake it all off. Elizabeth was a wonder, he thought, striding up the street with the sea-wind behind him. Queer that none of the other chaps had had the nerve to make love to her. Of course, she said herself she was too brotherly for them. But she had fallen for him all right, all right.

At the moment he was filled with passionate gratitude towards her. She was the biggest success he had ever had. She was one of those superior people who understood books, and yet she hadn't turned him down. Far from it. He was the first man she had ever fallen for.

He studied the figure of a girl coming towards him, her head down against the wind. Showed up a girl, that did. Elizabeth was as well made as any of them. God, he was glad to be well out of the time when he couldn't look at a girl without thinking there was only a skirt between him and her. Elizabeth had saved him from that.

Not consciously in words, not even in half-glimpsed images did he recognize Elizabeth as anything like an anchorage or a haven for his storm-driven life, but the feeling which was swelling his heart as he neared home would have engendered such a conception in a more articulate person. He was only aware that he had never felt like that before about any girl. As he fitted his latchkey in the door he was excited because he was to see his wife immediately, and his disappointment was all the more overwhelming when he found the drawing-room empty. The mistress, said Mary Ann, rushing from the kitchen, had left word she was sorry but she had to go out for tea. 'With Mrs Doctor Scrimmager,' added Mary Ann of her own accord; 'at least they gaed out thegither.'

'I'll mak' you a fly cup for yoursel',' she offered.

'No, no, Mary Ann; you'll never get a man if you offer him nothing but tea,' said Hector. 'Tell the mistress if she comes back before me that I'm away to the Club for something better than tea.'

Mary Ann giggled. A heartsome young man, the master, and with a wee spark of the devil in his eye; just what a man should have.

The wee spark of the devil in Hector's eye was occasioned by a curious blend of emotions. Because Elizabeth had gone out he was not only disappointed, he was resentful with the same kind of resentment a child feels when it has hurt itself and its mother does not pick it up. He was also irritated

because it was Mrs Scrymgeour whose company Elizabeth
had preferred to his; he disliked Mrs Scrymgeour and wished
that.his wife were less intimate with the woman. At the same
time he was conscious that he was a man, a swaggering,
independent creature, and he was pleased to have an
excellent excuse for flourishing his masculinity in despite of
Elizabeth. He would go to the Club and have a high old time
with the fellows. He was popular in the Club. He might, in
fact, make a night of it. It would serve Elizabeth right.

On his way to the Golf Club he passed close by the lighted
windows of number seven Balfour Terrace, where Mabel was
sitting alone at tea, turning over the new magazine the
perusal of which was to lead her imagination to startling
conclusions a little later in the evening.

Next day the wind had increased to a storm; the thunder of
the breaking grey sea could be heard in the High Street, and a
relentless rain stung the faces of the goodwives as they
scuttled from one snug shop to another doing their shopping.

Mrs Hector Shand was standing at her drawing-room
window gazing at the low clouds racing behind the few
leafless trees of her garden. The prospect was bleak, but
Elizabeth, being accustomed to unkind weather, was not
depressed. She was planning to take a run on the links, for
when a strong wind blew she could not help taking to her
heels and following it.

But the front-door bell rang, and almost immediately Mary
Ann's voice cried: 'The mistress is in here, Miss Shand.'

Aunt Janet was breathless; she tumbled rather than
walked in, clutching a sodden umbrella and a brown-paper
parcel.

'Oh, my dear!' she exclaimed. 'Oh, my dear!'

'She's heard about it,' said Elizabeth to herself, feeling
trapped.

Aunt Janet was brimming over with solicitude; she had
obviously come to comfort and to exhort, to investigate and
bewail the scandal.

'What a terrible thing!' she cried, endeavouring to seize
Elizabeth's hands at the same time as Elizabeth tried to take
the parcel and umbrella from her. 'What a dreadful thing!
Oh, I'm *so* upset. Where is he?'

'Come and sit by the fire,' said Elizabeth; 'let me get your wet things off.'

'I was sure I should find you in. I said to myself: "The poor child will be mourning her heart out." Is Hector upstairs?'

No, he's gone out to the football match.'

'But, my dear Elizabeth!'

'It's dreadful weather for standing about, I know. *I* shouldn't spend a wet afternoon like that —'

Aunt Janet's visibly increasing distress broke off Elizabeth's sentence.

'That's not what I meant at all – not at all.'

Janet put a hand on the younger woman's knee.

'My dear, how do you know he won't go and get drunk again? Why did you let him go? I heard all about this dreadful affair of last night —'

'How did you hear about it?'

'But, Elizabeth, it's the talk of the town. I heard about it from at least three different sources.'

'Oh, I suppose so. I didn't think.'

'And now you say he's at a *football match*.'

'He won't be tackling people there,' said Elizabeth, laughing. 'And he won't get drunk, Aunt Janet, for he promised me—'

'I was sure of it. I was sure you would lead the poor boy in the right direction.'

'Besides, it wasn't so bad, not so very bad, from what I can make out. They were all rather well on, and Hector was practising Rugger tackles. It was quite an accident that Hutcheon got his collar-bone broken.'

'But, my dear, I heard that young Hutcheon was brought home in a dreadful state, simply covered with mud and blood.'

'Then they must have been scrumming in the street. Still, I'm sure it was only a lark. It's easy to break a man's collar-bone when you pitch him over; I've seen Hector do it before.'

'Hector doesn't know his own strength. Well, my dear, it's a mercy you can take it so calmly; but really, my dear, I am *so* distressed. I was told that they were swearing and blaspheming in the street in the most dreadful manner, wakening people out of their beds.'

Elizabeth repressed a smile.

'I don't believe it'll happen again,' she said. 'Hector's terribly ashamed of himself.'

'It mustn't happen again, Elizabeth. You must do all you can to prevent it.'

'Well, last time I told Hector I would go down to the Club and drag him out by the hair of the head if he did it again, and this time I have threatened to go down and get drunk beside him—'

'But, my dear Elizabeth! I know you're only joking, but really!'

'Why, what else could I do?'

Aunt Janet was genuinely shocked.

'My dear, I don't think you quite realize . . . Hector isn't like other young men who can take a drink or leave it. His father literally died of drink, and Hector is so like him. In every way. Whisky is dangerous for him.

'Aunt Janet,' said Elizabeth, becoming earnest, 'I do know all that. Hector has told me everything about himself.' (Things he wouldn't tell you, she added silently.) 'But surely I'm not a kind of policeman keeping guard over him, am I? He's so ashamed of himself that it wouldn't be fair to take advantage of him and tie him down with promises. I don't want to say to him: "You mustn't do this, or that." Why should I? It was of his own accord he promised me he wouldn't get drunk again; I didn't ask him to promise anything. And that's much the best way, I'm sure.'

Aunt Janet shook her head. 'I hope, my dear, I only hope you're right, but I'm afraid you're not. We all hoped that marriage would settle Hector, but I know John isn't at all pleased with his work, and this is the second time already that Hector has been violently drunk since you were married.'

Is it my fault? thought Elizabeth, her temper rising.

'Hector likes excitement,' she objected. 'Perhaps he needs it. He hasn't been accustomed to office work, and there isn't much excitement to be got in this town. As for me, I can go for long walks and read, but Hector —'

Nonsense! said Janet Shand to herself angrily. She was angry with Hector too, but Elizabeth had no right to be so slack with him. She had no sense of her duties to her husband.

But her anger lessened as she peered at the girl's face. In spite of her casual, cheerful air Elizabeth was looking worn. Aunt Janet recovered herself.

'Well, well, you look as if you hadn't slept,' she said as kindly as she could. 'When did Hector come home, my dear?'

'Not so very late – about one o'clock. But we didn't get to sleep till after five.'

Elizabeth stared into the fire and suddenly smiled, reminiscently, it seemed to the watching old woman. She felt a pang of jealousy. Hector had been used to confess his sins and seek absolution in her lap; but now he was in the power of this strange girl.

'You have a great influence over him, my dear Elizabeth,' she said solemnly. 'You must try to use it properly.'

'He has a great influence over me, Aunt Janet.'

Janet Shand asked the question she had been longing to ask for months:

'Why did you marry him, Elizabeth?'

Elizabeth's blush mounted as usual till her ears were burning. She hated it; she wished she could control her blood.

'Because I was madly in love with him – and I still am, and I shall be always.'

Her answer was almost defiant.

The short winter afternoon was rapidly waning, and Elizabeth still stared into the glow of the fire, the shadows darkening around her. She saw there the glow in her own heart.

'I know what you mean,' she added in an abrupt voice. 'Lots of people have said it to me. I'm supposed to have brains, and Hector has none, not the academic kind, at any rate. I have the knack of passing examinations; Hector hasn't. I like to read all kinds of books; Hector never opens a book if he can help it. What can we have in common, people wonder. That's the superficial point of view. What do these things matter? They're all second-hand. What we read or don't read makes no difference to ourselves. The real *me*,' she struck her bosom, 'is made of the same stuff as Hector —'

She broke off as abruptly as she had begun. She could not explain it to Aunt Janet. They were both wild and passionate; they wanted the whole of life at one draught; they would sink or swim together. Images flowed through her mind: in the air or under the sea or rooted in the earth she saw herself and Hector living, growing, swimming, breasting the wind together. She thought of his wide shoulders, his strong neck, his swift and lovely feet. . . .

'What have brains to do with it?' she asked, looking up. 'It's a miracle, Aunt Janet; a miracle that sometimes takes my breath away. Whatever made him fall in love with me, I often wonder. . . .'

She smiled suddenly, and touched Aunt Janet.

'You can't explain away a miracle, can you? A miracle swept us off our feet, and we got married because we couldn't help it. That's the answer.'

Much of what Elizabeth had refrained from trying to express was none the less transmitted to the old woman on the other side of the fire. She had lived so long on vicarious emotion that it had become her one solace, and she was grateful to Elizabeth for the thrill she now experienced. Her gratitude submerged her resentment.

'I love him, too, Elizabeth,' she said, wiping her eyes. 'But you have the greater influence over him, I am sure. If you would only use it!'

'When you are driven by a strong wind you can't *use* it, Aunt Janet!

'But, my dear Elizabeth —'

A note of helplessness sounded in Aunt Janet's voice.

Elizabeth suddenly felt exasperated. She sprang to her feet.

'You don't believe in us! You don't believe it has any meaning! You're only thinking of the little things, like keeping house and coming home at ten o'clock —'

'But surely you want Hector to get on in the world,' protested Aunt Janet, whose head was whirling. 'I only want the best for both of you.' She was crying.

Elizabeth's emotion transformed itself again.

'My dear, my dear,' she coaxed, kneeling before Aunt Janet, 'don't worry, don't worry. We'll be all right. There's something in both of us.'

She petted the old woman for some minutes. Then, still, kneeling, she went on: 'To tell you the truth, I don't like Hector's getting drunk any more than you do. But I think I understand it. I might do the same myself, if I had been accustomed to it as he has. What good could it do to coerce him? He'd only be angry with me. It would destroy the unity between us. Give us time, that's all. We'll both grow in grace. Don't you see? I feel that so strongly that I know I must be right.'

She went on soothing Janet, who was wiping her eyes again.

They were both startled by the ringing of the front-door bell. It was now almost dark.

'Whoever can that be?' Elizabeth started to her feet.

Mary Ann, mindful of her manners before the minister, ceremoniously announced:

'Mr Murray.'

William Murray came in eagerly, carrying a small book, but hesitated when he found he could barely discern his hostess by the flickering light of the fire.

'Hello!' said Elizabeth. 'I'm afraid we're rather in the dark here. Wait a minute and I'll light the gas.'

'I hope I haveh't disturbed you.' The minister hung back.

'Not a bit,' said Elizabeth, striking matches. 'I'm very glad to see you.'

The gaslight flooded the room with brightness, submerging along with the shadows Elizabeth's glowing sentiments. The minister sat down. Elizabeth looked gay.

'We've been having an argument. Should one coerce other people for their good? Which side do *you* take, Mr Murray?'

The minister smiled because Elizabeth was smiling at him. Mrs Hector stimulated him pleasantly.

'I should need to know something about the circumstances,' he said.

'Oh, Miss Shand says: yes, one should force other people

to do things, and I say: no, one shouldn't. Tell us what you think.'

'Well,' said the minister, 'do you know, I should never *force* anybody in anything. But surely one person can *influence* another? In fact, I think we all influence each other, whether we ought to or not, and perhaps whether we know it or not.'

'Ah, but that's a different thing' and 'That's just what I say' broke simultaneously from Elizabeth and Janet.

'To force ideas or conduct on another,' went on the minister, 'is egoism; but to influence another, if it's done in – in love,' he stumbled over the word, 'is surely the highest altruism?'

'Altruism my hat!' retorted Elizabeth, to Aunt Janet's horror. 'How can it be altruism if we influence other people without knowing it.'

'I should have said rather that we influence other people *more* than we know.'

'Then we can't take much credit for it, can we?'

'Perhaps there's something in that.' The minister was thoughtful. 'We all transmit rays of which we know very little. Or, rather, they are transmitted through us.'

'I agree with you there,' said Elizabeth unexpectedly. 'And that's just why we shouldn't interfere with them.'

'But if there were no interference, if we allowed the unknown influences free play, would you not agree that the world might be flooded with – with love?'

Again the minister stumbled over the word.

'In that case, I should look out for a Noah's Ark.'

Aunt Janet looked from one to the other in bewilderment. Elizabeth laughed.

'I feel contradictious,' she said. 'I think we might dilute our arguments with tea.'

She wondered, with an inward chuckle, as she pulled the old-fashioned handle which jangled a bell in the kitchen, whether the minister too had come to condole. But that wasn't like him, she decided; and in that she did him justice.

Mabel Shand, however, who was then on her way towards number twenty-six High Street, was coming expressly to gloat – which is another form of condolence. She thought

that Hector would certainly be at home, and that she would
have an opportunity to pay off old scores. She promised
herself she would not leave him a leg to stand on.

'Where's Hector?' was her first question when she was
shown in. She was surprised to see the minister; he seemed
to be very chummy with Elizabeth, she noted. Aunt Janet
there too, of course, waiting to enfold the sinner in her
benevolent arms. Elizabeth was almost indecently gay; she
did not seem to care a rap.

'Hector? Oh, he's out at the football match.'

'Is it safe, do you think, to let him go out to football
matches?'

'He won't scrag anybody, if that's what you mean.'

Mabel's dislike of Elizabeth was beginning to be returned.

'But that, it seems, is just what he does do,' murmured
Mabel.

'My husband nearly killed a man last night,' said
Elizabeth gravely addressing the minister. 'At least, that's
what people seem to think. Should I keep him forcibly in the
house to prevent him from committing murder in the high
streets?'

The minister was embarrassed. He recollected that Sarah
had spoken to him of some scandal concerning Hector
Shand. But Mrs Hector, for all her gravity, still had a
twinkle in her eye; she was obviously dangling bait in front
of him. Yet he could not rise to it with the lightheartedness
he had felt before Mrs John Shand came in.

He murmured something about his argument in favour of
influence.

Mabel laughed a little.

Elizabeth turned her back on her sister-in-law.

'I was only teasing,' she said. 'It's not so bad as that. Will
you have some more tea? Is that my Maeterlinck you've
brought back? What do you think of *Wisdom and Destiny*? I
had an idea it would appeal to you.'

'Yes, yes.' His embarrassment still persisted. 'I like some
of it very much.'

He could not discuss the book just then.

The real reason of his embarrassment was that the
presence of any lady member of his congregation reminded

him that he was the minister. In speaking to Elizabeth he quite forgot the minister in the man, an experience so unusual that he found it delightful. But his present constraint brought back his formal vocabulary and he said:

'I really came to ask you to take a stall at the Christmas sale of work, which is run by the ladies of the congregation.'

'What?' said Elizabeth, open-mouthed. 'Me?'

Mabel laughed again. 'You're one of the ladies of the congregation, Elizabeth, although you don't seem to know it.'

'Yes,' said the minister. 'Mrs John Shand is kindly taking over the sweet stall, and I thought – I imagined a gift-book stall would be very suitable for you.'

'That's the very thing for her, Mr Murray,' said Aunt Janet heartily. She was glad to see that Elizabeth's pertness had not offended the minister, and it pleased her to think of Hector's wife taking a dignified place at a church function.

'Oh, Aunt Janet,' interrupted Mabel, 'that reminds me, you'll give me some jam for my stall, won't you?'

Mabel and Janet began a lively exchange of confidences about jam and marzipan sweets, under cover of which Elizabeth said to the minister in a low tone:

'I couldn't possibly do it. I wish you wouldn't ask me. I'm no good at things of that kind.'

William Murray got up to put his teacup on the table, and remained standing beside her. His constraint vanished.

'I wish you would try,' he urged, bending down.

'I don't feel like a lady of the congregation.'

'It's not really in that sense that I ask you to come; it would be a great pleasure to me to have you there.'

The yearly sale of work made him feel nervous and distracted. Elizabeth's presence would in some way be a support to him. 'I'm no good at things of that kind either,' he added, 'and we should help each other out.'

Elizabeth smiled up to him as he bent confidentially nearer to make this confession.

'If you put it like that,' she said.

It was at this moment that Hector Shand, having let himself in, walked into the drawing-room.

In spite of the fresh air with which Calderwick was liberally supplied he did not feel much the better of his afternoon's outing. He was already dissatisfied with himself when he went out to the football match, and neither the weather nor the bad play of the local team had relieved his dissatisfaction.

At the close of play, mindful of his promise to Elizabeth, he had refused the invitation of several friends to 'have one' at the Clubhouse, and as the men of Calderwick were as self-conscious about their drinks as about their women there had been a considerable amount of chaffing when he said with attempted heartiness: 'No, I promised the wife.'

All the way home his grievances harassed him. John had jumped down his throat that morning. Calderwick was a one-horse town where a man couldn't enjoy himself without everybody kicking up a fuss. Damn it all, a fellow had to go on the loose sometimes. A fellow couldn't be mollycoddling about his own fireside all the time. All very well for Elizabeth; she had her books; but it gave him a pain in the neck when he tried to read a book.

His head ached and there was an evil taste on the back of his tongue. As his physical misery increased his dissatisfaction with himself, his sense of failure threatened to overwhelm him completely. The one thing he needed was to lay his head on Elizabeth's bosom, as he had done to his comfort in the small hours of the morning. He hurried on, and almost burst into the drawing-room.

His quick eye at once caught the picture of Elizabeth and the minister smiling intimately to each other, while Aunt Janet and Mabel were talking in a corner. Half of him seemed to rise inside and choke in his throat, while the other half sank clean through the pit of his stomach, leaving him hollow and sick. The figures in the room changed their positions like puppets while he stood there glaring.

The look in his eyes made Mabel forget her intention of teasing him. Better go at once, her social sense warned her. She hastily put on her furs.

'Glad to see you enjoying yourselves,' said Hector at last, removing his eye from Elizabeth but making no attempt to come farther into the room.

Elizabeth felt and looked bewildered.

'We're only having tea,' she said. 'Here's your cup.'

'I'm afraid I must go now,' put in Mabel quickly. 'Good-bye, Elizabeth; good-bye, everybody. It's good-afternoon and good-bye in the same breath to you, Hector, I'm sorry to say.'

Hector had moved his lips once or twice as if swallowing, and he now turned to Mabel with exaggerated *camaraderie*.

'Not a bit of it, Mabel. I only looked in to say I wasn't having any tea. I'll come with you.'

'Why, where are you going, Hector?' cried Elizabeth.

'To the Club,' said Hector, without looking at her. 'So long, Aunt Janet,' he went on. 'See you another time. Sorry I can't stop. Come along, Mabel.'

The door shut upon them. Elizabeth found herself filling a cup with hot water instead of tea.

'Oh, I'm sorry,' she said in a flat voice.

Then she suddenly burst into tears.

'Go away!' she sobbed. 'Go away! Both of you.'

With another sob she rose and rushed out of the room.

To his own amazement the minister's first impulse was to rush out after her. He was literally upset; everything within him felt topsy-turvy. Little enough had been said, but Elizabeth's agitation seemed to him natural and his own not less so. Something evil had struck into the very heart of the room like an invisible thunderbolt and had scattered the peace of all the people in it. Yet he was amazed to find himself involuntarily springing to the door.

Janet Shand caught him by the sleeve. Tears were streaming down her cheeks, but her voice was harsh and angry. 'Let her go!' she said. 'You can't do anything with her. Nobody can do anything with her. She'll be the ruin of him yet.'

William shook his arm free but stood irresolutely shifting his feet while Janet Shand sank into a chair crying: 'My poor boy! My poor, poor boy!'

William Murray could not bear to see anyone in tears; and it was not only because he was a minister that he felt obliged to comfort those in disress. On this occasion, however, his own distress was so immediate and unexpected that his instinctive attempt to comfort the old woman was awkward and perfunctory.

He found himself outside on the pavement with some confused idea in his head that Miss Shand had sent him out to find Hector and bring him back. He started off mechanically with long strides, but the street was so thickly crowded with Saturday-nighters that his impatience drove him into the roadway. He ejaculated irrelevant words as he walked. 'No, no,' he said, and 'Evil, evil.' The rain had stopped, but the storm was not yet spent; high above the blue arc-lamps of the High Street a wild scud of clouds was flying over the waning moon, and, as if driven by the same force, the minister flew along the street below.

Blindly he turned out of the High Street. He wanted to get hold of the man. Had Janet Shand asked him to catch Hector Shand, or had she not? Anything might happen, she had said, with Hector in that mood. His fists clenched and unclenched as they swung. His heart was pounding; little pulses hammered in his eyes. 'Evil, evil.'

In the side-street where he now was, a dark street indifferently lit by gas-lamps that flung yellow rings upon the wet pavement, the minister suddenly came to himself, and leaned against a wall. He was possessed by evil, his body was shaking with anger, his fists were thinking of hitting Hector Shand, of hitting him and hitting him until he crumpled up. The last time he had been so invaded by anger was as a boy of fourteen when he had seized a bully at the school and pounded his head against a window until the window smashed in. His remorse afterwards, and his terror of the murderous fury that had thrilled him, had converted him to that contemplation of the eternal love of God in which he had found serenity. Not until this day had the devil entered into him again.

He walked to and fro between the two gas-lamps, filled with an anguish of shame. He a minister of the Gospel, a servant of Christ! He stood on the edge of the pavement and stared at the wall, a high, well-built wall enclosing a garden. Its regularly cut stones were so smoothly fitted together that there was neither handhold nor foothold all the way up to the top, although the stones were greenish with age. The minister stared at it as if obsessed.

Smooth, blank, and yet frowning, the wall stared back at him. The minister shut his eyes as if the sight of the wall had become intolerable. 'O God,' he prayed, and again, and again: 'O God,' the simple incantation with which the soul seeks to recover a communion it has lost.

When he began to walk again it was at a more sober pace. He had sinned. He had met evil with evil. One should overcome evil with good. One should be sorry for a man like Hector Shand, not murderously angry with him. At any rate, he was in no fit state to pursue the man; he could do nothing spiritually effective; he felt spent.

But young Mrs Hector was sobbing her heart out. He shivered a little as the remembrance of her tears called up the scene again. It was dreadful to live with evil in one's own household. She had in her husband the same kind of problem that he had in Ned. They needed all their strength, both of them. . . . They must help each other. . . . And for her sake something ought to be done at once. Something had to be done if only to relieve the oppression round his own heart. . . . The minister decided to ask John Shand to go himself and fetch his brother home.

'Is Mr Shand in?' he asked the maid, wearily supporting himself by the iron railing. 'Can I see him privately for a few moments?'

The girl hesitated.

'Is it Mr John Shand or Mr Hector?' she said.

'Are they both here?'

'Yes, sir.'

The minister swayed a little.

'Oh, then it doesn't matter; it doesn't matter,' he mumbled, and turned down the steps again.

The sound of a gramophone followed him, as the astonished maid peered after him.

'Losh keep's a'!' she said to herself as she shut the door.

Sarah Murray observed her brother's dejection when he came into the sitting-room, where she was knitting by the fire.

'What's the matter, William? Didn't you see Mrs Hector?'

'Yes.'

'Is she going to take a stall, then?'

'I think so; yes, I believe she will.'

Sarah knitted on in silence. If William wouldn't tell her she wasn't going to ask.

'Supper's nearly ready,' she said finally.

'Was Ned all right at tea-time?' asked William, without lifting his head from his hand.

'Not so bad. That's to say, he never said a word.'

'He *is* better, Sarah, don't you think?'

Sarah scratched her head with a knitting-needle.

'You can't call it a way of living to lie in bed every day till dinner-time and sit up every night till two in the morning and never set a foot across the outside door,' she said sharply. 'The only difference I see is that I've got the upper hand of him now.'

'What makes you think that, Sarah?'

'I've *daured* him,' said Sarah. 'Ever since one night I went into his room and stood up to him. He knows now that I can stand up to him, and we've had less trouble ever since. There's no more word of Teenie giving notice, nor there won't be as long as I'm in the house, and Ned knows it. So I just let him lie in bed in the mornings; it keeps him out of the way. I believe, William, that it's yon breakdown of his he fashes himself about: I think he can't account for it. So I rub that into him between times. . . . It's just pure daftness to put up with him,' she added angrily. 'What kind of a life is it for a laddie of his age? He's just been pampered in this house. But you won't find strangers willing to do that. It might do him good to be living away from us. Except that I don't see what kind of a job he could possibly be any good at.'

'You're wrong there, Sarah; he's a very able fellow, Ned.'

'He is, is he? Pity his ability can't be turned in a more useful direction. . . . I must say I don't think much of intellect,' finished Sarah. 'People who can pass examinations often don't seem to be fit for anything else.'

If that was a furtive fling at Mrs Hector Shand it missed the mark; William seemed not to have heard it.

Sarah collected her knitting and went to see about supper.

Ned came down to supper and sat silently hunched over his plate. William was uncommonly silent too, and Sarah felt a little sulky as she filled the plates and passed them down. She could not help wishing for once that she had a sensible man like John Shand in the house. William was all right, of course; but he was in a queer mood. He had been having queer moods lately. And he was seeing a good deal too much of that young Mrs Hector. What had happened to-night, she wondered.

After supper, as Ned was sliding out of the door, William called: 'Ned!'

Ned paused suspiciously.

'Won't you play me a game of chess!'

'No, I'm busy.'

Ned pulled the door behind him with his usual force but the usual slam did not result, for William had caught hold of it.

'What are you busy at? Mathematics?'

Ned thrust his head in and jerked a thumb at Sarah.

'Needn't think you're going to copy *her*,' he said.

'I was only asking,' said William gently, 'because I'm interested. I know you're a wonder at mathematics.'

'*She* thinks she knows everything,' said Ned, still glaring at Sarah.

But he did not go.

'I'm not doing mathematics; I'm writing a story,' he shot out suddenly.

'A story?' William was pleased.

Sarah shrugged and began to collect the dishes.

'A story,' said Ned emphatically. 'About the world as it should be. Every house in all the towns empty. Nothing but cats and dogs. No *women*.'

His eye was still fixed on Sarah's back as she vanished into the kitchen. Then he looked doubtfully at his brother.

'I'd like to see it,' said William eagerly. 'May I come up?'

'What d'you want to see it for, all of a sudden?'

Ned's face was twisted with suspicion; his eyes had a dull, guarded look.

How thin the poor fellow's getting! thought William, and he put his hand on Ned's shoulder.

'My dear lad,' he said, 'my dear Ned, just because you're my brother.' He let his hand lie, endeavouring to convey his affection through the contact.

Ned shook it off furiously.

'Who do you think I am?' he shouted. 'Jesus Christ?'

He spat venomously in his brother's face and slammed the door.

## THREE

Elizabeth was still lying on her bed when Hector came home. She could see a patch of the night sky through the window. She had long stopped sobbing, and in the centre of the black cloud which encompassed her world a nucleus of calm weather was forming. She stared at the patch of sky; there was enough moonlight to illumine it faintly; clouds seemed to be marching over it to an unheard processional music, punctuated now and then by a star. What a fool she was, she thought. The love between Hector and herself was as enduring as those stars behind the fugitive clouds.

Her heart leapt as she heard him come in. He had not stayed at the Club, then; he had come back to her. She half turned, listening; his feet seemed to be mounting the stairs into her very bosom.

'Elizabeth!' he said, opening the door. His voice was humble. She sat up and held out her arms in the darkness.

'My darling, my darling,' she said.

With inarticulate murmurs they caressed each other. The bliss of relaxation began to steal over Elizabeth, the peace of reunion, but Hector was still clutching her tight and pressing his face against her. She stroked his cheek.

'How could you do it, my love?' she asked.

'I was just mad with jealousy,' said Hector, still clinging. 'Jealous of that damned snivelling sky-pilot. I couldn't help it, Elizabeth; it just came over me, and I felt mad.'

She kissed him on the forehead.

'But you *know*, don't you, that you needn't feel jealous of anybody?'

He shook his head vehemently.

'But you *do* know,' she insisted. 'You're a part of myself. I simply couldn't fall in love with anybody else.'

'I'm always afraid of losing you,' said Hector, his voice muffled in her dress. 'I'm no highbrow; I can't talk about books and things; and some day you'll turn me down. . . . I deserve it,' he went on, lifting his head. 'When I think of all the girls I've turned down I feel that you're going to be my punishment for the lot.'

Elizabeth's spirits were rapidly rising; she shook him a little and said: 'Oh, you silly ass!' Then she kissed him full on the mouth. They lay for some time without speaking.

'All the same,' said Elizabeth at last, 'I'm glad you didn't stay at the Club drinking yourself dottier.'

'I didn't go to the Club,' said Hector, twisting and untwisting a piece of her hair. 'I – you won't forgive me if I tell you, but I must tell you.'

Elizabeth drew away a little. She had forgiven him; she didn't want confessions; she was beginning vaguely to dislike Hector's insistence on lengthy confessions.

'What does it matter?' she said. 'The only thing that matters is *this*.'

'It does matter.' Hector's voice was sombre. 'You don't know what an out-and-out rotter I can be. I went down the back lane with Mabel, and I was feeling so mad, and she was jawing at me about behaving myself better, and I knew what a little bitch she was, and her arm was always coming up against mine, and – well, I just took hold of her and kissed her as hard as I could.'

'What?' said Elizabeth incredulously. 'Mabel? Did she let you?'

'She liked it all right, you bet your life! She pretended she didn't. But I was — Oh, hell, when I'm in that state I *know*, I tell you, and I just knew she was itching for it.'

'Well,' said Elizabeth, 'is that all?'

Her voice was quite cool.

'That's about all,' said Hector.

He was beginning to feel relieved. Elizabeth wasn't going to cut up rough after all.

'I swore I'd paint the town sky-blue scarlet unless she asked me in for a drink, and I gave her a lot of slosh about her influence over me and all that, until she nearly purred. So I went in with her and had a drink, and we danced a bit —'

'Have you been there all this time?'

Hector stopped in surprise at the sudden sharpness of the question.

'It's not so very late,' he said. 'John —'

Elizabeth pushed him away and sat up sobbing:

'That's all you care, is it? That's all you care. You go out leaving me heart-broken, and then you go fooling with Mabel for hours and hours, leaving me – leaving me —'

All the rage and self-pity that had apparently vanished was closing over her again.

'I had to tell you, don't you see?' Hector kept on repeating. 'I *have* to be sure you won't turn me down.'

He felt rather helpless; he had not expected her to be quite so jealous. He said so.

'I'm not jealous!' shrieked Elizabeth. 'It would never come into my head to be jealous of anybody, let alone Mabel. I think jealousy is idiotic. I'm simply *angry*, because you could go out and enjoy yourself after hurting me so much.'

'The hell you are!' Hector began to feel angry too. Damned unreasonable, he thought.

Elizabeth slapped the hand he was trying to caress her with.

He got off the bed.

'I might as well go and get roaring drunk,' he said, making for the door.

Elizabeth sprang after him. 'If you do,' she said, 'I'll come and get drunk too.'

Her threat sounded like mere bravado even to herself. A sense of weakness came over her.

'Don't go,' she said. 'I can't do without you.'

The reconciliation made them very happy. It also blinded them to the real issue between them which had obtruded itself nakedly enough in their quarrel, and as they sat cheek by cheek agreeing together what fools they had been their unanimity was more apparent than real. Elizabeth meant that she had been a fool to be miserable at all, since their love could never die, while Hector meant that he had been a fool to be jealous of a half-man like the minister. Elizabeth was now ready to regard Hector's sojourn with Mabel merely as an attempt to distract himself from his unhappiness, and

Hector was ready to look on Elizabeth's friendliness to the minister as the polite amiability of a hostess; but they did not recognize that in so construing each other's actions they had each left out a good deal of the truth.

'We need a change of some kind,' said Elizabeth finally, after turning over in her mind the various circumstances preceding the outburst. She was glad to lay the blame of it on Calderwick. 'Let's take a day off to-morrow.'

But perhaps it was an obscure sense of some change in herself that prompted her to use these words, for in the small hours she awoke with an anguished feeling that she was lost and no longer knew who she was. She had been dreaming that she was at home, but now the window, faintly perceptible, was in the wrong place, and she knew without seeing it that she would collide with unfamiliar furniture were she to get out of bed. There was sweat on her brow and her heart was thumping; the world stretched out on all sides into dark impersonal nothingness and she herself was a terrifying anonymity. She took refuge in a device of her childhood. I'm me, she thought; me, me; here behind my eyes. Mechanically she moved her arm and crooked her little finger as she had often done before. It's me making the finger move; I am behind my eyes, but I'm in the finger too. . . . But the clue she was striving to grasp still eluded her, and if she could not seize it she would be lost for ever. When she was almost rigid with terror the name 'Elizabeth Ramsay' rose into her mind, and the nightmare vanished. Her body relaxed, but her mind with incredible swiftness rearranged the disordered puzzle of her identity. She was Elizabeth Ramsay but she was also Elizabeth Shand. Hector was there. She put out her hand and gently touched the mass of his body under the coverings on the neighbouring bed.

Elizabeth Ramsay she was, but also Elizabeth Shand, and the more years she traversed the more inalterably would she become Elizabeth Shand. Those years of the future stretched endlessly before her; with that queer lucidity which is seldom found in daytime thinking she could see them as a perspective of fields, each one separated by a fence from its neighbour. Over you go, said a voice, and over she went, then into the next and the next and the next. But this was no longer time or space, it was eternity; there was no end, no goal; perhaps a higher fence marked the boundary betwen life and death, but in the fields beyond it she was still Elizabeth Shand. She was beginning to be terrified again, and opened her eyes. Mrs Shand, she said to herself. It was appalling, and she had never realized it before.

Hector's quiet breathing rose and fell like an almost imperceptible ripple of sound. He was sunk beneath the waves of sleep, she thought, flying as usual from metaphor to metaphor; he was gathered up within himself like a tightly shut bud, remote, solitary, indifferent. He was stripped of everything that made companionship possible; he was now simply himself. You are a part of myself, she had told him, but was that true? When she had first emerged from sleep she had had no consciousness of him. In the ultimate resort she too was simply herself.

She was now wide awake, and she lay staring into the darkness seeing the separateness of all human beings. But as if they had gone round an immense circle her thoughts came back to the question of her own identity. Elizabeth Ramsay she was, but also Elizabeth Shand, and she herself, that essential self which awoke from sleep, had felt lost because she had forgotten that fact.

Elizabeth liked to find significance in facts, but she confused significance with mystery. The more mysterious anything appeared to her the more she was convinced of its significance. The change in her name which she had hitherto lightly accepted now seemed to her of overwhelming importance.

Hector, separate as he is, she argued, would not be sleeping so quietly if he and I were not in harmony. So even in sleep, that last refuge of the separate personality, there must be some communion between us. He rests in me and I in him. In a sense therefore it is true that we are part of each other.

She sat up in bed and bent half over him. He was curled up on his side, facing her, and she could just discern the outline of his cheek beneath the darker hair. A great tenderness towards him flowed through her. She could not live without him. She was not only herself: she was herself-and-Hector.

Their quarrel had ended, she remembered, when she had abandoned her pride and told him she could not do without him. Pride is the stalk, she said to herself, but love is the flower. Give up the old Elizabeth Ramsay, she told herself, emotion sweeping her away, and became Elizabeth Shand.

She lay down again. She must learn to be a wife. Was that what Aunt Janet was driving at?

It was a long time before she fell asleep. But she fell asleep smiling.

## FOUR

On Sunday mornings in Calderwick the streets are hushed; no whistling of baker is heard or monotonous jangling of coal-bell; the very dogs, furtively let out for a run before church time, slink more quietly along the pavements, missing the smells and sounds of weekday traffic. On this Sunday morning both sky and earth were new washed and sparkling after the storm; the air was unseasonably mild, and the people of Calderwick, as they struggled into their Sunday clothes, felt that it was real Sabbath weather.

At a quarter to eleven the church bells began to ring. With an effort one could distinguish the various bells – the four United Free, the Congregational, the Wesleyan, the Baptist, the Roman Catholic and the Episcopal bells – but all were overborne by the peal from the Parish Kirk, which rang out irregularly, gaily and yet commandingly over the town. The Parish Kirk had the only peal of bells in Calderwick, including the great bell whose deep note rang curfew every night at ten o'clock: the single tones of the free-lance churches could not but sound tinny in comparison.

In response to the summons doors opened in every street, and streams of soberly clad people began to converge in the middle of the town, where the river of churchgoers flowed strongly down the High Street, overbearing with ease a small cross-current setting towards the Plymouth Brethren. Like other large rivers it divided again near the end of its journey, and drew off congregation by congregation, leaving the main wash of the flood to spend itself in the spacious dusk of the Parish Kirk.

St James's United Free Church, where Sarah Murray was already at her post in the manse pew, was a small building holding about six hundred souls. It was lined and seated with pine-wood in a cheerful shade of yellow; it had an organ with painted pipes, a canopy of stars shining on a blue sky above the pulpit, and windows filled with lozenges of transparent coloured glass, red, yellow, blue and an occasional purple, which combined into geometrical patterns if one looked at them long enough. High up on the wall immediately facing the pulpit was the large white dial of a clock. It was not true to say of William Murray, as Mary Watson did, that he preached with his eye on the clock, for although he gazed at the clock face he never noticed what hour it registered. He stared at the expressionless white circle because it helped him to forget the rustlings and coughings in the congregation below, and through a kind of self-hypnosis helped to lift him into a transcendental world favourable for sermons.

On this Sunday morning the minister was paler than usual, climbed very slowly up the pulpit steps, and seemed to have taken a vow not to look at his congregation. Once he cast a hasty glance at the Shand pew, then during the hymn he looked steadily again in the same direction; there were only three figures in the pew, however – John Shand, his wife and Miss Janet Shand, in her best toque. But he gave out his text in a firm voice: 'Matthew, chapter five, verse twenty-two: "Whosoever is angry with his brother without a cause shall be in danger of the judgment . . . but whosoever shall say, Thou fool, shall be in danger of hell fire."'

When the rustling of turning pages died down the congregation began to sit up. The way in which he had said 'hell fire' gave them a shock. Mary Watson twisted round to look at the clock, put a cinnamon lozenge into her mouth, and prepared to listen.

Because hell fire was not to be taken literally, said the minister, one dared not assume that it did not exist.

Mary began to nod her head emphatically, and kept on nodding it. This was something like. What had come over Milk-and-water Willie? His een were fair blazing.

'Cut off from the communion of God and cast into outer darkness,' said the minister. There was a desperateness in his voice which thrilled his hearers.

It was a pity that Elizabeth and Hector did not hear that sermon; he was never to preach another so good.

Hector and Elizabeth were escaping on bicycles, pedalling along the upland ridges to the north of Calderwick where wide fields sweep down in bare curves to the sea-cliffs and on the other side thick forests of pine run up to the flanks of the mountains. Rain never lingers on these sandy roads and winter takes little from the austere beauty of the landscape. Elizabeth and Hector tinkled their bells merrily as they ran down a slope towards a foaming brown torrent that was carrying its load of rain to the sea. Elizabeth gazed at Hector's broad shoulders receding in front of her. It pleased her to recognize that he was both stronger and heavier than she was. That helped her to be Mrs Hector Shand.

Next day she was still happy and humble. Her new mood of dedication led her after breakfast to darn Hector's socks 'exactly like a wife', as she said to herself. In the afternoon she avoided Emily Scrymgeour and went down to the sea.

The sand was firm and level; the sand-dunes had been curved by the wind as by a slicing knife into clean, exact curves; the long tawny grass above was matted and tufted like the sodden fell of a weary animal. The land was still and quiet, but the sea had not yet forgotten its rage. There was a deep swell, and the smooth backs of the rollers heaved to an incredible height before toppling and plunging in cataracts of foam. Elizabeth turned her back upon the land and revelled in the recklessness with which the walls of water hurled themselves headlong. Shock after shock of the plunging monsters vibrated through her until she was lashed to an equal excitement and hurled back again the charging passion of the sea. That was the way to live, she cried within herself. Hector and Elizabeth Shand together would transform the world.

Characteristically she did not remember that although she had turned her back on the land it was still there, quiet and unshaken.

After her orgy by the sea Elizabeth felt the need of making a large decisive gesture. She took the longer way home, which led past the manse of St James's, and pulled the bell loudly at the manse door. Teenie dumbly opened the sitting-room door for her and vanished. There was a figure in the dusk beside the window curtain, and Elizabeth, still panting for immediate action, rushed towards it crying:

'Oh, Mr Murray, I've come to apologize. . . .'

Ned stepped forward, and Elizabeth's ears burned. At the same time she felt that Ned's thin white face was pitiful, and her heart nearly died away when he said: 'So I'm not to be kicked in the gutter like a dog and left lying?'

'You?' said Elizabeth. 'No, never.'

They stared at each other.

'I saw you get the Dunlop Medal,' said Elizabeth suddenly, in a breathless voice. 'A lot of us went in to see the Math. show and I saw you get the Dunlop Medal.'

'Of course, I remember you,' said Ned. He waved an arm. 'Please take a chair. What are you doing here?' he went on. 'Got a job?'

'No, I'm not working.'

This answer seemed to please Ned.

'So I'm not the only one,' he said. 'I'm staying here with my brother; he's a minister, you know. I might have been a minister too, but they never let me take Hebrew. . . . There's always something.' He bent forward confidentially and tapped on the table. 'The thing to do is to keep dodging. Keep dodging, for they're cunning. They'll get you if they can —'

The door opened, and Ned's expression changed in a flash. His face, which, as Elizabeth noted with a sinking depression, was essentially handsomer than his brother's, twisted until it became mean and ugly, he contracted his shoulders as if ready to spring and snarled rather than said: 'Good God!'

William Murray came in quietly, as if nothing had happened. He greeted Elizabeth almost with coldness, and sat down. Ned was still glaring at his brother, and Elizabeth's mouth dried up as she looked at him. She could think of nothing to say.

William's voice said politely: 'This has been a lovely day, hasn't it?'

'Glorious,' she answered quickly. 'I've been down to the sea. It was – it was glorious.'

Ned rose and stood at the window with his back to them,

jerking his head round from time to time with an uneasy twist as if his collar irked him.

'When the sun began to set,' Elizabeth babbled on, 'the foam caught all the colour, first rose and then lavender. And the lip of each wave spilled over the sand was opalescent. And just beneath the top that curls over, you know, the light shone pure green through the water.'

Ned turned swiftly.

'Do you know what I saw in the paper this morning – this very morning?'

His voice was harsh. He came back and leaned over the table.

'A butcher found a little stray kitten in his shop and chopped off his front paws and threw it out. A little stray kitten. Chopped its paws off.'

'Oh no!' cried Elizabeth.

'I'll let you see it in the paper.'

Ned began to shake out a newspaper with exaggerated gestures.

'Mrs Shand doesn't want to hear about it,' said William.

Ned stiffened.

'Mrs Shand?' he said. 'Mrs *Shand*? That's not your name.'

'I've married Hector Shand,' said Elizabeth faintly, because even as she said it she felt that it should not be said.

Ned flung down the paper.

'Trickery!' he said. 'I knew it. The same low cunning! But too obvious, madam, too ob-vi-ous.'

He thrust his face into Elizabeth's with a sudden sneer, and then as suddenly marched out of the room with his head in the air, slamming the door.

The minister propped his elbows on the large table and covered his face with his hands.

Before Elizabeth could do anything Ned's head popped in again.

'The worst of the lot,' he said, 'is Hector Shand.'

He slammed the door, and reopened it immediately.

'He'll wait for you at a back door,' he said, 'and stick a knife into you!'

This time he could be heard tramping away from the door and up the stairs.

William Murray had not moved.

'Mr Murray!' said Elizabeth in a low voice sharpened a little with fear. 'Mr Murray!'

The minister removed his hands.

'You're not afraid of him, are you?'

'I shouldn't be, I know. Oh, it's not *him* I'm afraid of; its the state he gets into that frightens me. I mean, that a human being should be able to get into such a state. I thought at first it was pitiful, but it's more than that.'

She was twisting her fingers together.

'How can such a thing happen?' she said. 'What does it *mean*?'

'I am beginning to think,' said the minister with cold precision, looking at his hands, 'that it means hell fire. Ned is in hell.'

'You mustn't say that.' Elizabeth rose to her feet. 'That's what you mustn't say.'

The minister shrank; he looked weary

'What else?' he muttered.

'I don't know what else. . . . But that makes it seem hopeless. There *must* be some way. . . . You can see that he was meant to be different.'

'Did you know him at the University?'

It was Elizabeth's turn to shrink.

'Not exactly,' she stammered. 'I knew about him, of course. He was a nice boy.'

'And now this.' The minister looked up fiercely. 'The love of God has been withdrawn from my brother.'

Elizabeth sat down again. She felt suddenly both assured and eager.

'I'm not religious in the ordinary sense,' she began. 'I don't think I'm a Christian. I don't believe in your heaven and hell. I believe in something that flows through the universe. When I'm in touch with it I know at once; I feel happy; I feel I can do anything. You can call it God if you like. I have just found it again after losing it for months. It can be lost and found. It's not a permanent state like heaven or hell. Your brother has lost it and why should he not find it again?'

The minister covered his face again, and muttered something undistinguishable.

'It's not outside, it's *inside* oneself. And yet it comes suddenly, as if from outside. You must know what I mean, or you would not be a minister.'

William Murray stared at her.

'You are right,' he said. 'I would not be a minister if I did not know it.'

'It's what makes life worth living,' said Elizabeth, her face glowing.

It occurred to her on the way home that she had forgotten to apologize to the minister. The apology, however, no longer mattered. They had gone far beyond that.

## FIVE

On the following Thursday Hector was surprised to find on his office desk a note from Aunt Janet asking him to come in to see her on his way home in the evening. When he saw the envelope he had a vaguely guilty feeling, but even after reading its contents he could not think what was in the wind. Probably nothing much. Perhaps she only wanted to talk over John's extraordinary invitation to Lizzie. Queer old card, John. Hector looked at him with the secret satisfaction he had felt all the week and reiterated to himself: 'I've kissed *your* wife, you old pi-jaw, and that's more than you can say to me!' He wondered for a second or two if Mabel had said anything to Aunt Janet, and even though he was sure that she was not such a fool he had an uneasy conscience when he met his aunt.

'Haven't seen you for a long time,' he said in a loud, affectionate voice. 'Been too busy all week being a good boy. Let me see, yes, Monday, at home canoodling the wife; Tuesday, pills at the Club and *no* drinks – home at ten o'clock; Wednesday, canoodling the wife again, and this is Thursday. See the wings beginning to sprout just where my back tickles?'

Aunt Janet patted him fondly. But he knew his aunt, and he knew that something was bothering her. He sat down and pulled his chair plump in front of her, then, taking her hands in his, he said: 'Cough it up, Mumsie. Anything you don't like about your little Hector?'

The pressure of Aunt Janet's fingers responded as he had expected to the name she liked best to hear him use, and which he never used before others.

'I want to talk to you about Elizabeth, Hector,' she said.

Hector's relief was as great as his astonishment.

'About Elizabeth? What's she been doing?'

'Oh, nothing – nothing that means anything at least. She's a dear girl, Hector, and I know she loves you, but she's just a little thoughtless. Thoughtless, that's all. She doesn't know how people look at things. And Mabel and I have agreed that perhaps a few hints from you would help her more than anything we could say.'

Hector's eyes darkened.

'Mabel's a little cat. I'd like to know what *she* can find to pick on in Elizabeth.'

'Yes, yes, I know, I know. Mabel has her faults, I don't deny it. But she has more *experience* than Elizabeth, dear. In some ways Elizabeth is very young for her age. For instance, at the University slang and student manners are all very well, but they don't do in a place like Calderwick, Hector.'

'Has she been saying damn or something like that?' Hector was grinning.

'It's much more serious than that, my dear. Although that's bad enough. You now what a position the Shands have in the town, and I will say this for Mabel, she keeps up her position wonderfully. But Eizabeth seems to be quite unconscious of it. It appears she has been quite rude to some of Mabel's friends – not unkind, you know, but thoughtlessly rude; and she goes about a great deal with that Mrs Scrymgeour. Mabel and I don't think Mrs Scrymgeour is a good influence for any young woman. Of course, Dr Scrymgeour is a good doctor, and Mrs Scrymgeour goes to church and all that, but the nice people in this town don't think very much of her, and Elizabeth is being tarred with the same brush. Little things, Hector, little things; like running about without gloves and saying damn, and screaming with laughter in the street like a mill-girl – all little things, Hector, but they count for a great deal. Mrs Scrymgeour is not the companion for Elizabeth. She spends all her time gossiping in shops, I hear. Well, Elizabeth's father was a small shopkeeper himself – I don't like to remind you of that, but —'

'Stuff and nonsense! Elizabeth has nothing to do with that. I'm damned lucky to have her for a wife, Aunt Janet.'

'I didn't mean that, Hector. It's so difficult. What I mean is that she doesn't *know*, she has no standards to tell her that gossiping with tradespeople isn't the right thing for a Shand. Not that she's a common girl, at all —'

'See here, Aunt Janet, you're backing the wrong horse. Elizabeth has more brains in her little finger than Mabel ever will have in her whole body.'

'But that's just why she needs guidance, Hector. If she weren't a very unusual girl it wouldn't matter so much. It's just because she doesn't think of the little things that somebody must do it for her. And it's not only Mrs Scrymgeour. . . . The town is beginning to talk about the way she's been going about with Mr Murray. Every day this week, Hector.'

'The town has a damned impudence!' Hector scowled.

'She's told me all about that,' he went on. 'The sky-pilot's in trouble, and Elizabeth is doing her best for him and his measly brother. I don't say they're worth it, but that's no reason for blackballing Elizabeth.'

'I know, I know; but then people are *like* that.'

Aunt Janet saw she would have to produce her trump card after all.

'And with my own eyes, Hector, I saw something I hoped I wouldn't have to mention. There was a meeting on Wednesday afternoon about the sale of work, which is on the 20th you know, and I saw Elizabeth sitting so close to Mr Murray at one point that one of her feet was between his. I know that others saw it too.'

Hector no longer grinned; he laughed, perhaps too loudly.

'Sure you weren't seeing double, Mumsie? Was it only tea you had at the meeting.'

'My dear Hector, you don't need to tell me that Elizabeth didn't intend it: I am sure she didn't even notice it. And that's just the point. She must be taught to notice these things.'

Aunt Janet was in her most earnest mood, but she failed to get a serious reply from her nephew. When he suggested chaining up Elizabeth with a padlock during his absence if John would do the same for Mabel she began to grow angry.

'These things may not matter very much among men, although I should have thought that no decent man would like to see his wife making a fool of herself, but they matter very much among women.'

Women be damned, thought Hector.

He was perturbed, both by Janet's disapproval of his wife and by her indignation. Her anger always made him feel uncomfortable, but when it was visited on his own head he could allay the storm by a confession and penitence which finally brought absolution. Her anger with Elizabeth merely confused him; he did not know what to do.

'What's more,' added Aunt Janet, 'this ridiculous idea of John's is going to bring Lizzie here, and Elizabeth will be exposed to *her* influence next. If you don't put Elizabeth on her guard – you don't know Lizzie, of course, but I do.'

Aunt Janet's shake of the head relegated Lizzie to unmentionable depths.

Hector, like all the other men of his acquaintance, accepted unthinkingly the suggestion that women were the guardians of decorum – good women, that is to say, women who could not be referred to as 'skirts'. Good women existed to keep in check men's sensual passions. A man, driven by physical desire, they argued, is mad and reckless, and his sole protection from himself is the decorum of women. They believed that any decent man would afterwards be grateful to a woman who had prevented him from seducing her. It is possible that 'the weaker sex' – a phrase constantly on their lips and in their minds – was an accusation against women for not being entirely exempt from frailty. At any rate, Lizzie Shand used to tell her friends that in Scotland man's chief end was to glorify God and woman's to see that he did it.

Hector's emotions, therefore, as he listened to Aunt Janet's strictures on Elizabeth's want of decorum were disquieting and profound. He felt much as the driver of a high-powered locomotive would feel on being assured at the top of a steep decline that his brakes were defective. His business was to drive the engine; the brakes were Elizabeth's concern, not his; but if she could not do her duty as a woman he would leave the rails and wreck himself fatally.

Hector Shand was not extraordinarily stupid. This apparently logical division of duties between the sexes seemed natural even to clever men in bigger towns than

Calderwick. Still more surprisingly it was accepted with pride by accomplished women, who devoted all their ingenuity to putting on the brakes as frequently and as smoothly as possible.

Because Hector's confusion was painful to himself, and because he felt that women knew their own affairs best, he repeated with increasing energy 'Women be damned!' as he made his way home. He had been struck, too, by Mumsie's reference to the approaching arrival of Lizzie. What could have come over John? He supposed that, after all, John had not wholly escaped the herditary weaknesses of the Shands, and that his weakness was coming out in queer spots, the old hypocrite!

But Elizabeth was so happy to see him that he began to feel resentful of Aunt Janet's insinuations. Elizabeth was all right.

'Been to see Aunt Janet,' he said carelessly. 'She's in an awful stew because Lizzie's coming.'

'Oh, Hector, I'm looking forward so much to seeing Lizzie!'

'Whatever for?'

'She sounds exciting. Besides, just think of meeting another Elizabeth Shand! Elizabeth Shand by birth and Elizabeth Shand by marriage – it gives me the queerest feeling. It's like seeing yourself in a mirror for the first time.'

'By God, I hope not! According to Aunt Janet, Lizzie's a worse Shand than I am. Aunt Janet hates her like poison. A sneering, godless bitch, that's what she is. Probably drinks like a fish. I shouldn't wonder. Lying about in the streets of Monte Carlo most likely and damned glad to come here for a decent meal. I wouldn't have believed it of John. Aunt Janet thinks he must have sent her money to come with. I wonder what his little game is?'

'You just swallow whatever Aunt Janet says. I don't believe a word of it. My opinion of John has gone up ever since he asked her.'

'I don't swallow everything Aunt Janet says. What have I been doing this last hour but contradicting her to her face?'

Elizabeth was amused.

'Have you been sticking up for yourself?'

'No, I've been sticking up for you.'

'For *me*?'

'It's all that little wretch Mabel,' said Hector hastily. 'She's been spinning yarns to Aunt Janet about you. I told her they were yarns.'

'What yarns, Hector?'

'Oh, yarns about you letting Mabel's dignity down in Calderwick.'

'I like that! Mabel!' Elizabeth's tone was scornful enough.

'And Aunt Janet was begging me to save you from the Scrymgeour female.'

'Oh, I know all about that,' said Elizabeth, her nose in the air. 'Mabel's set are always trying to have a dig at Emily Scrymgeour. I even heard Mrs Melville calling Emily vulgar because she nods and smiles to her own maid when she meets her in the street. And I said in a loud voice that I'd stop and pull my Mary Ann by the tail if she were to pass me without seeing me. They didn't like that.'

She added with a laugh: 'I'm glad you kissed Mabel. It makes me feel more equal to her.'

'Kiss her every day in the week to please you,' offered Hector.

Elizabeth settled herself on his knee and pulled his hair.

'I'm being a good wife this week, am I not?'

'A peach of a wife, I don't think! What about your scandalous goings-on with the sky-pilot? Aunt Janet was telling me about that too.'

'Why, what on earth could she have to tell?'

As lightly as possible Hector retailed the incident reported by Aunt Janet, exaggerating his aunt's horror. Its effect on his wife was not at all what he had expected.

Elizabeth was more of a prude than either of them realized. She had freed herself only partially from the prevailing suggestion that sex was shameful. If in the beginning she had not enjoyed Hector's first kiss so much that she was convinced of her great love for him she would have been ashamed to remember it. She had never been accustomed either to give or to receive caresses, and it was only with Hector, her lover and her husband, that she could feel unashamed of her body.

But because she set love above marriage she thought herself broadminded, and other people, including Hector, accepted her at her own valuation.

She was flaming with rage and shame.

'But Aunt Janet *knows* me!' she repeated. 'How could she ever think of such a thing?'

Hector followed her about.

'I told her it was all rot,' he kept saying.

'But that she should *think* it, Hector. What can one do with people who have such dirty minds. And she *knows* me; it isn't as if she didn't *know* me.'

That was the sore point for Elizabeth. She began to think that she must be vulgar without realizing it if other people could believe such things of her. Vulgarity was a word she despised, but it had the fascination of mystery. It made her feel woolly-headed, she used to say, because it was so meaningless. Did she lack something, she now asked herself, that everybody else possessed? Had she a blind spot?

With a fresh access of shame she remembered how less than a week ago she had opened her heart to Aunt Janet. Surely, she told herself, surely anybody who wasn't an utter fool would have realized then what kind of a woman Elizabeth Shand was. If one were to be misunderstood like that the only thing to do was to keep oneself to oneself. It was she who had been the fool to trust Aunt Janet so much.

She felt inclined to avoid everybody except Emily Scrymgeour. As for the minister – she had said already all she could say to him: one could not go on repeating oneself interminably.

'They can all go to the devil!' said Elizabeth to Hector. 'The Murrays too, for all I care. And I'm damned if ever I'll attend another Ladies' Work Party!'

The intensity of his wife's resentment assured Hector more than ever that Elizabeth was right. She wouldn't let him down.

## SIX

Mabel was feeling restless. Calderwick was a dull little hole, she reflected, as she stood at the window playing with the cord of the blind. There had been rain all morning, and the roadway was full of irregularly shaped puddles through which there bumped an occasional tradesman's van. Drops of rain were still starring the puddles from time to time, and the laurustinus behind the railings was dripping. The room behind her was dark in spite of a fire, but it was too early to switch on the lights, and at any rate she was bored to death with the room. She had read the last magazine; she knew by heart all the bits of music on the piano; she was fed up with the gramophone; it was too wet to play golf, and nobody was likely to call. Apparently the only thing that attracted her interest was the acorn-shaped wooden bob at the end of the blind cord.

Mabel was not the kind of woman to escape from her boredom by considering it as an objective phenomenon. Is it a peculiarly human affliction? she might have asked herself. Are cats ever bored? Would a child be bored if its parents left it alone on a desert island? None of these questions occurred to Mabel. It did not strike her that boredom was a remarkable state in a world full of things to smell, to touch, to taste, to listen to, and to think about. She assumed – and she may have been right – that the laurustinus was as bored as she was, and that the patient grass in the park opposite was bored by the rain.

She did not even wonder why she was bored. She knew. John, her husband, was too dull and elderly for her. He went to the office every day; he came home for meals; he went to church on Sundays; he kissed her every morning and every night; he gave her money when she asked for it. He wouldn't dance; even the records he liked to hear on the gramophone were boring things without a decent tune; he wasn't interested in her friends, and, in general, he was just a bore. Mabel let go the acorn bob so that it hit the window-pane with a sharp rap.

The only person he was really interested in, she thought, was his precious sister. And he was getting grumpy because he hadn't heard yet whether she was coming or not. But if Lizzie Shand were in the south of France why on earth should she come to Calderwick in the middle of winter? Mabel had seen posters advertising the south of France, and as she gazed out of the window she noted that Calderwick was colourless – grey skies, grey pavements, grey people. She herself would become grey in the course of time. Sarah Murray, she thought with a flash of spitefulness and horror, was grey already, inside if not out, although she was only a little over thirty. Mabel looked down at the silken sleeve of her rose-coloured gown. Then she walked deliberately up to her bedroom, turned on the lights and drew the curtains.

Nearly an hour later she was standing with all the frocks she possessed scattered around her, hanging over chairs, and lying on the bed. Her hair was a little ruffled; her cheeks were glowing. She had tried the frocks on, every one, but she had now come to the last of them, and she did not know what to do next. She was no longer bored, however; she was pleased by her own prettiness, and with renewed self-confidence she began to approve of herself in other aspects also. For instance, she had conscientiously done her best for Hector.

Any other woman might have led him on after that sudden kiss in the back lane; it was nearly a whole week ago, but she still remembered the thrill that ran down her spine when he kissed her. A heartless woman would have made a fool of him; a prig would have told her husband; but she, Mabel, had magnanimously used her power over him to keep him out of temptation. Nor had she told Aunt Janet of her favourite's lapse; she had instead urged on Aunt Janet the necessity of making Elizabeth into a better wife for Hector. She and Janet between them, she had suggested, could turn Elizabeth into more of a lady and less of a vulgar lump. Hector should be grateful. Why not pay a call at number twenty-six, just to show Elizabeth that bygones were bygones? She hadn't seen either of them since that last Saturday. It was nearly half-past four now; Hector would be at home by five; they would all have tea together.

The last shreds of her boredom vanished into the wardrobe with her frocks. John could have tea by himself. She was going on an errand of mercy, as it were, and even wifely duty had to give way to larger issues, had it not? She put on her pearls.

The acorn bob hung listlessly at the window of the empty drawing-room.

Both Mr and Mrs Hector Shand were at home when Mabel was shown in. Elizabeth was coldly polite, but Mabel had expected that.

'Got up to kill, aren't you?' said Hector, almost savagely. She laid her coat over his arm almost as if she were laying herself, he thought, and seizing her hat he brutally clapped it on his own head. The plume of cock's feathers streamed out behind his ear.

'All I want are a few kiss-curls,' he said, his eyes glittering as he looked at Mabel, 'and then I could play the peacock as well as any of you women.'

Mabel gave a little scream of concern.

'You'll ruin my hat, Hector! Take it off.'

'You deserve to have it ruined.' Hector twirled the hat on his hand.

Elizabeth was still cold.

'Put Mabel's things on the sofa,' she said. 'And ring the bell for another cup, please.'

Hector sniffed loudly as he sat down again.

'Been drenching yourself with some kind of stink, haven't you? All the street-walkers do that. I thought you were a respectable married woman?'

He had reverted to his old habit of baiting Mabel, but he was doing it with more venom than before, thought Elizabeth. She began to think he was going too far in his merciless criticism of Mabel's clothes, voice, manner, and conventional standards. Mabel was showing more and more resentment. No wonder.

Mabel too was aware that there was a new undertone in

Hector's railing. It annoyed her, but it fluttered her with an excitement that was quite pleasurable. At any rate, Hector did not bore her as John did. . . . She was conscious of her own lithe figure under the rosy silk of her dress, and of her long, well-shaped legs.

'By the Lord!' said Hector, 'I'll have to thread pink ribbons through my pants, or something. If respectable married women can doll themselves up like that, I don't see why respectable married men shouldn't put up something of a show.'

Elizabeth smiled, but she was not amused by the duel.

Their voices got sharper and sharper. Mabel finally shed all her dignity and put out her tongue: and the more hoydenish she became the more quiet and detached was Elizabeth's attitude.

When Mabel rose to go Hector growled:

'I suppose you expect me to take you home in all this rain?'

'You forget, Hector, we're dining with the Scrymgeours to-night: there's no time to spare,' put in Elizabeth.

'Thank God for that,' said Hector. 'The *Scrymgeours*, Mabel, your particular friends, did you notice? We're having dinner with them.'

'You were awfully rude to her,' said Elizabeth, trying to laugh, when Mabel had departed, cock's feathers and all.

'She went off in a huff all right,' Hector's voice was complacent. 'She deserved every bit of it after the things she said about you to Aunt Janet.'

Mabel was annoyed at first as she picked her steps in the dark wet streets. It wouldn't have taken Hector a quarter of an hour to escort her. He was deteriorating. Aunt Janet was right in thinking that Elizabeth would be the ruin of him. Dining with the Scrymgeours were they? Indeed!

She was still smarting from the lash of his tongue. But, incomprehensibly, Hector's rudeness was less offensive than Elizabeth's stupid attempts to palliate it. A phrase from one of her magazines came into her mind as she noted the rustling of her own petticoats: 'the delicious *frou-frou* of femininity'. Elizabeth had none of that, not a particle of it. She perceived suddenly that Hector had been gibing at her femininity in order to save Elizabeth's face.

He's beginning to feel that Elizabeth is a great lump, she said to herself.

She felt younger, more alive, and, on reflection, pleased with the openness of Hector's tactics. He was hard and aggressive; she liked men to be hard and aggressive. She preferred people to be successful rather than sentimental. He was an unscrupulous brute, of course; but she had the whip-hand of him, no doubt of that. John would turn him out of the mill at a word from her. His boldness in the circumstances was not unpleasing.

'Well, little woman?' said John, beaming upon her and showing his strong teeth. 'Where have you been to in all this rain?'

John's contentment was soon explained. He had received by the evening mail a letter from his sister, who was coming on the thirteenth.

'Next Saturday,' said John, rubbing his hands. 'Thirteen was always Lizzie's lucky number, she used to say.'

Mabel curled her lip as she went upstairs. John was growing positively soft.

'I'm so tired,' he had said, yawning and stretching his arms. 'I'll be glad when the week's over and it's Sunday morning again.'

Thank goodness, thought Mabel, it's only Friday night.

Elizabeth was puzzled by the fact that she had felt like a wet blanket during Mabel's visit. She had actually discovered herself feeling outraged by the childishness of the other two, and she had never before regarded herself as definitely grown-up. Was this a part of the process of becoming a wife?

Surely I'm not going to turn into a walking Morality, she thought impatiently. I don't like disapprovers. But if she refused to disapprove, she could not deny that she was disquieted. In Hector's rudeness to Mabel there was something that she did not like.

'I don't know what came over you,' she said to him. 'You made me quite uncomfortable. Suppose I had been going on at John like that, how would you have felt?'

'Grand! I'd have backed you up for all I was worth.'

Elizabeth had to laugh.

'I dislike Mabel too much to chaff her,' she said. 'I suppose that's it. It was really comical how ladylike I felt!'

The Scrymgeours rarely gave dinners, partly because Dr Scrymgeour liked to be left alone at his own fireside and partly because his practice was so extensive that his presence at home could not be guaranteed. But Emily was longing to show off her husband to her new friend, and Elizabeth was now so intimate with Emily Scrymgeour that she felt almost a proprietary interest in the doctor. She was, in fact, identifying a part of herself with Emily, exactly as she had identified a part of herself with Hector. In consequence she thought it absurd of Hector to say he did not like Mrs Scrymgeour; he would like her well enough when he got to know her.

The doctor's wife was a small neatly made woman with large vivacious eyes of so dark a grey that they looked black. Her abundant black hair was glossy, her skin of a smooth pallor which remained impervious to the climatic effects of Calderwick, her quick hands short-fingered, nervous and capable. Her tongue was as quick as her hands, but she had a warm voice and the confiding manner of a child, although she was a good ten years older than Elizabeth.

She had comforted Elizabeth by assuring her that most of the other women in the town were dreadful sticks who hadn't two ideas among them.

'And they're all so frightfully pi,' said Mrs Scrymgeour, 'not like you and me.'

It was a relief to pour into Mrs Scrymgeour's ready ear a confession of inability to be interested in such topics as the winter underwear of husbands and how to keep darns from being scratchy. Mrs Scrymgeour agreed too that whist drives were awfully boring.

'I go to some of them, of course – good for my husband's practice. But they're glad when I stay away, if you know what I mean. I'm such a good player, and it sounds a dreadful thing to say, but most of them are terribly greedy for the prizes.'

Mrs Scrymgeour's method of rearing her child was sniffed at, it appeared, by the Calderwick ladies. She was suckling it herself.

'They think that's so vulgar,' she confided to Elizabeth.

It was also considered undignified for a doctor's lady to push her own perambulator, and no argument could have more effectively secured Elizabeth's constant attendance.

Her friend's manner in shops filled Elizabeth with envy. She had a special crony behind every counter on whom she lavished her bright smiles and who was rewarded for extra attentiveness by confidential gossip. Portly grocers carrying reserved baskets of large eggs came out in their aprons to admire the baby while Elizabeth held the perambulator, and even Mary Watson smiled, although she nodded her head vigorously and said: 'That bairn o' yours is far owre spoilt.'

The care bestowed on the upbringing of young Teddy surprised and fascinated Elizabeth. The doctor, it appeared, was always firing off new theories about the child's development, and these his wife retailed to Elizabeth with great vivacity. She was proud of her husband, and had a fine sense of showmanship.

'But he never screams!' Elizabeth had remarked one day. She had had a vague idea that babies screamed incessantly.

'Oh, doesn't he! He screams for his milk all right. You should hear him.'

'But he never screams while he's out,' persisted Elizabeth.

'Why should he? His little tummy's happy, and he trusts the whole world – even Mary Watson.'

'Da-da,' said the baby.

Mrs Scrymgeour remembered the doctor's latest discovery and expounded it. The baby was saying da-da at present because his teeth were beginning to push through, and his attention kept returning to that part of his mouth. Before that he said ba-ba and boo-boo because his attention was concentrated on putting his lips together, on sucking; and still earlier he said goo-goo, and gay-gay, and gi-gi.

Mrs Scrymgeour bent over to her baby with each new sound and the baby chuckled as if at a great joke.

'And he said that because he was attending to swallowing his milk, guggling it down, which must have been about the first thing he had to learn,' she concluded in triumph. 'Isn't he a nut, my Jim?'

To see a pattern suddenly emerge in life where no pattern was discernible before is one of the keenest of human pleasures, and Elizabeth was thrilled by this orderly explanation of a baby's random sounds. But Mrs Scrymgeour had not finished. She chuckled like her baby and glanced sideways at Elizabeth, saying: 'Of course, it wasn't only swallowing he had to learn in the beginning. When you take in food you have to let it out at the other end, too: and so Teddy used to attend to both ends; he used to grunt at both ends simultaneously.'

Their laughter rang out in the street and even passers-by smiled.

'And Jim swears that the only thing which keeps us from speaking with our tails as well as with our mouths is insuff – insufficient apparatus.'

They both held on to the perambulator, weak with laughter. The baby joined in.

It was simple and pleasant laughter, but Mrs John Shand had not thought so. She had wrinkled her pretty nose in disgust as she saw her sister-in-law making a spectacle of herself with the Scrymgeour woman, and crossed the street to avoid meeting them.

A vulgar creature, she said to herself. It would not be long till Hector's eyes were opened, for, in spite of his faults, he was, after all, a gentleman.

Elizabeth, however, had no misgivings as Hector sat down beside her vivacious friend. She turned expectantly to Dr Scrymgeour.

The doctor looked tall beside his wife, but small beside Hector. He had the slightly explosive manner of the shy man who is daily forced to overcome his shyness. His head was broad rather than long, with a wide forehead that was the first thing one noticed about him. Its width was accentuated by the parting in the middle of the fair hair above it, and it made the rest of his face at first sight insignificant. But his blue eyes were keen, Elizabeth discovered, and his lips, although thin, were beautifully cut. In repose they lay folded upon each other like the lips of a child, she thought.

The promise of that wide forehead attracted her, for she was naïve enought to believe in foreheads as an index to intelligence. She did not think it necessary to stumble over preliminary nothings, for Emily, with her delightful directness, had introduced her husband with these words: 'You can tell Elizabeth the worst, James. I've given you away completely already.' Yet the doctor evaded her with generalizations when she asked him point-blank for some more of his theories about the upbringing of children. His smile was nervous, it even verged on a giggle: he had false teeth, too, and although she tried to be tolerant Elizabeth disliked false teeth.

She felt balked.

Her identification with Emily made her feel humiliated as well as balked. If he tells Emily why shouldn't he tell me? she thought, and the only possible answer seemed to be that he did not consider her to be sufficiently intelligent. Perhaps he was afraid she would be shocked. For the first time it occurred to Elizabeth that a capacity for being shocked argued a lack of intelligence. This new idea excited her, as new ideas always did, and she turned to the doctor, with an imitation of his wife's most arch manner, crying: 'I believe you are afraid of shocking me, but you know it's only stupid people who are ever shocked! Besides I know all about Teddy speaking at both ends—'

The corners of the doctor's mouth went up.

'Emily's too fond of that story,' he said.

'What story?' called Mrs Scrymgeour across the table.

Elizabeth answered her and Emily laughed heartily. Elizabeth glanced at Hector to share her enjoyment with him. To her surprise he looked almost sulky. He shot one glance at her which she could not interpret and crumbled his bread.

'Teddy is illuminating a great many phrases and attitudes for me,' went on the doctor. He began to giggle again.

'Why do the ministers speak of the "milk of the Word"?'

'Do tell me.'

'Watch any baby sucking,' said the doctor with glee, 'and you'll see it.'

'Oh do tell me!'

'When Teddy sucks he puts all his energy into it—'

'Hear, hear!' from Mrs Scrymgeour.

'And that makes him clench his fists and bend his arms in

and draw up his knees. Now the flexion of the arms brings the fists close together. Turn him up endways in that position and he would be kneeling in prayer. Sucking the milk of the Word. There you have it. Isn't it illuminating?'

'What a *lovely* idea!' Elizabeth forgot all about Hector. 'Drawing comfort from Heaven like a child at the breast.'

'There's the Milky Way up in the sky too,' added the doctor. 'The first god must have been a mother-god. Yes, yes.'

He was fingering his wine-glass.

'Bottle-feeding,' he fired out suddenly, with another giggle, 'will probably mean the end of religion.'

'James!' said Mrs Scrymgeour in delight. 'That's a new one!'

'Well, your bottle-fed baby sees the milk going down in the bottle until there's none left, and he knows that it's empty. He can't have the same emotional satisfaction as a child sucking at the breast, which is an apparently inexhaustible source of comfort. Communion with nature, you know, and all that. Your bottle boy isn't likely to grow up a mystic.'

'I shall put Teddy on a bottle to-morrow,' declared Emily.

'I wish I had some proof . . . statistics of bottle-fed infants. . . .'

The doctor shook his head in comical rue.

'Nobody draws up the kind of statistics I want. But if religion knew its business the Pope would issue a Bull forbidding feeding-bottles. On the other hand, you would have the rationalists financing feeding-bottles.'

He broke off, chuckling, and drank his wine.

Mrs Scrymgeour was radiant. Her husband was going through his paces very well, and Elizabeth looked as if she were enjoying herself. The doctor relinquished his wine-glass and applied himself to a highly decorative sweet which Elizabeth was privately attempting to analyse and deciding to acquire from Emily's book of recipes. Mrs Scrymgeour turned the full broadside of her charms upon Hector.

But although Elizabeth was stimulated by the doctor's remarks and preoccupied with the sweet, she was at the same time trying to ignore a certain uneasiness in her spirit. There was something in what had just been said that threatened danger to her inner life.

'Don't you believe in religion, then?' she asked.

The doctor seemed embarrassed again. . . . Apparently he did not like serious questions.

'Er–er a childish way of comforting oneself, don't you think?'

'But how can one live without it?'

Elizabeth was genuinely shocked at last, and since something she valued was in danger she did not stop to reflect upon stupidity and intelligence.

'Oh, well, one does, doesn't one?'

'I don't mean conventional religion, going to church, and that kind of thing. I mean precisely that capacity to draw comfort from the universe, that mystical communion you were speaking of. Don't you believe in that?'

'Er–no,' said the doctor.

He looked at Elizabeth, then he looked away.

'I believe many people feel such a communion,' he added, 'but it isn't what they think it is.'

'But if I don't believe what I feel,' burst out Elizabeth, 'what *am* I to believe?'

Dr Scrymgeour carefully spooned up the last of his sweet and said nothing.

'You take all the poetry out of life,' murmured Elizabeth.

The doctor brightened and laid down his spoon:

'I haven't a grain of poetry in me.'

Elizabeth stared at him, and saw again that his lips were cut like the petals of a flower. Her blank horror was invaded by a secret sense of superiority. He did not understand himself.

'Perhaps you have more poetry in you than you guess,' she returned, smiling, and for the rest of the evening she refrained from lapsing into seriousness.

'Well,' said Emily, whirling round upon her when she went upstairs for her wraps, 'well, what do you think of my husband?'

'I think he's a darling.'

'Isn't he clever?' said Emily, with satisfied triumph. She then handed Elizabeth a compliment: 'He's a shy creature, you know, and he doesn't usually trot out his pet ideas before company. He must have liked you.'

'Do you know,' said Elizabeth, flattered, 'he has such a lovely mouth that I couldn't keep my eyes off it.'

'Better not tell Mr Shand.'

It occurred to Elizabeth that she ought to return the lead and ask for a verdict on Hector, but Emily had already screwed down the gas. Elizabeth obediently went downstairs.

But when Hector was fumbling with the latch-key at their own door she was appalled to hear him say: 'Thank God, that's over!'

'What's the matter, Hector?' she called, pursuing him into the drawing-room, where he was striking matches. She thought that he was jealous, perhaps, and perhaps even a little excited with wine.

'I can't stand that woman,' retorted Hector, pitching his coat on a chair and unwinding his muffler. His nose was very high and haughty.

Elizabeth's eyes widened.

'She was very nice to you.'

'Nice to me! Huh! Expects every man she meets to eat out of her hand, doesn't she? Bloody bitch, that's what she is. Thinks everybody's going to fall for her. She makes me sick.'

Hector stuck his pipe between his teeth and reached for the tobacco-jar.

'But heaps of people like her.'

'You bet your boots they don't,' said Hector through his clenched teeth as he stuffed his pipe.

'Oh, nonsense, Hector; I know they do.'

'She only tells you they do. I tell you she would turn any decent fellow *sick*.'

'I can't see what's the matter with her.'

'The matter with her,' said Hector between puffs, 'is that she's all my eye. I'd like to smack her skinny little bottom good and hard.'

Elizabeth burst out laughing.

'Is that all you have against Emily, that she's too skinny for your taste?'

'No!' said Hector, with unexpected ferocity.

Elizabeth, however, went on laughing. Fresh from a new environment she had not yet accommodated herself to the familiar room and all that it connoted. At the moment she was not a wife.

'Oh, Hector, didn't you once tell me you couldn't look at a woman without thinking of going to bed with her? It's not really Emily's fault if you think she's too skinny.'

'If you must have it,' said Hector, rising and standing on the hearthrug; 'I don't think she's the kind of woman you should associate with.'

'Indeed!' Elizabeth sobered all at once. 'And why?'

'Look at the kind of talk she hands out. Tells me her baby's first sense of beauty comes from feeling her breasts. Feeling her breasts, she tells me! Might as well ask me to feel her bubs and be done with it. And her husband's no better.'

'Do you mean to tell me that you were shocked?'

'I should damn well think I was.'

'You've said many worse things to me.'

'Not before other people.'

'And you've done many worse things.'

'Damn it all, haven't I been sorry for them? What's that got to do with it?'

Hector too was defending something he valued that he felt to be in danger. He was particularly indignant that it should be threatened by a woman, since women were its natural defenders.

'You're a stupid fool!' cried Elizabeth, her eyes hard.

'Go on.' Hector was grim. 'Go on. Spit it all out.'

Elizabeth remembered her wifehood. She went up to him and locked her hands round his unyielding arm.

'Don't you see, Hector, don't you see, darling, that it's simply stupid to be shocked at things?'

'I may be stupid, but I don't see. I'm only thinking of you,' he went on less grimly. 'I don't want my wife to be an easy mark for other people to sneer at, and that's what will happen to you if you get into that woman's habits.'

Elizabeth unloosed her hands.

'The Scrymgeours are the only intelligent people I've met in Calderwick. I intend to go on being friendly with them.'

'Intelligent be damned! Don't come with that highbrow stuff to me.'

'I'm not going to stultify myself, not even for you. You can do what you like about it.'

'So that's that,' said Hector in a stifled voice. He did not know the meaning of the word that Elizabeth had brought out with such a grand air, and his ignorance made him savage.

'That,' responded Elizabeth, 'is that.'

She felt such a cold ferocity in herself that she was frightened. This was like none of their previous quarrels. There were tears in her eyes as she walked upstairs, but they were tears of mortified pride, not of wounded love. How dared he dictate to her what she was to think? Stupid, sulky fool. He was as bad as Aunt Janet. She grew hot again as she remembered how near she had been to asking Emily: 'And what do you think of *my* husband?'

Disjointed sentences started up in her mind. She walked about the bedroom saying, 'Oh, my God.' Then she flung herself on the bed and stared dry-eyed at the wall. She was terrified at herself. 'If I don't believe what I feel what *am* I to believe?' she had said to Dr Scrymgeour. And at the present moment what she felt was that she didn't give a damn for Hector.

Hector poured himself a glass of whisky and gulped it down. As he found himself biting on his pipe-stem so fiercely that he was afraid he would break it he emptied out his pipe and lit a cigarette. . . . The cigarettes and the glasses of whisky went on in an uninterrupted chain.

So that was that. She despised him for a stupid fool. Now he knew where he stood. Nothing more to expect.

Using words he didn't understand, by God! And all he asked for was a little decency.

Hard lines on a poor devil who was only trying to do the right thing. Trusting to his precious wife to help him not to make a bloody mess of his life and she turns round and sneers at him.

What the hell was the use of trying?

As the whisky diminished in the decanter Hector more and more savagely shook himself free from the entanglements he felt irritating him. His love for Elizabeth was one; it only put him in the power of a woman who despised him. His love for Aunt Janet was another; it only related him to a code of prohibitions which he could not observe unaided. Elizabeth and Aunt Janet stood on either side of him demanding what he did not have, for he had neither intellectual freedom nor moral constancy. His slighted vanity, his wounded love, and his morbid feeling of insufficiency filled him with pain and dull rage, and he turned that rage upon the two human beings who stood nearest to him.

Damn all women, he said to himself as he emptied the decanter. He had come to no other conclusion: he was very drunk and intensely miserable.

When he finally stumbled upstairs in his stockinged feet a reek of whisky came with him. Elizabeth was undressed and lying in her bed with her face to the wall. She was very rigid, but he was too drunk to suspect that she was awake. She could hear him disentangling himself from his trousers; he was obviously attempting to make no noise. Suddenly she did not know whether to laugh or cry. His physical presence had thawed that terrifying ice about her heart. Almost palpably she felt her love for him joining them together again. . . . Hector put out the light and crawled groaning into bed. Elizabeth turned round and stretched out a hand in the darkness as if across a gulf that could still be bridged.

Her hand touched him lightly. He shook it off, growling: 'Leave a fellow alone, can't you?'

She turned her face to the wall again and wept quietly, while Hector dreamed that he was dead, lying on a bier in a place that looked like a church, and that Elizabeth and Aunt Janet in deep mourning walked up the aisle to look at his body.

## SEVEN

Saturday was Mary Watson's busiest day. Coats hadn't been going so well this winter as they should have done, but at last they were beginning to sell, and she was kept hard at it running upstairs to the mantle showroom.

'I'm fair run off my feet,' she complained, slumping on to a stool covered with black American cloth. 'That Mrs McLean is just like the side o' a hoose; there's not a coat in the whole of my stock that'll meet across her, and I've had every single outsize off the hangers. I'm fair worn out.'

Her first assistant made no comment. She got on very well with Mary chiefly because she was taciturn.

'There's Jeanie come back,' she said after a while, as the door opened with a rattle and a stumble of feet came down the steps.

'Ay,' said Mary dryly, 'Jeanie's a handless and footless creature. She'll come a clite on her head one of these days. . . . Is all the messages done? Has she ta'en Miss Reid's trimmings yet?'

'No' yet.'

'Jeanie, you've to take this down to Miss Reid the dressmaker. And on the way back ye'll speir at the manse for Mr Murray, and say that Miss Watson would like to see him at once. At once, mind ye.'

Mary allowed herself a few minutes more on her stool. She was indeed weary. But the chief cause of her weariness she was keeping to herself. No need to make a scandal in the town, although the scandal was bound to come unless a miracle happened, she thought bitterly. Well, she would try the minister first.

Jeanie's scared little voice piped its message at the manse door. When she stumbled down the shop steps again she elbowed through a throng of customers and hovered uneasily at the back until she could rid herself of the answer.

'Miss Murray said to say the minister was writin' his sermon and she couldna disturb him, but he would come as soon as she got at him.'

'Tchuk, tchuk,' said Mary.

Writing his sermon on a Saturday afternoon! When he had the whole week to do it in! She was indignant.

When, nearly an hour later, William Murray diffidently appeared Mary was more than tart.

'It's to be hoped the Lord answers prayer quicker than his ministers,' she said. 'I might have been dead by this time for all you kenned. But I've noticed that folk that hasna muckle to do take the whole week to do it in.'

The minister inquired what service he could render.

'I canna tell you here,' said Mary. 'Come into the storeroom. Na, ye're that late it's just on tea-time: I'll walk hame wi' ye mysel'.'

'Has anything happened to your sister?'

'You may weel ask, you that hasna been to see her for months and months.'

A ready answer, a bit of fencing, would have refreshed Mary, but the minister was in no condition to give battle. Since that terrible evening when Ned had spat in his face he had indeed driven the devil out of himself, but the house of his spirit although swept and garnished was still empty. God had forsaken him. Prayer had been unavailing; the sky was merely indifferent sky; he himself was nothing but a vessel of clay, a wretched body of flesh and blood that felt both night and morning as if it had swallowed an enormous cold grey stone.

This oppression in the region of your solar plexus, somebody might have told him, is only a derangement of your sympathetic or your parasympathetic nervous system, my dear fellow. You have had some emotional shock, that's all. It is a salutary experience if you face it frankly. Revise your hypotheses. Some of them must have been wrong, for the world is exactly the same as it was.

It is doubtful whether that would have comforted William Murray. Like Elizabeth, and, incidentally, like his

brother, he believed in the last resort only what he felt. But
the interpretation he had put on his own feelings for so many
years had lulled him into such security, had flooded his
world with so much sunshine, that he was unfitted to discard
it. Ask a man who has been capsized in a cold sea, apparently
miles from land, to believe that he never had a boat and that
he must have swum out there in a trance, and the task will
not be less difficult than that of persuading William Murray
that his personal assurance of God's support had been for
nearly twenty years a delusion. Your swimmer will believe in
the non-existence of a boat only if he awakens to discover, for
instance, that he is not swimming, but really flying in the air,
or pushing through a crowd; nothing less than the shock of a
similar transposition, an awakening into a different kind of
consciousness, could revise William Murray's conception of
God.

As they walked through the darkening streets Mary told
him her tale. It appeared that on Friday, the day before, she
and Ann had quarrelled. They were aye quarrelling, that was
nothing unusual, but this time Ann had taken some notion
into her head and had locked the house, snibbed the windows, and refused to let Mary in at night. Mary had trailed
back to the shop and slept in the mantle showroom, and
cleared it up so that the lassies suspected nothing when they
came at eight next morning. She had made an excuse to slip
out for a bite or two in the forenoon, and she had eaten a
dinner at the nearest baker's. But this was Saturday night;
she couldna sleep in the shop and bide there all Sunday; and
would the minister do something with Ann? 'She can hear
you fine through the keyhole. I gave her some fleas in her
lug, I can tell you. But not a word to anybody, Mr Murray; I
dinna want this to be the clash of the town. I dinna want to
have the door forced.'

'But surely,' said the minister (people who defend an
indefensible position always begin with 'surely'), 'surely
Miss Ann didn't do it deliberately? She may be lying helpless.'

'Preserve us a'!' said Mary slowly, nearly stopping.
'You've kent my sister Ann for twa years and yet you say
that! You're a bigger fool than I took you for. . . . Dinna

mind my tongue,' she went on quickly, 'I canna help laying
it about me. But Ann! She's been a hard and cantankerous
woman all her life, Mr Murray. The de'il kens who would
have put up with her the way I've done. She plagued my
mother to death when the poor woman was lying bedridden;
mother didna dare to move a finger in her bed or Ann was at
her like a wild cat for ravelling the bedclothes. She was the
same when she was a lassie. . . . Many's the skelp across the
face I've had from her, the ill-gettit wretch. Father widna
have her in the shop; he said she would ruin his business in a
week with her tantrums, and yet she was better to him than
to anybody. And since father died she's led me the life of a
dog, Mr Murray. I sometimes dinna ken how I've managed
to keep going.'

It may have been the darkness of the small streets and the
impersonality of a silent and only half-visible companion
that encouraged Mary to be so confidential. She had never
told so much about herself to anybody. Depressed as he was
William Murray could not help feeling vaguely that after all
there was much to be said for Mary Watson, and that the
goodwill he liked to postulate in everybody was not lacking
in her, but only hidden away. His mind was not clear enough
to let him perceive that her aggressive attitude towards the
world was a kind of self-defence, but he was sorry for her.

'I've aye tried to be respectable,' said Mary. 'I've done my
duty; nobody can say I havena done my duty. But this last
carry-on of Ann's fairly crowns a'. This is the first time I've
had to ask help from a single living being, Mr Murray.'

William Murray was touched by this confession. It did not
occur to him that Mary so fiercely resented the necessity of
asking help that she might not be grateful afterwards to the
helper.

'We all need help sometimes,' he said, to himself as much
as to her. Perhaps in turning to God he had turned his back
too much on his fellow-men. God must be present in all His
creatures. . . . In Mary Watson, for instance, in Ann
Watson . . . even when He gave no sign of His presence,
even when the soul felt empty and forlorn. . . .

It was only one's consciousness of God that was intermit-
tent. . . . Elizabeth Shand has said something like that. . . .

His mind kept returning to Elizabeth Shand, as if warming its numbed faculties at a fire. He had not seen her for some days: he hoped she would be in church to-morrow. God was not a mere person, she had insisted, not a limited creature with fits of bad temper who sulkily withdrew Himself from His children; the fault is in us, she had repeated, if we feel ourselves cut off from God, and that alone should keep a man from falling into despair, since faults can be discovered and corrected. That was one-half of what she had pressed so urgently upon him: it was the half from which he drew some comfort. The other half of her argument was a doctrine he would not admit, that God existed not in another world, but in this very material one. 'We shan't discover God anywhere if not in ourselves,' she had said. 'I don't believe in your separation of the body from the spirit. I can't think of my spirit without feeling that it's even in my little finger.'

No, no. William Murray knew that the body and the passions of the body could darken the vision of the spirit. In itself the body was nothing but darkness. That was what oppressed him so much.

'We all need help,' he repeated to Mary Watson, becoming aware that she had stopped speaking and was expecting an answer.

'Tits, man,' she retorted, 'you said that before. That'll no' get Ann to open the door to us.'

'I'm sorry,' said the minister. 'I was thinking of – I was thinking, Miss Mary – that—'

'What you are going to say to Ann?' demanded Mary.

The minister did not know what he was going to say to Ann. He had a confused hope that God would put the right words into his mouth.

'As I was saying,' said Mary, with marked emphasis, 'it's no' so easy to get her oot; I just canna bring the police, even if I wanted a scandal, for the hoose is hers, no' mine. The shop's mine, but the hoose is hers. She hasna a penny piece besides what I give her, but the hoose is hers. Father willed it like that. And what she wants is to make a scandal; just that, just that. She's waiting girning behind that door for me to break it open, and then she'll have the police on to me; I ken it fine. Brawly that. Ay sirs!'

'Surely she's not counting on that. . . .'

Mary snorted and turned up the lane towards the cottage. The nearer she got to the gate the more she ceased to believe that the minister would be of any use at all.

'It's the fear of God you have to put into her, mind you that,' she said, opening the gate and preceding him along the garden path.

The cottage was in darkness save for a feeble light shining through the blind of the kitchen window.

'She's in her bed,' said Mary in a loud whisper. 'That's the light from her bedroom shining through the kitchen. Chap at the front door as hard as you can.'

She pushed him past her, and stealthily pried at the lighted window.

'It's snibbed,' she whispered. 'A' the windows are snibbed. Chap at the door, man, I'm telling you.'

In the mirk of that winter night William Murray, as he rapped firmly with the cold iron knocker on the door of the little cottage, felt incongruously that he was making a last trial of his faith. It was not in a great arena that he was to be proved worthy or unworthy, not even in a despairing battle for his own brother's soul, it was in knocking at a door trying to persuade one bitter old woman to give shelter to another. The cottage itself reminded him of the text with which he had been wrestling all the week: 'But if thine eye be evil, thy whole body shall be full of darkness.' The kitchen window was a dim and evil eye; the cottage was, like himself, a body full of darkness. He rapped once more, and remembered again how Ned had spat in his face. A shrill scream followed his rapping, which he recognized although it was intercepted by the door, and he could make out slow and shuffling footsteps. Ann was not helpless, then: she was able to walk.

'Cry through the keyhole,' urged Mary, but the minister remained upright and silent as the footsteps became more audible.

There was a sound as of unlocking, and a scream: 'Wha's there?'

He nearly jumped: the voice came not from behind the

door but from the kitchen window to his right. Ann had
stopped there, unsnibbed the window and opened it a little
from the top. He could see her dark outline.

'It's me, Miss Ann: Mr Murray.'

'What were you wanting?'

'I want to talk to you.' The minister's voice was gentle,
but firm.

'Come back the morn then: I'm no' wanting anybody the
night.' The window shut with a bang.

'Eh, the obstinate wretch,' muttered Mary. 'Try her
again; chap on the window; go on, man; go on.'

The minister walked to the window and rapped on it. Ann
was barely discernible inside. His sympathy for her welled
up again.

'She shouldn't be shut up all alone like this,' he muttered,
and rapped more insistently than before.

Ann came closer to the window and peered through the
glass as if she were spying into the darkness behind his
shoulder. For a fleeting second William Murray thought of a
human soul in captivity, peering into the unknown through
the dim glass of its conciousness: Ann's situtation was too
like his own not to disturb his emotions. He rapped harder
still, crying: 'Let me in.' Standing there in the loose soil of
the garden bed he felt an infinite pity for both of the sisters
and for himself.

Ann suddenly undid the window and thrust out her head.
Although her face was only a few inches from his she
screamed at the highest pitch of her voice: 'Come back the
morn, I tell you! I have to keep the hoose lockit – for a
purpose. I'm no' safe from my sister Mary if I open that door.'

Her remarks, like her glances, were fired into the
darkness behind him.

William Murray put up a hand and held the window down.

'Come, come, Miss Ann,' he said coaxingly, 'that's not
the kind of woman you really are. I know you better than
that.'

Ann seemed not to hear a word. She had no desire to
appear a saint, she merely wished to prove her sister a devil;
and she suddenly cut clean across the minister's cajoleries by
screaming: 'I see you! I see you, you jaud! Come oot frae

ahint the minister! Ye needna think I dinna see you. I'll let
the whole toon ken hoo you've treated me, so that I have to
lock myself up in my very hoose to be safe from you!'

'Nonsense, Miss Ann! No, no – you'll just injure yourself—'

The minister's voice was drowned by Mary's energetic
reply:

'Lock yersel' in then. Bide there. Not a penny piece will I
give you—'

'I'll let the whole toon ken it, then. On Monday I'll awa'
into the poorshoose, and what'll you have to say to that?
Better to live in the poorshoose by myself than to live wi'
*you*. Mary Watson's old sister in the poorshoose! They'll ken
you then for what you are, my leddy.'

Mary was tired, disappointed and angry.

'Ye cunning auld deevil,' she retorted, 'I'll set the police
on you, that's what I'll do. It'll be the police office and no'
the poorshoose for you, and that this very night, as sure as
my name's Mary Watson.'

'This is my hoose. The police canna take a body up for
locking her ain hoose door. Na, they canna!'

'They can take a woman up for keeping what's no hers.
You've a' my gear in there, and my fur coat and my —'

Ann had disappeared with a thin satirical chuckle. Mary
darted to the window and began to throw it up.

'You're a fushionless fool o' a creature, are ye no'?' she
said to the minister. 'Ye might at least help me through the
window.'

Before William Murray could move Mary was thrust back
by some large soft object which fell on the ground. Rapidly
after it came a succession of things, scattering in the
darkness.

'My fur coat, ye deevil!' he heard Mary cry, half sobbing,
and then he saw her clutching Ann by the hair and shaking
the older woman to and fro over the window-sill. Ann began
to scream. Instead of desisting for fear of scandal Mary
tugged the more furiously; she was as if transported out of
herself. The minister at first felt almost suffocated at the
sight of the two women worrying each other, and then the
inert mass in his bosom seemed to burst into flame.

'You call yourselves Christians,' he found himself crying, as he held Mary at arm's-length. 'I'll cut you both off from the communion of the Church – both of you, do you hear? I'll blot your names from the Church books. I'll expel you publicly from the congregation!'

He almost flung Mary away from the window.

'Open that door at once, Ann Watson,' he continued, 'or I shall proclaim you from the pulpit to-morrow.'

His own vehemence amazed him, even while he exulted in it. This time his anger gave him no sense of sin: it was like a clean flame burning up dross, and like a devouring flame it swept the two women before it.

Ann groaned as she shuffled to the door, but the key grated in the lock, and the minister stalked in.

'Let us have a light,' he said.

Ann's fingers were shaking, but the minister avoided looking at her.

'Go and put on a wrap,' he said, 'while I bring in your sister.'

Mary was sitting on the ground where he had left her. She was crying. She had not cried since the day of her father's funeral.

'Go inside,' said the minister coldly. 'I'll pick up your things.'

He groped in the flower-bed, which was now faintly illuminated by the paraffin lamp in the kitchen. A fur coat, a hat with hard jet ornaments, two black kid gloves, a flannel nightgown and, gleaming in the dark soil, a large gold watch with the glass smashed he collected one by one, shook the damp earth from them and took them into the cottage.

Mary was sitting at the table, her head supported on her hands. She had unpinned her hat. He noted that Ann was in her bedroom and that Mary had stopped crying. For the first time in his life he felt scornful of tears: his old susceptibility was gone. He noted simply that she had at least stopped crying.

'Get me a Bible,' he said, in the same cold, authoritative tone, laying his armful on the table.

Mary looked up and saw the watch.

'It's broken! Father's watch, and she's broken it! Fifteen

years I've had that watch —'

He silenced her. What were fifteen years compared to eternity?

The minister picked up the watch, and when Ann reluctantly appeared, in an ancient dressing-gown, he made it the text of his sermon.

On earth, he told them, what is broken can be repaired, but although mended it can never be unflawed again. A moment, a second, suffices to smash for ever what has for years been intact. How much more irrevocable is a break in one's relations with God! What is done can never be undone, never; even repentance cannot undo it. . . . The least of our actions is of eternal significance. . . .

The more he berated them the more they felt involuntarily drawn together. His insistence that they were both equally wicked exacerbated but united them. It was the threat of expulsion from the Church that had cowed them, and they now submitted to his exhortations from fear rather than from conviction.

Mary was the first to fidget.

'I have to get back to my shop, Mr Murray.'

'Your shop! You should be thinking of your immortal soul.'

'My shop canna wait.' The ban was lifting from Mary. Her immortal soul could wait till the morn, she was thinking, but Saturday was Saturday and *not* Sunday.

Ann exchanged a look with her sister, a look which said plainly: Get him out of here.

'I'll mak' you a cup o' tea before you go to the shop,' she offered.

'Aweel,' said Mary, rising, 'we've had it out, now, and I dinna think we'll flee at each other again for a while, Mr Murray. If Ann has ony mair o' her tantrums I'll let you ken.'

'Me! It's no' *me* has the tantrums—'

The minister rose quickly, clapped on his hat and marched out into the night without another word.

Half frightened the two sisters looked at each other.

'Na, he'll no',' said Ann abruptly. 'He's no' like us. It winna last.'

She hobbled to the fire and drew the simmering kettle on

to the middle of the range. In response to this generous action Mary cleared her things off the table, merely compressing her lips as she looked at the condition they were in, and shaking them out ostentatiously before taking them into her room. A tacit truce was thus concluded.

Common sense had triumphed over rage and tears.

We're queer folk, reflected Mary, as she went slowly back to her shop. Queer, dour folk, the Watsons.

That evening had brought her closer to her sister Ann. She actually felt the better for it.

The minister also was feeling the better for it. Although he had departed in impatience the heavy oppression which had weighed so long on his bosom had discharged itself like a gun with the flash and explosion of his attack on the two sisters. As if he had finally vaulted an obstacle he had balked at for years, William Murray was exhilarated and wondered at his previous foolishness. It now seemed to him that he had been faint-hearted all his life. He had made himself spiritually sick by evading the fact that God's anger was as real as God's love. The old ecstatic serenity was gone, but in its place he felt a tense determination to fight the battle of the Church. Instead of spreading himself anonymously into the universe, as if he were a quiet wave lapping into infinity, he recognized himself now as an individual with a definite place in the world; he was a minister, backed by that authority and prestige of the Church which, for the first time in his life, he had invoked, and invoked successfully. His appeal to the Church had been involuntary, almost unconscious; its very spontaneity convinced him that it had been prompted by God Himself.

Anger was at times good and necessary, he said to himself, as he walked home buoyantly. It was weakness to be too sympathetic. In his sick state he had sympathized too much with everybody: for instance, he had sympathized with both Mary and Ann Watson, first with one and then with the other, and yet they were both in the wrong – not to be sympathized with at all. Christ had driven the money-changers out of the Temple, and had spoken to devils as one having authority. That was the right way with those possessed of a devil.

He remembered suddenly how Sarah had said about Ned: 'I've *daured* him.' She was right. One could not create light without dispelling darkness. For years he had shut his eyes to the fact of evil; but now he had heard the word of God, and he would deal faithfully with evil wherever he found it. He had awakened out of his sleep. 'Wherever I find it,' he said, opening his own front door.

The wall in front of William Murray was no longer smooth, without handhold or foothold, no longer blank. It now had both lights and shadows on its surface. He could climb it.

## EIGHT

When Elizabeth Shand awoke in the morning Hector was still asleep. He was facing her as he lay, but his head was half-buried in the pillow and little of him was visible save his tumbled hair and closed eyes. The terrible sensation Elizabeth had of having dropped down a bottomless chasm began gradually to fade before the reassuring familiarity of Hector asleep in the next bed. She could not see his face, but she knew that his body was the same body it had always been; behind those closed lids the same Hector must exist. If once she had been daunted by the aloofness of her sleeping husband she was now comforted by it. Asleep, he was still her sweetheart, unchanged by the conflicting storms of yesterday, sunk into the most profound part of himself, which, of course, was the essential Hector, the Hector who loved her and whom she loved. Their quarrel of the night before seemed irrelevant as she lay looking at him. She remembered how she had told the minister that she could not believe in the separation of the spirit from the body; and now she thought that it was when most completely sunk in the body, as in sleep, that the spirit was most itself.

Quietly she crept out of her own bed and crawled in beside Hector. Let him awaken to find her close to him, she thought. Surely there was some current of invisible force which flowed in an unbroken circuit around them as they lay motionless together, a healing current, she thought, which would bear away all their differences. She felt his eyelashes stir on her cheek, and pressed him to her in a passion of tenderness.

If Hector was surprised to be awakened in this fashion he did not show it. He rubbed his cheek on hers and kissed her tenderly enough. Even the reek of stale whisky did not annoy Elizabeth; she was both exalted and contrite, and she dismissed all scruples as unworthy. But Hector had a fiendish headache, a rotten headache; that damned whisky couldn't have been good stuff. Elizabeth got up and fetched him two aspirins in a glass of water.

'You're much too good to me, Elizabeth.'

Did this protest mean that Hector felt himself fettered by his obligations to her? She did not stop to wonder.

Her mood, persisting until next day, which was Sunday, inclined her towards going to church, and she was a little surprised and touched by Hector's ready acquiescence.

Whenever they went to church they sat in the Shand pew, and after the morning service all the Shands strolled home with Aunt Janet, and returned by way of Balfour Terrace, where John and Mabel took their leave and Elizabeth and Hector, waving good-byes, went back to the High Street alone.

John, being the senior Shand, sat at the outside end of the pew; Hector was next to him, then Elizabeth, Aunt Janet and Mabel. Elizabeth found it possible to smile on both the other women, but unconsciously, after the first silent greeting, she edged towards Hector and away from Aunt Janet. She found herself also regretting that she had cut off her intercourse with the minister merely because of Aunt Janet's scandalmongering, and she waited eagerly to catch his eye and send him a message of reassurance.

The minister walked up to the pulpit with his usual solemnity, with even more than his usual dignity. His glance crossed Elizabeth's once, but his blue eye flashed such a cold strange gleam that she felt snubbed. Perhaps he resented the way she had dropped him?

She forgot this personal question in her amazed disapproval of the sermon. She could not know that William Murray had sat up until far into the morning reshaping that sermon to fit his spiritual rebirth into the Church. Where was his sympathy, his tolerance? she asked herself. The man was thundering theology from the pulpit; splitting hairs, logic-chopping. Far above the heads of his congregation, anyhow, thought Elizabeth scornfully, looking round at the vacant or sleepy faces. He was now proving to them that the existence of good connoted the existence of evil; this world was a world of both good and evil, unlike the Kingdom of God, which, when it came, would be neither good nor evil, but equally beyond both, transcending both. Meanwhile, because on earth we had intuitions of good, we must admit also intuitions of evil.

'The metaphor of darkness, like all metaphors, misleads our childish minds,' said the minister. (Was that meant for her? thought Elizabeth.) 'We fold our hands passively and wait for the sun to dispel the darkness of evil, when we should be fighting it, driving it away, casting it out, as Christ cast out devils.'

In her mind's eye Elizabeth suddenly saw Ned's distorted face, and her heart grew heavy with a feeling of doom.

'The Church, as the visible body of Christ,' preached the minister, 'is an alliance against the powerful forces of evil. Alone, we cannot fight evil; it is too strong for the individual; we all need help in the struggle, and so we are banded together to form a Church. Who is not for us must be against us. . . .'

Elizabeth, more and more confounded, leaned forward in the pew and rested her chin on her hands. The man was actually talking about original sin. What had happened to him? What was he going to do to Ned?

'The body in itself is evil,' insisted the minister, 'until we deliberately consecrate it to God.'

Elizabeth sat back with such violence that she dislodged a Bible from the shelf in front of her and sent it clattering to the floor. She wished she had the courage to rise and con-tradict the minister on the spot. . . .

Aunt Janet was offering her a peppermint.

'Don't you feel well, Elizabeth?' she whispered.

'Me a peppermint too,' whispered Hector, grinning.

Aunt Janet rustled the little paper bag. Elizabeth turned fully round and looked at the clock to see how much of this apalling sermon was still to come.

She would not listen any more. The odour of peppermint and cinnamon, the incense of a Scottish Presbyterian church, floated around her. Sucking her hard peppermint, she stared at one of the windows, combining the little panes of glass into squares and diamonds of colour. Let him stew in his own juice, she thought angrily. Let him take a whip and beat the devil out of Ned if he chooses; it's none of my business.

The congregation stirred; the sermon was finished; everyone stood up to sing the final hymn. Elizabeth kept her mouth shut. She would never, never go to church again, let the Shands say what they liked. She wasn't going to have all that theological tapestry hung between her and the universe.

Slowly and sedately they moved out in the throng.

'Did you feel ill, Elizabeth?'

Aunt Janet was at her ear, solicitous.

'No, I was only angry.'

'Angry, my dear?'

'Angry with all the nonsense Mr Murray was talking.'

'I thought it was a very good sermon, I'm sure. Didn't you think so, John?'

'A very good sermon,' said John.

'Well,' Elizabeth laughed a little, 'I think it's awful to have to listen without being able to contradict. I wanted to answer back.'

She turned round, looking for Hector as usual, but was surprised to see him walking off with Mabel. It was extraordinary. He had never done that before.

She could not help watching the two figures in front. Mabel walked very well; she had an elastic step; her very back looked gay. She and Hector were laughing. It was queer, she commented to herself, that the sight of Mabel and Hector exchanging badinage should rouse in her the same feeling of disapproval that had invaded her the other day. She felt grown-up again, relegated to the background with the sober adults, as it were, while the children frolicked along in front. It puzzled her.

John seemed to be amused at something. Whatever it was, he checked himself from putting it into words. But the twinkle in his eye suddenly delighted Elizabeth as she caught it.

'Your beard twinkles when you smile, John,' she said, feeling audacious. 'The point of your nose twinkles, too. Look at it, Aunt Janet, doesn't it now?'

She had never before suspected that she could venture to chaff John, or that he would like it. Apparently he did like it, and her grown-up feeling vanished when she discovered that John was an excellent victim of teasing. She forgot that for a second or two she had resented being left to his society. Behind a cross-fire of personal remarks she escaped for the moment from her anger with the minister, her forebodings about Ned, and her uneasiness with regard to Mabel and Hector. In spite of his beard, and his size, John was not so very grown-up after all.

'I was afraid of you at first because of your beard,' she confessed, 'but now I see that you are only hiding behind it.'

When Aunt Janet was safely within her own front gate Elizabeth found herself still beside John.

'You know my sister is coming on Saturday?' he said suddenly.

'Oh yes,' cried Elizabeth. 'I'm looking forward *so* much to meeting her.'

'I think you'll like each other. I couldn't help laughing when I saw you fidget so much in church; she used to do exactly the same.'

'Did she want to answer back too?'

'She always did,' said John gleefully.

Elizabeth's heart leapt. 'Is she at all like me?'

'No, not at all. She's more like Hector, I must admit. But, although you may not care to hear me say so, she's much better-looking than Hector.'

'I'll let you say so as much as you please. When does she arrive on Saturday?'

'I think she's to travel overnight from London coming in here about ten o'clock. Hasn't Mabel invited you and Hector to come to dinner on Saturday night to meet her?'

'No, not yet —'

'She'll probably do it before you go home. We'll have a jolly evening.'

John actually hummed a little song to himself. That finally broke down the frail wall of Elizabeth's discretion.

'Do you know, I think I must have several blind spots,' she said, 'I'm only finding out now what you're really like.'

John smiled half-shyly.

'I've decided that your bark is worse than your bite, John.'

'How do you know that?'

Elizabeth laughed; her eyes sparkled.

'I'm learning sense. I used to judge people entirely by what they said; but now I know that it's the person behind the words that matters. When you like people it doesn't matter very much what they say.'

'I thought you liked Murray?'

'That's a shrewd hit,' said Elizabeth, with a rueful grin.

John grinned back. 'And yet you were nearly jumping out of the pew at him this morning.'

'I couldn't help it. But I'm sure it's because he himself has changed that what he said annoyed me. Something has changed him. I'm afraid of what he might do. . . .'

'How's that? I thought myself that he seemed to be coming to his senses. He's been mooning about for years in a kind of dream, quite off the earth; and this morning I thought he had wakened up.'

'I liked his dream better. . . . I don't want to be brought down with a thump on to solid earth. Besides it wasn't solid earth, John. It was only logic. It was husks for the prodigal sons and daughters, that's what it was; and who has a right to say that we are all prodigals and must be fed on husks?'

John did not answer at first. Then, with an appeareance of lightness, he said: 'Oh, well, after the husks comes the fatted calf, you know. We'll have that next Sunday.'

Elizabeth realized with a stricken feeling that he had applied the parable to himself and his sister.

'I'm for the fatted calf all the time,' she said as heartily as possible, and dropped the discussion, feeling clumsy and foolish.

When they all halted at number seven Balfour Terrace she could not resist slipping her arm inside Hector's, as if it were necessary to let Mabel see that Hector had been merely on loan. In this graceful position they both accepted Mabel's invitation for Saturday night to meet Lizzie.

As they turned home Hector disengaged his arm. Men and women in Calderwick certainly never walked arm-in-arm by daylight, but Elizabeth quite unreasonably felt chilled by his action.

'You ran away and left me,' she said.

'Oh, Mabel wanted to tell me about the car she's going to get. She screwed it out of John this morning.'

'A car! How lovely.'

'I'm going to teach her to drive it. We're going up to Aberdeen some time this week to buy it.'

'You know, John really is a dear,' said Elizabeth suddenly, apparently ignoring Hector's statement. 'I've only just found it out.'

'John? He's a swine.'

'No, he's not! How can you say such a thing?'

'I suppose you're going to call me a liar, are you?'

'What's the matter, Hector?'

'Oh, nothing. I suppose you think I've bloody well deserved all I've got from John?'

'I don't care whether you did or not. He's certainly different now.'

'Hell of a difference!'

'People *do* change, Hector. It's queer that they do. I suppose we all do. . . .'

'Well, I'm not going to *argue* about it.'

The tone of Hector's voice as he said 'argue' conveyed that he had had enough of argument with Elizabeth, and reminded her, with a shock, of their previous argument. All her uneasiness came back, and her thoughts congealed like a crust over her feelings, so that she did not venture to say another word. They walked on in a silence that grew more oppressive the longer it lasted, and it lasted until they got home.

The invisible barrier between them seemed to cut across the table as they sat at dinner. Elizabeth was scrupulously polite in offering more helpings, and Hector accepted them with equal politeness.

'What are you going to do this afternoon?' she asked. On Sunday afternoons they had always gone out together, but to-day she was determined to thrust no assumptions upon Hector.

'I think I'll run up and see Hutcheon.' Hector's tone was quite careless. 'He's got a small car – a beauty – and I'd like to have a shot at driving her somewhere this afternoon, to get my hand in.'

In other circumstances Elizabeth would have cried, 'I'm coming too!' but she only looked at her plate and filled her spoon with exaggerated care. In another moment her emotions would break their crust and come bubbling up. . . . Hector felt the imminence of the outburst, and he laid down his napkin.

'I'd better be getting along,' he said, 'or Hutcheon will be gone. Excuse me, please.'

Elizabeth had learned a few things that Sunday morning, and in the afternoon and evening she learned something more. Her first lesson was that in the absence of Hector her painful agitation subsided with incredible quickness. Half-an-hour after his departure she was able to sit down to a book by a philosopher called Bergson, whom she had discovered just before leaving the University and who excited her. The second lesson for the day was that the same agitation returned with the same incredible suddenness the minute Hector set foot again within the house. She seemed to have become two separate persons, one of whom was calm and confident in Hector, while the other was childishly, almost hysterically, affected by his presence.

All the understanding excuses she had found for him during the afternoon, all her quiet resolve to find a harmony which should include both her love for Hector and her good opinion of John, all her faith in the underlying permanence of that love, disappeared when he came in, as the clear reflection in a still pool disappears when the mud at the bottom is stirred up by a stick.

The whole of Elizabeth's world was in flux, although not exactly as Bergson had declared it to be, and instead of regarding the phenomenon with scientific interest she felt as if she were drowning in it.

## NINE

Elizabeth, governed as she was by images, thought of herself and Hector as the terminals of an invisible and powerful current which ought to flow unimpeded from one to the other. Hitherto she had not imagined that a distortion of the current could distort the terminals also, but in the next week she grew more and more baffled by the effects of the distortion upon herself. Whenever Hector spoke to her a lump rose in her throat; his approach seemed to graze an intolerable wound; and the more grimly she told herself that this was absurd and petty the more she was bewildered by her own spurts of resentment. On the other hand, whenever he ignored her or turned away in impatient anger her resentment was lost in a self-pity that sometimes passed off in a fit of submissive tenderness towards her husband and sometimes drove her sobbing to her bedroom. She could never tell what she was going to do, and in none of her actions was she recognizable to herself except during Hector's absence. As soon as he left the house she would stop crying and say: This is not me! What *have* I been doing?

These more stable moments emerged like rocks once the waves of emotion were spent. They might have served Elizabeth as a basis for self-examination but, being young and indeterminate, she preferred to gaze with increasing bewilderment at the cross-currents of the sea. Elizabeth had a habit of turning her back on the land.

Hector was less bewildered because he was deliberately drifting, and in doing so he was perhaps subserving a deeper purpose. The ports we try to make by tacking may be less salutary for us than those to which we drift. There may be no such thing as chance in human conduct. Hector, at any rate, although unhappy, was less surprised by the estrangement

than Elizabeth. It seemed to him now that he had foreseen it
all along. It served him right, he thought, for marrying a
woman supposed to be brainy; she was bound to despise
him sooner or later. He could not forget her contempt; he
kept worrying it like a dog at a bone. For a few hours on the
day after their quarrel he had apparently forgotten it, but it
had been only temporarily buried beneath a load of depression, and now he was turning it over so often that there was
no chance of its disappearing. His persistence in dragging it
to light was indeed so obstinate that there must have been
some other motive at work which he did not surmise. In
vain Elizabeth tried to assure him that she was sorry, that
she hadn't meant it, that it was too absurd – he refused to be
placated. It began to look as if he were clinging to an excuse.
That was perhaps what bewildered Elizabeth most.

She was incapable of realizing that she had failed him in
something essential, and he was too inarticulate to make it
clear. Even when he said, 'You don't give a damn for
decency, so why the hell should I?' she was merely angry.

So Hector drifted deliberately, even defiantly, as if he had
argued the situation to some such conclusion as this:
Elizabeth should have steered him on his course; she should
have guided him into the haven of respectability; and if she
refused, if she unshipped the rudder and flung it at his
head, whose fault was it that he drifted?

Moreover the current that was bearing him away had
been pulling at him ever since his marriage. In becoming
estranged from his wife Hector was only doing what the
whole of Calderwick expected of him. Wives, in Calderwick, were dull, domestic commodities, and husbands, it
was understood, were unfaithful whenever they had the
opportunity. Hector also had the reputation of being the
wildest daredevil in the town, and in the Club, where every
man liked to be thought a bit of a gay dog, his prestige was
enormous. His prestige was now likely to increase still
more, for he spent every night in the Club getting drunk.
When he was not at the Club or in the office he was flirting
with Mabel. Because of Elizabeth's inexplicable failure as a
wife he could not hope to rival John as a respected citizen,
and to captivate John's wife seemed an alternative way of

getting even. Mabel was asking for it anyway, he told himself.

It is difficult to see what current could have carried Elizabeth away had she too been minded to drift. In Calderwick wives are not so well provided for as husbands. Wives in Calderwick, for instance, do not forgather in drunkenness, so Elizabeth was denied that relief. Nor could she count on support from Aunt Janet; she could not, indeed, count on any of the women she knew except Emily Scrymgeour. The only thing she could have done was to be unfaithful to her husband, but for a Calderwick woman to do that is not to drift: the whole social current sets the other way. Mabel was not drifting towards Hector, for instance; she had no intention of leaving the social current; she was only swimming a little against it to try her strength, to give herself something to do. There was no easy drift to which Elizabeth might commit herself except the traditional stream of respectable wifehood. Both as a member of society and as an individual she was more buffeted than Hector.

For the first day or two she took long, solitary walks, seeking an assurance from the sea, the grass, and the leafless trees in the little valleys that she was still the same Elizabeth. The house seemed to be agitated by stormy emotions, but out of doors, she thought, in the slower, larger rhythm of the non-human world, she would again find herself, and, in consequence, find Hector too. She laid her hand on the smooth trunk of a large beech and looked up through its rounded boughs at the grey sky. It was a wise old tree, she thought, sixty years old perhaps, maybe a hundred; she had watched its leaves change from green to russet, and now she could almost feel the warm life withdrawn into its trunk, which in spring would flow out again into a thousand buds. An old, old tree, but it would put out silky new leaves, with downy edges, leaves so young and tender that one would hesitate to touch them. . . . Sudden tears filled her eyes as she thought of the spring buds; it was an intolerable thought that such young things should bourgeon only to be burned in the fires of autumn and stripped from the boughs by savage winds. We are like the leaves, she thought, and when we flutter from the tree we think it is freedom, but it is death.

She stood there, with the palm of her hand pressed on the smooth grey bark, and stared at a world that was filled with death. Everything died. Everything *could* die. It was intolerable. How could she have been so unthinkingly happy in such a world?

She fled back to the town, where mortality crowded together and roofed itself in from the terrible emptiness of the sky. Men and women were incredibly pathetic, she thought, or incredibly courageous. But, in comparison with death, of what importance were their silly little notions of right and wrong? What did it matter if Hector thought the Scrymgeours indecent? How could she bother to be angry with him when he might die?

The thought of Hector dead haunted her all the rest of the afternoon. The physical presence of living people usually keeps us from inflating their images with sentimentality, but when the objects of our desire are removed from us in space or time their images can shrink or swell disproportionately; and as Elizabeth in her imagination was removing Hector to a point much farther away than the office, where he was presumably detained, his image became gigantic, filled with all the qualities her frustrated tenderness longed for. By five o'clock she was sitting at the tea-table waiting for him in a state of almost painful anticipation. At half-past five she made tea and drank it by herself; his absence had become a voluntary absence, and his image began to shrink; the sentiment which had sustained it flooded back upon her until she had to get rid of it in an outburst of tears, after which she lay on her bed in cold despair. Hector had dwindled into nothing; he was worse than dead to her, for there was no consoling image left. She felt as if it were she herself who was dead.

When Hector came in, some time after midnight, she turned her face to the wall. He was very drunk.

Next day she shrank from going out. But she could not settle; she wandered from the window to the bookcase, and from the bookcase to the window again, forgetting her book. The certainty of death made everything irrelevant and trivial. Born to die, she said to herself. She might equally well have said, Dying to be born, for what she was gazing at was the winter death of the garden, but her eye was prompted by the apparent deadness of her own heart, where no quickening movement promised new life. The end of Hector's love for her seemed like the end of the world.

Elizabeth was a victim of her upbringing as well as of her temperament. From her earliest years she had been subjected to the subtle pressure of the suggestion that a husband is the sole justification of a woman's existence, that a woman who cannot attract and keep a husband is a failure. That some such theory should emerge in a society which regarded the sexual act as sinful was inevitable; one cannot train women in chastity and then expect them to people the world unless the sinfulness of sex is counterbalanced by the desirability of marriage. In Elizabeth's case temperament had modified tradition so far as to set romantic love as well as marriage on the other end of the lever depressed by sex: marriage alone without love would not maintain the equilibrium. One might admit that the odds were heavily weighted against her.

Her restlessness was perhaps a symptom of vitality. At any rate, after walking round and round the drawing-room she went on an impulse into the kitchen, where the strong-armed and red-headed Mary Ann was singing as she washed up dishes. Elizabeth, as Mabel said, had simply no idea how to treat a maid; she was incapable of keeping her own place, and therefore unfit to keep other people in their places.

'Well, Mary Ann, are things looking up?'

'First rate, mem. . . . I had a rare time last nicht.'

Mary Ann beamed, and plunged into the soapy water again.

'Here, give me a dish-clout and I'll dry the dishes. I can't settle to anything this morning.'

'You're looking tired,' said Mary Ann, with affectionate concern. 'Dinna you touch that dish-clout. I should have had thae dishes done lang syne. I'll no' be a minute. And then I'll make you a cuppie o' tea, will I?'

'You think a cuppie o' tea is a cure for everything, Mary Ann.'

'So it is,' said Mary Ann stoutly. 'Gi'e me a cuppie o' tea and I dinna care what happens next.'

Elizabeth sat down on the kitchen table.

'How's the lad getting on?'

'Eh, fine, I tell ye. He's coming on. He gi'ed me a pickle sweeties last nicht. I gi'ed him one on the lug he wasna looking for.'

'Aren't you afraid to hit a policeman, Mary Ann?'

'Me? No' me. A polisman's only a man-body, especially if he's your lad. A bit dirl on the lug's good for them.'

'What did he say?'

'"You're a daft besom," he says, "Mary Ann," he says, "but I like you for it," he says, rubbing awa' at his lug. "Do you ever think about me?" he says, the great soft gomeril. "Whiles," says I, "but no' aye!" That gi'ed him something to think about. "Whiles," says I, "but no' aye!"'

Mary Ann chuckled as she cleared the dishes away. Elizabeth sat lamely on the table, realizing that good-humoured banter can be as efficient a barrier to intimacy as the most discouraging aloofness. She did not know how to begin confiding in Mary Ann.

'Now for the cuppie o' tea.'

Mary Ann bustled to the stove.

'All right, Mary Ann.' Elizabeth slipped off the table. 'Bring it into the drawing-room.'

Her half-conscious wish to talk to somebody became a definite desire to consult Emily Scrymgeour. She felt that she was blindly going round and round in circles and that talking to a third person might clear her vision. Since that unlucky evening of the dinner-party she had not seen Emily, but that active lady had already guessed something of what was happening. Scandal in Calderwick percolates at first by a kind of osmosis from one mind to another long before it becomes current, and various people had remarked Hector's frequent appearances in Mabel's new car and his increasing devotion to the whisky at the Club. In fact, Emily was waiting for her friend's confidences.

'I'm sorry for her, mind you,' she said to the doctor, 'but she's such a queer mixture that she'd shy off if she thought I was trying to poke my nose in too far, even although she thinks the world of me. She's really very reserved – like you.'

That judgment would have amazed Elizabeth.

'She takes the wrong things too seriously,' said the doctor. 'Bound to get hurt.'

'Jim! And you've only seen her once! You *are* a clever wee man, you know. It isn't everybody can get a husband like *you*.'

This complacent reflection was never absent from the background of Emily Scrymgeour's thoughts, and made her tolerant of other wives' difficulties.

Elizabeth did not suspect that she was falling like a seed into a carefully prepared bed when she walked into Emily's drawing-room, apologizing diffidently for her defection of the past week. She did not realize it even when Emily sent Teddy out with Peggy the maid, averring that she had so much sewing piled up in the basket that she could not afford to go out, and that anyway it was better to sew with somebody to keep one company.

'Don't you hate sewing and darning?' said Elizabeth.

'No, I love it. Haven't you ever seen my white embroidery? I like working with my hands and I make all Teddy's clothes myself. Look at the design on this romper. . . .'

'I wish I was some good at sewing,' burst out Elizabeth. 'I can't even knit.'

'Your hands look capable enough,' returned Emily, working busily with her own quick short fingers. 'I hate to see women with helpless-looking hands, but yours aren't like that.'

Elizabeth, thus admitted to the same pinnacle of womanliness as her friend, squirmed there in silence for a minute and then abased herself.

'My hands are all thumbs, Emily, in every way. You don't know what a fool I am.'

Her voice roughened as she said this, for she was executing one of those complicated manœuvres of which the human spirit is strangely capable. Her vanity and her love were hurt, her pride was bewildered, and she had a longing to weep on Emily's shoulder; but at the same time she could not abuse her husband to anybody, and the only alternative was to abuse herself. The savage roughness in her voice was caused by anger, and as she started up to walk about the room her anger increased. She was contemptuously furious with herself.

'A fool!' she kept on saying. 'A damned fool!'

'It's unlikely that you're the only fool in the world,' said Emily, laying her work aside. 'People do quarrel with their husbands,you know.'

She laughed at Elizabeth's startled face and patted the sofa, on which she had expressly seated herself.

'Don't prowl like that, but come and sit down and tell me all about it. I've been married for eight years, Elizabeth.'

'How did you know?'

'It's not difficult to guess, is it? What else could it be?'

'Oh – anything. I'm an ignorant fool, I tell you. I never suspected that I was a half-wit, and it's unpleasant to discover it.'

'Do you think I'm a half-wit too?' said Emily, smiling.

'I think you're the only intelligent woman in Calderwick.'

'Do sit down and be sensible.' Emily was still smiling. 'What you really mean is that you didn't learn at the University how to manage a husband.'

'I haven't learned how to manage *myself*; that's what's bothering me.'

Elizabeth ceased prowling, and looked directly at her friend.

'I feel that myself has let me down. I don't know at any minute what damned silly thing I'll do next. Yes, I have quarrelled with Hector, but that's not the worst of it. The worst of it is that I haven't sense enough to know how to set things right. Emily, I can't speak to him without bursting into silly tears.' This was the most revealing speech that Elizabeth had ever made, even to herself, and for a moment she had the feeling that something within her was struggling into consciousness, some recognition of an incompatibility too fundamental for compromise.

Emily brushed it away.

'You take the wrong things too seriously.'

'Do I?'

'Of course you do. You are turning a simple quarrel into something much too tragic. My dear Elizabeth, I've known you for long enough to see that.'

'Do I?' repeated Elizabeth. Almost absent-mindedly she

sat down beside Emily, and leaned forward, clasping her hands together.

'It's not such a simple quarrel,' she said suddenly. 'I don't think he loves me any more.'

'What makes you think that?' Emily quietly resumed her sewing. To herself she said: Aha! Now we're getting at it.

'Because if he loved me as – as I love him,' Elizabeth's voice faltered, but she went on, 'he couldn't keep things up against me the way he does. Emily, if you love a person you *love* a person, no matter what's said or done. Quarrels are only on the surface —'

'That may be true of women, but men are different. Now, listen to me.' She checked Elizabeth's protest, laying a hand on her arm. 'There's a lot of nonsense being talked about the equality of the sexes, chiefly by mannish women. I'm not a mannish woman; I don't believe in them. Men and women are quite different. I'm going to talk to you very frankly. Hector is the first man you ever slept with, isn't he?'

Elizabeth nodded, blushing.

'But you're not the first woman he ever had.'

Elizabeth's blush deepened.

'Of course you're not. It doesn't mean so much to him as it does to you. It's you who will have the babies. That makes a big difference, don't you see? Every wife has the same handicap in her relation to her husbnad. Marriage for a woman, my dear, is an art – the art of managing a husband – and that means not taking his passing phases too seriously. Strategy is what you need, and tactics —'

'I want to live with Hector without any tactics,' broke in Elizabeth. 'I want to live with him and just be myself.'

'But you can't,' said Emily firmly and decisively.

'Then I'll run away.'

Emily pulled her down again on to the sofa.

'That would be the silliest thing you could do. Where would you go?'

'I can teach,' said Elizabeth stubbornly.

'No school would take in a woman who had run away from her husband.'

'I could take my own name and leave Scotland.'

'I thought you said you loved him?'

Elizabeth hid her face in her hands. There was a long silence.

Waves of self-reproach were rising higher and higher in Elizabeth, and the unspoken thing which had been struggling into consciousness was finally drowned.

'I do love him; I do love him,' she whispered. Without removing her hands she added: 'I've been thinking all the time about his love for me, not about my love for him.'

Emily patted her shoulder and said nothing.

'He's miserable too,' whispered Elizabeth. 'He gets drunk nearly every night.'

After some minutes she sat up, with a bright eye, and looked at her friend:

'I've been a bad wife, Emily. Thank you, very much, for clearing me up.'

'What about some tea?' said Emily briskly.

Elizabeth could not help laughing.

'All crises in women's lives seem to be punctuated by cups of tea,' she said.

Later that evening Emily sat on the rug by her husband's knee and told him about her successful management of Elizabeth: 'Don't you think I was right?'

The doctor in his thin voice said: 'You should have told her to have a baby.'

'So I did, after we had tea. I told her a baby was a wonderful thing for making a man human. Aha!'

She pinched the calf of his leg.

'I suppose,' said the doctor, 'you didn't think of asking her how they got on in bed?'

'She'd have been dreadfully shocked if I had. Besides – I shouldn't think there would be any difficulty there – her husband's a Shand.'

'Their reaction times may be different,' said the doctor.

'Jim,' said his wife, 'what a wee devil you are!'

Elizabeth had yielded herself to the stream of traditional wifehood, and the boat of her soul no longer rocked. She had but one course to follow – to devote herself to her husband, to love him selflessly, exacting nothing and giving much. She had been a bad wife, and now, God helping her, she would be a good wife.

A cynical observer might have remarked that she was now inflating with sentimentality her own image instead of Hector's and setting it up in the role of Noble Wife. Yet these wind-blown puppets of our imagination play more than visionary parts in the drama of the soul, and have the advantage of being able to collapse suddenly when the need for them is over. Elizabeth, hidden within the self-made figure of the Noble Wife, was shielded for the time from social disapproval as effectively as a pneumatic tyre is shielded from the bumps of a hard road. Moreover, she now presented the comforting appearance that Hector expected of her.

She must have known this instinctively, for she first bathed and powdered her face, and then put on her prettiest frock. In Calderwick at that time it was considered slightly improper to powder one's face by day, but Elizabeth excused her daring by reflecting that darkness had already set in, although it was not yet five o'clock. She inspected herself in the glass and added a string of coloured beads, signs of dawning femininity which might have pleased her sister-in-law.

She then put on a hat and coat and left the house with a quick, firm step. She could not wait for Hector; she was going to the office to bring him home. This time she would not burst into tears when she saw him. No wonder he got fed up, she told herself; any man would be fed up with a wife whose nose was always blobby.

The image of the Noble Wife was growing rapidly in size. Unconsciously, without words, Elizabeth was adding to the number of its attributes.

The perfect wife was not only selfless and loving – she was sympathetic, understanding, tactful and, above all, charming. . . . She must always be pretty – no, not pretty, Elizabeth did not aspire to prettiness – she must always look 'nice'. The *frou-frou* of femininity was beginning to rustle round Elizabeth. Here, too, was the cloak of charity which should cover her husband's many sins, while her devoted love sustained and comforted him. . . . Elizabeth was not far from the final dogma that woman exists for the sake of man. She was going beyond her teacher, Emily Scrymgeour, who believed only that woman should pretend to exist for the sake of man.

There is, however, a keen ecstasy in renunciation. We must not pity Elizabeth as she makes her way upstairs to the inner office of John Shand & Sons; she is transfigured by happiness. All the doubts that have vexed her for the past few months appear now as selfish hesitations: she feels that in spite of herself she has been miraculously led from one stepping-stone to another until she has emerged from the fog of uncertainty to find herself safely across the Rubicon in the full sunshine of wifehood.

Some of that sunshine was needed in the inner room where Hector was still sitting at his desk. He was alone: John had been out all day at the farmers' mart, for it was a Friday, the weekly market-day of Calderwick. The outer office was empty, except for Mason, the head clerk, who was nervously hovering about his desk, and peeping every now and then through the glass partition to see if Mr Hector wasn't thinking yet of going home. Mason had never known the junior partner to sit so long in the office.

For hours Hector had been humped over his desk in listless depression, drawing lines and diagrams on a bit of paper. He had put in what he called 'a thick week', and the defiant recklessness that had carried him along was now ebbing away, leaving behind it disgust and staleness. There were heavy black pouches under his eyes, and his mouth was drawn tight as if he were afraid it would fall out of control were he to open it. One could almost see the inchoate sagging outline of the form that might be his at the age of fifty, the ghost of the father, Charlie Shand, horribly incarnate in the flesh of the son.

Whether this illusion of Charlie Shand's presence was the cause or the effect of Hector's thoughts it is impossible to say. His father was haunting him. He was going the same way as the old man, he thought, jabbing furiously at the paper: drink and women, drink and women; and he would end in the same way. Might as well be dead. He saw himself again lying on a bier in a place that looked like a church.

That might be the best thing for all concerned. He was sick of everybody and sick of himself. Might as well *be* dead as feel dead.

He hadn't a dog's chance in Calderwick. The place was too full of his father. . . . He shuddered and shut his mouth more tightly than ever, while he drew aimless little pictures down the side of the paper. Then he set to work drawing a ship, a child's ship, with masts and sails growing out of a rudely sketched hull. He became absorbed in it, and after he had finished the sails he put in a solitary figure in the bows, and then printed a name on the stern, ELSA. Elsa? There was another queer word struggling in the back of his mind, Koben, Kjobben something, and a doubling, a thickening of shadowy images, as if he were retracing some experience he had had before. . . .

His mouth fell open. He had seen the ship *Elsa* in the harbour, with foreign fellows jabbering along her deck, and from that day to this he had not thought of her until his pen had printed the name. The rope curling on the quay beside him. . . . Better to drown in the open sea than in a stagnant dock. . . .

He sat motionless for a while, with a new feeling springing up within him, a feeling faintly like hope. He was superstitious; he believed in omens; and the ominous dream of his own death had oppressed him heavily. This ship, he felt sure, was a sign. A sign of what?

His mind suddenly cleared, and he knew as well as if he

had thought it out that he would take ship for some far-off country, Australia or Brazil or the South Seas. He would sign on as a sailor, a cattle-man, anything: the voyage would take months, months of hard work far from pubs and women; at the other end there would be at least one's pay, and a week or two of glorious rioting in a new country. Somewhere in the South Seas. He had had enough of the North.

Hutcheon's people were shipping agents: young Hutcheon would help him to do it and would keep his mouth shut. He would sign on to work his passage. He still had over two hundred and fifty pounds of his own: that would help to start him in something at the other end: or he could ship again for another voyage somewhere else if there was nothing doing where he landed. Clear out! By God! he would.

He sat staring into vacancy, lost in his dream, voyaging into that unknown which put Calderwick in its right perspective, reducing even John to a fat, foolish puppet whom it was absurd to take seriously. He had been too young, too raw, when he was shot out to Canada; he had not seen how unimportant the family was, how little Calderwick mattered; but this time he would stand on his own feet. He snapped his fingers. The ghost of his father wavered and vanished from his brain.

Hard work, hard physical labour, and then a spree; that was a life he could enjoy. In Calderwick there was opportunity for neither the one thing nor the other: all a fellow could do was to soak himself rotten in the rotten Club, and then addle himself still more on an office stool, or go to church on Sunday like a good little boy and be jawed at by all his family. . . . An uneasiness began to disturb him: he jabbed at the paper again. Well, let them think he was a quitter – a natural, heaven-born quitter: if that was his line he would follow it out. To hell with them all!

A noise outside made him start. He sat up and moistened his dry lips; he became conscious that he wanted a stiff whisky. He looked at his watch; it was past five o'clock. Old Mason must think he'd turned damned industrious. Hardly had the thought shaped itself when he was again startled. Wasn't that Elizabeth's voice?

In the few seconds during which he sat staring at the door
before it opened he was, as he would have termed it, in a blue
funk. He had avoided thinking about Elizabeth while
dismissing her from his life, as he had avoided thinking
about Aunt Janet, or even Mabel. By lumping them all
together as 'women' and putting them in the same phrase as
'drink' he had escaped the necessity of considering them as
individuals. Even now he was unwilling to think of Elizabeth
as Elizabeth. His sense of guilt and his resentment at feeling
guilty, which combined to produce the blue funk, threw up
another impersonal phrase. 'Just like a woman. Just like a
woman,' something muttered savagely at the back of his
mind as he sat with jaw set and eyes fixed on the door.

It is much easier to dismiss people from one's business
than from one's life. The absolute importance of money is
impressed on us both directly and indirectly with such force
that it seems a final argument to say that So-and-so costs us
too much; even So-and-so sees the force of it, although he
may resent dismissal. Money, after all, is money. But we do
not feel with the same conviction, with the same prospect of
general approval, that we are, after all, ourselves, and that if
So-and-so costs us too much he must be thrust out of our
lives. Civilization, in binding us to one another with a solid
wall, turns into ramshackle structures the private dwellings
of our spirits; we lean lopsidedly upon each other and
hesitate to complain of encroachment, or to refuse support
even when the rooftree is cracking under the strain. We rely
more and more upon the wall of civilization to stave off
collapse, and less and less upon ourselves. In fact, we live so
much upon the wall and so little in ourselves that we do not
often know what condition our house is in, or whether it
needs repairs.

Hector's decision to rid his house of encumbrances and to
repair it was so recent, and apparently so spontaneous, that
he could not justify himself, and it was natural that the
arrival of Elizabeth should put him in a blue funk. She was
ushered in by Mason, who was relieved to find that there was
a comprehensible reason for Mr Hector's waiting so long in
the office. Mason's eye was rather appealing, and Hector,
glad of a diversion, answered the unspoken appeal.

'We won't be a minute, Mason,' he cried, hastily rising. 'Get me my coat, will you?'

To Elizabeth he said nothing: he could not think what to say, but stood leaning his hands on the desk. Without noting whether Mason had shut the door again Elizabeth ran towards him. 'My dear love,' she said, 'my dear, dear love.'

Hector, armoured in the conviction that she despised him, had been hard to her. He had returned an equal coldness and silence to hers, and had been infuriated by her tears, which he interpreted as reproaches. But she came towards him now with such tenderness in her eyes and in her voice that he was taken off his guard, and before he could stop her she had her arms round his neck.

'My dear love,' she said again, with a vibration in her voice which he had never heard before. He remembered that her bosom was comforting, his head sank, his arm went round her, and for a long minute they embraced each other. When he tried to lift his head Elizabeth stroked it and whispered: 'I've come to tell you I've been a bad, bad wife, and now I'm going to be a good one. My darling, my darling.'

His eyes blurred and he put out a hand to steady himself against the desk. He was damned tired, he remembered. Elizabeth felt the almost imperceptible droop of his body and for the first time since coming in she looked at his face. His eyelids were wet. She kissed them, but he kept his eyes shut.

'I'm damned tired, Elizabeth,' he said.

She took his coat from Mason, who was coughing in the doorway, found his hat, and led him downstairs. They walked home arm-in-arm, closely pressed together.

Elizabeth did not suspect that the tears in Hector's eyes might have been tears of disappointment. She felt tender and protective towards him, as if he were a baby she must foster and encourage, and the strength of her feeling at the moment excluded any doubt of its necessity. The perfect wife is bound to assume that her husband requires her devotion, that without her he would be 'lost'. This traditional and easy attitude fits loosely over the real problem, the problem of one individual's relationship to another, and conceals its shape exactly as the cloak of charity conceals failings.

But Hector surrendered himself without resistance to his wife's devotion. He had been unconsciously reaching for that cloak of charity ever since his marriage. Time after time he had confessed his sins in Elizabeth's lap as if she were his mother, but he had never got the desired assurance that whatever he did she would still be a mother to him. That assurance was now hovering around him at last as he sat in the arm-chair before a glowing red fire and let Elizabeth put on his warm slippers for him.

And yet he felt miserable. The spark of hope in his breast seemed to have been blown out. He tried to excuse himself.

'I've been thinking all day what a rotter I am. . . . Going the same way as the old man did, Elizabeth. You won't let me come to that, will you?'

Elizabeth sat on the padded arm of the chair and took his head on her bosom. Her face shone with exaltation.

'No, I won't let you. I love you more than anything in the world – more than myself even. I've just discovered that.'

'Keep me off the drink, Elizabeth. . . .'

She kissed him on the forehead.

'I promise.'

He suddenly lifted his head.

'And make me a good boy for ever and ever. Amen.'

His tone was bitter, almost savage. Elizabeth peered into his face.

'What is it?' she said half under her breath.

He buried his face in his hands. Elizabeth knelt beside him and tugged at his wrists.

'What is it, my love? Hector, I want to help you.'

She clasped his wrists and caressed them. Strong arms, she thought, sliding her fingers and the palms of her hands down his arms; strong arms, with their short black hairs, and their sinewy hardness under her soft palms.

'I'll make you happy,' she said. 'As happy as we were at first. . . . Us two against the world, Hector. We'll show them. . . .' She went on caressing his arms, but a strange anxiety was spreading in her heart. Hector's face was still hidden: he made no response to her assurance. She felt as if she were desperately fanning an extinct fire.

'I'll do anything you like, Hector. I tell you I've been a

beast to you, but it's going to be different. . . . I'll give up Emily Scrymgeour. I'll behave like a *perfect* lady, except when we're just together, us two. Us two, Hector. . . . I'll back you up all round. . . .'

'For God's sake, shut up!' said Hector. Then seizing her hands he laid his forehead on them and groaned: 'No, I didn't mean that. I didn't mean that.'

Elizabeth's lips trembled, but she made no sound. She could feel Hector's eyelashes quivering on her fingers, and she pressed her hands closer to his face to stop that fluttering. She bowed her head upon his and, still on her knees, began kissing the back of his neck.

The scent of peat and tobacco smoke from his tweed jacket, the thickness of his black cropped hair, the strength of his neck and shoulders inflamed her senses. After weeks of estrangement they were so near to each other that all this misery seemed to her suddenly an absurd irrelevance. She tried to force her hands from Hector's grip. Laughing, she struggled with him.

But Hector held on to her wrists as if they were straws and he a drowning man. The softness and warmth of her caresses and of her body drew him towards her almost irresistibly, and yet he resisted with all his force. He had the feeling that if he yielded now he would be bound for life to the fate he had escaped in imagination that afternoon.

Elizabeth, still laughing, sank back on her knees. She did not take Hector's resistance seriously.

'Let me go,' she said.

He tightened his grip.

'Listen. . . .'

Elizabeth looked up in alarm. His eyes were black and sombre.

'Let me go,' she said in a sharper voice. 'You're hurting me. Let go!'

Hector set her free at once, and she sat on the rug chafing her wrists.

'Will you let *me* go?' he said, and as if this unequivocal statement had broken a dam his words came rushing out in a whirling flood, tossing at Elizabeth's feet the sediment of his despair.

'Damned, mean, narrow little world, Calderwick,' he finished. 'I'm done for if I stay in it any longer. I've got to clear out. Will you help me? Will you back me up, Elizabeth?'

Elizabeth sat staring at him.

'Go away?' she said. 'Without me?'

She seemed to herself to be shrinking and dwindling to a vanishing point on the hearthrug, her voice was small and forlorn.

The sweat stood on Hector's forehead.

'Don't you see,' he said, 'if I go, I don't know where I might land: I can't risk taking you —'

'But I can risk going!' cried Elizabeth. 'I'd go with you to the end of the world.'

'But I mean to work my passage. . . . I can't afford to take you.'

He bent forward and took her hands again. 'Don't let me down, Elizabeth. Back me up. I'll find something for both of us. . . . If I don't get out —'

He shuddered.

'You must go,' said Elizabeth. 'Of course you must go. Haven't I always wanted us to go to Canada or somewhere? But why can't I come too? I'll work at anything, Hector. I'll wash dishes. I'll scrub floors —'

'A fellow can't let his wife do that.'

Elizabeth sat still for a moment. Then she began to laugh hysterically.

'What's the matter?' said Hector. 'Stop it, Elizabeth: stop it, for God's sake!'

Elizabeth's laughter wavered into a shrill sound and died away.

'I *am* your wife,' she said. 'Am I not? I *am* your wife, Hector. I'll be a good wife. What do you want me to do?'

'I want you to wait for me,' Hector bent and unbent her fingers. 'I don't know where I'm going yet. But when I find a place fit for a woman —'

Elizabeth felt the idiotic laughter bubbling up inside her once more. She clenched her teeth on it. Shut up, she said to herself. I'm not me. I'm a wife, a woman, who has to have places that are fit for her.

'But what am I to do while I'm waiting?' she said aloud.

'I thought – I thought that perhaps you could live with Aunt Janet. . . .'

Hector had a momentary fear that Elizabeth would perceive that he was improvising. He was very grateful to her when she looked up quietly and said: 'I'll wait for you, Hector, as long as you like. I love you, and I shall always love you. But I won't be a burden on anybody! I'll find a teaching job, somewhere. After all, I'm a highly qualified young woman: it would be absurd of me to sponge on Aunt Janet.'

Hector was ashamed.

'I don't like doing it,' he muttered. 'I've two hundred pounds. I'll leave you a hundred. . . .'

'Nonsense! You'll need as much as you can scrape together. Where did you think of? . . .'

'Anywhere. . . . South Africa, Australia, Brazil. Pick up any chances going.'

Hector was surprised to find how reasonable and practical his adventure began to appear when it was looked at steadily. His sense of guilt evaporated.

'After all,' said Elizabeth, 'all this furniture was given us by Aunt Janet, and we can't fling it back in her face without an explanation. We must have it out with her, and with John too.'

'John won't raise any objections if you don't.'

Hector stared at his wife after saying this. A murky corner of his brain seemed to clear up. She was backing him; she was standing by him; and because she was backing him he wouldn't have to sneak away like a coward. She was taking all the moral responsibility off his shoulders.

'By God, Elizabeth,' he said, 'you understand me better than anybody!'

It was a sincere tribute to the impersonation of the Noble Wife. A lump rose in Elizabeth's throat, but she returned his look unwaveringly.

There was one curious consequence of this interchange. Both Hector and Elizabeth felt embarrassed when they kissed each other.

## ELEVEN

On the same Friday Ned Murray was sitting over his midday dinner, which, as had become his custom, he devoured alone after his brother and sister had left the room. The manse cat, a large black-and-white creature cherished by Teenie the maid, was sitting on the floor beside him, receiving portions of fish which Ned laid down with his fingers on the carpet.

The meal was usually conducted in silence. Teenie brought in the dishes, set them dumbly on the table, and forced herself to walk back to the kitchen instead of running. On this day, however, when she saw him feeding the cat so kindly she ventured a remark as she set the pudding down.

'Tam's in luck to-day.'

Ned looked at her hastily. There was still a remnant of fish on his plate, which he had intended to give to the cat, but he now crammed it into his own mouth, without a second glance at Teenie who was waiting to remove the plate. Thomas, a wise cat, knew that the piece of fish should have been his, and laid a paw on on Ned's knee with an inquiring mew. Ned flung his knife and fork down with a clatter, pushed the cat away and started to his feet crying: 'Self, self, self! That's all you think about, is it?' Thomas, in amazement, paused for a moment, and then as Ned continued to berate him fled to the kitchen.

Ned turned upon Teenie.

'I might have known it. Another dodge. You're all trying to live off me, the cat and all of you! Get out, do you hear? Get out!'

He pushed the palpitating girl into the kitchen, slammed the door upon her, locked it and put the key in his pocket.

Having staved off aggression from that quarter he made himself finally secure by carrying his pudding up to his own room, where he locked himself in.

Sarah emerged from the sitting-room across the hall when she heard him go upstairs, and made for the kitchen. To find her kitchen door locked against her angered her more than such a trivial incident might warrant, and she rapped upon it loudly, calling: 'Teenie! What's the matter, Teenie? It's me: open the door!'

Her anger increased to fury as she stood there holding the door handle, listening to Teenie's muffled explanations. She felt that the whole economy not only of her household but of her life was in jeopardy. It was with a feeling of 'now or never' that she mounted the stairs, saying to herself: I'll sort him.

She rattled Ned's door, crying: 'Give me the key of the kitchen door at once, do you hear? At once, or I'll bring the police to you.'

Her voice was hard and full of decision: it betrayed no doubt of her ability to enforce her will, and its conviction penetrated to Ned. The door was unlocked and flung open. Ned glared at her, but he retreated a step, although he said: 'Your impudence is beyond bounds. This is *my* room.'

'Give me that key. How dare you intefere with Teenie?'

'How dare she and all of you interfere with me?'

'Hold your tongue!' shouted Sarah. 'Give me that key!'

It was the first time that she had ever shouted at her brother, and her passion seemed to sober him.

'Oh, get out,' he said in an exasperated but normal voice. 'There's your key.'

He flung it on the table and Sarah pounced on it.

'If I find you doing such a thing again I'll – I'll thrash you within an inch of your life! And I'll have you jailed.'

'Get out, get out,' repeated Ned, in a reasonable enough tone, urging her to the door as if she were demented and he in full command of his senses. 'Get out of this; I have some work to do.'

'Kindly give me your pudding-plate.'

'Oh, take it, take it, take it. Is there anything else you want?' inquired Ned ironically.

'No nonsense from you, and don't you forget it, my lad.'
Sarah slammed the door behind her and marched downstairs again. She freed her kitchen door and said to Teenie:

'He won't do that again. Don't you worry; just leave him to me.'

Then she did an unheard-of thing: she invaded the study.

William was finishing a sermon on the text: 'Though He slay me, yet will I trust in Him.' The God of wrath and the God of love were incomprehensibly one and the same; it was not for His children on earth to question His doings. . . .

The Book of Job lay open on the desk befor him; he was sitting with an idle pen, staring at a certain verse.

'I must speak to you, William,' said Sarah.

William's heart contracted. Some fresh trouble?

'Put your pen down and listen to me.'

What had happened to Sarah? William turned round in his chair.

Sarah was sharp and concise. This kind of nonsense could not go on, and she would not allow it to go on. To his astonishment William discovered that his wrestlings for the soul of his brother were included in Sarah's definition of nonsense.

'Either you leave him alone,' she said, 'or you back me up in my treatment of him.'

William began to grow angry. He found it easier nowadays to transform heaviness of heart into anger.

'Do you know what you are talking about, Sarah?' he said sternly.

'I think I'm the only person in this house who has any sense at all of what I'm talking about. You've been preaching to Ned about sin and prayer and the will of God, and the only result is that he's ten times worse than he was. You just drive him past himself, and it's me who has to suffer for it. Arguing with him about sin isn't of the slightest use: what he needs is discipline, not argument. I'm going to discipline him, and I want you to leave him alone.'

'It's my duty,' began William, 'as a minister of God's Church' he was going to say, but instead he turned to the desk again and hid his face in his hands. What was his duty?

Was Ned visited by God's wrath because of some secret sin?
Or was the visitation incomprehensible, as in the case of
Job? Ned had a lively conviction of other people's sins, but
not of his own. All Ned wanted, he said, was security,
justice, a right place in the world; and was it his fault that the
world conspired to defraud him of that? Logically, William
was no match for Ned, who could twist any of his arguments
by the tail. He had finally preached contented submission to
the will of God, resignation, acceptance without murmuring,
but that had only roused Ned to frenzy, so that for a whole
day he had done nothing but bang in and out of the study,
screaming forth blasphemies againt the God of his
brother. . . .'

Sarah relented when she saw the minister hide his face.

'There might be a time for that kind of thing, later,' she
conceded, 'but he's in no condition for it just now. What he
needs is firm handling, as if he were a bairn. I'm going to
make him get up for breakfast, and dress himself decently.
And I'm going to cut off the gas at the meter at eleven o'clock
every night. A regular way of life —'

She broke off. Her resolution was not sufficient to enable
her to finish her sentence. A regular way of life is the first
duty of a Christian, she was thinking, but William, she
knew, would not agree with her. Men got such queer bees in
their bonnets; even the best of them.

William still sat motionless.

'You said before – don't you remember? – that I was quite
right in standing up to him.'

Sarah was insensibly taking up the defensive.

The minister roused himself with a sigh.

'Yes, yes: you're right to a certain extent, Sarah. . . . He
must learn to live in this world as well as in the other.' He
smiled a little wryly. 'But washing one's face and putting on
a fresh collar every day is only cleaning the outside of the
platter after all.'

'It's at least a beginning,' said Sarah, turning to go. 'And
it's the only way that some bairns can be brought up to
understand that there must be order in the world.'

The door closed behind her, cutting her off, but leaving
the last sentence still hanging in the air.

Order in the world? Did William really believe that there was perceptible order in the world? What he believed was that God pervaded the world; but more and more he was being driven to acknowledge that God's order was beyond human comprehension, although not beyond human faith. 'Your God allows mean cunning,' Ned had said. 'Your God allows sheer cruelty. Your God allowed Christ to be crucified, and still allows it.' Ned was blind to everything but the evil in the world. . . . There was one remark of his which persisted at the back of William's mind. 'Your God allows brute savages like Hector Shand to do things to people that I wouldn't even think of, and then gives him a job and a wife and a home. . . .'

He had not known what answer to make, for he too felt there was evil in Hector Shand.

Strangely enough, although Ned was becoming more and more exasperating, the minister was now convinced that there was real innocence in the boy. He was not evil in himself. He was twisted with fear, but he was not evil. Ned was a queer tangle of odds and ends, like the reverse of a pattern which might never be discernible this side of the grave, but which one felt was there. God's pattern, thought the minister.

He summoned to his recollection what he could remember of his brother's life. It was not much. There were six years between them – a large gap when both were young. He was at the University when Ned was at school: and he was in orders when Ned came to the University. But there was one domin- ant characteristic in all he could remember: Ned's amiability, gentleness, docility – whatever it was, it was an almost excessive mildness of temper. Ned had been tied to his mother's apron-strings until she died. He must have been about ten at that time.

The minister sighed, and followed in his memory the phantom of his mother. She had been gentle too; gentle and frail; uncomplaining under the harsh and somewhat frac- tious rule of her husband.

An odd thought struck him. Sarah was always like father, he said to himself in surprise, and Ned and I were like two different versions of mother. . . .

The more he brooded on this resemblance between himself and his brother the more agitated he became. It was as if he were resisting with all his might the temptation to catch hold of an idea which was struggling for recognition. How could there be a fundamental resemblance between two people whose vision of life was so different? Ned's vision was a nightmare; by an unhappy fatality he saw nothing but evil in the world. It was an impossible nightmare; one could not go on living in it; and yet the minister suddenly comprehended with agony that the nightmare closed round Ned with an immediate certainty that prevented him from questioning its truth. It was as real to him as water closing over his head. But if Ned were like a man weighted down so that his head was just under water, with a little readjustment could he not be as easily cradled on the top of the sea, and would he not then be exactly like his brother?

The minister swerved away from the implications of this admission, and forced his mind back to Ned. When waters are closing over his head a man can think of nothing but himself: he cannot be gentle and amenable; he must insist that his feelings are of the first importance, and that he is suffering; he must be in a state of terror. All that was true of Ned. Nor is a man necessarily a devil because he is drowning and clutches at other people and curses God. An infinitesimal readjustment to bring his head above water will suffice to restore his natural gentleness.

The verse in the Book of Job detached itself once more from the page:

'O that one might plead for a man with God, as a man pleadeth for his neighbour.'

Oh, that one might!

What was this sea that closed over Ned's head and for so many years had cradled himself in security?

The point of the idea had at last pricked the minister's consciousness, and he started. Ned saw nothing but evil around him, and for years he himself had seen nothing but good. He had believed in a consoling dream exactly as Ned was believing in a nightmare. Was the dream as false as the nightmare? Or were they *both* real?

The minister felt as if he were on the verge of a sickening abyss.

When he recoverd himself he said aloud: 'Neither heaven nor hell. Or both heaven and hell?'

He remembered, as if from a far-off world, that he had once guessed at a final state of being where there was neither punishment nor forgiveness, neither good nor evil. . . . But that must be on the other side of death. . . . On this side of it both heaven and hell were real. You could not have one without the other: you could not live without admitting both. That had been forced upon him.

They must be real. They must be real. But God was incomprehensible.

'O that one might plead for a man with God, as a man pleadeth for his neighbour.'

But one might not. Sympathy was unavailing. That, too, he had had to learn.

The minister offered up a prayer to the incomprehensible God he acknowledged, asking that his feeble spirit might be sharpened and hardened to do God's work as a faithful member of His Church.

Later he finished his sermon.

# PRECIPITATION

## ONE

'And my cats?' said Madame Mütze, pausing on the terrace. 'You will be good to them while I am away, Madeleine?'

'Bou Di,' said Madeleine, the tears running down her broad cheeks. 'But I shall fatten them up for the return of Madame. Madame is too good to all the creatures.'

'If it comes very cold leave the little shed open for them.'

Madame looked up the valley towards the col, which was powered with snow. Behind the long low house the hillside rose steeply, thickly grown with thorny scrub, in which sheltered the stray cats who so mysteriously appeared every morning at the back door of the Villa Soleil. The sky was grey. Madame turned slowly round and looked over the sea, marvelling as she still did after three years at the persistent blue of the water in spite of the grey sky above it.

In her childhood she had imagined heaven as a space of luminous blue, behind the bright blue sky of the hymn, and the magic of that infantile heaven still cast a glamour over the Mediterranean; for the sea remains changeful and mysterious even to those who are disillusioned about the sky. Yet although the sense of magic suffused Elizabeth Mütze when she looked at the blue sea her characteristic passion for analysis insisted that a colour so independent of the sky must be caused by minute particles of some kind held in suspension in the water. In another person the analytical passion might have dispelled the sense of magic, but Elizabeth Mütze had preserved them both; and on this dull day she wondered as usual whether it was limestone or salt in the water that made this southern sea so magically blue whenever one looked at it with one's back to the sun.

She turned to Madeleine again.

'Au revoir. Madeleine, I shall return soon; in three weeks,

perhaps two, if I am very frozen in Scotland.'

That Madame should be going to the ends of the earth in the middle of winter! Madeleine's protestations broke out anew, but her mistress laughed and said: 'Be at ease. I shall return long before the snakes come, Madeleine, and that is what you really fear, is it not?'

A broad smile irradiated Madeleine's tears.

'But it is true, that about the snakes! Madame is learned; she does not believe it; but it is true!'

Madeleine's husband, the old Antoine, carried Madame's suitcase to the carriage, in which the young Antoine was already cracking his whip. It was not far down the winding hill-road to the station; Madame's seat was booked, she had nothing to do but to think. Madeleine, craning her neck after the cloud of white dust, said to herself: The poor Madame, she goes away to forget.

Elizabeth Mütze might have said that she was going to remember. The two halves of herself which Karl had held together were now falling apart again. When she first met him, ten years ago, she had told him that she was like an ill-regulated alarm clock; the hour struck at the right time, but the alarm did not go off until days after, when it was too late. The hour was now striking for her departure to Scotland; the mechanism ticked correctly; her luggage, her tickets, her seats, were all booked; the carriage was creaking down to the station; but she felt as if she wre going only a few miles away, and when the alarm did go off, days – or perhaps weeks – later, everything would already be changed and irrevocable.

This time-lag in her feelings had become painfully evident since Karl's death. She thought she had squarely faced the likelihood of his death; she had seen it coming for long enough to be prepared; she had discussed it with him calmly. When he was dead she had closed his eyes and given the necessary orders with a fine fortitude that was the admiration of her friends. All was over, she told herself, and thought that she knew exactly what that meant. But a month later the alarm had begun to go off. A voice within herself cried passionately night and day: You did not tell me it would be like this! And she could only grieve, and found no answer but that she was apparently as blind a fool at thirty-nine as she had been at nineteen.

Yet age made a little difference, she thought, sitting composedly behind the young Antoine. At nineteen Elizabeth the first was at least thrilled by the events into which she so recklessly plunged Elizabeth the second; at thirty-nine Elizabeth the first was *blasée*. She ought to have been excited over her return to Scotland; an absence of twenty years was no trifle; but she felt as if she were only stepping into the train for Monte Carlo. . . .

And yet, as usual, Elizabeth the first had no hesitation. To go back to Scotland was the right thing to do. One should have a standard by which to measure one's growth. In returning to the home of her childhood and stormy girlhood she would perhaps find out where she now stood. Karl had been her measure for so long that without him she was lost. Madame Mütze settled herself in the corner seat and wondered whether everyone had as cold and imperative a monitor as she had within herself.

When she was a little girl Elizabeth the second had been, if anything, a few moments the quicker of the two, and Elizabeth the first was restricted to making sarcastic comments. It was in her teens that the sarcastic devil had taken the lead, and by the time she ran away from Calderwick with Fritz Elizabeth the second was toiling well in the rear, and all her agony had not availed to change events.

Nor did it now avail. Karl was dead and buried, Elizabeth reiterated to her other self. The clear, firm contours of the land she had been living in had made her beliefs sharp and concrete. None of your Celtic twilights, said Elizabeth the first grimly, looking out of the window at the well-defined planes of the landscape and the houses. In the south of France appearance *was* reality. Karl was dead and buried. Life went on. Moreover it was only fools who needed to be reminded of that, she told herself. The one grossly obvious fact about life was that it went on, on and on and on. Life was like roulette; if the stakes were never removed from the encumbered table the game would have to stop. Karl was merely a stake.

You are making phrases again, protested the other voice.

I'm telling you the truth, she answered. . . . This craze of humanity for preserving the last resting-places of its dead is going to have queer results in another half-million years. What will the living do when the cemeteries of the dead are spread over half the habitable globe? Find a new theory, I suppose, about the Day of Resurrection.

However divided one may be, to travel alone in an express train induces a sense of singleness. The multifarious world, so inexorably receding and renewing itself on both sides of the train, compels the lonely spirit by contrast to become aware of its integrity. Long before she reached Saint-Raphael Elizabeth Mütze had ceased to debate with herself, and had given herself up to the impressions which flowed upon her from outside. Like the thrust of a pin helping forward one by one the cogs of a reluctant wheel, each new vista moved her thoughts a little further from her painful obsession with the dead by forcing her to realize the living.

The solitary passenger has a peculiar, almost a god-like, detachment from the lives through which she flashes; then, if at any time, she can contemplate individual destiny *sub specie æternitatis*. She can see without being seen and without responsibility for what she sees. Children stop playing in the dust to wave a hand; startled small animals lift their heads; in one continuous movement she experiences countless disconnected existences, bound to their environment and changing in nature, in occupation, as that changes. Thickly cultivated ground, lonely waste, wayside village and spreading city all spoke to Elizabeth Mütze in their own voices as the train sped on, and by the time that darkness fell she had become a passive listener.

Here I am, she said to herself, walking up and down the platform at Marseilles, and that is the last irreducible fact. Karl was, and is not. All these people simply are. *Why* they are, and *how* they are, is of no conceivable importance; it is sufficiently remarkable that they *are*, that they exist. It is most extraordinary that I exist, that I am here, walking on a platform in a city called Marseilles.

She slept in the train more soundly than she had slept for months. When she awoke the passivity of the night before was faintly irradiated by a more positive feeling, as if to the statement 'Here I am' she had added a hesitating query: 'What next?' The fields and houses running past no longer beat into her consciousness; she sat gazing at them only half-seeingly. Now and then something caught her attention, a receding line of swaying poplars, or the silhouette of a hill, but what she chiefly observed was the gradual thickening of the air, the encroaching clouds that brought the level sky closer to the earth and spread a veil over the sun. It was nearly two years since she had been even so far north as Paris; four years since she had been in London; twenty years since she had been in Scotland. The clear, sharp contours of the land were softening into a blur in the hazy atmosphere; presently it would be raining; but she assured herself that her stark vision of facts would never be dimmed, no matter what happened to the landscape.

Yet she did not now repeat with savage vehemence that Karl was dead. Instead she brooded over the years that they had spent together. What had she brought out of them besides the elemental consciousness of being alive and the determination to face facts? Karl had always told her that she was an extraordinary combination of scepticism and vitality. 'I look for what is true,' he had said in delight, 'and you leap like a tiger upon what is *not* true. So we correct each other.' She had leaped like a tiger on many of his theories. . . . Madame Mütze found herself smiling. Karl invariably looked at facts as if they were hieroglyphs, and his divination in reading the ciphers was sometimes marvellous. A great part of that, at least, he had left behind him, in his seven books. 'Meine sieben Sachen,' he had said, laughing, a fortnight before he died, 'they are literally all I have to show.' He had written them since meeting her and – how characteristic that was! – he had written them in his study surrounded by mountains of reference-books, without once visiting the countries whose ciphers he unriddled. Her vitality, he had said, was all he needed to provide him with vegetative material on which to feed. . . . Women were like grass, he said; they were the fundamental nourishment. . . . Anonymous nourishment, thought Madame Mütze, remembering how she had objected to this description. Karl had always explained her elaborately to herself; but he had explained

himself too; he was able to say at any point precisely what
influences were affecting him, and she had never subscribed
to his explanations. Still, Karl survived in these seven books,
and she survived only in herself. She had nothing else to
show. Was she, then, mere pasture on which an imaginative
man could browse?

I wish I could really *see* myself, she thought, gazing out of
the window. I can see other people clearly enough; myself I
cannot see. I know nothing about myself, except, simply,
that I am here and going to Scotland.

Karl had been amusing about Scotland. 'I have never been
in Scotland,' he had said loftily, 'but I know that you cannot
be Scottish. No, it is impossible. You have the rational
scepticism of a Latin, and the temperament of a Latin. That
is why you had the sense to run away from Scotland, my
Elise.'

Karl should have written a book about the primitive
people of Scotland, she thought with a spurt of amusement.
He would have inspected their mythology as if they were
Tlinkit Indians. He would have explained their ideology to
them. Ideology was a favourite word of his.

What was the ideology of Scotland? Looking back,
Elizabeth Mütze strove to revive her memories of the little
town in which she had been born and brought up. For years
before she ran away she had lived in a state of perpetual
resentment, it seemed to her, but there was no bitterness in
the recollection. It was like looking through the wrong end of
a telescope at something so distant that it became
impersonal. Her emotions remained untouched.

Yet why had she written to her brother John? She had
regretted the letter as soon as it was posted. It was a capitulation to all that she had run away from. It had seemed to
make her marriage vulgar. The people in Scotland would
never understand that marriage; she had not attempted to
explain it to John; she could barely explain it to herself. At
the time she had thought it amusing to end with marriage
instead of beginning with marriage; and she and Karl had
laughed over it once the argument was settled. She was
herself surprised at the curious ferment of feeling it caused in
her some days afterwards, a ferment which brought up from

the depths of her nature the desire to let John know, and, less excusably, the desire to let Aunt Janet know. It was partly devilment that had prompted the letter, the devilment of a schoolgirl. Madame Mütze was ashamed to remember it.

Karl had also written to his people in Mecklenburg, and he had neither excused nor regretted his letter. My parents love me very much, he had said, and they will continue my allowance to my widow, which they would not have done to my friend. Neither the genuine sentiment nor the equally genuine element of calculation had disturbed Karl; presumably Germans had a different ideology. . . . Or was it merely that Karl was a different kind of individual? As soon as she had posed the question Madame Mütze realized how absurd it was. One could not classify people in that way. Karl was a German, but not a typical German; she was a Scot, but not a typical Scot; had one really explained anything by saying that?

In Scotland, at any rate, she would find out how far she had progressed. She smiled again at her assumption that Calderwick had stood still for all these years while she had been moving swiftly. Could one ever correct the delusion that life decreased in importance and intensity the farther it was removed from one's own immediate neighbourhood? One's very eye fostered such illusive analogies; the fences and telegraph poles next the train appeared to be moving at great speed, while the trees in the middle distance were slower, and those in the farther distance stood still, like Calderwick.

But if Calderwick had also progressed how could she measure against it the changes in herself? There was some conspiracy in the nature of life which would always prevent one from seeing oneself clearly against an unchanging background. That was in itself a kind of proof that nothing stood still, whatever one's illusions.

Madame Mütze was not in the mood to protract her journey by lingering in Paris or in London. One did not dally with the spoon when one took a nauseous draught, less than ever when one had deliberately prescribed it for oneself. She was an excellent traveller, and she conveyed herself ruthlessly from train to steamer, from steamer to train, and, crossing London by night in a taxicab, settled herself to sleep in the Scottish express. The comfort of her present journey was in sharp contrast to her flight to London with Fritz so many years ago. What a disappointment London had been to her then in the smoky grey morning after a night spent in a crowded huddle on a third-class seat! She had expected a city of palaces, in wide and beautiful streets; and her first vision had been of dusty litter, grime, and staring advertisements of Reckitt's Blue. She remembered that pang of disappointment much more clearly than her growing disappointment with Fritz.

This time there would be no disappointment at the end of the journey. She had ceased to believe in miracles.

The train attendant spoke to her in a precise Scots accent. 'Two minutes past ten,' he said, in an almost defiant tone, when she asked the time of their arrival in Calderwick. 'But you'll have to shift out of the sleeper at Dundee, about eight o'clock.'

He said that as if it gave him a kind of satisfaction to put passengers in their place, looking through his spectacles with a shrewd, defensive glance. Take it or leave it, he seemed to be saying. Elise Mütze's charming air left him unaffected. She could not help smiling as she locked the door upon him. Compared with the young Antoine or the old Antoine he was an ungracious figure, although probably more efficient than they were. It was the tone of his voice that did it – a thin, dry, blighting intonation which suddenly re-created Calderwick for her.

*Br-rr-rr!* she said to herself.

But although she lay down with confidence in her ability to sleep soundly she was disturbed by dreams. Something within her was uneasy and apprehensive. One of her dreams woke her up. A voice, a dry Scots voice, was saying: 'You'll be exactly as you were before, only the inconvenience will be removed.' It was a surgeon, she realized: an operation had been performed; something had been cut out of her, and they were just going to remove the bandages, saying that it was all healed up now, when she awoke trembling because she was afraid to see the scar.

Her dreams were rare but vivid, so vivid that it was

difficult to believe them unreal, and for a second she felt her body, thinking that the bandages were after all removed, and yet the scar was not there. The same confusion of categories led her to assume for a moment that she was travelling through France towards Menton, and that Karl would laugh when he heard of her absurd dream. But Karl was dead and she was doomed to travel at great speed backwards through her life, as if she were reversing a spool, until she was shot out again at her starting-point, a resentful girl of nineteen brought back to an angry home.

Through these shifting planes of unreality her mind hurried, looking for solid ground, and came to rest on the consciousness that Karl was indeed dead. The uncertainties of her half-dreaming state resolved themselves into a regular rhythm of the engine beating out: Karl – is dead; Karl – is dead; and Elise Mütze buried her face in the pillow.

She awoke finally when the train jolted into the Waverley Station at Edinburgh. The Scots voices in the corridor and on the platform caught her ear, and she pushed aside the blind and peered out. The morning was still dark, but under the lights she had glimpses of what seemed to her large and brosy faces; while a diminutive boy was calling down the platform a cry she seemed to remember: 'Chawk-olit, Edin-burry rock.'

Forgotten scenes were knocking at the door. I must not miss the Forth Bridge, she said to herself, and became aware that she was excited at the prospect.

The excitement remained, even when the looming spans of the Forth Bridge ceased their recurrent flicker. With every mile the countryside grew more familiar as the day slowly broadened, and she sat gazing at the farm-lands, at the absurdly small grey cottages, without any of the philosophical detachment which had immobilized her in France. She paused only once to reflect that it might have been different had she been coming back for good, but that to a visitor everything remembered was delightful.

Before they crossed the Tay Bridge the attendant reminded her that she would have to change, and told her he would get someone to help in carrying her suitcase. He seemed more human. The *blasée* part of her shrugged, and thought: He's expecting his tip. But even as she tipped him, lavishly, she smiled upon him with direct friendliness; the cynical voice of experience was overwhelmed by an assurance that it was she who had altered, and not the man; she had moved from one frame into another, and her judgments were prejudiced in a different direction. She judged the man more truly, she thought, in her present mood than in her past one; her foot was on her native heath, and unconsciously her estimates of human worth had changed.

Yes, it was like moving off one shelf on to another.

Her excitement became painful as the train neared Calderwick. Every inlet of the grey North Sea, every little bridge and clump of trees woke memories. She admitted to herself at last that what had brought her home was her need for John's affection and her conviction that it remained unshaken after all those years. His letters left no room for doubt. John's affection might not enable her to see herself more clearly, but it gave her an immediate sense of her own value. That was what she needed. She was leaning out of the window when the train puffed into the windswept station of Calderwick. For the moment all the various personalities in Elizabeth Mütze were fused into one.

## TWO

From the beginning Madame Mütze's appearance in Calderwick produced effects she never guessed at. John was the only one of her circle who was not thrown off balance. As soon as he saw her he knew that his heart had been right; it was impossible that Lizzie should ever be anything but just Lizzie.

'You are exactly the same,' he said as they clasped hands, and he meant it honestly.

Mabel, however, peeping through the drawing-room window to see what she had to expect, was staggered. Arm-in-arm with John the most elegant woman she had ever seen was mounting her front steps. She met her sister-in-law effusively, almost obsequiously; clothes such as hers, worn as she wore them, exacted deference. Mabel capitulated on the spot. But her capitulation meant more than mere homage to superior taste and knowledge. Here was a woman who had committed the unpardonable sin, and instead of being made to repent in a tawdry equivalent for sackcloth and ashes she had prospered, and not only had she prospered, she moved with assurance and distinction, as if no breath of derogation had ever dimmed her lustre. She must have made a brilliant marriage, thought Mabel, observing with one swift glance after another the details of the newcomer's toilette. She sighed with happiness as she promised herself a long, *long* talk with her new sister.

'It seems absurd to call you Lizzie,' she said. 'You don't look in the least like a Lizzie.'

'Most of my friends call me Elise.'

'Elise!' chuckled John. 'I thought it was Mrs Doctor Bonnet, with a bee in it.'

John acquired importance in Mabel's eyes that morning.

Elise (she loved the name Elise) was apparently devoted to
him: and although Mabel ran about in her sister-in-law's
wake she never quite caught her up; it was John whose
company was preferred. But Mabel did her best. She consulted Elise upon every detail of the dinner for the evening.

'Who's coming?' said Elise.

Mabel was apologetic.

'I'm *so* sorry, we asked only Hector and his wife. Aunt
Janet's coming for tea. But we'll have a real party for you
next week, won't we, John? Let's give a dance for Elise.'

'I'd forgotten about Hector,' said Elizabeth Mütze. 'I
didn't realize that I had so many connections, John.'

John's gaiety clouded for a moment.

'Hector's only your half-brother.'

'And Aunt Janet's only my half-aunt. Aunt on the father's
side but not on the mother's.'

They looked at each other and laughed.

In spite of the laughter Elizabeth Mütze was determined
to allow no claims upon her except John's. As soon as they
walked out of the station – for she had insisted on walking –
she knew that she had returned to John but not to Calderwick. Calderwick had shrunk incredibly; it was like some
clean and quaint Dutch town, she observed; where had it got
that smack of the Dutch? Everything seemed to be in
miniature: the little market-square of the High Street, the
gabled houses, the short, straight little streets running
downhill towards the sea. It was all the same, yet not the
same, and by labelling it Dutch she kept it at a distance.

'I know what everybody's saying,' she remarked. 'They're
saying: "Eh, that's Charlie Shand's wild dochter come
back!"'

A faint uneasiness disturbed her. If she allowed it, Calderwick would reduce her too in size until she was merely
Charlie Shand's wild daughter again. Within the first ten
minutes she had found out what she wanted to know, that
the second half of her life was of much more value to her than
anything in the first half. Except for John. It was at that
point that she slipped her arm into his.

Elizabeth Mütze's determination to keep Calderwick in
the proper focus as a *genre* picture which she could inspect

with detached interest was perhaps what baffled and fascinated Mabel. It baffled Aunt Janet also, but without fascinating her. Janet Shand came to tea, as a concession to family feeling, but she came amply clothed in the righteousness of disapproval. Her niece's clear, amused eye seemed to strip her naked. Janet felt a little helpless because Mabel had apparently gone over to the enemy, but she returned several times to the attack.

'I'm glad to see you're wearing mourning, at least, Lizzie.'

'Oh, this isn't mourning: I wear black sometimes because I look well in it.'

'That's real lace, Elise, isn't it?' broke in Mabel, who had been eyeing the ruffles at her sister-in-law's neck and wrists.

'Quite real. I'll allow you to call it demi-mourning if you like, Aunt Janet, if it's a comfort to you. Eminently suitable for a demi-mondaine, don't you think?'

She regretted this remark as soon as she made it, but Aunt Janet seemed not to have understood the word.

'What is it they call you now – Mrs Moots, or something like that?'

'Frau Doktor Mütze. I'm really a German now, you know. Karl thought it better for me to take his name rather than my own, for, in German, Shand means disgrace.'

Elizabeth Mütze laughed merrily. But Janet Shand went away trembling with indignation. Lizzie was as heartless and unprincipled as ever. Although she was nearly sixty-four Janet still believed that the good were rewarded and the wicked punished not only in the next world but in this, and Lizzie's apparent immunity from punishment upset her. She also blamed Mabel bitterly for her defection; it was disloyalty to all respectable women to countenance such a creature as Lizzie. Her only consolation was her belief that Lizzie would yet come to a bad end. Lizzie was worse than her father, and despite her strong affection for Charlie Janet acknowledged that he had deservedly come to a bad end.

Mabel marvelled more than ever at her sister-in-law as she watched her fencing with Aunt Janet. Elise seemed to come from a world she could only surmise, a world where morality, as she knew it, was superseded by something else.

'Tell us about all the things you've seen and all the people you know,' she begged. 'You must have met lots of interesting people, Elise.'

There were times, Mabel suddenly realized, when Elise was uncannily like Hector. She was much smaller of course, but she had the same neat hands and feet, the same quick movements, and at this moment she had the same devilry in her eye, although her eyes were a clear grey and Hector's a dark hazel, so dark as to be almost black. Mabel bridled a little in response to the queer smile and the wicked look in her sister-in-law's eye.

'Of course, if you don't *want* to tell me, don't. I suppose you think I'm not able to understand,' she said, like a huffed child.

Elise flickered her eyelashes. 'Nonsense, Mabel. I don't know where to begin, that's all. Besides, although I've met lots of queer people, I've met none queerer than myself.'

Her smile broadened and became frank as she caught her brother's eye. John leaned back in his chair and guffawed. It must be admitted that this constantly recurring situation was trying for Mabel. She controlled herself admirably.

'Begin where you left off, when you came here, Elise. Tell us about your house, for instance.'

'My house? It stands nearly at the top of a hill, and there's a terrace with great brown jars on it, full of geraniums. Not genteel geraniums; masses of them, cascades of them. And from the terrace you look up the valley towards grey craggy mountains, and down the valley towards the sea. . . . Italy is on my left and France on my right, and the Mediterranean is my washpot. . . . And seven stray cats come every morning to my back door.'

John smacked his thigh.

'She could never go down the street without speaking to a cat!' he said.

'It's an interesting question,' went on Elise reflectively, 'this question of the relationship between humans and animals. . . . I can comprehend why I like cats, but why they like me remains a mystery.'

'You feed them, don't you?' asked Mabel.

'That doesn't explain why they all come walking with me

whenever I go up the hill. I never feed them at the top of the hill. They don't go up there by themselves, either; but every time I go up, one after the other joins me until I have the whole cortège frisking beside me. . . . It's the companionship they like. . . . They get it from nobody down there except me. . . . But why should they like it? It must be a give-and-take, but a give-and-take of what?

She had fallen, insensibly, into one of the musing discussions she used to have with Karl.

'There are snakes up on the hillside too,' she added. 'Oh, grass snakes, quite harmless and rather beautiful; as thick as my wrist. They come in the summer – I don't know where they spend the winter. Madeleine, my maid, swears that they all come looping down from the mountains in the early summer, and vanish there again in the autumn. At any rate we had a couple on our land all last summer, and every time Madeleine had to cross the hillside I had to escort her, because she's convinced that snakes follow up women in the hope of sucking milk from their breasts. She has the most gruesome stories of young mothers falling asleep and wakening to find a snake suckling them! Madeleine is nearly fifty, and twice as broad as I am, but she wouldn't go to the wash-trough if I didn't come with a stick to fend off the snakes. She's full of queer superstitions about animals, almost all of them about the peculiar dangers women run. She thinks that men haven't nearly as much to fear. It must be a very old belief, as old as the affinity between Eve and the serpent; but it's not a belief in companionship; it's a sexual fear of some kind, perhaps —' She broke off suddenly.

'But you're not interested in that kind of thing. You must excuse me. . . .' She glanced at them, smiling. John was tugging his beard with a puzzled look in his eye. He was really wondering how Lizzie had managed to remain the same creature as the little girl who had believed in magic and had tended bruised bees in a paste-board hospital, furnished with flower-heads and lumps of sugar: but his puzzled expression misled his sister. Mabel, she divined, was merely bored; the superstitions of maid-servants did not interest her; but John, she thought, was troubled because of her queer ideas. . . . Oh, Karl, Karl! what shall I do without you? the other voice cried suddenly within her.

'My husband had a passion for myths and legends and superstitions. . . . I must have got into the habit of talking about them,' she said, and immediately thought: What a fool I make myself appear, aping the dutiful wife! Is this the effect of Scotland?

'Will you give me a cigarette, John, and a light?' she asked, producing an amber holder from her handbag.

'I suppose everybody smokes on the Riviera?' said Mabel enviously.

'Don't you? Give your wife a cigarette, John. I'm sorry mine are all finished: I must get some more.'

John offered his packet to Mabel, with a half-doubting, half-roguish expression on his face. Mabel laughed, and took one, feeling very daring.

'I know how to smoke all right,' she said, cocking her eye at John as she puffed while he held the match. 'I used to smoke them on the sly behind the bushes at Invercalder. You never knew that, John, did you?'

'Bou Di!' said Elise, sitting up in her arm-chair. 'Is it still very wicked for a woman to smoke a cigarette in Calderwick?'

'Of course it is.' Mabel blew out smoke. 'It's not *done*, my dear Elise.'

'I can only suppose, then, that a cigarette has a suggestive shape and that when a man sees a woman sticking a cigarette into her mouth —'

John looked embarassed: Mabel giggled. But Elise was furious with herself for not having said outright what she meant.

'It's not funny,' she said. 'I didn't mean it to be funny. The idea that it's unchaste for a woman to smoke a cigarette is on a level with Madeleine's superstitions about snakes.'

Mabel as well as John now looked embarrassed. A little leaven may leaven a whole lump, but when it is a moral process the leavening may take a long time. Even although she had decided that it paid to be like Elise, even although she had determined to be like Elise, Mabel felt uncomfortable.

Elise, however, suddenly chuckled and lay back again in her chair.

'Upon my word,' she said, 'here am I glowering in your drawing-room, John, just as I used to glower when I was fifteen. I'll tell you what's the matter, it's Aunt Janet. She's brought it all back to me. She used to put me in a dumb rage from morning till night, Mabel, and I find the old rage rising up again.'

'I don't remember that it was ever a very *dumb* rage,' said John.

'Yes, it was! It seethed inside me for weeks before it boiled over. I remember thinking,' and she laughed, a clear laugh, purged of resentment, 'that for Aunt Janet the world was nothing but one enormous fig-leaf! And I thought of pointing out to her that one is entitled to the fig-leaf only *after* eating the apple from the tree – not before. However I—'

John knew very well what she was hinting at. In picking that German fellow she had picked a sour enough apple from the tree of knowledge of good and evil, and surely she might have the decency to admit that it had set her teeth on edge. The very thought of it had set *his* teeth on edge. He liked Lizzie to be light-hearted and audacious; her audacity thrilled him; but, after all, there was a limit.

Elise observed his uneasiness.

'I've shocked John again,' she said. 'I always did. But you like being shocked: you know you do.'

Of course he liked it. John smiled at her. Yet his uneasiness persisted. Lizzie's freedom of speech was exhilarating, but she had upset him once by showing that it could lead to freedom of conduct, and now he realized that he could never again trust her completely. Lizzie had come back exactly the same Lizzie that she used to be, and in bringing back the old delight to him she had brought back the old problems.

To disapprove, to check Lizzie's exuberance, was as difficult and as necessary as it had ever been. There was a limit; of that John was convinced; a firm line of demarcation ought to be drawn: but how insubstantial, how elusive did that line become when scrutinized closely by the dazzling searchlight of Lizzie's gaiety!

'It's Aunt Janet's fault,' said his sister, 'if I have a passion for tearing off fig-leaves. . . .' To herself she added: That must have been what Karl meant when he said I pounced like a tiger on what was *not* true. Fig-leaves!

An incongruous but relevant memory intruded itself, of a statue she and Karl had chanced upon in the Salzkammergut, a statue representing the Trinity. God the Father, she remembered, had a long beard and a cock eye: God the Son was wearing the dove of the Holy Ghost in place of a fig-leaf. Aunt Janet would like that statue, she thought. . . .

She glanced round inquiringly, and Mabel found an ash-tray for her.

'Thank you. Would you mind very much if I had a bath now and took a rest before dinner?'

'You won't have very long,' said Mabel. 'The Hector Shands will be here in about half-an-hour.'

'I think you'll like your namesake,' John put in. 'I've seen her smoking a cigarette.'

Elizabeth Mütze stood still.

'My namesake?'

'Hector's wife. Her name is Elizabeth. Elizabeth Shand.'

'How dare she?' said Elizabeth Mütze.

## THREE

Elizabeth Mütze lay in the bath sniffing at a clear, maroon-coloured piece of soap. It was like John, she thought, to stick to the soap they had always used as children. She had no doubt that the violet-scented soap was Mabel's, and the plain soap John's. So damned healthy. . . . He was just the same. He had always liked her, and yet he would have preferred her to be plain Jane and no nonsense. He was just the same: terribly moral, terribly sensible. . . . She could twist him round her little finger up to a certain point, but beyond that point—Schluss! Beyond that point John was quite impervious to argument. It was queer that he, the brother, should be so bound to the moral code while she, the sister, followed her own line. The sheep and the goats again. . . . The one could never have any but a purely sentimental attachment to the other. . . . Affection plus disapproval was of no bloody good to anybody.

I shall clear out immediately after Christmas, she thought, pitching the maroon piece of soap into the soap-dish. Any attempt of mine to hang on to John is damned silly. Surely I can stand on my own feet?

This assertion of herself was followed by a slight shock as she remembered that she had a namesake in Calderwick. Another Elizabeth Shand in the family seemed an insult, as if an interloper had pushed her out of place. Yet what place had she in the family after all? Why should she care how many provincial nonentities assumed her name and style? Elizabeth Shand! She said it aloud, with exaggerated scorn. Thank God I'm not Elizabeth Shand any longer! she added, climbing out of the bath and towelling herself furiously.

If she stayed long in Scotland she would have to live on the defensive. That was, of course, an admission of weakness.

She had not expected to resent Aunt Janet so much. Damn the woman!

Here I am glowering again, she said, laughing a little as she lay down on her bed. The relaxation of her limbs relaxed the tension in herself and she continued to smile as she shut her eyes. Let them all sit in judgment: there was no gaol to which they could consign prisoner at the bar. Aunt Janet's morality was a fiction; it had no relation to the one important thing in life, the integrity of the spirit. What was it you used to say Karl? *Integritas, consonantia, claritas.*

She rested for a time on these cool words. . . . And yet, she thought, absurd as it is, I find it trying to be treated as a fallen woman.

Her smile became mischievous. She continued her inaudible conversation with Karl:

Aunt Janet despises me as a prostitute. Mabel envies me as a successful prostitute. John worries about me as a prostitute turned respectable, who may lapse again at any moment. Not one of my kin can accept me as I am . . . as you did.

The smile faded from her lips, and she was lying very still on the bed when Mabel herself knocked on the door, crying: 'Aren't you ready yet, Elise? Can I come in?'

Elizabeth Shand, meeting John's kind eyes in the drawing-room, felt guilty. Her courage was screwed up: she was ready to tell John that Hector wanted to go away, and that for his own sake he must be allowed to go away, but Hector had objected to her telling John that evening.

'No, no, damn it,' he had said, 'I want to enjoy myself to-night. Time enough to burst it on him in a day or two.'

The knowledge that he was going to be quit of everybody in a short time exhilarated Hector. He had no consequences to fear: whatever he said or did would be wiped out by the simple act of departure; and he found that he did not care what other people might do or say. He was even prepared to have some fun with his disreputable sister. 'Let's all go on the blind together,' he said to Elizabeth: 'let's make a night of it.'

Elizabeth could not approve of his recklessness, for she was too deeply committed to the responsibility she had assumed. The Noble Wife must help her husband to be his best self, not his worst; she must form him, and that, of course, meant that she must reform him.

Elizabeth's voice was a little sharp as she refused to consider the possibility of making a night of it. It would only make John angry, she said: and it would be bad policy to make John angry.

Hector, knowing instinctively that the greater the sin the more effective is subsequent repentance, waved her argument away. If old John were in a paddy he'd be all the more pleased to get rid of the villain. 'He'll even pay me to clear out if I play my cards well enough.'

Yes, thought Elizabeth tartly, but what about *me*? She did not elaborate the thought; she even stifled it: she must not think of herself, she must remember only that she loved Hector. Yet the look in Hector's eye as he spoke of playing his cards well alienated her; and the boisterous manner in which Hector and Mabel greeted each other alienated her still more. For a moment Elizabeth wished that Hector were already out of the country.

Mabel ran upstairs to summon her sister-in-law and, left alone with John and Hector, Elizabeth felt awkward. With the departure of Mabel, Hector seemed to think that social interest had also departed. He turned over the gramophone records, whistling a tune as if there were nobody but himself in the room. For the first time since coming to Calderwick, instead of wondering whether she was a credit to Hector Elizabeth began to wonder whether he was a credit to her.

A little reflection might have shown Elizabeth what was happening to her, but incipient reflection and dawning doubt alike were caught up and blown into nothingness by the entrance of Elise.

The eye sees what it looks for, and Elizabeth was looking for her other self. Had it been a man whose arrival she was expecting with so much interest she would have been embarrassed by that interest; had it been a man who now came into the room she would have been afraid of her own emotion; but since Elise was a woman Elizabeth did not know that she actually fell in love with her at first sight.

Elise, cool and sparkling, noted that it was Mabel who

showed off Hector, and that it was left to John to bring forward the shy, large, awkward creature who called herself Elizabeth Shand. She examined her namesake with a satirical eye: one of these earnest women who don't know how to do their hair, she decided, and turned to Hector again with unconcealed surprise.

'I should have guessed you were a brother of mine even if I had met you at the bottom of the sea.'

She stared at him frankly.

'What a curious experience it is to meet someone so like oneself!'

'You're not very like each other, really,' put in John.

'Oh, but I think they are,' cried Mabel.

'Well,' said Elise, 'it takes the conceit out of me to find that I am merely a family type instead of an original model.'

But even as she said this she was discovering that Hector's mouth was different from hers: the lips were less finely turned, and opened over slightly irregular teeth: it was a larger mouth, too, a less discriminating mouth, a weaker mouth than hers.

'You're both black Shands,' said John. 'I went through all the family papers and albums when our father died, and I found that it was our father's grandmother on his father's side who was the first of that type in the family. But it's only a general family resemblance.'

'Black Shands?' commented Elise. 'I suppose Black Sheep is what you really mean, John?'

'How did you guess it, Elise? Hector is a double-dyed black sheep.'

Mabel's playful, provocative tone perfectly underlined her meaning, which was further emphasized by the hand she laid on Hector's shoulder. She wanted to let Elise see that she, too, had a way with men. Hector, who was a little taken aback by the elegance of his half-sister, welcomed Mabel's gambit with relief, and followed it up so thoroughly that the room was presently dominated by their brisk exchange of invective, which was kept up even after they were all seated at table.

Elise was half exasperated and half amused. She thought that they were both 'showing off' before her. How was the wife taking it? she wondered, and stole a glance at her.

Elizabeth Shand's eyes were cast down: it was impossible to tell from her face what her feelings were. A real Scottish face, Elise thought, all nose and cheek-bones: the black Shands were certainly of an entirely different type. 'That great-grandmother of ours,' she said to John, 'the first black Shand, was she a Scot, do you know?'

Her eyes were still resting absently on the face of the other Elizabeth, as if it were merely an exhibit in a museum of Scottish faces, but she was startled by the change which flitted over it when she began to speak. The girl lifted her eyes as if with an effort, as if a weight had been holding her eyelids down, and looked straight across the table at her. Elise almost jumped: the eyes were so intensely alive, the expression in them so completely altered the whole face. She felt unexpectedly embarrassed, as if she had been caught prying.

'There was a kind of suggestion, not certain enough to be a tradition,' said John, 'that she was partly a foreigner – an Italian or a Spaniard or something.'

'Ah!' Elise smiled. 'That might explain a lot.'

She deliberately included Elizabeth in her smile, and received another shock. The girl blushed.

Does she never open her mouth? Elise wondered. Is it shyness, or is she indulging her sense of power by keeping out of the conversation?

Aloud she said to John:

'This interests me. Have I inherited more than just the features of my outlandish great-grandmother? Am I to suppose that I'm not a free individual, but a victim of heredity, John?'

John was disconcerted by the question. He was inclined to agree that she was a victim of heredity, and to make excuses for her on that score: but he knew that nothing used to enrage Lizzie so much as having excuses made for her.

'No, no—' he stammered.

'What? You don't think that our great-grandmother, who may have been a wild baggage, is responsible for my being such an unsatisfactory sister?'

'And Hector an unsatisfactory brother,' interposed Mabel.

'Tut!' said John. He was annoyed. 'There's only a general

family resemblance between you and Hector: it means
nothing, absolutely nothing.'

He said this with all the more conviction since he was
uneasy in his mind: the unpredictable waywardness of his
sister was in some respects too like the unreliability of
Hector. 'Nothing at all,' he repeated.

'I think it does mean something,' said Elzabeth Shand, in
a low, hesitating voice.

'That's no compliment to you,' Hector turned to Elise.
'Elizabeth knows what a bad lot I am. Don't you,
Elizabeth?'

'Elizabeth may not know what a bad lot *I* am,' said Elise
wickedly, keeping her eye on the embarrassed girl. 'Some
are born to be black sheep' – she indicated Hector – 'some
achieve it' – she rolled an eye at Mabel – 'and some have it
thrust upon them' – she looked at Elizabeth and John – 'but
I am the three in one, and the one in three.'

She was so droll that everybody laughed. Like a good
player, having secured the attention of her audience, Elise
exploited it to the full. Her light, sarcastic self was escaping
successfully from the other self within her, which could not
believe that Karl was dead. Her mind was alert and cool,
pinking its objects neatly, like a rapier. These objects for
the most part were human oddities whom she had met in
nearly every corner of Europe. Elise was a good mimic and
represented their differing accents with spirit.

Mabel was delighted to hear at last the word 'baroness',
which Elise used with apparent unconcern.

'So there she was, sitting up in bed; and she had staged
herself gorgeously, with a crimson cushion behind her and an
enormous parasol spread over her head. "I expect him in two
minutes," she said, "my dearest Elise, will you tie this over
the light to make it more flattering?" And "this" was a pink
silk nightgown. Of course, I tied it over the light for her.'

'Was she a real baroness, Elise?' said Mabel eagerly.

'Well, her husband was a German baron. She herself was
a Hungarian. She couldn't speak English at all, and the man
in this case was an American who spoke neither French nor
German, so that was why I had to interpret. "Tell him," she
would say, "that he is a volcano." "Tell her that the volcano

is an extinct one." "Ah, tell him that I know there is a glow kindling beneath the ashes." "Huh, how kin she tell that? Kin she tell how far a frog kin jump?"'

'Were you her companion?'

'I? Of course not. I was merely holidaying in the same hotel.'

So her sister-in-law really hobnobbed on level terms with baronesses, thought Mabel.

'Women who are convalescent in bed always seem to be amusing,' went on Elise. 'There was an American woman I met in Vienna, a huge, jolly creature, with a fist like a ham, and a voice like a fog-horn. In her clothes she was majestic and somewhere between fifty and sixty; but in bed with a pigtail over each shoulder she was just fifteen. I used to take in cups of tea to her while she was indisposed, and one day she said to me:

'"Why doesn't the doctor ever come in to see me?" She meant my – Karl – and I said: "I suppose he's shy of coming in while you're in bed," and she returned: "Tell him that if he comes into *my* room he'll be as safe as if he were in God's pocket."'

Elise laughed and held out her glass to Hector for refilling.

Hector had been filling his own glass very frequently, and while he replenished Elise's he gave her a confidential leer.

Elizabeth, on the other side of the table, noted that. Of course he was thinking that his sister was 'hot stuff' and that they would probably get gloriously tight together. She felt that this unspoken assumption could not but annoy Elise and make her withdraw into silence and she wanted Elise to go on talking, it did not matter about what. She plunged into the first sentence that occurred to her.

'I suppose you speak German very well, Elise?'

'I do know it pretty well.'

'It's an awful language though, isn't it? I had to get it up a little to read some notes on texts. They call a girl "it", don't they?'

Elizabeth stopped breathlessly, for she was overwhelmed by the conviction that her remarks were banal. Elise, however, set down her wineglass and took up the subject.

'Yes, a nation must be held guilty of its language. And

they don't call only a girl "it", they call a woman "it". "Das Weib" is a worse offence than "das Madchen", for it hasn't the excuse of being a diminutive. "Das Madchen" can be passed, for, after all, they say "das Bubchen". But to take "Weib" and subject *her* to a grammatical gender is purely pedantic. Is there another language in the world which makes a woman neuter? I could swear there isn't. Latin, French, Italian. . . ? I don't know any others, but I'm sure there isn't. What an indictment! Oh, I must point that out to some of my German friends!'

Elise looked pleased.

'It's the finest example of pedantry that I've ever met. . . . The rule is everything, the fact nothing. . . . As if there shouldn't be exceptions to every rule! . . . As if the right end of a word were more important than the right end of a woman!'

Elizabeth was delighted. How deftly Elise had caught the clumsily thrown ball, and how skilfully was she turning it round!

'So you think the psychology of a nation could be deduced from its language?' she asked.

'Not by me,' said Elise coolly. 'I should suspect myself of merely confirming my own prejudices. I can't track down ideas: I have to wait until they strike me. I knew – someone – who could shut himself up in a room and hunt ideas like big game. But I always suspected him of collecting only the horns and the skins. . . . I distrust any systematic interpretation of everything.'

'But, Elise,' cried Elizabeth, 'everything has a meaning if one looks at it. Everything implies everything else —'

Her mind was in a glow and thoughts were crowding upon her, as if she had pulled the end of a skein which was going to unwind until the whole of life was explained.

A daisy in a field, she was thinking, isn't just a daisy; it's the meeting-point of an infinite number of cross-sections of the universe.

'I dare say,' Elise interrupted her. 'But how do you know it's a true meaning? One of the things I liked best about Ilya, the Hungarian I was telling you about, was that she always said: "Life has no meaning, none at all. But I find it very enjoyable!"'

She gave her brother a smile, and Elizabeth, with a sense of rebuff, realized that Elise had not forgotten the rest of the company, and that she had. She was silent for the rest of the dinner.

They all removed to the drawing-room, and Hector, kicking rugs aside, began to dance extravagantly with Mabel to the gramophone. Elizabeth lingered beside Elise and John, praying for a chance of getting Elise all to herself. She wanted to communicate to the other woman her own fervour, and at the same time to relate it to everything in heaven and on earth. Whenever Elizabeth had a strong feeling she was impelled to give it a cosmic background. Yet, in spite of her excitement, she feared that Elise would find her dull. She had said nothing to interest the newcomer; nothing at all; she had only listened. . . . If she had not been so inexperienced Elizabeth might have known that everything comes to her who listens. She was, indeed, a gifted listener. Elise had already become aware that she was drawing vitality from the silent girl. What Elizabeth had said was negligible, but the warmth that streamed from her had given Elise a curious feeling of trust. One could trust this girl, she thought, without defining more closely in what respect the statement was true. Besides, Elise had once quoted to Karl, 'I am like a match; I must have a box to strike on,' and in Elizabeth, her namesake, she now perceived a very serviceable box.

'Come and sit beside me, Elizabeth – unless you want to dance with John?'

'Don't *you* want to dance with John?'

Elizabeth shyly slipped into the proferred seat. She did not want to dance. She did not want to be reminded that Hector and Mabel, having opened the door, were now glissading into the hall outside, like a pair of children. She wanted to thrust Hector out of her consciousness, but she felt a certain inexplicable anger against him, an anger which extended to Mabel. Elise had opened to her a world of escape from Calderwick, a world sparkling with interest which convinced her that she had been stagnating in mind if not in heart ever since coming to Calderwick, and, without suspecting for a moment that Elise had cut herself to the quick to achieve her apparent detachment, she envied her that detachment and was prepared to regard Hector as an encumbrance. Yet she was angered to see how well he and Mabel danced, and how closely they held each other.

John, too, was angered. His wife was almost flouting him in her disregard for propriety. He tugged at his beard, but he tried to look genial. The fellow, after all, was Elizabeth's husband and his own half-brother. Thank God, he thought, neither Elizabeth nor Elise seemed to take their behaviour amiss; perhaps there was nothing in it, after all.

Elise looked at him with an air of mischief.

'This kind of dancing is too expressionistic for John, isn't it, darling?'

'Too shameless,' growled John.

'But dances are always inspired by love or war,' went on Elise, 'and in either case, you know, a flank attack is the most successful.'

Elizabeth laughed, a clear spontaneous laugh.

Perhaps Elise had been deliberately testing the girl; at any rate when Elizabeth laughed without any undertone of disapproval her sister-in-law joined in the laugh with obvious satisfaction.

As far as Hector was concerned, the evening fizzled out lamentably. He had managed to kiss Mabel twice in the hall, but she was not sporting enough to keep it up, and he had to return in her wake to the family group. Elise, probably discouraged by John's unamiable temper, had not got drunk with him, although she had been friendly enough. Elizabeth had been a bit on her high horse, especially on the way home. And although she had made it up with him, and let him into her bed, there had been a something.

There was indeed a something, which Elizabeth recognized at first as the persistence of the embarrassment that had recently arisen between her and Hector whenever they kissed each other. Her body craved his embraces, but when he was in her bed she felt that a great part of herself withdrew from the physical contact. Her mind, too, was in a ferment, as if her encounter with Elise had roused a long-dormant faculty; scraps of the evening's conversation darted into her head and out again, followed by brilliant and exhaustive supplementary discussions of everything that had been touched upon; ideas branched and grew in all directions; the significance of heredity, of language, what she ought to have said about the meaning implicit in all things, beginning from the daisy in the grass – in short, her conjugal embarrassment was complicated by a bad attack of *esprit d'escalier.* Her mind kept flying away from Hector, and even from herself; it was no longer Elizabeth who put her arm round Hector's neck, it was a wife embracing a husband.

Her mental activity, however, was not the cause of the embarrassment, of this partial withdrawal. Something had been lacking ever since she had agreed to Hector's going away. The glamour had vanished, the deep, passionate excitement that had made her shut her eyes whenever Hector kissed her. And to-night her eyes were far from shutting. She despised her body; it had still turned to Hector although she herself resisted; her arm had snuggled of itself round his neck although she was cold to him. She despised Hector for flirting with Mabel, a shallow, commonplace pretty doll, and when she compared him with Elise he himself seemed shallow and commonplace.

It was the thought of Elise that gave poignancy to this contempt. It was because of Elise that she was ashamed of Hector. It was through Elise's eyes that she now looked at herself and her husband and despised herself for having fallen in love with a man who had neither wit nor brains, a man whose sole social accomplishment, flirtation, was crude both in its technique and in its objects.

Elizabeth disentangled herself from the sleeping Hector and climbed into his vacant bed. Oh, I am a fool, she said to herself, turning over and over between the cold sheets. She could not shut her eyes and sleep; she could not shut her eyes to anything. She was a fool. But how? And why? She took the wrong things too seriously, Emily Scrymgeour had said; and now, contrasting herself with Elise, she found herself stupid, heavy, clumsy and solemn; she wasn't even pretty like Mabel. She fell into an agony of humility.

But if she judged herself so worthless what right had she to despise Hector? What was it in herself that sat up aloft and belittled these two living creatures, herself in one bed and Hector in the next? What was it that tempted her to despise her body? Had she not always found a magical satisfaction in the thought that she was in her own little finger, her toes, her thighs, her belly, and her breasts? She ran her hands over her body. You are me, she said, repeating the statement again and again as if it were an invocation. She had cried out upon William Murray for saying that the body unsanctified by God is evil, and now she had herself fallen into that heresy, the heresy of thinking that the body, when some part of oneself holds aloof from it, is the wrong-doer. . . . Her arm, when it ached to snuggle round Hector's neck, was it in the wrong because something in herself rejected the action? Or was it her arm that was innocent, and her contempt, her withdrawal, her sense of shame, were they not evil? The spirit denounced the body as evil; could not the body also denounce the spirit? She had been despising Hector, envying Elise, abusing Mabel and belittling herself; if *that* was not the sin against the Holy Ghost, what was it?

Elizabeth went on stroking her body, almost mechanically. She herself, body and spirit, was also, like the daisy in the field, the meeting-point of an infinite number of cross-sections of the universe. But, unlike her, the daisy was folded up in a simple unconsciousness of its position. A daisy would never be ashamed of itself. . . .

As she lay quietly alone in bed an image of herself grew before her, hovering in space, an extended, shadowy image, clearly defined at each extremity and thickened into obscurity in the middle. It was an overlapping of vibrations rather than a solid form, and the vibrations extended beyond the farthest stars. One end of this shadowy projection had long, slow, full waves; that was the body and its desires. At the other end were short, quick waves; these represented the mind. And the space in between, she asked herself, the thickened obscurity, what was that? Muddle and confusion of forces, in which she was now involved? She strained to hold the image, waiting for illumination, but it changed; the middle portion condensed into her own shape, but the two ends diffused themselves throughout space, as if her head and her feet had spread into infinity. At the same time Elizabeth felt in her feet that desire to run which she had had so often, ever since childhood.

The firmness of sandy soil, the coolness of short grass on the naked foot-sole, the wet softness of drifting leaves in a ditch, all the sensations her feet had ever experienced, seemed to become a part of her again, and drew her down through her feet until she was the earth and all that grew upon it. Her blood ebbed and flowed with the tides of the month and the tides of the seasons, and she was no longer separate in her own body but a part of all life. And suddenly, as if she had broken through a barrier, in that world she found Hector. She remembered his grace and strength in running, his rejoicing head cleaving the waters of the sea, his quick eye and hand controlling a frightened horse; his neck was a column, his thighs were grand like trees; her body tingled with the remembrance of his body. All that she had not felt when he lay so recently beside her thrilled through her now; the glamour came back; and she knew that she had done wrong to be ashamed of him. She saw with immediate clearness that it was only inside a room, in the world of talk, of articulate expression, that Hector was trivial. Out of doors, with no roof but the sky, he was like an impersonal force. In loving Hector she had loved something transcending both of them.

The life which had streamed out through her feet, as if into a sea out of which all creatures rose like waves, returned upon itself as she lay rigid and flowed up – up, like sap rising, until she felt as if her head were branching. This was the other end of her vision, and she knew what it represented. It was the world that Elise had recalled to her, the world of thought, of ideas, spreading into vast impersonal abstractions which made another infinity.

And that was the world in which Hector had no part. . . . And between the two, stretched as if on the rack, lay the shape of Elizabeth Shand.

## FOUR

# I

Sarah Murray no less than William was being forced into a fatalism regarding Ned, but for different reasons. It had taken only two days to make a breach in the fortifications of her disciplinary theory. She had discovered that discipline depends eventually on might even more than on right, and within the four walls of the manse it was beginning to look as if might and right were on opposing sides.

On Friday night, as she had threatened, she had cut off the gas at eleven o'clock, after giving Ned fair warning. She ought to have gone to sleep with a quiet conscience, but she found herself lying listening in the darkness to the unceasing prowl of Ned's feet, up and down, up and down. There was something terrifying in the fact that he was not daunted by the darkness, that he had not taken refuge in bed. It suggested to Sarah that the darkness within Ned, to make him capable of disregarding the darkness around him, must be tenfold the blacker of the two.

After a long interval she heard the scrape of a match and the clatter of feet upon the narrow stairs. She half raised herself. Where was he going? Down into the dining-room. What was he doing, prowling about downstairs? But the doors and windows were all locked; the cupboards were shut up: there was nothing he could despoil except a tin of biscuits; and it was hardly likely that he would go out into the streets. She made herself lie down again.

He was walking up and down the dining-room between the table and the door. She could not help hearing him. Monotonous, insistent, his feet sounded first on the carpet and then on the boards. Should she go down after all and order him to bed?

Her disinclination to rise made the first small breach in her system of discipline, for of course it was absurd to have anyone prowling about in the small hours and she ought to have insisted on his going to bed. But she was so tired. Confused dreams ensnared her; the more she swept out corners the thicker she became entangled in cobwebs, and finally an enormous, hairy spider crawled over her shrinking body. She twitched and moaned, but she was asleep, and Ned remained downstairs.

On Saturday morning Sarah felt more irritable. Ned had got at the biscuit tin, and apparently he had been drinking water out of a broken cup; there were burnt matches all over the floor of the dining-room and the kitchen, and it was impossible to surmise at what ungodly hour he had gone to bed. But he must get up for breakfast all the same. . . . Sarah pounded on his door and then marched in.

Ned was lying on the bed in his shirt and trousers. He had kicked off his slippers, and thrown his collar on the floor, but these were all the preparations he had made for sleep. His unshaven chin looked dirty, and even in sleep his mouth was wry as if he had drunk a bitter draught.

Sarah shook him.

'Get up! It's breakfast-time.'

'What the hell!'

'Get up! It's breakfast-time. You're to come downstairs to breakfast like everybody else.'

When she and William were nearly finished breakfasting Ned had burst in upon them, in his socks, shirt and trousers exactly as he had tumbled out of bed, unwashed and unkempt.

'Go and wash yourself and put on a collar and tie before you get your breakfast.'

With a malevolent glance at her, but without a word, Ned had sat down as he was and seized the loaf in his filthy hands. So the issue was joined; the battle of wills begun.

Sarah had not spared herself. She heaped as much abuse upon Ned as he did on her. But she had been weakened by the look of sick distaste on William's face. Much good William was; he only got up and went out of the room. She was angry with William; he ought to have backed her up instead of tacitly agreeing with Ned's reiterated: 'Virago! Virago! Virago!'

The battle had raged all day. At dinner-time Ned was still unwashed, still without his collar and tie; and at tea-time, and at supper-time; and it was to be presumed that he would go to bed again in the same condition. But that was not what disturbed Sarah most. What disturbed her was that she was beginning to fear Ned. His voice had gone on all day like a saw; but towards evening the saw had taken on a sharper edge. He had turned upon her the very threats she uttered the day before. 'I'll thrash you within an inch of your life,' he had said, and 'I'll inform the police of the way you are treating me.' She had never seen him look so ugly. Even in his socks he towered above William, and she knew he was strong. Before he went up to his room Sarah felt that if she were for a second to relax the tension in her backbone he would be at her throat. She had let herself down to his level; and now that his first surprise was over he was emboldened, she felt, to attack her as an equal. For the first time in her life Sarah Murray locked her bedroom door from the inside. On the Saturday night she hardly slept at all, and heard Ned not only descend to the dining-room as before, but come up again towards three in the morning. She heard him say, as he passed her door, 'I want to know the truth, the truth,' and the savage despair in his voice struck to her heart.

Next morning, it being Sunday, she surrendered. She did not waken him at breakfast-time, but fed William and herself in the quiet peacefulness appropriate to the Sabbath. She established another record in her life by absenting herself from morning church, since Ned had not awakened by the time the bells were ringing, and she was afraid to leave him in the house with Teenie.

It had come to that. Sarah was trembling and afraid. There had been a moment on the previous day when Ned had grasped the bread-knife and her knees had knocked together. Ought she to have mentioned it to William? Her anger against William rose again. In his own way he was almost as bad as Ned. She felt resentful even of the fact that he had escaped to church, while she had to stay at home and face it out.

But life must go on, even in a manse on a Sunday. Although at the moment she should by rights have been sitting in the manse pew Sarah could not sit idle in her chair at home. She would help Teenie with her dishes since, of course, she could not sew or darn on the Lord's Day, and the idea of reading the Bible gave her a slight nausea. Without being aware of it, she was really angry with God as well as with William. . . . When Ned was about she had more faith in the police than in God, in the law of earth than in the law of heaven.

The two women were still in the kitchen when a noise on the stairs made them both stiffen.

'He's got up,' said Sarah dryly. 'Make the tea, Teenie.'

She carried a pile of dry plates to the cupboard and set them down on the shelf without a tremor. Yet her heart was fluttering queerly, though her hand was steady. She would not ask Teenie to do anything she was afraid to do herself, and so she could not send Teenie in with his breakfast. Methodically she began to arrange a tray.

The suspense before an expected blow falls is more painful than the blow, and Sarah thought that the time during which she arranged the breakfast-tray and waited to hear Ned slam his way into the dining-room behind her appeared long only because of her suspense. In reality Ned had passed the dining-room and was now at the front door. If he had gone quickly Sarah would not have been in time to prevent his going out, but he was walking slowly, as he had come downstairs, pausing now and then to mutter. Sarah suddenly heard him speaking to himself in the hall and darted from the kitchen through the dining-room without stopping to think.

Ned, in his dirty shirt and trousers, was opening the front door with a slow, abstracted movement, as if he were somnambulizing.

'Where are you going, Ned?' cried Sarah in a voice more anxious than sharp.

'I must go and apologize to Hector Shand.' Ned's voice was reasonable, even mild, but curiously remote. That gave Sarah courage. She sprang to the door and shut it.

'Hector Shand's in church.'

She stood with her back to the door. Ned did not seem to see her.

'I must know the truth, the truth. I must see Hector Shand.'

He began to tug at the door apparently without noticing her.

Sarah turned the key behind her and drew it out of the lock. Her personal fears had vanished, swallowed up by a greater, nameless fear as she looked at his dull remote eyes.

'The door's locked,' she said, trying to keep her voice from shaking. 'And Hector Shand's in church. Wait till the church comes out.'

For a moment it looked as if the mask of remoteness were to be broken up by a violent spasm of anger. Sarah repeated over and over again, 'Wait till the church comes out,' and finally Ned turned in the same meandering, absorbed fashion and drifted into the sitting-room. Sarah sagged against the door, but immediately recovered herself when she saw Ned trying the latch of the window. She opened her mouth to scream, but only a hoarse sound came out:

'Teenie! Teenie!'

An equally hoarse whisper answered her:

'What is it, Miss Murray?'

'Run for the doctor. Quick. And then fetch Mr Murray. Get him out of the church. Get John Shand too, quick. Lock the kitchen door and take the key with you. Quick.'

She followed Ned and spoke to him as if to a small child:

'Never mind the window, Ned. Wait till the church comes out and then you can go by the door. You're too early —'

She repeated these simple statements again and again, although she felt that the wheels racing madly in Ned's brain could not be controlled by anything so pointless as her words. Yet they were the only tools she had. . . .

The cogency of words is at all times mysterious, and perhaps the tone in which they are uttered has a more direct effect upon the hearer than the meaning they convey. A dog, for instance, will wag his tail when he is told in a kindly tone that he is a dirty scoundrel. These overtones or undertones of the spoken word are so potent even in human intercourse that precision in the use of language is almost impossible.

Sarah was right; mere words, however reasonable, however clear, might convey to Ned the exact opposite of their intention, or might convey nothing at all.

But there was something in her voice for which she had not allowed, and which penetrated to Ned. In spite of his size she could not help feeling that he was a bewildered child, and her heart swelled with an unfamiliar emotion when he turned obediently from the window. She remembered what a good child he had béen, what a good boy, and it was with real kindness in her voice that she said: 'Besides, it's raining, and you would catch your death of cold like that.'

After a moment's irresolution Ned sat down at the piano and began to play.

## II

On that same morning, after her vision of the night, Elizabeth woke with a sense of freedom. Mary Ann in the kitchen, hearing the sounds of romping in the best bedroom, smiled and sang as she laid the breakfast-table. The master and the mistress had made it up thegither, she thought, and the house would be itself again. It was a cold, rainy morning, but the merry skelp of feet on the floor above her head was as good as a blink of sunshine.

How easy it is to be happy, thought Elizabeth. She even particularized the thought, adding: How easy it is to be happy with Hector. It was as easy as in the first days of their courtship and marriage. She gazed with affection at him as he put on his collar; how lovable was the strength of his neck and shoulders! She was happy with that thrilling, apparently unmotivated happiness which, for so long as she could remember, had from time to time irradiated the world for her. It was a condition that arose spontaneously; it seemed to flow in upon her and through her, and had no perceptible connection with daily routine. It transfigured even ordinary objects and events, as moonlight transfigures a landscape, and with the same large carelessness as moonlight obliterated all sense of difficulty, of the incongruous, the impermissible. It fell upon Elizabeth most frequently when she was gazing into the gulf of the sky, or at the sea; but it had surprised her also in the enclosed haven of a summer field as she lay among flowering grasses, watching a minute insect climb a jointed stalk; and there were rare days, as now, when she woke to find it already in her heart. Her vision of the previous night had evoked it, she knew; and she thought, too, that she knew from which of the two infinities it sprang; it was not born of the head.

Her preoccupations of the past weeks sank into triviality. She had found herself again, and she was as happy as in the first days of her love for Hector, but, she told herself, it was a more informed, a better-grounded happiness. She no longer expected him to fill the whole world; he had his own kingdom; and instead of despising him for what he was not she rejoiced in him for what he was.

It must be admitted that Elizabeth remembered only the two extremes of her vision; she ignored the middle region in which was condensed the shape of Elizabeth Shand – the region, it may be presumed, of daily life, within which fluctuate the conventions that seek to form it. Between poetic passion and intellectual passion there lies a difficult and obscure space, in which many people spend their whole lives. . . .

Elizabeth, however, ignoring this middle region in which she was conventionally a wife in a tradition of wifehood – forgetting, that is to say, the burgh of Calderwick and all it stood for – was radiantly happy on this Sunday morning.

Hector announced that he wasn't going to church. In spirit he had already said good-bye to Calderwick, except for a few private qualifications, and refusing to go to church was a symbolic gesture. He would smoke his pipe and read the Sunday papers; he might even toddle down and pull Hutcheon out of bed.

Elizabeth laughed. 'I wouldn't go to church either if I didn't want to see Elise,' she said.

It was almost a point of honour. 'Shall I see you at church?' she had asked eagerly, and Elise, shrugging her shoulders, had answered:

'Church? Oh well, I never miss my cues.'

It would not be fair not to turn up at church after pledging Elise like that. Whether Hector came with her or not didn't matter. Whatever Hector did on the surface of life was now gloriously unimportant. The universe would have to be rent to its foundations before she and Hector were separated. He might leave Calderwick – he should leave Calderwick – but she would go with him, or follow him after a brief, impermanent interval of time. Measured by eternities their absence from each other whether she went to church or Hector to the South Seas was momentary and insignificant.

Under her own umbrella Elizabeth became a drop in the river of bobbing umbrellas that slowly flowed along the pavement of the High Street towards the churches. Elizabeth felt kindly towards the other umbrellas; they were all gong to worship the same God as herself, even although they had a partial and limited idea of the cosmic force which she acknowledged as the Godhead. She wished that people were not divided off into congregations; how much more sincere and moving would be a service if it were shared in by the whole populace of the burgh assembled in a gradiose and shadowy building! In a small church like St James's one was too conscious of the individual members. Elizabeth yearned for a tribal gathering of vast proportions, the vaster the better.

John was guarding the end of the pew, with Elise next to him. Mabel and Aunt Janet were sitting beyond Elise. After a moment's hesitation Elizabeth slipped in between John and his sister.

Elise sat looking round her with interested eyes. What a queer experience it was to be once more in the poky little church where she had suffered so much in childhood! She could even identify some of the people, grown older, but still sitting in the same pews, still clad in decent black. The same ornate chandeliers. The same flat white clock face. The same hideous yellow pine seats, and awful terra-cotta pillars painted behind the pulpit. The only difference was the presence of a small pipe-organ, each pipe decorated with squiggles of gold and terra-cotta, in front of which sat an organist embroidering a slow march with flourishes of his own devising. Elise remembered the old precentor with his tuning-fork; he was better than this.

She had almost forgotten that there was a beadle, who solemnly bore the big Bible up the pulpit steps and then stood at the foot of them awaiting the arrival of the minister from the vestry. It was not the same beadle; old Mr Webster was probably dead. . . . He had a comfortable, motherly wife who kept hens and always had fluffy chickens to show little Lizzie Shand. . . . Dead too, probably – all dead.

Elise began to feel as if she were in a churchyard. Each pew was a memorial to some dead member of the church; the blanks in the seats she remembered were more numerous than the survivors. The manse pew was quite empty. . . . The last minister she had 'sat under' was an unctuous vulgarian whom she had christened 'Pecksniff', and Mrs Pecksniff and all the little Pecksniffs used to fill that pew. How Pecksniff used to strut down to the pulpit, his black robe billowing behind him! And what a sermon he had preached after attending an elder's death-bed! Elise smiled; she would have enjoyed that sermon better now than in her younger days; she had now a more catholic taste in absurdity.

The minister was coming. The organist surpassed himself in a final flourish. The minister's gown hung lank; it did not billow like Pecksniff's. He held it closely round him with one hand; he stooped slightly as he walked. But quite a young man! Why did he walk like an ancient? A young man, and a hungry face. Poor devil, thought Elise. . . .

The rustling of pages began, and the organist pulled out stops. Elise recollected that she had no Bible, and rummaged in the shelf below the reading-board. All the old Bibles seemed to be still there; she examined first one, then another, and finally with a strange exultation drew out her own, dog's-eared and rusty, the very Bible Aunt Janet had given her on her tenth birthday. She opened it and stood up when the others did, but it was not the text of the psalm she was looking at, it was the straggling scrawls covering every blank space at both ends of the book. Her name, Lizzie Shand, and sometimes Elizabeth Shand, was repeated over and over in every kind of writing, sometimes sloping forward, sometimes backhand, with prim letters or curly letters, never twice the same. On one page was boldly written:

Black is the raven,
Black is the rook,
But blacker the Devil,
Who steals this Book.

And under that was drawn a skull and crossbones.

For a moment or two Elise felt not that the long-vanished Lizzie Shand was a ghost, but that she herself was the ghost of that impetuous and resentful small girl. The small girl's emotions touched her again; she was no longer coolly amused at the paltry ugliness of the church, the narrow complacency of the worshippers, she was both furious and miserable at being forced to take part in the service. Her one positive conception of God that He was a miracle worker, an omnipotent magician, had been shattered on the day when she had prayed Him to turn her into a boy and nothing had happened. The God that remained was merely an enforcer of taboos, and a male creature at that, one who had no sympathy for little girls and did nothing for them.

The psalm was finished, and Elise sat down, having travelled in two minutes from one century to another with a glance at John's beard. Elizabeth Shand, Gott sei Dank, was only an uneasy ghost between the boards of her Bible.

But another Elizabeth Shand had grown up meanwhile. Elise turned her head again, this time to look at the girl beside her. She had a vague idea that this Elizabeth Shand had sung heartily every verse of the psalm.

That was somehow out of character. . . . Elise felt, irrationally enough, that the resentments of her own youth should have passed on to the next generation of girls. Young things who did not know themselves were always at a disadvantage, and young girls faced with the traditional doctrines of the Church were at a special disadvantage. They ought to be resentful. And yet this young Elizabeth Shand had apparently accepted the old tradition; and these small children fidgeting on the next seat would in their turn grow up and fill the same pews, and believe in the same old – Or would they? Could such a hocus-pocus of nonsense prevail over human intelligence for ever?

The young Elizabeth Shand caught her eye and smiled, irrepressibly, it seemed, as if she were bursting with happiness. Elise again felt the curious warmth that streamed from her. The girl had vitality, at any rate; perhaps she was not imposed upon after all. She did not look as if she were.

An odd memory darted into her mind. She had found one Sunday two lines in a book of devotional poems she was set to read and had outraged Aunt Janet and delighted John by quoting them gravely at all times. What were they?

To me, to all, Thy bowels move;
Thy nature and Thy name is Love.

She shook with sudden mirth, and took out her handkerchief to stifle it.

John at the end of the seat tried hard not to smile. Lizzie had one of her old giggling fits; she always had them in church, the besom! How little she had changed! He hunted in his pockets for a peppermint; he always used to slide one into her hand when she giggled. She turned imploring eyes upon him above the handkerchief, but he had to shake his head. Not one, in all his pockets.

Elise bit her lip, struggling to control herself, but Lizzie Shand, although bidden to vanish, was a persistent ghost.

The jet bugles in Aunt Janet's bonnet trembled. Her face was very red. She had peppermints in her pocket, but she would have died rather than pass them to Lizzie. Mabel was surprised to see Elise forgetting her dignity. She felt a little superior and also a little nearer to her sister-in-law, less disposed to be snubbed. Elise had her weak points too. And after all, her past was *not* irreproachable although she had been clever in surmounting it. Mabel sat up straighter. Elizabeth the younger smiled openly. . . . The impish ghost of Lizzie Shand had apparently brushed against all of them, in spite of Frau Doktor Mütze.

The giggling fit left Elise as suddenly as it had seized her, but she too was no longer quite the same woman who had entered the church. Not only in memory but in feeling she had identified herself with the life of Calderwick, and in that brief moment, far beneath her consciousness, something had germinated.

But the unease in the Shand pew seemed to have spread

through the congregation. For a shocked second Mabel thought that all heads were turned in their direction. She was immediately reassured, however; it was the beadle everybody was regarding as he made his way on tiptoe down the passage towards the pulpit. The minister had just finished a prayer and was about to read the chapter from the Old Testament, but the beadle mounted the steps, passed him a piece of paper, and tiptoed creakily back.

A wave of expectation rippled through the church. Somebody ill? Somebody dead? A doctor or a relative urgently asked for? The minister looked upset. He sat down for a minute and buried his face in his hands. The congregation stopped rustling and sat in breathless stillness.

William Murray stood up, holding on to the book-board of the pulpit. He spoke in his ordinary voice, not his pulpit voice, and that struck many of his hearers as sacrilegious:

'There will be no further service. . . . I have had bad news; I must go home at once.'

Without another word he shut the Bible and descended the pulpit steps.

An excited buzz in which there was a note of indignation filled the church even before he had disappeared, and many were so busy whispering that they did not observe the beadle coming round to the Shand pew. But when John Shand got up and went out the buzz swelled in volume.

'What a like thing!' said Mary Watson to the people in the pew behind her. 'Not even a benediction. It's not decent.'

Most of the church members were of the same opinion. Nobody wanted to be the first to rise. The congregation had attuned itself to reverence, and its mood had found no communal discharge.

Two events stood out in the general uncertainty. Young Mrs Hector Shand and that sister of John Shand's, that hizzy – ay, she had had the face to come back – rose together and went out with unseemly haste, as if it were not the House of God they were leaving. Almost at the same moment the organist, with the satisfaction of one to whom a great moment has come, moved to the organ and began to play a doxology reserved for special occasions:

    Now to Him who loved us, gave us
    Every pledge that love could give. . .

Waveringly at first but finally united the congregation sang it through.

## FIVE

'Don't distress yourselves,' was John's parting admonition at the vestry door before he caught up on the minister and the manse servant.

A half-apologetic glance at his sister excused himself for having included her in advice that was really intended for the younger Elizabeth. Elizabeth was, indeed, extraordinarily agitated. Elise had marked the girl's agitation as she started to her feet in church, ejaculating something about Ned, and took to her heels. That was partly why she had followed her; partly too because she was both curious to know what had happened and thankful for a pretext to leave the church. Elizabeth had darted round the corner of the street to the little door giving access to the vestry, and all she had said was: 'I'm sure it's Ned. I know it's Ned.'

'What Ned?' asked Elise, but got no answer, for at that moment the two men and the maid appeared, and Elizabeth, disregarding John, flew at the minister with the accusing question:

'What have you been doing to Ned?'

John's intervention had saved what might have become a painful scene, thought Elise, as she drew her sister-in-law away, for the minister's defiant attitude could have been expressed in the Biblical words, 'Am I my brother's keeper?' and Elizabeth seemed to be primed for an explosion. The girl was full of surprises, thought Elise, with a half-smile, as she remembered her dumb shyness of the previous evening.

The wind had veered a point or two towards the north; the grey clouds were breaking up and blowing over a pale, cold blue sky; only the puddles with their ruffled surfaces told of the morning's rain that had driven in from the North Sea. It was towards the shore of the North Sea that the two women now turned as if by consent, although hardly a word was spoken.

Salt spindrift and an occasional fan of sharp sand stung their faces when they came out on the dunes. The sea was choppy and fretted with white caps; no whalebacked billows heaved from the horizon as on that day when Elizabeth had exulted in their power; the water looked cold and ugly, except towards the north where the broadening space of clear sky spread a greenish light over the bay and outlined the headland above it.

'How clear the light is over there!' cried Elise. 'Look, you can see every tree on the skyline.'

'You can see more than trees,' said Elizabeth, with a curious bitterness. 'There are the chimneys of the asylum William Murray is going to send his brother to.'

'Well, why not? Why are you so angry about it?'

'Because I'm sure he's pushed Ned over the edge. Weeks ago he said Ned was in hell, and since then he's been preaching hell fire and the wrath of God and original sin. What nonsense, what damnable nonsense!'

'In that case the brother will probably be better off in the asylum than in the manse.'

'Oh, Elise!' the girl's voice broke. 'Can't you *imagine* what it must be for a sensitive and nervous boy to find himself in an asylum for the insane? If he was bewildered and frightened before he'll be a hundred times more lost and terrified in the asylum. How is he to know that the world isn't cruel if he's kept under retraint? What can he find to believe if it's suggested to him on every side that whatever he thinks and feels is mad? And could he believe anything madder than that God punishes people by putting them in hell? If Ned Muray is to be shut up in an asylum I think William Murray should be shut up too.'

'If all the people who have delusions were to be shut up in an asylum there wouldn't be many left outside.' Elise was quite cheerful. 'Come and walk on the sand; it's too cold to stand still.'

'But why should Ned be singled out then? He's not really insane; he doesn't imagine that he's Napoleon or Alexander the Great or anything like that; he's only afraid that everybody's against him, that people are mocking him and trying to hurt him.'

'Perhaps they are. I've known people who attracted ill-treatment as a horse attracts flies. It sounds to me as if he were the kind of person who asks for insults. He'll be safer in an asylum. I am much more interested to know why you feel so strongly about him.'

'Wouldn't it upset you to hear that a young man you knew was being sent to an asylum?'

'I shouldn't be *angry* about it.'

'I *am* angry,' confessed Elizabeth. 'It's such a shame. It's such a waste of good material. . . . He was one of the best mathematicians at the University.'

'Even that doesn't move me to anger. I am prepared to be sorry for him, and to be sorry too for that poor devil, the minister, whom you were so ready to scratch.'

Elizabeth was silent for a moment. Then, almost in tears, she said:

'Don't laugh at me. I know I'm a muddled creature. But I am angry – I *was* angry, rather, and I don't know why.'

'I have found,' said Elise slowly, as if she were choosing her words, 'that anger – or resentment, which is the same thing – is a symptom of weakness in oneself, a sense of being at a disadvantage. My weakness is usually a susceptibility to public opinion. I try to cure myself by seeing the absurdity of public opinion when it is judged at the bar of my own reason. But I don't see what public opinion has to do with your anger in this case; for you are resenting an action in which you have apparently no part. That's what interests me.'

It was a long time before Elizabeth spoke again.

'I do have a part,' she said in a low voice. 'It's myself I am angry with; you are right.'

Elise made no comment. But Elizabeth could not leave the matter there.

'I have a bad conscience about Ned,' she burst out. 'He was a queer, solitary creature at the University. You know, in a university the effect of a crowd of students is exhilarating, but frightening too. Everything you do is done against a background of people your own age. Especially in a small university like ours. Even walking down the street isn't

simply walking down the street; it's more like walking down
a stage. You have to harden yourself against the crowd, or
pander to it, and enjoy it. I did both. Never mind that. . . .
But Ned Murray never pandered. Apparently he didn't
harden either, although he might have armed himself in
conceit because of his class record. . . . He simply hid. He
slinked. He scuttled round corners. . . . And so they ragged
him. He had a chest of drawers and a table piled against his
door; he was as frightened as that. . . . And they pulled him
out. He screamed until they had to gag him. . . . They
shaved half his head and nearly drowned him in a fountain. . . . If people did that to me I think I'd want to kill
them. And yet I laughed. I knew about it beforehand and I
was amused. I heard about it afterwards, and I said: 'Well
done!' And now I know what a dreadful, horrible effect it
must have had on a nervous boy like Ned Murray, and . . .'

She was crying.

Elise patted her arm.

'I've *helped* to send him to the asylum,' sobbed Elizabeth.

'If you had made a public martyr of yourself and objected
beforehand, would the ragging have been prevented?'

'I don't know. . . . I d-don't think so.'

Would Hector have refrained from being the ring-leader if
she had objected? Elizabeth could not tell. But somebody
else would have led the attack at some other time. . . .

'If a boy insists on being like gunpowder waiting for a
spark the spark is bound to come, sooner or later,' said Elise,
'whether from your hand or another's.'

'But one should help other people and not hinder them.'

'In the long run one can never help other people.'

Elizabeth wiped her tear-sodden face and looked up.

'What?'

'People can help themselves only,' affirmed Elise with
decision.

'That's what I used to think, that one was separate, but
now I know it's not true, Elise! That doesn't go deep
enough. We're only separate like waves rising out of the one
sea. Last night I saw it and felt it so clearly, the oneness
underneath everything – and I knew that religion and poetry
and love were all expressions of that oneness. . . .'

Elizabeth had taken Elise eagerly by the arm, as if she would communicate her vision by contact as well as by speech. She poured out her sentences in a rush of words, forgetting herself in the urgency of her gospel.

'That's the oneness beneath us, out of which we rise, and there's another above us to which we grow, the oneness of intellectual truth. . . . It made me so happy; it cleared up something for me that I've always felt and never understood. And this morning I was at peace with the whole world because of it. And now – I can't go back on it. I can't shake off all responsibility for Ned. And that's partly, too, why I was so angry with William Murray; instead of preaching the real religion that strengthens the sense of oneness he was preaching separateness; he was cutting Ned off; he was turning what should have been a source of strength into a bugbear. . . .'

*Exaltée*, thought Elise, walking on in silence. There's something wrong here. Yet she sees through her own eyes, at least.

'Have you considered,' she said aloud, 'that this missionary zeal of yours would saddle you with the responsibility for every deranged and unhappy person in Calderwick – not to speak of the whole world?'

'No, Elise, that's absurd. I'm not really absurd. I'm concerned only with people I know, with people I meet, with people on whom I have some personal effect.'

'A limited liability company. . . . Well, I don't feel inclined to be a shareholder. Your universal sea out of which we all rise is too featureless for me. If I have risen out of it, which is possible, I'm not going to relapse into it again. The separate wave-top is precisely what I am anxious to keep.'

She looked up at the strong contour of the headland, brooding now in an almost animal solidity against the lucent green sky. Her thoughts were light and clear again; she felt revivified, as if new strength had been given her, and words came to her of their own accord:

'I maintain myself in the teeth of all indeterminate forces. This wave-top, this precariously held point of separateness, this evanescent phenomenon which is *me*, is what I live to assert. . . . And I should like to know why *you* want to drown yourself?'

For drown yourself you will, if you go on like that, she added mentally.

'It's not drowning,' said Elizabeth earnestly. Her tears had stopped. 'It's diving for something. Yes, that's what it is. Life is such a muddle, Elise – at least for me. I haven't your sureness. And the ordinary conventions haven't any meaning for me; I must dive for my own religion, my own meaning. Some day I shall find it. I think I have found some of it.'

She looked into Elise's face and smiled, the same shy smile of the night before.

'Do you know, in spite of what you say, you have helped me a great deal, Elise? You're the only person I've ever met who understands what I'm driving at, even although you don't agree with it.'

Elise too smiled.

'I understand it to some extent because I went through something like it myself. But that was before I was fourteen. Fourteen is the right age for missionary fever. You ought to have got over it long ago.'

All the way home Elise turned over in her mind the thought that something must be wrong between Elizabeth and Hector. One didn't dive into general love for humanity if one had a firm title to the love of one man. Not in her experience.

They were an ill-assorted couple, no doubt. . . . Elizabeth was intelligent, but innocent, whereas Hector! Probably the first man who ever kissed her, thought Elise, with a half-scornful, half-sorrowful smile. It wasn't her business anyhow.

## SIX

Teenie the maid had called in at the doctor's house on her way to the church, so Dr Scrymgeour was the first to arrive at the manse. Sarah was in the dining-room, watching the street from the window. Ned was still playing the piano, but his playing had become more vehement, more bizarre, and every now and then she could hear him rise from the piano and walk about the room. She tapped loudly on the window as the doctor emerged from his car, and when he turned to peer at her she waved her hand and ran to the door. This effectively hindered him from ringing the bell.

Sarah opened the door with as little noise as possible.

'Come in,' she whispered. 'Don't let him hear you.'

'A grand clatter he makes on the piano-keys,' said the doctor, sitting down at the dining-room table and drawing off his gloves. 'Now, what is it, Miss Murray? I got a message that you were frightened for your life. . . .'

Sarah hurriedly related the gist of what had been happening in the house for the last few weeks. . . . She hoped that the minister and John Shand wouldn't come in before her recital was finished, for she couldn't resist getting in a few flings at William.

'If I had Ned to myself I think I could manage him, Dr Scrymgeour, but there's Teenie – she's worse frightened than I am – and there's William, and he just drives Ned from bad to worse with his preachings, and, to tell you the truth, I'm fair worn out with it all. I thought I was at the end of my tether this morning when I sent for you, but the laddie hasn't been so bad since then. If he's handled like a bairn he can be managed; it's when William tries to reason with him that he gets past all bounds.'

'But the minister wasn't in when you sent for me, Miss Murray.'

The doctor looked at her keenly.

'No!' admitted Sarah; 'it was a new ploy of Ned's that frightened me. He was trying to get out into the street in his old shirt and slippers, saying he had to apologize to Hector Shand. . . . But I wiled him away and he began to play the piano, and he's been at it ever since.'

'M-m, yes.' Dr Scrymgeour rubbed his chin. 'I can hear him all right.'

Ned broke off short at that moment, and walked up and down the sitting-room arguing something in a high, excited voice. . . . Then as suddenly as he had left off he plumped down on the piano-keys again.

'Apologize to Hector Shand? What else did he say, did you notice?'

'He was roaring in the night, and this morning too, that he wanted to know the truth.'

'Ay, poor lad . . . poor lad. The truth's a kittle business, even for the best of us, Miss Murray. He doesn't sleep well, does he? More or less excited all the time?'

'He dozes off in the early morning and sleeps till twelve o'clock if he's left. But he never stops speaking to himself or roaring at us all the rest of the time. . . . I don't know how he can keep it up. It wears me out just to hear him.'

'Has he ever mentioned Hector Shand before?'

'Not that I can remember. But they were students together, of course.'

'Has he threatened anybody with violence?'

'N-not exactly. . . . I *was* frightened for a minute yesterday. . . . But he wouldn't lift his hand to folk, not really, Dr Scrymgeour. . . . He was always such a gentle laddie. He never used to say "No" to anything or anybody!' Sarah wiped her eyes. She was herself surprised at the excuses she was putting up for Ned.

'Quite so,' said the doctor. 'Quite so. And now he won't say "yes" to anybody or anything. . . .'

'But it canna last, doctor!'

'It may not last for very long. . . . We'll hope not. . . . But human beings are thrawn, Miss Murray.'

'Is it just pure thrawnness?'

'No, no, that's hardly what I meant. Let's say "persistent" instead. We couldn't go on living if we weren't persistent, you know. . . . And this laddie seems to have a lot of strength.'

'But why, doctor, why should he carry on like this? It's not common sense.'

'Not even the most sensible body is all common sense, Miss Murray. There's not much common sense about some of the things we keep in the wee corners of our minds. Eh?'

He darted his 'Eh?' at her with a kind of giggle, and at that moment the front-door bell rang.

Sarah flushed a dull red and went to open the door. It was John Shand and William, of course; she ought to have been looking out for them instead of listening to the doctor. Ned, of course, had heard the bell. He had stopped playing. Would he come out?

'Whisht!' she said sharply, indicating the dining-room door. 'In here.'

She shut the door behind her, and stood against it to keep Ned out should he try to come in. William looked 'raised', thought Sarah, as if he had been quarrelling with somebody. Her eyes rested on John Shand with a certain satisfaction. John Shand had more sense than any of them.

She repeated again her account of Ned's doings that morning, addressing herself more and more exclusively to John.

When his brother's name cropped up John Shand's face darkened.

'What has Hector been doing? Why should there be any mention of *him*?'

'Probably no reason at all,' said the doctor. The confidential manner in which he had spoken to Sarah had vanished; he was now cold and brief.

'Delusions, you think? But why my brother rather than somebody else?'

'The connection may be of the slightest, Mr Shand. The patient's statements can hardly be accepted as facts, although they may provide clues to his mental state – very tangled clues.'

'You think my brother – is insane?' asked the minister in a strangely dry voice.

'It's a difficult word. A border-line case, perhaps. But I think he should be removed for treatment. The sooner he's away from here the better.'

The minister nodded.

Sarah swallowed something. 'It's my fault,' she said, 'for getting frightened this morning. . . . But I'll not be frightened again. Couldn't you give him some medicine, doctor, and leave him here for a while till we see?'

'It'll take a few days in any case, for I see no need of an emergency certificate. . . . But I think, Miss Murray, you would be well advised just to let him go. . . . He's been getting worse instead of better for all these months he's been at home.'

'Do you think *we* are to blame?' asked the minister in the same dry voice.

'There's no question of blaming anybody,' said the doctor, with a hint of surprise. 'This is a case for investigation and treatment, not for blame. . . . Could I see the patient now, do you think?'

Sarah found that this was the moment she had been dreading.

'I'll come with you,' she said.

William Murray remained standing where he was.

'Perhaps I'd better slip away now,' said John. 'I wouldn't have come, you know, Mr Murray, if your sister hadn't sent for me.'

'It was very good of you to come.'

John Shand, feeling more and more embarrassed, picked up his hat and umbrella.

The minister turned round and arrested him with a question:

'If it was *your* brother, Mr Shand, would you send him to an asylum?'

'I should do what the doctor advised. . . . Certainly — What's that?'

There was a scuffle and a woman's shriek from the hall. Still holding his umbrella John rushed out, and saw Ned Murray pushing the doctor by main force to the front door.

'Out of this house! Out you go!' he was repeating in a clipped, harsh voice, apparently exasperated beyond endurance.

'Oh, John!' called Sarah, clinging to Ned.

John dropped his umbrella, seized Ned and held him pinned by the arms. He was the only man there who was physically a match for Ned, gaunt though the boy was, and he had to exert all his strength to keep him prisoner, for Ned kicked and struggled and spat with vindictive fury. Hard kicks on the shinbone are bad for the temper, and John began to twist Ned's arm behind him.

'You bloody coward!' screamed Ned. 'Where's the police? Open that door and bring the police!'

Sarah was now hanging on to John.

'Oh, dinna do that. Dinna hurt him,' she was sobbing.

'Lock him in the sitting-room,' said John, addressing the minister. 'Take the key from the inside and I'll push him in.'

Ned kicked at the locked door until the wall beside it shuddered and a picture fell on the floor with a crash. The minister stood as if paralysed, then wiped some spittle from his face with his handkerchief. John Shand was dusting his trousers violently.

The doctor drew Sarah into the dining-room.

'It's an emergency case, after all. He'd better go this afternoon.'

Sarah braced herself and stopped trembling:

'He'll never go of his own free will. I dinna want an open scandal, doctor.'

'I'll send down two powders as soon as I get home. Put one of them in his dinner, or in anything he'll eat: the whole of it, mind. That'll settle him. I'll send full directions.'

'Yes.'

Sarah followed him. Once in the hall, where Ned's deafening assault on the sitting-room door made it difficult to hear oneself, she seemed suddenly to lose her temper. She flung the door open, and literally hustled out the doctor and John Shand, slamming the heavy door upon them.

Then, without a word, she unlocked the sitting-room door, pushed it open a little way, and stood back.

Instead of rushing out headlong, as she had expected, Ned drew himself up in the doorway. He was panting and dishevelled; his eyes were enraged; but he was more 'on the spot', Sarah said to herself, than he had been earlier in the morning.

'Cowards. Sneaks. Lowest cunning. Brute ignorance. . . .'

Sarah turned abruptly and marched into the kitchen. She neither knew nor cared what William was to do. She could hear Ned's voice rising in pursuit of her:

'My sister. My *sister* turns them on to me.'

John Shand's hat was still on the dining-room table where he had dropped it. With a vicious baff of the hand she sent it flying to the floor.

In the kitchen she locked the communicating door, sat down on a chair and burst into tears, awkwardly comforted by Teenie.

## SEVEN

The manse was extraordinarily quiet. Teenie had washed the dinner-dishes and had gone home, as usual on Sunday; the minister had driven off to the asylum with Dr Scrymgeour and Dr Macintyre, following the ambulance, and Sarah was sitting alone in the house. The winter afternoon was closing down; in another hour it would be quite dark. The small fire in the sitting-room grate between its restraining bricks lipped and leapt up the chimney, and the only other sound was the ticking of the marble clock.

The stillness, although it enfolded Sarah, began to oppress her. She did not now need to stretch her ears listening for Ned. Ned had been carried out to the ambulance like a dead log, and she it was who had doctored his food for him. . . . Where would they all have been without her?

Sarah's lower lip trembled and she began to smooth her black skirt over her knees. Ay, she always had the heavy end of the stick. And in spite of all she had done it was her that Ned blamed and would go on blaming: 'My *sister* turns them on to me.' Not a word to William.

It was her that Ned had abused most hatefully all these months . . . all these months. And what had she ever done to the laddie except try to guide him for his good? She had taken up from her dying mother the burden of looking after him and of standing between him and his father. She had darned and mended and cooked and washed and pinched and scraped for all of them – for her father when he was bedridden and ill-tempered; for her brother William in his manse, and for Ned all the time; even when he was away at his classes she had sent him his clean clothes and a cake and scones every week, every single week.

Thankless work. Ay, thankless work. Sarah's lip trembled still more. Not one of them valued what she had done. Ned least of all. And now, at the end, they had forced her to be a Judas. She it was who had called in the doctor and put the powder in Ned's soup.

But she had called in John Shand too, hoping against hope that he at least would be able to manage Ned. . . . And all he had done was to hurt the laddie. . . . Not one of them knew how to do it except herself, and she was tired out. . . . None of these men could stand from Ned the half of what she had stood, for all their size and strength. . . . If it wasn't for the women the world would be in a gey queer state. And the women got little credit for it.

Ay, well, she would do her part, as she had always done, thanks or no thanks. She would have to economize more than ever now, for how was Ned to be paid for in the asylum? Of course they couldn't let him be a pauper patient. . . . Still, he wouldn't be wasting the gas and coal at home.

This return to the more practical side of life comforted even while it challenged Sarah. Ned, after all, had been a burden, and he need not have been a burden; he could have been earning his own living. A certain sympathy for William began to trickle back into her heart; William had had them all to carry on his back. If it hadn't been for William they wouldn't have had a roof over their heads. William was a half-wandered creature himself, and he couldn't help it if he didn't know what was the best way to handle Ned. He was better than John Shand, whom she had held up to herself as a model man. Her sense of humiliation and failure concentrated itself into a rage against John Shand which deepened until it drew off all the overflow of her emotion.

What right had he to look so embarrassed when he came in, as if he thought she had no business to summon him to what was a family affair? He might have remembered that she wasn't the woman to do things for no reason at all, and that there was perhaps something he could help her in. . . . He hadn't thought of her feelings at all. . . . Besides, he was William's leading elder. . . . That was another reason. . . . She had expected something more from the man than brute force. But when it came to the bit that was apparently the only answer he could make. . . .

She was almost glad that Ned had shown so much violence. That had at least given John Shand something to do. She would never call him in again, never. She and William would shoulder their own burdens in future.

Sarah rose to her feet and poked the fire until it blazed, in defiance of all housewifely principles. Her lip no longer trembled. She would be beholden to nobody.

And for a start she would redd up the house. John Shand's hat and umbrella had already been dispatched to him by Teenie. He needn't bother; it would be a long time before she sent for *him* again. . . .

Sunday or no Sunday, she would clean the scuffed paint on that door. She would not be reminded at every turn of what had happened in the morning. If folk could kick paint on a Sunday, folk could clean paint on a Sunday. She fetched a bottle of paraffin and some rags. . . .

When she had done her best with the door she went up to Ned's room with a set face, cleaned out the grate and put into drawers and cupboards every vestige of her brother's recent presence.

She had barely emptied the ash-pail, downstairs, when the bell rang, and to her surprise Dr Scrymgeour came in with William.

'I thought I would just look in and tell you that it's all right, Miss Murray. Your brother'll be well looked after. . . . Dr Eliot out there is a good man, you can depend on him to do everything that can be done. . . .'

The doctor suddenly smiled his nervous little smile, and said: 'Besides, I want to be sure that you're all right. . . . You've had a trying time, and I think that you'll be none the worse of a tonic, Miss Murray – if you don't mind my saying so.'

'Me?' said Sarah. 'A tonic?'

She was 'black affronted', as she said to William afterwards.

The doctor turned to William:

'Your sister's a gallant woman, but she mustn't be allowed to wear herself out. . . .'

This unexpected commendation had a strange effect on Sarah. She began to cry.

'There, there,' said the doctor. 'What did I tell you? A wee bottle of tonic, Miss Murray. I'll write the prescription now. And see that you don't pour it down the sink when you're feeling prideful. Keep it going until I give you leave to stop it. Where's my pen?'

'Come into my study, doctor. You can write it there.'

The doctor's eye rested for a moment on the minister's face and looked away quickly. The doctor's fingers replaced the fountain pen in the pocket where they had discovered it. The doctor's legs carried him towards the study, unwillingly, but obedient to something within the doctor's skull. However nervous one is, one cannot leave a fellow creature to drown in imaginary waters.

'Tell me,' said William Murray in a shaking voice, 'as a medical man, tell me honestly all you know about my brother's derangement.'

'And what good,' countered the doctor sharply, 'would it do you if I did, Mr Murray?'

'I want to know is there a reason for it?' said the minister. 'A medical reason? Something you can put your finger on? Something that's definite, like a microbe —'

'It's not infectious, man, nor hereditary. You gave us all the medical history of the family yourself; you know well enough it's the first case to occur. And, speaking as a medical man, I wouldn't commit myself until he's been thoroughly examined – maybe not even then.'

'But you think it possible that there may be a physical reason for it?'

'There's bound to be ultimately a physical reason for it, as you put it, but whether we know enough to identify it and set it right, Mr Murray, is beyond me to say. A wee bit chemical change somewhere, a lack of balance in internal secretions, an exhaustion of nervous tissue – it may be something that's been going on for years, and it may not. Some idiosyncrasy in an organ the size of a pinhead may be at the bottom of it, Mr Murray. . . . I–I–I think I know what's bothering you – and this is not speaking professionally – you were too anxious this morning to know if you were to blame in any way, Mr

Murray. There's no single individual now living that could have caused or hindered this breakdown in your brother. You needn't reproach yourself.'

William Murray stared haggardly at his comforter.

'But his fears, Dr Scrymgeour, his suspicions, his – his – lack of faith —'

The doctor checked something that was on his tongue, and then said suddenly: 'That persecution mania nearly always accompanies obscure breakdowns. It's one of the symptoms. Considering the long biological history of man, and the fact that herd animals nearly always reject their sick, it's not surprising if an unhappy human being fears that he's to be rejected by his herd. We haven't outgrown our origins, Mr Murray, and I doubt if we ever will. . . . All communities persecute, and in that light persecution mania is reasonable enough.'

'So Ned's fear is a fear of the evil in the human heart?'

'You can put it like that.'

'But all disease doesn't lead to that fear, Dr Scrymgeour.'

'No, I grant you that. But a certain kind of obscure disease leads to it, as I said: cases that we call mental.'

'But it's not a disease of the *mind*, doctor. Ned's mind is acute enough. . . . He's a brilliant mathematician.'

'Um,' said the doctor. 'Well, call it a disease of the ego then. There's not much room for the ego in mathematics. You can't put into a formula a single half-hour of your own life, whether you call it $t1$, or $t2$, or $t3$, or $t$ anything. And from something Miss Murray said I suspect your brother's ego has been ailing for a long time. She told me he never could say "no" to anything or anybody. That's an abnormal timidity, and looks like a constitutional or acquired defect going back to childhood.'

'But he hadn't this fear then!'

'I'm afraid I can't agree with you, Mr Murray. It may have been gathering all these years till it had to burst out. There's maybe more hope for him now that it's come to a head.'

'But, doctor, there have been lifelong invalids who — Don't you see that one couldn't fear evil in others unless there was evil in oneself?'

'Oh ay,' said the doctor. 'We're all human.'

'These dark places in the soul – these are what I should be able to illuminate – these are *my* concern, doctor, as the obscure diseases in the body are yours, and that's where I may have failed my brother . . . that's where I may help him, if I can. . . . I thought you might tell me. . . .'

'Havers, man!' said the doctor firmly. 'Listen to me. I said, and I say it again, there's no single individual now living could have caused or hindered your brother's breakdown. I'll go further, and say that our imperfect civilization may have been partly responsible for your brother's breakdown. We're all reared on fictions from the breast up, and it's more than one man's job to undo the effect of these fictions, especially if they're working on an ego with some possible deficiency in its make-up. You've done all that you can do for your brother in putting him in charge of experienced medical men. You're more than twenty years too late for anything else.'

'You leave no room for God, Dr Scrymgeour.'

The minister said these words almost in a whisper.

The doctor shrugged his shoulders and took out his pen.

'Here's your sister's prescription, Mr Murray,' he said.

## EIGHT

There was one shop in Calderwick that kept its doors open on Sundays. Even without that distinction to emphasize its alienation from a Presbyterian community the shop would have been at once picked out as an exotic by the casual visitor, for it was painted in three colours like a Neopolitan ice, and the outlandish name of Domenico Poggi appeared above its doorway. The majority of the citizens – especially the other shopkeepers – regarded the portly Domenico as a son of Belial and spread tales about him that amply justified their disapproval. Domenico indentured his shop assistants and house-servants from his native land and oppressed the poor creatures, it was said, as if they were slaves, giving them no wages but blows, working them twenty hours out of the twenty-four, and keeping them in an unimaginable state of filth. Mrs Poggi was rarely seen, for she was always big with child, but she was often heard screaming in one of the back rooms above the shop, where Domenico was supposed to thrash her black and blue, and on one occasion, it was said, she had tried to poison him. The children, it was reported, hated their father like the very devil, and now that they were growing up he did not dare to abuse his wife so violently as at first, but everybody knew that the whole Poggi family lived in constant strife. In short, had Domenico sold Bibles he would not have escaped calumny in Calderwick, for he was a foreigner, he had not been settled above twenty years in the town, and he was making money. His business, however, was of a kind that lent itself to denunciation by the godly. He pandered to whatever lust for pleasure survived after a hard day's work in the mill hands of both sexes and the plough-men who came in on bicycles from the country districts. As an alternative to the muddy gutters of the High Street

Poggi's gaudy establishment competed successfully with the public-houses, where no social or other intercourse was encouraged between the sexes. Poggi supplied drinks that made up in colour and variety for their presumably non-alcoholic content, ice-cream in cones and wafers, fried fish and chips, liqueur chocolates, cigarettes, billiards (in a back room), dancing (also in a back room) and pornographic postcards (in a remote corner of a back room). An automatic musical instrument liberated gay, tinny snatches of Italian opera, still further exciting senses already stimulated by Poggi's bright lights, red and yellow paper chains and shining mirrors. His clients were not ungrateful; unlike the more respectable citizens they took the alien to their hearts and referred to him affectionately as 'Podge'.

Poggi's children, black-eyed, black-haired, with finely drawn eyebrows and splendid teeth, spoke with the native accent of Calderwick. Some of them resembled their father, looking like Japanese dolls in childhood and growing into lowering and sullen young ruffians; but two or three 'took after' their mother, who was admittedly a 'bonny creature' when she first arrived in Calderwick as Domenico's girl-bride. The eldest daughter, Emilia, now seventeen, was almost beautiful, with cheek-bones, jaws and chin subdued to a pure oval uncommon in Scotland, and was a favourite even with her father, who trusted her alone of his numerous progeny to take charge of the shop in his absence.

On this Sunday morning, Milly Poggi, perched on a stool behind the cigarette and chocolate counter, was opening her heart to two lady friends. Business was always languid on a Sunday morning, and the shop seemed to be still yawning after its late dissipations of the previous night; the floor had not been swept, nor the small tables wiped; it was obvious that Domenico was not yet out of bed and that his slaves knew it. Milly would hardly have been so candid had her father been within earshot.

'Some blinking old Italian I've never set eyes on,' she concluded. 'I'll see him far enough first. I'll rype the till and run awa' wi' Charlie.'

Becky Duncan, her chum, gazed at her with awed eyes.

'I believe you would,' she said.

But her elder sister, Bell, whom she had brought in to see Milly, laughed scornfully:

'Hear the young things blethering! You've a hantle to learn yet, you twa.'

Milly and Becky, who were jealous of Bell's prestige and experience no less than of her real fur coat, turned upon her fiercely:

'We ken as muckle's you do, and as muckle as we *want* to ken.'

'Wha's this Charlie, then? Has he ony siller?'

Bell fingered her pearl brooch as she asked the question. Milly's reply came hot and quick:

'I'm no' the kind o' lassie that takes siller off a man.'

'The mair fool you, then, to make yourself so cheap.'

'I dinna make myself cheap, Miss Duncan, and I'll thank you to remember that this is my father's shop —'

'Haud your tongue, Bell; you're off your eggs and on to chuckie-stanes,' interposed the young Becky. 'Charlie Macpherson's been at Milly for months to run awa' and marry him.'

Bell tossed her head and shrugged her plump shoulders.

'And if he has siller he'll no marry her, and if he has nae siller the mair fool her.'

She shook off her annoyance at being, as it were, bearded by these young and ignorant creatures, and with maternal solicitude added:

'Dinna say I didna warn you. Once a man gets what he wants he flings you off like an old glove. Even if it's been force-wark. Maybe you dinna ken what force-wark is. I said you'd a hantle to learn.'

Milly, whose ambition it was to become Mrs Charles Macpherson of the fish shop, and to push a baby round Calderwick in a perambulator, like any other respectable married woman, began a swift reply, which was suddenly checked by the shadow of a customer darkening the doorway. Bell nipped her young sister's arm and turned away to look at a showcase, muttering:

'Govey Dick, if it's no' Heck Shand!'

Hector Shand, having sat for an hour and a half on Hutcheon's bed while his host shaved, dressed and discussed under oath of secrecy the possibilities of working one's passage on a cargo-boat to South Africa, or even Australia, was sauntering home with one hand nursing a pipe, and the other in a pocket, when the open doorway of Poggi's reminded him that he was nearly out of tobacco. A certain respect for himself as a potential magnate of Calderwick had kept him hitherto from entering Poggi's shop, but on this morning he had no hesitations.

Milly Poggi, he thought, scanning her as he gave his order, was a damned good-looking kid. He had heard a fellow at the Club lamenting her inaccessibility; apparently her father was always just around the corner with a belt. That wouldn't have frightened *him* off when he was younger. One could do a lot across a counter.

He leaned on one arm and cast a roving glance round the notorious establishment, pleasantly titillated by the sense of being in what was, for Calderwick, a den of vice. The same fellow who had spoken of Milly had shown him one of Poggi's celebrated four-leaved-clover postcards. As he looked at the low-hung doorway leading into the back premises, where he had heard these and other aphrodisiacs were distributed, Hector had a faint recurrence of the thrill that the smelling of the corks from his father's whisky bottles had given him as a child. Milly, picking up the half-crown, warm from his trouser-pocket, that he had thrown on the counter, could not keep her eye from sparkling and her mouth from smiling. She knew that Hector Shand had been packed off to Canada four or five years ago because of Bell Duncan, and if Bell herself made no move towards him she would say: 'There's an old friend of yours here, Mr Shand' – if only for the pleasure of seeing Bell disconcerted. Bell wouldn't have turned her back on him like that if she had been sure of a greeting.

But Bell, having settled her hat by the reflection in the glass showcase, faced round with great composure and said: 'You didna expect to see *me*, did you?' holding out her hand at a fashionably high angle.

Hector took the hand and swept off his hat before he recognized the speaker. But when he did recognize her he shook her hand again. It was a warm, plump hand, a hand that snuggled when one held it.

'I didn't know you, Bell, you're such a toff.'

Although Hector rather self-consciously collected his small change without making further advances, Bell felt reassured and confident after that handshake.

'I've just come down for the week-end to see ma mither.'

'Ay,' said Hector. 'You're fine and braw. Better-looking than ever, Bell. What have you been doing with yourself?'

'Oh, I've been getting on AI. I've been a barmaid in Glasgow. Plenty o' siller in Glasgow.'

Bell tossed her head and pulled her fur coat over her bosom. Hector's eyes followed her movements, but he rattled his change in his trouser-pocket and said nothing.

'I hear you've been getting on AI too,' she went on. 'You're in the mill now, aren't you?'

Hector's dark eyes began to glitter.

'No thanks to *you*, Bell,' he said, moving nearer until he almost touched her.

Bell slowly flushed up to the eyes, but she stood her ground.

'We'll let that flee stick to the wa',' she said. 'You were aye a deevil, and ye're just as muckle o' a deevil as you ever were.'

'So you didn't come to Calderwick just to see me?'

'Hear him!' Bell was growing shrill. 'I came to Calderwick, Heck Shand, to say good-bye to ma mither. . . . I'm sailing for Singapore on Friday.'

Hector Shand stared at her without moving, and his eyes no longer glittered. The unaccustomed flush subsided from Bell's cheek.

'Singapore!' he said at last. 'Have you got a lad out there?'

'I wouldna go the length o' my foot for any lad. My eldest brither's out there, and he's started a bar, and he's sent me my passage money, and more forbye.'

She pulled Becky forward.

'This is my young sister and you can ask her if you dinna believe me.'

Becky giggled with embarrassment. Hector picked up his packet of tobacco.

'Sailing from Glasgow?' he asked.

'Ay, Friday.'

'How long are you in Calderwick?'

'I'm going back to Glasgow the morn's morning.'

'Come here a minute, Bell.'

Hector beckoned her to one of the small tables, where Becky and Milly could not overhear what was said.

Bell tossed her head again, with a side-glance at the two flappers, to see that they were properly impressed, and minced her way across the shop.

'Come out and meet me at the old place to-night,' urged Hector.

Bell looked him in the eye.

'I'm no' so green as I used to be.'

'Nor me either.'

Hector smiled upon her.

'You used to like me well enough,' he added.

'I liked you owre weel, Heck Shand, and fine you kenned it, and you were for flinging me awa' like an auld glove, and that's the truth of it. But you'll no' get the chance to do it again.'

'Bell, as sure's death, you'll not be the worse of it if you come out and meet me to-night.'

'It's owre cauld, and wet forbye; this is no' the middle o' summer.'

'Bring an umbrella, and I'll see that you're not cold.'

He was grinning now.

'It would be a lark, Bell, for you and me to have a walk and a crack together.'

'Ach, away with you!' said Bell, thinking with a kind of rueful scorn that she still appreciated the hint of a dimple he showed when he smiled.

'Meet me at eight o'clock, in the old place. I've something to tell you, and something to ask you. Bye-bye!'

His broad shoulders darkened the doorway again, and he was gone.

'He's just as daft about me as ever he was,' said Bell loftily to the two younger ones.

## NINE

The church bells began to ring for the evening service, and John Shand hastily stopped the gramophone. Before he could put into words, however, the inquiring look he gave his wife and his sister they both protested, one from either side of the fireplace.

'No church! Oh, no, John, no, John, no!'

'This is the only evening we're likely to have Elise to ourselves; don't let's waste it on church.'

Mabel thought she had put that in rather neatly, in case Elise *should* suspect that one hadn't invited people because – well because one didn't know that Elise was so presentable.

'A nice quiet family evening,' she went on. 'That will be lovely. Put on another record, John.'

'No, the church bells would spoil it.'

Elise swung her feet down and made room on the sofa. John closed his new cabinet gramophone – the only one in Calderwick – and sat down beside her.

'That was Bach, wasn't it?' said Mabel, laying down her magazine.

'No, Beethoven.'

'I'm sure you told me last week it was Bach.'

Mabel was cross. She didn't like to be caught out by John.

'I wonder if the *Ninth Symphony* has been recorded,' interrupted Elise. 'When I lived in Germany I went to hear it every March. The concert season always finished up with the *Ninth*. I must try to get it for you, John, when I go back.'

'It's not listed in this country, so far I know. I've never heard it.'

'Oh, Elise, you mustn't speak about going back. You've only just come.'

'I feel as if I'd been here for months – you've made me so much at home.'

Did the second half of her sentence save the first half? Elise wondered.

It was true. That Sunday afternoon in the Shand drawing-room had given her the illusion of having been there for an eternity. Generations of dead-and-gone Calderwickians were approvingly ranked behind everything that John or Mabel said and did; the *clichés* might have sounded differently in an age of bustles and side-whiskers, but the sentiments, Elise was sure, had been the same. . . . There was nothing so immortal as respectability. . . . All the pre-Mabels must have found something or somebody every day to be 'not quite nice', although they probably used another adjective, and the pre-Johns must have judged everything by its reliability or some equivalent term.

On the whole, John was better than Mabel. He had a real feeling for music, although he was starved of good music in Calderwick but for his gramophone. And he had affections strong enough to puzzle his principles, strong enough to have kept his sister alive in his heart and imagination long after his conscience had cut her off. A queer kind of immortality, thought Elise, a simulacrum of herself that would go on existing even if she were to die to-morrow – a simulacrum that might become a family legend if John had any children.

She looked up, but contented herself with thinking instead of uttering the question: Why haven't you any children? Mabel had a beautiful body; her children should be shapely. John was strong and healthy; his children should be sound. They were the very people who should have children; they were nothing if they were not links in a chain. . . .

'How would you feel, John, if you had a daughter exactly like me?'

The question delighted John – perhaps the supposition delighted him even more.

'Now, how in the world did you get to that from Beethoven's *Ninth Symphony*?'

'It made me think of immortality.'

That was only half a prevarication, for Elise realized that all day the great chorus,

> Seid umschlungen,
> Millionen,

had been singing itself at the back of her mind, even while her thoughts were running on the linkage of one generation with another, and now she found ideas crowding upon her that must have been hiding behind the music.

After translating the words of the chorus she said: 'It's a grand surge of sound, and because it's a surge of human voices it hits you directly on the solar plexus and drowns your separate self and sweeps you away on a broadening tide of anonymous emotion – and that's one way of extending oneself, by losing one's personality in the flood. Then there's another way of extending oneself – by multiplication, by producing children who produce more children, and so on. But there's a risk in that of transmitting family rather than individual characteristics, so that you, for instance, might have a daughter like me. That was how I came to it, I suppose.'

She knitted her brows and went on thinking aloud:

'But neither of these extentions satisfies the conscious part of me, which wants to extend itself for ever lengthways; to be me and to go on being me. Of course, that's why people believe in personal immortality. . . . And yet I can't believe in it. . . . And yet Beethoven still lives in his music, although he's dead, and millions of people now walking about don't live in anything at all—'

She stopped suddenly, for she perceived that she was on the point of telling Mabel and John that they were as good as dead.

'If I didn't believe in personal immortality,' said John gravely, 'if I didn't believe in another world that this, I'd throw up the sponge.'

That's what's wrong with Lizzie, he was thinking; that's why she's so flighty and unreliable; she's got no hold on anything. His heart grew heavy.

'You don't surely think that people should do exactly as they please?' he asked.

'For myself I think so, but not for other people,' said his

sister, smiling. 'Or rather, I think that people should all *think* what they like, and not take their thoughts ready-made from any source whatever.'

John shook his head.

'You would put an end to all authority and tradition.'

'I should *digest* authority and tradition. I should extract the grain of truth from the husk of symbol and digest it.'

John shook his head again.

'But I put more faith in human nature than you do,' insisted Elise. 'The result would be a better and not a worse standard of conduct. I would neither sacrifice myself to others nor others to myself. That's walking on a razor-edge, or course; a kind of balancing trick that needs courage. But better than walking along a chalk-line like a hen, even although it brings one ultimately to the same goal.'

'I think I'll stick to the chalk-line, Lizzie,' said John.

Elise looked at Mabel, who was again hidden behind her magazine. A pert and fresh-coloured girl's face was on the cover. Mabel wasn't listening. Elise permitted herself a dig at John.

'And then, if you bump into me, you can always point to the chalk-line, can't you, as a proof that you're right and I'm wrong?'

'Especially when I bump into you,' amended John.

Elise half turned towards him and said in a low voice:

'Then why did you invite me to Calderwick?'

John did not look at her, but put his hand over hers and squeezed it. They both kept silent for a few minutes. Elise removed her hand at last.

'All the same, John, I wasn't wrong. You mustn't draw lines for me. I could never have stayed in Calderwick. . . .'

John remained silent, watching the fire.

'I realized that clearly in church this morning,' said Elise. 'You know it's much more difficult for a thinking girl to swallow tradition than for a thinking boy. Tradition supports his dignity and undermines hers. I can remember how insulted I was when I was told that woman was made from a rib of man, and that Eve was the first sinner, and that the pains of childbirth are a punishment to women. . . . It took me a long time to get over that. . . . It's damnable the way a girl's self-confidence is slugged on the head from the beginning.'

John chuckled a little at that.

'You used to bully me from morning till night,' he said. 'A boy needs *some* tradition that will back him up where girls are concerned. I know I used to curl up inside every time I had to pass girls giggling in the street.'

'I didn't bully you, John, did I?'

'You didn't suffer from lack of self-confidence, anyhow,' grinned John.

'But I did suffer, all because of superstitions that are long out-of-date and still perpetuated. I *did*. It came over me this morning in church, I tell you, all-of-a-sudden-like.'

'Was that what you were giggling at?'

Elise told him what she had been giggling at, and John was surprised into such mirth that he forgot his concern for his sister's lack of belief in authority.

'Poor Murray,' he said, when his laughter had subsided. 'It's just as well you didn't go to church to trouble him to-night. He's had trouble enough for one day.'

'Elizabeth poured out her heart to me about it. She's a strange girl, John; I think there's a lot to her.'

Mabel looked over her magazine.

'Elizabeth?' she queried. 'She's one of the stodgiest women I know. I can't think what you see in her.'

'I like her too, I must say,' said John, with vigour. 'And she's far too good for Hector. But wasn't it surprising how she attacked poor Murray at the vestry door? I didn't think she would have flown at him like that, and just *then*—'

'What struck me,' put in Elise, 'was that she spoke to him as a human being, not as if he were a figurehead. . . . I bet you nobody else in his congregation does that.'

'Why, she *is* rather like that. A kind of simplicity – very charming.'

'I don't suppose Elizabeth knows it's a gift,' Elise commented.

'It isn't a gift,' said Mabel. 'It's the complete lack of any social sense.'

Elise leaned back on the sofa and thought deliberately: Elizabeth is the most interesting woman I've met for years.

She had just discoverd it, to her own surprise, as if Elizabeth had gone on growing within her since they last met. And she recognized, too, that the chorus from the *Ninth Symphony* which had been haunting her had been released by Elizabeth's words of the morning: we're only separate like waves rising out of the one sea.

> Seid umschlungen,
> Millionen,

hummed Elise to herself. That chorus, she thought, is the nearest I can get to religious feeling, I suppose. And it isn't anything but mass emotion. . . .

Elizabeth gets more out of *hers* than mass emotion, she went on thinking. To her, it isn't merely an indulgence. She hurls herself into it impetuously. . . . But how alive she is! She goes on living in me and excites me to rhapsodizing about choruses before John and Mabel. . . . She's more alive in me than I am in John.

John would embalm me in his affection, she thought, like a fly in amber, immortally preserved in the heart of his immortal respectability. All he asks is that I should make him laugh occasionally – pipe a merry tune in my little cage.

'Some more music?' said John hopefully, preparing to rise. 'I've a very pretty thing of Mozart's you haven't heard.'

Affection plus disapproval, repeated Elise to herself, is of no bloody good to anybody. She regarded John affectionately, none the less, as he wound up his other canary, the gramophone. But her attitude could not have been represented by William Murray's text: 'Though He slay me, yet will I trust in Him' – a text which the minister at that very moment was elucidating with fervour, even with passion, his eyes fixed on the unresponsive white face of the church clock.

## TEN

The events of the morning had agitated Elizabeth, and her talk with Elise had only partially allayed her agitation. But for the rest of the day she had no chance to review her feelings and come to terms with them. Hector was too full of his own plans, too restless, too exhilarated: he scrambled over the surface of her attention like an excited child. In most cases of distress surface distraction has its uses, for it may divert the mind from premature interference with the deeper emotions, and if Hector had not distracted her Elizabeth might have had instinctive recourse to one of those games that involve the movement of cards, or pawns, or fragments of words, and hold the attention without disturbing the feelings, or she might have spent the time reading a novel, an occupation which, it is alleged, supplies the same need.

Hector's exhilaration had appeared at the luncheon-table. He came home full of a new project recommended, he said, by Hutcheon: he should make for Singapore and reconnoitre from there. Hutcheon knew somebody who had made money there out of a café-bar. Hector could look round a bit and put his money into anything that would pay.

Neither Hector nor Elizabeth had much knowledge of Singapore, but their ignorance did not hinder them from crossing and recrossing it on imaginary tracks until a map of their mental meanderings would have looked like a piece of cross-hatching. Conversations which take the place of dominoes or patience can be as intricate as any game, and demand ingenuity rather than knowledge. They were both confident in their ignorance, Hector because he was genuinely reckless, and Elizabeth because she did not expect the universe to go bankrupt and dishonour the promissory note she had drawn on it. Had she known, however, that Hector was proposing to himself a departure to Singapore on the Friday of that week, in four days' time, her confidence might have wavered. To Elizabeth a month or six weeks seemed a long time, just as two hundred pounds seemed a large sum of money, but her courage might have contracted in proportion had the month on which she reckoned been reduced to four days. Perhaps that was why Hector refrained from reducing it. What she didn't know, he thought, wouldn't hurt her.

While running riot hand-in-hand with Hector over the Straits Settlements Elizabeth had glanced now and then at her own plans. She would, of course, find a job in an English school. On the very next day she would consult the advertisements in the English newspapers at the Public Library. Strangely enough, the prospect of teaching in a school for young ladies in an unknown country exhilarated her, and she thought that she understood Hector's exhilaration because she shared in it.

After supper, however, Hector vanished immediately, saying he must discuss the project further with Hutcheon, and Elizabeth was left to herself. Her mood darkened at once, as a landscape darkens when the sun is veiled, and her thoughts flew back to Ned Murray and William.

Ned Murray was in the asylum. Coming home with Elise she had met John Shand, hatless and perturbed, and what he had to tell distressed her now even more than it had distresed her then. Her imagination credited Ned with the despair of a young child torn from his familiar nursery and thrust into a blind cell with no one to hear his cries. A vague feeling of guilt oppressed her, as if she ought to have done something, and could have done something, to prevent it.

Yet, in spite of her self-accusation in the matter of Ned's ragging at the University, her feeling of guilt remained vague and would not attach itself to a definite act of omission. She could not fix on anything that she might have done or said. Why, then, did she feel so guilty? Elise, for instance, had been very cool and sensible about it. . . . But then Elise had not been mixed up in it. . . .

In thus admitting to herself that she was mixed up in it Elizabeth was brought up short. If she were involved at all it could only be through her relationship to the minister. She was assuming, in fact, that she was so intimate with William Murray that her actions might have affected his. . . .

Elizabeth's ears began to burn. She recollected that once or twice during that week when she had walked so often with the minister she had fancied – but no; it was impossible. He liked her and she liked him, that was all. She shrank from imputing to William Muray an inclination to fall in love with her as if it were the imputation of a crime, so strongly was she influenced by the code in which she had been brought up. And she shrank with equal dismay from the suggestion that she might have encouraged him by her unreserve. Elizabeth was far from being an emancipated young woman. She remembered her own horror at Aunt Janet's insinuations. It was vulgar to think such things. It was vile. William Murray wasn't that kind of man. . . . They had got on very well together, that was all, until he began to say such dreadful things about the body being unsanctified. . . .

Elizabeth's hair almost crisped on her head as she realized how well William Murray's sudden denunciation of the body fitted in with the theory she was trying to discard. If he *had* found himself falling in love with her he was bound to experience a revulsion from physical passion. He must have struggled against it. She remembered that cold flash of his eye from the pulpit. . . .

There was shame on every side, however she tried to evade it. If she were mistaken, if he had not fallen in love with her, he might have misinterpreted her kindness to him exactly as she was now misinterpreting his kindness to her. . . . Perhaps some of the malicious gossip had even been retailed to him, and that was why he had looked at her like that. . . .

The blood in Elizabeth's head rushed back to her heart; she felt cold and faintly sick. It is extraordinary how the mere hint of a sexual relationship can distort the image of one's fellow-creatures. But for her gratuitous sense of shame Elizabeth would have perceived, as she had once done, that William Murray's character contained no conventional malice, and that even if he had been told that Mrs Hector was setting her cap at him he would have scouted the suggestion.

Elizabeth's fear that she had been unwomanly may, indeed, have sprung from something in herself she did not suspect. The crimes one imputes to others are usually crimes of which one has secret and often unsuspected knowledge, and it is permissible to infer that Elizabeth was secretly attracted to William Murray. That would partly explain her unaccountable feeling of guilt. It would explain, too, why she suddenly rebutted with fierceness the very idea of flirting with a minister. A man who despised his body! A man who could preach hell fire! With this denunciation her sense of guilt vanished, and was replaced by scorn. In merely entertaining the possibility of such romantic, if not vulgar, nonsense she was letting herself down to the level of Calderwick.

For perhaps five minutes Elizabeth looked steadily at Calderwick, seeing it with the depressing, prosaic bleakness of a winter noon under grey skies. Life was terrible when the transfiguring glow vanished from it. Whatever she did in Calderwick would look ugly in that bleak grey light. . . . Thank God, she was going to leave the town!

Almost as Elise might have done she shrugged her shoulders. Calderwick was to blame, not she. She had done her best. Elise was right; she should not take the fate of the Murrays so much to heart; it was their own concern.

With the thought of Elise an infiltration of colour, of warmth, irradiated the landscape again. It did not occur to Elizabeth that her attachment to Elise could infringe upon her loyalty to Hector, and so in considering Elise her vision was not distorted by shame. One can surmise that for that reason alone Elizabeth would always be more at her ease with women than with men, unless she were to outgrow the half-conscious taboos of her youth.

Her sense of guilt had vanished, at any rate. But she was left with a new problem. Was Elise right, then, in her other contentions? Was it not only undesirable but impossible to love one's fellow-creatures, to identify oneself with them? Was that oneness of which she had dreamed – that oneness of the earth-life, that ecstatic communion with all living things – nothing but a lie? Was she fooling herself? Was Calderwick, in fine, a fair sample of the world?

It was a pertinent question, but she did not put it fairly. To her the choice seemed to lie between a world transfigured by the warm glow of feeling and a bleak grey world in which isolated objects harshly repelled each other. She was young and warm-hearted; there could be no question on which side her choice would fall.

She began to walk up and down as her imagination kindled again. She caught at her love for Hector and concentrated on that as one concentrates rays with a magnifying-glass, until the flame rose up and once more the grandiose images she lived by illuminated her mind. She was linked mystically to her husband by nothing less than a universal force. Their love was like the sea, the mountains, the rushing wind and the evening stars. It was drawn from the source of life itself, and would bear them up through every vicissitude. On a billow so enormous they could both ride out of Calderwick without any risk of not being eventually cast up together on some more fortunate shore. . . .

'The lunatick, the lover and the poet . . .' It is to be feared that it was the light of the moon in its full splendour that was now intoxicating Elizabeth.

## ELEVEN

By Monday morning the clear space of sky in the north-east had spread southward far beyond Calderwick, and looked as if it were to maintain itself, promising days of light frost and sunshine, nights of hard frost and brilliant stars. A delicate rime picked out with white crystals every blade of grass in John Shand's garden, and each twig, each branch, each stiff leaf on the evergreen bushes, was similarly outlined by pale, unemphatic but crystalline sunlight.

'I had forgotten that you had light of this quality in Scotland.' Elise turned from the window to the breakfast-table. 'It's hard light, like the light in the South, and it shows up the shape of things.'

Did it reveal the fact that the edges of her thoughts were becoming blurred? She felt curiously soft and impressionable that morning.

'What are you thinking of doing today, Lizzie?'

'I've no idea. What's the programme, Mabel?'

Even while she politely included her sister-in-law Elise, trying to sharpen herself, commented inwardly that Mabel expected and actually liked to be pointedly included in a conversation.

Of course, said Mabel, she had no plans; of course they would do whatever dear Elise preferred.

'I thought that perhaps you would like to come and see over the mill this morning?'

Elise cocked a laughing eye at her brother.

'With all my heart! I know you want to show it off.'

John cleared his throat.

'Mabel thinks the mill a messy place. . . . You won't mind, my dear, if Lizzie leaves you and comes with me?'

Mabel, it appeared, would mind; she had never said the

mill was messy; naturally she would like to accompany Elise. . . . But, of course, if Elise would rather go alone . . .

An hour later, as she sat waiting in the drawing-room for her sister-in-law, Elise permitted herself further sarcastic observations. Women like Mabel were the very devil. This simple visit to the mill was now turned into a kind of social function, a diversion provided for a guest by a thoughtful hostess, and the hostess was busy, no doubt, dressing the part. She doesn't even know she's acting, thought Elise, recalling her own excellent but always conscious performances on the social stage, and recognizing that it was years since she had last done that kind of thing. Like other insincerities social hypocrisy had faded so imperceptibly out of her life with Karl that she had hardly realized its departure. . . .

Her thoughts were softening again. It was a queer world they had lived in together, she and Karl. Elise bent closer to the fire as if in the hope that its glowing heat would scorch her eyeballs dry. For with a sudden rush of tears, as if congealed and frozen feelings had thawed, the flat line-drawings of memory, which she had thought were all that was left to her, took on flesh and blood, and in an instant were corporeally real. She did not *remember* sitting in the same room as Karl, she *was* in the same room as Karl. That moment was real to her as a dream is real to the dreamer: the very richness of its content showed her the emptiness of mere memory, and how much she had lost of which she had barely been aware. . . .

It passed as suddenly as it had come, long before Mabel opened the door. Elise sat alone again, shaken and weeping, in a palpable fog of sentiment, a fog in which every shape was blurred, a fog peopled by ghosts that had inexplicably drunk blood, a fog that she made no effort to dispel, even after she had calmed herself.

Mabel had indeed dressed herself for the part with extreme care; she had even pinned a red chrysanthemum in the collar of her coat; and she looked so youthfully pretty that Elise was touched. After all, she thought, dressing-up and make-believe are a comfort to bairns – especially in a dead-alive hole like this. Her moment of transfiguration had left Calderwick more drab than ever, and she was sorry for those who were doomed to live in it. Yet before they had walked a hundred yards the keen air began to blow away her depression, while at the same time she found herself stepping carefully over the well-earthed joins between the irregular grey-blue slabs of paving-stone, exactly as she had done in her childhood, and was both disturbed and amused by the discovery. She sniffed the salt tang in the air.

'There's always a sea-wind blowing in Calderwick.'

'It takes the curl out of my hair,' complained Mabel. 'I have to be always washing out the stickiness. You'll find that too, if you've forgotten.'

'I have forgotten a great deal. . . . *Br-rr-rr*, that's a seeking wind!'

They were glad to whip round into the shelter of the mill-yard, where some carters were beating their arms across their bodies like flails. Mabel picked her way among the round cobbles, holding her skirt high, without a glance to right or left, but she knew how many men were in the yard, and if she did not peer up at the office windows it was because she divined at least one pair of eyes behind them.

As they paused inside the doorway of the shadowy main building Hector came clattering downstairs in high feather.

'Here we are, ladies! Come up into the office.'

Hector's exhilaration was probably caused by the weather: like the children in the streets he ran faster and shouted louder because of the frost and the sunlight, thought Elise, touched for the second time that morning by the youthfulness of her relations. Yet, as she went round the mill beside John, she observed that there was more in Hector's exhilaration than mere youthful well-being. His quick eye was less guarded, and he was openly, even shamelessly, flirting with Mabel, who grew every minute pinker and more girlish. Following John up a wooden ladder leading into a loft Elise cast a backward look at the other two, and for the life of her could not avoid giving a smile of comradely appreciation as she caught Hector's eye. With excessive pantomime he blew her a silent kiss to which she returned a wave of the hand. It was not until a few minutes later that she remembered with rueful dismay that the couple whose flirtation she had encouraged were John's wife and Elizabeth's husband.

Emboldened, perhaps, by her obvious appreciation Hector and Mabel had removed themselves on tiptoe from the foot of the ladder, and Elise found herself alone in the loft with John. With some idea of covering their escape and also, inconsistently, of comforting John, she launched into warm praise of all that she had seen in the mill.

'You've made it twice what it was in father's time. I can see that, John.'

'The business is as sound as a rock now, although trade's bad in general. I've been offered the chance of capitalizing it on a bigger scale, as a limited company. . . . Of course, if I did that, I should be the chief shareholder: I should keep it in the family, Lizzie.'

His dream was coming true. He had his sister beside him in the citadel of his achievements, and in the fostering warmth of her admiration John blossomed until he opened out into vainglory:

'It's been an uphill fight, Lizzie, I can tell you. For years it was touch and go—'

But at that height John stopped, suddenly conscious of danger. It would never do to draw Lizzie's attention to the difficulties he had had. . . . What on earth was he thinking of? He felt confused by his own carelessness, and would not allow his mind even to formulate the fear that Lizzie would mention her supposed share in the mill.

Elise, however, desiring only to tease him a little now that he was boasting, rushed full upon the subject: 'Capitalizing, did you say? You'll have a fat tummy before you know where you are, and you'll be grinding the faces of the poor as well as corn! I'll have to keep an eye on you. Shall I be entitled to a seat on the Board?'

Human spirits have a mysterious faculty of communicating even unformed thoughts, and perhaps Elise's question was not so fortuitous as it seemed, perhaps she was beginning to read the thought that was arrested by fear in the bottom of John's mind. He could not hustle it away quickly enough, and had such a guilty expression on his face that Elise laughed. 'Oh, John! You look as if you had been caught cheating. Have you been pocketing some of my income all these years?'

The flush of distress deepened on John's brow, but he struggled to smile. Before he could say anything, however, the unconscious process of transmission was completed and Elise had read off the message.

'John!' she said, seizing him by the arm. John tried to meet her eyes frankly. 'You've been paying me money out of your own pocket all this time.'

John succeeded in smiling.

'Well, why not?'

Elise stood looking at him without a word. Then she laid her cheek on his arm and said softly: 'My dear, dear John. My dear, dear John.'

It was, after all, one of the most exquisite moments John had ever experienced.

'Do you mean to tell me,' said Elise after a while, 'that at the same time as you disowned me you began to support me?'

'I didn't see what else I could do, Lizzie.' They were sitting side by side on a couple of sacks. 'I didn't know but what you might be in Queer Street.'

'In Queer Street I should have been many a time if it hadn't been for my quarterly cheque.'

She relapsed into silence, while John patted her hand.

'I *did* wonder a little,' she brought out at last slowly, 'why I should suddenly have an income I had known nothing about, and why it should be paid before I was twenty-one, but Tom Mitchell was so positive about it that it was easier not to wonder. . . . I knew you had just taken over the management, and I thought perhaps my share had been allotted at the same time. . . . Oh, I think I must have shut my eyes wilfully! . . . There can't have been any money to spare at that time, John?'

John refused to speak. Elise leant over and kissed him.

'Don't say anything to Mabel,' he said presently. 'She doesn't – nobody knows except Tom Mitchell.'

'I wouldn't have believed you could be so close about anything! Your face gives you away completely, John, when you have a secret.'

'Only to you, Lizzie. There's nobody else knows me so well as you do.'

'I verily believe that's true. Isn't it queer?'

'It's only natural.'

But Elise did not reciprocate by telling him that nobody knew her so well as he did. She looked absent, as if she were still digesting what she had learned.

'I won't offer to pay you back, John,' she said suddenly. 'There's no need of that between you and me. But I won't take any more, indeed I won't. I've got more than enough money. Karl's people are rich, and I have a very adequate allowance from them, besides the royalties on his books. And there's something else; something you won't approve of, I'm afraid. Two years ago I made a grand haul at Monte Carlo – and I still have most of it.'

'Gambling?'

'Gambling on the wicked green tables, John. I had phenomenal luck. I think it was fifteen hundred I made.'

John gasped.

'I never knew anybody like you, Lizzie. Never.'

They both laughed, Elise first and then John, louder and louder, and as they laughed the tension of the last half-hour slackened off, the bitterness of John's twenty years' regret vanished, and Elise felt in her heart a native warmth that had been for months unfamiliar to it.

Their laughter became almost hysterical. In the middle of it a hallo came up the ladder and Hector's head appeared:

'Aren't you ever coming down, you two stick-in-the-muds?'

He gaped when he saw them, and shouted to Mabel at the foot of the ladder: 'Gone dotty up here, both of them.' But as he looked at Elise he said to himself: 'She's a sport. I've a good mind to tip her the wink about everything.'

Hector had divined a new mother-confessor in his new sister.

TWELVE

At about five o'clock on the same day Elise, attending to
Mabel's guests at tea, watched them as if the drawing-room
were a tank of air in which samples of humanity had been
enclosed for her inspection to help her in solving the riddle of
existence. For if Karl's death had impaired the visible structure of her life John's few words in the upper loft of the mill
that morning had brought it about her ears. On the platform
at Marseilles she had rejected as irrelevant the question: To
what end does one live? – contenting herself with what
appeared the irreducible minimum: the fact that one lived
and would go on living; but that apparently irreducible
minimum, that stark assertion of herself, had enclosed an
element of pride, the pride of the independent creator who
looked at her own work and found it good. During the
afternoon before the tea-party guests arrived that pride had
been squeezed out of Elise to the last drop. The house of
which she was so proud had been built only in the hollow of
John's hand. It was as much by the grace of John as by its own
qualities that it had maintained its equilibrium. Elise felt as if
she stood now on the bare ground of existence, uncertain
whether she could claim anything as her own achievement.

To what end, then, to what end? Was the question perhaps
less irrelevant than she had decided?

Any valid answer to the question, What is the end of
human life? must be true for everybody, Elise reflected. The
lowest common measure of any assortment of people might
provide an answer – the lowest common measure, for
instance, of Mrs Mackenzie, Mrs Gove, Mrs Melville and
Miss Pettigrew. . . .

As if her fate depended on the result of her observations
she watched the ladies in Mabel's drawing-room. Like her-

self these women were economic parasites, absolved from
struggling for the means of life and presumably free to follow
its ends. What did they live for?

Elise smiled, for at the moment the chief end of life for
these ladies seemed to consist in being 'upsides with each
other', and in effacing the impression made by Mrs Smith
who had been boasting of her success in breeding Cairn
terriers. Against the Cairn terriers Mrs Mackenzie set her
son, who was to be a civil engineer; Mrs Gove extolled her
own dog, a Shetland collie, who was as intelligent as a child;
Mrs Melville described two Chinese jars she had recently
inherited, and Miss Pettigrew mentioned the part she was to
play in a forthcoming production of *The Mikado*.

Elise listened and watched. No; she had not misjudged
them. Not one of the topics – neither the education of sons
nor the nature of animals nor Chinese art nor light opera –
was taken up; there was no exchange of information; any
objective interest that the ladies might have in these subjects
was not allowed to appear. They were absorbed in upholding
their status as successful people, with power over children,
dogs, objects of art and rival competitors. Personalities
spreading like trees, thought Elise, measuring their
importance by the size of the shadow they cast. . . .

And why not? It was the nature of life to push and grow, to
rise out of the jungle undergrowth, to overshadow rivals.
Even knowledge served that end at times, or else one would
not speak of 'mastering' it. . . . Mrs Melville, in spite of her
reticence, might conceivably know something about *'famille
verte'* and *'famille rose'* – and what did it matter whether she
did or not, if the end of Chinese civilization was to provide
her with a pair of fine jars for her mantelpiece?

To put it that way was of course absurd. Teleology led to
queer conclusions. Had canine and human life evolved
merely to enable Mrs Smith to breed Cairn terriers?

Elise shelved the intruding reflection that canine life –
perhaps all life – was extraordinarily accommodating in
allowing itself to be bred to a pattern.

To what end, she repeated – looking round the drawing-
room – to what end the pains and persistence of countless
anonymous generations, the faith, the philosophy, the sci-

ence of countless civilizations? To produce in this year of
grace in a room in Calderwick Mrs Melville, Miss Pettigrew
and myself?

The absurdity of the answer made it at least probable that
the question itself was absurd. . . .

No, she said aloud, replying to Mrs Mackenzie, she was
never sea-sick when crossing the Channel. No, it was not
because of any specific nostrum.

'My boy went over to Paris this last summer, and he was
terribly sick in the boat. He wasn't even able to take any
refreshment when he reached his destination. . . .'

Motherhood? queried Elise. The physical capacity for
motherhood was a common measure, perhaps the lowest
common measure, of all present. But like the urge for power
it was an attribute, not an explanation, of individual life.
From the racial standpoint, of course, it could be argued that
the individual existed to continue the race, that Mrs Mackenzie lived to produce her son: and from the standpoint of
Mrs Mackenzie's son that was doubtless an all-sufficient
reason. Any individual must feel that in producing *him* his
parents had amply justified their existence. . . . Teleology
was plausible when one looked backwards . . .

That's it, said Elise to herself. I believe I've hit it. Teleology works backwards but not forwards. . . . To look forward from the Chinese artist making his jars and to see at the
end of the vista Mrs Melville's mantelpiece is preposterous,
but to begin with the mantelpiece and trace events back to
the production of the jars is exciting.

'Do let us have some of your amusing stories,' interrupted
Mrs Melville. 'Mrs Shand tells me you have met so *many*
interesting people.'

Mabel and the other ladies looked expectant. Elise isn't in
form at all, Mabel was thinking; what on earth is the matter
with her? Is she going to let me down?

As she spoke, Mrs Melville exhibited her social smile –
that is to say, she narrowed her eyes, thrust out her chin,
bent her head sideways towards her left shoulder and
uncovered all her front teeth. Elise, pursuing problems in
teleology, passed no judgment upon Mrs Melville's smile,
yet an irrelevant breeze of fury rippled through her,

breaking up the dead calm in which she had been tranced. As if she were hanging on to a sail that threatened to belly out and carry her through the walls of the room Elise tightened her fists and knitted her brows, then rose quickly to her feet, saying: 'I have a headache. I'm afraid I must be excused.' For a second she regarded the company with an unseeing look, then she made a queer little foreign bow and walked to the door. Mabel tried to detain her with offers of aspirin, but Elise said briefly 'I have everything I want' and ran upstairs.

Once she had shut and locked the door the breeze of fury became a hurricane and Elise let it blow through her. In the body she was pacing only up and down the room, but in the spirit she was rushing furiously through space – or was it time?

'Anything is better,' she found herself crying, 'than that soft strangling.'

What soft strangling? Where did that phrase come from, and to what did it refer? 'I'm damned if I know!' she said, coming to a stop in the middle of the floor. Was it the fingers of teleology that had been loosened from her throat, or the fingers of Calderwick? 'I'm damned if I know!' she reiterated, and in that moment of consciousness she caught sight of herself in the long mirror.

One cannot look at oneself and remain angry; contrariwise, if one insists on remaining angry one cannot go on looking at oneself. Elise stared; the mirror was like a fog enclosing a ghostly image; gradually the image grew clearer, took shape, and Elise, breaking into a smile, said: 'Hello, Lizzie Shand! Where have *you* been all these years?'

The impetuous, resentful small girl who had hovered in the church and stepped with Elise over the paving stones of Calderwick had come back, and with her had come a passionate sense of individuality that required no teleological argument to sustain it. On the Marseilles platform it had been Karl's widow who tried to adjust herself, in the mill-loft it was John's sister, but the woman who now looked at herself knew that she was more than widow or sister or daughter. She had already caught up on the last week; she had perhaps caught up on the last twenty years as well. The

time-lag that had troubled Elizabeth Mütze was beginning
to shorten.

She was not to be explained away. She would have been
herself even if she had had to sing in the streets for a living.
The assurance that in essentials she had neither been planned by fate nor deflected by circumstance invigorated her.

Forty years, she thought, nearly forty years it's taken me
to find that out. A long and obstinate adolescence. . . . She
had been running away from things all her life. She had run
away from Calderwick – from Fritz – from Fritz's anarchist
friends in Brussels – from one city to another, from one
clique to another, from one job to another. I was never more
than a year in any town, she thought, until Karl cornered
me. And how she had run away from Karl!

During all these years she had struggled to keep herself
untouched by sentiment, fastidiously shaking herself free of
entanglements, pruning her own emotions and ruthlessly
lopping with the knife of reason every tendril that sought to
fasten upon her. That was the reason why her marriage was
put off and put off; she had feared for what she called her
independence; and now she realized, with a scorn of her
fears, that if Karl had not been dying she might never have
married him. . . . For years she had been strangling herself.

Her scorn, her aversion from her past cowardice, moved
her again to anger; again she paced the room; but there was a
queer gladness beneath the anger, and finally she said:
'Well! Now I've run away from a tea-party, and most
extraordinarily have cornered myself.'

When she went downstairs the guests had gone and Mabel
was petulant. Elise smoothed her sister-in-law's ruffled feathers and entertained the dinner-table with zest. Before the
fish came in she had already plunged into reminiscence: 'I
once knew a Professor of Demonology in Brussels—'

John laughed and was happy: his misgivings about Lizzie
had vanished, like smoke, in the fire of their mutual
affection.

But next day Elise surprised both John and Mabel by a
desire to spend the morning alone.

'I want just to potter today,' she said. 'I want to wander all
over Calderwick, down the High Street, round the harbour,

and into every hole and corner where I used to play.' Lizzie Shand, who had never picked up stitches in her life, was going to do nothing but pick up dropped stitches for three mortal hours. . . . She almost ran down the front steps.

## THIRTEEN

The bright frost still held, and Calderwick was beginning to
look parched as if in a summer drought; in the dried-up
roads the ruts were sharp and iron-hard; the depressions
where once puddles of water had stood were now covered by
thin brittle shells of white-bubbled ice beneath which no
trace of water remained. Young Mrs Hector Shand's inner
world, although still bright, was also beginning to look
parched. For, now that she was prepared to be supremely
happy beside Hector, it was becoming increasingly difficult
to find herself beside him at all. On Monday evening, after
office hours, he had vanished soundlessly from the house,
and did not return until midnight. On Tuesday morning he
dressed himself in his sports tweeds, announced that he was
going with some fellows to have a pop at a rabbit or two and
wouldn't be back till after dark, and, to use his own terms,
*did a bunk* immediately breakfast was over. Elizabeth, with a
cheerful air, set about buying small Christmas presents, but
she was perhaps unduly ruffled by a remark of Mary
Watson's. 'An' hoo's your man?' said that stern woman,
looking incongruous behind an array of Christmas 'fancy
goods'. 'He's like a' the men, I warrant; he needs a guid eye
kept on him.' Elizabeth thought she heard somebody giggle
in the crowded shop and went out with a hot face. To restore
her equanimity she walked down to the seashore, and after
aimlessly wandering over the crust of frozen sand began little
by little to quicken her steps as her imagination caught fire
again. It was so much easier to make contact with the present
Hector of her imagination than with the elusive Hector of
actuality.

When he came back, however, bringing with him a faint
chill from outdoors, a suggestion of withered bracken and

beech-leaves, Elizabeth rubbed her soft cheek against the stubble of his jaw, pushing upwards so that she felt the prickles, and pressing hard so that they hurt. She sat on his knee, contentedly sniffing the scent of peat and tobacco on his old jacket. His strong body, glowing after exercise, fascinated her; she punched and tickled him and finally kissed him on the neck inside his collar. But after five minutes Hector put her off his knee, lit his pipe, and began to fidget up and down the room. He declined to be entertained by a sing-song at the piano, and when Elizabeth proposed the cinema he said, although kindly: 'Don't feel like anything tonight, girlie.' Then, knocking out his pipe, he added: 'Think I'll take a turn down to the Club.'

It is arguable that the excessive omission of the first personal pronoun in conversation betrays an excessive consciousness of its importance. Elizabeth stifled a dawning resentment that might have brought her to this conclusion, and with a slight effort maintained her cheerfulness. But as she sat by the fireside she felt that the whole day had somehow been wasted. . . . She had not even seen Elise.

That night she was still more demonstrative towards Hector, and Hector, marvelling, commented privately that all women were hot stuff once they knew the ropes. She whispered in the dark that his hair was like grass, his shoulders, she said, running her hands over them, were mountain ridges; she clung to him until they were both stilled in sleep, folded in perfect conjugal amity. The invisible current flowed apparently unbroken around them.

Yet next day Hector proved as elusive as ever.

'No, I'm not going to the office,' he said, as he dressed. 'Told you I wasn't going back.'

'What'll John say?'

'He'll give me the sack, I hope and believe.'

He looked neither defiant nor apprehensive, and Elizabeth had to return his smile.

'Well, must you be sacked just before Christmas?'

'I can't stand being preached at, that's all, and I'm not going to give John the chance of preaching; he can sack me instead. Oh, I know *you* think he'll give me his blessing if I go on my knees to him—'

'I do believe if you went frankly to him he'd help you out—'

'Yes, with his foot.'

Hector's cheerful recklessness made his wife laugh.

'Let John give me the sack: that makes it all the easier for me to clear out.'

'But,' said Elizabeth, and stopped in perplexity. It *would* make things easier for Hector. But would it not make things more difficult for her?

Hector did not give her time to think it out. 'Ba-ba-ba-ba!' he said, whirling her round. 'You leave your Uncle Hector's cards where he likes to keep them – up his sleeve. Besides, who wants to go to an office on a fine day like this? I'm going to take all I can while I have the chance.'

'Chance is a fine thing,' quoted Elizabeth from Mary Ann's stock of sentiments. Yet she was uneasy. This new stroke of Hector's would cut the knot effectively; it was a bold stroke, a reckless stroke, and she could not but admire the recklessness of a man who deliberately and in cold blood gets himself sacked. Yet she was uneasy, as if she surmised that in cutting the knot of diplomacy Hector was severing himself from all other ties, including his tie to her.

After breakfast she ran into the kitchen to ask a trifling question or two, but Mary Ann prolonged the interview for nearly half-an-hour. Smiling, Elizabeth strolled back to smoke a cigarette with Hector and found that he had disappeared. He was neither upstairs nor downstairs.

Her uneasiness increased to apprehension, and she was disturbed by the sick, crawly feeling usually termed a sinking of the heart. But the doubts and fears stirring within her were like subaqueous creatures that could not push their heads through a mat of surface vegetation, so compact and impenetrable was the texture of her belief in the love between herself and Hector. She now stood by the window weaving new strands into that belief, designed to make it even more impervious, and the crawling fears gradually subsided.

Meanwhile Hector, with a pair of skates under his arm, was entering the garage off the High Street where Mabel's new two-seater was kept. He did not want to have Elizabeth hanging round. She was being damned decent to him, but he wanted to keep out of her way – just as he wanted to avoid Aunt Janet. Isn't it like women, he thought, to begin hanging round your neck as soon as you try to shake them off? All that he desired, for the two days he was to remain in Calderwick, was the sense of utter relaxation, of letting go, that was his conception of freedom; and, whether they knew it or not, both Elizabeth and Aunt Janet were always screwing him up to something. Women couldn't help it, he supposed. Mabel, in her own way, was just as bad, thinking she had an 'influence' over him. Unlike Elizabeth and Aunt Janet, however, Mabel need not be taken seriously. . . . She was just a skirt, and he rather enjoyed playing her up. Not a bad little skirt, either, if it wasn't for her ideas of being a somebody in Calderwick. He wanted to borrow her car, anyhow, and he wouldn't mind borrowing her company as well. If he turned up all ready at her front door she wouldn't be able to resist the prospect of skating on the Dish at Invercalder. Frosts in Calderwick never lasted for long, and if they didn't take this chance, he would tell her, they might never get another. She wouldn't know how true that was.

So on that Wednesday morning, about half-an-hour after John's punctual departure to the mill, a loud honking from the kerb drew Mabel and Elise to the window, where they perceived Hector clambering out of a car. He flourished a pair of skates and grinned. Mabel almost collided in the hall with her maid, to the maid's surprise, for Mrs John Shand did not usually answer the door herself.

Hector coaxed and argued, waving the skates; Mabel demurred and hesitated, with appeals to Elise; Elise smiled and shrugged her shoulders.

'And why aren't you at the mill? John was furious with you last night.'

'He'll be twice as mad tonight, then, for I'm going to skate on the Dish whether you come or not.'

'Do you like skating, Mabel?' Elise was driven at length to ask, amused by Mabel's determination to make her a party to the affair.

'I simply love it.'

'Well, then,' and Elise shrugged her shoulders again.

For the next few minutes Mabel pressed Elise for an assurance that she did not object to being left alone, and that she would not think it rude if Mabel deserted her. Elise stood the fire calmly, and in a few minutes more the last shot was discharged. Mabel went upstairs to dress.

'I think I'll go up to the High Street and ask Elizabeth to come for a walk,' said Elise, not without mischief, for she wondered how Hector would take her reference to his wife. 'Is she busy?'

But she was surprised by his enthusiastic assent. The very thing, he said; it would do Elizabeth good. Besides, there was something they wanted to consult Elise about. He meant to say, he himself was in a bit of a hole and would love to talk it over with Elise. The fact was, they were both thinking of clearing out. Leaving Calderwick. At least he was, and Elizabeth thought she was too. But he would spit it all out to Elise if she would meet him next day, say at the Pagoda Tearooms at eleven in the morning? There was a quiet corner there and over coffee he would tell her everything.

What woman could deny herself the pleasure of being told everything by a young man? The Elise who had first come to Calderwick might have done so, but not Elise in her present mood. Moreover she had not yet enjoyed the honour of being Hector's confessor: if it had been the third or fourth time of asking she might not have been so complaisant.

'Not a word to Mabel – or to John.' Hector put his finger to his lips, as Mabel's heels came click-clacking merrily down the stairs.

'Shall I mention it to Elizabeth?'

'Of course,' returned Hector. Her second probe, it seemed, had also failed to make him wince. Apparently the utmost confidence existed between Hector and Elizabeth. Or else he's quite indifferent to her, thought Elise, watching the two-seater drive away.

## FOURTEEN

## I

Elise's present mood, the mood that made her amenable to Hector's advances, was unprecedented in her experience. She had no resentment left. . . . It began on the morning when she pottered alone about the streets of Calderwick, giving herself up to caprice; loitering in odd little back lanes; staring into the small windows of shops that sold home-made brown candy, halfpenny boxes of sherbet and lucky-bags; peering between the planks of the jetty at the restless green water lifting and dropping the fans of seaweed that grew on every wooden prop; and even standing for a while in the shelter of a ruined sea-wall with a vacant eye on some shawled and scarfed children who were playing there with flat, wave-worn bits of glass and red brick. These clean little streets, that looked shallow because the houses on either side were so low, recovered something of what they had once held for her in the days when there were chickens or rabbits, it seemed, in every back-yard and slices of bread-and-jam at every back door. She was no longer detached from Calderwick and no longer contemptuous of it. She sat down for a few minutes on an ancient wooden seat that fronted a leprous blank wall, and remembered that the ugly wall provided an excellent surface for the rebounding of soft rubber balls, and that neither she nor her schoolfellows had ever seen that it was ugly. Children never co-ordinate what they see, she thought: every bit of a landscape or a town or a house front is as important to them as every other bit. . . .

That night she dreamed that she was sitting on a bank of shingle before a stretch of sand; far out the sea crawled sluggishly among sandbanks and children were trotting with mothers and nurses to be dipped in the shallow pools. A long, distant, menacing roar reverberated from the horizon, and Elise had time only to remember that heavy rollers were reported on the Atlantic – without surprise she realized that it was the Atlantic she was fronting – before an enormous, endless billow came blotting out the sky and broke over her head. With a start she awoke, confusedly thinking of the helpless children, still hearing the roar of a second billow mounting behind the first, and with fear leaping in her bosom. As she awoke to fuller consciousness the fear ebbed away, leaving her in a queerly lucid and calm impregnability. She did not open her eyes; she was aware of herself as one is aware of a steady light in darkness; she was an unassailable point within the compass of her body, the centre, as it were, of a dimly perceived circle. This central point, she felt, was beyond the reach of accident and passion; it could not be touched through injury to the body around it. Unmoved, assured, it could look fearlessly at anything.

In the morning the calm acceptance, the tranquillity, of that inmost self still remained with her. There was no resentment left.

Her new attitude combined incompatibilities, as if the lion and the lamb had lain down together. She saw Mabel's faults, for instance, none the less clearly, but she was tolerant of them; she could still make sarcastic private comments at Hector's expense, but she could not take sides against him; she did not like her family any better, but she felt no desire to fend off any of them, not even Aunt Janet. That was the most surprising consequence; she saw that Aunt Janet was a weak-minded, prejudiced old woman, and yet she did not resent Aunt Janet. The centre of one's being, apparently, was both tranquil and inclusive. It was only on the circumference that people stood shoulder to shoulder and rubbed each other up the wrong way. Those who lived in the centre of themselves could treat neighbours with all the courtesy traditionally accorded by one ruling sovereign to another.

But surely I shall begin to resent things again sooner or later, she thought, as she walked briskly towards the High Street after seeing Mabel and Hector disappear. Was it possible to go on living in the centre of oneself? Nobody could tell, she decided; for that clear-eyed, tranquil *something* in the core of personality might be a comparatively recent human development, unpredictable and unforeseen. What *it* would do if Mabel or John or Hector or Elizabeth asked for partisan sympathy she did not know, but she surmised that *it* would not be partisan. To that new self all triangles must be equilateral triangles. . . .

Elizabeth, although crammed with unasked questions seeking an answer, was shy and silent as they climbed the ridge to the south of the town on top of which lay a moor that blazed red in August and purple in September but was now merely bare scrub on black peat, pitted with pot-holes of water, black, too, with ice.

'Look at that crow.' Elise pointed to a large bird sitting solitary in a tree. 'How monstrously disproportionate he seems! All birds look much bigger when the trees are bare.'

'I never noticed that before,' said Elizabeth.

'No?'

Elise did not turn her head but went on gazing at the prospect before them. They were on the edge of the moor, facing north, on the rim of an enormous pie-dish of which one end was broken clean off where it met the sea. In the hollow beneath them lay Calderwick, with its spires and chimneys pricking up through a faint haze of smoke, and behind it the plough-land, cut into rectangles, tilted upwards towards the rim of hills. The masts of fishing-smacks could be seen lying along the jetty; the little river flowed invisibly along the foot of the ridge on which they were standing. It was a spacious and peaceful landscape, filled with light.

Elise, as she looked at it, was divesting it of civilization, restoring its forests, its swamps, its naked moors and sandhills. Unpredictable and unforeseen, she was saying to herself, thinking alike of the new self she had discovered and of the new character that humanity had impressed on the landscape before her during the past two thousand – four thousand – she did not know how many – years.

Elizabeth stood silent, gradually surrendering to the impersonal peace and beauty of the scene. To her, however, it was not impersonal, for she was peculiarly susceptible to the pathetic fallacy, and the quietness of earth and sky, their unassertive air of being there for all time, reassured and confirmed her faith in the permanence of human love and aspiration.

But neither speculation nor reverie could long outface the wind that blew upon them as cold and pure as if it came straight from the Pole. They stepped down from their hummock of peat and struck across the moor. Elise paused beside a bog-hole and said: 'How black that ice is!' Then, hacking on it with her heel: 'And how thick!' These idle words unbarred some limbo in her mind to which she had regulated everything unconnected with her recent speculations – or, indeed, they may have been scouts sent out by the temporarily forgotten prisoners.

'How stupid of me to forget!' she cried. 'I met Hector before I came up for you and he told me that you were both thinking of leaving Calderwick. . . .'

At a bound Elizabeth's shyness turned itself inside out and was revealed as loquacious confidence. The more she told Elise the more she found to tell. In the most innocent-looking streams of memory she discovered unexpected opinions, hard little judgments, as hard and clear as crystal, and she exhibited their facets with increasing enthusiasm. 'People become what they are expected to be, and Calderwick *expects* Hector to go to the bad.' That was one of them. 'In Calderwick I feel like a threshing-machine that gets only a little chaff to thresh.' That was another.

Elise, listening, discovered that Elizabeth's ideal of living was a perpetual intoxication by what she called the 'earth-life', that power which she had fantasied as coming out of the earth and spreading to the stars. According to Elizabeth this power, whatever its source, inspired all poetry, all love, all religion, and was markedly absent from Calderwick, or, at least, unacknowledged there. Elizabeth spoke as if it were the water of life, in the absence of which Calderwick was a desert of sand fit only for ostrich-like inhabitants to thrust their heads into. She conjured Elise to tell her that elsewhere the world was not like Calderwick, so arid, so desiccated into conventions, so removed from all that was spontaneous and natural.

When she was moved Elizabeth could be eloquent, and

her eloquence delighted Elise. It did more; it challenged Elise, as if she saw a vast force of water running to waste for lack of a channel. Her newly discovered, central self all at once found something to do besides contemplating its own impartial tranquility.

'Unpredictable and unforeseen' Elise had called it, and it now justified these epithets by exhibiting a desire to educate the young, or, at least, to inform the young that one need not be completely submerged even by billows rising from the sea.

Her opportunity came when Elizabeth, carried away by her own words, translated the 'earth-life' into cosmic terms, confounding God and Nature in one terrific rush through the universe.

Elise interrupted her by remarking that Nature was sufficiently condemned if it were true that one touch of it made the whole world kin. In any case, Nature was an anachronism in the present stage of human development, which had gone far beyond anything either planned or foreseen by Nature. Nature envisaged nothing but birth, survival and reproduction, and was no guide to mankind beyond these simple limits.

While we must struggle to live, said Elise, we have no uncertainty about what to do. But when we have once secured the means of living, when we have established ourselves and grown strong – when we have done, that is to say, what Nature expects us to do – then we are plunged into horrid uncertainty, then we have to grope, tentatively; we grope into absurd blind alleys, sometimes; we take up hobbies: we collect stamps, for instance, or breed Cairn terriers; but too often, having no further obstacles to overcome, we merely fabricate new obstacles to keep ourselves busy, because an immediate obstacle makes life look easy. . . .

Mankind, said Elise, groping like this in the dark, helped only by the infernal adaptability of Nature, had created the arts and the sciences out of a void. The adaptability of Nature was itself an argument against following Nature; Nature was fool enough to follow anything. One should ask only: Is this intelligent? and never: Is this natural? People who urged intelligent men and woman to go 'back to Nature' were merely imbecile, in Elise's opinion. It was no use trying to drive either oneself or Calderwick back to Nature; if one wanted to drive anywhere it should be towards a more enlightened understanding. . . .

In short, civilized mankind was what it was, good or bad, mainly through its own efforts, and might develop in the most unexpected directions if it were encouraged to trust its intelligence and to outwit Nature wherever it could.

Elizabeth, startled, provoked and stimulated, convinced as she was that in any argument one need only go 'deep' enough to find fundamental agreement, protested against the use of the expression 'to outwit Nature'. Could one not rather say 'to transcend Nature'?

No, Elise insisted on outwitting Nature, saying with a laugh that that was how she felt about it. Nature was too strong, too cunning; one had to filch from her the energy for one's own purposes. Especially if one was a woman. It was not for nothing that old superstitions credited Nature with being more dangerous to women than to men.

Elise had suddenly remembered her maid-servant Madeleine and the snakes. . . . She had to tell Elizabeth about the snakes, and about Madeleine's fears, and about the possible symbolic meaning of those fears, and about the special difficulties that hampered women from girlhood. Conversation seemed inexhaustible. And in the heat of discussion Elizabeth quite forgot to ask where Hector was going when Elise met him. Nor did it occur to Elise to mention that Hector had gone with Mabel to skate at Invercalder.

'Marriages that need children to hold them together are merely copulations,' she was saying instead. 'The innocent child that reconciles his father and mother is made into one of Nature's panders; he's only asking for more brothers and sisters, the little brat.'

Elise was enjoying herself wholeheartedly; she was 'having her fling'. The apparent resentment which actuated her gibes was only apparent: she felt no bitterness. And in a pause of the argument she said, without premeditation: 'You and I, Elizabeth, would make one damned fine woman between us.'

## II

Mabel and Hector did not return until four o'clock. This protracted absence, whether foreseen by Nature or not, had certainly not been foreseen by them. It had come about so 'naturally', however, that Nature might well have had a hand in it.

The Dish was a small, deep lake in a fold of the hills behind the village of Invercalder, some five miles from Calderwick. It was much in use for curling, for it lay high enough to ensure ice in a cold spell and it was so still, being sheltered by larches at its open end, that its ice was like glass.

Hector's strong and supple body adjusted itself with apparent effortlessness to every kind of rapid movement; he was swift and graceful on skates as he was in the sea or on the football field. Mabel, although a practised skater in the best Invercalder style, had never attempted to dance on skates as she was now required to do, and in every sense was swept off her feet by her partner. In vain she tried to attribute her admiration of him to the fact that he looked so much more of a gentleman than anyone else on the lake; the touch of his fingers, the strength of his arm, the recklessness in his eye all excited her as no lady should ever be excited.

Naturally, therefore, when they called at the Mains of Invercalder to see her father before going home and found that brosy man just sitting down to his midday dinner, Mabel was not unwilling to join him and put off for a while the inevitable return to decorum.

'Hoots,' said Mains, 'the broth's just coming in, and there's plenty o' a'thing. Bring twa chairs inowre, Nell.'

Mains, Mabel's father, was a large, long-limbed man, with a red face, a slow voice and no regard for the proprieties. He was a widower of long standing, and a succession of housekeepers came to the farm and went again, usually with alimony. The present incumbent, Nell, as Mains informed Hector with a jerk of the thumb and a slow wink, after she had discreetly removed herself, was 'the grieve's dochter frae Nether Calder. A fine lassie. But she's like the lave o' them: I doubt she'll no' be muckle use to me in a whilie. God kens how *you* manage to get awa' wi' it, Mabel; twa years married an' no sign o' a bairn yet.'

'Wheesht, father,' said Mabel calmly, unfolding her napkin. Perhaps the most admirable trait in Mabel's character was the calmness with which she accepted her father.

There was a firm affection between them. Her mother she barely remembered: a pretty young creature, to judge from her wedding photograph in a stiffly bunched dress with a rose at her bosom and incredibly innocent eyes. Mabel had created a legend of refinement around her mother's photograph, and, supported by that, met her father's frankness with equanimity.

The Mains of Invercalder was a prosperous, well-stocked steading. The farm-house was a tall, white-harled building with a gable-end at right angles to the main structure, and an ample carriage-sweep. Behind it stretched an array of byres, barns and stables. Mains was a noted breeder of cattle and horses as well as a successful grower of wheat. From so much engendering of animal life a strongly sensual atmosphere hung over the farm, an atmosphere which the conversation of its master did not dispel; and after a generous dinner followed by whisky and an inspection of Mains' young horses both Hector and Mabel were kissing-ripe.

Mains, clapping his hat on his head, departed finally to a remote part of the farm, leaving them alone together in the darkness of the empty stable where the little Singer was garaged. It was only natural for Hector to clasp Mabel tightly in the most alarming embrace she had ever experienced in reality or in imagination. They were both moved by a craving as immediate and apparently as simple as hunger or thirst.

Its apparent simplicity was, of course, profoundly treacherous. The sexual instinct has such complicated emotional effects on men and women that its masquerade as a simple appetite ought not to be condoned. Mankind has an inkling of this fact, and much ingenuity is applied to shielding the young and inexperienced from the bewildering effects of sex. It is thus of some interest to know what particular consideration saved Mabel from the technical

surrender of her virtue. It was not her marriage vows, as one
might think, nor a conviction that sexual indulgence was
wicked in itself: it was the sudden recollection that she had
people coming to tea and whist.

But she could not really forgive Hector. Whether she
could not forgive him for his attack on her or whether, as
Elise suspected when Mabel tearfully confided in her, it was
his abandonment of the attack she could not forgive, it
would be difficult to determine.

## FIFTEEN

Elizabeth, happy and hungry after her walk, was not disturbed by Hector's absence as she might have been had she known what he was about. Her faith in the natural, the spontaneous, the unrestrained, was still bubbling up like a fountain, and the force that made it play was the force that had brought her and Hector together, and would keep them side by side, she thought, until the end of time, for it was inexhaustible. One could not measure it and draw it off for irrigation, as Elise insisted. No, no, Elise; one did not measure and calculate one's life. One did not cut and prune oneself; one simply grew. One grew and took one's chances.

That sounded reckless enough, but Elizabeth was not genuinely reckless. She thought herself daring, as she thought herself broad-minded, whereas her courage and her broad-mindedness were ideal rather than actual, the outlines of an imaginary structure not yet filled in by experience. In following what Elise called Nature Elizabeth was following what she conceived to be God, consequently in taking her chances she was taking what she conceived to be ultimate certainties. The seed has the same faith when it is in the ground and begins to grow; even if it finds itself growing in a cellar it does not abandon its faith without a struggle; and should it be tough enough in its kind, as a bush or a tree, it will break its prison by virtue of its faith. That instinctive faith governed Elizabeth, and although it cannot be called recklessness – for genuine recklessness can be found only in the human consciousness, while Elizabeth's faith is common to all plants and animals – it inspires actions that usually pass for reckless.

Elizabeth, however, being more than plant or animal, was fated to have her faith disciplined. She could not, as she imagined, escape pruning. There are people like Elise who prefer to do their own pruning; there are many who submit to pruning by others; there are a few, like Elizabeth, who do not know that pruning is inevitable and do not foresee that their eager growth will be broken off by circumstance – pruned raggedly, that is to say, instead of cleanly, by the apparent cruelty of chance instead of by design; a bruising and breaking of shoots that inflicts more pain than the quick cut of a knife; although, if the tree survives, the fruit that is formed may be none the worse.

In marrying Hector Elizabeth had entered upon a discipline that was to bruise her much as the discipline of the Church had bruised the minister. In either case a wide, formless, ecstatic feeling was being forced in an unforeseen direction by what one may call hard facts.

On this afternoon, however, Elizabeth, being not yet so hard pressed as William Murray, sat dreaming beside the fire. Her mind no longer leapt up to meet Elise's sallies; she was brooding instead on the charm of Elise herself. That a woman could be so lovable and so wrong-headed! When Dr Scrymgeour said he had no poetry in him she was sure that he belied himself, and she was equally sure that Elise belied herself in railing at Nature.

Elizabeth now felt a warm, protective tenderness for the wrong-headed creature. In spite of her years and her undeniable dignity Elise was so small, so vivacious and so impertinent! And she had run away from Calderwick with a married man. . . . And now she said that Nature was an anachronism. The besom! said Elizabeth, with a slow smile of appreciation.

Gradually she ceased to say to herself: Elise is charming; or: Elise is a besom; she merely thought: Elise is here, in Calderwick; and as she thought it her smile grew drowsy and contented. When Emily Scrymgeour came bustling in upon her she felt exactly as if she had been caught in private drug-taking.

'All alone in the dark?' said Emily. 'I've only looked in for a minute or two. . . .'

Elizabeth lit the gas, for it was dusk although only three o'clock, and disentangled her visitor's fingers from the corkscrewed strings of half-a-dozen small parcels.

'I never knew anybody like you for wee boxes and wee parcels, Emily.'

'Christmas presents – or they're going to be when I'm done with them. My dear, I've simply had to *fight* my way out of Mary Watson's. The shop's clucking like a hen-house; half the town's in there. I've had a whole half-hour of intensive scandal.'

'What about?'

'Now, just fancy anybody asking that! About the Murrays, of course. The Reverend William shouldn't have walked out of his pulpit without any formalities; he may have to walk out of it for good. Do you know what Mary Watson says? "Flying in the face of the congregation as well as in the face of God." She's got her hackles up properly. She says Ned's madness is a judgment on the minister. If he has the nerve to show his nose at the sale of work on Saturday I pity him.'

'But that's abominable!'

Elizabeth started up in anger. Calderwick and its damned prejudices! What else could the minister have done but leave the pulpit? He was too upset to be anything but natural.

'I heard that you were there,' Emily's tone was sly. 'I heard that you and your new sister bounced out of the church like two rubber balls. But Mary Watson doesn't lay the blame on *you*; she's willing to put it all on Miss Shand.'

'Aunt Janet? What's she got to do with it?'

'No, no; your sister-in-law. Isn't she a Miss Shand?'

'My dear Emily, she's a Frau Doktor. A widow.'

'A widow! Did she marry the man then?'

Elizabeth began to grow red.

'She married a famous scholar recently.'

'Aha! Now, that's what I call a clever woman. So that's why she came back, is it?'

Emily Scrymgeour, although she was also small, vivacious and impertinent, suddenly appeared so much inferior to Elise as to be insignificant. From that moment Elizabeth would have sacrificed Emily Scrymgeour, together with the whole of Calderwick, as a show-offering, if not a burnt-offering, before Elise. But what she said was: 'Oh, nonsense,

Emily; don't be silly. Elise isn't that kind of woman at all. I admire her immensely. I like her *very* much.'

*O sancta simplicitas!* one might have said to Elizabeth. *That isn't the way to allay one woman's jealousy of another!*

'I'm sure she's all you think her. . . . Of course she's ever so much more interesting than us old-fashioned housewives in Calderwick,' said Emily. For two pins, she was thinking, for two pins she would get Elizabeth off her high horse by just telling her—

What could she have told her? An important addition to the volume of scandal, some information about the movements of a certain Bell Duncan. . . .

It was unfortunate that William Murray had dismissed his congregation so prematurely, thus letting loose upon the High Street three-quarters of an hour before their usual time a body of experienced scouts whose eyes had raked Poggi's shop through its ever-open door.

But Elizabeth of her own accord climbed down from her high horse, and the information was not passed on. Emily did not want to forfeit any advantage she had in Elizabeth's regard. She reverted to the safer topic of the minister.

'Jim said to me yesterday that he wouldn't wonder if he had William Murray on his hands as well as the brother. He said they were both – now what was it? – "over-valued neuropaths". Isn't he a little terror, Jim?'

When she got home she appealed for approval to the little terror.

'You do think, don't you, that I was right in not telling Elizabeth what they were saying about her husband?'

'Let ilka herring hang by its ain tail,' was the doctor's comment.

'I've just had Murray at me again,' he added. 'He's trying to torment me as well as himself. . . . "Man," I said to him, "considering your profession, there's only two alternatives before you, and you'd better swallow one of them and be done with it."'

'What were the alternatives, Jim?'

'Ah, I didn't tell him that.'

'But you can tell *me*?'

'Well . . . he's bound to swallow one of the God plusses.'

'What on earth—?'

Emily's eyes danced, and she laid down her sewing.

'He's asking himself two questions about his brother's condition: first, could God have prevented it? Now, that can be answered in the positive or in the negative: God plus, you see, or God minus; second, could human agency, including himself and the poor laddie, have prevented it? Man plus, we'll say, or Man minus. But that's two gey awkward questions to put side by side, for being a minister he's bound to say "God plus" to the first and that brings him hard up against it whichever way he turns. . . . It's a fine problem. . . . But he's one of your born God plussers and there's nothing that can be done with *them*,' said the doctor.

## SIXTEEN

## I

Three confessions in twenty-four hours, thought Elise, looking gravely at Hector. Yesterday morning, Elizabeth; in the evening, Mabel; and now Hector.

She had looked at him with grave attention ever since he began talking; she did not appear shocked or angry, but neither did she seem to be sorry for him. Hector was a little nonplussed.

He drank off another cup of coffee. His head needed clearing. He had had a good few drinks the night before, after being turned down by Mabel. . . . He wished to God that Elise would say something.

It was absolution, of course, that Hector wanted, not a judicial summing-up; and Elise, who knew that, kept her observations to herself. She was also wondering why this spate of confessions had broken over her. Three confessions in twenty-four hours. . . . Was it a consequence of her own *Aufklärung*? Did the dispassionate, central self attract confessions?

Hector's confession had begun as a compound of excuse and self-accusation, but the excuses had tailed away and the self-accusation had mounted in enormity under the grave eyes of his listener. He had spent his whole life, she discovered, either in lifting women's skirts or in hiding behind them, and the one habit accused the other. He should confine himself to the first, she thought. Probably that was what he *would* do after leaving Calderwick.

'Well,' said Hector, making an effort, 'what do you think about it?'

Elise's hand moved towards her handbag and drew back again.

'What do you think about it yourself?'

'Calderwick's a damned rotten hole, and the sooner I'm out of it the better.'

'I think you're right in going,' said Elise quietly.

Hector snatched eagerly at this morsel of approbation.

'I knew you'd understand. Damn it all, Elise, *you* didn't regret leaving Calderwick, did you?'

'No,' said Elise, adding, with a smile: 'I mean to do it again.'

'Elizabeth,' said Hector, and stopped. That was the snag; yes, that was the snag. 'She's going too,' he said, and stopped again. Then he plucked up courage. 'John damned well *ought* to support Elizabeth until she gets a job; he's done the dirty on me often enough.'

'Don't you worry about Elizabeth,' said Elise. 'I'm going to look after her.'

This resolve, which had sprung fully armed from her head on the previous evening, still surprised Elise, as the appearance of Minerva must have surprised the Father of the Gods, and, like Minerva, it was helmed and weaponed to resist attack.

It was Mabel's confession that had evoked it, and in especial her half-angry, half-ashamed indictment of Hector as the kind of man who couldn't stick to any woman. Yes, Elise agreed; he was probably the kind of man who needed a wife to run away from. 'But it's more exciting to be married to a man like that than to John,' wailed Mabel, luxuriating in her self-sacrifice. If only Hector had been the senior partner, or had some money! She frankly called John an old stick and Elizabeth a great lump. Her one consolation was the probability, to which she returned, that Hector could never stick to one woman, not even to a pretty woman.

A 'transient', said to Elise to herself, suddenly remembering her early twenties. In Brussels she had studied the tenets of the Saint-Simonians, amongst others, and had accepted Enfantin's classification of temperaments. 'Permanents' and 'Transients' they had called them in Brussels . . . in those days when one believed in categories. . . . Elise smiled at the recollection; she had begun as a 'transient' herself, and ended up as a 'permanent'. But there was not much likelihood that Hector would ever follow her example; he was a natural 'transient'.

And Elizabeth—?

Again Elise felt compassionate towards Elizabeth's youth and ignorance. She did not know what she was heading for. Her vision of life was almost sublime in its credulity. . . . One ought to do something about it.

Mabel's sobs grew more infrequent; she wiped her eyes and sat up. 'I never want to see him again,' she said. 'He's not worth it. I want to get away from him. . . . Oh, Elise, couldn't you take me back with you when you go?'

It was at that moment that Minerva, fully armed, astonished Elise. She found that she had decided to take Elizabeth back with her. . . . And to make things fair all round she would give Hector some money.

This resolve withstood attack, and it withstood what was more disturbing, the aloofness of her isolated, central self. . . . Within its citadel that self refused to approve or disapprove. She might be doing a magnanimous thing, or she might be simply stealing the girl. In supplementing Hector's two hundred pounds, which Elizabeth had mentioned with such pride, she might be paying back part of her debt to John, or she might simply be buying Hector off. . . . The central self was not moved by such arguments as: 'Freely ye have received, freely give.' Inclusive and impartial, it refused to decide which of the two interpretations was right – foster-mother or kidnapper, generous philanthropist or payer of hush-money.

'Why, child, you would be bored to death in my house,' she said to Mabel. 'I don't keep rich young men on tap. . . . You had much better get John to take you south.'

Mabel's troubles weren't worth bothering about. They would solve themselves once Hector was gone. But that was just when Elizabeth's troubles would begin. . . .

'Don't you worry about Elizabeth. I'm going to look after her,' said Elise.

Hector was loud with surprise and gratitude.

'That was the one snag,' he said. 'That was really what I wanted to sound you about. Although, mind you, I think

I've managed to get the sack from John, and he'll probably feel responsible for Elizabeth.'

'Have you got the sack?'

'Haven't been to find out yet. I expect it's waiting for me in the office.' Hector grinned. He was beginning to feel reassured.

'Did Mabel?' He cocked an eyebrow at Elise.

'No, she hasn't told John. I don't think she will. But the next time John abuses you she won't contradict him.'

'They can blacken me as much as they like; I don't give *that* for them now.' He snapped his fingers.

As he sat there exulting in his freedom – for he had shelved all his responsibilities – Hector was a sample of genuine human recklessness. Elise recognized the quality; she had it herself. It was a readiness to throw up everything, to break all ties and disappear into the unknown, trusting neither in chance nor in Providence. . . . In her present mood she stigmatized it as cowardice, but she recognized it with a certain sympathy. The two black Shands were not unlike in some respects.

This reflection made it easier for her to open her handbag and produce the cheque. That cheque had worried her. . . . She could not afford to shower upon Hector and Elizabeth all the money she had received from John during twenty years. . . . After some hesitation she had compromised on three hundred pounds for Hector, with the reservation that he might have some more later. . . . But she wouldn't tell him that.

'It'll take perhaps a fortnight to cash,' she was explaining. 'You must not tell anyone about it, not even Elizabeth.'

Elizabeth would be off to Singapore too if she knew there was so much money. . . . Elise could not entirely stifle a sense of guilt.

Hector stared at the cheque as if it were a warrant for his death. He did not touch it. Without looking at Elise he said between his teeth: 'I'm going to-morrow. I've booked my passage. I'm going with that girl I told you about – Bell Duncan.'

Elise clasped her hands tightly.

'Does Elizabeth know?'

'No.'

Elise leaned forward a little. As she moved Hector looked up.

'Yes,' he said. 'I'm a cad.'

'Don't be melodramatic,' said Elise coolly. 'How queer!' she was commenting. 'Nature is definitely melodramatic – like this.'

'I'm leaving Calderwick to-night,' insisted Hector. 'I'm sailing third-class with Bell Duncan.'

Elise unclasped her hands and leaned back. She saw that there were beads of sweat on Hector's brow. How irrelevant it all was. . . . What did it matter whether he went now or later, with this girl or with another?

The central self was faintly bored by such peripheral matters. It was also rather bored by sex. . . . If all people were to live in the centre of themselves, Elise suddenly realized, the human race would soon die out.

With that her last resistance to the transaction vanished. Her sense of guilt had already vanished. All she had to do was to get rid of Hector as quickly as possible.

'Pick up that cheque,' she said. . . .

## II

At about twelve o'clock Hector Shand came out of the Pagoda Tearooms with a cheque for three hundred pounds in his pocket and an urgent desire for a drink. The sky was darkening with clouds; the wind had shifted a point to the east; the frost was slackening, and the air was raw. There might be snow before nightfall. Hector turned up his collar and made for a bar.

When he came home for lunch he was effusive, almost maudlin; but he was sober enough to remember that he had vowed to conceal the cheque from Elizabeth, and to have her informed that he was booked for Singapore next day.

'I shall stop the cheque at once if I find that you have broken your promise,' Elise had said, shaking back the white ruffles from her wrist as she lit a cigarette.

But one couldn't just cough it up over the luncheon-table, ducky. . . . Poor Elizabeth. Poor lil Elizabeth; a no-good husband; a rotten husband. Do you still love your Uncle Hector?

Elizabeth tried to laugh him off, and when that failed, to scold him off. He had some food and sobered up a little; but his melancholy deepened as he grew sober, and after lunch he flung himself on his knees with his face in her lap.

'I'll never be any good, never.'

Stroking his hair, Elizabeth passionately denied that mistakes were irretrievable or failings ineradicable.

'You'll forget all about me when I'm gone, and serve me right,' he mumbled.

Never, oh, never! How could he even *think* that? The tears started to Elizabeth's eyes. She forced his head up and saw that his eyes were also wet.

'Here we are,' said Elizabeth. 'You and I, under this roof, and it might be any roof in the whole wide world and we should be just the same to each other. . . .'

Hector raised himself and buried his face in her breast, holding her tightly.

'Oh, Elizabeth!' he muttered. 'Oh, Elizabeth!' Had it not been for some malice, some dirty trick of Fate, he felt, how happy they might have been.

Outside, the first flakes of snow, so light and small that one could hardly call them flakes, were thickening the air and driving almost invisibly past the window.

Hector kept his face hidden.

'I've something to tell you. . . .'

'What is it?'

She could feel him draw a shuddering breath, and she laid her hand on his shoulder.

'I'm booked to go to Singapore to-morrow, and I have to leave Calderwick to-night.'

'To-night! Oh, Hector!'

## SEVENTEEN

## I

A vacant body – that is to say, an idle body – often denotes an active mind, and there are people who hold the reverse to be true. Of these Elizabeth was probably one, for she helped to pack Hector's effects with a fury of activity that must have been designed to prevent thought. As he rejected one thing after another which her solicitous hand had tucked into corners Hector wondered how he had ever imagined that he could slip out of the house unobserved, or, on the pretext of a mere week-end in Dundee, carry off the two large suitcases which he had prescribed for himself.

It may have been because the snow was now falling thick and fast that he tried to dissuade Elizabeth from coming with him to the station. But if he was afraid that she would embarrass him by weeping on his bosom, as some return for the tears he had shed on hers, he must have been pleased by the propriety of her demeanour on the platform, especially as Hutcheon was also present.

Elizabeth was cordial to Hutcheon. Perhaps she had been suspecting him as a Mrs Harris to Hector's Sairey Gamp; his presence, certainly, relieved her mind of something she could not quite define. His awkwardness did not surprise her; he had always been ill at ease while talking to her; she could not imagine why.

On this occasion, however, Hutcheon's awkwardness was the dissimulation of something like panic. He exchanged a quick glance with Hector and almost imperceptibly jerked his thumb towards another part of the platform. There were few people travelling by so late a train, and these were mostly huddled in the shelter of the newspaper kiosk, for the platform, though roofed, was open at both ends, so that the station was a funnel for the blizzard. The light, too, was dim. But Hector's keen eye descried the cause of Hutcheon's panic, a slim young girl in a mackintosh carrying what appeared to be a pasteboard box tied up with string. Shortly afterwards he walked Elizabeth down to the far end of the platform and there slipped his arm around her and gave her a kiss. When they came back Hutcheon was holding the pasteboard box.

Elizabeth saw it. But even if she had questioned it she would have answered herself that Hutcheon had retrieved it from one of the seats where he had left it lying, and that it probably enclosed some foolish parting gift for Hector.

Becky Duncan, having given up the package and watched it go into Hector's compartment, ran home to report that Heck Shand's wife was actually down at the station, and that Jim Hutcheon had 'snickit' the box out of her hand before she could say Jack Robinson. Mrs Duncan pursed up her mouth and said: 'Ay. Ay. Imphm. Just that. Oh ay!' – remarks which were highly non-committal, and could scarcely have provided a foundation for the rumour that was to run through Calderwick that very evening. Her next-door neighbour, who was in the kitchen sharing a fly cuppie of tea with her when young Becky returned, nodded her head more but said even less, except when she asked: 'What was in the boxie?'

And although Mrs Duncan gave an inventory of all she had put in it – item, a shortbread, item, a Scotch bun, item a pound of black buckies – a local sweetmeat – and several fal-lals my lady had left behind her – it is not easy to see how that list of innocent Christmas comforts sent by a mother to her daughter could possibly justify the positive statement retailed within two hours all over the town that Heck Shand was off to Singapore with Bell Duncan. One can explain it only by admitting that the Scots are a highly intelligent people.

Jim Hutcheon, however, left alone on the dark platform with Elizabeth when the train had thundered away, showed little of his native intelligence. He was tongue-tied and he looked stupid. In reality, he was both sorry to lose Hector and envious of his luck. To him, as to Hector and to most men of that age, any place east of Suez spelt enchantment. The Singapore of Hutcheon's imagination was constructed on the same principles, and ministered to the same needs, as Domenico Poggi's gaudy establishment in the sober High Street of Calderwick.

But he could not enlarge on it to a respectable married woman, least of all to one whose husband had set off in questionable company for that delectable land. He was a nice lad, young Hutcheon, and he was tongue-tied beside Elizabeth. With her he could not pursue those never-ending speculations that had kept him and Hector awake for hours, such as: is it true that a woman never forgets the first man she sleeps with? or: is it true that a stallion or a gelding can swim for hours if need be, while a mare must inevitably fill up with water and founder? . . . He could not even ask Mrs Shand to come and have a drink.

Elizabeth was melancholy, Hutcheon tongue-tied, and so these two children of a romantic age walked out of the station on either side of a wall of silence. At the mouth of the entry leading up to her house Elizabeth said mechanically: 'Goodnight, Mr Hutcheon.' Then, with one of her abrupt and disconcerting movements, she thrust out her hand and shook his. 'You'll miss him too,' she said and, turning away, ran up the 'close' to her own front door.

If she had not run away Jim Hutcheon might have said something. As it was he went off into the snow thinking that it was really a bit thick of Hector. . . . What would she feel like when she found out?

There is an undercurrent of kindly sentiment that runs strong and full beneath many Scots characters, a sort of family feeling for mankind which is expressed by the saying: 'We're all John Tamson's bairns'; and it was perhaps a touch of that sentiment which made Hutcheon sympathetic to Elizabeth in spite of his prejudices as a man and a friend. It is a vaguely egalitarian sentiment, and it enables the Scot to handle all sorts of people as if they were his blood relations. Consequently in Scotland there is a social order of rigid severity, for if people did not hold each other off who knows what might happen? The so-called individualism of the Scots is merely an attempt on the part of every Scot to keep every other Scot from exercising the privileges of a brother. We should misunderstand Calderwick as completely as Elizabeth did if we did not recognize the sentiment underlying its jealous distinctions, its acrimonious criticisms and its awkward silences.

One must admit that a stranger would find it difficult to recognize. He would observe that Mrs Duncan of the Fisherrow could not aspire to official acquaintance with old Mrs Macpherson of the fish-shop in the High Street, and that Mrs Macpherson in her turn was ignored by Mrs Mackenzie the fish-merchant's wife, but he could not know that each of these ladies took as much personal interest in the others' doings as if they were sisters. Mrs Mackenzie sails past Mrs Duncan in the street, but she has just spent an hour discussing Bell Duncan over a tea-table, and has finished up by saying: 'I'm sorry for Mrs Duncan; she seems a decent body.' There is nothing that concerns young Charlie Macpherson that the other two mothers do not know, and if they were to meet on a desert island or in an English town they would fall upon each other's necks. The acrimonious tone of Mary Watson's voice, which offends the outsider, is exactly what she employs in speaking to her sister Ann, and John Shand treats his brother Hector as he would treat any of his men. The whole of Calderwick is bound together by invisible links of sympathy. . . . It is not everyone who can live without embarrassment in a Scots community.

So Elizabeth, shutting her front door behind her, thought herself alone in her castle, but if she was alone anywhere it was in a castle in Spain. From kitchen to kitchen shawled wives were running with the news that Heck Shand had gone off by the six-o'clock train on his way to Singapore with Bell Duncan, and one after the other they said: 'Isn't it terrible for his wife, poor lassie?' By eight o'clock in Elizabeth's own kitchen Mary Ann Lamond was listening to her mother, who had arrived out of breath and covered with snow, saying: 'They tell me . . .'

'I dinna believe it!' cried Mary Ann. 'And you can tell them that from me. The mistress hersel' was down at the station. "It's very sudden, Mary Ann," she says, says she, "but we've had it in mind a long time," she says.'

'Aweel,' returned her mother, 'I had it from Mrs Ritchie, and she had it from Mrs Beattie, and she had it from Mrs Kinnear, and she had it from Mrs Pert, that bides next door to the Duncans. And you ken yoursel' that Bell and him were seen thegither on the Sunday.'

No messenger ever proved his credentials more thoroughly. Mary Ann laid her head down on the kitchen table and blubbered.

She assumed at once, as everybody did, that her mistress was betrayed, and with the heroic spirit of a Mrs Partington keeping the Atlantic at bay with a mop she set herself to isolate Elizabeth from the rumour.

'You'll no' be going out today?' she said next morning, setting down the breakfast teapot. 'A body canna see an inch in front of their nose, the snow's that thick. Just you bide by the fire, and if there's anything you want tell me and I'll run out for it.'

Elizabeth propped up a book against the milk-jug. It was like a return to student days, she thought, and there was something pleasant in being on one's own again. . . . She had fifty pounds, more money than she had ever possessed at once. . . . There were three vacancies in English schools that she had already applied for. . . . And Hector would make a fortune for both of them. . . .

Her eyes suddenly overflowed. But though one or two tears rolled down her cheeks and her mouth twitched a little Elizabeth went on reading. She had 'had her cry out' during the night and was determined to be sensible. It was only her silly eyes that wept a little now and then because Hector had not let her go with him to Singapore.

Silly fool, said Elizabeth in a rough voice, and turned another page. She had nothing to cry about and plenty to do. She must interview John – that would be easy – and Aunt Janet – that would be difficult. In the three or four weeks remaining to her she must settle up the house and come to some arrangement with Aunt Janet about the furniture. Worst of all, she must explain the whole affair to her parents, who had never approved her marriage to Hector because he was not, as they said, a godly man.

It was a strange thing that Elizabeth, who was willing to

explain herself by the hour to Elise, had always shrunk with impatient irritation from explaining herself for even five minutes to her father and mother. She scowled a little as she thought of it.

The snow was indeed as thick as Mary Ann had said, and it was driving before gusts that sounded eerie in their violence. As she looked out of the window Elizabeth felt isolated from the whole world, secluded behind thick veils of snow. But it was not unpleasant. . . . She remembered all at once that this was a Friday, a market day, and that John would be up in the farmers' mart. She could not go there looking for him. . . . Put it off, said a voice, put it all off, keep today for yourself.

When she was a small girl it had often amazed her parents that Elizabeth could shut herself off with a book so completely that even shouting failed to arouse her attention. She sat down now by the fire with *Pride and Prejudice*, and in ten minutes was utterly absorbed.

## II

Meanwhile rumour had begun to percolate from kitchens to drawing-rooms, and the news that Hector had gone off arrived at number seven Balfour Terrace together with the day's bread. Mrs John Shand was both dismayed and flattered when she heard it: dismayed because Hector had gone off with such a common girl and flattered because she thought he had done it for her sake. It was just the kind of thing that would happen in one of her favourite stories, when the villain with the heart of gold sacrifices himself to save the heroine's honour. . . .

Frau Doktor Mütze was less pleased.

'It is all over the town already?' she asked, with some tartness. 'This might be the African jungle, the way news travels.'

Yet she was relieved. She could now be open and above-board with Elizabeth. She could now say, in effect: Hector is a worthless creature; forget him, and come with me. Salutary medicine for Elizabeth – but bitter, bitter as death, Elise suddenly realized, remembering all that Elizabeth had said to her. . . . Elizabeth's feelings struck their roots deep; they were no hardy annuals like Mabel's. . . .

Elise looked at the falling snow, then went quietly upstairs and put on stout shoes and a thick travelling cloak. The sooner the better, she said to herself, feeling as if she ought to take a small black bag with her, like a physician.

She arrived at Elizabeth's door fifteen minutes after Emily Scrymgeour. Mary Ann, barring the door with a brawny arm and a firm statement that Mrs Shand was not at home to anybody, had been no match for the agile little wife of the doctor. She jinked round me as if I was a lamp-post, thought the discomfited guardian, sitting in the kitchen and stretching her ears to listen if the mistress was greeting. But when the door-bell rang again she made no effort to keep out the newcomer. This visitor was one of 'the family'; and although Mary Ann, a true daughter of Calderwick, had never heard the phrase 'it's not my place to do so-and-so' she knew that it would be exceeding her powers to turn away 'the family'.

The mistress was not greeting; she was even smiling. More and more disconcerted, Mary Ann closed the drawing-room door and retired to her kitchen in bewilderment.

But Elizabeth too was bewildered. Emily's commiseration was so very excessive. Emily was so incredulous when she was told that Hector's departure was a planned affair, approved and abetted by Elizabeth. 'I took him to the station myself,' Elizabeth was saying when Elise appeared. She was beginning to feel impatient; why should Emily Scrymgeour insist on her sitting in sackcloth and ashes, so to speak? She hailed Elise with joy and proudly presented her to Mrs Scrymgeour. 'My next-door neighbour, who is almost angry with me because I'm not in tears. . . . I suppose you've heard too that Hector went away last night? When I told you about it on Wednesday I didn't expect him to go *quite* so soon.'

Something in Elise's cool glance might have offended Emily, or perhaps she was only jealous because she had not enjoyed Elizabeth's confidence while the other had. At any rate she looked as sharp and dangerous as her favourite weapon, a needle.

'Well, thank goodness there are some things *I'm* too old-fashioned to countenance,' she said, looking first at Elise and then at Elizabeth.

Elizabeth straightened herself.

'What do you mean, Emily?'

Elise turned her back and drummed on the window-pane. Emily Scrymgeour's short nervous fingers worked over each other as if they itched.

'You know very well what I mean. I mean that I don't approve of married men running off with girls. And if their *wives* encourage them to do it I say it's a disgrace to womanhood. You should be ashamed of yourself, Elizabeth Shand.'

Elizabeth bounded from her seat with a dark flush on her brow and set herself between Emily and the door.

'You don't get out of this room until you take that back,' she cried. 'What do you mean by your vile insinuations? What the hell do you mean?'

Elise turned round:

'Let her go, Elizabeth. Let her go, I tell you. There's more behind this than you imagine.'

She walked forward slowly until she stood before Emily Scrymgeour, her face grave and quiet.

'I think you'd better go,' she said. 'Please.'

Then she continued towards the door and, throwing it open, stood waiting.

Emily Scrymgeour went.

Elise shut the door and looked at Elizabeth.

'Hector,' she began. Then her compassion for Elizabeth obscured her judgment.

'There's a rumour in Calderwick that Hector has gone to Singapore with a girl called Bell Duncan,' she said.

'But that's absurd,' returned Elizabeth, in the same quiet toner. 'That's just the kind of thing they *would* invent in Calderwick.'

'I think there's no doubt that the girl is on the same boat.'

'How do you know?'

Elizabeth's tone was still quiet, but she began to shiver and caught at a chair.

Elise said nothing.

'Elise! For God's sake, tell me the truth! I must know exactly.'

'Her mother says so.'

'That's no evidence,' said Elizabeth, her teeth chattering. 'That's no evidence at all. I must get at the truth of this. I must get at the t-truth. Can't you *see*, Elise, I must get at the truth. She may have followed him. I know all about her. She may have gone after him deliberately. Even if she is on the boat I don't believe Hector knew. . . .'

Elise sighed, and said what she had been trying to escape saying:

'He did know, for he told me yesterday morning that he was going with her.'

'He – he told you?'

'Yes.'

'And you d-didn't tell me?'

'No.'

'My God, why not? I could have stopped him. Why not? Why didn't you tell me? I can't help my teeth chattering, Elise, but I'm quite calm: I'm not going to make a fool of myself—'

With that Elizabeth pitched in a dead faint on the floor.

## EIGHTEEN

A mere fall of snow could not keep Sarah Murray indoors, for the sale of work was to be opened next day and she had to spend the morning and afternoon in the mission hall of St James's supervising the reception and arrangement of goods. It needed someone in authority to keep the stallholders from poaching each other's show pieces. Sarah had tried to organize the sale in what she called 'a business-like manner', but although she had put up labels identifying Mrs Gove's stall as Fancywork and Mrs Mackenzie's as Woollens she knew that, left to themselves, these ladies would soon make the labels look silly. The consciousness of being the supreme judiciary, the manse delegate, gave Sarah an added firmness and impartiality; she was a good administrator and she enjoyed her day's hard work.

When she came back towards five o'clock she found the minister's lunch still untasted on its tray.

'Has he never stirred, Teenie?'

'No, Miss Murray.'

Sarah clicked her tongue on the roof of her mouth. 'He should never have gone out there yesterday,' she said. 'But he wouldna be advised.'

All day William Murray had sat at his desk with his head bowed on his hands. The minutes slipped past him irrevocably; one by one they slipped away, and, once gone, he knew that they were irretrievable. Outside, the snowflakes slipped past the window, and the minutes were light and unnoticeable in their passage like the snowflakes, but each one of them was a doom, and the sum of them was a man's destiny. That was the mystery. Time, so fleeting that one could never arrest it, was weighted with eternal consequences.

Last Sunday he had committed Ned to the asylum, and, whatever happened, that Sunday could never return, that deed could never be undone. Lord, forgive me, he cried, for I knew not what I did!

Thursday was visiting day at the asylum, and he had insisted upon seeing his brother. If Ned had received him with curses he could have borne it, but with a young beard on his thin face, weeping and wistful, he had plucked at his sleeve and begged to be taken home. 'Out of the question,' said Dr Eliot firmly; 'quite out of the question.'. . . . What is done can never be undone. One by one the irrevocable minutes pass. . . .

And what was to keep a man from making a false step? How could he know if it was God or the Devil that prompted him? How discriminate between righteous anger, for instance, and unrighteous? There was no answer to that, save the conviction, now pressing heavily upon the minister, that both kinds of anger were of the Devil: a conviction for which his own feelings were the last authority. Since allowing anger to invade him under the pretext of driving out evil he had known the calm of determination but not the peace of holiness. . . . And yet God was a God of wrath as well as a God of love.

The minister agonized with himself until, weary and famished, he sat in a kind of stupor, holding his heavy head in his hands. Once or twice he muttered: 'The Lord's will be done.' He desired to sleep and to forget.

Sarah went into the study and touched him on the shoulder. He did not move. She shook him gently.

'Come to your tea, Willie.'

It was many long years since she had called him that. The minister stared at her and then pushed his hair back confusedly.

'I think I've been alseep,' he said.

He staggered as he got up, for his legs were stiff. How long had he been sitting there? And what strange dream had he fallen into? A yellow river, as broad as the eye could compass; turbulent water yellow with fine mud; and he careering down the middle of the stream on something resembling a large wooden tea-tray, perfectly round, with a hollow in the

middle on which he had to balance himself. . . . One false
step, and he knew he would be lost in one of the dimpling
whirlpools around him. And all he had to steady himself by
was a straight short pole. . . . The shape of his curious vessel
made it impossible to steer in any direction; he had to follow
the current as best he could. He had an idea that the river was
in China, but that, at the same time, it was the river of the
will of God. . . .

He had never been in China, but he was certain, in that
moment, that the yellow river he had seen was a real river.

He washed and brushed before he sat down to the tea-
table, and he looked almost cheerful as he took his cup from
Sarah. The dream was a kind of answer. . . . There was
nothing to be done but resign himself, as many greater than
he had done, to the will of God. An Oriental philosophy, no
doubt.

William Murray set his cup on the saucer and stared at
Sarah.

'I've had such a queer dream,' he said, 'about China and a
tea-tray—'

'You would be dreaming about your tea,' said Sarah, 'and
no wonder.'

The minister smiled, shook his head, and said nothing
more. When he was finished with the meal he asked for his
outdoor shoes.

'Where are you going in all this snow?'

'This is my night for visiting old Johnny Pert.'

'Johnny Pert's not dying yet, and he can do without you
to-night. You're not fit to go outside the door.'

'I must do my duty by the folk in my charge,' said William
in a mild voice, 'so long as I'm their minister, Sarah. It
wouldn't be kind to disappoint the old man.'

'Kind!' Sarah exploded. There were folk one should be
kind to, and there were folk one shouldn't be kind to, for
they just took advantage, like that Johnny Pert, and, indeed,
all the Perts, who hung on to the minister merely for Church
coal and Church poor-box funds, and were always making a
poor mouth about themselves—

'And who is to judge them, Sarah? Not I, not I. . . . I
can't even guide myself, far less others.'

'And you'll not let yourself be guided,' snapped Sarah.

'I'm learning,' said the minister, putting on his coat.

The blast whirled right into his face when he opened the door; it was blowing straight in off the sea with such a drive of snow that one could hardly see the next lamp-post in the street. The minister bent his head forward and plodded into the heart of it. Old Johnny Pert lived in one of the tenements in the Fisherrow, the nearest approach to a slum that Calderwick could show. It lay round the corner from the harbour; one had to go straight down Dock Street and then bear to the right. . . .

The flurry of snow and wind made the town strange and ghostly; the force of the elements reminded the minister of the torrent force in the yellow water of his dream; but this time he was striving against the current, not carried away by it. When one had an objective one could guide oneself. What was God's objective? To what strange purpose did He hurry His children along the stream of Time? The minister did not know. . . . All he could say with certainty to his congregation was that one should not wreck one's neighbours in the river. . . . Little children, love one another. . . . And even that had not availed with Ned.

He braced himself against the stronger gale that shrieked from the estuary and met him with full force in Dock Street. The darkness of the river-mouth, like an encroaching hand, here seized upon the town, blotting out the whirling battalions of snowflakes. Now that he could no longer see them the minister felt more acutely how the snowflakes pelted into his eyes, and he screwed his face up till his eyelashes met. He wished he had taken a walking-stick. He could have used it, like the pole in his dream, to keep his course even. A queer, queer dream. . . . Hurried on, irresistibly, on the tide of God's will to what unknown sea? . . . The Pacific, of course, thought the minister, almost smiling in the darkness. The sea of God's peace. . . . He stumbled, staggered, and then stumbled again.

## NINETEEN

The postman left a flat basket of snowdrops that Mabel had ordered from Dundee for her stall at the sale of work.

'Aren't they lovely!' she said. 'I wonder where they come from.'

The snowdrops were tied in tight little bunches, with a ring of dark ivy leaves around each boss of flower-heads. Elise bent over the basket and picked out four bunches.

'I'll buy these from you now.'

'Oh, take as many as you like, Elise; never mind the money, it's only for Foreign Missions or something. . . . There's the telephone!'

Mabel's voice sharpened as if in fear:

'What, John?' she said. 'What? What? Oh, my God!'

She turned to Elise.

'John says Mr Murray's been found drowned in the dock. They think he missed his way in the storm last night.'

Two startled faces looked at each other.

'Poor devil,' said Elise.

'There won't be any sale of work,' said Mabel. Her lip began to tremble. She sat down and cried into her handkerchief.

'I'm – I'm frightened,' she sobbed. . . . 'I hate anybody I know to die. It makes me so frightened.'

'Poor, poor devil,' said Elise, thinking of the young minister's thin, hungry look. She walked to the window and looked at the round blobs of snow capping the evergreens. The hungry sheep look up and are not fed, she said to herself.

Mabel mopped her wet cheeks. 'I don't see why people need to die before they're old. It's – it's so *mean*.'

So meaningless, thought Elise, still looking out of the window. Even if one has found a central self, to have it blown

274

out like a candle in the dark. Not even burned down to the butt.

'What will poor Sarah Murray do?' said Mabel. 'She won't have a penny.'

Elise made a little impatient movement. Life was too short for that kind of thing. Elizabeth – yes; Sarah Murray – no. She didn't want to hear about Sarah Murray's sorrows.

'She hasn't anybody in the world but her brother Ned, and he's in the asylum.'

Mabel's voice was awe-stricken.

Elise turned abruptly and picked up her snowdrops: 'I'm going to see Elizabeth.'

Elizabeth – yes, because that's my caprice, she thought, walking rapidly up the street. And Sarah Murray – no; because that's my caprice too. . . . I decline to pad my actions out with reasons. I can find myself a dozen reasons on either side, and I decline to do so. . . . That's what it has come down to. It's more honourable to strip one's actions bare, to say: 'Yes, I want to do that; no, I don't want to do the other, and any motives I might allege for either action are probably spurious, so I shall leave them out.'

'How is your mistress, Mary Ann?'

'She's just aye sitting on the sofa, mem. She'll no' gang to her bed. She's had a cuppie o' tea, but she'll no' eat a bite.'

Elizabeth was sitting staring at the floor with her hands clasped between her knees. When Elise came in she looked up, and pressed her finger-nails into her knuckles: but she sat there dry-eyed and mute, as she had done the day before; the only difference was that she was more white-faced.

It's time to shock her out of it, thought Elise.

'William Murray was found drowned this morning,' she said quietly, standing before Elizabeth with the snowdrops in her hand. 'In the dock.'

A long and difficult tremor shook Elizabeth; she looked desperately at Elise and then flung herself round with her face to the wall and sobbed.

Elise sat down and caressed her.

'That's better,' she said. 'That's better. Cry, my dear; cry.'

'Oh – oh,' moaned Elizabeth.

Elise began to stroke her gently, rhythmically; and after some time the sobs ceased to be vehement. Elizabeth caught Elise's hand and pressed it to her face without lifting her head from the sofa-cushion.

'You're so good to me,' she muttered. 'And I was a brute to you yesterday. I couldn't help it, Elise; I – I couldn't help it.'

'You *were* rather a brute. I felt quite worn out by the time I got home.'

'But what's the use? I can't feel that there's any use in anything. I might as well be dead. . . . The minister is in luck,' whispered Elizabeth. She began to cry again. 'Is he dead? Is he dead?'

'He missed his way in the storm last night and fell into the dock.'

'That too,' muttered Elizabeth. 'Why not? Why not?'

'Why not what?'

'I fainted yesterday,' said Elizabeth, her face still turned to the wall. 'I never fainted before. I felt a queer something rising up, and I said – *I* – that I wouldn't make a fool of myself, and my own body, that I have lived in all my life, that I have trusted as myself, let me down. . . . I loved Hector. I trusted him as myself, and he let me down. . . . I believed that there was a God somewhere, and that He was in the stars and in myself and in Hector's love for me' – she began to sob again – 'and He has let me down; and if the sea in Calderwick harbour, in his own town, can deceive and drown William Murray, why not? Why not?'

In a minute or two she began again, in the same harsh, quick voice: 'I've been sitting here since yesterday, seeing it all, over all the world. Everything we trust in lets us down. . . . People build their houses on a green hillside, and laugh in the sun and praise God, and the hillside opens between the hearthstone and the door and swallows them up. Why not? . . . The ox shelters under a thick, tall tree that it has known in the home field since it was a calf, and the lightning splits the tree and the ox together. Why not? . . . I've seen all that – and worse – since yesterday, sitting here. Everything dies, everything *can* die, and why should William Murray not be drowned?'

'Amen,' said Elise. 'You wouldn't listen to me yesterday, but you must listen to me now. Who are you that you should *not* be let down, as you call it, by the chances and accidents of life? Who are you that you should *not* be let down by your feelings and your blood and your nerves and your reasoning, like any other human being? The marvel is not that we are fallible and foolish, but that we have the wit to see it and to go on in spite of it. We are burdened with error and prejudice, like a rich field covered with stones, and the marvel is not that we stub our toes against the stones, but that we have sense enough to clear them away – even if we clear only the little patch that is ourselves. And even then, I have realized, we clear it not only for ourselves, but for the toes of other people who come after us. . . . I don't know whether there is a God or not, but I do know that there is humanity, that there is a rich field, and that there are tons of stones to be cleared away. . . . And I think,' concluded Elise, 'that you should regard Hector as something that had to be cleared out of your patch. Of course you loved him; of course he loved you; but it was only nature, it wasn't anything more. . . . You fell in love with his body and pretended to love his mind, or his spirit, or whatever you call it. On the whole, that's better than falling in love with a man's mind and pretending to love his body. . . . I did that once. . . . Some day I'll tell you the story of Fritz. . . . But you can't expect, brought up as you have been, to find that the first man who attracts you is your mate for life. You were too hungry when you met him, that was all. That's nothing to be ashamed of. . . . And I think that you are ashamed to admit to yourself that you hung your dreams round the neck of a man who didn't want them.'

'No!' cried Elizabeth, her face still buried in the pillow. 'That's not it,' she said, lifting herself a little. 'I failed him and myself too. I let myself despise him and scorn him. . . . Something in me hit out at him, and I let it. And then I knew that I had done wrong, but it was too late. . . .'

'Well, that may happen to anybody,' said Elise coolly. 'You have learned something. You can't live with a man you don't respect.'

'Oh, Elise—'

Elizabeth sat up and looked at her friend.

'That's the worst of it . . . I can. Even though I *know* he's gone off with – that girl – and she had him before I did – my arms are aching for him now.'

She burst into tears again, but this time, thought Elise, they were healing tears.

She rose and took off her hat and cloak.

'I'm going to put these snowdrops in water,' she said.

## TWENTY

Fifteen days later an express train from Paris to Ventimiglia carried two women passengers travelling together. At first glance they were remarkably unlike: the elder and smaller of the two was elegant and assured, with a cool eye and a humorous mouth; the younger was a tall, awkward, shy creature who shrank into herself when she thought anyone looked at her. But the face was strong, thought a fellow-passenger as he looked again, although of an uncompromising gravity – only a woman so young could look so serious – and in time would be better worth modelling than the other. A good face for a sculptor in another few years. . . . Were they Russians? he wondered, and was extremely surprised to hear them exchange a remark in English.

They did not exchange many remarks, for they were alike in being silent. Elise was contrasting her present journey through France with her last, and her infrequent glances at Elizabeth contained surprise as well as satisfaction. Here she was, returning with a brand-new daughter, or sister, or wife, or whatever it was, having carried her off like a second Lochinvar. She had not anticipated that when she went up to Calderwick. . . .

At least I kept my head to some extent, thought Elise; I actually left Mabel and Sarah Murray behind!

She mused over the difference betwen Calderwick as she had found it and as she had left it. Was it entirely a subjective difference, a measure of the difference in herself? In Calderwick she had knitted together the two halves of her life, and the town as well as herself appeared to have a new harmony, a new humanity; but was it not essentially the same that it had always been? . . . Perhaps. . . . She remembered Mary

Watson's face on the day of William Murray's funeral. . . .
Even when Elise first ran away from Calderwick Mary
Watson had been a grim character. But on William Murray's
funeral day the tears lay on her cheek as she said, humbly: 'I
think we all trauchle ourselves and other people ower
muckle.'

Perhaps the difference was not merely subjective. . . .
Life was unpredictable and full of surprising changes.

Had Aunt Janet changed? Elise recalled how she had last
seen her aunt straying aimlessly around the house, picking
up trifling articles which she carried absently from one room
to another and hid behind cushions. Had she not always tried
to hide things behind cushions? . . . People said that Hector's last escapade had 'broken' her; but was she really
changed?

Mabel had been shaken up, but would go on much the
same. John too. He was sound and sweet at the core, thought
Elise; she would not have him change. . . . That hard-faced
spinster, Sarah Murray, seemed to have a grudge against
him, even although he had installed her as Aunt Janet's
companion, and John bore it with amazing patience. . . .

Well, *I* have changed, thought Elise, giving Elizabeth
another quizzical glance. Perhaps it was only tart, unripe
characters that changed as they mellowed. I have a lot of
mellowing to do yet, she decided, with a sudden chuckle.

What was to happen next she simply did not know. When
she rediscovered Lizzie Shand she had thought that a final
revelation, but almost immediately she had gone on to
discover Calderwick, and then she had found her central,
dispassionate, impregnable self, and then she had found that
the presumably final impregnable self tended to become a
little inhuman, and that if one listened exclusively to its voice
one remained perched on a high fence without any incentive
to descend on either side of it. . . . But she had descended,
flouting the impartial self, and somewhat petulantly had
declared that in the end one acted on caprice, on naked and
unaccountable caprice, and that it was dishonest to pretend
otherwise . . . and, presto! within half-an-hour she had
burst into surprising eloquence about stones that had to be
cleared away from the toes of future generations. . . . And

she meant it too. There was something in it. She had not thought it out yet, but she felt it might be her *Gebiet* to clear away stones of prejudice and superstition so that other girls might grow up in a more kindly soil. And Elizabeth would help her . . . until she fell in love with somebody the exact antithesis of Hector. . . . But that might take years.

Elise looked out of the window. Her eye fell full on a square white house with a roof of thick tiles, thick and curved, as if they were halved flowerpots, fitting loosely one upon the other, tiles that had once been red and were now bleached in parts to a calcareous whiteness, thick, casual-looking, familiar tiles. . . .

'Elizabeth!' she said, leaning forward. 'This is the Midi!'

'What are those twisted little stumpy dwarf trees?' said Elizabeth, pointing to them.

'Vines,' replied Elise, with great content.

Vines! thought Elizabeth. She had never imagined that vines looked like that. . . . She had imagined something more lush . . . not this dry, bright landscape with those gnarled little trees, that looked as if they had been maimed and tortured. . . . Crippled, like herself.

'This is the South,' said Elise, smiling.

A good many miles nearer to Hector. . . . Elizabeth turned her face aside again; her mouth trembled, and her eyes overflowed.

A step paused at the door of the compartment, and a fresh, jolly voice cried: 'Jesus, Maria, Joseph! Du, Elise?'

'Ilya!' said Elise. 'What are *you* doing here?'

Ilya came in, with loud vociferations of pleasure. She had curly yellow hair, Elizabeth saw, and bright little blue eyes, twinkling above powder and rouge. . . .

'Does she understand German?' asked Ilya, indicating Elizabeth. 'No? Well, my dear Elise, you have run away with her, you say? Have you then given up men?'

With every word Madame Mütze felt Calderwick receding farther and farther, for Ilya's conversation travelled even faster than the train. . . .

# MRS RITCHIE

# Contents

# BOOK I: THE CHILD

The Child: God of my Fathers, an abyss
has opened between me and myself.
The Answer: I clove that abyss.
The Child: How shall I Bridge it?
The Answer: Throw a tight-rope across it.
If you fall, you fall.

## ONE

The school building hummed and vibrated, for it housed
an orchestra of nearly three hundred young human souls.
From the infants' department, where raps on the knuckles
were given with a knitting-needle, to the sixth standard
room, where the head-master's leather tawse lay openly
on his desk, the strings of life were muted but humming
in a deep accompaniment to the shriller notes of the
class exercises, a vibrating accompaniment which flowed
through the stone walls into the road outside. That road
turned down from the town's main northern highway with
a business-like air which would have deceived anybody, so
confident was the sweep of its kerb and the smoothness
of its wide concrete paving. It would have deceived
anybody, far less Jim Rattray, whose bemused feet had
of themselves a tendency to shuffle down any broad and
easy road. He was far enough from the White Horse Inn
to have forgotten where he was going, and he followed the
hypnotic curve of the kerb until he came to the school.
The humming vibration in the air soothed him; he leaned
against the school wall and swaying almost imperceptibly
hummed an accompaniment of his own: 'Dee-dee-dee-dee,
dee-dee-dee'; his eyes were shut and his face peaceful in
the spring sunlight. Tree-shadows striped him; he was as
unconscious of his broken shoes and sackcloth apron as if
he had been naked in some primeval forest; he might have
been listening to the faint, far-off drumming of happy fists
upon ape-like bosoms.

But suddenly the steady rhythm of the school broke and
became a confused roar, as of a charging herd. Something
black and bulky began to stir in Jim Rattray's midriff: the
enemy were coming. He clenched his fists, seeking for a

3

branch, a stone, to hurl upon them; and when they roared around him:

> 'Jimmy Ratt—att—airy,
> Teapot nose,
> One two three and
> Away he goes,'

he too roared, and shook his empty fists. His enemies ducked beyond reach and chanted again:

> 'One two three and
> Away he goes.'

'Mary Rattray! Annie Rattray!' cried a shrill voice. 'There's yer faither!'

Mary Rattray charged straight into the pack of boys, cuffing and hitting out: 'Leave my faither alane! I'll blood yer noses for ye if you dinna leave my faither alane.'

Jim Rattray opened his eyes.

'C'wa hame, faither,' said his daughter, pulling him by the sleeve. 'Man, it's denner-time.'

Annie Rattray hopped on one foot from the kerb to the roadway, her long pigtails flapping. She did not approach her father and her elder sister, but when they lurched together up the hill, taking the middle of the road, she followed at a distance, walking carefully along the kerbstone. Her short, sturdy figure had a compact and almost prim look in contrast to the shambling limbs of her father and the long-leggedness of her sister, but in spite of her careful walk there was a black and bulky rage within her. To think that he had come to the school and shamed her there before everybody! She walked with her eyes fixed on the narrow kerbstone so that she might not see her father. To come to the school, of all places! The very pavement she was walking on, the new school pavement made of superior concrete slabs, fitted in exact squares, dotted like heckle biscuits—that very pavement cried that it belonged to a world which was not her father's, but was as far removed from it as from the broken cobbles in the mud of Mill Wynd where the Rattrays lived.

She would never forgive him. Or Mary. To come to the

school in that state, and then Mary to take his arm! All very well for Mary, who got out of everything by shouting other people down: Mary wasn't at the top of her class; Mary had little to lose; Mary was just a black.

A black, that was what she was, and her father, yes, and her mother. A fine family to be born into. Worse than the blacks of Africa or America.

In Calderwick at that time any detrimental was referred to as a 'black.' But the blackness of James and Mary Rattray did not show in their complexions; they were sandy-haired, freckled, big and bony, with long limbs and large feet. Annie herself was the black-haired one: she had crisp thick black hair that swung far below her waist in two pigtails, pigtails so long that they looked a little ridiculous on such a small girl. Her pigtails were her pride, just as her short stature was her grievance, and perhaps it was sheer will-power that had driven them so far down her back, for although Annie Rattray's legs were short, her spine was long and in every joint expressed resolution and endurance.

Worse than the blacks of Africa or South America. A vivid picture flashed into her mind of her father and Mary cast out into that land of desolation which the teacher had said was called Tierra del Fuego because of its pitiless cold. Annie Rattray saw a flurry of snow over ice-bound wastes on which her father and sister were cowering with nothing on them but a scanty animal skin apiece, fastened by the paws over one bare shoulder. She changed the snow into sleet and then into hail: her rage drove the hail until it was lashing her father and her sister on their naked, shivering bodies. This eased her feeling of suffocation. The black and bulky oppression in her middle was now discharging itself, running up her spine, her neck, into her lower jaw which was thrust forward and rigid: if she had allowed any sound to escape it would have come out as a hiss. The inaudible hiss of her rage and of the hail driven before it gave her a pleasure so keen that it suddenly inverted itself, so to speak, and she herself was exposed to the lashing hail. She walked erect, exulting in the sting of it, while the others were beaten to the ground, and it served them right.

Annie Rattray was only eleven and three-quarters, and

she knew nothing of her remote ancestry, but the defiance
that now stiffened her spine was not unlike the defiance
of some ancient champion challenging men and gods to
break him. She marched along, stiff-backed and staid; just
an ordinary little girl, one would have said, in a dark blue
pinafore and black-ribbed stockings pulled up over her
bony knees, with a checked canvas school-bag swinging
from her left shoulder. But anyone who looked twice
at her might have remembered the upright, rectangular
forehead and the pointed, obstinate chin that made her
face disproportionately long; the length of the face, the
length of the pigtails, the length of the back were all absurd
in so small a girl with such short legs and little feet. Her feet
seemed to have eyes of their own, for she was still walking
very precisely along the kerb although she had long ceased
to remark it. There must have been something royal in her
feeling of exaltation, for now she saw herself as the queen
of that far-off, savage land; and so that she might the better
enjoy her absolute power she stopped the hail. Hers was no
longer a mere power of resistance, but a power of life and
death over her subjects. She was more devastating than
any hail. They crawled before her—father, mother, sister
and schoolmates—while she sat on a throne with a whip
in her hand and her feet on the naked back of a brown
slave. Just as it came up her back she would kill or spare,
and she cared less than nothing for what anybody might
think. What did they matter to her? She was the queen.

'Well, Annie, I didn't think *you* were a dreamer.'

Annie's dream folded its shining wings and plunged with
lightning speed into some hidden abyss, taking with it the
flicker of anger roused by the interruption. It was a prim and
respectful Annie who raised her eyes; for this was Miss Julia
Carnegie, her Sunday-school teacher. Miss Julia, Annie had
been told, was the youngest of the three Miss Carnegies, but
to a girl of eleven all the Miss Carnegies seemed old, tall
and formidable. They were real ladies who did no work:
they had a highly polished table in which one could see
one's face, and two maids in cap and apron; Miss Susan,
moreover, was hung with little gold chains and padlocks,
while Miss Julia actually wore pearl ear-rings. Annie swung

one pigtail forward so that Miss Julia might notice how clean her hair was; last Sunday Miss Julia had detected a louse on Tina Gove, but she would never find a louse on Annie Rattray.

Miss Julia was wearing the ear-rings and a cameo brooch; she had a parasol, too.

'Just coming home from school?'

'Yes, Miss Julia.'

'What standard are you in now, Annie?'

'Standard five, Miss Julia.'

'That's a high standard for such a little girl.'

Annie flushed, and Miss Julia smiled.

'You're a good little girl, Annie; I'm sure you're a great help to your poor mother.'

'Yes, Miss Julia.'

'Well, I'll be seeing you on Sunday, I suppose?'

'Yes, Miss Julia.'

Miss Julia nodded pleasantly and walked on, but Annie's feet now lagged, for her dream had vanished and she was nearing home.

When she went down the step leading into the dark kitchen everything was as she had expected. It was her mother's ironing day, and piles of roughly dried clothes lay all about in confusion, clothes that Mary and Annie would have to deliver on the morrow, dragging the heavy basket between them from door to door. Mrs Rattray, small and spare, was standing in the middle of the floor, with her hands on her hips as if to keep unbroken the circuit of her nervous force, while Jim Rattray leaned against the mantelpiece, very unsteadily, for he was trying to empty the dottle out of his cutty.

'I'm sick of the very sight of you—and this only Thursday,' said his wife.

Jim, by attending to something within himself, managed to perceive her voice as an unpleasantly shrill but meaningless sound.

'Dee-dee-dee, dee-dee-dee,' he hummed, knocking his pipe on the bars of the grate.

But the cutty suddenly broke. Jim, still swaying, looked at it for a moment, during which his wife laughed ironically.

Something black and bulky began faintly to stir in his midriff; his hands clenched on a fragment of his cutty and with all his force he threw it at her. Then he said: 'Och, to hell,' and lurched out of the door into the wynd, where his back found a familiar wall, and he shut his eyes and resumed his 'Dee-dee-dee, dee-dee-dee.'

Mrs Rattray said:

'You lay the table, Mary; there's twopenny pies, they're in the bag on the dresser; and you, Annie, gather thae claes on to the bed. Quick, now.'

Annie closed her mouth firmly, cleared the bundles of shirts, sheets, drawers and towels off the chairs, off the floor, and ranged them neatly on the bed in the corner of the kitchen. She would get out of this hole one day; see if she wouldn't!

## TWO

When Annie Rattray was born she took it for granted, like
other infants, that the whole world was her heritage, and it
was with placid dignity that she lay in her narrow wooden
cradle. Her innate majesty, however, was soon smacked,
silenced and snubbed into bewilderment, a bewilderment
that passed through fretfulness into settled resentment
when she discovered that to be Annie Rattray was to
be of no account whatever. By the time she was eleven
her heritage had shrunk so much that she had barely
room to take up her stand upon it. As a Rattray she
had no prestige in the community of Calderwick. As a
young Rattray she was, indeed, entitled to house-room,
clothes and food in the basement occupied by her parents
in Mill Wynd; yet even that title was an inherited debt
rather than an endowment, for her mother never ceased
to remind her that she must repay the cost of her keep as
soon as she was able; while to the general world beyond
Calderwick, had it observed her existence, she would have
appeared simply as an immature female, a potential link
between two generations, and she would have received
little consideration on that account, since the breeding of
citizens was not regarded as a contribution to the national
wealth. And yet Annie Rattray was fiercely aware of herself
as Annie, an individual human being with every right to be
Annie; indeed, she was inwardly aware of nothing else. At
the age of eleven she was like a leaf that had curled into a
tight spear instead of expanding a sensitive surface to sun
and air and rain; a closed, secretive creature, cherishing a
private dream of supremacy.

But had she not playmates? Was she not at school? She
had been attending school for six years, and of course she

had played with other little girls; yet it would be truer
to say that she had played among other little girls. In a
small enclosed square of concrete adjoining the big girls'
playground, an enclosure bounded by the school lavatories
and the infants' building, Annie Rattray had whipped her
top among twenty little girls whipping tops, all in a kind
of backwater, an apparently fortuitous eddy of little girls
circling in the shallows on the verge of the river. In that small
enclosure they were drawn together as if for security, and it
was certainly some need for security that made them all do
the same thing at the same time, now spinning tops, now
bouncing balls, now playing hopscotch; for although they
seemed to be engrossed in a common occupation, each of
them was isolated in a separate dream, a dream, perhaps, of
achieving equilibrium in an unstable and incomprehensible
world. When one is seven or eight the motives of the
larger humans who prescribe one's behaviour are still
incomprehensible, arbitrary, and possibly malicious; the
unstable top is less elusive, for its spinning can be controlled
to a dreamlike equilibrium; the rolling ball is less elusive, for
it can be bounced on a chosen spot; the game of hopscotch
is less elusive, for its scheme is clearly outlined in chalk on
the concrete and all that one needs is a firm balance on one
leg. In the emotional bewilderment of childhood a sense of
persecution can easily arise, and to be like other children,
to be doing the same thing as other children, is a magic
that lulls one into security and keeps off the nightmare of
isolation. But the separate dream persists.

It persists even when one emerges into the larger yard
and joins in a general game like hide-and-seek. For the
real meaning of hide-and-seek lies in the hiding, in the
secret withdrawal: it is the 'hiders' who genuinely enjoy
themselves; the 'seekers' have their office forced upon them
by failure, and it is an unpopular office. The separate dream
can persist until the sense of isolation becomes acute and
one child after another sees itself in fantasy detached from
its family, from its playmates, as a changeling or a martyr,
and from this forlorn position begins to reach blindly for
support. Many children at this time attain their highest
pitch of imaginative passion, for the gathering force of

puberty has not yet drawn them into the middle of the stream, and it is in the middle of the stream that dreams can be lost for ever in some inaccessible part of oneself.

On the day when her father came drunk to the school Annie Rattray's private dream rose to a terrifying intensity of self-assertion. The only prestige she could imagine was that of ordering people about, but it was nothing less than an absolute despotism that she dreamed of then, a power of life and death over others. On that day her dream of simple and savage supremacy reached its highest point, and as if it had beat its head upon a roof it dropped exhausted. Annie got up next morning with a new feeling of desolation, a sense of hopeless discouragement. What was the good of dreaming herself a queen? It was Annie here, and Annie there, and 'You shut up!' and 'You clear tha'e dishes before you stir a step to school.' 'I'll no'! I'll no'!' she shouted, but Mary hit her round the ears with a wet dish-cloth and her face was all begrutten when she came into the playground.

She stood there miserable and bewildered among the chaos of flying legs and voices. Annie was small for her age, and could not run fast enough to distinguish herself, nor did she enjoy being impounded as a recruit in the singing-games, for she found it pointless to go round and round without ever being chosen out. If only she could stand for once in the middle of the ring and sing: 'Father, mother, may I go? On a cold, cold frosty morning!' But it was always Mary who did that. It was Mary's loud tongue that dominated the playground, and Mary's long legs that caught everybody up . . . The girls were playing bar-the-door now, scuffling and shrieking and flying helter-skelter. Annie stood by the shed at one side of the yard and surveyed their aimlessness with hostile eyes, as a stranded mariner on an island peak might watch the gyrations of savages in the sea around him.

The school bell rang, ting, ting, ting, Ting, sending rhythmic waves of order through the playground chaos. Class by class, wave by wave, the girls surged into the school building and filed off into their class-rooms, into their seats. Annie tossed her head as she led her file of followers, for she was top girl in standard five and sat at the end of the back seat. Now she was in her rightful place at last.

It was Friday morning. Arithmetic test cards, and then geography. She would have the test card finished first, except perhaps for Bob Craigie, who was top of the boys, and Mr Laing would give her the answers and let her go round the girls checking what the others had done. Correct or Wrong, there was no ambiguity about that, a big C or a big W on each sum. There was no silly choosing-out in arithmetic. Even Mary's sums would have had to be marked wrong if they were wrong, which they would most likely be. Annie regretted that Mary was in a higher standard; she would have given anything to be able to score a huge W on each of Mary's answers, just to teach her what was what, just to show her that there were other arguments than wet dish-cloths.

'Please, sir, I'm finished.'

Annie's straight, narrow body thrilled with triumph as she stood up and thus announced that she had beaten everybody again. Mr Laing perfunctorily checked her answers; he expected them to be right; the class expected them to be right, and Annie expected them to be right. He scored five C's one after the other, and handed her the key-card with the answers, as usual. This was the culminating point of Annie's school week, when she went round armed with the card of authority, dispensing strict and impartial justice. Two and two made four, whatever anybody said or did: the world of knowledge was impersonal, enduring, raised above the transiency of daily life into precision, into dogmatic certainty.

The test cards were collected, the marks noted on a register. Mr Laing shut his book into a desk and took up a pointer. The capes and rivers of Europe, if you please. Hands shot into the air, fingers cracked loudly, and every time a cape was wrongly named Annie Rattray leapt in her seat, quivering with eagerness to show that she knew them all, she could beat everybody, she was the best scholar in the class, perhaps in the whole school. Then the map of South America was hoisted over the map of Europe, and in a rhythmical chant the whole class recited the capes and rivers of South America, led by the teacher. Annie sat swaying her body in time to the chant in a kind of ecstasy, hypnotized by the steady repetition of indisputable facts, all labelled and laid up for ever in some treasury of knowledge, neatly docketed facts, irreducible facts about which there could be no question, facts the possession of which brought one marks and more marks and more marks.

Her excitement in proving her mastery over these facts made her forget the hollow discouragement that had assailed her in the morning, yet when the eleven o'clock interval cast her out into the playground again she was once more inexplicably dejected. In the class-room one knew where one was, but in the playground there was a queer reversal of everything—as if the real life of the class began outside the school door, and knowing the capes and rivers of South America did not matter at all. The triumph of beating everybody else should have persisted; it should have supported her and raised her like a queen in the playground; but she was pushed, jostled, cannoned into, mocked for her slowness, ignored. Annie retired to the railings and leaned on the ledge beneath them; she even shut her eyes and tried to invoke the vision she had experienced yesterday, when she was a queen with her foot on the back of a slave, on the back of her sister Mary: she could remember all the details: she could remember the hail, the exultation, the feeling of dominance, but it was like reading about it in a lesson-book; the authentic, convincing thrill would not run up her spine. Her dream was broken, and she felt as if it were broken for ever.

So it happened that Annie Rattray turned more and more to the ordered life of the class-room, where a ladder of visible achievement was set up for her to climb. Her starved self-importance, her hunger for prestige, drove her up from rung to rung, and as the ladder was one which nothing but a hunger for prestige could induce a child to climb, Annie's teacher regarded her efforts with satisfaction. She had the proper competitive spirit that made his task relatively easy; he was grateful to her, and awarded her high marks in everything. At the end of the school year, when she was just over twelve, Annie Rattray won a prize for general proficiency. Perhaps Mr Laing had a moment of compunction as he thought how ignorant she was of her destiny as a woman; at any rate the book he selected for her was a well-bound manual of cookery in clear print. On the first page was an inscription: 'Presented to Annie Rattray by the School Board of Calderwick, Jubilee Year, 1887.'

The prize-giving day was a great occasion, for there was also a Jubilee Procession in which all the school-children marched. In her best frock, singled out for distinction as a prize-winner, Annie recaptured to some extent the triumph of feeling herself a queen, and her ambition flared up in an ephemeral, fierce blaze that, like the Jubilee bonfire, made more palpable the darkness preceding and following it.

Her best frock was doffed, the procession was over, and Annie became once more an insignificant unit in the holiday crowds. But the prize-book remained, laid high on a shelf in the kitchen beside the Bible. Annie never went through the kitchen without looking up at it, as one might lift his eyes to the hills. That it was a cookery-book and not a story-book disappointed her not at all; she had never owned a story-book, and a wreath of laurel would have served equally well and could not have been more irrelevant in the Rattrays' kitchen.

## THREE

Annie could remember few details of that summer before or after the one great day on which she got her prize. The school vacation, like other vacations, was a holiday only in name for the Rattrays; the influx of summer visitors brought more work into Calderwick, and Mrs Rattray kept Annie busy helping her with the extra washing that she did to oblige the boarding-houses. Mary took a temporary job as an errand-girl in a draper's shop, and James Rattray did casual labour carting sand from the shore to the docks. The northern summer that year hung a crystalline, transparent veil of light over the bare and reticent contours of the dune-land around Calderwick, and a whispering wind from the sea ruffled the sharp bent-grass and the fragile harebells that rose from among dwarf thyme and eyebright, but Annie noted none of these things; indeed, she did not even note the washing, wringing, ironing and folding of clothes that filled so much of her time. She was living in a state of suspended animation until school should begin again, and it was only her prize-book that nourished her spirit in the meantime. She was sullen and aloof; sometimes she played hopscotch by herself on the pavement, once or twice she searched for four-leaved clovers in the grass of the drying-green, but she spent most of her spare time sitting kicking her legs on a wooden bench that stood on a waste patch of links near Mill Wynd. There she sat, kicking viciously, perhaps driving her foot through the faces of her mother, her sister and her father; but although her expression was inscrutable she was aware all the time that her prize was lying secure on a high shelf in the kitchen.

On Sundays, however, Annie revived a little. Sunday-school did not offer such a wide field for one's prowess as day-school did, but to go to Miss Julia's class was better than nothing. It was a class of only eight girls, and it was abominably like the playground in having arbitrary standards of value: a starched petticoat or a new Sunday hat or a fresh lace frill conferred more distinction than a mere capacity to recite the Shorter Catechism and two verses of a psalm; and a young Rattray, even in her Sunday best, was no match for the others in finery. But Miss Julia herself was on such a high social pinnacle that she could ignore the pretensions of her scholars, and Sunday after Sunday she praised Annie's impeccable memory. Besides, in her grave voice Miss Julia told stories about heathen customs abroad and the dreadful things that savages did before they were converted to Christianity. Annie liked to hear about the black slave-gangs, and the floggings, and the lions that sprang out of the tall jungle. She was particularly struck with the story of an escaping slave-mother who was carrying her baby on her back and met a lion face to face; the woman raged and scolded and abused the lion with such vehemence that the creature retreated in bewilderment before her fury, step by step, while she shook her fist at it, until the jungle grass closed on it again and the slave-mother reached the mission station in safety.

But the tight little spear of Annie's life aimed its point steadily towards the day on which school began again, and on that day, as she took her seat in the sixth standard, she felt as triumphant as if she had shot time on the wing. The headmaster himself taught the sixth standard, and to be at the top of the sixth standard was to touch the pinnacle of distinction in the Townhead School. The ex-sixth standard, although it shared the same class-room, could be left out of account, since it was composed of boys and girls who were merely waiting for their fourteenth birthdays to release them, boys and girls whose interest was already turning to the mill or to the shop that was to receive them in a month's time or in six months' time when their names would be crossed off the register. The ex-sixth standard was, as its name implied, a class that had abdicated the throne; a class ripe for revolution.

To repress these malcontents of the ex-sixth, severe

discipline was needed. The headmaster who ruled them had to have an eye like a hawk, a face of iron, and a ready tawse. Mr Boyd, the headmaster of the Townhead School, fulfilled these requirements. It was said that he burned his tawse in the fire to make it sting hotter. As he called the roll the new sixth standard sat rigid and silent; one does not whisper or shuffle in the presence of an autocrat who has been a bogy during the whole of one's school life. But a smile fluttered round Annie Rattray's mouth, and she could not help tossing her pigtails back and looking across the large room to the bench where Mary sat among the ex-sixth pupils. This was a more exciting situation than any she had yet experienced in school, and somewhere within her Annie felt a stirring of her old force. She would get the better of Mary at last. Her slate was clean, her books were unopened, her pencils sharp. And as she regarded the closed impassive face of the headmaster, with its pointed iron-grey beard, her heart suddenly turned over with an unaccustomed flutter, turned over in her bosom like a water-lily leaf, and in that moment of fear and longing the tight green spear of Annie's life began to uncurl.

It was a slow and at first an imperceptible process. She was aware only of a new pleasure in her work, because she desired to win Mr Boyd's approval as well as to beat the others. But it was as if her desire had thrown out invisible filaments which felt every motion of that aloof mind behind the teacher's desk. At first she bestowed anxious pains upon the achievement of the smaller perfections demanded by the headmaster; he did not have to rap more than once with a ruler upon her copybook, saying sharply: 'Do you call that an s?' Every one of Annie's letters after that was punctiliously closed and rounded; nor did she forget the double line neatly ruled beneath the answer to a sum. It was not enough in Mr Boyd's class to submit work that was correct, everything had to be ruled and spaced and finished off. A straggling column or a blotted word was as disgraceful as a glaring error in calculation or in grammar. But soon, guided by those filaments of desire that followed the lines of her mentor's thought, Annie began to take pleasure not only in the ordered setting-down of work, but in the ordered

relation of facts to a system. She delighted, for instance, in
that unravelling of sentences which was called general and
particular analysis; upon her slate she would rule the single
columns and the double columns with a grave intentness
that was already more than the mere pleasure of possessing
knowledge. And it was not only the general principles of
grammar that Mr Boyd revealed. Every Friday afternoon
he gave his classes an hour's lecture on flowers, or stars
and planets, or coal, or frost, and from these lectures
there emerged a world in which everything was ordered,
logically ordered and reasonable. Mr Boyd tied up all the
untidy ends of life and bound them to a vast trellis-work of
inviolable reason, a trellis-work which, as he was careful to
point out, was not created by man, but was inherent in the
constitution of the universe.

It was only during the lecture-hours on Friday that the
headmaster allowed himself to relax into enthusiasm, and
these were the hours in which Annie was most thrilled. She
sat still as a mouse, with her dark eyes fixed on the teacher's
face, and the words 'law' and 'duty' fell into her mind as if
they were personal gifts from Mr Boyd.

She had no need now to search for four-leaved clovers
or to feel miserably isolated even in the playground. Who
walked in the light of the headmaster's favour walked as with
God, and the playground was only a part of his kingdom.
For she had secured the head's reluctant favour. He was
undemonstrative and sharp as ever, but the class soon noted
that Annie Rattray never got the tawse and was never set
in a corner with her face to the wall. That she did nothing
to merit reproof did not matter; auld Boyd was capable of
giving 'palmies' to a whole row of innocent scholars if he
heard so much as a single whisper rise from their bench
while his back was turned. On one or two occasions he had
actually commended Annie's work as a model to the class;
and that in itself was enough to label her as 'Boyd's pettie.'
The pride and warmth of her earlier dreams encompassed
Annie once more; but now she was not a pretended queen
tyrannizing over imaginary slaves, she was the first favourite
of an actual and rather grim despot.

## FOUR

From what source do human beings draw their inner
assurance? It is not easy to tell. Mary Rattray, certainly,
seemed to draw assurance from the mere fact that she
was alive. She seemed to have no consciousness of failure;
reproof and discomfiture rolled off her, as her mother
said, like water off a duck's back, and she forgot buffets,
whether literal or metaphorical, as soon as they were given
or received. Annie beat her in every class examination that
the sixth and the ex-sixth standards shared in common,
but she remained unmortified. To try to hold Mary down,
Annie finally decided, was like trying to sit on a wind-bag
that one could neither prick nor burst.

Mary dominated the playground as much as ever. In that
chaotic whirlpool she always bobbed up on top. If she made
a mistake or forgot the next verse in a singing-game she
would cry: 'Och, let's play another,' and even in the full tide
of one song she could initiate a contrary movement that after
a little hubbub overbore and carried away opposition. Yet
she did not think of herself as a leader; her predominance
was unconscious, apparently instinctive. The wind blew
her whither it listed, and most of the girls were blown
with her.

To discipline Mary in school needed a strong hand.
Mr Boyd relied on the tawse, whose five leather fingers
symbolized the hand of justice, more potent, more impersonal and more dignified than the bare human hand. The
tingling, smarting pain of the tawse should have stimulated
Mary's awareness of authority both in knowledge and in
conduct. The headmaster even jerked her wrist up with a
pointer just before he brought down the tawse, since she
had an expert knack of dropping her hand suddenly at

the moment of impact so that the blow was cheated of its force. And yet it was Annie's awareness of authority that was stimulated rather than Mary's; she followed the downward fall of the tawse with avid satisfaction, a satisfaction that was much more subtle and enjoyable than the simple pleasure of smacking Mary's face in private. But as Annie's alliance with the headmaster strengthened she began to dislike seeing Mary get 'palmies.' To be out on the floor for punishment was to be a centre of attraction, even although it was blows that one attracted, and Annie felt that her sister should receive no kind of attention at all from Mr Boyd. Mary was just showing off, and it would be a good day when she was fourteen and the school was rid of her. The only thing to do with the like of Mary was to put her out and shut the door upon her.

On Mary's fourteenth birthday, therefore, Annie had a special feeling of communion with the headmaster, and when the afternoon session came she even thought that she could detect a certain satisfaction on Mr Boyd's face as he ticked Mary off on the last register that would record her attendance. In a dreamy, contented vacancy Annie sat waiting to answer her own name when it was called out; an unnecessary formality, since Mr Boyd must be as aware of her as she was of him, yet a pleasant one. It gave her a thrill to hear Mr Boyd's voice repeating her name and her own voice following so close upon his. It was like a meeting, an overt act of recognition that was at the same time unsuspected by the rest of the class.

'Annie Rattray!'

'Here, sir.'

'Stay behind at four o'clock.'

Annie started in confusion. The headmaster was already closing the sixth-standard register. She did not know whether she had dreamed that sharp command. But Mr Boyd never repeated an order and never explained himself, so in her agitation she did an unheard-of thing; she turned and whispered a question to the girl beside her. The sibilant sound provoked an answering hiss from the outraged headmaster; he fixed Annie Rattray with a black look and said: 'Silence there!' Annie's heart grew

faint and small with fear and longing. Her cheeks burned
for the rest of the afternoon, and by four o'clock her knees
were weak.

'Did Boyd say I was to wait behind at four?'

She got the hurried question out at last, and her neighbour
looked surprised.

'Ay! Did you no' hear him?'

Annie stood miserably beside the headmaster's desk while
the others filed out, and she felt as if Mr Boyd were going
to expel her as well as Mary. A conviction of unnameable
guilt towards him rose from somewhere within her; in her
secret thoughts she had taken his name in vain, and he who
divined everything was now going to call her to account.

'What do you want to do when you leave school?'

Annie lifted her eyes to the point of Mr Boyd's grizzled
beard. The blood that had ebbed to her heart now flushed
her pale long face and confused her mind.

'You're not going into the mill like your sister?'

'No, sir,' whispered Annie.

'Speak up. Have you thought of what you would like to
do?'

'Yes, sir.'

'What, then?'

In that moment Annie realized her temerity. She had
as good as confessed to Mr Boyd something she had not
dared to formulate even to herself, for it was like equalling
herself with a god to say that she wanted to be a teacher. But
Mr Boyd must know her secret. Who could hide anything
from him?

Her face was hot, but she spoke up clearly enough:

'I'd like to be a teacher, please, sir.'

'You know that means going to the Academy?'

The headmaster's well-schooled voice expressed no surprise. His calmness braced Annie.

'Yes, sir.'

'You know that there are fees to be paid at the Academy?'

Annie twisted her hands together and said nothing. Of
course she knew. Like all the Townhead children she
despised and envied the Academy pupils, and although
she had never yelled after them: 'Academy puddocks!' she

had been glad to hear others do it. Of course she knew that they paid fees, the gentry puddocks. But how could she hope to get her mother to pay the fees?

'Don't you know that you could get a bursary?'

'No, sir.'

'There are bursaries of ten pounds and eight pounds offered by the School Board. The bursary competition is in June. I don't usually encourage girls to attend my bursary class, but I have decided to give you the chance. If you wish to attend, come here next Monday morning at eight sharp. There will be three boys and yourself in the class. If you go to the Academy you can become a pupil-teacher in four years, and a bursary would cover your fees there and most of your books. Tell your mother that and bring me an answer from her tomorrow.'

Annie's prim walk broke into little breathless runs as she went home. She could go to the Academy! She could really become a teacher; she, Annie Rattray, Annie Rattray! The repetition of her own name was like an invocation, and she ran unseeing past a knot of girls, among whom was her sister Mary. A skirl of derision arose: 'Boyd's pettie! Boyd's pettie!' and suddenly she was seized from behind by two strong arms. Annie struggled in fury:

'Let go! Let me alane!'

'What was auld Boyd sayin' to his pettie?'

'Never you mind. That's my business.'

Her ferocity freed her from Mary's grasp, for she fought like a mad creature. Mary snatched away her slate, on which the home sums for next day were written out, but Annie wrenched it back. Mary, however, had found time to spit accurately in the middle of the sums, and triumphant hoots followed Annie as she raced home.

Mrs Rattray was sitting in a chair by the fireside. It was not ten minutes since she had come in from the wash-house that she shared with the other families in the tenement; she had been turning the wringer all afternoon and her back was aching.

'Is that you, Annie?' she said, looking up. 'Set the tea, will you; the kettle's near boiling.'

Annie dumped her school-bag on the floor and breathlessly poured out all that Mr Boyd had said.

'The Academy! Losh keep me! And do you think I'm gaun to break my back working to keep *you* at the school?'

'But the bursary would pay for it all—'

'The bursary wadna pay me for your keep. *You* at the Academy? It's no' even as if you were a laddie. Na, na, my leddy, the minute you're fourteen you gang to a job, or else you'll gi'e me a hand here wi' the washin' and the hoose.'

'I'll no'! I'll no'! I want to be a teacher—'

'Not another word, now. Not another word. I'll hear nae mair o't. Not another word, Annie Rattray. You lay that table and stop your greeting, or I'll gi'e you something to greet for!'

Annie's hands clenched, seeking to close on something, to hurl something at her mother. She kicked at her school-bag and then stooped to pick it up, but as she stooped Mary came flying in, and it was Mary who got the weight of it full in her chest. The books scattered, Mary staggered, and Mrs Rattray, darting out of her chair, gave Annie a stinging buffet on the side of the head.

'Take that, you ill-gettit deevil!'

'I'll bash your face in!' panted Mary.

With a howl that was more animal than human Annie rushed into the other room, crashing the door behind her, and cast herself upon the bed. The rage in her midriff was so bulky, so oppressive, that she could no longer stand upright; she needed to extend herself flat, to let that suffocating tension find its discharge unhampered by the force of gravitation. With her teeth she tore at the coverlet, with her feet she kicked against the iron foot of the bedstead; millions of years earlier some ancestor of hers might have wreaked the same uncontrollable fury in the same way upon the body of a victim.

This passion within Annie obliterated the neat scheme of rational activities which her mind had been following under Mr Boyd's guidance, submerging it as a volcanic flood might submerge an intricate system of linked waterways. And the revulsion that ensued, the ebb that set in towards some dark subterranean chamber in the bowels of the volcano, drained dry what was left of the waterways, so that they were mere gaping cracks in a barren waste, where the water of life no longer flowed. Annie's head and her feet were growing cold and colder, her face was pressed into the quilt, and her contracting energies ebbed as if into a bottomless pit of darkness where Annie Rattray became almost anonymous and where the whole world of school meant nothing at all. What were facts about exports and imports? What did two times two matter? What were law and duty and the right classification of categories? Words, mere words, empty cracks in a barren landscape. Annie Rattray, as if presaging what was to happen, had hurled away her bagful of school books, and now she was withdrawn into a darkness where the sole reality was the assertion of a primal self that was no Rattray and hardly even Annie, a self that acknowledged nothing but its own will to be.

The more complex the personality the less easy it is to withdraw into that primal self. Perhaps the ease with which Mary flowed in and out of it accounted for her instinctive assurance; Mrs Rattray was never far away from it; but James Rattray could not find his way back into it without the help of alcohol, and Annie was more surely his daughter than she knew. To submerge her consciousness, to forget her pride, to relinquish her insistent personal self she needed the force of passion. The force of passion had now drawn her down, and she lay there, spent, but renewing herself at some inexhaustible source of energy.

In the kitchen Mrs Rattray and Mary made tea and sat down to a comfortable meal. The flow of passion had merely refreshed them: Mrs Rattray's back felt the better for it, and Mary, by the time she had washed up the dishes, had forgotten Annie's fit of temper and Annie's absurd ambitions; she had others things to occupy her, for she was going into the mill next Monday. And her father came lurching into the kitchen in a befuddled condition, and Mrs Lamont from next door came in to borrow a cupful of sugar, and Mrs Rattray and Mrs Lamont together berated Jim, and Jean Lamont was coming in at eight o'clock, and the kitchen was filled with warm, stirring life.

It was late in the evening when Annie emerged from the

bedroom, blinking a little and pale with cold. She looked
at her slate; Mary's spittle had blotted out the sums so she
could not work them out. She regarded the blotted sums
with indifference, but the sight of Mary's spittle roused a
feeling of cold fury. Her majesty had been insulted, her
Annie Rattrayship had been spat upon; she herself was
more important than all the sums on earth, and she was
going to assert herself as never before, not in the trivial
world of school, but at the very centre of the world. Mary
was not in the kitchen, but Annie calmly washed the slate
clean and with the same calm coldness demanded that her
mother should give her something to eat.

This unnatural calmness lasted until she got into bed,
and she was lying stiff and rigid when Mary tumbled in
beside her. The contact of Mary's body roused her, and
she gave her sister a vicious prod with her elbow:

'You keep to your ain half o' the bed.'

'Academy puddock!' retorted Mary, settling herself to
her easy and immediate sleep.

Annie pressed against Mary's backbone with cold hostility. Whenever Mary shifted in her sleep, even a fraction of an
inch over the imaginary line that Annie had drawn down the
centre of the bed, Annie firmly thrust her back and tightly
grasped her half of the coverlets, for she was beginning to
shiver. Something was changing horribly from thick to thin
in her head, and then swelling again into awful thickness.
Thick—thin—thick—thin, and her teeth were chattering.
She tucked her feet inside her nightgown and hunched up
her knees close to her chest. That was how Mary always
slept, closed up like a penknife. It was difficult to keep to
one's own half of the bed when one curled up like that, and
on principle Annie usually slept extended at full length.
Tonight, however, she closed in on herself, curling up as
if to protect her defenceless belly, like a hedgehog; and as
if the focus of her life had descended towards her belly
her thoughts had become darker, simpler, more nakedly
savage. When at length she fell asleep she dreamed among
other things that she was walking on thick clear ice, beneath
which the faces of her mother, her father and Mary looked
up at her. She stamped upon them.

## FIVE

When Annie got up she dressed, as usual, beneath her flannelette nightgown, turning her back on Mary, until she had on her bodice and petticoat, then she slipped out of the nightgown. She washed her face and hands at the kitchen sink, moving the porridge pot aside to get under the tap, which was a curved pipe resembling the crook of a shepherd's staff. Then she unplaited her hair and brushed it. On this morning she stood in front of the glass and looked at herself as she brushed. So that was Annie Rattray. Annie Rattray was behind those dark eyes; it was Annie Rattray who stood there enveloped in a mantle of long black hair. She brushed more and more slowly, peering at herself. Everybody grew hair and had two eyes. Not even an Academy puddock had more than two eyes and two hands, and there was not an Academy puddock who had longer or thicker hair. It shadowed her as with darkness. But there was the shadow of another darkness still hanging about the girl, and perhaps that was why she peered at herself so intently. For the first time in her life she was examining herself as a human being seen from outside.

Why should Annie Rattray's bonny hair be tied up in pigtails? It may have been a decision to throw off other shackles that prompted her to think this question. She took the bits of scraggy black ribbon that usually bound the ends of her pigtails and looped her hair with them at each side, leaving it to flow free over her shoulders.

Her breakfast plate of porridge was waiting on the kitchen table. Mary choked on a mouthful of tea when she saw her sister's new style of hairdressing.

'Have you gane gyte?' demanded Mrs Rattray.

26

'It's *my* hair,' said Annie coldly, 'no' yours.'

'It's me that'll have to get the lice oot o' it when you come back from school. Awa' and plait it up this minute. Save us and keep us, do you think you're gentry?'

Mary, still choking, snirted tea over the table:

'Maybe she thinks she'll get a lad.'

'You and your lads. A fine time that was for *you* to come hame last night. You needna think you can bide oot after ten o'clock just because you've left school.'

'Och, awa',' said Mary, reaching for the teapot which was sitting on the hob.

'I want a cup o' tea, too,' said Annie. 'If Mary can get tea so can I.'

'Tea! What next? Awa' and plait your hair up. Do you hear me?'

Annie lifted her eyes and eyed her mother with that naked look of equality which passes so rarely from child to parent. There was something else in the look, too—a cold gleam that unaccountably fluttered Mrs Rattray a little. She began to think her daughter was fey.

'If I canna be a teacher,' said Annie, 'I'll do what I like wi' my ain hair.'

'Then you can get the lice oot o' it yoursel'!'

But this retort was a surrender, and Annie knew it. She felt that she was on a new footing in the world as she made her way through the streets towards the Townhead School. She did not dawdle, but she looked at nearly everybody: mill-girls hurrying back to their second shift of work, shopkeepers standing at their doors, clerks diving up closes to mount the stairs to some office, women with net bags choosing vegetables for dinner, a minister on a bicycle, scores of boys and girls on bicycles all converging on the Academy, errand-boys with baskets, a grocer's assistant in a white apron, and a girl carefully balancing babies' bonnets on little hat-stands in a draper's window. Annie looked at each of them with a cold, measuring glance. Tall or short, fat or thin, rich or poor, they were all just human beings like herself; she was as good as any of them and better than most.

The bell was beginning its ting, ting, ting, when she

reached the playground, and she had just time to find
her place in the file. 'Eh, look at Annie Rattray!' said a
girl behind her, and there was a suppressed giggle. Annie
marched into the classroom, very erect, and swirled her
skirts a little as she sat down, shaking out her hair at the
same time. The moment had come. What would Mr Boyd
think of her hair, and what would he do when she told him
that she hadn't done her home sums? With her new coolness
she stared at him; he was just a man, too, although he was a
headmaster. Whatever he knew about sums and grammar
and geography and the motions of the planets he was just a
man, and went home to his dinner, and was maybe raged
at by his wife for being late.

'Annie Rattray!'

'Here, sir.'

But he did not look up from the register book. Annie
whispered to the girl beside her: 'I havena done my home
sums,' and, right enough, like a shot, Mr Boyd flashed a
black look at her and said: 'Silence there!' Annie must have
been fey, for the gritty tone of his voice did not frighten her;
she shook out her hair again and sat up with an expression
of conscious innocence.

Slates were clattered and laid on desks. Annie laid her
blank slate before her. Should she get up and tell him before
the whole class, or should she wait till he came round to
inspect the sums? She made up her mind to wait; this was,
in some curious way, a private affair between herself and
the headmaster.

Mr Boyd read out the answers to the sums; slate pencils
squeaked as the pupils marked a C or a W on each, and
then the slates were turned round to face the headmaster's
critical eye. He would take off a mark, or two marks, or even
all five, as quick as look at you, did you but have ill-made
figures and uneven lines.

Annie held up her blank slate bravely enough. But
Mr Boyd at close quarters was a formidable figure. Her
heart turned over as he said: 'What's this? Where are your
sums?' and it was in a small voice that she answered, without
looking up: 'Please, sir, I didna do them.'

'Why not?'

Her overnight assurance began to return:

'Please, sir, my sister Mary spat on them and rubbed them out.'

She lifted her eyes for a fleeting glance into his; her heart beat hurriedly, her face reddened, and she dropped her eyes again.

Mr Boyd was called 'an inflexible disciplinarian,' and it may well be asked: What hidden fear made him so strict? Were his principles like a child's tower of bricks that could be made to topple at a touch? How could he assume—as he did—that the four-square structure of law and order, which he believed to be the very masonry of the universe, rested solely on the pillar of his will, and that if he failed to uphold his will even against one puny scholar the whole fabric would collapse? The answer lies perhaps in the fact that human life is transient and mortal, while the human spirit cries passionately that it is immortal and that its works endure for ever. A man who is but a man is cut down like the grass; the place where he has been will know him no more. But a man who dedicates himself to be a pillar in some temple of the spirit has raised himself into eternity, and he must believe, he must believe with passion, not only that the temple is eternal (inherent in the constitution of the universe was Mr Boyd's way of putting it), but that his support of it is not unmeaning, that he is an indispensable part of its structure. If a headmaster is not really supporting the weight of the universe the temple of law and order is an insubstantial fantasy and he himself is but a mortal man; the very slates that his scholars present for inspection have been quarried from a hillside which has survived generations of men like him. Beside the hard, resistant surfaces of those slates he is a soft, vulnerable creature exposed to accident and disease, doomed to decay and to be forgotten, a man cowering under the shadow of death.

Now Annie Rattray's fleeting glance at the headmaster was a naked look of equality, a look that said: 'You are not a headmaster, you are a man, a human being like myself.' Mr Boyd's fear of death stirred and quivered; he became instantaneously a rigid pillar of authority. His well-schooled voice was cold and impersonal:

'Stand out there.'

Annie trembled. She was projected, unknowing, into the age-old conflict between the mortal flesh and the aspiring spirit; she was being launched as a missile at a rigid, unyielding structure raised by the fears of man. She was not even a grown woman, she was an immature girl, and the combat was perhaps unfair; at any rate she trembled with dismay, although she had come so recently from that dark chamber where life affirms itself nakedly as the vehicle of its own meaning and where the structures of the spirit are discarded as superfluous.

Mr Boyd disdained to repeat the order; he passed on to inspect the other slates, and Annie forced her reluctant legs to move. She advanced to the middle of the floor and stood there with her back to the class. Now they could all see her hair. It was really beautiful hair, long and crisp and rippling; the class was free to admire it now that Annie Rattray, 'Boyd's pettie,' was standing on the floor waiting for the tawse.

There was a subdued rustling that stiffened into absolute silence when the headmaster returned to his desk. The expectancy in the room stretched like an overstrained cord and snapped when the first sharp lash of the flat leather fingers descended on the hand waveringly held out to receive it. The fear of death, the whole weight of authority, was in that unerring blow, and when it descended upon Annie Rattray's hand the class was jubilant. Served her right for sucking up to auld Boyd. Annie's immunity from punishment had rankled in the minds of her school-fellows and made their own submission to the tawse look like disgraceful surrender; but now that authority was once more vindicated as an irresistible and impartial force their self-esteem was restored.

Three times the tawse came down with a crack like the lash of a whip, and when Annie stumbled back to her seat, nursing a swollen palm, her return to the body of the class was symbolic as well as actual. The others had rejoiced over her punishment, but she was now one of themselves; it was with a new feeling of fellowship that they made room for her to pass.

Annie sat down and struggled to swallow her tears. She would not let him have the satisfaction of seeing her cry. The throbbing pain in her hand was almost intolerable, but she would endure it to show that Annie Rattray was the stronger. What right had he to strike her because of a few sums? She herself was more important than all the sums in the world. He had no right to do it, even if it had been her fault that the sums were not done, and it wasn't her fault. The headmaster was wrong, perversely, maliciously, cruelly wrong, and it was Annie Rattray who was right in spite of everything. She was no longer dismayed; she was furious.

## SIX

During that day Annie Rattray went down three places in class. Her inattention and insubordination exasperated but did not really surprise the headmaster. He had seen too much of that kind of thing. In the sixth standard pupils were apt to turn insolent, especially the girls, and a girl's insolence was more difficult to check than a boy's. Girls were more—more—what were they? The headmaster's mind shied away from the question with a spasm of irritation; they were simply more exasperating. Girls were all right up to the age of twelve or thirteen; after that, Mr Boyd felt, they should be sent somewhere else, to learn cooking and sewing.

Annie felt furious, but not disgraced. In some strange way the plane of her interests had shifted; to challenge the headmaster had now become much more important than to please him. Moreover, her new attitude was tacitly approved by the rest of the class. The very fact that she was sitting in the middle of the bench instead of at the end of it gave her a warmer and more secure feeling—as if she were bolstered up by the others. On that first day of her new life she did not herself write notes to other girls—a forbidden pastime—but she passed on notes when she was asked; she lent a rubber to a girl beside her, although she was punctilious about getting it back; she even watched a game of noughts and crosses carried on under cover of the desk.

In the playground, too, there was a difference. Perhaps the absence of Mary accounted for it, perhaps it was the result of Annie's punishment, or it may have been due to the simple fact that skipping-ropes had come in and that the whole class was needed 'to keep the pottie boiling.' A long clothes-line was brought out, and Annie found herself

ducking and leaping over it at the heels of girls she had
hated. Helter-skelter they went flying in an endless chain,
one after the other, through and out again; after that they
did 'going to market,' and finally 'all in together.' A high
March wind blew out their petticoats and made the rope
curl like a breaking billow; their blood raced as fast as the
cloud-masses in the sky. And when the bell rang at the end
of the play-interval and Annie came back to her seat with
the others, her long hair tatted and tangled in elf-locks,
she was suddenly aware that the schoolroom smelt stale
and stuffy—a stale, stuffy, limited place, and her palm
no longer smarted and her fury was gone. She felt more
than ever the equal of auld Boyd, if not his superior, and
when she stood up to answer a question she looked at
him boldly. With a twitch of irritation the headmaster's
hand closed on the pointer he was holding, though his
face remained impassive. He said curtly: 'Sit down.' But
his voice was always curt. With another challenging look
Annie sat down. A cat could look at a king.

The same invisible filaments with which she had formerly
searched the mind of her preceptor now conveyed to her the
fact that nothing exasperated auld Boyd more helplessly
than just to be looked at like that. He couldn't give you
palmies just for *looking* at him! Annie went on looking.
She looked at his hair, at the point of his nose, at his
beard, his tie, his buttons. Her voice was exaggeratedly
respectful, even gentle, when she answered him, but her
eyes were bold and unwavering. Mr Boyd began to stare
over her head when he addressed her, and he addressed
her less and less often. In a few days he was ignoring her;
he bestowed neither praise nor blame, and marked her work
in silence.

Meanwhile Annie felt more and more at home in the
playground. Skipping-ropes stayed in fashion a long time
that spring, for the weather was cold and blustering, and
skipping induces warmth. The skipping games became
more and more intricate, until at last 'double dutch' came
in. For 'double dutch' one doubles the long rope so that
its two halves rotate simultaneously in opposite directions,
making a spinning teetotum of rope. To keep one's footing

in life is not more difficult than to keep one's footing in double dutch, which is done at high speed and makes the soles of the feet burn. After a few days of intensive double dutch the general interest in skipping began to wane. The rope, however, asked to be used, and a game called 'Runaway Slaves' was proposed. Annie found that this game excited her with an eager vehemence, especially if she was one of the two girls at either end of the rope. The rope-carriers, whose movements were thus restricted by the length of the line between them, were the masters, and it was their business to round up the masterless slaves and trap them one by one in the coils of the rope. The flying slaves enjoyed the game intensely; they shrieked and ran in all directions while Annie and her assistant stalked them over the playground. But Annie's enjoyment was of a peculiar intensity. She could control the rope adroitly and she acted to perfection the part of a savage master. The more she scowled and gritted her teeth at the slaves the more they shrieked with delight. Now she shortened her grip on the rope, restricting still more her own freedom, to leave the end loose for whizzing round her head. 'I'll skin the hide off o' you when I get you!' she cried, and the runaway slaves nearly died of laughing.

Annie's straight, narrow personality was rounding itself a little, and her straight, narrow body was rounding itself too. Her renascence was progressing, although she did not know what was happening to her. The new life which had begun for her on that evening when she lay passive in the darkness was opening out in obedience to the universal law that turns children into adolescents and gives them a chance to be born again. Annie had begun to be born again in that moment when she descended into the dark chamber where life affirms that it is important in itself, an affirmation which gives the young infant its innate dignity and the woman her strength to bring forth life and to rear the generations of men. But because Annie Rattray was what she was, because thirteen years of struggle lay behind her in which her consciousness of herself had hardened and toughened until it was like a sharp, aggressive spear-point, she had no intuition that her strength was lent her by a force that had nourished millions of creatures before her and would nourish millions after her; she had little sense of kinship even with humanity and no premonition of the many ways in which human life can find expression. For her there was only one expression of life, and that was herself. She was her own ultimate value. The spear-point that was Annie Rattray had learned to do nothing but assert Annie Rattray, and even when it began to put out leaves, to open out in adolescence, it was to form those leaves on its own pattern, like spines of furze. So the adolescent Annie Rattray who whizzed her rope in the playground was very like the childish Annie Rattray who dreamed her dreams of domination, except that she had a new, instinctive assurance.

A month or two later a still more thrilling game was invented, and when Annie was given the chief part to play in it she took her pre-eminence for granted. In some roundabout way a few garbled facts about mesmerism had reached Calderwick, and one or two of the bigger girls brought this knowledge to school. It was secret and somehow guilty knowledge which could not be communicated in the playground, but was whispered in the road outside, and not immediately outside the school, but farther down the hill, where the pavement came to an end and the road narrowed to a lane between high green banks. Seven conspirators gathered there round Tina Gove, a thin girl whose eyes seemed to be popping out of her head with excitement: 'And then he waves his hands afore your face, like that, and then you fall down, and then you dinna ken anything you do after that, for you're in the blues, and when you waken up again you dinna ken what's happened, and he can make you do what he likes.'

A delicious terror invaded them as they listened. They all wanted to be mesmerized, to surrender themselves to a dark, irresponsible force and to waken up again with a clear conscience. Conscience is reluctant to go down into the dark cave, but if conscience can shut its eyes and be put to sleep what an adventure the self may have! It can discard all the burdens of civilization and return to a passion that is old and strong as the earth. Their terror was both fear a longing. But who was to be mesmerized first? Who was to go down into the darkness?

Annie Rattray, of course!

Annie stood on a hillock where there was soft grass to tumble on. Hands were waved before her face and she squinted her eyes towards her nose, concentrating her force until something black and bulky grew in her midriff. Then with a shriek she toppled sideways, getting up on the instant like a maddened fury, her fingers clawing the air and a strange hiss coming out of her mouth. The more she mauled and clawed at her companions the more real did her simulated passion become; she leaped and yelled like a maniac, and the others fled, their knees loosening, shouting 'Murder!' For in the dark cave one moment of feeling is the same as eternity, and all divisions, all edifices of the mind and the spirit are sucked into that whirlpool, and hatred is indistinguishable from love, and fear from longing, and life is one with death. So they ran shouting 'Murder!' and their knees sank and failed, and Something swooped upon them and they died rejoicing in life. It was a terrifying and glorious game.

Months ago, ages ago, Annie had been marooned on a peak of isolation, looking at savages tumbling in the sea, but now she was herself cleaving that sea and swimming mightily with the roaring of many waters in her ears. One by one she caught and conquered the creatures around her, and when the last of them was thrashed and floundering, lo! she floated serene and dominant, unquestioned, unrebuked, upon a submissive element. She sought her tussock of grass again, shut her eyes, and said in a weak, gentle voice: 'Where am I?'

'She's comin' oot o' the blues!'

'Hoo do you feel, Annie?'

'Dod, you gi'ed me a richt dunt. My leg's black an' blue. It's the black an' blues you must have been in!'

'She disna ken what she did. You dinna ken that you dunted Tina's leg, do you now?'

Annie sat up and shook out her hair. 'No,' she said, in the same weak voice. 'What did I do?'

'Dod, you nearly rove the claes off my back,' said Tina Gove. 'Me next, you lassies; it's my turn next.'

'Na, it's me next!'

The conspirators had now become devotees with a rage for self-immolation. Tina shouted the others down; it was her right to be chosen next, for she had revealed the mystery in the beginning, and it was she who had mesmerized Annie Rattray so successfully. It was now Annie Rattray's turn to put Tina in the blues.

But it is not given to every one to go down into the dark cave and ride the whirlpool. Tina began to giggle hysterically. Instead of attacking others she had to be slapped on the back, and her giggles turned into a burst of weeping, and it was as if a spell were broken; the game was over for that day.

Next day, however, they stole away at four o'clock to play it again in secret, and the day after that, and the day after that. None of them could go into the blues so successfully as Annie Rattray, and more than one girl confessed to her in private: 'Mind you, I was real frichtened at you, Annie Rattray.' Annie's performance became more and more impressive; her voice, when she 'woke up' on the tussock, was weaker and gentler than ever, and she never forgot to disclaim all knowledge of her actions during the frenzy. But one afternoon a petulant cry was raised: 'Och, awa', you've torn my frock,' and this was followed by the accusation: 'You're ower rough, Annie Rattray.' Through this breach in public confidence another aggressor boldly pushed her away: 'Och, she's juist like her faither when she has the blues.' Tina Gove giggled and began to pipe up:

'Annie Ratt-att-airy,
    Teapot nose—'

Something black and bulky rose suffocatingly into Annie's throat; her hands clenched, seeking a branch, a stone, seeking some extension of herself that could blast and slay her enemies, but her fingers closed on nothingness, and so it was her naked fist that landed in Tina Gove's face. Then she turned and ran off down the lane.

Nobody attempted to follow her.

## SEVEN

A simple passion of rage leaves the quick of oneself unscathed; the rage finds relief in action and is discharged; the self can coil itself up and renew its strength. But however one may writhe in a passion of misery the sword-cut is not healed that divides oneself from oneself. Annie's rage only nerved her hands to clench themselves and her legs to run faster and faster down the lane, and with every stride it found relief; yet the misery that beat upon her heart and her temples as if it would burst the confines of flesh and bone could find no ease, although it turned round and round upon itself unceasingly.

And that roundabout of misery was accompanied by a childish tune hammering persistently on four notes:

> 'Annie Ratt-att-airy,
> Teapot nose,
> One two three and
> Away she goes.'

The maddening, catchy tune was wound up inside Annie's head as if she had a hurdy-gurdy on her shoulders.

> 'Annie Ratt-att-airy,
> Teapot nose—'

That kept time to her steps, however fast she ran, and her loudest sobbing could not overpower it.

Yet all the misery that swirled inside her, filling, it seemed, every crevice of her body, stopped at the frontiers of that body and had no existence at all beyond the tenuous covering of her skin. On either side of her woebegone figure the grass grew unheeding; leaves were opening,

38

seeds sprouting; lively birds fluttered out of the hedge, and over the hedge a man was whistling as he harrowed a field, stepping out behind a pair of broad-backed brown horses. Annie's sobbing became still louder and more desperate as if to force her wretchedness upon an indifferent world. But her misery remained Annie Rattray's misery. Life, in its protean fullness, had cast up impartially bird and tree, horse and man, Annie Rattray and her father, and it was unconcerned if one of its creatures chose to be miserable. This bright indifference outlined Annie's isolation, and as her awareness of it grew her rage slackened and her misery swelled into self-pity.

For she was deeply humiliated. When her mother quashed her ambition to become a teacher she had been furious but not humiliated. When the headmaster lashed her with the tawse she had been dismayed but not humiliated. On these occasions something had given her assurance to feel that she was right and that it was the others who were wrong. But now she had been wounded in the quick of that self-assurance and she was humiliated. In affirming herself she had apparently affirmed that she was her father's daughter, and all her narrow personal pride was in revolt.

To have a rudimentary personal self, a simple, undifferentiated consciousness, has its advantages. Mary Rattray, for instance, would not have been humiliated by the accusation that she was like her father; she might have laughed or she might have knocked many heads together, but she would not have been miserable. Annie Rattray's vitality had a more difficult course to run; her insistent personal self was now in revolt against that other self which had surged up within her like a drunken frenzy. She might as well have been drunk! She had been mocked exactly as her father was mocked! She writhed in misery, and the misery swelled into self-pity. Poor Annie Rattray, she thought; poor Annie Rattray, who was never allowed to do the things she wanted to do . . . Poor Annie Rattray, who only wanted to go her own way, and everybody tried to drag her down . . . Poor Annie Rattray, who could do things so much better than anybody else and yet never got a chance . . . Poor Annie Rattray, who

ought to be admired and respected by everybody. It was
a shame!

But beneath Annie's self-pity something ruthless was
happening. The indulgence of pity may be a concession
by one part of the self to the ruthlessness of another part,
for one can shoot an animal dead and feel pity for it at the
same time; and if Annie's tears began to flow more easily
and more pitifully it was because she was weeping for a loss,
for the loss of something that her pride was forcing her to
discard. She did not suspect that what she was discarding
might have more value than what she meant to attain, but
she wept for the loss of something that had meant much to
her, so much, indeed, that even these tears were perhaps a
dangerous concession.

She wiped her eyes on her sleeve. The mechanical roundabout of misery was ceasing; the feeling of wretchedness, as
if it were shrinking downwards, had subsided into a patch of
greyness and sickness about her stomach. Annie stretched
herself, rising on tiptoe, with her arms flung above her head,
seeking to rise above that patch of misery and let it sink
into oblivion. Some hope of this kind may have first made
man aspire to stretch towards the sky and walk upright; all
the children of men, at any rate, are lured by upwardness,
and when she caught sight of a wooden bridge over the
railway track towards which her blind flight had brought
her, Annie set off at a run to climb to the top of it. Hooking
herself on to the lattice-work she stared down at the long
perspective of the rails. The patch of grey sickness within
her did begin to sink, but it sank at an alarming speed;
her stomach seemed to be floating downwards, drawing
her irresistibly after it, and in sudden terror she clenched
her fingers and clung to the wooden slats. Something was
luring her to let go and fall down; it may have been her
self-pity that was so dangerous, and now she dared not
indulge in concessions, she had to be altogether ruthless.
Stubbornly she clung to the lattice until her head cleared
and her eye steadied itself by following the dwindling rails
to their distant goal, the toylike platforms of Calderwick
station. It was as if she herself had arrived at some invisible
station, and she loosened her hands from the lattice-work

and stood upright on the bridge, ruthlessly determined that she would never again suffer humiliation.

The pride of the eye carries the spirit effortlessly over leagues of ground which would make a painful and toilsome journey for the body. Annie gazed at the straight, inviolate track of the permanent way and her mind was blank, but her spirit followed her eye along promised lines of certainty cutting through the bewilderments of life. She stood very straight and her misery dissolved and vanished. Then as if dreaming she lifted her face to the wide sky overhead.

A feather of cloud at which she was staring changed from rose to grey, and Annie realized all at once that the sun had nearly set and that she did not know how long she had been standing there. A strand of hair which blew across her face surprised her; she had forgotten that her hair was no longer tied in pigtails. What had come over her to do all these silly things? The red eye of the sun peered from a rift in the clouds, and as if a ray had penetrated her, Annie felt that God was looking at her, and almost in the same moment she knew that until this very evening she had been giving herself to the devil. It was the devil who had led her into humiliation. And because the wages of sin is death it was a last temptation of the devil that had nearly drawn her to fall from the bridge. The solemnity of death and the solemnity of God—or were they one and the same?—filled the darkening world around her, and she was hushed in awe, uplifted in spirit as in body. It was not yet too dark to discern the roofs of Calderwick in the distance, huddled round the steeple of the Parish Kirk, a tall, graceful steeple which soared above the humbler human dwellings as a witness that God was greater than any citizen of Calderwick—greater than Mr Boyd, greater even than the Provost who had come to the school on Prize Day. And He had singled out Annie Rattray . . .

Somewhere up there, beyond the sunset clouds, He was thinking of Annie Rattray . . . Our Father which art in Heaven. In that moment of exaltation Annie discarded her earthly father for ever, and the isolated dream that had cut her off from the others at home in Mill Wynd now rose and joined her to the skies.

God was her Father. In Mill Wynd she was a changeling.

Did the wide vault of the sky suddenly seem too high and
too remote? Or was it that the gathering shadows reminded
her of the devil? Annie shivered slightly, and with a last look
at the railway track descended to earth, walking soberly as
befitted a daughter of God.

## EIGHT

But her sober walk quickened, for she was a long way from home and the void of the night was already encroaching on field and fence, hedgerow and tree, turning them into unfamiliar looming shapes. It was as if the light of reason were vanishing from the world, as if the blurred and darkening shapes among which she moved might themselves begin to move, might thicken and grow around her into a monstrous brood of devils. The eye of God was shut and she was drowning in darkness as a sleeper drowns in a nightmare, and as a sleeper hurries trains of thought through obscure byways, seeking the glimmer of reason, so Annie blindly retraced at a run the track she had so blindly followed. It was with a gasp of relief that she saw the far-off gleam of an outpost light twinkling from a solitary cottage, for where humanity can build a roof to fence out the night the human spirit is emboldened to fence out its own darknesses, and as Annie passed the cottage her devils retreated into the waste behind her. The track widened into a road that led into the town, into the heart of the town where the house of God rose so fearlessly, enclosing for itself a larger space of night than any human being could master. Annie did not dare to look up at the top of the steeple, she followed the sparse gas-lamps along the familiar pavements; and even Mill Wynd, dark as it was, appeared to be a shelter, a solid rectangular stronghold of rational and ordered life.

But when she stepped down into the kitchen her face closed and became a cold white mask, and she remembered that in this house she was a changeling. The kitchen was full of those same monstrous shapes that had grown out of the hedges, and they were no longer dumb.

'Is that you, Annie? You're late.'

Mrs Rattray, tying on a clean apron, came round the corner of the table.

'Your kipper's in the oven. I'm awa' ootbye to ha'e a crack.'

She bustled out, but the kitchen was still overfull. Mary had propped the looking-glass beside the gas-jet in the middle of the mantelpiece and was taking out her curling-pins and combing out the frizz. All day in the mill she wore her curlers beneath a man's snouted cap, but now she was preparing for the High Street evening parade, and Jean Lamont from next door was sitting on the bed waiting for her. Jim Rattray, in his shirt-sleeves and braces, was sprawling in the big chair by the fireside, smoking his cutty and watching Mary.

'Onything wi' breeks on,' he said, and spat on the hob.

Mary had a curler in her mouth, but Jean answered for her:

'No' you, Jim Rattray, onywye; you're ower auld.'

'Ower auld, am I? Dod, I'll gi'e you a dry shave for that.' He laid his cutty on the hob and dived behind the table to get at Jean. Mary screwed herself half round to watch them, her eyes twinkling. With a closed, cold face Annie drew her kipper from the oven and sat down to eat it at the farther end of the table. She would not raise her eyes to see the scrimmage on the bed, but she could hear it. Jean Lamont was skirling and kicking as the man's unshaven bristle was rubbed first on one of her cheeks and then on the other.

'Help! Murder!' screamed Jean. 'He's kittlin' me!'

'Jab a hatpin intill him,' advised Mary.

Annie went on eating her kipper, with her eyes lowered; she pulled the needles of bone out of her mouth and ranged them on the side of her plate.

'Would you, you limmer?' said Jim. 'I'll jab *you* in a minute.'

The scuffle recommenced, but Jean suddenly grew angry:

'Haud aff, there; nane o' that! I'll tell Mrs Rattray on you.'

Mary burst into skelloching laughter as she combed out the last of her fringe, and hummed loudly the refrain of a song that was the most recent libel composed by the mill-workers on their employer:

> 'Was ever seen in a' the toon
> Sic bow, sic fiddle?'

Then, laying down her comb on the mantelpiece, she called out:

'Barley, you lads, barley now. I'm ready, Jean.'

'He's lowsed doon a' my hair.'

Jean sat up sulkily, pinning her hair under her hat, and Jim got to his feet, yawning: 'E-e-ech.'

He reached for his cutty and spat on the hob just as Annie lifted the teapot off it. She could see the round blob of spittle frothing up and drying and shrinking into a crackling film. That was what hell would be like; her father and Mary and Jean Lamont would parch and crackle like that on the hob of hell.

'You're to wash up the dishes, Annie; mind you that.'

'You mind your ain business and I'll mind mine.'

'Yeh-eh!'

Mary stuck out her tongue and cleeked Jean by the arm. They swirled out of the kitchen, out into the night, into the dark places.

Jim Rattray settled himself in the chair, stretched his long legs in front of him and yawned again. Annie stood up and began to clear the fishy plates from the littered table. Everything was dirty, befouled and besmeared; the devil had left his prints all over the kitchen. She piled the dirty dishes on the sink, filled an enamelled basin with hot water from the kettle, and began violently to wash off grease-marks and thumb-stains, scouring, rubbing and scrubbing the devil away. When all the crockery was clean she turned the basin bottom up and Jim Rattray's legs slipped still farther across the hearth and his head nid-nodded on his chest. Annie looked at him as she took a damp clout to wipe the table, then she scrubbed at the stretch of American cloth until its peeling surface curled away from the network of dirty cracks. She looked at him again, and as if the sight of him suggested that the room needed sweeping out she took a broom from behind the door and began to sweep, poking and knocking under table and chairs. She swept round his feet and under his legs, then she paused and stood looking down at him. She could see his brow under its mat of sandy hair, his long red nose pitted with large pores, his ragged sandy moustache beside which the cheeks were grained with dirt under their stubble, and the furrows on his brow were dirt-engrained too. A button was missing from his shirt and the gap bulged as he breathed, showing a tangle of short yellow hairs on his chest. Annie suddenly felt sick. These hairs looked as if they had a life of their own, growing like alien, indifferent grass on that breathing body: like the stubble on his cheeks they would go on growing as if the devil were in them, even if they were to be shaved off each Sunday. The sickness that turned her stomach was a sickness of fear, not of misery, but she recognized it as a warning that the devil was astir, and she looked at her father's grey worsted foot as if she expected to see a cloven hoof. James Rattray, her father, was asleep in darkness with the devil, and the devil, as everybody knew, was hirsute all over . . .

Annie's sickness grew into terror as she realized that after all she had not found God soon enough; she was herself already marked with the mark of the devil, and now she must always keep herself covered up. Her long pale face flushed with shame and she averted her eyes from the sleeping man. She began to sweep again, and the tufted grey fluff under the bed clung to the broom-head as if it too were a devil's growth. Nobody should fall asleep in a kitchen, she thought, nor should there be any beds in a kitchen; the living-room at least should be kept wakeful and clean, whatever might invade a bedroom. But she had done what she could. As for Mary's comb, with the broken hairs still sticking in it, that was Mary's business; it could just lie on the mantelpiece.

Annie Rattray washed her hands under the tap, rinsing them again and again, before she sat down at the table to do her school homework. Parsing and sums were like a barrier between herself and the devil; they belonged to the world of clean wakefulness, not to darkness and dirt; and she suddenly understood why the headmaster detested dog-eared pages, and why a blot was more disgraceful than an error. The headmaster was revealed as an ally, and she finished her tasks with scrupulous neatness; perhaps he would recognize with pleasure that she had at last come over to his side. She must find some way of living in light and cleanliness, and now it seemed monstrous that she had lost the chance of becoming a teacher . . . What had bewitched her? She should have ignored her mother's objections. It was the devil himself who had seduced her into thinking that it was unimportant . . . But she must find some other way out; she could not, she would not, stay at home after leaving school, nor would she go into the mill. Annie propped her chin on her hands and stared at the wallpaper, where large, blowsy, faded brown roses alternated with what appeared to be tall green reeds, just like tawny lions' heads thrusting out of the jungle . . . Annie stared them down as the slave-mother Miss Julia talked about had stared down the lions; she, too, would reach the mission station in safety, and Miss Julia would tell her how to do it . . .

Mrs Rattray came in and Annie closed her books, put the pen and ink on the shelf, and went off to bed, for her mother was unhooking her bodice and her father was awake and letting down his braces. She was no longer terrified, for there was always the mission station and Miss Julia and the headmaster; yet she had the devil's mark upon her and she must be hidden in bed before Mary arrived. For it was not only the bed in the kitchen that was a nest for the devil; all beds were dangerous, and she must guard herself well . . . Here in the bedroom, where only a candle was keeping the devil at bay, she must go down into the darkness of sleep. Annie hurried into her nightgown and buttoned it up to her throat. Perhaps she could leave the candle burning? Or put her head right under the bedclothes? But the devil was everywhere, and now she remembered a text from Sunday-school: The devil walketh about like a roaring lion, seeking whom he may devour. Where was God? she thought in panic. He must protect her while she was defencelessly asleep in the darkness. Annie had never said her prayers before going to bed, but now quite naturally she went on her knees and repeated the Lord's Prayer. That would sanctify the bed, and she must climb in quickly, before the efficacy of the prayer could wear off . . . Yet she remembered that it was the front of the bed she had prayed over, Mary's side of the bed, and so she got out again, pulled the bed out from the wall and knelt down on her own side of it, in the small space between the mattress and the wall. She repeated the Lord's Prayer again, adding: 'O God, help me!' and this time she had a feeling of assurance. She could venture to go to sleep. God had singled her out, and on the Judgment Day she would sit at His right hand, while her father and her mother and Mary would be cast into hell.

## NINE

Annie plaited her hair in two long pigtails next morning. There were black rings under her eyes, but she had escaped the devil, although she had some confused recollection of struggling in her sleep to run away from Something that was pursuing her.

'You look mair wise-like wi' your hair oot o' your face,' commented her mother. 'I thocht you'd get tired o' hunting for lice.'

How stupid the unenlightened were! Annie disdained to make any reply and set off for school resolutely enough, although she did not know how God was to help her to get the better of Tina Gove. Her chance soon came, however, and it enabled her at the same time to show the headmaster that she was once more prepared to acknowledge an alliance with him.

'Please, sir, Tina Gove's playing at x's and o's under the desk.'

Yet Mr Boyd remained unfriendly. He gave Tina Gove the tawse after one sharp look to verify that Annie was telling the truth, but at the same time he said: 'Attend to your own work instead of to what your neighbours are doing.' This threw Annie into unexpected confusion; she screwed down the corners of her mouth and did not look up even to see Tina Gove getting her well-deserved palmies. Did the headmaster not understand that she was threatened on all sides by the devil and that she simply had to be watchful? He had as good as told her to mind her own business, and certainly it wasn't her business whether Tina Gove went to hell or not; to make certain that she herself didn't go to hell was as much as she could manage. But surely one could never be safe so long as other people encouraged the devil? She had only been trying to do her duty. She had only been trying to help.

Her confusion deepened into resentment. Mr Boyd had mistaken her zeal for impertinence, as if an encroachment on his sole authority undermined instead of strengthening the power of God. Of course he did not yet know that Annie Rattray had become a daughter of God. She watched him as he gave a dictation to the ex-sixth at the other end of the room, and her face assumed the expression of one who is martyred for righteousness' sake.

She wore the same expression when Tina Gove, who had sobbed convulsively all morning, attacked her at eleven o'clock in the playground:

'You clype! You mean bitch! I'll ca' your face into the middle o' next week!'

Annie's hands clenched, but instead of trying to murder Tina Gove she kept a grip on the devil, and referred the matter to a higher consciousness.

'You hit me, and I'll tell Mr Boyd on you.' Then, as her righteousness rose triumphant, she added:

'And it would set you better no' to swear.'

'Wha's swearing?' demanded Tina. But her eyes were uneasy, and Annie pressed her advantage:

'You were. And what's mair, I'll tell Mr Boyd aboot "the blues"; it was *you* that started them.'

'Och, c'way, Tina; dinna you speak till her,' and hands plucked Tina away, hands whose owners had shared in the game of 'the blues.' 'Dinna ha'e onything to do wi' her; she's turned into a clype.'

They drew away from Annie as if she infected the air, and, although she had triumphed, she retained the look of a martyr.

For the godliness to which she had committed herself required unceasing vigilance and self-sacrifice, and on its altar there had to be laid the hirsute offspring of the devil, passions slain in their infancy. But although Annie's pride made the offering, girt like a priest in the garments of religion, there was no attendant congregation of subservient worshippers to confirm that high office, nor was the altar raised up to be seen of men from afar. At that time Annie had to be priest, victim, altar and congregation within herself; it was not surprising that the look of martyrdom should settle on her face and that she should make her garments of righteousness as conspicuous as possible.

So that evening, after her day of isolated martyrdom, Annie closed her eyes in the presence of her family and said grace to herself before beginning tea. That was what Miss Julia did when the Sunday-school class had their annual tea-party. And now for the first time Annie understood the significance of the act, for food must go down into the belly where the devil has his stronghold. It was like saying a prayer before getting into bed; and she waited until Mary came into the bedroom before repeating 'Our Father,' which this time she repeated aloud. Mary had skirled with derision at tea-time, and now she cried: 'Holy Annie! Great snakes!' But Annie lay down composedly on her sanctified half of the bed, and did not even prod her sister with an elbow.

To resist and exorcize the devil at home was easy enough, his machinations were so obvious, but in school Annie's task remained difficult. There was a perplexing ambiguity about Mr Boyd's attitude. She watched him at first with a jealous eye, for it was just possible that in setting himself up as an arbiter of her conduct he was serving some strange altar that was not dedicated to the God she had found. Perhaps he thought that if she were not to be a teacher she had no claim to eminence. If that were so, if he thought the passing of examinations more important than the service of God, he was no better than a whited sepulchre in that starched dickey of his. Mr Boyd maintained order and wakefulness in school, but what did he do when he got home? And Annie could not help thinking, as she looked at him, that on his chest too the devil's hairs were growing, and that if it were not for his starched dickey and high collar he would be another Jim Rattray.

She did not recognize that this new problem was an old one, originally suggested by the devil—the problem whether Mr Boyd was a man or a headmaster—but although it continued to perplex her as a problem she came tentatively to be on the side of the headmaster. After all, one could not imagine Mr Boyd in shirt-sleeves; the starched dickey was a symbol of his official life. From nine until four daily his was not a private, personal world into which the devil could enter; the devil, however ubiquitous, could not peep through the analysis of a sentence or find his way into the workings of a sum. Words and figures might indeed be used for the devil's purposes, but Mr Boyd's business was only to give his scholars the rules of knowledge; how they applied the rules was not his concern. It wasn't Mr Boyd's fault if Mary Rattray sang lewd songs in the mill, although he might not approve; and perhaps he had rebuked Annie Rattray's crusading zeal because she was trying to bring into a lower court questions of conduct that could be settled only in some higher court—in Sunday-school, for instance. For all his authority, the best that Mr Boyd could do was to produce teachers, not saints, and Annie restored her self-esteem by reflecting that God had preserved her for the higher vocation of the two.

It was the Bible that she now looked at in passing through the kitchen, and not her school prize; it was in the church and the Sunday-school that she sought to win distinction. Annie Rattray now went regularly to St James's Church on Sunday mornings, and occupied one of the two 'sittings' rented by the Rattray family in a side pew near the choir. It was fitting that workaday clothes should be discarded, that one's Sunday undergarments should be of clean white instead of flannelette and striped cotton, even that one's hair should be covered with a Sunday hat. Annie thought that men were allowed to take their hats off because their hair was cut short; indeed, the most respectable men, the elders and deacons, were usually bald-headed—a signal triumph over the devil. In the house of God Annie felt herself exalted in a community of saints and martyrs, and as she sang 'Nearer, my God, to Thee,' she knew that words and music were here put to their crowning use, the service of God, a greater and higher service than anything Mr Boyd could achieve. Annie's eyes were now fixed on the minister as once on the headmaster, and she was convinced that the Reverend Mr Hay looked at her with special intimacy. But she felt a hesitation, a kind of disappointment, whenever she passed the door of the Parish Kirk on her way to St James's, for it

looked almost as if St James's Free Church were only one
of God's lesser houses, and Annie wanted to be a privileged
member in the highest and biggest household of all.

This, however, proved to be another temptation of the
devil, and it was Miss Julia who made it clear. In her
gravest voice she said: 'Annie Rattray has just asked me
what is the difference between the Established Church and
the Free Church. I thought that all of you would know that,
but I see that I must tell you. The Established Church is
certainly a Christian church, but it falls into the error of
submitting to dictation by the State. The Free Church
acknowledges only the authority of God, and its ministers
are *not* paid by the State. It is a really *free* church, Annie;
that is the difference.'

Miss Julia's tone as she conceded that the Parish Kirk
was a Christian church reminded Annie of a previous lesson
on 'Hymns and their Authors,' in which Miss Julia, with
the same intonation, had conceded that John Wesley was
a good man although he was a Methodist. So it was not
enough to be a Christian; there were apparently Christians
and Christians, and one needed to be as good a Christian
as Miss Julia before one could discriminate properly among
them. Annie now knew what was the right attitude to take
towards Mr Boyd: he was a good man, although he was not
the best kind of Christian; like the Parish Kirk, he had the
appearance of loftiness, but, like the Parish Kirk, he was
subservient to the secular power. She looked at Miss Julia
with increased respect. Next morning she felt a forgiving
patronage towards the headmaster; his lack of perception,
his cold indifference to the most important issues of life,
arose from his lack of freedom, from his incapacity as a
paid servant of the State to lead an independent life
responsible only to God. But St James's was a really
*free* church. Miss Julia's grave, impressive voice haunted
her memory. Miss Julia was a really free and independent
Christian; Miss Julia was a real lady, who lived a Christian
life behind a peculiarly solid and respectable front door;
Miss Julia drew to herself all the tangled strands of Annie's
perplexities and ambitions. If she could but quit Mill Wynd
for ever on the day when she left the Townhead School and

enter into a Christian household like Miss Julia's, Annie felt that she would enter into a securer, larger freedom; the lions would be banned from the mission station and the dark devils of night and chaos would be roofed out. She decided to ask Miss Julia for a place in her household. With that decision Annie's interest began to recede from school, so that when she sat at last in the ex-sixth standard she looked forward to the day of her release as eagerly as any of the unregenerate sinners beside her, and her defection appeared no more laudable to the headmaster than that of the others.

'Annie Rattray!'

'Here, sir.'

He ticked off her name for the last time with a certain grim satisfaction.

# BOOK II: THE GIRL

The Girl: A hand has been stretched out to me.
The Answer: Take it.
The Girl: But if I lose my balance?
The Answer: Shake yourself free.

## TEN

The three Misses Carnegie lived in a house that had been their father's and their grandfather's before them; the only other survivor of the family, Mr William Carnegie, had generously conceded the old house to his unmarried sisters and set up for himself in another part of Calderwick. He could afford to do so, for he had inherited the large wood-yard by the river and a fair amount of house-property in the town, while it was unlikely that his sisters would ever marry, Miss Carnegie being now sixty-one, Miss Susan fifty-eight, and Miss Julia, the youngest of nine, already forty-seven. Her elder sisters regarded Miss Julia with indulgence, even with compassion, as being still subject to the weaknesses of female nature which they themselves had now surmounted, and the vigorous authority which they claimed and exercised was not allowed to be her right. The delicacy and propriety of Miss Julia's conduct were all that might be expected from a lady dedicated to the domestic altar and the sacred hearth of home; she never by word or look provoked discord between herself and her sisters, and submitted amiably to their direction as her dear mother, whom she so much resembled, had submitted to the direction of papa. Papa's functions had been neatly divided between the two elder women: Miss Carnegie ruled the household and paid the bills, while Miss Susan brought into the home a breath of the outer world, for she attended every auction sale in Calderwick and the neighbourhood, shod in stout boots and carrying a thick walking-stick. Miss Julia's maternal duties, unhappily incapable of any but vicarious fulfilment, were supplied by the care of her Sunday-school class, eight girls whom she watched over devotedly, seeking to elevate their minds by

frequent reference to a future state of eternal bliss. As
Mr Wordsworth so beautifully put it:

> A simple child
> That lightly draws its breath,
> And feels its life in every limb,
> What should it know of death?

Miss Julia, in her most grave and solemn voice, remedied
the lack of that knowledge in her simple children, reminding
them that they were future wives and mothers, and candidates for immortality; that they might be destined to
watch over the couches of the sick and dying, perhaps to
perform the last sad offices for their own parents, sisters
and children, and that they themselves would sooner or
later taste of death, the common lot of mortals. Miss Julia
herself was moved by these mournful reflections, for she
often thought with sorrow that it would be her lot to close
the eyes of dear Susan and dear Matilda. Not being a
heathen, however, Miss Julia was not depressed by such
thoughts; she was rather moved to a deeper thankfulness
for her present blessings, and especially for the Providence
that had placed her in a Christian home and taught her to
expect paradise hereafter.

On an evening in April 1889, Miss Julia Carnegie was
sitting alone in the drawing-room when the parlour-maid
announced that a young person giving the name of Annie
Rattray wished to speak to her. Mindful of her sacred trust,
Miss Julia laid down the book of poems by Bishop Heber
and said: 'Show her in here, Betty.' 'In *here*, m'm?' queried
the parlour-maid, who was a pert creature; but receiving
only a grave confirmation of the order Betty had to usher
in the young person in question. Miss Julia greeted her
with an affectionate welcome, for Annie Rattray was one
of her most promising pupils, diligent, respectful and
conscious of her relation to the Author of her being. It
appeared that the dear child, standing, as she did, on the
threshold of life, and being instructed of the trials and
temptations that awaited her in this world, had come to
her preceptor for guidance and counsel. What can better
avail to call into action all the faculties of the soul than

to be consulted by a young immortal needing care and instruction, a young immortal, too, belonging to the sex on which the evils incident to human existence fall with peculiar force? Miss Julia's heart yearned over Annie. To wish to become a domestic in some Christian family, what a proper ambition for a young, unprotected female! For in Annie's case the shelter of the paternal roof, alas! offered no protection from the contamination of the world, in spite of her poor mother's self-sacrificing devotion. Annie had not been blessed, like Miss Julia, with an exemplary father whose conduct admitted none of the vices that were too common in the other sex. Coming from such a home, what remarkable propriety of feeling Annie Rattray displayed! Miss Julia flattered herself that she was in some measure responsible for this gratifying state of things; the good seed sown on Sundays was bearing fruit.

'My dear Annie, I cannot find words to express my gratification that you should consult me, and that you should display such very proper sentiments. I agree with you that employment in the mill, or in a shop—even a high-class ladies' establishment—is not desirable. Only in a Christian home can a young girl learn her proper duties to society and to her Maker, and fit herself to be a credit to her sex in her domestic relations. I shall make it my business to inquire in the town for a suitable situation; my recommendation, I think, should carry some weight, and I shall have no hesitation in recommending you whole-heartedly. I am sure you will make a *very* good maid, Annie, when you are properly trained.'

Annie twisted her fingers together, embarrassed, doubtless—as who would not be?—by such august approval.

'On what date do you leave school?' Miss Julia drew her private diary from a pocket, and poised the small gilt pencil.

'On the twentieth of May, please, Miss Julia. But please, Miss Julia, could I not . . . could you not . . . I'd rather come to *you*, Miss Julia, than to anybody else.'

'To me?' Miss Julia was startled and flattered by this unexpected appeal. How touching it was to have evoked such affection and confidence! The dear child!

'I had not contemplated . . . I can promise nothing until I consult my sisters, Annie . . .'

But Miss Julia's smile betrayed that the idea was not unwelcome to her. What a treasure Annie would be! And how pleasant for all of them to have in the kitchen a young female of such admirable character! How easy it would be to train her in the faithful discharge of her duties! Mrs Bruce would doubtless be glad to have an extra pair of hands at her disposal, and in time Annie might even rise to be parlour-maid . . . she was very intelligent and had an excellent memory.

'Our staff is a modest one, Annie; we have only a cook and a parlour-maid, who does housemaiding duties as well . . .'

A pert creature, Betty. Dear Susan was perhaps a little ill-advised in her preference for smartness in a parlour-maid. But if Susan could insist on retaining Betty, there was really no reason why she herself should not have a protégée of her own . . .

Miss Julia dismissed Annie Rattray graciously, with a definite promise that her application would be earnestly considered and a reply dispatched at the first possible opportunity, and after the door had shut upon her interesting visitor relapsed into a pleasant reverie. How amply one was rewarded for devoting oneself to the improvement of the young! Miss Julia thanked the Almighty for this proof that her life in this vale of tears had not been spent entirely in vain, that she had been enabled to exercise an influence for good and thus to fulfil the noblest function of her sex.

Miss Julia's plea for the engagement of her Sunday scholar was received with some surprise by her sisters, but eventually looked upon with favour. Miss Carnegie inclined to think that Mrs Bruce, the cook, would be spared many laborious ascents of the stairs if a willing young girl came into the house, and Miss Susan, knowing her favourite's dislike of the dustpan and broom, agreed jovially that Betty would be thankful to get out of some of the dirty work, the hussy! With great tact they agreed to let Miss Julia herself send the message conveying to Annie Rattray her good fortune, and Miss Julia was sensible of having achieved a new status in the household, which threw her into a delightful flutter of anticipation.

## ELEVEN

Annie and Mrs Rattray carried a small wooden trunk between them to the Carnegies' house on a mild evening in May, and almost as inconspicuously as the trunk the new maid slipped into her place in the household. Miss Julia herself conducted Annie upstairs to the attic she was to share with Mrs Bruce and Betty; a neat single bed, with snowy sheets, had been set up for her in a corner, and she was entitled to two drawers in a tallboy beside it. When Annie had ranged her underwear in these drawers beside the new caps and aprons Miss Julia had given her she felt even more secure than when the shining, solid front door had closed behind her so massively yet so quietly; the drawers of the tallboy were also massive and they slid smoothly home, presenting an impenetrable front of grained and polished wood. It was as if she herself were enclosed in a dedicated, private sanctuary, as if she had walked out of a life of weekdays into an enduring Sabbath—not the precarious, open Sabbath that stretched to the sky, but a Sabbath roofed in like a church against the incalculable forces of night. Annie shut her trunk upon the few garments left in it, pushed it under her bed—a bed to herself!—and descended to the kitchen.

Here there was plenty of ordinary weekday bustle, for Betty was laying the table in the dining-room next door, and Mrs Bruce was peering into saucepans and lifting dishes out of the oven, but on the shelves and at the back of the great kitchen dresser a hierarchy of shining pans and dish-covers maintained a Sabbath-like specklessness and immobility. That Sabbath order, one felt, would soon be re-established in the whole of the kitchen, and Annie set to work cheerfully enough on the bowls and moulds

and other cooking utensils which Mrs Bruce required her
to clean.

'That's that, then,' said Betty, smoothing her starched
apron. 'What's your name, lassie?'

'Annie Rattray.'

'Mine's Bet Bowman. Ha'e, would you like to have a
look at the table? Dicht your hands and come through
wi' me.'

'She'll do no sic thing. You finish washing up, Annie.'

Betty tossed her head: 'You dish up the dinner, then,
and dinna keep me waiting.'

Annie bent over her wash-basin in non-committal silence.
Betty was friendly in her manner and Mrs Bruce unfriendly;
Betty was starched and glossy and neat, Mrs Bruce flushed
and a little dishevelled. But there were Christians and
Christians, even in this house, apparently; it would be as
well to wait and see whom Miss Julia favoured.

The gong was sounded and a rustling next door
announced that the ladies had come in. Smartly, efficiently,
Betty appeared and reappeared between courses, saying little
and whisking off with a dispatch that encouraged Annie to
side with her. Betty, after all, neat and jimp in her uniform,
stood very near to the ladies in the dining-room, while
Mrs Bruce and Annie had to stay in the outer court of the
kitchen. When the dining-table had to be cleared Annie was
allowed to help the parlour-maid, and she discovered that
this same dining-table was the hallowed, polished mahogany
on which the annual tea of the Sunday-school class was set
out. Her new familiarity with it came as a fresh proof that
she was being initiated into a higher life, and her respect
for Betty increased.

But with the laying aside of her duties, when the three
of them sat down to supper in the kitchen, Betty became
all at once Bet Bowman, a girl who might as well have
worked in the mill beside Mary Rattray. She winked at
Annie when, grace being over, she was discovered with her
mouth full of unblessed bread and butter. Her irreverence
towards God included a lesser irreverence towards her
mistresses, the three Misses Carnegie, whom she referred
to as 'auld runts,' and 'a pack o' auld maids'; worse still,

she persisted in holding up to ridicule Miss Susan, whose admitted favourite she was.

'She's aye runnin' to the watter-closet when she's no' runnin' to the sales,' said Bet Bowman, finding some obscure satisfaction in accusing her protector of incontinency.

'Haud your wheesht!' said Mrs Bruce. 'You may be a good parlour-maid, Bet Bowman, but you're a bad, bad lassie.'

It was dreadful to find the devil behind a starched apron—as if one had discovered the devil behind the headmaster's starched dickey—and Annie was thrown into confusion. She herself had the mark of the devil on her body, behind the decent striped frock, and who knew where he might be lurking even in a Christian family behind a solid, respectable front door? A Christian had to be suspicious, a Christian had to watch for the devil through a thousand loopholes, and perhaps Mrs Bruce had been justified in her unfriendly and suspicious reception of a newcomer.

Annie was still confused when they filed into the drawing-room for family prayers. She could not help regarding Miss Susan, for instance, with suspicion, for Miss Susan had a great black moustache on her upper lip, and if the devil could display himself on her very face the solid gold chain she wore might prove an insufficient fetter. Miss Susan had a gold chain on one wrist, too, a massive gold chain with a padlock, as if she felt a need to fetter the devil strongly; that padlock somehow suggested a bond between Miss Susan and Betty, the two-faced parlour-maid, who was now kneeling so primly beside a chair. Miss Susan's resonant voice rang out boldly, too boldly, as if she were bidding for God's favour at an auction-sale. Annie rose from her knees feeling almost afraid to peep at Miss Julia. But Miss Julia looked exactly as she did in Sunday-school, and smiled very pleasantly in answer to Annie's frightened glance. That made the drawing-room once more a consecrated place, a room free from the sordid business of daily life, a veritable Sabbath room to which one penetrated after labouring through a week of ordinary rooms, and Annie dropped a deep curtsey to Miss Julia as she went out to get her candle and go to bed. The devil might be more ubiquitous than she had thought, but with Miss Julia's help he could be kept at bay. She remembered that she was to have a bed to herself, without a corner in it where the devil would find harbourage, and she went upstairs feeling that she would rest in the Lord. When Bet Bowman ran up behind her, carrying a stone hot-water bottle and crying: 'If I canna ha'e a lad I maun ha'e a pig,' Annie turned from her coldly. Bet Bowman's bed was a hotbed for the devil—fancy having a pig in May!—and the space that separated Annie's bed from hers marked the distance that all true daughters of God had to keep between them and the children of the devil. Annie turned a contemptuous shoulder to Bet as naturally as if all her life had been spent in snubbing other people, and it was with cold, disapproving, contemptuous eyes that she watched Bet Bowman throw her clothes in a heap on a chair and drop her stockings on the floor. Bet's tidiness, Bet's fastidiousness, were merely a plaster laid on like an apron, and were as easily detachable.

That seemed to clear up Annie's confusion. The devil was not really clean, not really tidy; one had only to watch him closely enough to see that his assumption of virtues was a sham. And Annie blew out her candle and settled herself to sleep with the conviction that nobody would ever discover *her* to be a sham, not if she challenged the whole world to do it.

## TWELVE

Annie set herself to sweep and scrub and scour with a thoroughness that shamed the devil and won even Mrs Bruce's approval.

'I ha'e nae patience wi' lassies that canna work except when you keep an eye on them,' she admitted, 'but I'll say this for you, Annie Rattray, you're a good worker.'

Bet Bowman, on the other hand, went into hysterics over the length of time that Annie spent on her tasks. 'Awa' and clean oot the closet,' she would cry, 'and that'll learn you to be quicker, for Miss Susan'll be in on you in twa ticks.' Yet she was glad enough to let Annie dust the drawing-room. 'A fyky, wearisome job,' she said; 'it fair scunners me.' So Annie shook out the ball fringe along the mantelpiece, flicked the dust from the satin antimacassars, and wiped the leaves of Miss Julia's palms. There were three kinds of these 'parlour palms,' and although Annie never learned their names she knew them intimately: one with darkish ribbon leaves, one with fans of sharp, lance-like leaves, and the third, reminding Annie of a Bible illustration, with a crown of glossy, five-pointed leaves above a tall, slender stem. This Biblical palm, which was really a castor-oil plant, set a seal upon the drawing-room; looking at it Annie felt awed by the sacred aloofness of the sanctuary in which it grew. For the drawing-room remained a Sabbath room although she entered it daily and although it gave her more work than all the other rooms put together; and sometimes, as she stood in contemplation before the Bible palm, Annie thought that it was a room in which the angels of God might have felt at home.

The Misses Carnegie, too, regarded the drawing-room as a place apart, where the elect sat with folded hands.

Miss Carnegie cast up the household accounts in her bedroom; she would not have dreamed of doing them in the drawing-room. Much as a devotee might hang offerings on an altar Miss Susan brought home 'finds' from the sales and set them in the drawing-room. Miss Julia painted her favourite arum lilies on every flat surface that could be decorated, and cherished an ambition to grow a real arum lily in a pot in some corner of the drawing-room. An arum lily, to Miss Julia, suggested the drawing-room as it suggested a church; the pure flawless white of the spathe was so holy and the pure gold of the spadix so like the sceptre of God. Miss Julia thought that when she was dead she would like arum lilies on her coffin, but it did not seem incongruous to have them painted on the drawing-room fire-screen and on the drawing-room antimacassars. Indeed, nothing in the drawing-room seemed incongruous to any member of the household, with the exception, perhaps, of Betty Bowman; and at first, not even to Annie, who had to dust and arrange them, did the multiplicity of knick-knacks and ornaments appear other than harmonious. It was left for a later generation—the generation in which Annie's children grew up—to look at the parlours and drawing-rooms of that age with different eyes.

The drawing-room in the Carnegies' house, in short, was not a room, but a symbol. Reduced to its simplest terms, what it symbolized was the age-old desire of humanity to avoid the isolation of independent thought by gathering round a family hearth. This traditional sentiment in favour of family life gathers the members of a family round a hearth that is at the same time an altar, for the family becomes a prototype of some universal family which has God for a Father, and thus Miss Julia's fire-screen is naturally an altar-piece, and the Carnegies' drawing-room becomes a kind of Christian equivalent for the household shrine. But no symbol remains simple throughout the ages, and the Misses Carnegie were not only Christians, but heirs of the Reformation; they were Protestants, and not only Protestants but Presbyterians, and not only Presbyterians but adherents of the Free Church of Scotland—a secession

within a secession from the universal family Church of the
Middle Ages. Thus they had inherited not only a broad
human desire for security in the bosom of a family,
but an exclusive and isolated private relation to God
which undermined that security. For a private relation
to God brings inevitably a private relation to the devil;
the isolated soul is equally at the mercy of both. God
becomes a threatened, that is to say, a vengeful God,
while the devil becomes more and more a menacing,
insidious figure; and whether they will or not, seceders
find themselves encamped in a position that is exposed on
both flanks, so that they dare not let anything pass without
first asking whether it comes from God or the devil. And
the devil is so cunning that the brightest colours, the most
alluring scents, the most seductive shapes must be suspect
unless they are obviously dedicated to a moral purpose;
consequently in the Carnegies' drawing-room the colours
were of a restrained soberness, the pictures were religious
or allegorical, the photograph albums looked like family
Bibles, sacred songs lay upon the piano, and books of pious
verse were arrayed on the small tables. One would have
said that the devil was effectually banned. Annie Rattray,
however, had really progressed farther than her mistresses
along the dangerous path of secession, for she had discarded
her own family, a step that a Miss Carnegie could never have
taken in any circumstances; and although she revered the
drawing-room she began to discover that there were things
in it, relics of past generations, apparently, of which she
did not approve and which she would have relegated to an
attic—such as a pair of naked men in bronze controlling
fiery bronze horses, and two vases with almost naked
nymphs painted upon them. Annie always turned these
vases round until each presented to the eye nothing but an
innocent spray of flowers; she could not do anything with
the bronze men, but she did not dust them so thoroughly
as she might have done. Miss Carnegie's crochet cottons,
too, were kept in an octagonal box-table, the top of which
was an inlaid draught-board. True, the draught-board was
never used, and Miss Carnegie's crochet could not be called
worldly since she crocheted nothing but little mats for the

drawing-room tables, yet Annie felt that the draught-table should have been excluded.

The drawing-room, however, was more than a sanctuary of Christian family life, more than a sober Presbyterian retreat from the seductions of the devil; it was also a room inhabited by women who were morbidly modest. Perhaps the renascence of family sentiment, in itself a bulwark against the threatening advance of intellectual emancipation, was responsible for this excessive modesty, since an exaggeration of sexual differences provides a constant titillation within the home that may help to retain the vagabond male within its precincts. In spite of its soberness, then, the drawing-room displayed an exaggerated modesty derived from its owners, who buttoned themselves up to the neck in tight-fitting bodices revealing the contours of their busts, and draped themselves down to the toes in skirts that emphasized the size of their buttocks. Whatever could be draped in the drawing-room was skilfully draped. The mantelpiece was draped with dark green plush and edged—perhaps not fortuitously—with ball fringe; the small tables were draped with dark green covers edged with ball fringe; the rosewood grand piano was draped with a Paisley shawl; the arm-chairs were discreetly draped with anti-macassars on top of their covers and broad valances at the foot; even the freedom of the door was hampered by a curtain of green plush edged with ball fringe. Only the draught-table and the thin, unvoluptuous legs of the small chairs were left undraped.

Moreover, the Misses Carnegie were not only women, they were ladies whose forebears had been wealthy for two generations. Their grandfather, by virtue of the same dangerous individualism that had made him a member of the Free Church with a private relation to God, had amassed a private fortune as a timber-merchant; his sawmill and woodyard were still flourishing in Calderwick. Along with a portion of his wealth the Misses Carnegie had inherited something else—the obligation to demean themselves in such a way that the world must approve their sudden rise to eminence; the obligation to be ladylike. They had to advertise their refinement and their wealth as well as their moral and religious principles. That was why there was a grand piano in the drawing-room and a litter of fragile but expensive knick-knacks on the occasional tables, which were themselves fragile and expensive. One of these tables was reserved for silver articles that were kept in a state of high polish and never put to any use. There was no æsthetic principle involved in the arrangement of the little boxes, baskets, bells, pagodas, candle-snuffers, paper-knives and curlicues that lay on the silver-table; the silver-table served the same purpose as Miss Julia's pearl earrings, and it could not have been for æsthetic reasons that she wore those, her ears being both large and red. A pagoda of ivory had a table to itself along with some carved African elephants; but these probably represented Miss Julia's interest in foreign missions rather than her degree of refinement. Nor were the sausage-like pads refined that were stuffed with sawdust and laid along the window-sashes, yet they gave the drawing-room its last touch of exclusiveness, for they excluded the common air.

Annie dusted and polished and tidied daily in the drawing-room, and imperceptibly the various influences which had created it sank into her personality. Little by little, too, she came to associate particular objects in it with one or other of her mistresses. The bronze men restraining their horses with fluttering bronze reins suggested Miss Susan and the fettering bracelet she wore; the draught-table and the silver-table were Miss Carnegie's, as were also the velvet-and-silver photograph frames. The piano, the books of poetry in limp leather bindings, the ivory pagoda beside the ebony elephants, and, of course, all the palms and arum lilies, were Miss Julia's.

Annie revered Miss Julia.

## THIRTEEN

It was not many weeks before Miss Julia rewarded Annie for her devotion by borrowing her from Mrs Bruce on Tuesday afternoons to help with the missionary work. Miss Julia organized collections for the London Missionary Society as well as for the Foreign Missions of the Free Church, and the London Missionary Society in its gratitude sent up batches of books for distribution to the successful collectors. These books were now unwrapped on the dining-room table, and Annie helped to check the list of collected moneys and to assign the prizes.

They were handsome books, rather thin, but large and well illustrated, with one of the most telling illustrations repeated in gilt upon the cover. This year's books were all about India; last year's had been China and the year before that Africa. Miss Julia had a whole row of them on a shelf, and she very kindly offered to lend one to Annie.

'Please, Miss Julia, can I have Africa?' Annie asked, for she saw upon its cover a slave-mother shaking her fist at a lion, the very slave-mother whose history Miss Julia had related in Sunday-school. There were other similar marvels in the book, Miss Julia assured her; it was full of lions, witchcraft, ordeals by poison, terrible beasts of prey and no less terrible superstitions. Africa was indeed a Dark Continent, and Miss Julia's voice took a deeper, a more solemn note as she expounded to Annie the degradation of the torrid zone. The map of Africa became a dark blot on the round belly of the earth, a devil's mark upon the belly of the earth. Annie and Miss Julia drew closer to each other over the polished table, and in their virgin minds hippopotami rolled their vast bulk, crocodiles heaved their obscene heads, insatiable lions sprang from cover, and cruelty, lewdness and murder roamed unchecked. It was a hot, savage night of lust that Miss Julia called up, as if tropical sunlight were a darkness that quenched the flickering ray of the human spirit, and the fervour of her imagination was not less startling than the unexpected, burning spear which the arum lily raises from its bridal spathe. The devil himself peered out from the tangled bush of Africa and dark motions in the undergrowth marked his attendant lions.

There is a saying: 'Who sups with the devil must have a long spoon,' and certainly Miss Julia showed Annie how to sup horrors with the devil by using a spoon long enough to keep him far away in Africa, or India, or China. One's blood might thicken and one's knees loosen, but it was a righteous indulgence, for even as one supped with the devil one praised the self-abnegation of the missionaries who were spreading the Light in these dark regions. Nor did Miss Julia confine herself to fantasies; she was indefatigable in presiding over the making of clothes for the poor, naked savages, and looked forward to the day when there would not be one undraped child of darkness left in the whole of the mission field.

Annie enjoyed these Tuesday afternoons. She had plenty of work to do, for besides the collecting-lists there were the garments to be cut out for the church ladies who sewed them on Wednesdays, and seams had to be pressed and rolls of material checked. Annie worked busily and listened to Miss Julia as she described the horrors of heathendom. The support of foreign missions, Miss Julia thought, was a holy duty that should especially commend itself to the female sex. A woman's place was certainly the home, but without in any way quitting their proper spheres women could quite well exert themselves to influence a larger circle than that around the domestic hearth . . . Look at the dear Queen, how truly she was the Mother of her People!

With an insistent anxiety Miss Julia proved again and again that a woman could be a mother in spirit although she was not a mother in fact. And through all her tortuous self-justification there ran the praise of self-abnegation, of self-sacrifice, as if the assertion of the self were one of the worst temptations that could beset a woman, and as if perfect motherhood involved complete self-effacement.

Annie listened in silence, but confusion began to invade her mind. Miss Julia spoke with authority, and yet the queenliness of self-abnegation was not the queenliness of which Annie Rattray had dreamed . . . But Miss Julia said the influence of a good woman was the most powerful on earth; every great man in history had been inspired by some noble woman, and the sanctity of family life, on which all true righteousness depended, was committed exclusively to the hands of the female sex. It was a great, a solemn destiny to be a woman, and every woman must therefore be more scrupulous in moral and religious obligations than any member of the opposite sex . . .

Miss Julia never forgot that Annie was a young female immortal committed to her charge, and she repeated assiduously those sentiments which were designed to keep her pupil in the straight path of female propriety. In other words, by a natural transition, Miss Julia led Annie from the sultry passions of heathendom to reflect upon her own sexual functions as a potential wife and mother.

## FOURTEEN

The influences of the drawing-room and of Miss Julia's
obsession with sex were further strengthened by Bet
Bowman's taunts. Annie was finding it easier and easier
to express her contemptuous disapproval of Bet Bowman
without saying a word. The curled lip, the shrugged
shoulder, the deaf ear are more effective than words,
and Annie's self-righteous silence exasperated Bowman
sufficiently. 'You're getting a face on you wad turn milk
soor,' she said. 'You'll be anither auld maid like the lave o'
them in this house.' In season and out of season she flung
at Annie's head a song which had for its refrain:

> 'O-oh dear, what shall I do
> If I die an auld maid in a ga-arret?'

These taunts about old maids increased the confusion
in Annie's mind. For in the kingdom of heaven, towards
which she was striving, there was no marrying or giving
in marriage—did not the Bible say so?—and in her retreat
from the lower regions she was undoubtedly coming nearer
and nearer to a spiritual garret if not to an actual one. And
yet while one remained on earth 'old maid' was a term of
reproach, and marriage was a Christian sacrament, and a
good woman had to have a family over which to exert her
influence. It was obscurely confusing, and Annie's ordered
categories were tangled up. For marriage was associated
with the devil's mark upon one's body, and how was one
to keep the devil out of it? Besides, the taunt of 'old maid'
cut clean across all divisions between good and evil; it was
an irrelevant taunt, and Annie saw no way of countering
it. Theories which accounted for everything else failed
completely to take the sting out of Bet Bowman's words.

74

For instance, one could righteously condemn Betty's private untidiness on the assumption that it betrayed her bondage to the devil, since the devil is incapable of consistent virtue; on that assumption it is clearly reprehensible for a parlour-maid to keep her own things in a state of fiendish disorder. Yet even Mrs Bruce, when she declared that the contents of Betty's drawers in the tallboy looked like nothing but fish-guts, was left speechless by the retort: 'I'm no' one o' your auld maids. And you needna tell me you're no' an auld maid either, for a'body kens that your man ran awa' after you hadna been twa months married, and he's never come back to this day, and no wonder! Life's no' worth living if it has to be a' tidy.' And in a way that admitted of no further argument Betty slammed the offending drawers shut.

Annie could not rescue Mrs Bruce; she could not think of anything to say, and had to content herself by looking like one who is martyred for righteousness' sake. But Bet Bowman's taunts stung her as no sneers at her righteousness could have done. One might be as righteous as Miss Julia and yet remain an old maid, and to remain an old maid was obscurely disgraceful. It was a perplexing dilemma.

About this time Annie began to be troubled by nightmares. Bet Bowman, as was to be expected of such a devil's buckie, was an unquiet sleeper, and at some hour in the dead of night her swaddled hotwater pig would fall thumping on the floor, awaking Annie with a start. In the morning Annie forgot her dreams, but at that hour in the night she would start awake in terror, pursued by some horrible monster that was moving behind her in an impenetrable darkness of undergrowth or of deep water, a resistant darkness through which she had to fight her way, struggling, while the monster—was it a lion?—gained upon her stride by stride, until she awoke with her ears buzzing and her mouth dry with fright. Or she was being forced up a long and narrow passage where the walls closed in upon her, with monstrous shapes on her heels, and she would awake groping in her bed for some way out. The terror of these nightmares did not abate even before the name of God. Annie would lie shaken and trembling for what seemed long hours before she was calm enough to pray to God and fall asleep again. Strangely enough, if she happened to think of Miss Julia, whose bed-room was just under the floor, her terror faded more quickly. Miss Julia's presence was nearer and more comforting than God's. It was as if she were being tormented by something which had nothing to do with her private relation to God, something which was both obscure and irrelevant, like Bet Bowman's taunts, and yet could not be swept aside.

It accompanied her even to St James's Church, where the congregation were gathered together as brothers and sisters in the Lord, and where thoughts about old maids were surely out of place. On Sunday evenings Annie and Mrs Bruce sat at one end of the Carnegies' pew, divided from the three ladies by a small round pillar no thicker than a lamp-post. Annie sat close to the pillar, for Miss Julia was on the other side of it, and she could smell the Sunday perfume of Miss Julia's gloves and handkerchief. The Carnegies' pew was luxuriously cushioned in red cloth and was fitted with a private box for Bibles and hymn-books; it was one of the superior pews in the church and was set well back from the pulpit. In such a pew Annie Rattray should have been content to feel herself more intimately a daughter of God than when she had to sit on the bare pitch-pine in the cheap side pew by the choir railing. Yet even there, on her red cushion, sitting between Mrs Bruce and Miss Julia, she found herself thinking that the Carnegies' pew would have gained in dignity had there been an elder at the end of it instead of Miss Susan. Miss Susan's black moustache and stout walking-stick were poor substitutes for an elder's beard and an elder's silver-handled umbrella. Not even Miss Susan, who tramped about to auction sales just like a man, could stand beside the collection plate at the door or carry round the bread and wine on Communion Sundays. Looking at the ranks of serried Christian families, each one decently disposed in its pew with a husband and father, probably an elder or a deacon, guarding the entrance, so that every gangway was fringed with solemn men in black broadcloth, Annie felt that the red cushions and the perfume on Miss Julia's gloves could not make the Carnegies' pew anything but an open and unguarded seatful of old maids . . . Any matron in the church, sitting comfortably beside her lawful husband, could despise Miss Carnegie and Miss Susan Carnegie and Miss Julia Carnegie—three old maids.

Annie sat up more straightly on her cushion, and moved a little farther away from Miss Julia. The Carnegies' pew was in a commanding position; one could see and be seen. She would let them all see that *she* wasn't to be despised. *She* wasn't an old maid. Nobody should be able to point the finger of scorn at *her*. And the next time Bet Bowman said 'auld maid' she would answer: 'You're anither.' Besides, she would say: 'It's better to be an auld maid and get to heaven than to marry a black and be a black yourself and go to hell. Set you up,' she would say, 'you and your auld maids; you've had a lad for a gey long time and he hasna offered to marry you yet, and if he did he's juist a black, anyway . . .' For Bet Bowman had a sweetheart, a grocer's assistant from the High Street. On Sunday evenings Bet went out ostensibly to the Parish Kirk, but Mrs Bruce and Annie had their suspicions about that. It was not divine service for which Bet exchanged her domestic service on Sunday evenings; no, she prinked herself up for man, not for God; and when she stood whispering with a lad at the back door it wasn't from the Kirk they had come, more likely from the Muckle Howe on the links. 'Bet Bowman should think shame o' hersel',' Mrs Bruce had said more than once . . . Annie remembered her father giving Jean Lamont a dry shave on the kitchen bed. Kissing and cuddling were disgraceful unless you were married. It was like getting into bed without saying your prayers . . . Maybe when you got married the devil's mark faded away.

Annie looked again at the decent fathers and mothers of families sitting so majestically around her. Would they dare to come to church if they had commerce with the devil? It might not be safe to marry an ordinary man, but if one married an elder or a deacon surely one would be armoured against the devil and his suggestions.

## FIFTEEN

On that Sunday evening in church Annie had moved away from Miss Julia, and now she was divided from her by more than the thickness of a pillar. She had the strange feeling of looking at things through two eyes that would not focus, and her mistress's Tuesday confidences only increased the discrepancy.

Miss Julia's stock of mission stories had come to an end, but she was unwilling to renounce the pleasurable excitement she had experienced in telling them, and her conversation now was becoming undeniably confidential and intimate. She had a sense of guilt in being so intimate with a servant, even although Annie was her equal before God, and she would break off abruptly whenever one of her sisters chanced to come into the dining-room. Indeed, Susan had burst in one day just as she was on the point of telling Annie that a gentleman had once proposed to her and that she had considered it her duty to refuse him because he was not a Christian. Susan had interrupted her only in the nick of time, and Miss Julia had felt as she used to feel when dear papa caught her reading a novel. Since then she had tried to be severely impersonal, and fell back on discussing with Annie those extracts from the daily newspapers which Miss Carnegie and Miss Susan permitted their younger sister to read; but the personal note *would* intrude—the dear child was so devoted to her—and, after all, was she not entitled to give her charge the benefit of her experience?

'There is a new spirit of self-seeking arising in the country, Annie,' she said one day. 'You will not have heard of it, but there is a great strike in London. The dock-labourers are refusing to unload even food from the ships. I don't think it could happen in Scotland, for Scotland is still a God-fearing

78

country. But the English working-men are drinking and gambling so much, I hear, that they can think of nothing but getting more money for themselves . . . And a Roman Catholic cardinal is actually encouraging the men to strike! I wonder—can it be a Catholic plot to upset Britain?'

Miss Julia's eyes brightened. Rome was the Scarlet Woman, and whenever she thought of Rome Miss Julia thought of pomp, idolatry and seduction. The Roman Church was a good substitute for heathendom, and in her 'solemn' voice she began to recount its errors. It was an institution that drugged its worshippers into acquiescence by a cynical exploitation of sensuous, even theatrical effects—crucifixes and altars with wax candles and incense, Miss Julia had heard, which was even more stupefying than tobacco or—or—what was that drug?—hashish. 'They don't dare to let their people read the Bible for themselves,' said Miss Julia, working herself up. 'Roman Catholics have to believe only what the priest tells them. The priests set themselves up between the congregation and God. My dear Annie, we are greatly privileged in belonging to a Church that recognizes every worshipper's right to private communion with the Almighty.'

This assertion of individual rights, had Miss Julia been capable of regarding it objectively, might have appeared to her as dangerous as the self-seeking of the English working-classes, for it was part of the same historical process. But she went on to remark that the English Church was nearly as bad as Rome—from what she heard—and that it was no wonder if the English took to drink and gambling, or if a cardinal should think that England was ripe for Roman intervention. The English chanted set prayers in an artificial voice instead of speaking simply and directly to God, and their churches, too, were bedizened with crosses and candles. The one thing they did *not* do was to worship the Virgin Mary; otherwise they could hardly be called Protestants at all.

The worship paid to the Holy Family, had Miss Julia been capable of regarding that objectively, might have appeared to her as desirable as the reverence she herself felt for Christian family life. But it was in complete unconsciousness

that she passed over to Annie her conflicting prejudices:
it was wicked to worship an idealized mother, but one
must worship the ideal of motherhood; it was wicked
to recognize any authority save God's, but one must
submit to those in authority, provided that they were
not priests. Annie's confusing sensation of being out of
focus became intensified; her first simple dilemma—wife
or old maid?—was turning into a many-headed monster of
a dilemma, and to help herself she fixed her mental eye on
one half of Miss Julia's statements while ignoring the other
half. And when Miss Julia, perhaps unwittingly drawn to the
question by her hot championship of a God who excluded
the feminine attribute of motherhood, presently asked: 'By
the way, how is your dear mother?' Annie in her confusion
told a deliberate lie. 'My mother's very well, thank you, and
wishes to be kindly remembered to you.' It was a black lie,
for Annie had not once returned to Mill Wynd to see her
mother or her father or her sister.

'I hope she will be spared to you for many a day. You'll
miss her when she's gone, Annie. I know what that means,
for I am the youngest of our family, and I have seen so many
of my near and dear ones pass over to the other side. But
we shall all be united in God, I trust, when we rise again
on the Last Day.' Miss Julia took out a fine handkerchief
and dabbed her eyes.

Annie's discomfort and embarrassment were not entirely
due to her mental confusion, or to Miss Julia's show of
emotion, or to the prospect of facing her family on the Last
Day. She had told a lie, and terror was mounting within her.
On the Last Day when she stood before God a Voice would
cry aloud: 'Annie Rattray told a deliberate lie to Miss Julia.'
And for that lie she might be hurled into hell . . . Annie felt
as if she were tottering on a tight-rope over an abyss. Had
she taken a false step, or was there still time to retrieve it?
Could she clutch at Miss Julia's hand and confess her sin
and find her balance again? But suddenly, as she looked at
Miss Julia, she knew that it was of no use to confess the lie
to her; she had a momentary but keen intuition that Miss
Julia was more confused than herself, and her pride forbade
her to humiliate herself before such a person. A muddled

old maid! If she had told a lie it was because Miss Julia was
not capable of understanding the truth. If she had told a lie,
confession to Miss Julia might appease her conscience, but
it would destroy her pride. If she had told a lie, the matter
was between herself and God . . . no priest was needed.
And had she really told a lie? Could she not make the
lie a truth by going to see her mother that evening? In
that moment Annie took a farther step away from Miss
Julia along the dangerous path of independence. It was her
own conscience that had to guide her—Miss Julia had said
so—and although many things that Miss Julia said found
no ratification in Annie's heart this doctrine of the soul's
single responsibility to God, and to God alone, penetrated
into her heart as well as into her head and joined itself to
the private dream of supremacy which had never ceased
to inform the very core of her personality. Annie was once
more securely poised on her tight-rope.

'Yes, Miss Julia,' she said, with downcast eyes.

After tea she begged half an hour's leave from Mrs Bruce
to go to see her mother. For the lie, even though it were an
expedient lie, must be cancelled; her conscience told her
that. Annie's conscience and Annie's pride were entering
into a strange alliance, for she was inclined to feel angry
with God because He had permitted her to tell a lie. Little
by little she was inverting her attitude towards God. On the
railway bridge she had felt uplifted because He had singled
her out, but now she was beginning to feel that she had
singled Him out, and that He had no right to fail her.

The basement kitchen in Mill Wynd looked as if all
these months had left it unchanged, except that it was
smaller and more noisome than Annie remembered it.
Mary was titivating her hair at the glass on the mantelpiece, Jim Rattray was lolling beside the damped-down
fire, Mrs Rattray was taking off her apron to run outbye
and have a crack with somebody.

'I was just wondering when you'd have the grace to come
and see if we were living or dead,' said Mrs Rattray. 'Do
you like your place?'

'Ay,' said Annie.

'Are you getting on weel?'

'Ay,' said Annie.

'I'll warrant they're pernickety, the three madams?'

'No' very.'

'I'm hearing they have a grand piano?'

'Ay.'

'Wha plays on it?'

'Miss Julia.'

'Do they have a late dinner at nights?'

'Ay.'

The catechism was a long one, and Annie continued to answer in reluctant monosyllables. But presently her mother said:

'Weel, it seems to agree wi' you fine; you've grown fatter; you're no' sic a skinny-ma-link as you were.'

'High living,' put in Mary.

'Have you gotten your first quarter's wages?' asked Jim.

'Ay,' said Annie.

'Let's see a bawbee or twa o't; I could be daein' fine wi' some siller.'

'It's in the Savings Bank.'

Jim laid down his cutty and turned round:

'In the Savings Bank!'

'Ay.'

'Here's your faither been oot o' work for near three weeks,' cried Mrs Rattray, 'and you never sae muckle as thocht o' bringing a sixpence into the hoose!'

Annie said nothing.

'But you could maybe speir aboot a job for him in the Carnegies' yaird?'

'I wadna like,' said Annie.

Jim was still staring in amazement at his daughter:

'In the Savings Bank! And you no' sixteen yet! Dod, you'll be a naggin' bitch, just like your mother.'

Mrs Rattray turned on him:

'And what wad *you* do wi' the pickle bawbees, tell me that? You canna get the drink fast enough down your gullet. The lassie has a perfect right to bank her bit money.'

'It was Miss Julia banked it for me,' said Annie.

'Ay weel, I thocht you hadna the gumption to do it yoursel'. Are the Carnegies no' gaun awa' for a holiday?'

'No' yet. There's a lawyer cousin coming for a whilie.'

'Whatten a cousin will that be, now?'

'I didna speir.'

'You didna speir, and you wadna like, and you dinna ken! You've turned gey mim among your three auld maids.'

'I'd better be getting back,' said Annie. 'Mrs Bruce'll be needing me.'

Mrs Rattray's voice became falsely hearty:

'Ay weel, it's a good place you've gotten; see and stick to't. Tell Miss Julia I asked to be kindly remembered to her, and Mrs Bruce too.'

Annie was startled, and her resentment at her mother's comments gave way before a rush of exultation. God had put the very words into her mother's mouth! She hadn't told Miss Julia a lie after all; she had only anticipated the truth. On the Last Day, when she stood before God, her record would be unblemished. And that meant that she could depend on herself, for God must be guiding her . . .

Mr Boyd's assertion that law and order were inherent in the constitution of the universe, her own intuition as she stood on the railway bridge that there were lines on which one's life could move with certainty, Miss Julia's repeated assurance that the individual soul was in direct contact with the Almighty—all these ideas were fused together in the heat of that moment, and Annie sped back to the Carnegies' house in a glow of triumphant power, exactly as if she were an engine driven by God along lines securely laid down since the beginning of the world, an inviolate track that led straight to heaven.

## SIXTEEN

But Annie's journey to heaven was bound to be a solitary journey. For death is a solitary adventure, and any journey towards a heaven in the sky must first pass the frontier station of death. Moreover, only those who profess themselves aliens on this side of the frontier may pass it successfully, and where all are strangers it is best to keep oneself to oneself. Annie did not accept this isolation without a struggle; it grew upon her almost imperceptibly at first; finally it even terrified her, so that she was tempted to abandon her singleness.

She was aware of it in church, for instance, when she felt uneasy instead of secure in the fold of the congregation. The six hundred eyes that seemed to be fixed on her in derision as she sat in a defenceless pewful of old maids belonged, after all, to people who were booked for heaven by the same train as herself. Yet she had an intuition that the tickets, although booked by the Free Church, carried no guarantee of safe arrival, and that many of her fellow-passengers would be turned back. She preferred, as it were, to stray along the corridor by herself, seeking a favoured place farther forward, as near as possible to the invisible Driver. And this she could better accomplish in the privacy of the Carnegies' house, especially when she was alone in the drawing-room, in which she now spent more time than ever.

She began to cold-shoulder her nearest fellow-passengers; they were light-minded, all of them. Yes, even Miss Julia; for although she did not go flying here and there in search of auction-sales, like Miss Susan, she had a regrettable habit of strolling aimlessly down the High Street every morning, literally walking the streets and exposing herself to the devil.

Miss Julia was also aware that these strolls needed some apology, for she never left the house without advertising some excuse for her departure, explaining that there was something she lacked and must seek outside—what could it be? 'I'm just going out to get another ball of cotton,' she would conclude, or, 'Dear me, I find I must take this brooch to Mr Aitken to have a new pin put on.' Annie received the apologies without comment, but she felt that Miss Julia had no call to go gadding. Within the four walls of the house she herself was content to remain, and it was only the like of Bet Bowman who would complain that the place was like a family vault, and that another year of it would be the death of her. Within the four walls of a Christian house one could be as if alone with God.

But the very intensity with which Annie experienced the presence of God brought her rapidly to the discovery that its solemnity was one with the dread solemnity of death. There were nights when she awoke with a start in the darkness, quaking with the fear that she might die before morning—nights when God was no longer securely and warmly enclosed within herself, nor even roofed in under the spire of a church. In the featureless vast of the night God's infinite majesty escaped all bounds, even those of distant heaven, and came close upon her, pressing her to insignificance; and whatever the certainties of her soul, her body in those terrible moments knew only the certainty of death. It was a fear in which all lesser fears were swallowed up; it was like a flood loosed upon her to which she could oppose nothing save a pin-point of agonized consciousness. That fear could not be exorcised by Miss Julia's presence in the bedroom below; nothing, it seemed, could exorcise it, and all that Annie could do was to endure it, setting her teeth, with a grim satisfaction in the thought that if she could endure that she could endure anything.

Her solitariness at these moments was absolute, and that gave her a steel-like hardness of resistance. On Sundays she looked the matrons of the congregation full in the eye. But an apparently insignificant occurrence relieved her constriction, and became Annie's first temptation to stray from the single, narrow path she had set herself to follow. The Carnegies' cousin arrived for a fortnight's golfing holiday. He proved to be a cousin on the mother's side, and a lawyer—a douce, quiet body, said Mrs Bruce, and an awful nice mannie. Annie did not think much about him on the Saturday evening when he came, but next day in church she was amazed at the sense of relief that pervaded her whenever she looked at him, sitting there so spruce at the end of the pew, with his good black coat, stiff white collar and smoothly brushed grey head; she felt proud to be in the same seat with a man who was so reverend and respectable. The whole pew seemed to be blooming with an unusual softness and grace; even Miss Susan looked less defiant, for she was wearing a veil that hid her moustache, and with her ample curves and the thick gold chain on her bosom she might have passed for the decent, kindly wife of the man beside her. As for Miss Julia, she had donned a split-new toque with purple velvet flowers in it.

Annie turned several times and peeped round the pillar to satisfy herself with the sight of the lawyer. Some sternly watchful eye in the back of her head began to close drowsily, and she dropped into a reverie. By the time the sermon was ended she was feeling warm and happy, although she had not heard a word of it, and when the precentor raised his tuning-fork the hymn that was sung made her heart turn over in her bosom:

> Faint not nor fear,
> His arm is near.
> He changeth not, and thou art dear . . .

Annie stopped singing and bent her head over the hymn-book. It was a clear sign from God, a sign that one day she would sit in church beside an elder who was her lawful wedded husband, a dignified and honoured partner in a dignified Christian marriage. Her fear of death, her fear of the terrifying, featureless God Who pressed so close upon her in the night, went up like a fume on the music of the hymn; it was as if a constricting, endless ring had gently uncoiled into a spiral, pushing Death and that terrible God of Death into the far depths of the sky, leaving only an accessible, friendly Father within her reach, a Father Who did not insist that His daughters must be old maids. She went to bed that night without any terrors.

The new liveliness and warmth that had stirred in the pew on Sunday filled the house during the course of the lawyer's visit. On weekdays, it was true, he was not so reverend, for he wore a golfing suit covered with wide brown checks, and Annie disliked those checks as she disliked cross-purposes. Bet Bowman, on the other hand, ran about with a grin of pleasure whenever the checks appeared in the dining-room, and her main burden was: 'Eh, isn't it fine to have a man aboot the hoose!'

'He should wear his decent blacks,' insisted Annie. 'Thae checks look like a mill-lassie's shawlie.'

What else, of course, could one expect of a suit that was used for the golf, for divagations over the wild waste of the links, where the Muckle Howe drew Bet into its sinister hollow on Sunday evenings? Those wild and shaggy dunes were more inimical to modesty than paved streets; and yet perhaps a man-body could risk his modesty more safely than a woman, and if he was busy thrusting a wee white ball into a hole he was kept out of other mischief. Had it been Miss Julia, or even Miss Susan, now, who put on a checked suit and went out daily with a bag of golf-clubs there might have been cause for scandal. But the lawyer was a decent man in spite of his golf, and although Annie regretted the brown checks she was pleased to feel his presence in the house. Everybody was pleased. Miss Susan, to be sure, was hard put to it, for she dared not pull the upstairs watercloset plug while a man was within hearing, and so she was compelled to come through the kitchen to the back yard. But that only added to the graceless Betty's pleasure, and in any case Miss Susan enjoyed having the lawyer to argue with at table. Miss Carnegie showed her pleasure in a characteristic manner; she abused the kitchen staff for hanging out underwear to dry in the back yard, on which the spare bedroom window looked out. 'Drawers and nightgowns hanging there under the man's very nose!' she said indignantly. 'Whatna kind of house will he think this is?' Miss Julia, too, was pleased, and in the evenings sang songs of Mrs Hemans's which had been lying forgotten inside the piano-seat. But it was Bet

Bowman, after all, who got the most fun out of the visitor, and this brought her into open collision with Annie.

The lawyer was always down for breakfast at least half an hour before the ladies. He accused his cousins of laziness, lying abed so late. How was he to guess that they were listening anxiously behind their doors, drawing their dressing-gowns close, to hear him go downstairs before they ventured to the bathroom? Betty knew, however, and she took full advantage of the situation.

'Here's your porridge,' she would say, 'you'd better sup them now, for the leddies tak' a long time aboot their affairs.' Or she would remark demurely: 'Dinna be late for your golf the day. I canna think what Miss Susan's daein' upstairs a' this time, I'm sure.'

One morning when Betty came giggling into the kitchen to report what she had just said Annie flared up in sudden anger: 'A fine way to speak to a decent man! You're just like an animal, Bet Bowman.' The parlour-maid flared up in her turn: 'You keep a civil tongue in your heid when you speak to me. If I get any o' your impidence, as sure's death I'll get Miss Susan to give you the sack!'

'And as sure's death I'll tell Miss Susan what you've been saying aboot her—'

'Haud your tongues, the pair o' you,' said Mrs Bruce. 'If anybody gets the sack it'll be you, Bet Bowman, for your ill-scrapit tongue.'

Bet Bowman, like a tap that could not be turned off, went on muttering about folk who wad have you think that butter couldna melt in their mouths but had drucken faithers and came out of homes like pigsties. These thrusts, however, did not pierce Annie's armour, for she was no longer Jim Rattray's daughter, and she was already regretting that she had not left Bet Bowman to the vengeance of God. 'As sure's death!' Bet had said, and God might have struck her dead that minute . . .

The lawyer, decent man, would have been amazed to learn that the kitchen was divided against itself on his behalf, and that Annie Rattray felt a proprietary interest in him and his Sunday blacks. Had he known all that he stood for in Annie's mind he would not have donned the brown checks

so lightly nor would he have bestowed a special half-crown
on Bet when he went away. This last unwitting action of his
roused in Annie all the jealous wrath and disappointment
that conjugal infidelity provokes. She was angry with herself
for having hung her dreams on such an unworthy figure,
and as for Bet, she was sure that the anger of God must
strike down Bet Bowman; as sure as death.

This unmerited rebuff threw Annie again into her
constricting solitude, and she was again obsessed by
thoughts of death and the Judgment. If only God would
strike down Bet Bowman, she thought, He would still be
her Father and she would have a foretaste of her final
triumph. It was Miss Susan who was suddenly struck
down, however, some months later, and the vicariousness
of this punishment bewildered Annie at first. Yet there was
some kind of a devil's bond between Betty and Miss Susan,
and it certainly served Miss Susan right that she should
come to grief while attending a farm roup. If an outraged
stot knocked her down and broke her leg for her it was
a judgment of God on her for being there at all . . . She
would never be able to walk five miles again, and hirpling
to church would set her better . . .

Miss Susan was brought home in a turnip-cart and
hoisted upstairs by two embarrassed men who stank
of cow-dung and defaced the stairs with their dirty,
tackety boots. Annie scrubbed the paint white again,
and thought that it was just like Miss Susan to bring
the stink and dirt of a farm-yard into the house. But Betty
actually blubbered, and Miss Susan sent her sisters out
of her bedroom with a flea in their lugs and demanded
Betty—Bet Bowman, if you please!—to wait upon her. It
was obvious that they both knew that Miss Susan was
in a sense taking Bet Bowman's punishment upon her
as well as her own . . . The secret bond was becoming
apparent.

Betty came and went with a new importance and a show
of solicitude for her patient that did not deceive Annie.
'Internal injuries, the doctor says, as weel as the leg . . .
Puir auld creature.' And of course Betty supported her
accomplice in her refusal to have a nurse. 'I can gi'e the

creature the bed-pan as weel as onybody,' she declared. 'But, oh, mind ye, she's sair hurt.'

Miss Julia, indeed, feared the worst for her sister. 'In the midst of life we are in death, Annie,' she said; and even Miss Carnegie found it difficult to get through the chapter which she read at family prayers instead of Miss Susan, her chin trembled so much. Only Bet Bowman remained undaunted: 'Die? She'll no' die o' a bit dunt.' But Annie knew that the guilty Bet was trying to minimize Miss Susan's punishment for her own sake. The day came when Betty was thrust out weeping, and a trained nurse took charge and kept the patient drugged with morphia. The whole house was hushed and the imminence of death brought God very near. It seemed almost sacrilegious to make a sound of any kind. And when it was reported downstairs that Miss Susan had 'slippit awa',' Annie was shocked at the snivelling noise Bet Bowman made.

They were all permitted to look at Miss Susan in her coffin. Among the white frills the dead woman's face was strangely chapfallen and the blunt nose was sharpened so that it hardly looked like Miss Susan at all, but Annie's heart fluttered painfully when she saw the familiar black moustache, blacker and more conspicuous than ever, the enduring mark of the devil upon the cold clay of the corpse. Miss Julia had massed arum lilies around the coffin, but in that moment Annie realized that they were quite in vain; it was only Miss Susan's body that was quiet and serene, and not all the affection of her sisters could stand between her and the wrath of God. Annie's terrifying sense of solitariness rose round her again like a wall of ice, and when she was cowering in bed she had the odd, inexplicable fancy that if Miss Susan had only married the lawyer she would not have grown the moustache and it would have been all right.

The lawyer cousin came to the funeral in his decent blacks, along with Mr William Carnegie and an array of other gentlemen. Bet Bowman peeped from under the kitchen blind to see the cabs and had to be pulled away from the window by Mrs Bruce. 'You heartless hizzy!' said the cook. 'Her that's awa' no' cauld in her coffin yet, and you peekin' oot at the gentlemen!' 'Miss Susan was the only one I aye liked,' blubbered Bet; 'she was the only one in this house that aye had a cheery word for a body.' Annie drew down the corners of her mouth. What a liar and hypocrite Bet Bowman was! And she needn't be hoping to catch the lawyer's attention, he hadn't so much as looked her way this time. He had not looked Annie's way either, but little she cared for that. He was just a silly body who would give half-crowns to a limmer like Bet.

But the limmer got more than a crown out of the lawyer's visit on this occasion, for when he read the will it became known that Miss Susan had left fifty pounds to Betty. Fifty pounds! And yet Annie was less surprised than Mrs Bruce. She had always known that Bet and Miss Susan were in the one cart, and she was not surprised, no, she was not surprised. Mrs Bruce herself would hear no disparagement of the dead: 'Her that's awa'' would think that Miss Carnegie would be making some provision for me, you ken; and maybe she will, I'm no' saying. I'm no' lippening to it, you ken, Annie, but her that's awa', puir thing, she would be thinking that naebody else would gi'e that Bet Bowman a bawbee, except only hersel'...'

But fifty pounds! And only twenty-five pounds for Mrs Bruce, who had served the dead woman for fifteen years and more! Five pounds to Annie Rattray was equitable enough, but to leave Bet Bowman fifty pounds! If I was Bet Bowman, thought Annie, I wouldna touch the money, I would give it to foreign missions or something ... Annie shuddered at the memory of that black devil's mark on the dead white face; no, she would not touch her own five pounds, she would offer them to Miss Julia for the missions. It was money that needed to be sanctified, if ever money did.

Miss Julia, however, put her hand on Annie's shoulder and said: 'It's like you, my dear, to make such an offer, but this is a sacrifice that the Lord does not demand of you ... You're a dear, good girl, Annie—' She broke off and began to cry, still keeping her hand on Annie's shoulder. 'Oh, Annie, Annie,' she sobbed, 'when Matilda goes I shall be left all alone...' Annie was deeply embarrassed. The pressure of Miss Julia's hand was like a demand for sympathy, but

no amount of sympathy would make her any the less alone
on the Judgment Day, and she would have to stand alone
before God even if she had had twenty sisters. Not even if she
had a husband to keep her company in the night could she be
anything but alone when the night of death came upon her
. . . A flicker of anger shot through Annie's embarrassment.
She felt like saying: 'This isn't Christian-like behaviour!'
Her shoulder grew hard and resistant under Miss Julia's
pressure; she would have liked to shake off the hand that
rested there. Miss Julia was behaving like a silly bairn. Annie
felt like saying: 'I'll give you something to greet for!' But her
embarrassment kept her silent, since it was just possible that
Miss Julia was really crying because her sister had gone to
hell and she lacked the courage to admit that she knew it.
Miss Julia, after all, was not such a good Christian as Annie
Rattray.

## SEVENTEEN

So Annie's silence affirmed the solitariness of Miss Julia, the solitariness, indeed, of every human soul, herself included. Miss Julia's vague resentment of it made her extremely dignified; she dabbed her eyes and said: 'Go upstairs for my smelling-salts, Annie.' The alacrity with which Annie went reinforced her mistress's dignity, and for the rest of that afternoon Miss Julia Carnegie issued commands instead of sentiments, and reflected, not without pride, that if dear Susan were watching from heaven she would approve.

But the knowledge, conveyed by Annie Rattray's hard, unyielding shoulder, that she was solitary began to weigh on Miss Julia. Matilda was growing quite deaf and had to be shouted at; she had failed much since Susan's illness and sometimes seemed to forget that Julia was there at all, as if she had taken leave of both sisters on the day that Susan died. There were long hours during which Miss Julia sat alone in the drawing-room doing nothing. Annie continued to present a wall of rectitude that baffled advances. She was perfectly respectful and even submissive, saying, 'Yes, Miss Julia,' with proper meekness; yet it was the submissiveness of a flexible but restraining corset. All her life Miss Julia had been morally corseted, first by her father and then by her sister Susan, and now Annie Rattray was implacably supporting her in her duty as a Christian lady. Miss Julia involuntarily sat up very straight and became more dignified in manner when she was directing Annie, but she was doing less and less of the actual mission work, and sometimes she grew peevish, making Annie do a seam twice or scolding her sharply for some trifling disarrangement of the paper scraps on which the collectors' lists were noted. These lapses she tried to atone for afterwards by praising Annie lavishly, but her sense of dissatisfaction grew.

In the kitchen Annie's silent rectitude was not so formidable, since Mrs Bruce depended on no approval save Miss Carnegie's, and Bet Bowman, as everybody said, was neither to hold nor to bind now that fifty pounds were coming to her. She made no secret of her intention to give notice and get married as soon as she got the money, and it became tacitly accepted that Annie, despite her youth, was to be promoted in her place. It may have been in anticipation of this step, or simply because she felt more adult than Miss Julia, that Annie decided to put up her hair. She coiled her two long plaits round the back of her head, and the mass of braids gave proportion to her long profile. She made quite a handsome young woman, with her clear pale skin and her dark eyes and hair; she was slim but not scraggy, and while she was sitting down appeared taller and more dignified than Bet Bowman. It was only when Annie stood up that her impressiveness fell away, for her legs were still too short and her feet ridiculously small. But she was as neat as Betty, if neither so tall nor so smart, and with her skirts down to her ankles she looked all at once more like twenty than fifteen.

'Why, Annie, you've grown up,' said Miss Julia. There was something peevish in her tone, as if she saw a ruthless individuality emerging out of the comfortable levels around her. Yet one could hardly accuse Annie of anything definite; she was quietly ruthless, if she was ruthless, and her rectitude was unimpeachable. Miss Julia could not dismiss a servant for rectitude, a spiritual daughter of her own, too, from her own Sunday-school class, but there were times when she said with curious emphasis: 'I'm sure I don't know what I'd do without you, Annie.'

Perhaps in obedience to Annie's inaudible suggestions Miss Julia turned at first to the most blameless occupations during the idle hours when she sat in the drawing-room alone. She read her Bible diligently, for instance, and marked with red ink all the promises she could find in it. Not without reason, however, had Annie distrusted those morning strolls in the town, for there came a day when

Miss Julia, having tracked down every promise in the Bible and feeling the need of fresh reading-matter, entered the Calderwick Subscription Library and thereafter spent much of her time in a most regrettable fashion. The recollection of what her papa and Susan had said about novel-reading should have deterred her, but it only succeeded in making her remove the novels in the evening to her bedroom so that Annie might not find them lying in the drawing-room next morning. And if she did discover in the fiction she read ruthless young heroines asserting themselves unduly, she was at least comforted by the inevitable triumph of sentiment in the last chapters, and could assure herself that the dear child had meant no real harm. Nor can it be denied that after weeping copiously all morning over the pathos of an innocent mother sundered from her own child Miss Julia felt more competent to deal with Annie Rattray in the afternoon.

Bet Bowman's wedding-day arrived. She had the grace to invite both Mrs Bruce and Annie to the ceremony, which took place in a hotel, a licensed hotel, Annie noted, thinking to herself that the devil's fifty pounds would bring its due crop of troubles, for the lad that Bet was marrying was employed in a licensed grocer's shop, and if their married life started with port wine and whisky at the wedding it wouldn't be long in going downhill. Annie herself had expended some of Miss Susan's legacy in buying a wedding present, a framed engraving showing a lion and a lamb being led by a little child—an excellent picture to serve as guide for a newly married couple; but after the wedding she said to Mrs Bruce on the way home: 'A corkscrew would have done them better.'

It was the first wedding Annie had ever attended, and the chief impression that she carried away with her, although she said nothing about it, was that a bride was of surprising importance, not only in her own eyes, but in the eyes of everybody. There was no more 'Betty' or 'Bet Bowman' or even 'Mrs Reid'; it was, 'Isn't the bride looking sweet?' and 'You're a friend of the bride's, aren't you?' Almost as if merely by marrying Andrew Reid, who was, if not actually a black, the most ordinary of ordinary grocer's

assistants, a figure who served you with butter and sugar
across a counter, Bet Bowman had entered a higher rank,
where she was removed from all humiliation; almost as if a
wedding-ring were a kind of halo. And Annie had to appease
herself by remembering that nobody was too high for God to
reach. Still, the bride's importance rankled. It was somehow
unfair. Annie was reminded of the resentment she used
to feel when Mary dominated the playground; indeed,
Mary and Bet were not unlike each other in some ways,
and wriggled into prominence by the same unfair and
arbitrary means. It was not much consolation that she was
returning to a building within whose walls she had earned
promotion and real prestige; it was too like a return to the
class-room after the hollow dejection of being passed over
in the playground in favour of someone like Mary, and for
a little while Annie felt as if she were twelve again.

'The bride looked real fine in her braws, though,' said
Mrs Bruce.

'They'll be flung into a drawer like fish-guts the night—or
on the floor,' said Annie viciously. 'And I'm jalousing that
there would be not a button on her under-bodice, nor a
string to her petticoat underneath the braws.'

Just a plaster, she kept thinking. Just a starched apron
on top of muck. Mary and her curlers a' ower again.

Annie's promotion had come as pat as promotion in
school. Miss Julia had found herself incapable of saying
'No' when Annie offered herself as house-parlourmaid in
Betty's stead. Annie was young, but she looked older than
she was; she knew the ways of the household; she was neat
and efficient; she got on excellently with Mrs Bruce, and
Miss Carnegie, who disliked changes, was accustomed to
her. In her Sunday-school voice Miss Julia said: 'I trust
you will like your new duties and responsibilities, Annie.
Of course it will mean your giving up the mission work,
but I do not want to be selfish.'

'I think I could still do the mission work,' was Annie's
firm reply.

A fine mess of it Miss Julia would make without her. And
she would be able to manage all the work, for she was twice
as efficient as Bet, since her neatness and her method were

not put on and off like an apron. As for Miss Julia, she was losing whatever wits she had ever had.

This was painfully evident at the railway station one day when Annie attended Miss Carnegie and Miss Julia to the train for Edzell, where they were to spend a fortnight in furnished rooms. Miss Susan Carnegie had gone on a much longer journey with less fuss. But then Susan had always bought the tickets and booked the corner seats and super-intended the porters whenever the Carnegies took one of their rare journeys by train, and Miss Carnegie was really too deaf and frail now to battle with these difficulties, so that Julia Carnegie found herself forced, to her dismay, into unfamiliar responsibilities. Or was it more than the mere train journey that appalled her? Was she involuntarily reminded of that other journey to the inevitable frontier station of death? Miss Julia, at any rate, was as much obsessed by thoughts of death as if her ticket for Edzell had been a ticket for heaven. She would not sit in the last carriage in case there was a collision from behind, nor next to the engine in case it ran off the rails; no, no, Annie, in the middle of the train, if you please. And are you *sure* that this is the right train?

'Yes, Miss Julia,' said Annie for the fourth time. 'I asked the guard.'

But it is of such dreadful importance that one should take the train for the right place—not for the Other Place—that one needs reassurance from no less than the Master Himself.

'Have you asked the stationmaster, Annie?'

Annie grew impatient. There was only one railway that went to Edzell, and this was it. And in any case a board affixed to the train said 'Edzell' as plain as the nose on your face. She helped Miss Carnegie into a compartment in the central carriage, where there were no rear-guard or van-guard risks to be run, and she insisted on Miss Julia's getting in.

'Have we got everything, Annie? Are you sure nothing has been forgotten?'

One dare not forget a single item of the outfit that one may need at the other end . . . Is there nothing, nothing

at all—some little duty, some little kindness, perhaps—that
has been overlooked? Now, at the very last minute, there
is still time, but time is slipping dreadfully away and soon
it will be too late ... Is there nothing? Are you sure
nothing has been forgotten? This searching of conscience
is a complicated and subtle matter, and Miss Julia's flurry
was excusable. One must repair even at the last moment
any remembered omission ...

'Annie, don't forget about the eggs. Oh, Annie, if there
are any letters—'

'It's all right, Miss Julia; I have the address.'

But Miss Julia's agitation was too profound and obscure
to be allayed by merely practical answers. And she wanted
to be regretted by those she was leaving.

'You are a treasure, Annie,' she said at last. Domestic
treasures are not laid up in heaven, however, and Miss
Julia had rebutted her sister's suggestion that Annie might
be useful in Edzell. Miss Julia was leaving her treasure
behind ...

'Thank you, Miss Julia. You're off, now.'

'We'll send a telegram to let you know of our safe arrival!'
called Miss Julia, as the train moved away.

Ah, if one only could!

## EIGHTEEN

The Misses Carnegie retired to bed early in the evening and Mrs Bruce was usually asleep by the time that Annie came upstairs. As she turned off the small gas-jets behind her the house, too, went to sleep, storey by storey, until her candle, shining through the topmost window, was like a wakeful eye above a sleeping body. Thus every night, at least, Annie Rattray became the head of the house; and even after her candle was blown out, when the wakeful eye was shut, she retained her sense of possessing the whole sleeping mass beneath, for she could journey through every room in her mind knowing that each piece of furniture stood precisely where she had decreed. Yet her control of the house was continually menaced, and although in bed she could indulge to the full a satisfaction in the orderly subservience of her territory, that territory, narrow as it was, could not be kept inviolate.

It was not that Annie relaxed her vigilance. By day she guarded the house-door and by night she watched from her attic, and yet confusion slipped in. Miss Julia smuggled novels past her and Miss Carnegie spilt tea over the bed-clothes, to say nothing of visitors, unsummoned by Annie, who omitted to wipe their shoes on the mat and hung dripping mackintoshes in the hall. Miss Carnegie alone was as bad as a poltergeist, for she stayed in bed till midday and often left her work-table in the wrong corner of the drawing-room. Annie would have liked to forbid the two Carnegies to move a single article from its place in the drawing-room, and she showed open displeasure if she found in the morning that a table had been set before the fire or a chair pushed back. Worst of all, however, were the clocks, that ticked on in every room of the house as if to spite her; for she was now twenty, and if she spent another six years in that house she would be an old maid—she would be on the shelf.

To be laid on a shelf, remote from the world like a Bible high above the confusion of a kitchen, was a premature anticipation of heaven which Annie felt she had not willed. It was almost as if God had shelved her, as if the triumphal journey heavenward that she had so confidently begun had come to a standstill at some intermediate station, for even the Judgment Day was no longer so imminent, and at the age of twenty Annie seemed no farther on than she had been at fifteen. There was nothing to mark her progress, if she was journeying heavenward, and perhaps her insistence that the house furniture should be literally immobile was an attempt to convince herself that she was receding from earth to heaven at lightning speed, at a pace so swift that she could see everything maintaining the same position for ever and ever; perhaps it was the only alternative to admitting that she herself was standing still and that time was racing past her.

Quite rightly Annie diagnosed that her stagnation came from the heart and not from the head. It was the drawing-room that was at fault, not the attic, and whenever she had to knock for admittance at the drawing-room door a spasm of irritation shot through her. What was the use of her keeping the drawing-room clean and holy if Miss Julia sat in it all day reading trash?

'It's no' like a house of your own,' she grumbled to Mrs Bruce.

'Guidsakes, lassie, you couldna keep a house of your own ony cleaner!'

'I could sit in the drawing-room mysel'.'

'You think ower muckle o' yoursel',' said Mrs Bruce dryly.

Annie turned away in dudgeon. She was the only person in the house who was young enough to be of some use to God, it seemed to her; the others were no longer capable of serving Him. Of what use was Miss Carnegie to God? She hardly even went to church nowadays. And it was impossible that Miss Julia's muddling with the missions could be counted as effective service, nor could she exert any influence for good on her Sunday-school class after reading rubbishy novels all the week. But it was not merely that they were useless, the two old maids; they were like a spot of decay that threatened to spread. The insidious influence of the devil was poisoning the whole house, from the drawing-room outwards. Annie's prayers, when she knelt by her attic bed at night, became fiercely insistent, with a fierceness that resembled anger.

She began to hate the long wooden shelves in the kitchen, which were so high up that she could not reach the top row of saucepans without climbing on a chair. Mrs Bruce was growing stiff in the joints and could no longer take down the heavy pots, so that Annie was always being interrupted in her proper work to rax down this, that and the other.

'I'm sure I dinna ken why you have sic a spite at the shelves,' said Mrs Bruce. 'You're souple enough to climb on a chair.'

Annie blazed up in wrath, for her spite at the shelves did not bear questioning.

'Folk have no business to make shelves so high up,' she insisted, and the heat of her rage blew in upon Miss Julia in the drawing-room, who, poor lady, desiring only to shelter herself behind *East Lynne*, was glad to promise new shelves at a more accessible height. 'I'll tell Johnny Ritchie to see about it,' she said.

Johnny Ritchie, the joiner, knocked at the kitchen door a few days later and came in silently with his large tool-bag, which was gey like a muckle fish-bag, thought Annie. Had she not summoned him herself she would have resented his entry, but she said merely: 'Dinna you make a mess on my clean floor. Here, I'll spread a newspaper for you.' She knew Johnny Ritchie by sight, for a turn of the head brought him into view every Sunday in church. He was a small man, a little taller than Annie, with absent blue eyes and a drooping brown moustache.

'I'll no' need the paper,' he answered, 'I'm only gaun to measure for the shelves. Where do you want them?'

He knelt in the corner of the kitchen, slowly and carefully marking off measurements. Annie was surprised to see how

big his hands were, and for a moment she stood looking at
them: brown, knotted, gnarled hands, much too big for a
wee man like Johnny Ritchie.

'The auld shelves are ower high,' she said.

'Ay.'

He did not even turn his head, and Annie went briskly
away. When she came back he had gone.

'He's a quiet bit creature, that,' she said to Mrs Bruce.

'He's a real douce body,' agreed the cook. 'I kent his
mither fine.'

'Oh?'

'She died when he had juist left the school; he couldna
have been mair than fourteen. Na—let me see . . .'

Mrs Bruce pulled the years to pieces, like bits of wool
for a rug, and rearranged them in a pattern.

'And that was how it was,' she concluded. 'She died and
the bairnie died too, and they were buried in the one grave.
And Johnny Ritchie never spoke word to his father from
that day till the auld man's last day on earth.'

'He doesna look like that kind o' a body,' said Annie
thoughtfully. 'But he has great muckle hands for a wee
man.'

'Oh, ay, he's a skilly joiner . . .'

Johnny Ritchie's father, Annie remembered, had been an
elder, a buirdly, big-nosed man, with a white beard. And he
and Johnny had always sat at opposite ends of the pew . . .
Dod, that was something like! For seventeen years they had
sat there every Sunday and had never spoken word to each
other . . . Johnny had left his father's house and lived in
lodgings, fending for himself until he had set up on his own
account in his father's old workshop. That quiet bit man!

She looked at him with new interest when he came
bringing the shelves next afternoon.

'You'll need the newspapers the day,' she said. 'I
winna have any scuttering about on this floor, mind
you that.'

She felt quite jocular as she spread the newspapers: this
Johnny Ritchie who had stood out against his father could be
so easily ordered about. Where did he conceal his strength?
Was it in his hands? She noted the easy assurance with which

those hands grasped the hammer and drove the nails home.
Every nail went where he meant it to go, and went far ben,
thought Annie. Yet, when the shelves were finished, Johnny
Ritchie humbly shook the litter together on the newspapers
and crumpling it into a ball said: 'Where'll I put this? I
havena made muckle mess.'

Annie felt like laughing; the man looked as if he were
afraid of her!

'Here give it to me. I dinna trust you no' to drop it.'

She smiled as she said it, and a faint, uncertain smile
wavered in Johnny's eyes. With even more briskness than
usual Annie seized the crumpled ball of paper and shavings
and conveyed it out into the yard, then she took a broom and
swept the corner clean where Johnny had been working. He
picked up his woven tool-bag and stood hesitating, as if he
almost felt compelled to offer her that too.

'Ay weel,' he said.

'Bide and ha'e a cup o' tea,' interposed Mrs Bruce. 'The
kettle's on the boil.'

'Tits, man,' said Annie, 'put down your bag. It's near
five, and the tea'll be ready in twa ticks.' This invitation
surprised herself as well as Mrs Bruce, for Annie never
encouraged visitors.

'Ay weel.' Johnny slowly set the bag on the floor again.

'That's richt,' said Mrs Bruce. 'Draw in your chair.'

'You're real comfortable in here,' said Johnny, his absent
blue eyes fixed on the shining array of dish-covers and
saucepans.

'Clarty but cosy,' came Annie's laughing reply, and
Mrs Bruce looked up in renewed surprise:

'You needna say that, Annie Rattray; I dinna ken a house
in Calderwick that's keepit as this house is keepit.'

'But it's no' like a house o' your own,' went on Annie
recklessly. 'Is it, Mr Ritchie?'

'I bide in lodgings,' he said.

Mrs Bruce filled the teapot and hooded it in the woollen
cosy, then she folded her hands:

'Will you say grace, Mr Ritchie?'

Johnny Ritchie ducked his head over his plate so that
the grace he muttered was nearly inaudible behind his

moustache, and yet the level syllables spread in a quiet pool of peace round the table, or so it seemed to Annie. It was almost like sitting in a kirk-pew with Johnny Ritchie at the end of it . . .

Mrs Bruce took up the conversation and the teapot as if there had been no interruption:

'And you wi' a fine bit hoosie out the road yonder! Man, you should think shame o' yoursel', biding in lodgings.'

Johnny Ritchie shrank, and his eyes wandered uneasily to the door, while his right hand grasped a knife.

Annie was feeling brisker than usual, and quicker in the uptake. As unerringly as she had once divined the headmaster's feelings she now divined Johnny Ritchie's, and she came to the rescue:

'Ay, you'll be ready for a scone and butter. You'll no' get scones like Mrs Bruce's ilka day.'

She put a floury scone on his plate and pushed over the butter so that he could use the knife he had grasped. Johnny Ritchie felt vaguely grateful.

'Ay,' he said. 'Oh ay. She's no' verra guid at the scones, Mrs Napier.'

He cut the scone neatly and jabbed the knife into the butter.

'You'll need mair butter than that,' said Annie. 'Ha'e, tak' that.' And she put a large swatch of butter on Johnny Ritchie's plate.

'Losh keep's!' it was on the point of Mrs Bruce's tongue to say, 'you're making geyan free wi' the butter, lassie. What's come ower you?' But her sense of hospitality constrained her to cry instead: 'You can think a lot o' yoursel', Johnny Ritchie; it's no' a'body that Annie here would help to butter. She's mair likely to shut the door on folk than to ask them in.'

Johnny Ritchie looked at Annie again.

'I'm a bit like that mysel',' he said. 'Maist folk—'

He stuck in embarrassment, and again Annie helped him out:

'Maist folk juist want to poke their noses into what doesna concern them. I like to keep myself to myself, Mr Ritchie.'

She tossed her neat head above the glossy starched collar of her neat black dress. Johnny Ritchie's eyes rested on the smooth, shining plaits, where not a hair strayed out of control. Annie Rattray's gown sat jimp to her figure, every button in its place, and her starched cuffs were as immaculate as the collar. She looked as if she had arrived at certainty; her movements were decided and exact, and she knew her own mind, he thought, and did not fear to speak it out. Not like himself, haunted as he was by fears and questions . . . Johnny Ritchie began to stir his tea, and he kept on stirring and stirring as if he were going round and round a point that could not be settled.

'Mrs Napier's no' juist a grand cook, then?' asked Mrs Bruce.

Johnny's spoon stirred more slowly and stopped. 'She does awa' no' sae bad,' he admitted, and then the faint smile rose in his eyes again; 'but she's a lukewarm kind o' body. Ay, she's like the Laodiceans, you ken, neither het nor cauld. She lets the broth cool in winter and then in summer I canna get a drink o' cauld watter frae her; it's aye juist lukewarm, like the broth and the tea, and the shaving-watter on Sunday mornings.'

'But that's nae comfort for a hard-working man!' Mrs Bruce was scandalized. 'Can you no' tell her to heat the broth up?'

'I hardly ever see her,' confessed Johnny. 'She sets my things on a tray in the lobby and chaps at the door and nips awa' afore I can open it.'

'I never heard the like! What ails the woman? She's a widow, is she no'? I mind her man . . .'

Johnny drank his tea, leaving the spoon in the cup, while Mrs Bruce traced the history of Mrs Napier's man. He wasn't interested. Mrs Napier herself was well enough, for she left a body alone . . . True, she could never make up her mind to anything so definite as hot tea, and he remembered her alarm one Sunday morning when he had put his nose round her kitchen door to ask for the loan of a kettle . . . Dod, the woman had looked as if she didna ken what a kettle was, far less where one was to be found!

His eye ran again over the shining order of the kitchen

he was in now. The precision of it was fascinating—a place for a'thing, and a'thing in its place . . . This kitchen was like an answer, while Mrs Napier's kitchen was only a hopeless question.

'A snod bit kitchen, this.'

It was to Annie that he said it, for she had the same precision and certainty as the kitchen. He had as good as said, 'A snod bit lassie.' And he felt almost as if he had committed himself and as if Mrs Bruce had noticed it, for she intervened:

'You would be a lot better in your ain house, Johnny, wi' a guid, comfortable woman to look after you.'

He was at once on the defensive:

'It would cost mair. There's the rent o' the bit hoose, you see; that brings me in something.'

'Oh ay; there's the rent. That's true. Imphm.'

'And I can do the repairs mysel'; forbye, the Reids are good tenants.'

'The Reids?' said Annie. 'No' Bet and Andrew Reid, is it?'

'Juist that,' Mrs Bruce assured her. 'That bonny cottage out the road, that Bet and Andrew Reid are in, that's Johnny Ritchie's.'

A slow flush rose into Annie's cheeks and burned there for the half-hour during which Johnny sat beside her at the tea-table. She knew Bet Reid's cottage; it was not far from the Townhead School, and she had passed it every day when she was a schoolgirl. A bonny cottage, with a porch and a bay-window and a garden—not a potato-patch, but a garden with a bordered path running down to the railing; none of your common cottages with a front door opening straight on to the road . . . And that bonny cottage, which she could not bear to see Bet Reid inhabiting, belonged to this quiet bit man at her elbow!

A house of her own, a decent Christian marriage, a triumph over Bet Reid—all that, all she could desire on earth, was sitting at her very elbow, and yet she dared not simply put out a hand and grasp it! The flush burned more hotly on her cheek-bones, for she was shaken by fear and desire and pride and humiliation. It was as if God Himself had set this chance at her elbow. Why should she not be able to take it? Why not? She sat in a fluttering uncertainty that was almost shame, telling herself that it was a bonny come-down for Annie Rattray to think of setting her cap at a man. For even the humiliation of being an old maid was less crushing than the shame of being cried down as a forward hussy. And the gossip of Calderwick loomed before Annie like a featureless, shadowy monster that the spear of her will could not pierce because it was as intangible as a cloud and as formless as the sea; a black, shadowy monster that threatened to close over her head and smother her in shame if she moved so much as a finger to get down from her shelf before a man picked her off it.

And yet she was in danger of slipping. For the devil himself was awake and stirring in Annie, as a lion might shake the tall grasses in the jungle before springing into the open. The fluttering of her blood told her that if she only let herself go she could pounce upon Johnny Ritchie and carry him off. Once, for a brief period, she had abandoned herself to darkness as to a submissive element, and could she not do it once again, only once, this time avoiding the black monster of shame into whose maw she had so unskilfully fallen seven years ago? A house of her own! A decent Christian marriage! No scandal could touch her once she had achieved that . . . Before she even knew that she had yielded to temptation Annie found herself saying in a small, gentle voice, the same weak, gentle voice with which she had disclaimed responsibility for 'the blues' on her tussock of grass: 'Try another scone, Mr Ritchie.' And she laid the scone almost tenderly on his plate.

## NINETEEN

Now Johnny Ritchie was a man who spent many hours rocking in a small boat on the estuary, with a can of mussels at his feet and his lines trailing in the tide-water. He had been too long a fisherman to think of himself as a fish; he was accustomed merely to let down his lines of inquiry, and it did not occur to him that he himself might be an answer. So he rose to Annie's bait unwittingly.

Yet he would not have done so had he not thought, like every fish, that he was getting something to his advantage without committing himself. It was pleasant to meet with warmth and gentleness; it was pleasant to be told to his face by Mrs Bruce that he was weel-kent as the best joiner in the town; it was comforting to hear from a trig lassie like Annie that the shelves were a grand job of work. And Johnny thought that Annie was the madam to know good work when she saw it; ay, that she was . . . And when he let slip that he had a fancy to set up as a cabinet-maker, for there was more money in that than in simple joinering, it was heartening to hear her say: 'I wonder at you, Mr Ritchie, that you havena done it long ago, and you so skilly wi' your hands.'

Johnny Ritchie twice said: 'Ay weel, it's time I was awa',' before he could bring himself to leave. And he stepped out along the street with a longer stride than usual, and his spine, that for some years had been growing into a curve like a question-mark, straightened itself a little. A door had been opened to him that was not opened to any chance-comer; for she was a bit of a madam, that Annie, with her starch and her pernickety ways, and she was more likely to shut the door on folk than to ask them in, yet she had made him kindly welcome, and had said: 'Haste you back!' when he went away.

But if he did not recognize the bait, still less did Johnny Ritchie divine the hook. He thought it was simple friendship that made Annie smile and nod to him in the church door as the congregation came out; and when Miss Julia Carnegie sent for him again to put a new door in the yard shed, and yet again to repair the planking in the floor of Annie's attic, he did not suspect that Annie was the instigator. He began instead to think more of himself, both as a man and a joiner, under the steady flow of her encouragement, for no decent man, when a woman invites him to cock himself up and push himself forward, refuses to credit himself with virility. Johnny Ritchie found it natural to progress from nodding and smiling at the church door to convoying Annie and Mrs Bruce a bit of the way home, and the convoys grew longer, until it became a matter of course that he should drop in on a Sunday evening after church for a bite of supper.

These were pleasant suppers. There was always a little daffing about the immaculate order in the kitchen, and Johnny had to wipe his feet extravagantly on the mat before coming in, for Annie asserted that men were clarty creatures, bringing dirt in with them and leaving disorder behind; and there was more daffing at table, for Annie took it upon herself to teach him not to stir his tea for so long and not to leave his spoon in the cup while he drank it. 'I'll mak' a man o' you yet,' she said, and the threat sounded playful rather than sinister. None the less, the suggestion of matrimony began to pervade the air, especially when the cabinet-making was discussed, for by this time it was openly understood that Johnny Ritchie was a dovering kind of body, who had to be forced to make up his mind, and he began to feel uneasy, as if he were being urged against his will into a settled establishment.

It became clear that his uneasiness was not without grounds. 'A cabinet-maker,' said Annie, 'ay, and why not a deacon in the kirk as well? There's waur men than you that are made deacons.'

Johnny cleared his throat: 'Oh ay. Imphm. Ay, but they like deacons to be married men . . .'

'Weel,' said Annie, 'weel?' Johnny had to avoid her eye. 'Forbye,' she went on, 'it's no' very respectable for a decent man to be aye living in lodgings.'

This assumption, that a decent man should not be served by hireling women, that a bachelor's life was raffish as well as comfortless, flattered but disquieted Johnny Ritchie. It came into his mind again when he went home after lingering for an hour in the Carnegies' pleasant kitchen. He hung up his cap on its usual peg and felt his way along the dark lobby to the door of his room. The winking red light of the wee fire in the grate flickered into the lobby and revealed a trayful of crockery sitting on the table opposite his door. The sight of that tray irritated Johnny unaccountably; the woman might have jaloused that he wasna in the house, and had no need to let his tea sit there for an hour, getting colder and colder. A plate of watery haddock was set on top of a jug containing water that had once been warm; a naked brown teapot smelt nauseatingly of strong, cold tea when he lifted the lid. An hour, at least, it had been sitting there; the woman didn't care whether he was in or out.

He lit the gas-jet and carried the tray to the kitchen door. Mrs Napier jumped up in wordless fright as her lodger came in without knocking and slammed the tray on her table. 'You should surely ken whether a man's in or out,' he said roughly, and this unusual roughness from Johnny Ritchie frightened her even more, so that her hand fluttered to her throat. 'It's no' me she thinks about, it's my money,' grumbled Johnny, shutting the kitchen door, and he grew angrier as he felt that Mrs Napier regarded his entry into her kitchen as an unwarranted intrusion into the private parts of the house. He was entitled only to what he paid for . . . 'Dod,' said Johnny, stumbling back along the hobby, 'dod, they're no' far wrong; it's almost like living wi' a hoor.'

But what was a man to do? Tramp the open roads and sleep in a common ditch? No, he was a decent man and wanted to live in a decent fashion; he wanted to feel that there was a place which he alone could fill

. . . But not his own house—anything but that. Not the house where his mother had lain dead, with the usurping infant dead beside her; not the house where he had heard her screaming—screams that had gone through him like a knife; and although that was eighteen years ago Johnny cowered as if he could hear them still. The wages of sin is death. That awful sentence echoed through his mind, as it had echoed for all these years; and to touch a woman and get her in the family way was a sin that could bring death, an awful death, a death of screaming agony . . . What was a man to do?

With a feeling almost of desperation Johnny Ritchie escaped into the summer twilight and got out his wee boat by the shore of the estuary. It soothed him to sit above the dimpled water that was so mysteriously full of fish. There was no finality about the sea; there was aye mair fish in the sea than what came out of it. A man could go on fishing and fishing and never exhaust the possibilities of that inscrutable, mysterious mother of life . . . Maybe he could just go on as he was. He had managed for a good many years . . . Dod, if it came the length of marriage he could aye run away . . . Hoots, there was nae question o' marriage.

Next Sunday evening he appeared as usual at St James's Church, and with his usual friendliness met the kindly welcome extended to him by Annie and Mrs Bruce. Annie asked if she might take his arm, on the pretext that the pavement was too uneven for her high-heeled shoes, and Johnny complied, telling himself that her cleeking of him was just a friendly dependence on his strength. But beneath this compliance Annie sensed the deeper resistance to her advances, and she became so set on overcoming it that she forgot her lingering fear of gossip and her dread of the devil . . . The man must, must, must be brought to a point . . . Would she actually have to cuddle him?

She tried the indirect method first. She displayed an interest in his buttons; she parted his hair; she bought him a pair of slippers and put them on his feet herself, after making him take off his shoes. The grey worsted socks he wore were gey like her father's, but Annie slid on the

slippers caressingly. She hung a new tie round his neck.
The only thing left her to do was to hang herself round
his neck. And still Johnny Ritchie was not brought to a
point. Annie's temper began to suffer. Mrs Bruce, who
had begun to make jocular references to Johnny, hinting
that Annie might do worse for herself, learned to hold her
peace after having her nose nearly snapped off, and told a
crony of hers that she only encouraged the man about the
kitchen because she would be thankful to see the back of
that Annie Rattray.

But one evening as Johnny was letting himself into his
room something brushed against his leg. 'Is that you,
Mirren?' he said; 'ay weel, guid pussy, guid pussy; c'wa'
in then.' Mirren, Mrs Napier's cat, a grey tabby with a small
anxious face and a large long body, padded after him to the
fireside and mewed. 'Ay, but there's nae haddie the day;
it's eggs this time,' said Johnny, scratching her beneath the
chin. 'You dinna like egg, Mirren. Ha'e, there's a bittie
bread-and-butter.'

Mirren sniffed at the bread-and-butter and left it lying;
she was restless and sprang up on the bed, where she turned
round several times, padding down a hollow for herself.
Johnny Ritchie, having finished his tea, sat down in the old
chair by the fireside, a wide-bottomed chair with broken
springs and a turkey red cushion to fill up the sagging seat.
He set his feet on the fender and took down his pipe from
the mantelpiece, feeling that his lodgings were well enough
after all, and that Mrs Napier was a woman who left a man
alone. Here he was as snug as if it were his own fireside, and
he had even a cat to sit beside him without having to take
any responsibility for her . . . He looked round for the cat:
'Na, na, Mirren, come oot o' that. You can get in ahint
me here; there's plenty room on the chair.'

He patted the cushion insistently, and Mirren, quitting
the bed, jumped on to his knee, purring. Johnny lifted her
awkwardly and plumped her on the turkey red cushion
behind him. The cat snuggled down between the man's
back and the curve of the chair; she nosed under the
tail of his coat until it lay over her like a blanket; her
claws stretched and drew in again, and her purring made

a pleasant accompaniment to the rustling of the man's magazine. Johnny had acquired a bundle of tattered *Strand Magazines*, ninepence for the lot, and he liked to thumb them over, studying with especial interest the 'Illustrated Interviews,' which admitted the reader to intimacy with famous men and women, an intimacy achieved by photographs revealing 'The Drawing-room,' 'The Hall,' 'The Dining-room.' To 'The Bedroom' neither Johnny nor any inquisitive outsider was ever allowed to penetrate, for the chastity of life had to be preserved, but Johnny's bachelor eye was content to feast on the lavish upholstery of the less private domestic interiors. He was interested in furniture, all the more as he had nearly decided to set up as a cabinet-maker, and the furniture of the great and famous was more than ordinarily interesting.

Mirren's purring grew louder, and she shifted behind him, turning and twisting; her hind legs kicked against him.

'You'll ha'e me oot o' the chair, Mirren,' said Johnny, skipping 'The Billiard-room' and turning to 'The Boudoir.' He reached one hand behind him and patted the cat on the head. Mirren's purring grew hoarser and became almost a snore.

'Dod, you're geyan pleased wi' yoursel',' said Johnny. At that moment the flap of his coat, just below the left-hand pocket, heaved in a strange manner, as if something were squirming beneath it, something that could not possibly be one of Mirren's legs, and as Johnny stared at it for a second of startled dismay the blunt head of a newly-born kitten poked out from under it.

'God! She's kittled in my very pocket!'

The *Strand Magazine* fell on the fender, and Johnny Ritchie sprang to his feet, gaping at the family interior posed on his own chair. Mirren's third kitten was just being born and she was too busy to look up, but her hoarse purring never stopped.

'In my very pocket!' repeated Johnny. 'That cowes a', Mirren.'

He stood silent for a few minutes, then gently put a finger

on one of the kittens. Mirren licked the finger with her rough tongue and shifted a little into the hollow he had vacated.

Johnny Ritchie ran along the lobby and opened the kitchen door without stopping to think that he was intruding:

'Mirren's kittled in my chair, Mrs Napier . . .'

'Oh, dear! What a like thing!'

It was only then that Johnny grew embarrassed.

'And you sitting in it!' said Mrs Napier, standing help-lessly beside the complacent mother.

'She keepit on purring and purring. How was I to ken? She never stopped . . . Dod, she just purred and purred, and I just thought she was geyan weel pleased wi' hersel' . . .'

'Oh, Mr Ritchie!'

'Have you a box for her?'

'Ay—she—there's the box she aye has for her kitlins; it's in the cellar . . .'

Johnny Ritchie carefully lifted the cushion—cat, kittens and all—into the wooden box and carried it into the kitchen.

But he did not sit down again in his chair. The horsehair stuffing stuck out in stiff coils from a great rent in the seat-cover, and he stood looking at it, smiling and shaking his head with the bewilderment of one who has discovered something unexpectedly pleasant; he gazed at the horsehair stuffing as if it were a miraculous secret that had just been revealed to him.

For the cat had kept on purring all the time . . . Not a whimper, not a cry; she had simply purred and purred as if she were highly pleased . . . She had purred and licked his finger. An innocent look came into Johnny Ritchie's blue eyes, and he stood, surprised and pleased, as if the sword of the archangel had been lowered to let him pass into a lost Eden.

After a time his lower lip quivered, and all at once slow tears began to trickle down on to his moustache. He turned and leaned his face on the mantelpiece . . . 'Oh, mither, mither!' As if the tears had unsealed some old bitterness and washed it away Johnny realized that he need not have felt so hard against his mother. She had died in child-bed, but she had not died in sin; for child-bed was innocent, innocent . . . Mirren's in the right o't, he kept thinking; Mirren's in the right o't . . . He had been wrong; it was the bitterness of his jealousy and his loss that had made his heart hard, and his misery had turned into a misery of condemnation . . . How often had he told himself that if she had not died he would never have forgiven her . . .

He blew his nose and sat down in the chair, staring into the fire. Dod, Mirren was in the right o't. His heart swelled with vague tenderness; women, ay, women and innocent bairnies . . . There were as many folk in the world as there were fish in the sea, and they hadna all been born in sin; it wasna possible. A hoor, now, that would be different . . . But with a decent woman, that would be finding innocence instead of losing it . . .

'Ay weel,' said Johnny at last.

He looked into the kitchen to pat Mirren on the head, and went for a dander under the stars. Annie Rattray, now, she was a decent, kindly, snod bit lassie . . . she knew her own mind and had no daft-like fears and notions. Ay, she was a good lassie, Annie; a man wouldna go wrong wi' her. The bit hoose was a kindly enough hoose; he had been happy in it when he was a bairn . . . It was a kindly hoose for bairns, wi' the garden and a' . . .

Annie knew that there was a difference in Johnny Ritchie the next time she saw him. 'He has a saft look in his eye,' she said to herself, and the flush burned on her cheek again. He was coming to the point after all, and she slipped round to the other side of Mrs Bruce as they walked home.

'No' needin' my arm the nicht, Annie?'

'Na; no' me.'

Her voice was almost tremulous, and she ran up to her attic when they reached the house.

She was as trig as ever when she came down into the kitchen, but very pale.

'What ails you the nicht, Annie?' said Johnny.

'Nothing.'

Perhaps Johnny had given Mrs Bruce a wink. At any rate, Mrs Bruce made some excuse to leave them.

'Annie,' said Johnny Ritchie, 'Annie——'

She burst into tears, and he put his arm round her.

'Ay weel,' he said, patting her tenderly, 'ay weel.'

Annie dried her tears and looked up.

'Johnny, I've—I've mair than thirty pounds saved in the bank,' she said.

# BOOK III: THE WOMAN

The Woman: I must be the
best tight-rope walker in the world.
Look, I am more than half-way across,
although the rope shakes.
The Answer: I am shaking the rope. If you fall, you fall.
The Woman: It is my Enemy who shakes the rope.

## TWENTY

In the second week of October 1896 Annie Rattray and
Johnny Ritchie were married in the Carnegies' drawing-
room. Miss Julia was as pleased about the wedding as
if she were marrying off a daughter, and insisted on
providing a sit-down tea in the kitchen afterwards, where
she graciously invited the company to feel at home, and
told the bridegroom once more that he was getting a Perfect
Treasure of a wife.

But for a Rattray wedding it was not a very homely affair.
Annie's demeanour was so distant that Mrs Rattray found
it difficult to assert her rights as the bride's mother, and
Jim Rattray, who clapped the bridegroom on the shoulder
and jerked a thumb towards the pub round the corner, was
even more severely snubbed, so that he grumbled: God
Almichty, this is like a Band o' Hope meeting!' Mary and
her husband, Chay Stott, one of the town scavengers, a
good-natured man with a cowlick plastered on his forehead,
had their hands full with their two children, sticky brats
who picked the sugar whorls off the wedding-cake and
upset their milk over the table-cloth. Indeed, the bride
had cause to be ashamed of her relations; they showed
up badly beside the bridegroom's quiet, genteel cousins,
the four spinster daughters of an ironmonger in Dundee,
who were well enough off to come to Calderwick for the
wedding and stay the night in a temperance hotel. But
when Annie stood up in the drawing-room beside Johnny
Ritchie, with the youngest of the spinster cousins, Lizzie
Jane, supporting her as bridesmaid; when she looked down
at the spray of maidenhair and white chrysanthemums, so
elegantly sheathed in silver foil, that pranked on the silk
front of her bodice; when she held out her finger for the

ring that was to make her Mrs Ritchie, she felt uplifted far
beyond her family, uplifted beyond even the Carnegies and
the other guests, whose faces were indistinguishable outside
the nimbus that surrounded her, for she was the bride, the
bride! The ring was slipped on, the magic circle that fenced
her off from humiliation; her hand closed on it. She was
safe at last and beyond the reach of all of them. It was as
if she stood again on a bridge with her head in the skies
and a shining track before her, but this time the track rose
from earth to heaven, straight up to the right hand of God,
and her foot was securely set upon it.

She still felt aloof, even when she was sitting in the kitchen
at table between her husband and the minister. But she had
only to remain quietly on her chair, for she was waited on
hand and foot like a queen. 'Sandwiches for the bride! Tut,
tut, you must eat something,' said the minister, and 'Tea
for the bride, Mrs Bruce,' cried Bet Reid. 'She'll no' need
any sugar wi' it the day.' Through the blinding nimbus
Annie became aware of Bet Reid, into whose shoes she
had twice stepped—first the parlour-maid's job and now
the bonny cottage . . . but she would be the owner of the
cottage while Bet Reid had only been a tenant . . . 'I only
hope,' Bet was saying (the hypocrite!), 'that you'll be as
happy in your wee house as me and Andrew have been,
Annie—oh, I beg pardon, Mrs Ritchie, I mean.'

'Thank you, Mrs Reid.' . . . Yes; Mrs Ritchie to you and
everybody else from now on; no more of the Annie, if you
please . . . And the bride laid her hand on the table and
looked at her wedding-ring, then she glanced round the
kitchen. This was the last time that the old and the new
would be so tangled together. When Mr and Mrs Ritchie
stepped into the cab that was to drive them to their home
the last thread would be snapped that bound Mrs Ritchie
to her old life, to her servitude as a parlour-maid, to her
humiliations as a spinster Rattray. She regarded her mother,
her father, her sister; they were almost unreal. She could
not hear the meaningless words they were shouting across
the table. They had to be asked to the wedding because
marriage was such a queer mix-up of God and the devil;
the minister and Jim Rattray both had to be there, both had

to be there . . . The figures around the table became still
more unreal, and the conversation loudened and died away
like a far-off buzz, like the far-off drumming of approving
fists upon ape-like bosoms . . .

'Open the window, the bride's in a dwam!'

'It's the excitement.'

'How do you feel now, Annie?'

That was Johnny Ritchie's voice, and it seemed strangely
irrelevant; surely it should have been a girl's voice. And
Annie should reply: 'Where am I? . . . What did I do?'

'Do you feel better now, Mrs Ritchie?'

That was the minister. Annie opened her eyes; she knew
now where she was. Whatever might happen, she had been
solemnly married in the drawing-room, and here was the
minister . . .

'Thank you,' she said in a weak, gentle voice. 'Thank
you, I'm all right now.'

But Johnny Ritchie was glad when at length he and Annie
were settled in the cab, shaking grains of rice out of their
hats. It was a pity the minister had gone away so early, for
the bride's father had found the back-door and had returned
stinking of whisky, and the bride's sister and Mrs Reid had
sent obscene jokes flying across the table, like pellets of filth
bespattering the innocence of a decent marriage. Johnny
Ritchie brushed the rice off Annie's boa with irritation.
That kind of thing might have been expected from the
men, but not from women, married women too—mothers
of bairns . . . His mother would never have done it, nor
his Annie, and his irritation vanished in a vague swell of
tenderness.

'Never you mind them, Annie,' he said, taking her
hand in his.

'I'm no' minding them.'

They sat in silence as the cab whirled them through the
High Street, out the North Road, past the broad, cemented
pavement that turned down to the school, right out to the
bonny cottage. Johnny assisted his wife to step down and
she walked firmly up the path to the front door. She was
the mistress of this house; she could go in and out as she
pleased and sit in the parlour whenever she liked.

'Wipe your feet on the mat, Johnny Ritchie!'

'This'll be a michty clean house, I'm thinking,' retorted
Johnny, with a grin.

'I'll no' let a Rattray set foot across the door,' said
Annie.

The cottage was in apple-pie order. Annie had spent the
last few days in putting everything to rights. Much of the old
Ritchie furniture was there, brought down from the garret
where it had been stored. Johnny had discovered in himself
a tenderness for it that would not let him discard anything
still capable of being patched and repaired; he had gone over
the chests and the chairs, the tables and corner cupboards,
until the old was as good as new. It was only the big things
they had had to buy: a wardrobe, a kitchen dresser, a double
bed; and of these only the bed was split-new an enamelled
black iron bedstead with bright brass knobs at the corners.
Johnny Ritchie could easily have got a bedstead as good and
half as cheap at an auction-sale, but he had got it into his
head that a new bed was the right thing. So there it stood
in the front bedroom, a new, innocent bed covered with a
white honeycomb counterpane.

Johnny Ritchie wiped his feet on the mat, then he hung
up his coat and hat in the lobby and vanished shyly into the
kitchen leaving Annie to enter the bedroom alone. But she
lingered in the lobby and opened the parlour door first. Her
parlour . . . Mrs Ritchie's parlour; her very own Sabbath
room where not a speck of dust should lie. The opening
of the door sent a waft of air into the cold, still room;
the green balls fringing the low-hanging table-cover stirred
and swung, and in the bow-window the five-fingered green
leaves of the palm stirred too, an authentic palm, gifted,
together with its real brass pot, by Miss Julia . . . Annie softly
closed the parlour door and went into the front bedroom to
take off her hat and mantle.

The stretch of white counterpane looked enormous.
Annie turned her back on it and put her garments in
the wardrobe. But the bed filled nearly the whole of the
room; one could not ignore it. Mrs Ritchie must get into
that bed beside Mr Ritchie and somehow contrive to pay
the devil's price without falling a victim to the devil . . .

Annie stood fingering her wedding-ring. A decent Christian marriage was more than a sanctuary from the world; it was a perpetual assertion of God in the very darkest and most devil-haunted cavern of life . . . She had to put out a hand to support herself on the chest of drawers, for an oppressive fright was beginning to constrict her breathing and she was afraid that she would faint again, this time on the very top of the marriage bed. To faint away and to waken up after the deed was done, as if on a tussock of grass, would be an easy way out, and yet Annie fought down her fear, for the price, she felt, had to be paid with open eyes; she dared not swoon away lest the devil should tip up the scale and claim her wholly, body and soul.

Above the bed hung an old text that had come down from the garret, Thou God Seest Me, printed in solemn black letters beneath a largely opened eye whose rays spread into the remotest corners of the white rectangle. And at each of the corners the plain black frame made a cross. Her inner eye must be as that eye of God; like His it must penetrate to the remotest corners of her body, unsleeping, vigilant, irradiating the whole of it so that it became a fit garment for a daughter of God.

She came into the kitchen pale but smiling a little. Johnny had already put on his slippers, those slippers she had given him, it seemed so long ago, and was sitting in his chair at the cheek of the fire, facing the low easy-chair that had been his mother's and was now his wife's. The whole kitchen shone and winked in the gaslight, from the waxed green linoleum on the floor to the saucepans on the handy shelves Johnny Ritchie had put up and the dish-covers on the big dresser that stood so conveniently near to the sink. Everything was in its place, and as Annie tied a white apron round her neat waist Johnny Ritchie felt that he had come home at last.

Because he did not know how else to express his exhilaration he chaffed his wife:

'I dinna believe you ken where the tea's kept, Mrs Ritchie.'

'I ken fine where everything is,' she replied, whisking a kettle from the hob to the fire. 'But whether I'll be able to lay my hand on anything the morn's morning after you've been through the house is mair than I can tell. You men are clarty creatures, even the best of you.'

A cold supper had been arranged for them on the table, and was covered by a cloth. Annie felt that for this one evening at least Johnny should do all the work.

'You can tak' the cover off,' she cried. 'I'm going to do nae mair this night . . .'

'Are you tired, Annie?'

'Ay, a wee thingie tired, maybe.'

But as they ate the supper they went on daffing, with a growing note of challenge, as if each was daring the other to something. And after supper, forgetting her vow of idleness, Annie plunged the plates into hot water, and as she stood there, with both her hands immersed, Johnny Ritchie clipped her round the waist and kissed her on the cheek.

'That's no' fair, Johnny Ritchie,' she said, nudging him off with an elbow, but her protest sounded unconvincing; it was rather as if she had willed that the man should attack her when she was defenceless.

Johnny kissed her again.

'Haud off,' said Annie. 'Tak' and dry the dishes.'

'Ay weel,' said Johnny, 'a man's guid for something, it appears; I can dry dishes as weel as ony auld wife.'

He seized a wet plate with a flourish of the dish-cloth.

'You'll break it!' cried Annie in alarm, and at that moment the plate slithered to the floor and crashed. Annie gave a little scream.

'Och, there's aye three things has to be broken,' said Johnny Ritchie, 'and that means only twa mair to be broken in this house——'

He stopped suddenly as if embarrassed and bent to pick up the pieces.

'You've begun geyan early,' said Annie, in a queer voice. He swept up the splinters and took them out to the bucket.

'I'll forgive you this time,' Annie had said finally.

Johnny was still embarrassed when he came back, and Annie's heart, that had jumped and fluttered ridiculously at the noise of the crash—as if a broken plate was anything to be fleggit at!—was still pounding unevenly in her bosom.

'Ay weel,' said Johnny, poking the fire vigorously, 'ay weel . . .'

'Is everything locked up?'

'Ay, a'thing but the front door . . .'

He took his big watch out of his fob and began to wind it up. Annie untied her apron and folded it over and over. Neither of them looked at the other, but Annie's apron took a long time to fold; she shook it out and folded it afresh long after Johnny's watch was wound up, and he stood waiting as if in an agony of expectancy. Would she say the word? Would she free him from this suggestion of guilt? Would she open for him the gate into the innocent Garden of Eden? Would she draw him to her in tenderness?

Annie laid the apron over a chair-back. 'Will we no' put up a bit prayer?' she said, almost in a whisper.

Johnny took her hand and pressed it.

'You do it, Annie,' he said.

'It's a man's place to do it,' she answered.

'Baith of us thegither,' pleaded Johnny.

'It's your place to do it,' insisted Annie.

Still keeping her hand in his he went down suddenly on his knees; they knelt on either side of a chair and Johnny Ritchie stammered a few words of entreaty to God. In the silence that followed he brushed his hand once or twice over his eyes.

When they rose up he said: 'I'll lock the front door. I'll no' be long after you, Annie.'

Annie went out silently.

Johnny Ritchie stood in the lobby with the big key in his hand, absently unlocking and locking the front door several times. Then he put the chain up across it and returned to the kitchen.

After waiting for fifteen minutes by his watch and the kitchen clock he tapped on the bedroom door: 'Can I come in? Can I come in, Annie?'

'Come in!' a tremulous voice replied.

She was lying in bed with the sheet up to her chin.

'I'll just take my things to the kitchen.' He screwed down

the bedroom gas to a 'peep' and went out on tiptoe with his night-shirt. When he came back Annie's face was hidden, and he turned the gas out and climbed in beside her . . .

Would she not say something? Would she not make a move? But Annie seemed scarcely to breathe. 'Ay weel,' said Johnny at last, putting an arm over her shoulders.

Annie set her teeth. Now she must be vigilant; now she must keep unsleeping that wakeful eye which was open somewhere in the top of her head . . . Her heart was trembling and pounding. The devil was stirring in her bosom; but she must not give way to him, she must keep her head . . . Thou God Seest Me . . . Oh, would it soon be over?

'Annie!' said Johnny Ritchie, and then, almost despairingly, 'Annie?'

But the warmth, the answering, absolving tenderness that he was entreating remained locked away and inaccessible, locked up like the prim, clean house, and to the door that guarded it Johnny Ritchie could not find the key. He was an intruder, a defiler, leaving unwanted filth behind him . . . He lay guilty and forlorn beside his rigid wife. Was this all? he asked himself. Was this all?

And Annie was asking herself the same question, but she was asking it with surprised relief.

The price was paid.

## TWENTY-ONE

Annie lay wakeful, at first in still triumph, but soon disquieted by sharp questions that kept growing in her mind like clusters of spears. Had she forgotten anything in the ordering of her house? Could she have overlooked a corner in which dirt might gather? Would she be, after all, a laughing-stock to her neighbours? What if her father, Jimmy Rattray, came drunk to her door—how could she keep him out? It seemed as if she would never fall asleep, and when the wakeful, anxious eye did shut at last, her spirit was still searching through labyrinthine ways for that clear track of certainty which it had missed, that track which ran like a ray of sunlight straight up to heaven. She turned her back on Johnny Ritchie, and in his sleep he pressed closer to her, for the sense of guilt was still vaguely troubling him and he wanted comfort and reassurance; his arm went round her body and his hand rested beneath her breasts. The warmth of his body against her backbone, the caress of his hand on her bosom, sent a deep drowsiness through Annie's questing dream; the blank walls that baffled her branched into tall hedges, flowered into arbours, drowsy arbours where one might sink backwards deeper and deeper into an acquiescent bliss, backwards into a blind, inverted world where no eye opened, where face was not opposed to face nor breast to breast, an old, instinctive world, older even than the Garden of Eden. But Johnny Ritchie, vaguely troubled by guilt, desired his wife to meet him face to face: his breast yearned for hers, and his desire brought him out of sleep into a half-wakefulness; he tried to turn her round. Annie's dream of sinking into bliss became a fall into a pit of shame; she struggled to regain her footing, and her struggles were a frantic escape from jeering tongues.

from pointing fingers. She awoke, pushing Johnny Ritchie desperately from her; and even when she remembered that she was married to him the hostility remained in her body although her voice was the voice of a dutiful wife. 'I'm sorry, Annie; I couldna help it. Oh, Annie, I'm sorry,' Johnny reiterated, and his supplicating apologies were taken as a matter of course.

But in the morning, if he felt cold and despondent as he huddled on his breeks in the kitchen before a fireless hearth, he repented of his despondency after the sticks had begun to crackle and Annie had drunk the cup of tea he took in to her. For she was as brisk as a bee, and she served him his breakfast piping hot, and the porridge was smooth, without a single knot in it, and the bacon was crisply fried. After his pleasant meal he had to walk no farther than down to the end of the tattie ground at the back of the cottage, where he was building a new workshop big enough for the cabinet-making. There he planed and hammered and sawed all morning, and as naturally as he had patched and repaired the chairs from the garret his thoughts patched and repaired his marriage. It wasna so bad. Probably women couldna be expected to enjoy that kind of thing, not decent women, anyway; and Annie had been real forgiving about it. A man had to be thankful if a woman put up with him; and he might have done a lot worse, for she was a trig lassie and a grand worker . . .

Yet that evening, as he sat by his own fireside, Johnny Ritchie could not help saying: 'We just need a wee cat now, Annie. I could get a kitlin from Mrs Napier.'

'A cat!' said Annie. 'I dinna haud wi' animals about the house. They just bring in dirt and disorder, and they make dirt, too, and slaister their hairs ower everything. Na, dinna you try bringing any cats in here, nor dogs neither.' And so Johnny had to be apologetic again. For it was only fair that Annie should have her say about the house; it was she who had all the work of it. She couldna be expected to allow a disorderly house . . .

The apologetic habit grew on Johnny, and as the weeks added up to months his very walk became deprecating. That may have been what Bet Reid observed when she said scornfully to Andrew: 'There's Johnny Ritchie dovering past the window. He hasna been married three months and he's got the legs o' an auld married man already.' 'Ay, you limmer!' said Andrew, 'and I've been married on you for five years, and what about my legs?' 'G'wa' wi' you; you're no' married on a nasty, stuck-up, mim-mouthed, prideful bitch like Annie Ritchie.'

Bet Reid's verdict, however, was not the verdict of the congregation of St James's, where Mr and Mrs Ritchie appeared twice every Sunday and on Wednesday evenings at the prayer-meeting as well. The St James's members said that it would be a good thing for the kirk if all young married folk were like Mr and Mrs Ritchie. In St James's it was known that Mrs Ritchie was a great worker for the foreign missions and that Mr Ritchie was spoken of as a likely deacon. The congregation looked at Mr and Mrs Ritchie sitting so doucely in their pew, and it was pleased with what it saw.

Indeed, the Mr Ritchie who appeared in church was very different from the Johnny Ritchie observed from her window by Bet Reid. In the first place, he was rigged out in his Sunday blacks, and the mere donning of these ceremonial garments allayed Johnny Ritchie's self-deprecation. A coarse, blundering creature he might be; like every man, a secret sinner in his wife's bed, a guilty sinner towards God, but in his Sunday best he was acceptable in the house of God, and might hope for grace and salvation. In the second place, Annie's attitude towards him altered subtly in the neighbourhood of the church and became positively meek and dependent as they entered the church door. At home, Annie's prestige in the eyes of the world depended on herself and her own housewifery, and Johnny Ritchie was merely a tolerated intruder upon her domestic order, but in church her prestige derived from the fact that she was the wife of Johnny Ritchie, a visible pillar of the ecclesiastical fabric, a man who might become a deacon or even an elder, a man who sat by right at the end of the pew and was the head of the family. And so while Mr Ritchie fixed his wistful blue eyes on the minister's face, lest he should miss a single hint of salvation, Mrs Ritchie

kept her eyes modestly cast down, regarding her Bible or
her gloved and folded hands, the pattern of a Christian
wife. Mr Ritchie saw only the minister, but behind her
cast-down eyelids Mrs Ritchie was aware of the whole
congregation, knowing that as Mrs Ritchie she presented
a flawless front in the same place where as Annie Rattray
she had felt exposed to derision. Mrs Ritchie did not fail
to be grateful to God, and she included Mr Ritchie in
that gratitude. She leaned upon her husband's arm in
the decorous, slow-moving throng that quitted the church
when the service was over; her smile was gentle, her gloved
hand timid, her voice small and unemphatic when she
exchanged greetings with the new acquaintances she was
making among the congregation. And the matrons of St
James's approved the bride, and when they went to drink
tea with young Mrs Ritchie they reported that she was a
grand manager and that you could eat your dinner off the
floor of every room in her house.

    In later years, as she looked back on those first six months
after her marriage, Mrs Ritchie was inclined to believe them
the happiest of her life. For during that time she enjoyed
as it were the best of both worlds, even although she and
Johnny had not much money to come and go on, and
had to look at both sides of a penny before spending it.
For Johnny Ritchie was master of his workshop and she
was mistress of her house; they were at nobody's beck
and call, and were entitled to hold their heads high in
Calderwick. She was able to keep her own house more
scrupulously than she had ever kept the Carnegies' house;
it was speckless and, except in the kitchen, immobile—as
if the timelessness of heaven had settled upon it. And as
the cottage, although it kept itself to itself behind its railing,
had its place and number in the North Road of Calderwick,
so Mr and Mrs Ritchie, although they were independent,
had their place and honour in the social life of the town.
There was an atmosphere of hope and progress about these
months, which was intensified by the feeling that this was
an historical year, the year of Queen Victoria's Diamond
Jubilee.

    Annie Ritchie could remember only one thing that

troubled her then—no, two things—Johnny's fishing and
the garden. Ay, they were really one thing, for she wanted
Johnny to dig the garden in his spare time and he wanted
to go fishing. She could never bring herself to grub among
roots and dark, earthy-crawling things in the garden; it was
like uncovering something that should be left covered up.
To thrust tools into mother earth was a man's job, not
a woman's, and Annie looked at the tangled thicket of
berry bushes and sweetbrier as if it were the obscene,
lion-haunted scrub of the African wilds. It was Johnny
who should penetrate into that, not her; it was a man's
business to keep the garden trim. On the other hand, the
sea could not be trimmed by man or woman, for it was an
unchancy, treacherous, wild monster, and what for Johnny
Ritchie wanted to sit rocking on the welter of waves behind
the river bar she could not understand; the pickle o' fish he
brought home werena worth it. He might be drowned, lost
in some dark deep where the light of God could never reach
him . . . Poor Johnny was uncommon obstinate about it, she
remembered, but she didna give in, for she knew she was in
the right. And then the Lord opened his eyes at last, for he
came home and found her greeting her eyes out one day,
and that was bad for her in her condition, and he promised
there and then that he wouldna leave her for the fishing any
more. Aye, these were the happy days before John Samuel
was born . . .

For although Mrs Ritchie kept herself to herself even in
bed, even in her husband's embraces, it became clear by
the month of April that she was with child. It was as if
something in her own body had stolen a march on her,
and Annie did not at first know what to think. But she
had kept her eye single and full of light, as the Bible
commanded; she had not given way to the devil, no, not
once; and if this was not the handiwork of the devil it must
be the hand of God. The matrons of the congregation had
no doubt that it was a sign of God's favour, although even
among them there were some who shook their heads and
said: 'Ay, Mrs Ritchie, you'll ken you're living now. Wait
till you have a hantle o' bairns and your house'll no' be so
perjink.' My house will be kept in order, thought Annie,

for all you say; *my* bairns will be dedicated to God from before their birth . . .

Yet as her pregnancy advanced Mrs Ritchie had to stay indoors. She missed the Jubilee celebrations, and could not even go to church. That troubled her a little. There was such a queer mix-up of God and the devil in all this business; it would have been a comfort to take her unborn child to church. She sat in the parlour instead and read the Bible, especially the Book of Samuel. And she decided that if the child was a boy he should be christened John Samuel.

As for Johnny Ritchie, he was nearly out of himself with joy. For his wife must have accepted him after all; her pregnancy was proof of it. His guilt was transmuted into innocence; his seed was made flesh, like the Word of God. He grew very tender of his wife, and reflected, with round, bewildered eyes, that it was a queer division of responsibility. In bed it had to be all his doing, but after that his wife did all of it . . . Well, that was obviously how things were meant to be.

## TWENTY-TWO

# I

As October came on and the time of her deliverance drew near Mrs Ritchie not only sat more and more in the parlour by herself, brooding over the Bible, but repaid Johnny Ritchie's tenderness with increasing irritability. For there was no evading the fact that something was happening inside her which she had not willed, although she was compelled to acquiesce in it. Her life had been thrown out of proportion; the unknown was bulking too largely; and to redress the balance she was forced to be doubly vigilant, doubly sharp. In spite of her condition, too, she insisted on cleaning the cottage from floor to ceiling, although it was already shining with cleanliness; the kitchen flue, she pointed out, had to be swept, for it must be choked with soot, and that meant turning the kitchen upside down, anyhow, so the whole four rooms might as well be done. She was in that frame of mind which desires hard, clean surfaces and hard, definite edges. The slow, rounding process of which she was the vehicle maddened her by its indefiniteness, its inscrutability, its slowness; she desired only its final certainty, the definitive act that would mark the end of it. At least she would not let the furniture in her house be blurred by drifting impalpabilities, and she dusted over and over again the chairs, the chests, the pictures on the walls and the leaves of the palm-tree. She shook out the dust from the ball-fringe on the parlour mantelpiece with irritated impatience. All these bobbles were simply a trap for dust; and she had half a mind to strip the mantelpiece bare, to fold up the table-cover and put it away in a drawer, to burn in the kitchen fire the tall, feathery grasses that filled the vases. And every day she quarrelled bitterly with Johnny Ritchie over the dirt he brought in on his feet.

'This house'll go to rack and ruin while I'm on my back,' she complained, 'what between you and Mrs Lamont and my mother . . .' For that was another grievance; her mother had to be admitted into the household, since somebody would be needed to cook the meals and tend the fires after the child was born. And the midwife was that same Mrs Lamont who lived next door to the Rattrays in Mill Wynd, so that the taint of Mill Wynd would be all over the house. It was just like letting a slop of dirty water come in through the front door. Annie's resentment gathered head; she nagged at Johnny and at Johnny's dirty boots, and at the holes he wore in his socks, and at the stains on his working trousers. She seemed to have a spite against his legs, for after looking at him one night as he stood miserably in his night-shirt before climbing into bed she said sharply: 'A night-shirt's no' decent for a man with hairy legs'; and next day she banished him and his legs to the small spare-room bed, pleading that she could not bear to see him sleeping peacefully on the pillow beside her while she herself could find no ease either lying down or sitting up.

When Mrs Rattray took up her quarters in the spare-room Johnny Ritchie was shifted to the horsehair parlour sofa. And it was on the sofa that he was lying, cramped with the effort not to fall off, when his wife's labour began, shortly after midnight.

'Tits,' said Mrs Lamont, filling a kettle in the kitchen, 'we'll manage fine. The doctor'll no' be needed for a whilie yet . . . But you can g'wa' oot and fetch him.'

Johnny ran for the doctor and ran back to announce that he was coming. He ran into the kitchen, where he was shooed out again into the lobby. In the narrow lobby he collided with the doctor and took refuge in the parlour, where it struck him that Annie wouldna like to see her sofa looking so ravelled, and he spent some time in straightening the blankets and hiding his night-shirt under a cushion. His hands trembled so that the night-shirt would not tuck in; first a sleeve and then a tail hung out. Johnny had to ram

the rumpled mass deep into the cavity between the head
of the sofa and the upholstery of the seat, and he rammed
fiercely, for it was somehow important that not an inch of
that night-shirt should be visible.

The door opened behind him. 'Would you like a cuppie
o' tea?' said Mrs Rattray.

'Ay, oh ay; I'm just coming,' he said apologetically, and he
tiptoed behind Mrs Rattray until he was past the bedroom
door. But as he went into the kitchen he heard a groan
issuing from the bedroom, and his face whitened:

'She—she's doing awa' a' right?'

'Losh keep me, the man's trimmlin'! Ha'e, you sit down
and drink your tea, Johnny. Annie's daein' fine; she's no' the
first lassie that's had a bairn, and she'll no' be the last.'

Johnny drank some tea, but choked on it when a moaning
cry came from the bedroom, followed by a louder scream.
He set his cup down on the table instead of on the saucer and
fled out of the back door, down the tattie patch, right down
to his workshop, where he tore at the door until the lock gave
and he could get inside and lean against his working bench
with both his hands over his ears. Annie wasna the first lassie
that had had a bairn, no, nor the first that had had a bairn
in that room, and his memory brought up two coffins laid
out side by side, a large coffin and a pathetically tiny one.
'O God,' cried Johnny Ritchie, 'dinna let her die!' And
that prayer became a wordless entreaty which insensibly
spread and darkened about him until it was an entreaty
for the redemption of his own failing soul. For if she were
to die his guilt would remain unabsolved and could never
be absolved, never . . . there would be no redemption for
him; he would never be able to touch a woman again, and
he would have to carry his burden of sin to the grave. So
Johnny huddled over his working bench, waiting for his
wife to deliver him. But in the recurrent agony of her pains
Annie had forgotten that she was Mrs Ritchie. It was Annie
Rattray who was holding on grimly, desperately, setting her
teeth to endure the pain as she had once in imagination
endured the lashing of icy hail on her naked body. And
it was an anonymous being, a primal self that was hardly
even Annie Rattray, who was uttering these screams and

fighting to get rid of something, to make an end, to finish, to accomplish some definite though difficult task. 'That's it!' said Mrs Lamont. 'That's it, now! That's my good lass.' But the woman on the bed needed no such encouragement; she was a woman of resolute will and endurance; she would fight to the bitter end.

## II

Mrs Rattray came plowtering down the garden with a lantern.

'Are you there, Johnny Ritchie? The de'il tak' you, man. Where are you? Johnny Ritchie! Hey, Johnny Ritchie! Come in and see your bonny bairn!'

Johnny Ritchie lifted his head from his hands and tottered out, dazed and half frozen.

'Is the bairn dead?'

'Dead, you muckle gowk? It's a bonny laddie, as like yoursel' as it can look—'

'And Annie?'

'The doctor's gi'en her something to mak' her sleep. Losh keep me, man, come inside and dinna stand havering there. It's bitter cauld.'

Johnny Ritchie stood in the kitchen looking down on his son, who turned his head from side to side and let out a thin wail, not unlike the mewing of a kitten. Johnny held up his own big hand, red with cold, and gazed first at his own fist and then at the infant's.

'My fingers are ower cauld to touch him.'

But he went on peering at the miracle which lay before him, and his blue eyes softened and he looked surprised and innocent, as if the archangel had lowered his sword to let him pass into a lost Eden.

## III

Annie Rattray woke up, amazed at her own weakness and at the pain she felt when she moved. Her hair was in two long pigtails, but the bed was strange. And what was Mrs Lamont doing in her bedroom?

'You've had a good sleep. Would you like to see your bairn? It's a fine laddie.'

'My bairn?'

'Nine and a half pund weight. Born at half-past six. You did gey weel, Annie; that's what comes o' having a big enough bum,' said the midwife, and shouted:

'Mrs Rattray! She's wakened up. Bring the bairn in!'

Mrs Rattray came in dandling a red-faced infant with a round head that rolled a little from side to side, helplessly, an incredibly tiny round head.

'Ay, noo! Ay, noo-na! You ken your granny, do you?'

'That's not yours, it's mine,' said Mrs Ritchie. 'Give it to me.'

John Samuel Ritchie knew that he belonged to his mother, although at first he was inclined to grasp the relationship by the wrong end and assume that his mother belonged to him. This mistake was natural, for he thought that all his sensations were his mother: it was she who sometimes made him feel warm and dry, and sometimes cold and wet; sometimes she let him lie still, and at other times rocked him or rolled him over and turned him up; it was she who changed bewilderingly from a brightness that made his eyes blink to a darkness that lulled him to sleep. But he soon learned that the soft white shawl was a less important manifestation of the maternal environment than the soft white skin of a round bosom which, just when he was beginning to feel forlorn, never failed to yield him the living connection he sought. And a certain regularity in the phases of his environment enlightened his bewilderment: the rolling and turning, for instance, usually followed the cold and wet and was succeeded by the warm and dry; the round white bosom always appeared at the same height; it was always after the same interval that he was lifted and laid into the ambient liquid warmth which seemed to him familiar and natural. John Samuel Ritchie, who was a placid and stolid infant, accepted it all, and began to discriminate until he identified the looming, moving object attached to the round bosom and the impelling hands as being more particularly his mother, more his mother than the shawl was, or the cradle, or the bath. But because he was slow to relinquish an impression he did not quite abandon the belief that his mother extended all around him, and indeed had not abandoned it when he died some twenty years later.

He was a healthy, well-made child, and Mrs Ritchie was

proud of him. She kept him so clean that Bet Reid declared: 'Annie Ritchie's bairn doesna dare to wet his hippens.' He was a credit to her, as everybody told her, and until he was nearly three months old she did not suspect that he could have any sin in him. But at that tender age John Samuel exhibited to his mother the fact that he was potentially a man, and although he was unconscious of offence his mother was shocked and uneasy. It didna seem natural in so young a bairn. Could it be that in this flesh of her flesh, bone of her bone, the devil had after all found a lodging? A smart slap descended on John Samuel from the all-providing maternal hand, and he screamed his protest at being given what he did not want. This outburst of temper confirmed Mrs Ritchie's fears, and she indignantly covered him up and left him to scream.

Before he was weaned John Samuel had learned to expect slaps and shakings, and by the time he was crawling he had learned to accept them. He still crawled hopefully after his mother, however. One never knew; this time she might not shut him in his high chair and tell him to sit still and keep clean. But as his activities extended, his mother's temper became shorter. Whatever he made for—the coalbucket, the dust-pan, the stones on the back garden path—she was sure to head him off, and John Samuel learned to confine himself to the long narrow lobby, where he rolled empty cotton reels to and fro and watched the front door in case it might open.

Johnny Ritchie, who was now a deacon, had nothing to say when Annie pointed out that the child must be brought up in the fear of God. He was beginning to realize that although John Samuel might be innocent enough to absolve his father of any guilt in begetting him he was yet a human infant and subject to original sin. Johnny furtively gave sweets to John Samuel after he had been smacked, but always at a decent interval after the smacking, and usually in a corner of the workshop where his wife could not see the transaction; and when he and Annie knelt by their bed at night to say their prayers he always put up a special prayer for his son.

The shortness of Annie's temper may have derived partly

from her second pregnancy, for when John Samuel was two years old, just about the time that Britain was declaring war on the Boers, a daughter was born to the Ritchies. She was christened Sarah, after Johnny's mother, and Annie, after her own mother, and was as unlike John Samuel as she could be. John Samuel had Mrs Ritchie's dark eyes and hair, but his round head and face resembled his father's; Sarah Annie was born with a thatch of golden down on her head like a duckling and she had Johnny Ritchie's blue eyes, but from the beginning the women who looked at her prophesied that she would grow up the living spit of her mother. She was a restless, fractious child, and where John Samuel had lain placidly under his blankets Sarah Annie screamed and kicked off all coverings. Mrs Ritchie was worn nearly to a shadow, she complained, between the two of them, what with Sarah Annie screaming the house down and John Samuel dragging lumps of coal over the kitchen floor. The boy had a trick, too, of standing staring at the baby, especially when she was being put to the breast, and his mute, persistent stare embarrassed and irritated his mother, so that one day before feeding the infant she turned him out of the kitchen into the back garden. John Samuel beat with his fists on the door, crying: 'Let Johnsammo in! Let Johnsammo in!' and his sobbing and yelling went on unceasingly while Mrs Ritchie was coaxing milk into Sarah Annie. By the time that the baby was laid down, she, too, screaming, Mrs Ritchie was twittering with rage, and she took John Samuel by the ear and locked him in the coal-cellar, saying: 'You can scream there as much as you like.'

When Sarah Annie had fallen asleep Mrs Ritchie unlocked the coal cellar. To her disgust she found that John Samuel had been sick over the coal and over himself. He was an unsavoury object, more like one of her sister's children than hers, and she scrubbed him and hustled him into clean garments, and tied a fresh pinafore round him. Then she set him on a chair and lectured him about the black devil within him, whose blackness she could not scrub away, and the hell that might await him when he died, a hell from which she would be unable to save him. Her voice shook and her face paled as she disclosed the horror of the pit into which a human soul could fall, and John Samuel was terrified, so terrified that he could not even bleat.

For many hours afterwards Mrs Ritchie was filled with a gloomy solemnity; the Day of Judgment, that had receded from her imagination, towered once more above her, and when she knelt by her bed at night she thought fearfully of the narrow bed in which she would lie at the last, and felt as if the sleep that was awaiting her might be the awful sleep of death. Folk as young as she was could die. Bob Craigie, who had gone into the bursary class when she couldn't, was dead just the other week—killed in South Africa by these savage Boers. From the dark blot of Africa death might spread and spread until it came even to Calderwick and stretched a long finger into the houses and stopped the life of young people as well as old; it would need only one touch and Annie's beating heart would stop like a run-down clock. And what would happen then? Her spirit, lonely and shivering, would have to leave its house and stand exposed to the searching eye of God. Thou God Seest Me. A Christian ought to remember that every night before lying down to sleep; and so Annie, kneeling by her bed, committed herself to God as she would commit herself to Him on her last day.

But the rehearsal of death is more difficult than any other rehearsal, and it is not so easy to assure oneself that the final performance will be all right. The chill of her fear certainly made the blankets seem warmer by contrast, and the apprehension of her ultimate loneliness made Johnny Ritchie's proximity welcome, but upon the Last Day of all there would be neither husband nor wife, neither parent nor child, and Mr and Mrs Ritchie, like their children John Samuel Ritchie and Sarah Annie Ritchie, would have to stand alone and be called to account before God. Sharp questions kept starting up in Mrs Ritchie's mind like clusters of spears, and this time it was not only the derision of her neighbours that pointed them, it was the derision, the contempt, of the congregation of saints and martyrs, angels and archangels, around the throne of her heavenly Father. What would they think of a woman who brought up her children so badly that they had to go to hell? The ultimate loneliness of the two children did not separate their mother from all responsibility, and if she did not do her duty by them so that they were a credit to her on that Day she would be mocked, she would be despised, she would be hounded through all eternity by the wrath and contempt of Heaven.

When a child clutches at his mother's skirt he is making a wordless prayer against that ultimate loneliness, a prayer for assurance that there is a living connection between him and her. Shall not a godly mother detach these clinging fingers? Shall she not, with her inner eye on that solitary responsibility of the soul to God, rebuke the lack of independence in her offspring? He is not to remain a child, for he must stand alone at the Judgment Day, and so she prises the fingers loose and sets him on a chair, with a sharp command.

As soon as his legs can carry him so far she sends him to church, with a spotless collar round his neck and a pair of gloves to keep his hands clean; he is led by his father, and looks neither to the right nor to the left, for a twitch of the hand recalls his attention. He learns to walk soberly, avoiding the mire that may tempt his feet; and although the stiff white collar chafes his neck and the gloves are tight on his hot little hands he must sit still in the house of God, even more still than in his mother's house, or he will fall into disgrace; he will have committed sin. For if it is dreadful to sin on a weekday, it is still more dreadful to sin on a Sunday, and the child, remembering the text above his mother's bed, Thou God Seest Me, bethinks himself that God's eyesight is even sharper in His own house than in an ordinary bedroom. So the child sits still, hardly daring to breathe, conscious only that there is a barrier around him which he does not understand but which isolates him even from his father, a barrier which rises impregnably every Sunday and compels him to be alone with the God he fears. The minister in the pulpit represents that God, and the child watches him closely; but although the black gown flutters and the two white bands under the minister's chin are in ceaseless motion, flying apart and falling together again, they tell the child nothing. He finds no clue even in what the grown-ups of the congregation say to each other at the church door after the service. They must know the significance of what they have been doing, for they are grown-ups, but their words are politely trivial; they say in voices which ring a little false: 'It's a fine day the day, Mr Ritchie,' or, 'Dreadful weather we're having, Mr Ritchie,' and the child, holding his father's hand, wonders if the weather is more especially God's weather on Sunday and if that is why the grown-ups insist on referring to it. But he is hurried from the house of God, which is in some strange way his father's house, and is brought back to number thirty-seven North Road, which is just as certainly his mother's house, for she calls out: 'Wipe your feet, the pair of you, and dinna bring dirt on to my clean floors.' And if in his relief at getting back to his mother's house the child clutches at her skirt, she prises his fingers loose and sets him on a chair, with the sharp command to sit still and be good.

John Samuel Ritchie's education has begun. His parents are doing their duty.

## TWENTY-FOUR

Surely, thought Mrs Ritchie, no parents ever did their duty better. And yet the more she struggled to keep the devil off the more cunningly did he beleaguer her. She began to discover that a fortified house challenges attack, that the more advanced towards heaven an outpost lies the more vigilantly it must be patrolled. The devil was lying in ambush just outside her front gate, ready to pounce upon John Samuel, for instance, when he went to school.

John Samuel was inclined to be a dovering body like his father, inclined to put off decisive moments—to cry: 'No' time yet, no' *quite* time yet, no' just this very minute.' But although that explained his reluctance to quit the house and his dislike of the punctuality with which his mother turned him out exactly five minutes before the school bell rang, leaving him barely time to run straight to school if he were not to be punished for lateness by the teacher, it did not explain, thought Mrs Ritchie, his reluctance to come back to the house again when school was over. No, that happened because the devil insinuated himself into John Samuel as soon as the front gate shut behind the laddie. For what else could induce John Samuel to come lagging home twenty minutes late for his dinner, with his collar muddy and his stockings torn, knowing, as he did, that his mother allowed him five minutes for the homeward run and that after dinner he must go to school again? Mrs Ritchie told him firmly, time and again, that if he took more than five minutes to come home he would be punished for it, and that if his clothes were in a mess he would be punished more severely, and yet she had to punish him nearly every day. Now, if the devil was strong enough to wile away a bairn who hated leaving his mother's house every morning, Mrs Ritchie must summon all her resolution to defeat him. The one thing that could guard the bairn was a habit of obedience, and so Mrs Ritchie told him: 'I'll teach you to obey me if I have to thrash you within an inch of your life.' He would thank her for it later on, she thought, wincing as the child's screams went through her head like a knife; he would be grateful when he was old enough to understand.

But Mrs Ritchie was not so simple as to think that the devil was checkmated merely because she thrashed John Samuel, nor even because she thrashed Sarah Annie too for bolting out of the back door like a rabbit whenever she found it open. (It was all very well for Johnny Ritchie to excuse his daughter by saying that she didna really disturb him in the workshop; Mrs Ritchie knew perfectly well that no man could get on with his work if a bairn was taigling after him, and that it was merely another device of the devil to draw her children from the security of home. A child that ran away as far as the workshop might run farther.) The whole population of Calderwick walked up and down beyond the bounds of the garden, and any one of them might be a vessel for devilish malice and hatred of the godly. So Mrs Ritchie was, in one sense, hardly surprised when Bet Reid marched in at the front gate one day and insulted her on her very door-step.

'No, I'm *not* coming in, Annie Ritchie. My Davie is in the class above your poor bairn at the school, and a' the bairns say that you lead the laddie a dog's life; and I heard him screaming mysel' yesterday, and the day before yesterday, and the day before that, and, as sure's death, if I hear screams like yon again I'll set the Cruelty man on to you. Mind you that, now. I've warned you, you wicked bitch that you are.'

Mrs Ritchie's long, pale face grew longer and paler:

'It would set you better no' to swear, Mrs Reid. I'm only trying to bring my bairns up to be decent and respectable, and to keep them from the gutter and from the likes of you. Get off my property, if you please.'

Mrs Ritchie advanced down the garden path, white and icy, without saying another word, and Bet Reid, red, voluble and still swearing, had the garden gate shut in her face. But Mrs Ritchie's icy dignity concealed a heart palpitating with fear and exultation; the Enemy was coming more into the open; she was in for it now. She was marked out as a martyr for righteousness' sake. Let them all attack her; she would show them that she was not to be downed.

When John Samuel came home that day, not quite so late as formerly, he received the thrashing he deserved, and, indeed, expected, but on top of it he got a long and searching lecture about hell and the devil. Mrs Ritchie saw, with triumph, that she was prevailing. John Samuel, sobbing broken-heartedly, promised to be good and to obey her to the letter.

'Then I'll no' need to thrash you any more,' she said, comforting him. 'I dinna want you to grow up to be meat for the devil, John Samuel; I want my laddie to be with me in heaven. And I'll give you an egg for your tea if you come straight home like a good bairn.'

'Ay weel,' said Johnny Ritchie, sighing heavily as he pushed back his plate. 'Ay weel, I've a lot o' work on hand; I'd better be aff.'

'Will you no' ha'e a bit ginger pudding?'

Her victory over John Samuel had made Mrs Ritchie's voice weak and gentle, yet Johnny Ritchie flinched when she spoke to him.

'Na; I hinna time the day.'

Johnny was getting careless about his meat, thought Mrs Ritchie; he was aye fleeing awa' to work at this, that or the other. But he was getting plenty of work, that was a good thing to remember; and if things went on like this the bairns would be able to go to the Academy after all . . .

Yes, the Ritchies were doing their duty, especially Mrs Ritchie. It was a pity she was so surrounded by enemies and had no Christian neighbours to encourage her. For although she was putting up a good fight Mrs Ritchie felt a need for encouragement. It was lonely work being an outpost, and so she slipped down to Morton the baker's at the corner of the street to ask if Mrs Morton would care to come all the way from the other end of the town to have tea with her next day. Morton the baker was an elder in

St James's, and his wife, good sonsy woman, never failed to say: 'I wish my bairns were mair like yours, Mrs Ritchie. I'm aye telling them that.' Nor did she fail on this occasion to remark: 'I never saw such weel-conducted bairns, Mrs Ritchie.' John Samuel and Sarah Annie, sitting each upright on a chair, hardly daring to breathe, gazed at their boots in confusion, but Mrs Ritchie's heart swelled with exultation. No, Bet Reid would find little support among the godly for her wicked, her unjustifiable accusations. 'They're no' sic bad bairns,' she replied modestly. 'I do my best for them, Mrs Morton; I keep them in about the house.'

Yet although Bet Reid had been routed from the doorstep and driven beyond the garden gate her poisonous tongue was certainly not silenced. From her parlour window Mrs Ritchie could see idle women, doubtless cronies of Bet Reid's, gossiping outside the gate, or even turning their heads to look at the house. It was always possible, of course, to scare them away by suddenly opening the front door and walking down to the gate; few of them stood their ground when Mrs Ritchie leaned over the gate and gazed up and down the North Road as if looking for somebody. But it was irritating to know that the dirty slime of slander was spreading around the house and that one had to be constantly sweeping it back into the gutter. There was something more that Mrs Ritchie could do, however. Out of pure friendliness she had been giving all her grocery orders to the firm that employed Andrew Reid, and she could now withdraw her custom. Nor would she hesitate to tell everybody the reason why. 'I cannot deal with a shop that employs such a godless man as Andrew Reid,' she would say. Indeed, she would make a round of shops, calling in at Morton the baker's and Ross the chemist's and Mary Watson the draper's, and they would all be glad to hear her news, for they were members of St James's Church and didn't hold with giving custom to Auld Kirk shops. Mrs Ritchie bestowed Sarah Annie, for this once, in Johnny's workshop, put on her hat and coat, took her basket on her arm, and sallied forth.

She did not scurry, although she was traversing hostile country, as she went down the North Road and passed Bet

Reid's house; she walked with stiff dignity, taking small, precise steps, and the starched collar round her neck kept her chin high. There was something irresistibly challenging about the small stiff figure, and Bet Reid, who ran into her in the street and was cut dead, could not help roaring with laughter. 'There's that Ritchie bitch on the war-path,' she said to the woman beside her, and Mrs Ritchie heard the loud remark. Her back stiffened even more, her chin went higher, and her round of the shops was longer and more exhaustive than she had intended. It was surprising what support she found, especially from Mary Watson, who said: 'You should be ashamed of yourself, Mrs Ritchie, that you ever spent a bawbee in an Auld Kirk shop, and it a licensed grocer's forbye, selling bottles of rank poison to poor creatures that would be better without it. A drop o' the Auld Kirk, they call it; weel, that lets you see what the Auld Kirk's like. And Andrew Reid will have something to answer for on the Last Day for all the drink he's served across that counter.'

Mrs Ritchie went home with her chin higher than ever, feeling that she had blazed a safe trail across a trackless jungle of wickedness in which enemies had been setting snares for her feet. But it was dreadful to think how much wickedness was in the world. And there were days on which her courage was not so high, when she was thankful to have her own house as a sanctuary—days on which she did not even go down to the garden gate, but contented herself with peering from behind the lace curtains that dropped like decent eyelids over the parlour window and the bedroom window to left and right of the door. Her long, pale face, peering from behind the curtains, thrilled the bands of noisy children that came along the road shouting from school, for it fitted a mysterious phrase that had become a catchword among them, a phrase of the moment which they shouted meaninglessly on all occasions: 'Face at the window!' They might have heard, or read on posters, that the melodrama, *The Face at the Window*, was being performed in the Burgh Hall, but the fascination of the phrase, the eerie hint of evil peeping through, was confirmed much more by the half-glimpsed face of Mrs Ritchie behind her parlour curtains than by the sinister face that scowled boldly at them from the advertising posters. Mrs Ritchie was a living bogy, a mother who half-killed her bairns, they had heard, and many of them went out of their way to pass her house and cry: 'Face at the window!' So the house itself, with its down-lidded eyes, came to look evil and mysterious to the children who passed it—as if the pale, peering face of Mrs Ritchie were the evil soul of the house peering out—and they kicked at the wooden posts of the garden gate as if they knew that an affront to the house was an affront to Mrs Ritchie. And indeed the spirit of Mrs Ritchie, the will of Mrs Ritchie, filled every crevice of that house, so that her own children would have thought as soon of disarranging their mother's features as of upsetting her furniture or insulting her gate-posts.

The impudent cat-calling of the passing gutter-snipes was another proof to Mrs Ritchie that the devil was beleaguering her house, and she had a double share of misgiving when Sarah Annie had to go to school as well as John Samuel. But the absence of both her children left the house peaceful; she was able to recapture that sense of absolute sovereignty which had made the first six months of her married life so comforting. Moreover, Sarah Annie was now big enough to walk to church, so that on Sunday the Ritchie pew was amply filled, and after a week of undisturbed diligence at home Mrs Ritchie could appear before the congregation in the house of God as an exemplary matron with an exemplary family. When the Ritchies walked in a sedate procession—first the children, then the parents—past the Reids' house on their way to and from church Mrs Ritchie did not turn her head to see if Bet Reid was at the window, but she knew that John Samuel's wide, starched collar and glossy boots and Sarah Annie's neatly brushed long fair hair and primly rolled umbrella were a challenge to the dirty brats that ran out and in of Bet Reid's kitchen. Sometimes she had the satisfaction of seeing Andrew Reid coming home from the Auld Kirk with his offspring, and she could truthfully say to Johnny Ritchie: 'It's a wonder Andrew Reid's no' black ashamed to be seen out with them.' They would be hanging on his arm, or punching

and scuffling and mudlarking behind him, the two girls with
tags of petticoat showing beneath their skirts, the boys with
muddy feet that looked as if they had been playing football
in the gutter with some old tin can. And Mrs Ritchie warned
her own children over and over again to have nothing to do
with those dirty, common children, the young Reids, but
to keep themselves to themselves.

John Samuel soon had reason to admit that his mother's
instincts were right, for one day as he was carefully picking
his steps on the way home Davie Reid pushed him slap
into the middle of a puddle and then taunted him by
chanting:

> 'Ritchie, bitchie, in a cage,
> If you touch him he will rage.'

John Samuel's distress grew so unbearable that he disgraced
himself by bursting into sobs and running away, whereupon
more young hooligans took up the burden of the song and
pelted behind him at full speed. Mrs Ritchie, as usual, was
waiting at the gate for her children, and at the sight of her
the pursuing pack scattered into the roadway, while John
Samuel clung to her skirt, almost past speech. 'You go
into the house, John Samuel,' said Mrs Ritchie. 'I'll sort
them for you.' She shut the gate upon John Samuel, but
instead of retreating into the house he stared over the bars
at his mother's triumph. For when she advanced into the
street, beyond the bounds of her own realm, calling upon
the culprits to stay where they were, not one of them but did
so, pinned to the spot by Mrs Ritchie's eyes and quailing at
the sound of Mrs Ritchie's voice.

'You muckle bullies!' she said, looking them up and
down. 'You should think black burning shame of yourselves. The headmaster'll hear about this. I know every one
of you, and you'll suffer for it, I promise you. Especially
you, David Reid.'

'It wasna me,' muttered David Reid, shifting from one
foot to the other. But John Samuel, regaining his courage,
cried from behind the gate: 'It was him!'

'I thought as muckle,' said Mrs Ritchie, nodding her
head, and then she turned her back on them and swept

John Samuel into the house. Sarah Annie, who had been hiding behind some other girls, one of whom was Betsy Reid, crept after her, awe-stricken. Even Dite Reid, it seemed, could not stand up to her mother . . .

That incident had some curious consequences. Mrs Ritchie went in person to see the headmaster, who not only gave David Reid the tawse, but sent a note to his father. Mrs Reid, who was as loud in her championship of the Ritchie children as in her detestation of the Ritchie bitch, gave Davie a severe dressing-down, and told her whole family that the Ritchies were to be pitied instead of jeered at for having a mother like that. She promised them, moreover, that when their New Year's party took place the very first children she would invite would be the two Ritchies, poor bairns. A thunderbolt could not have raised more dust in the Ritchies' house than that invitation when it arrived, for Johnny Ritchie actually opposed Mrs Ritchie's instant decision to refuse it.

'I take it very kindly of Mrs Reid to have asked them,' he said doggedly. 'She's no' sic a bad woman as you make out.'

Mrs Ritchie's reply was full of bitterness:

'I suppose you'll tell me next that the devil's no' so black as he's painted?'

'Ay weel,' said Johnny Ritchie, 'maybe no'. I ken that the bairns havena muckle pleasure in their lives, poor things.'

'Pleasure! Would you peril their immortal souls for the sake of one evening of what you call pleasure?'

Johnny Ritchie propped his head on his hands and sighed, but said nothing.

'Here have I,' said Mrs Ritchie, her voice trembling, 'slaved from morning till night to keep them decent, and you would let them go to that woman's house and learn to swear and make a mock of everything they've been brought up to respect! I'd rather see them dead and buried at my feet, Johnny Ritchie.'

'It mightna be a bad thing,' said Johnny Ritchie surprisingly, 'if we were a' dead and buried.'

'How can you say sic a thing?' Mrs Ritchie was now trembling violently all over, so that her teeth chattered.

'How dare you say sic a thing and God hearing every word you say, and you a deacon of His kirk?'

'Ay weel,' said Johnny, 'I only—'

He covered his face with his hands.

Mrs Ritchie steadied herself by gripping the back of a chair.

'You only want to see me dead and buried so that you can marry a woman more like Bet Reid,' she whispered. 'That's a' the thanks I get for doing my duty by you. That's a' the thanks I get for scrimping and scraping to make ends meet so that your wife and your bairns and your house are a credit to you. That's what a woman gets for marrying you—to be told to her face that you would like to see her dead and buried—'

For once in his life Johnny Ritchie achieved a decisive negative.

'No!' he said, looking up. 'That's no' true, Annie. I said no sic thing.'

'You said something gey like it, then. You seem to think that neither you nor the bairns has muckle pleasure in this house—'

'I only think that you're maybe a wee thing hard on the bairns, Annie.'

'Me hard on them? And me thinking of nothing but what's good for them! And me only trying to spare them suffering later on, in this life and the next! Ay, the next life, Johnny Ritchie, that you're forgetting; the life that goes on for all eternity.'

Mrs Ritchie's voice and body had ceased trembling; she seemed to tower above her husband.

'Ay weel,' said Johnny, 'I dinna think Mrs Reid's as bad as a' that.'

'But *I* say she is. *I* say she's sold to the devil, bound to him hand and foot, and has been for years, ever since I first kent her. *I* say that she's a godless, loose-living woman, and that my bairns will never set foot in her house with my consent, Johnny Ritchie.'

'Weel, I was only thinking they would enjoy a party; they've never been to any parties,' he mumbled.

'Parties!' Mrs Ritchie stared at him as if stupefied. Was

it a mere hankering for parties that had made him say such disquieting things? She felt as if a child had announced that he intended to commit a horrible murder and then had suddenly betrayed that he was ready to be bribed from his purpose by a gift of sweets, and that his words were not to be taken seriously. Johnny Ritchie was more of a child than she had ever imagined. Her whole body relaxed.

'Parties! Were *you* ever at a party when you were their age? I ken I never was. The first party I was ever at was Miss Julia's Sunday-school party, and I was ten year old by that time. I dinna ken what the world's coming to in these days, what with parties here and parties there. But if it's a party you're ettlin' for!—and a lot you ken about the upset it means in a house—if it's a party you're wanting!—you dinna mind if I work my fingers to the bone; but I tell you, I think of nothing but how to do the best I can for a'body, and I'll give a party here myself at the New Year. For into that woman's house my bairns will not go.'

And so because Davie Reid chanted a vulgar couplet at John Samuel's heels, a couplet for which Mrs Reid could not be held devoid of responsibility, Mrs Ritchie actually gave a Hogmanay party, and invited Mr and Mrs Morton and the four young Mortons. Supper was set in the kitchen, and the company played 'Hide the Thimble' and 'Twirl the Trencher' in the parlour; and John Samuel and Sarah Annie could hardly believe their eyes when Lizzie Jane Morton took the trencher into a far corner and then called out Mrs Ritchie's number, so that Mrs Ritchie had to swoop across half the room to catch it. Indeed, all who were present felt that Lizzie Jane Morton had a nerve.

As in duty bound, the Mortons gave a return party in a few days, and this time who should be there but Betsy Reid, the youngest of that graceless family. Lizzie Jane Morton's hand was again evident. For Betsy Reid and Lizzie Jane Morton and Sarah Annie Ritchie sat side by side at school, and it could have been no one but Lizzie Jane who had prevailed upon her mother to affront Mrs Ritchie with the sight of a young Reid. Mrs Ritchie, however, knew what was expected of a lady in another lady's house; she was stiff but gracious, and the incident passed off.

Yet who can divine all the consequences of an apparently
trivial incident? John Samuel Ritchie and Betsy Reid
showed off before each other on that evening; an innocent
enough parade, but one that was destined to recur again
and again, and to trouble Mrs Ritchie not a little in the
years to come. Mrs Ritchie, however, smiled genteelly
upon the antics of the children and thought only, with
some complacency, that the bairns were making more
free with Mrs Morton's house than they had dared to do
with hers.

## TWENTY-FIVE

Nobody dared to make free with Mrs Ritchie's house. The very smell of the green linoleum in the lobby reminded the children of their mother as soon as the door was opened, and if a chair had stood askew in one of the rooms it would have startled them as much as if one of Mrs Ritchie's round shining buttons had gaped from its buttonhole on her bodice. Indeed, the house was Mrs Ritchie and Mrs Ritchie was the house, as unshakable and permanent as if she were made of stone, with a solid roof on her head; a closed four-square family structure on which, it seemed, the winds of chance might beat in vain. From Mrs Ritchie the children and Johnny Ritchie went out into the world each morning; to her they returned for food, for clothing, for shelter, for sleep. On Sundays when Mrs Ritchie emerged from her house to go to church she seemed as strange to her family as a creature that had quitted its shell, and perhaps that was why she tried to armour herself completely before going out, covering her hands with gloves and her face with a black spotted veil.

During the week Johnny Ritchie merely slipped into the house and out again, leaving money behind him, but on Sundays he took on a new stature, although in fact his shoulders were now so rounded that he looked no bigger than his wife. In his black broadcloth, with the gold watch-chain over his waistcoat, and a bunchy silver-handled umbrella in his right hand, Johnny Ritchie was as respectable a figure as any man in Calderwick, and the nearer the family came to church the more Johnny Ritchie breathed freely, as if he were escaping from confinement into a larger air. For he was a deacon of the church, while Mrs Ritchie was only the deacon's wife, and when he sat at the end of the pew as the visible head of the family Johnny's importance overshadowed his wife's as the spire of the church overshadowed the humble living-houses beside it. In church Mrs Ritchie's Sabbath meekness was so marked that not a single woman in the congregation ought to have suspected that the deacon was of no account in his own house, or that Mrs Ritchie was now convinced that her husband would never rise to be an elder.

For what was Johnny Ritchie but a grown-up bairn? A bairn who hankered for parties and used hard words with the irresponsibility of a child; a bairn who was not to be taken seriously; a bairn who happened to have the big, gnarled, skilful hands of a man. Sometimes, it was true, Mrs Ritchie felt the shadow of a fear crossing her mind whenever she noticed his big hands. But what were a pair of hands? It was only in the workshop that Johnny Ritchie's hands were formidable; they would never dare to pull down a house. And in the house of God Johnny Ritchie's big hands, Johnny Ritchie's moustache, Johnny Ritchie's black trousers had at least a representative value.

The deacon's importance lasted throughout the whole of Sunday, and Mrs Ritchie would not have forgiven him had he failed to accompany her on the usual Sunday afternoon walk through the cemetery. For the solemnity of God was one with the solemnity of death, and as no pious family would think of walking anywhere on Sunday for idle pleasure the only possible excursion was a walk to the cemetery with new flowers for the family graves. As soon as the children came home from Sunday-school the Ritchies set out sedately, two and two, over the crunching gravel of the cemetery paths, and after laying their bunches of flowers on the close green turf they sauntered in the adjacent alleys, renewing acquaintance with the living and the dead, greeting every one on level terms, saying 'How are you?' to the living and reading the inscriptions on the headstones that commemorated the dead. From these excursions Mrs Ritchie returned even more refreshed than from church, for to walk among graves was like a rehearsal of the Resurrection Day, and she knew that no one was more certain of heaven than she herself. Yet once or twice in the summer months she was prevailed on to attend an open-air afternoon service in a field near the links. It gave the children a kind of holiday feeling to worship God in the open air, and from the wooden benches that were ranged among golden tufts of ragwort one stood up to sing new songs—little-used psalms with long, swinging lines and newfangled mission hymns that would have sounded too breezy in church. Mrs Ritchie would even push her veil above her nose in order to sing better, and forget to rebuke John Samuel for staring at the ragwort instead of at the preacher.

In general, however, Mrs Ritchie disliked holidays, especially the summer holidays when the children were released from school. The rest of the year had its regular laws: school for the bairns, the workshop for Johnny Ritchie, and for Mrs Ritchie the recurring seasons of house-cleaning and jam-making; but in the summer holidays, fittingly called 'the break-up,' the days of the week were smashed into lawless fragments and only Sundays remained intact. Do what she would she could not keep her two children employed about the house during the holidays; first one and then the other would be off as soon as her back was turned, and goodness only knew what they did down at the docks or on the sands by the sea. Life was not meant for playing in the sun and scarting about in wet sand. Mrs Ritchie had to keep reminding John Samuel and Sarah Annie that they were not as the beasts that perish, and that it was a sinful waste of the time God had given them to spend it running about like demented beings among the gorse-bushes on the links. The months of July and August seemed to mock Mrs Ritchie; she could not help asking herself in anxiety: 'What will the harvest be?' as if she divined that all around her hidden seeds of evil were burgeoning in the shamelessly inviting warmth and fragrance of the high summer days, as if the sun drew out whatever heathendom was latent in Calderwick. There was no doubt that public life was growing more lax, more frivolous, especially in the summer, for the Town Council had begun to organize 'attractions' for summer visitors, and one never knew when the streets would not erupt into senseless parades of decorated bicycles or pompous processions, headed by the town band, towards some foolish regatta in the harbour. 'This town's going from bad to worse,' Mrs Ritchie complained to Mary Watson; 'folk seem to be thinking of nothing but pleasure nowadays, and I have my work cut out to keep my bairns off the streets. Hallowe'en guisers are bad enough without the Town Council going out of its way to encourage guising in the broad light of day. It shouldna be allowed in a respectable town.'

Yes, it comforted Mrs Ritchie to know that the unruly summer was past and that the days were drawing in for the winter; it was a comfort to see the snug house lit up and the bairns safely under its roof while the darkness beat vainly at the windows. Mrs Ritchie allowed them all the freedom they needed, and if anybody was tied to the house it was herself. Did *she* ever have the chance to go gallivanting to the Band of Hope on Friday evenings? As for penny readings on Saturday nights, no thank you; no bairns of hers would go out on Saturday nights to listen to trashy songs and comic readings and stot up against drunken ploughmen on the way home.

'But Lizzie Jane Morton's going!' cried Sarah Annie.

'I should have thought Mrs Morton had mair sense. Are you sure, Sarah Annie, that Mrs Morton kens where Lizzie Jane is going?'

'It was Mrs Morton hersel' asked me.'

'I thought better of her than that.'

Mrs Ritchie's lips made a thin line across her face. When Mrs Morton, urged by Lizzie Jane, actually came in a few nights later to beg that Sarah Annie might go to the penny reading, Mrs Ritchie's lips again closed in a thin line.

'The streets of Calderwick on a Saturday night are no place for bairns,' she said. 'I'm surprised at you, Mrs Morton, and you an elder's wife.'

'Tuts!' cried Mrs Morton, 'you keep your bairns ower close about the house. That laddie o' yours, now, you'll mak' a lassie o' him at this rate.'

'I ken what's best for *my* bairns, better than other folk,' responded Mrs Ritchie, so stiffly that Mrs Morton retired in a huff.

The children, bending over their homework at the kitchen table, heard Mrs Morton's protest. John Samuel kicked moodily at the table-leg. Mrs Morton, for once, was in the right of it. The house was for lassies, not for laddies. When he was a wee, wee laddie, he remembered, and had been turned out of the house to go to school, he used to comfort himself by thinking that his father, too, was forced to leave the house after breakfast, and that it was only lassies like Sarah Annie and mother who were allowed to bide at home all day. He used to feel that he was being pushed out into the cold, pushed out into loneliness, whenever the door shut behind him. Well, that was how he felt now whenever the door closed to shut him into the house; he was pushed into loneliness as if he were in jail, and outside in the streets the other laddies were playing bools or football, having rare larks, and here he was jailed in the house, with wood to chop and coal to bring in after his sums were done, and tomorrow morning he wouldn't be able to go for a hurl in Beattie's milk-cart because he had to brush the boots and peel the tatties before he got out to school, and it was a rotten shame . . . He kicked at the table-leg as if it had been his mother's shin, and she bade him desist with as much asperity as if it were.

On the other side of the table Sarah Annie was ready to blubber with disappointment and rage. The house was *not* the place for lassies, and it was sickening the way people went on about it. Lassies should play tig in the streets if they liked. Lassies should shin up lamp-posts if they liked. Lassies should go to penny readings if they liked. Lizzie Jane Morton went, but Lizzie Jane Morton's mother was a silly fool, all the same. As for Sarah Annie's mother, she took good care to do what *she* liked, anyhow. Grown-ups were just dreadful, awful! . . .

The children bent their flushed, resentful faces lower over their copybooks; they had no slates, for a more hygienic age disapproved of slates, and so the satisfaction of spitting was denied them. But the down-bent heads looked dutiful enough, and Mrs Ritchie made no move to seize her hair-brush and beat the devil out of them. The hair-brush, designed to control the wildness of nature, seemed to Mrs Ritchie a peculiarly fitting instrument for chastising her children, who were now too big to be beaten with the bare hand. Still, even a hair-brush was not so good as a leather tawse; and she had been heard to say that a tawse should be given to every mother as well as to every teacher.

Yet it was not chiefly the weight of Mrs Ritchie's blows that made her children outwardly submissive. John Samuel had struggled again and again to contradict his mother, but he always shirked the fateful moment even when a loud voice inside him was shouting No! No! Whenever his mother looked at him the loud voice died in his throat and a dreadful anxiety oppressed his chest; he felt that if he defied her the whole universe would come crashing down on his guilty head. Sarah Annie had no compunction about dodging her mother, but even Sarah Annie dared not defy her to her face; all she could do was to run out at the door whenever Mrs Ritchie was not looking. Even then Mrs Ritchie was usually a match for her daughter: she had once run half-way to school after her and brought her back by the ear, although the school bell was ringing, to put her nightgown tidily into the bag that should have received it. The straight, unyielding figure, the long, unyielding face of Mrs Ritchie quelled opposition and suffocated protest as if by releasing an irresistible blast of force. Instead of contradicting their mother, therefore, John Samuel and Sarah Annie propitiated her: John Samuel now stopped kicking the table and rose obediently to bring in a bucket of coal; Sarah Annie shook her long hair almost over her face and blinked the tears out of sight.

At Christmas and on Mrs Ritchie's birthday the children propitiated her with gifts, and, as if they understood that she was the house in which they spent their lives, they offered her the gifts a house might need—an embroidered table-centre for the parlour, which would please her better, they felt, than an embroidered collar for her black silk dress, or a pink glass vase for the mantelpiece, which adorned her more fittingly than any jewel. Some ornament for the parlour was presented year after year, and it seemed the most natural thing in the world that Johnny Ritchie, a fellow-inhabitant of the house, should subscribe the greater part of the price. He himself had no claim to receive parlour ornaments; for him the children expended their own carefully counted pennies in buying a tie or a handkerchief, or even, as happened on one poverty-stricken occasion, a card of brass studs for his Sunday dickey and collar. Johnny Ritchie always sat in the kitchen, anyhow; he never went into the parlour at all except on the evening of the annual Hogmanay party.

But the outward submissiveness of her family did not allay Mrs Ritchie's suspicions that the devil, no longer content to lie in ambush outside her front gate, was seeking a foothold in her very house. John Samuel was growing to a great size; already he was nearly as big as his parents, and his big feet, his bony knees, above all, his big hands, made Mrs Ritchie tremble for his immunity. She could not be certain that wickedness was not gathering inside him, and, as if to assure herself that what a young male accumulated was harmless, she turned out his pockets every night after he had gone to bed, especially his trouser-pockets. What did she expect to find? Mrs Ritchie did not know, but every night she turned out the marbles, the leather 'sookers,' the bits of string, the furred scraps of candy, the stumps of pencil that filled John Samuel's receptive pockets. Once she came upon a scrap of paper folded into a cocked hat, like a *billet-doux*, and when she smoothed it out she saw written upon it in a handwriting that was not her son's: 'Partan-face, ha, ha, what did you expect?' Mrs Ritchie flushed with indignation. Had the boy left it there on purpose for her to find? Was he sly enough to get somebody else to write the insult? She laid the scrap of paper on the mantelpiece and confronted John Samuel with it in the morning:

'A bonny-like thing to leave in your pocket for your mother to find. Who wrote it?'

But although John Samuel choked and flushed with shame he managed to bring out the word 'Nobody.'

Mrs Ritchie gathered all her forces: 'I *will* know who wrote that, John Samuel.'

The boy, still scarlet, said: 'It's mine, it's no' yours.'

At that moment, Sarah Annie, catching sight of the paper, snickered suddenly with laughter. Mrs Ritchie grew pale.

'Not a bite of breakfast will you get, the two of you, nor will you stir a step from this kitchen till I know the meaning of this.'

'Och awa',' said Sarah Annie, 'it's only a note from Betsy Reid.'

'From Betsy Reid?'

Sarah Annie nodded. With a convulsive effort John Samuel, for the first time in his life, burst through the ban of his mother's authority.

'You clype!' he said to his sister, and then: 'It's no business of anybody's. It's *my* note. You shouldna rype my pockets.' With that he slammed the kitchen door behind him.

Mrs Ritchie turned on her daughter:

'Now then, Sarah Annie, you tell me all about this at once.'

'Och, it's only a lark. Betsy Reid and him are aye chucking notes at each ither.'

'I'll see about it,' said Mrs Ritchie, folding her lips. She dished up the porridge and then, opening the kitchen door, called: 'John Samuel, come to your breakfast this minute!'

There was no reply. Had the laddie gone out without his breakfast? Mrs Ritchie opened the door of what had been the spare bedroom: 'John Samuel, come to your porridge.'

'I dinna want any porridge,' came in muffled tones.

'Very well; then you can bide there till you do.'

Mrs Ritchie turned the key in the lock behind her and came back to the kitchen, carrying it in her hand. Johnny Ritchie and Sarah Annie were sitting quietly at the table.

'Where's John Samuel?' asked Johnny.

'I've locked him in till he's in a better frame of mind. I'll not have any boy of mine standing up to me,' said Mrs Ritchie.

Johnny Ritchie plied his spoon more and more slowly, and by the time his plate was empty he was scraping it almost mechanically, sending the spoon round the bottom of the plate as he sometimes sent his teaspoon wandering round and round his cup. Was he listening at all to what his wife was saying? Mrs Ritchie did not know, and her uncertainty sharpened her irritation.

'It doesna do to be slack with a laddie,' she pointed out. 'I'm only thinking of his good. And what business has a bairn of twelve to be carrying on with lassies? At his age! And Betsy Reid, of all people; a lassie that's bound to go to the bad; a bold, shameless limmer to be writing notes to laddies! She's just her mother over again, I'll wager.'

'It's no' *her* fault,' objected Sarah Annie. 'She just does it for a lark. How can she help it if John Samuel's soft on her?'

'You hold your tongue, miss,' said the exasperated mother. 'Clear thae dishes off the table. Not another word, now, Sarah Annie.'

'But John Samuel's no' had his break——'

A ringing slap on the side of the head cut short Sarah Annie's attempt to assert herself, and as she washed up the porridge plates her tears salted the dish-water.

As if the sound of the blow had wakened up Johnny Ritchie he pushed his chair back and rose to his feet.

'I think the laddie had better have his breakfast and no' be ower late for the school,' he said.

'It's *your* business to speak to him, then. You just slide out of everything, Johnny Ritchie. It shouldna be left to *me* to keep John Samuel from going astray, and you a deacon o' the kirk. A bonny deacon, I must say.'

Mrs Ritchie had never before expressed so freely her contempt for the man, let alone the deacon. Johnny Ritchie's nose reddened and the veins started out on his forehead.

'Give me the bedroom key. There's to be nothing locked in this house unless I lock it. Do you hear that, Annie? Give me that key.'

Mrs Ritchie had caught up the key, but her eyes were fixed on Johnny Ritchie's big hands. The hands seemed to have a life of their own; they were clenching and unclenching . . . She threw the key on the table, and her voice was suddenly small: 'I'm only trying to do what's best for a'body. I dinna want to see my bairns go to the bad. I only want to see them grow up good Christians, Johnny . . .'

Johnny Ritchie silently picked up the key and went into the lobby. Mrs Ritchie came behind him, with short, faltering steps, and when the door was thrown open it was in a trembling voice that she said, as one speaks to a baby: 'Come out, now, John Samuel; come away out and sup your porridge, like a good laddie.'

'Dinna be a muckle gowk, man,' said Johnny Ritchie, and with a snuffle John Samuel got off the bed, walked with down-bent head into the kitchen, and sat down at the table while his mother poured out his porridge. But after he had eaten the porridge John Samuel was violently sick over the kitchen floor.

## TWENTY-SIX

When Johnny Ritchie came home that night he sat vacantly before the kitchen fire with the long poker in his hands, poking holes in the black bubbles that puffed out of the coal. A wee blue lowe started out among the yellow flames every time he poked a bubble, and a fresh black bubble welled up from the hole he had made, once, twice, but rarely thrice; at the third time of asking the coal-bubble usually hardened and went dead. Nothing could come out but what was there already; the life buried in a lump of coal could not engender new life, it could only exhaust itself. A bonny wee blue flame for a wee while, and then the dull red glow of a cinder, and then grey death. That was it. Johnny Ritchie dropped a fresh nut of coal into the grate, waited until it had caught alight and then began his poking anew.

He was beginning to hate furniture. The fresh fragrance of the wooden planks as he planed them was pleasant; it was pleasant to lay them together and contrive the joints and smooth down the surfaces; but once the chair or the bureau was finished it was dead for him, fit only to be sold into somebody's parlour. He made and sold things for parlours, and what for? To keep his own parlour intact, that parlour into which he never went if he could help it. He made furniture all day in order to have something to sell, and what for? To keep himself alive and his family, to buy things that other men sold to keep themselves alive and their families . . . And to live merely in order to sell something merely to keep on living to sell something more was fair ridiculous. Yet a man couldna live if he had nothing to sell . . . Ay, there were fish in the sea and tatties and turnips in the ground and apples on the trees, but Johnny Ritchie had to go on making chairs and tables, day in, day out, to fill other folk's houses, to clutter up other folk's rooms with lumber, to give other folk's wives something to do. His own wife at that moment was thinking more of the finger-marks on her parlour table than of him . . . What was the use of it? Johnny Ritchie poked in vain at an exhausted coal-bubble: red cinder, grey ash; that was all. It would be better to be dead and buried and at peace.

Annie was aye yattering about the life after death. Ay weel, maybe it was the one thing left to hope for. Imphm, many a man, no doubt, had been driven before him into the same corner, with the walls narrowing and narrowing until there was no way out except through the narrow gate of a coffin. And then, after that? Would there be salvation? Would there be peace? Annie was geyan sure that *she* would get to heaven, onyway, and she would see to it that heaven was kept up to the mark . . . That wouldna mean muckle peace, would it?

A wry little smile on the deacon's face disguised itself hastily as a sniff, and Johnny brought out his handkerchief and blew his nose to make the disguise more convincing. She would be wanting to ken what he was smiling at, and he couldna just tell her that he was thinking what a time the Lord God would have with Annie Ritchie keeping Him up to the mark in heaven . . . Dod, that was fair blasphemous . . . Johnny Ritchie coughed into his handkerchief and put it back in his pocket. No, heaven would be mair like the kirk, and Annie Ritchie would have to sing small in it; ay, that she would . . .

He began to poke at the coal once more. The best thing to do with life was just to bury it decently. The kindest thing one could do for any man was to hap him in his grave. Johnny Ritchie's thoughts recurred again and again to the quiet graves in the cemetery where his mother and father lay, and beside them the infant that had breathed only for an hour and had escaped the burden of life. He would just have to bide his time; that was all. There was nothing more certain than death. Folk were aye dying. The one thing needful was to make sure of the life after death, and for that, indeed, the time might be short enough . . .

The fact that Mr Ritchie was preoccupied with death made it unexpectedly easier for him to agree with Mrs Ritchie. Calderwick, she had said, was going from bad to worse, but now, it appeared, the town was going from worse to worst, to unspeakable infamy, and a destruction like unto the destruction of Sodom and Gomorrah might be expected. It was no longer a matter of sporadic bicycle parades and New Year drunkenness in the High Street; the municipality had actually rented a pitch on the links for the whole summer to a shameless troupe of performing pierrots, and, still more appalling, the Town Council had decided that the town band must play sacred music by the sea every Sunday afternoon. Sacred music! Mrs Ritchie's breath nearly failed her. There was nothing very sacred about a big drum, and it was every bit as irreverent to blow hymns through a farting brass trumpet as to sing sacred words to profane music, like the Salvation Army. What was the world coming to? she asked, and as a dreadful answer to her question she heard that Andrew Reid had been appointed manager of the Co-operative grocery store, with a house above the shop, on the best side of the High Street. Andrew Reid had turned Socialist some years previously, and that was no more than might have been expected; but that a man like him, a red-hot Socialist, should get a good house and a responsible job instead of being put in jail was enough to bring down the wrath of God upon Calderwick. And as if that were not enough, the next thing she heard was that the Reids were sending their two eldest boys to the Academy, paying for them, mind you!—and that the whole clecking of Reids would likely follow their brothers as they grew older. 'The world canna go on like this,' Mrs Ritchie said earnestly to her husband. 'It canna last. You mark my words.' 'Maybe no,' said Johnny, 'maybe no. Ay weel, maybe it's all for the best.'

It was now necessary to watch even more strictly over John Samuel and Sarah Annie. Since he had defied his mother for Betsy Reid's sake, even although the defiance had sickened him afterwards, John Samuel was openly sullen from time to time. As for Sarah Annie, one never knew what that lassie would be at next. The minute she was outside the house it would seem that she forgot her mother completely. 'I saw your lassie up at the top o' the outlook pole down by the coastguard's,' a malicious neighbour would cry, or, 'Your Sarah Annie's been playing fitba' wi' the laddies, Mrs Ritchie.' 'I'm sure you're mistaken; it wasna *my* daughter,' Mrs Ritchie would reply with great dignity. But the hair-brush was more frequently applied to Sarah Annie's temples and she was given all the scrubbing to do on Saturday mornings. Now what, thought Mrs Ritchie, what would keep Sarah Annie and John Samuel in the strait path of righteousness in an increasingly wicked world? It was perhaps a pity that Sarah Annie wasna a laddie too; for the safest, the securest, the most righteous profession of all was to be a minister of the Gospel, and a lassie couldna well be that. But John Samuel could become a minister of the Gospel, and that would make him safe both for this world and the next; while Sarah Annie, if she were to become a teacher, would simply have to lead a godly and sober life . . . Mrs Ritchie had a sudden vision of herself on the Judgment Day presenting to God Miss Ritchie, M.A., and the Reverend John Samuel Ritchie, M.A., B.D.—or even, who could tell? the Reverend Doctor Ritchie. Safe, safe for all eternity! And all the angels of heaven would arise and call Mrs Ritchie blessed . . .

'How much have we got in the bank, Johnny?' she asked, in the weak, gentle voice which she always employed in referring to money or to the church.

'Ou, no' so very muckle,' was Johnny's canny reply. He might leave money in the house every week—indeed, it was a steady dribble of money that the house took from him—but the reserve in his money-bags was his own private affair, and whatever his wife had a right to she had no right to draw everything out of him.

'Would we be able to send John Samuel to the Academy and the University?'

Johnny Ritchie took up the poker and began to make holes in the black coal-bubbles.

'Dinna sit dovering there wi' the poker. I asked you, could we send the bairns to the University? I was thinking that John Samuel might be a minister o' the Gospel. Man, put down the poker, can you no', and give me a civil answer!'

'Weel,' said Johnny Ritchie, but he did not lay down the poker, 'I've been thinking about things mysel' . . . I might set up as an undertaker. It's a good paying trade . . . Ay, there's a hantle o' money to be made in that line; folk are aye dying . . . Twa–three years o' that and I wouldna wonder . . . Ay, it might be managed.'

An undertaker! Mrs Ritchie looked at her husband with something like respect.

'I didna think you had that muckle sense. Ay, you could easy make coffins in the workshop.'

As if she recognized that this was Johnny Ritchie's final capitulation to her doctrine that life was nothing but a preparation for death Mrs Ritchie treated him with much more graciousness after he added 'And Undertaker' to the signboard on which was painted 'J. Ritchie, Cabinet-maker.' She found some reason now for looking askance at his big hands; it gave her a bit of a grue to think that these hands hammered coffins together and lined them with paper-frilling and disposed the dead decently in their private houses. These very hands might even be fated to lay her out in her own coffin . . . Mrs Ritchie never mentioned this gruesome feeling of hers to her husband, but then he did not tell her either what were his feelings as he buried, one after another, men and women whom he had known all his life. Was he burying something of himself at each funeral? Was he haunted by the memory of the coffins that he had seen in his own parlour? Did he remember the occasion on which he had said: 'It mightna be a bad thing if we were a' dead and buried?' The shadow of fear that crossed Mrs Ritchie's mind might have been cast by a black thought lying deep in Johnny Ritchie, but neither he nor she made any reference to it. When Johnny Ritchie had on his tail-coat and was conducting a funeral his wife became meek in her bearing, exactly as if it were Sunday and she was sitting in church.

John Samuel, however, had a horror of the coffins in the workshop. True, his father called them 'kists' or 'boxes,' and he could see for himself that they were made of ordinary wooden boards sawn and shaped by Johnny Ritchie. But they had each a lid, and that lid was designed to be screwed down close on some human face that was dead and white like the soft dead-white of the paper-frilling. There was no pushing that lid away, no crying out that it wasna time yet, no' quite time, no' just this very minute . . . The boy felt that in the dreadful instant when the narrowing crack shut tight and the coffin was sealed the soul must lose its last chance to linger by the body and was hurried off, as if by a policeman, to face its God. How could father make those close-fitting lids? How could he bring himself to screw them down? And how could mother fawn on the screwer-down of coffin lids with that sickening and ostentatious meekness? John Samuel thought more than once that when his mother was dead she would like fine to be the invisible policeman appointed by God to drag reluctant souls to the bar of judgment. What would she say, then, when it was his turn to die and everything that he had ever done came out?

On the solemn days when Johnny Ritchie had on his tail-coat and was conducting a funeral, when Mrs Ritchie was speaking in a small, meek voice and casting her eyes down, John Samuel Ritchie could not eat his dinner, and usually stayed away from the house as long as he dared.

## TWENTY-SEVEN

The funeral undertaking proved a prosperous business for Johnny Ritchie. He never mentioned his bank balance, but John Samuel and Sarah Annie got threepenny bits to put into the plate at the church-door on Sundays and Mrs Ritchie sometimes put a whole basket of strawberries on the table when they were in season. Had it not been for the malice and godlessness of the people around her, godlessness which infected even her own children, Mrs Ritchie would have been as happy as a respectable woman could be. She had the cleanest and best-kept house in Calderwick; her two children were free scholars at the Academy; her husband's silent, bowed figure was clad in its blacks nearly as often as if he had been a minister. She had risen high in the world for a Rattray; indeed she barely remembered her Rattray connections, and her children hardly knew their cousins by sight. From Mill Wynd, where Mary Stott and her scaffy lived, presumably in appropriate filth, two doors from the old Rattrays, it was a far cry to the North Road, and Mrs Ritchie saw no reason why the distance should be shortened by any bridge of good will. Her greeting of Mary, if ever they met in the street, had long been reduced to an almost imperceptible nod and a slight contraction of the muscles round her mouth.

Old Mrs Rattray, however, occasionally trudged out to the cottage and sat in the kitchen, darting her shrewd eyes into every corner, saying: 'I see you've gotten a braw new biscuit-box,' or, 'You've had the doors painted again'; statements which sounded like accusations. But when the children came home from school the disparagement lurking behind her words was enabled to come out into the open; John Samuel's shilpit white face, Sarah Annie's

gracelessness, or it might be Sarah Annie's genteel accent
and John Samuel's glowering stare, were fully commented
upon by their grandmother. The children suffered her
remarks in silence. But one day Sarah Annie flashed out
in fury when the old woman, punching her in the breast
like a chicken, inquired: 'Is there no' anything growing
there yet?'

'You're a nasty, dirty old woman, and we don't want
you here!' cried Sarah Annie, and with that the fat was in
the fire. Mrs Ritchie's level voice cut through her mother's
protests: 'I try to bring my bairns up respectable and decent,
which is more than you ever did for me. I'm not going to
have you dragging them down into the dirt where you
tried to keep me sticking.' Her voice began to tremble
with indignation and self-pity, so that both her children
were moved in a shamefaced way to be her champions.
Sarah Annie recovered her self-possession first. She opened
the door and, in her best Academy manner, said: '*Good*
afternoon, Mrs Rattray.'

Mrs Rattray drew herself up, her dark eyes snapping:
'You should think shame of yoursel', Annie Rattray. I
worked my fingers to the bone for you, and this is the
thanks I get for it! I only hope and pray that your ain
bairns will turn on you some day the way you've turned
on me, you ill-gettit, thankless limmer, setting yoursel' up
to be better than your ain mither. As for you,' she fired
at the girl and boy, 'thowless Academy puddocks that you
are, you havena the gumption between you to scart a sow's
lug, and you'll be as muckle use to anybody as twa bits
o' strae. You a minister!' she measured John Samuel up
and down, 'you lang dreep; a'e thump o' your neive on
the pulpit-brods and you'd be greeting for a poultice on
the sair place. And you a teacher!' she whirled on Sarah
Annie, who was still holding the door open, 'you impident,
graceless lump; you'll just be your mother a' ower again, and
she'll no' ha'e her sorrows to seek wi' you for a daughter,
and God pity the bairns you ever get to teach. I wouldna
own the like o' you; I would think black burning shame
o' mysel' if folk kent that you were sib to me. It's a good
thing you're no' called by the name o' Rattray.' With that

she marched out, leaving a queer stir of excitement in the Ritchies' kitchen. Mrs Ritchie was still white and shaking, and Sarah Annie felt a rush of sympathy for her mother; even John Samuel enjoyed a momentary sensation of being on equal terms with her. A wave of authentic, spontaneous emotion had drawn all three Ritchies into its current; they had been swept together through the one outlet that was permissible to them in that house, an outflow of righteous disapproval and denunciation. The relief to their bosoms was so great that they all felt invigorated. Mrs Ritchie lifted one hand as she stood in the middle of the floor: 'John Samuel, Sarah Annie, you'll remember, I hope, to my dying day that I've done my best by you; and as sure as I stand here God will requite that woman for her wicked words.' She left the kitchen with a solemn step, and the children avoided each other's eyes for a moment. Then they grinned with pure enjoyment. 'She'll no' come back here again,' said John Samuel. 'If she does, I'll spit in her eye next time,' said Sarah Annie.

After that day, however, Mrs Rattray officially ceased to exist for the Ritchies. She herself might have returned for another bout, but her daughter was implacable. Until then Mrs Ritchie had never quite succeeded in discarding her mother as she had discarded her father, for although she had found a new Father in heaven she had not discovered any celestial supplanter for her female parent; in a shamed, unwilling fashion she had had to concede that one's mother remained irrevocably one's mother. But now she had an excuse for a definitive break; and when some fourteen months later she received a message at the door from a breathless small boy that her mother had suddenly passed away in her sleep the news seemed almost irrelevant.

Yet although Mrs Rattray did not return to the house her influence remained in the family, unseen but powerful. The children had experienced the invigoration of sharing a strong emotion with their mother during their united resistance to the old woman, and they desired to enjoy it again, to be carried beyond themselves on a flood of invective. Their mother's God frowned upon all other demonstrations of feeling, for to open one's heart in joy to the world was to invite the devil, but righteous indignation was an emotion to which no blame could possibly be attached; it was highly commendable as well as enjoyable. And perhaps because she was now cut off from her mother Mrs Ritchie had to supply her own lack and permit her own passion to rise in her breast from time to time, for she answered the unspoken challenge of her children more and more frequently, overwhelming them, their associates, and the whole of Calderwick in forceful tirades of abuse. The air in the Ritchies' kitchen was thick with angry words, and as often as not Sarah Annie answered her mother's tirades with counter-tirades beginning in the approved fashion: 'You should think shame of yourself, mother . . .' True, her counter-attacks usually ended in tears, but she was beginning to learn the technique; she was well on the way to become a skilled Scottish flyter.

John Samuel also practised vehement denunciation of his mother, but he did not utter it within the house. The angry feeling boiled up from his breast, but the words choked in his throat before they could come out, cut off by the blast of his mother's anger as the tops of waves are cut off by a hurricane. He listened to Sarah Annie in fearful admiration; she was younger than he and yet had the strength to rise against the hurricane before being eventually beaten down. It was as if the girl generated within herself some of the same dreadful force that made him quail. When the air was thick with angry words John Samuel's lungs laboured as if he were in a medium too dense for him to breathe, and he thought that his father betrayed the same discomfort. Instinctively John Samuel realized that if he was to find support it must come from another woman, from a wind blowing in the contrary direction, in the direction towards which he wished to be carried. He did not exactly thrive on the angry excitement as his mother and sister did, but he was stimulated by it to flee outside the house.

A boy who is conscious of some barrier between his emotions and the utterance of them may well believe that he is excluded from all that is warm and intimate in the lives of other people. Wherever the sign 'Exclusive' is hung up he will blindly push to get on the warm side of it, pushing out farther and farther, in the belief that he is pushing himself in; but wherever he is he will feel left out of something. John Samuel had not been trained to discharge his feelings at all except in repudiation and denunciation; he had no experience in tenderness, in fostering courtesy, in sensitive vibration to beauty of sound or sight or touch; he did not know how to meet other people, how to accept the world, and he could not help feeling that he himself was not accepted, that all he could hope for was anger and repudiation. Yet he pushed out for himself, trying to get on the warm side wherever he felt excluded, and as for some years now the sign 'Exclusive' had been hanging for him above the door into the Reids' house, it was to Betsy Reid that he turned.

On the other side of the Reids' door all seemed to be warm and pleasant. Mrs Reid's voice, even in abuse, had a warm smile behind it, for the Reid children ran out fearless and smiling even when their mother called after them: 'I'll knock you into the middle of next week, you wee deevils!' John Samuel would have liked to stand outside the Reids' door staring wistfully in at the joyous hubbub of their life, but as he could not well post himself on their stairs he waylaid Betsy Reid on her way home from school. Soon they were meeting each other regularly in the crooked lanes that ran between the long gardens at the back of the High Street, crooked lanes that reminded John Samuel at times how crooked his paths were from the standpoint of his mother's undeviating rectitude. Betsy enjoyed the importance of having a secret sweetheart; she and John Samuel nudged each other and showered abuse on each other as a mark of affection. John Samuel called Betsy 'Partan-face,' in memory of the unlucky note that his mother had found, and Betsy, too proud to show tenderness except in the same mode in which she received it, retaliated with 'Pie-face Jock.' They stood together, giggling, at the foot of the stairs which led up to the house above the shop in the High Street, and presently John Samuel, his heart pounding with excitement, kissed Betsy somewhere on the cheek. A week or so later he nerved himself to buy a small silver ring with a heart on it, which Betsy Reid accepted and put on her third finger.

But that ring brought him as much agony as happiness. Whenever he met Betsy his eye travelled first to her ring-finger. Was she wearing the heart or was she not? He could never be sure of her; and one day, when she laughingly cried, after some back talk: 'Oh weel, that makes us quits,' John Samuel felt sick with fear. His distress astounded Betsy. 'You muckle gowk,' she said, 'I didna mean that I was quit o' you!' But her gay assurance did not lighten John Samuel's mood. His round face was set, and he braced an arm on the wall on each side of Betsy so that she was his prisoner at the stair-foot.

'Betsy,' he said, 'I'm fifteen. Will you wait for me till I'm twenty-one?'

'Och awa',' said Betsy, feeling uneasy as well as thrilled. 'That's ower lang for a promise.'

'No, it's no',' insisted John Samuel, with desperation in his voice. 'I'll no' be able to stick it out if you dinna promise me.'

'You're going to be a minister, are you no'? I dinna fancy mysel' as a minister's wife.'

'I'm—I'm—' John Samuel choked and then brought the words out: 'I'm *damned* if I'll be a minister! It's my mother threeps it down my throat that I'm to be a minister. Will *you* promise, if *I* promise no' to be a minister?'

'What will you be?'

'I could maybe be a reporter like your Andrew.'

'So you could! Andy has a fine time o't in Dundee; nothing but free dinners and free drinks, mother says—'

'Will you—'

John Samuel's persistence and Betsy's evasions were both cut short by Mrs Reid's voice from the top of the stair:

'Betsy Reid, come upstairs at once! Who is it you've gotten doon there?'

John Samuel was shrinking away guiltily, but Betsy called back:

'It's Jock Ritchie, mother. Can he come up?'

'Oh, it's you, is it, laddie.'

Mrs Reid's voice changed and became warmer as soon as

she addressed him, and John Samuel felt a rush of gratitude round his heart.

'Come away up,' continued the warm voice; 'you've never been in our house yet, and I'm sure it's no' for want o' the good will. Come away up, and I'll give you your tea. It's a long time since I had a good look at you.'

John Samuel went upstairs as into Paradise. And as if the Reids' house were indeed Paradise the lion and the lamb, so to speak, were lying down together on the hearthrug before the kitchen fire; a placid cat with its paws tucked in was dozing beside a black Pomeranian dog, and John Samuel, to cover his confusion, bent down and patted first one animal and then the other. The dog started up and sniffed suspiciously at him, but the cat lifted its head a little, blinked, and began to purr. Another rush of grateful feeling flowed round John Samuel's heart and he realized, to his greater confusion, that he was almost inclined to shed tears.

'I wish we had a cat,' he said, caressing the sleek head and back.

'That's Pootsie,' said Mrs Reid. 'A great, muckle, lazy brute, are you no', Pootsie? And this is Nigger. C'wa, Nig, give a paw, now; a paw!'

'Mother aye gi'es daft names to her cats,' observed Betsy; 'the last one we had was called Teetsie. And we've done our best to call this one Peter, but she Pootsie's awa' at it from morning till night, and now the creature's nearly as silly as its name.'

The freedom with which Betsy teased her mother, the good-natured laugh with which Mrs Reid accepted the teasing, amazed John Samuel Ritchie. And when Davie Reid and Sandy Reid and Andrew Reid their father came in for tea the cheerful give-and-take in the family amazed him still more. There were no averted eyes or downcast faces; no tongue was still for long; nothing was swallowed down but food and drink. If John Samuel was silent it was from sheer happiness, and after tea he blissfully played 'Newmarket' for matches with Betsy and Nell and Sandy and Davie, and he had luck with his cards and won an enormous pile of matches. Presently Davie looked at the clock and rose abruptly. 'Time I was awa',' he said.

'Are you off to the brig?' cried his mother. 'See and wrap yoursel' up, Davie; it's a frosty nicht.'

'Davie's daft on stars,' said Betsy. 'He's awa' down to the brig every night wi' a star-map or something. An essay by David Reid: 'The Stars in their Courses,' will appear in our next issue . . .'

'Is that the time?' John Samuel was startled. 'Mother'll be wondering where I am . . .'

''Deed,' said the warm, motherly voice of Mrs Reid, 'you can tell her you've been in good hands.'

David Reid was gone before John Samuel, a dovering body like his father, had summoned up the resolution to take leave. He ran on the roadway because his heart was dancing; he had been let in, he had been accepted by the Reids . . . Even by David Reid. John Samuel glanced up at the night sky. Above the dark silhouettes of the house there was a powdering of stars; the longer one looked the more stars there seemed to be. John Samuel knew the Plough and the North Star, but all the other twinkling points of light were uncharted for him. His steps began to lag, and presently he stood still, gazing, until he had a crick in his neck and a faint vertigo in his head. Away up there were worlds upon worlds, shining in calm remoteness; the sky looked infinitely deep, the twinkling points infinitely distant and multifarious. How could one know which star would receive one's soul after death? Or whether one would have to fly beyond the farthest star of all? They looked much more remote than the sun, anyway, much less alarming, less like the peering eye of God. John Samuel had a sudden hope that in the vast spread of that sky one might dodge from star to star for millions of years before being caught at last by an angry and outraged God. There might be a respite . . .

He began to run home. He was unpardonably late.

## TWENTY-EIGHT

At the close of day, the rounding of one little life between night and night, the faithful labourer comes home to his reward. In Scotland he is rewarded by a sumptuous array of good things on the table, for the importance of this meal, inadequately called 'tea,' is profoundly understood. To come home for tea is to finish one's earthly toil and enter into a foretaste of paradisal joys. Mrs Ritchie, preparing for this banquet, could have set on the table oatcakes, pancakes, cream scones, soda scones, bran scones, drop scones, potato scones or treacle scones; queen's rolls (locally known as cats' faces), cookies, paris buns or lemon buns; cinnamon biscuits, butter biscuits, heckle biscuits or German biscuits; shortbread or petticoat tails; sponge-cakes, queen-cakes, cheese-cakes or macaroons; or even a plateful of assorted 'penny fancies,' covered with sugar icing in all colours. Every baker's shop in Calderwick displayed this wealth of tea-bread beside the ordinary loaves of white bread that stood in rows on their flat soles of thick brown crust, their soft sides still smoking where they had been torn from their neighbours after coming out of the oven, their rounded crusty tops vaulted like brown roofs; generous loaves that one might cut in thick, level slices and spread with butter, jam or treacle to appease hungry children home from school who could not wait until their father came in at six o'clock. In Calderwick the bairns ran into the kitchen for such a 'piece'—a 'jeely piece' or a 'treacle piece'—and then ran out again to bite crescents out of it until the crisp crust could be nibbled, the square sturdy crust known as 'plain Geordie,' or the rounded roof-crust called 'curly Kate.' But it was years since Mrs Ritchie's children had been regaled with a 'piece' at four o'clock;

they were supposed to be too big for 'pieces' and had to wait for the appointed hour when Johnny Ritchie came in by the back kitchen door from the workshop. Nor did Mrs Ritchie approve the wastefulness and luxury of fancy tea-bread; the heavenly rewards she imagined were of a less material nature. A man should be thankful to come home to a godly, sober, economical household and to sit down to a tea with 'kitchen' to it, such as a tasty bit of fish, or eggs and cheese, without lusting after the ingenious products of a baker's fancy, the devices of a heathenish, confectioner's heaven. Occasionally she would set biscuits on the table, Abernethy biscuits or heckle biscuits, but not butter biscuits, which were hardly spare and dry enough eating to commend themselves to her.

On this day the finnan haddocks were ready in the oven and Mrs Ritchie was watching the clock. John Samuel had not come home yet, but if he were late for tea it would be his own fault and he deserved no consideration. As soon as the minute hand touched the hour she would make the tea as usual.

Johnny Ritchie came in by the back door and carefully took off his boots and put on his house slippers before crossing to the sink for a wash. He said nothing to his wife and she said nothing to him. The hand of the clock touched the hour and Mrs Ritchie filled the tea-pot and brought the haddocks out of the oven, then she sat down in her place at the table. Johnny Ritchie dried himself hastily. Sarah Annie, who had been brushing her hair behind the screen that divided her half of the bedroom from her brother's, appeared in the kitchen. The family was ready, and Mrs Ritchie folded her hands, waiting for her husband to say grace.

Perhaps because it was his only chance of speaking without fear of contradiction Johnny Ritchie had fallen into the habit of saying grace at great length. Mrs Ritchie sometimes could not resist chinking a tea-cup against its saucer as a sign to him that he was unduly exploiting a privilege and that it was time to stop. Today, however, she did not move until the Amen was reached, for she was hoping that John Samuel would come rushing in while his father was saying grace and so merit a double share of reproof. But there was still no John Samuel, and Mrs Ritchie frowned as she handed the cups of tea across the table. The tea was followed by the haddock. 'Pass the bread, Sarah Annie,' said Mrs Ritchie, and no further word was spoken for a long time. But when he pushed his haddock plate away Johnny Ritchie asked: 'Where's John Samuel?' The opportunity had now come to make common cause in denouncing somebody, and Sarah Annie instinctively seized it. 'He thinks just because he's a laddie he can do what he likes,' she put in bitterly, but her mother silenced her. The occasion was too serious for the indulgence of simple denunciation. John Samuel in absenting himself from family tea had absented himself from a religious festival, from an affirmation of family reunion in heaven, and had voluntarily cast himself into outer darkness.

'Has he no' been home at all?' asked Johnny.

'He hasna shown face here since he left the house at two o'clock.'

The dryness of Mrs Ritchie's tone intimated that John Samuel's guilt was past speaking of. There was no room for mercy. God is not mocked. Johnny Ritchie immediately perceived the gravity of the situation.

'But this'll no' dae; it'll no' dae ava',' he said, relapsing into his broadest Scots in his agitation. 'Where can the laddie be?'

'He deserves the worst thrashing o' his life, big as he is,' said Mrs Ritchie, 'for what he's needing is to be taught a lesson.'

'I doubt he's ower big for a thrashing . . . It's just thoughtlessness, maybe; he hasna noticed the time, maybe. But where on earth can the laddie be, and it getting dark?'

'Och, dinna fash yoursel', faither,' cried Sarah Annie, forgetting her genteel English in her jealousy, 'he's just gallivanting wi' Betsy Reid, I'll bet you anything you like.'

'With Betsy Reid!'

Mrs Ritchie rose up from her chair, stretching herself to her full height; her straight, narrow body in its close-fitting black dress looked like a black iron poker; only her head seemed to be alive, and the very hair upon it was crisped in horror.

'Then it *is* a thrashing he's needing,' said Johnny Ritchie, with unusual energy, pushing back his chair, 'and I'll see that he gets it.'

Mrs Ritchie still stood as if petrified; all the blood in her body was in her head, and her thoughts darted like lightning above the immobility of her limbs. Her son gallivanting with Betsy Reid after the way she had brought him up! After what she had told him of the Reids! Her son, dedicated to God, wilfully trafficking with the devil! Mrs Ritchie felt that if she did not control herself into rigidity a storm might break loose in her bosom that would drive her to commit some dreadful action, to wreak a terrible vengeance on the Reids and on John Samuel, to batter their heads into pulp and fling them in the gutter before the whole town of Calderwick. She stiffened her back; she stiffened her jaw; and instead of a hiss she uttered only a long-drawn, shuddering breath. The devil was trying to fight his way up within herself, but though every member of her family yielded to him she would not yield; and Mrs Ritchie raised her eyes to the roof as if in prayer. When at last she spoke it was in a small, stifled voice:

'No, Johnny Ritchie, it's mair than a thrashing he's needing now. I've told that boy, and better told him; I've thrashed him, and better thrashed him; he winna heed thrashings and he winna listen to reason, and from this day on I wash my hands of him.'

Slowly, because she could not yet trust herself to move quickly, Mrs Ritchie cleared the kitchen table, removing everything, even John Samuel's untouched cup and plate. Johnny Ritchie made a movement as of protest, but Mrs Ritchie stared at him with a cold, fixed intensity that made him shrink and feel guilty. The flicker of energy in his breast died down and he huddled in his chair beside the fire, looking up from time to time at the clock.

But as the hands of the clock travelled from seven to half-past, the energy flickered up again in Johnny, this time as a stirring of fear. Where could the laddie be? No respectable lassie would be out wandering with him from four o'clock until this hour of night, and Mrs Reid, who was a respectable woman after all, would never let any lassie of hers bide away from home until half-past seven. Perhaps some accident had happened? Would the police maybe come chapping at the door to say that John Samuel had been run over? A quarter to eight . . . and the laddie had had no tea.

Johnny Ritchie got up:

'I'm going to put on my things and gang to the police.'

'You dinna think——?'

Mrs Ritchie's dark eyes were inscrutable, but the rigid tension of her body relaxed as she looked at her husband. Johnny suddenly felt infuriated.

'I dinna think he's in jail, if that's what you're hoping for; it doesna seem to dawn on you that the laddie might be lying hurted in the road somewhere, you dour, unnatural woman.'

Instead of countering his attack with one of her usual tirades Mrs Ritchie controlled herself again and answered in a level, cutting tone: 'God forgive you for your wicked passions, Johnny Ritchie, and for your wicked words; for you ken as well as I do that I'm only thinking of the laddie's good, and that I'd rather see him dead and buried than a disgrace to the family. But he's nae mair hurt than you or me, anxious as you might be to think that he is. I ken fine what's happened to him: that woman Reid has got her hands on him, as she's been trying to do for years.'

'I'm gaun to the police, onyway,' said Johnny doggedly, struggling into his coat.

It was at this moment that John Samuel rang the front door bell.

Johnny Ritchie hurriedly unlocked the door, and when he saw his son he gave him a skelp on the head that sent the boy staggering through the lobby.

'Is this a time o' night to come home from the school?' he roared, following the culprit into the kitchen. But if Johnny Ritchie desired to make his son's reception hot in order to counteract Mrs Ritchie's coldness, neither the force of his blow nor of his voice proved sufficient to shield John Samuel from the icy chill that struck into him from his

mother's eyes. She was standing where she had risen from
her chair, and without moving she stared at John Samuel
until he flinched. Not until then did she speak:

'Where have you been, John Samuel?'

'At the Reids',' mumbled John Samuel, half turning
towards his father. 'They gave me my tea.'

'At the Reids'?' struck in Johnny Ritchie. 'And here have
I been thinking you were maybe run over wi' a car, and I
was just going to the police office to speir about you. And
you sitting jocose in the Reids' a' the time!'

John Samuel raised his eyes and looked frankly enough
at his father: 'I'm sorry, father. I—I didna think.'

'It's time you learned to think, then,' growled Johnny,
struggling out of his overcoat.

Mrs Ritchie had not moved. With the same coldness she
asked: 'And do you need four hours to take tea with the
Reids?'

John Samuel's eyes sought the floor again.

'No,' he said.

'What have you been doing?'

'Playing games.'

'What games?'

'Card games.'

'Card games! Playing at cards! The devil's picture-books.
It's a wonder you thought it worth while to come back to
a Christian house. You'll be telling me next you've taken
to drink.'

John Samuel remained mute, but his face flushed and
he swallowed in his throat.

'I have nothing to say to you, only this: the next time
you enter the Reids' house, the next time you disgrace your
father and me by taking up with the Reids, you needna
come back here. This is a godly Christian home——'

'Mrs Reid's house is a lot mair Christian than this is!
You make this house more like a prison than a home. I
never asked to have you for a mother, and I wish to God
I'd been born a Reid! I wish to God my father had never
set eyes on you!'

Mrs Ritchie's self-control almost deserted her. She
stepped forward with her hand raised as if to fell John

Samuel to the ground, and he, fending her off like a
cornered animal, flung her from him with all his force.
Mrs Ritchie tripped and came down, striking her head on
the leg of a chair. Sarah Annie burst into tears and ran to
lift her mother, while John Samuel, leaning on the table,
grew white and sick. Before he reached his wife Johnny
Ritchie gave his son another and more powerful skelp.

'You would lift your hand to your mother, would you?'
he said, and then, bending over his wife: 'Are you hurted,
Annie?'

Mrs Ritchie lay as she had fallen, looking dazed, but
when she was lifted into a sitting position she put her hand
to her head.

'Where am I?' she said, in a weak voice.

'Are you hurted, Annie?'

'Oh, mother,' cried John Samuel, choking, 'I didna mean
it. I didna mean it, mother.'

'I canna hear a word you're saying,' said Mrs Ritchie
peevishly, 'dinna deave me, roaring in my lug.'

'Sit in the arm-chair, mother,' said Sarah Annie.

'Ay,' replied Mrs Ritchie.

She was helped up and set in her chair.

'Mother,' implored John Samuel, 'I didna mean it! Say
that you ken I didna mean it.'

Mrs Ritchie waved him off.

'I winna listen to you,' she said, 'you can gang to the
devil your ain gait.'

'You'd better gang to bed, mother.' Sarah Annie assisted
her mother to rise, and together with Johnny Ritchie they left
the kitchen, shutting the door upon John Samuel, leaving
him, as it were, in solitary confinement, a matricide in
intention if not in fact.

## TWENTY-NINE

That night Mrs Ritchie could not sleep, for accusing voices rang on her inner ear and she dared not shut the wakeful eye that kept a light glimmering in her mind; to invite sleep was to invite a darkness in which the voices might grow into monstrous shapes. Yet she was in the right and the voices were wrong. John Samuel, as she had predicted, had been in the Reids' house all the time, mocking at his mother. She was right and it was wrong; it was spite and malice and lying slander to say—what had John Samuel said?—no, she wouldn't think of it. One should not listen to the devil. I will not listen to a word of it, she said to herself. It was Johnny Ritchie's fault that she had ever had any children. I'll have nothing more to do with him, she said; I'll have nothing more to do with any of them.

She shrank away from her husband, into the far side of the bed. It was a disgrace that there should be nowhere for her to sleep except in Johnny Ritchie's double bed. There should be a top storey to the house; every decent house had a top storey. There should be a bedroom at the top of the house, with a white narrow bed in it for the mistress, a bedroom from which her light could shine like a wakeful eye above a sleeping body. One should be able to escape from the lower regions, from the sinful life close to the earth. Not only a bedroom, but a parlour there should be, high up at the top of the house, where a Christian woman could find peace and solitude. Although even there, thought Mrs Ritchie bitterly, they would come deaving her, shouting through the door at her, miscalling her for trying to do her duty by them . . . She had paid too much attention to her family, that was all, and they would maybe begin to miss her when her body was lying in the grave and her spirit was released into heaven . . .

During the next few days her son, John Samuel, abased himself. He sat at table with his lip trembling, occasionally darting a look at his mother, but as she neither looked at him nor spoke to him he lowered his eyes again and stared into his plate. He avoided Betsy Reid after school and came straight home, haunting the house persistently, grovelling, so to speak, at his mother's feet, begging for a word of forgiveness. For all the notice she took of him he might not have been there at all. The whole family was subdued and silent. Johnny Ritchie and Sarah Annie did not speak except when Mrs Ritchie addressed some question to them, and they initiated no conversation with John Samuel, although, unlike Mrs Ritchie, they did not act as if he were inaudible whenever he did say something. But on the fourth day John Samuel's eyes had ceased to supplicate and were sullen. He stared at his mother when he got up after breakfast and said, suddenly: 'You grudge me my very porridge.' 'Will you have some more tea, Johnny?' was Mrs Ritchie's reply. John Samuel went out, slamming the door. At dinner-time he asked boldly for a second helping, forcing his plate upon his mother. She did not betray, even by a movement of the eye, that she was aware of it.

'Gi'e the laddie a second helping, Annie,' said Johnny Ritchie. 'This has gone far enough.'

Mrs Ritchie started. 'Oh, I didna hear you,' she said, in a thin, acid, sneering tone. 'There's no' muckle left. I was thinking of keeping it for soup.'

'Gi'e the laddie what there is; we're no' sae poverty-stricken as a' that,' said Johnny Ritchie. It was a funeral day for him. He was in his blacks; he could presume upon his wife's outward meekness and his voice had a commanding ring.

In silence and with careful slowness Mrs Ritchie scraped the dish clean, gathering up the remnants of the stew and spooning the last trace of gravy on to John Samuel's plate. In silence she handed the plate to John Samuel, who began to eat with a great show of unconcern. Presently he laid down his knife and fork. 'I canna finish it,' he said in a choking voice.

'I doubt your son's e'e's bigger than his belly,' remarked Mrs Ritchie, with the same thin sneer as before.

'I'm *your* son as well as my father's!' shouted John Samuel. 'What did you have me for? I never asked to be born in this house.'

'That's enough, now! I said already there's been far ower muckle o' this. I'll not have it. Do you hear me? Finish your dinner in peace, or leave it in peace, but let me have no more o' this,' said Johnny Ritchie, with unusual determination.

'I'll leave it, then,' John Samuel muttered.

'Dish up the pudding, Annie.'

'*I'll* dish it up!' Sarah Annie jumped to her feet.

'Sit down!' roared Johnny, striking his fist on the table. 'Dinna you start interfering. Dish up the pudding, Annie.'

John Samuel was moved to unwilling admiration. That was the way to speak to her. He looked up and watched his mother as she collected the plates with a stiff, queer slowness of movement. Her body seemed to be made of wood; it was thin and flat as a board—like a black plank for a coffin, thought John Samuel, shuddering. It seemed impossible that he could have been born from that dead, wooden body. He could see the whalebone ribs of her stays, front and back, beneath her black bodice. She was all whalebone and starch; even her neck was encased in a stiff, high collar. How could any man have fathered a child upon that stiff figure of a woman? Dod, his father had some courage . . . That was the way to speak to her.

Sarah Annie was snivelling now behind her hair. John Samuel felt a curious satisfaction as he observed her tears. If he had dared he would have exchanged a glance of understanding with his father; he would have said, with a jerk of the head: 'Women!' 'Oh, ay, that was the way to treat them.

But Mrs Ritchie said never a word. In silence she gave out the suet pudding, and in silence the family ate of it.

Silence settled upon the house. Mrs Ritchie spoke to nobody except when speech was unavoidable, and to all remarks addressed to her she answered invariably: 'I canna hear you,' so that the question or the statement had to be repeated in a louder voice, which made the silence more dreadful.

'Mother,' burst out Sarah Annie one evening, 'are you growing deaf?'

'You needna deave me, shouting in my lug.'

'Well, *are* you growing deaf?'

Mrs Ritchie looked at her daughter. There were tears in Sarah Annie's eyes, and Mrs Ritchie unexpectedly addressed her as an equal:

'I've had a roaring in my lug ever since I was knocked down. I wouldna wonder but what I am growing deaf.'

'Oh, mother!' blubbered Sarah Annie. 'Oh, mother!'

'You needna fash yoursel'; there's no' muckle that I want to hear, anyway.'

'You'd better see the doctor,' said Johnny Ritchie anxiously.

'I dinna want the doctor.'

'It's a muckle lie!' cried John Samuel, starting up from his lessons. 'She can hear if she wants to hear. I dinna believe a word o't.'

'You should think shame o' yoursel',' Sarah Annie attacked him; 'you think a'body's a liar like you.'

'Is there never to be any peace in this house?'

Johnny Ritchie rose from the fireside, still grasping the poker.

'You'd better ask *her*,' replied John Samuel, indicating his mother; 'if there's no peace in this house it's her fault.'

'I'll no' be here long to trouble you,' said Mrs Ritchie in her new, meek, sneering voice. 'I ken better than any o' you that I'm no' wanted here.'

The ticking of the kitchen clock sounded loud as the other three persons in the room stood still, frightened and embarrassed, staring at Mrs Ritchie's rigid back. Johnny Ritchie cleared his throat twice, but Mrs Ritchie did not move; he went softly back to the fireplace and softly laid the poker in the fender.

'I think you'd better see the doctor the morn's morning,' he said, sitting down in his chair again.

'I dinna want the doctor; I'll no' be an expense to anybody if I can help it.'

Johnny cleared his throat again:

'I've a good pickle bawbees saved up in the bank——'

'Oh, have you?' said Mrs Ritchie, still sneering. 'It's the first I've heard o't.'

'Annie, you ken fine I wouldna grudge you anything.'

'I canna hear what you're saying.'

Mrs Ritchie picked up her knitting. Johnny Ritchie's clenched fist opened on his knee with a helpless gesture. Sarah Annie shook back her hair with a violent movement and sat down to a school book, boring her fists into her temples and screwing her mouth tight. John Samuel, scowling and sullen, settled opposite her. A glacial silence fell once more on the Ritchies' house, broken only by the metallic clicking of Mrs Ritchie's knitting-needles and the mechanical tick-tock of the large kitchen clock.

But John Samuel, in the middle of a Latin sentence involving the subjunctive mood, suddenly looked up and glanced round the room, like the puzzled observer of a motiveless quarrel. He had a queer feeling of anonymity, as if he were a stranger in a strange land. This was not his home, surely? What had he to do with these other silent figures? It was almost a giddy feeling, a light feeling, as if, nameless himself, he could rise and float away into a nameless world; but as his eye fell on the long black back of Mrs Ritchie, sitting rigidly upright in her chair, he felt a check as sickening as the sudden check and jolt of an ascending lift that is jerked to a stop. Mrs Ritchie was not anonymous. John Samuel stared at her as if hypnotized. That was his mother, Mrs Ritchie; but she was not his mother; she was not Mrs Ritchie; she was a secretive, rigid, assertive individual called Annie. She sat there silently obstructing the comforting wave of anonymity that sought to roll through the kitchen and carry her family away to the ends of the earth; she sat there pinning each of them down to her barren, isolated rock; she sat there raising a barrier around each of them, cutting them off from the whole of humanity, shutting them within four invisible walls of silence. The sickening jolt that pulled him up short made John Samuel's blood beat thickly. Something had to be burst open, and he scowled at his mother's back as if he

would have liked to rip it up. If it were not for her he
would not have to be John Samuel Ritchie; if it were not
for her he might be anybody at all: he might be a stranger
who could stride into the house and shatter its silence and
stride out again without being called to account. He might
let himself go; he might lose himself . . .

But Mrs Ritchie did not move when John Samuel,
having finished his Latin prose, took his secret excitement
to bed with him. She remained immovable when Sarah
Annie said good-night in her ear, resting a hand on her
unresponsive shoulder. She sat still, knitting rapidly, and
Johnny Ritchie, watching the glittering knitting-pins, felt
that they were weaving an impenetrable web of flashing
light and clicking sound through which no words of his
could force an entry. He put out his great, gnarled hand
and seized the stocking.

Mrs Ritchie stared at the big hand on her lap as if it were
the hand of an unknown man. Then she looked up:

'Oh, it's you, is it?'

'Wha else could it be?'

Johnny felt a little stupefied and more than a little
alarmed.

'Annie,' he said urgently, 'you'd better see the doctor
the morn.'

'I winna ha'e ony strange man meddling wi' me.'

'I'm sure you're no' weel.'

'I'm as weel as ever I was, maybe better.'

'But you're going deaf.'

'And what if I am? It'll keep me from hearing myself
miscalled for trying to do my duty.'

Johnny removed his hand:

'I'll tell the doctor to come in, onyway.'

'If he comes,' said Mrs Ritchie, 'I'll shut the door in
his face.'

Her eyes looked at Johnny Ritchie with a cold, fixed
intensity that made him shrink as if a door had been shut in
his own face. In silence he rose and made his preparations for
going to bed. In silence Mrs Ritchie folded up her knitting
and followed him into the bedroom. In silence they knelt,
one on each side of the bed, as they had done for years, and

offered up separate petitions to God. In silence Mrs Ritchie turned her back on Johnny Ritchie and, lying on the extreme verge of the bed, rigidly extended, stared into the darkness, keeping at bay the monstrous accusing voices which sought to drag her down into nameless shame.

For that was the horror of it: the accusations were not formulated; the shame was nameless. She was jeered at, flouted, mocked, abused, but the voices did not tell her why . . .

# BOOK IV: THE WOMAN

The Woman: I have reached the other side.
God of my Fathers, where are you?
The Answer: Thou fool; I am in the abyss.
The Woman: I heard no answer. There is no one here
but myself.

## THIRTY

Mrs Ritchie closed down her defences. She had been wasting her life on ingrates, and now she would waste nothing more—not a word, not a gesture, not even a halfpenny or a heel of stale bread. What was hers was hers, and she would give nothing away; she had her own soul to save and she would save it.

She began to keep both the front door and the back door locked and bolted during the daytime. Johnny Ritchie had to knock on the kitchen window before she would unlock the back door to let him in from the workshop, and the children, coming home from school, had to ring at the front door and wait on the step until she had decided to hear the bell. Even then she would not open the door until she had put the chain across it, so that she could peer through a narrow crevice and satisfy herself that the would-be intruder was really her son or her daughter.

Her deafness remained obstinate. The doctor whom Johnny Ritchie himself escorted into the house to examine her shook his head; she refused to hear his questions and he could not discover if her father or her mother or any of her relations had ever suffered from deafness. Her prescribed a nerve-tonic and, murmuring about possible constipation, a purgative. But Mrs Ritchie—perhaps because she knew that constipation was a penalty exacted by her idea of civilization—Mrs Ritchie, who desired rather to ignore the lower regions than to correct them, to deny rather than to encourage her bodily activities, burned the prescriptions in the kitchen fire and added what would have been the price of the medicines to the secret money-box she was filling. Except that it condemned her family to wait shivering outside the door on cold, wet days, her deafness did not incommode the household; John Samuel, indeed, whether out of bravado or because it enabled him to break the freezing silence without incurring rebuke, professed himself delighted with it. He was now able to say things aloud behind his mother's back which a year ago he would not have dared even to think, and he and Sarah Annie could indulge in a guerrilla warfare of muttered recriminations which ceased only when their father came in. But although his increasing boldness provoked his sister it drew no acknowledgment from Mrs Ritchie. She gave no sign that she had heard a word of his protests except that once or twice when she admitted him into the house she looked at him with fixed hostility, as if to say: 'The day will come when you'll be shut out for good.' He could have sworn that his mother paid no heed to his comings and goings, his sayings and doings, provided that he appeared punctually at meals and went to bed every night at ten o'clock.

It was all the more of a shock to him when one day, as he was hanging his cap and overcoat in the lobby, Mrs Ritchie suddenly turned and came back towards him, saying: 'What was that I heard you telling me, John Samuel?'

John Samuel reddened: 'I was saying that it's time I had a latch-key. I'm sixteen and I want a latch-key.'

A latch-key! No wonder that Mrs Ritchie had not been able to believe her ears. A latch-key! A tool with which anyone could rape her house at any hour of the day or night! She looked her son up and down: 'You needna think that anybody's to come into this house unless I let them in myself. If it's loose living you're ettling for you can g'wa' and bide somewhere else. I'm not going to have folk gallivanting out and in of *my* front door as if I were a common randy like some I could name.'

'Mrs Reid's no' a randy!' shouted John Samuel.

'Indeed?' sneered Mrs Ritchie. 'I didna mention her. But if the cap fits——'

'Och, to hell!' muttered John Samuel. His mother's contemptuous look had stripped him of his assurance and he was again filled with the old, uneasy sense of guilt. Had she been watching him after all? Did she hear more than she let on? Was she just waiting to pounce on him?

'To hell with the old bitch!' he muttered in the kitchen, taking care that Sarah Annie should hear him.

'You're swearing,' hissed Sarah Annie.

'To hell with you, too!'

But his angry mutterings did not allay his uneasiness, and as he sat at table he could not help darting furtive glances at his mother's face. With every glance hope shrank and dwindled. Mrs Ritchie's smooth, tight braids, rectangular forehead, icily bright eyes, close mouth and long, obstinate chin showed no weakness, no indecision; even her ears, which were presumably incompetent, were well shaped and finely convoluted, lying complacently snug to her skull. It became incredible to John Samuel that he had actually pledged himself to have supper with the Reids on the morrow, that he had had the assurance to think he could ever escape. It was as if, travelling in an express train, he had conceived the mad idea of opening the carriage door and stepping out into a sunny field of grass. Whatever he did his mother's will would drive him on past all that his heart longed for, straight towards a pulpit in the United Free Church . . . If Mrs Ritchie were to find out that he was conspiring with the Reids to get a reporter's job on the Calderwick *Herald* that would be the end of everything; nothing would stop the unswerving wheels from grinding on over his body. John Samuel's spine prickled with chill fear; his throat tightened so that he could hardly swallow.

The bread was stale and hard, but that was not why he nibbled at it slowly, taking small bites all round the slice; he was trying to postpone the moment when it would be finished, as if it were a fate that his mother had handed out to him and that he could not stomach . . . Whatever he did she would put an end to everything . . . It was only in a cinema-film that one saw the rescuing motor-car come swooping across the road, overtaking the train, to receive the escaping hero through a carriage window, or the still more untrammelled aeroplane swooping freely across the sky to let down a rope for the hero to catch . . . Govey Dick! Fancy having the whole breadth of the sky to dodge about in!

John Samuel's imagination strayed through the pathless

sky, where no lines were laid down and a man could steer his own course . . . Why not? Why should it not be possible to dodge his mother and God through all eternity from star to star? But if there was no finality even after death there was no need to be scared by Mrs Ritchie's threats of definitive arrival . . . Govey Dick!

The boy's dark eyes, which were so incongruously like his mother's, became as bright as hers and his round face seemed to lengthen. He laid the half of his crust on his plate and pushed it away.

'That bread's as hard as a stone,' he said, in a loud, challenging voice.

'It's all you'll get,' snapped Mrs Ritchie, and in the tea-table silence her answer was as startling as his challenge.

'Father, are we that hard up that we need to eat the like of this?'

Johnny Ritchie's shoulders were now so bowed that he sat hunched over his cup, his chin sunk on his breast, but with an effort he lifted his eyes from the tablecloth and cleared his throat:

'Is that a' the bread in the house, Annie?'

'There's nothing wrong wi' the bread. I'm not going to have good bread wasted.'

Johnny Ritchie stared at her. His watery blue eyes looked tired, with grey pouches beneath them.

'I think you're maybe a wee thing ower careful.'

'How can I be anything but careful with everything being eaten up and no' muckle coming in?'

'I bring in plenty.'

John Samuel started to his feet, muttering: 'It's just sheer spite that makes her put down the hard ends. I bet there's a new loaf in the house.' He took the lid off the bread-crock:

'Ay, here's a fine new loaf that she's keeping till it's as hard as a stone too.'

He set an untouched loaf, still soft and almost warm, on the table.

'You'll spoil your stomach wi' that,' said Mrs Ritchie, with a thin, sneering smile.

'It's *my* stomach, and I'll spoil it if I like!' John Samuel was shouting now, bending over the table to yell in his mother's face.

'Sit down, man!' The plates dirled on the table as Johnny Ritchie brought down his fist. 'Is that a way to behave? Is that the way to speak to your mother?'

John Samuel sat down but his eyes were still bright. He hacked himself a doughy swatch from the new loaf and spread it thickly with butter. And while his mouth was full he startled the family again:

'Father, can I have a latch-key?'

'A latch-key? What for?'

'I have to be out late tomorrow night and I want to be sure of getting in again.'

'Where are you going to, the morn's night?'

'Committee meeting: football.'

He brought out the lie naturally enough, yet he could not make it other than brief. But he looked boldly at Sarah Annie, who was making incredulous mouths, and then shifted his gaze to meet his father's eye.

'You dinna need a latch-key for that,' said Johnny Ritchie. 'I'll see that you get in.'

'I'll be late.'

'You'll no' be a minute later than half-past nine, or I'll let you hear about it.'

'I'm the secretary,' said John Samuel firmly, 'and I have to write the minutes, and I'll maybe no' get off at half-past nine. But I'll be home on the stroke o' ten.'

(Govey Dick! To dodge them was as easy as winking, once you got into the way of it!)

'Half-past nine,' repeated Johnny feebly.

'I tell you I'll maybe no' manage half-past nine. But what for can I no' have a key?'

'The key's not to be taken from the inside of that door,' said his mother suddenly.

John Samuel began to shout again:

'The key will have to be taken out! I'm going to get a job! I'm sick fed up with this. I'm sixteen and I'm going to get a job as soon as I can.'

'What's a' this?' Johnny Ritchie roused himself again. 'Man, we're getting ready to send you to college.'

Mrs Ritchie sat still, with her fixed, sneering smile, and it was her smile rather than his father's question that the boy answered:

'I'm not going to college. I want to start earning my living. I winna have it cast up at me, day in, day out, that I'm an expense to anybody. Her and her hard ends o' bread!'

Mrs Ritchie said nothing.

'I dinna grudge the expense,' said Johnny Ritchie slowly. 'I thocht you were going to be a minister.'

'I dinna want to be a minister. I would rather be coffined than stuck in a pulpit.'

Mrs Ritchie, still smiling with her mouth turned down, nodded her head as if confirming a conclusion. She lifted her cup and saucer and set them on her plate. Then she looked straight at her son and said:

'The wages of sin is death.'

'That's no' true!' shouted John Samuel. 'You would like fine to see me dead and done for, but I'm going to get a job!'

Mrs Ritchie rose and began to collect the crockery from the table. John Samuel went on shouting:

'You would like fine to see me shut up by mysel', away from everybody, but I'm going to be in the thick o' things, I tell you ! You're no' going to keep *me* shut up inside this house or inside a pulpit. I'm going out to see things for mysel'. And there's a job I can get any day I like; and I'll get it, what's more, whether you like it or not!'

Mrs Ritchie removed the tablecloth. Johnny Ritchie got up, stiffly, and stiffly lowered himself into his old chair by the fireside. His face seemed more alive, as if some inner excitement had quickened it, but he did not look at his son. 'Whatna job were you thinking of, laddie? Your mother and me's no' that set on you going to college. Are we, Annie?' He had to repeat his question, loudly, before Mrs Ritchie replied:

'It's nothing to do wi' me. I'll take nothing to do with it. If he's no' to be a minister he can be a scaffy for all I care.'

'Ay weel . . . Ay weel . . . You wouldna think, now,

of coming into the business wi' me? I could do fine wi'
somebody to gi'e me a hand wi' the books.'

'No!'

John Samuel stopped short, for to his great surprise his
throat was tightening again, and he felt as if he wanted to
burst into tears. Why was he John Samuel Ritchie? Why
was he threatened on all sides by coffins?

'I'm going to be a reporter,' he said, but as soon as he had
brought it out he rushed from the kitchen to cast himself on
his bed.

'It must be the Reids that are getting him a job wi' their
Andy!' burst out Sarah Annie. Mrs Ritchie screwed her
mouth down a little more, but said nothing.

Johnny Ritchie suddenly looked old and weary as he
gazed into the fire, uttering: 'Ay weel . . . ay weel . . .
maybe no' . . .'

'Father,' cried Sarah Annie, 'dinna you mind. *I'll* gi'e
you a hand wi' the books.'

'You'll gi'e me a hand wi' thae dishes.' Mrs Ritchie's
voice was crisp, almost triumphant. Her son was not to
be a minister. She need not worry whether he would be
a credit or a discredit to her in heaven. She would never
see him there at all. He would have vanished into limbo.

## THIRTY-ONE

Mrs Ritchie's wisdom in raising a new inner wall to shut out her son was soon justified, for when he became a reporter he proved to be little more than a sewer through which the filth of the world poured inside the door of her house. His hours, to begin with, were disorderly. He might rush in for his dinner in the middle of the afternoon, between attending a flower show and bicycling to a farm roup miles away in the country, and although Mrs Ritchie merely left food in the oven for him she could not avoid some dislocation in the punctual routine of her days. But more disorderly even than his hours were the opinions he began to air; it appeared that he was always 'in the know' about something, and to his cynical inside information was added a defiant Socialism, which he must have caught from the Reids and from his chief, the editor of the *Herald*, who ran the paper on sound Liberal lines for its proprietor, but outside its columns made no secret of his own Labour sympathies. John Samuel behaved as if his profession licensed him to open all the doors that decency kept shut, and Mrs Ritchie sometimes felt as if she were living in a perpetual draught. For she could not help pricking up her ears whenever John Samuel announced that So-and-so was being sued for debt, or that there had been a high old row in the Town Council over some contracts, or that deep-rooted corruption had been unearthed in the transactions of the Harbour Board. She could not help listening and remarking that she had always believed So-and-so to be a spendthrift or that not a man in Calderwick was to be trusted; but before she knew what was happening next she was hearing loud arguments about the rights of Labour, about strikes and Trade Unions, and the high-handed oppression of Ireland—arguments in which John Samuel defended all resistance to authority and the law. Johnny Ritchie actually took up the arguments and debated points with his son, but it made Mrs Ritchie so indignant to hear disorderliness and rebellion even mentioned in her house that she often found her deafness no protection and had to retire to the parlour. John Samuel was as bad as a poltergeist, and had it not been for the comfort of sitting in her own parlour she might have imagined herself once more in the Carnegies' house, harassed and provoked by unruly malice that sought to disarrange the neat order she had decreed. For Mrs Ritchie regarded the law of the land as a projection of the law which she had set up in her own life, the control she had established over her own passions; the law was a sacred institution which existed to enforce upon other people the order to which she herself adhered, and to challenge it was heresy against Mrs Ritchie. She could not help believing that Labour and Suffragette and Irish insurrectionists should all be soundly thrashed and jailed. One did not sit and argy-bargy with the Serpent; one crushed it under foot as God had commanded. And here she was, driven out of her own kitchen by Johnny Ritchie and John Samuel, who were at it hammer and tongs over some wastrel called Jim Larkin, a name which should not fyle the tongue of any respectable Scot—an Irish wastrel, at that. And even when she went to her own bed Johnny Ritchie would be usurping more than half of it, curling himself up in a ball as her sister Mary had used to do. She had no peace or privacy anywhere but in her parlour.

Mrs Ritchie's knitting-needles rattled. Johnny Ritchie knew as well as anybody that right was right and that wrong was wrong, but he simply encouraged John Samuel to argue about it. If he had only the sense to hold his tongue! But Johnny Ritchie positively enjoyed the arguments; he looked forward to them, she could see that well enough; he provoked them, with his silly way of speiring: 'Ay weel, John Samuel, what's the latest iniquity of the capitalists?' Johnny Ritchie was aye ready to give away things instead of keeping himself to himself, and he was fairly revelling in the interchange with his son. A bonny pair! The one was as bad as the other. The one was as silly a bairn as the other. The one needed a thrashing just as much as the other. It wasna fair of God to let folk grow too old for a thrashing unless He meant to strike them down Himself.

But maybe God was just biding His time; and with this reflection, casting an eye at the clock, Mrs Ritchie jabbed her knitting-needles through the ball of wool and rolled up the shawl she was making. The Day would come when the heavens would be rolled up like a scroll and all sinners would be cut off from grace. Indeed, God had probably cut Himself off from them already and that was why so much lawlessness was starting up all over the country. Like John Samuel, the rebels were all shouting loudly because they felt God's silence. And if Johnny Ritchie continued to break that silence he too would be counted among the sinners.

Mrs Ritchie put out the gas and went into the kitchen. There was no sign of John Samuel. Johnny Ritchie was turning over a pile of battered old magazines that he insisted on keeping in the house.

Ay, Johnny was thinking, he had spent many an evening over them in his young days, before he was married. He had thought then that he was going to make grand furniture; he hadna learned then that the best thing to do with life was just to bury it . . . It made a man feel a bit wae to think that John Samuel, poor laddie, would come to that same knowledge in his time . . .

'Where's Sarah Annie?' demanded Mrs Ritchie.

'Ou, she's awa' to her bed.'

'And where's John Samuel?'

'He's oot.'

'But it's ten o'clock.'

'Ay, but he's oot at a dance.'

'At a dance! Did he tell you that?'

'Ay; he telt me he'd be late.'

'And you just said you'd bide up for him, I suppose?'

'No, I gi'ed him the key.'

'You gi'ed him the key! To go to a *dance*! I'm surprised at you that it was only your key you sent to the dance, and that you didna staucher out yoursel' to shake a leg. I suppose

it's the next best thing to coming home yoursel' in the sma'
hours to ken that your son'll be trying your key in the lock
o' your house. How do you think any decent woman could
sleep in her bed with the key of the house jigging about in a
godless, loose-living dance-hall? You're every bit as bad as
John Samuel, Johnny Ritchie, ay, worse, for at your time o'
life you should ha'e mair sense. You gi'ed him the key! To
go to a dance, save the mark! Is there nothing else you'd
like to gi'e him?'

'The laddie couldna get in if he hadna the key.'

'He could bide out, then, if he chooses to keep sic ungodly
hours. This is no' a disorderly house, but I must say you're
doing your best to make it one, Johnny Ritchie. I've washed
my hands o' John Samuel, but I must say I'm surprised
at *your* ongoings. You're worse than him—and he's bad
enough—colloguing with him in this kitchen behind my
back night after night.'

'I'm only trying to tell him the richt way o' things, Annie.
The laddie's no' a bad laddie——'

'The right way o' things is to learn him to bide at home
and honour his parents and no' yowl up in their faces. You
should learn him to hold his tongue. You should hold your
own tongue, for that matter. Whatna kind o' kirk would it be
if a' body was encouraged to rise up and argy-bargy wi' the
minister in the pulpit? And whatna kind o' Christian house
will this be if the bairns are encouraged to argy-bargy about
what's right and what's wrong? You should ken better, and
you a deacon o' the kirk. A deacon o' the kirk, behaving
like a silly bairn! It's nae wonder they havena bothered to
make you an elder.'

Johnny Ritchie's hands knotted themselves on the arms
of his chair. His official connection with the kirk was what
gave dignity to his life, that, and his hope of salvation in
the next world.

'Wumman,' he shouted, 'it's no' your place——'

'It's my place to tell you you're ower saft. You're ower
saft a' thegither——'

'God, what on earth possessed me to marry the like
o' you?'

'What did you say, if you please?'

Mrs Ritchie's voice had become thin and acid. She seemed to herself to be growing taller, and she could look at his knotted hands, she discovered, without the old flicker of fear. He wasna a man; he was just a dovering, thowless creature who had given his key, the mastership of his house, into the hands of his son.

Johnny Ritchie stared into the fire. He would not turn round and face her.

'What did you say, if you please?'

'I said, what on earth possessed me to marry the like o' you?'

'That's a Christian-like thing to say to the wife that has done her duty by you for seventeen years.'

'Awa' to your bed, wumman, and leave me alane, for God's sake!'

'You can take the name of God in vain, and you set yourself up to be a Christian? It's nae wonder your son swears at his mother. You'll be leading him round the pubs next. You're a whited sepulchre, Johnny Ritchie, and if I wasna a woman that did my duty I would let folk ken what kind of man you are—aye, the haill congregation, if they dinna ken it by this time. Man, did I say? A thowless, pithless, gaumless——'

'Will you gang to your bed and hold your bloody tongue?'

Mrs Ritchie turned her eyes to the ceiling:

'O Lord, dinna mind it against this house that siccan a word was ever spoken in it——'

Johnny Ritchie beat upon his forehead:

'You've driven me to swearing, and you'll drive me to murder yet,' he said in a stifled voice.

'I heard you,' said Mrs Ritchie. She was trembling now, but she remained upright. 'Ay, I heard your wicked words. And there's One above that heard them too, and they'll be written down for all eternity. But His hand is over me, and I'll live to see you get the wages you deserve.'

Johnny Ritchie buried his face in his hands and groaned. The black thought that had lain hidden in his mind had emerged at last.

'And I pray to the Lord that you'll repent of your

wickedness afore it's ower late,' went on the implacable voice. 'But as He is my Judge, this is the last word I'll ever speak to you, Johnny Ritchie.'

Mrs Ritchie was still trembling. She moved slowly out of the room. Slowly she shut the door.

Johnny Ritchie could hear her footsteps receding down the lobby. He heard her moving between the lobby press and the parlour; he heard the soft sound of bundles being dragged into the parlour—blankets? Was she making herself a bed on the parlour sofa? And finally he heard the loud turning of a key in the parlour door, a loud, emphatic, final click. What had he done? Would he ever win salvation?

He sat rocking his head in his hands. Would there ever be grace for him? Long, long ago, and yet it seemed but yesterday, in this very house he had lost his mother and with her his happiness, his guiltlessness; he had begun to sin then by hating his father, and now that he knew what it was to be a father he could understand how monstrous his hatred had been . . . But his father had been a dour man . . . ay weel, may be only a lonely man . . . a lonely man . . . For seventeen years, Annie had said; and it was for seventeen years that he had hated his father, sitting in the same seat with him Sunday after Sunday . . . Johnny Ritchie forgot his wife; he began to sob for the misery he must have caused his father to suffer, the lonely old man, sitting stark in his pew with his wife buried and his son hard and hostile to him. How could he have done it? How could he have been so hard and unforgiving? So hard and blind?

The sobs ceased as abruptly as they had begun and Johnny Ritchie sat huddled in his chair listening to the silence of the night. Above his head the clock ticked loudly; before his feet the flames in the grate whickered and died away. Folk hadna long to live on earth, and they wasted their years in being hard and blind to each other. Johnny Ritchie's heart was wae, not only for himself and his father, but for everybody . . . even for Annie Ritchie, his wife. He should have managed things better during all these years . . . Maybe she was right; he wasna muckle o' a man . . .

He sat staring into vacancy; the cinders fell in with little puffs and starts, and the red glow turned slowly into grey ash. After a timeless interval he heard footsteps coming briskly along the road outside, young, confident footsteps ringing on the pavement, and a clear whistle trilling a bold tune. The latch of the garden gate clicked and the footsteps came up the path. He rose to his feet and put out the gas; his candle was on the dresser as usual. He struck a match and lit the candle just as the key rattled in the front door lock, and John Samuel came in, humming:

> 'Talk of heaven, talk of bliss,
> Heaven is nothing to this.
> Yi–ip–I–addy–I–ay.'

John Samuel was astounded to see his father come out of the kitchen with a candle. Had the old man been waiting up for him? In the darkness and silence he felt bold and gay, on a level with his father:

'Were you feared I would bring a lassie hame?'

'I didna notice it was so late; I've just been dovering in my chair,' said his father.

Govey Dick! the old man looked grey and weary.

'You should have been in your bed lang syne,' said John Samuel.

'Ay,' said Johnny Ritchie, 'I'm just going.'

But at the bedroom door he added, without turning his head:

'Did you have a fine time at the dance?'

'Tophole,' said John Samuel.

The bedroom door shut.

## THIRTY-TWO

Mrs Ritchie got up very early next morning. She felt tranquil, even relieved, for on this night she had heard no accusing voices; but she could not enjoy her tranquillity until she had stripped the rumpled bedclothes off the parlour sofa. They made the whole parlour look unquiet and blowsy. She folded them up, slipped them into a corner of the lobby press, and, before going into the kitchen at all, swept and dusted and tidied the parlour until it was once more an immaculate sanctuary.

When her husband came to breakfast she turned her back on him and dished up the porridge without a word. But as nobody in the Ritchies' house ever wasted words on such superfluous greetings as good morning, neither John Samuel nor Sarah Annie noticed anything amiss. They were accustomed to silence at table. Mrs Ritchie spoke only once, and that was to bid Sarah Annie wash up the dishes at the close of the meal. Johnny Ritchie found his shoes brushed and a clean collar laid out for him to put on after breakfast; he put them on silently and went out to the workshop.

But by tea-time Sarah Annie, freed from the preoccupations of school, observed that there was a new tension in the house, that her mother did not even look at her father and left his few timid overtures unanswered. What was up? The worst of one's parents was that one couldn't just ask them what was up, as if they were ordinary people. Maybe they thought it indecent for children to ask personal questions; they were aye thinking harmless things indecent, at least mother was. Perhaps the asking of questions about what they had been doing to each other would be construed as what the Bible called uncovering their nakedness. Had they

been having a row in the night? Sarah Annie felt excited.
What had her father been doing to her mother?

As if Mrs Ritchie had divined her daughter's thoughts,
she brought up the question of indecency at once.

'You're getting ower big to sleep in the wee bedroom
with John Samuel. It's hardly decent, even though there
is a screen. Your father had better take your bed, and you
can come in and sleep with me.

Oho! said one part of Sarah Annie's mind, so that's that,
is it? But the other part of her mind flashed back at once:

'Why must it be me that has to shift? John Samuel could
shift into the big bed with father and you could sleep in his
bed just as well.'

'You're not to argy-bargy with me. It's better the way
I've told you, and never you mind why. Go and shift your
things into the muckle bedroom this minute. And you can
put clean sheets on your bed to be ready for your father.
I've spread the muckle bed ready for us two.'

Sarah Annie knew by the movement of her father's head
that this rearrangement took him by surprise. And yet a
minute later he had settled down again as if it didna
surprise him so much after all. What *was* up? They
must have had a terrible row to make mother shift him
out of the double bed, for she liked things to go on
the same for ever and ever, Amen. Father must have
answered back, thought his daughter, smiling. Dod, if
he had answered back that would explain it. Good
for father!

It was exciting to have changes. Sarah Annie ran to get
the clean sheets, and flung them friskily over her bed, with
such ample gestures that she had to push back the brown
folding screen. Father in her bed! What a lark! How would
he like it?

'Hullo, what's a' the steer?'

John Samuel came shouldering in, late for his tea, as
usual, and hunting for a clean hanky.

'Father's to sleep in my bed the night.'

'Crivvens! And you a Suffragette!'

'Oh, shut up! They've had a terrible row and mother has
chucked father out of the big bed.'

John Samuel whistled. 'He should have chucked *her* out. That's the way to treat a woman.'

'Och, you're aye trying to be funny. I tell you, it must have been a terrific row. She's no' speaking to him.'

'Yi-ip-I-addy-I-ay! I say, Sarah Annie, *you'd* better have a row with her next, and then she'll no' be able to open her mouth ava' . . . That's father in the same box as me, now. The brotherhood of man. United we stand——'

John Samuel snickered to himself and then coughed, flourishing his clean hanky.

'This segregation of the sexes has its points——' he began, and then snickered once more.

'As sure's death, you're a havering idiot,' said his sister. 'I dinna ken how Betsy Reid can put up with you.'

'Betsy Reid's a *nice* lassie,' retorted John Samuel, examining himself in the mirror as he put the handkerchief in his breast pocket. 'To the pure all things are pure. She's no' a Suffragette like you.'

'Yes, she is, then.'

'No, she's no', then.'

'Sut.'

'Not.'

John Samuel dodged a pillow and strolled into the kitchen for his tea, whistling loudly the dance tune he had whistled and hummed all day. His mother was not there. His father was sitting, looking shrunken, staring into the fire. John Samuel said: 'Hullo, father!' and peered into the oven for food. The old man's still gey grey about the gills, he thought; she must have been twisting his tail while I was at the dance, the nasty bitch. He should be damned glad to get out of sleeping with her.

'Where's mother?' he asked, as casually as possible.

'I dinna ken; maybe in the parlour.'

Poor old stick, thought John Samuel; his back is as round as a gird. What a life!

Johnny Ritchie would not speak. There was not a cheep to be got out of him, not even about Trade Unions. His son cast about in his mind for some topic to cheer the old man up, and partly out of mischief, partly out of an obscure desire to associate himself with his father, he hailed Sarah Annie's return to the kitchen with these words:

'Here, I say, I forgot to tell you. There's a Suffragette lorry come to the High Street.'

The remark was, as he had hoped, a spark to tinder. Sarah Annie was soon flaming:

'I can do things as well as you. I've a heid on my shoulders as well as you. I'm going to college, if you're not, and I'll earn my own living as well as you. Where's the difference?'

'You'll be looking for a man to keep you; that's one difference.'

'I'll do nothing o' the kind. I wouldna be beholden to any man. I'm never going to get married——'

'You'll no' get the chance. Nobody would want a Suffragette for a wife. It's only the women that canna get men that are shouting for a vote and asking for trouble.'

Sarah Annie was nearly crying with rage, and her rage was more than half bewilderment. She only felt with all her force that she was as much entitled as John Samuel to be considered an individual and had as much right to importance. She could neither understand nor counter the assumptions behind his arguments, for, like him—like nearly everybody else, in fact—she was incapable of disentangling the symbolic from the actual.

'They're not asking for trouble! They're only asking for a vote.'

'They're asking for a fight, and, by Jing, they'll get it! I'm going up to the High Street to see the fireworks.'

'I'm coming too, then.'

Johnny Ritchie roused himself:

'You're not to stir out of this house, Sarah Annie. I winna have a daughter o' mine mixed up wi' thae shameless hussies.'

'They're *not* shameless hussies.'

'It's only shameless weemen that would try to poke into men's affairs. You're ower young to understand thae things, but you're no' ower young to understand that no respectable wumman would be stravaiging the streets on a lorry. You're to bide at hame.'

'"Woman's place is the home,"' quoted John Samuel.

'"Awa' hame and rock the cradle." That's the stuff to give 'em!'

Sarah Annie's rage was now so great that she had a moment of illumination:

'You keep me tied to the house a' my life and I'll grow up just like my mother!'

'If you grow up as good a wumman as your mother——' began Johnny Ritchie, but Sarah Annie banged the kitchen door on his pious sentiment. She snatched her tammy from its peg and slammed the front door behind her.

John Samuel started up:

'Crivvens, I'd better keep an eye on her and bring her hame. There might be a row——'

'Ay, ay,' said Johnny Ritchie, half rising from his chair. 'It's ower chancy for a young lassie . . . I dinna ken what the lassies are coming to.'

John Samuel could not resist turning to shake his head at his father with a knowing look. 'Women!' he said, and ran out of the kitchen.

If there had been a row that evening in the High Street, if there had been the fireworks John Samuel anticipated, a small squib was still detonating all along the North Road. Sarah Annie, marching home at full speed, was arguing every step of the way. She broke into a run every now and then to escape from her brother, but he had the longer legs. 'The better to catch you with, my dear,' he said, skipping from the pavement to the gutter.

'Look here, I bet you wouldn't go and smash a window yourself.'

'Maybe no',' said Sarah Annie. 'But if the Suffragettes did it I would stick up for them. You think it's only men that can stick up for one another, but women can do it too.'

John Samuel snickered again. What an innocent she was! You never knew what she would say next. She had already given him a good one to tell the chief tomorrow: 'You think women should take everything lying down.'

'Go on, Sarah Annie; you dinna ken how funny you are.'

It was Mrs Ritchie who answered the bell, peering through the crack of the door at them.

'It's me, mother,' said Sarah Annie, her voice defiant and tearful. If her mother were to attack her next she didn't know what she would do.

'Where have you been, coming back at this hour on a Saturday night?'

'Aha!' said John Samuel. 'You may well ask.'

'But I didna ask you,' retorted Mrs Ritchie.

Sarah Annie walked mutely past her into the kitchen.

'She's been at a Suffrage meeting. Hasn't she, father?' cried John Samuel.

Now they would have to speak to each other, he thought; his mother would have to make common cause with his father over this.

'Fighting wi' bobbies and ploughmen,' he added.

Mrs Ritchie must have heard, but she turned her back on him and addressed her daughter. Nothing would induce her to say a word that might imply the existence of her husband:

'Wherever you've been, it's time you were in bed. I'll be after you in five minutes, and dinna let me find you anywhere except under the blankets.'

'I havena done my home-work——'

'That has nothing to do with me. Into your bed.'

'Awa' to your harem quarters,' said John Samuel genially.

And so it came about that Sarah Annie, instead of sympathizing with her father, went to her mother's bed in a blaze of resentment against all men, a blaze which lit up even Mrs Ritchie from a new angle, so that she appeared as the thwarted product of generations of masculine prejudice.

'It's the men's fault if my mother's like what she is,' raged Sarah Annie, getting into her father's half of the big bed. She was too angry to sleep, although she shut her eyes when Mrs Ritchie came in. Through her eyelashes she watched her mother undressing beneath her flannelette night-gown; goodness, with those plaits down over her shoulders mother looked quite young and different. It was so long since Mrs Ritchie had had a day's illness that Sarah Annie had forgotten those long black plaits. What did mother look like when she was my age, wondered the girl, and when

Mrs Ritchie had blown out the candle and said her prayers and climbed into the other side of the bed she plucked up courage to ask:

'Was your hair aye as long as that, mother?'

'Are you no' asleep? What did you say?'

'Was your hair aye as long as that?'

'Yes,' said Mrs Ritchie. 'Go to sleep.'

But the shortness of her tone concealed a certain gratification. She was inclined to be pleased with herself that evening, was Mrs Ritchie, and now she was inclined to be pleased with her daughter too. After all, she thought, Sarah Annie takes after me . . . And she's going to be a teacher . . . It was as if Sarah Annie would be the instrument, under God, of redressing the humiliations her mother had suffered in girlhood. Mrs Ritchie had the sudden conviction that in spite of her wildness Sarah Annie was to be depended on. And on this comforting conviction she fell asleep without once hearing the mocking voices of her anonymous accusers.

## THIRTY-THREE

The change in the sleeping quarters of the household altered the whole atmosphere of the house for the two young Ritchies as effectively as a new scheme of lighting alters the appearance of a room. But the mere interest of a change in the disposition of that changeless house did not account for all the holiday excitement that Sarah Annie felt when she woke up in the strange big bed, nor for the high spirits with which John Samuel watched out of the tail of his eye, the brown screen not having been replaced, his father struggling into a clean white Sunday shirt. They were both secretly thrilled by a sense of initiation into the life of their parents: Sarah Annie was filling her father's place and John Samuel, as he had said himself, was now in the same box as Johnny Ritchie. It was as if the separation of the parents satisfied some old desire in the children. John Samuel almost felt equal to slapping his father on the back. It was like children that his father and mother had quarrelled, and it was childish that they were not on speaking terms. He felt he would never be afraid of them again, and promised himself some fun in trying to trick his mother into speaking to the old man . . .

Their young excitement persisted even although Mr and Mrs Ritchie wore their unvarying Sabbath expressions. Sarah Annie gathered a bunch of lilac from the bush by the workshop door and stuck it in the middle of the breakfast table, and John Samuel pinched off a sprig to put into his buttonhole. The grown-up children, however, in their Sabbath blacks ignored the lilac, until Mrs Ritchie, serving up the ham and eggs, said to her daughter:

'There's nae room for that trash on the table; set it on the dresser.'

She filled each plate and passed it to Sarah Annie without comment, as if refusing further responsibility for it. In the same way she left her daughter to deal out the cups of tea. The look on her face announced that in pouring out the tea she was doing her duty as became a Christian—as she would do it, indeed, were she asked to pour tea for savages at a mission station in Darkest Africa—but that hand the cups to the degraded recipients of them she would not.

John Samuel smiled into his tea-cup. How long would she be able to keep it up? It was as good as a play to watch her. What would she do when it was time to start for church? His mother, however, had apparently thought out her plan of campaign. She appeared in the lobby, gloved, hatted, veiled and umbrella'd, at the usual time; even her threepenny-bit must have been ready in the palm of her glove, for she did not ask it from Johnny Ritchie. She said to Sarah Annie: 'Are you ready?' and walked off down the garden path on her absurdly small shoes without once looking at the two men. When John Samuel and his father shut the gate behind them the female Ritchies were already several yards down the street, and in that order the sexes proceeded to church and filed into the pew, Mrs Ritchie leading the way. She was determined, it seemed, to go through all the motions proper to Sunday without uttering a word to her husband.

John Samuel, divided between curiosity and amusement, watched her skill in greeting acquaintances at the church door after the service. She paused, shook hands, said a few words, and then slowly moved on as her husband came up, so that his salutations followed hers without overlapping, but with such perfect measure and timing that she appeared merely to be borne onwards by the crowd. There was nothing remarkable in the fact that the women of the family should walk separately from the men; indeed, it was the more natural observance in Calderwick, and it was only John Samuel who snickered to himself as he strolled beside his father in the wake of his mother's and his sister's skirts. The new grouping looked much better, he thought, for there had always been something ridiculous in the solemn bobbing of the small parents as they trotted behind their two tall children, but no outsider could have any conception how much funnier it really was. And he laughed again to himself as he thought of the walk to the cemetery in the afternoon, a walk which for a long time he had refused to join in. By Jing! for this one afternoon he would go too and back the old man up. By next Sunday they would be speaking again, and he must not lose this chance of a peep-show.

John Samuel was not disappointed in the afternoon's performance. Sarah Annie carried all the flowers and Mrs Ritchie stood at a little distance with an aloof air while her daughter and her husband laid the bunches on the two grave-mounds. But as they crunched their way soberly along the gravel paths, doing the usual round, the old discomfort oppressed John Samuel again; he could have sworn that the flowers on the graves were all decaying, that the graves smelt rank and the stones mouldy, that the black stuffs clothing the decorous citizens reeked of sweat and camphor. The old man surely had enough of graves and funerals all the week without needing to haunt the cemetery on Sundays as well. Death might be inevitable, but it was still far off, and as for the Judgment Day, that might never come at all. It was silly to live as his parents lived. John Samuel realized, with painful clearness, not only that he was growing up and felt himself on an equal footing with his father, but that he was unwilling to grow up into his parents' mode of living, that he was nauseated by it. If they were childish in one thing they were probably childish in others; and if his mother could take quite seriously this farce of not speaking to his father, probably most of the other things that she took seriously were just as farcical. All this decorum, for instance, was just a farce; all this Sunday observance, this insistence on respectability, this frowning at enjoyment, this droning of hymns to a farcical God of thunder and lightning and death. Life wasn't like that at all, as he had begun to find out in his job; there was ever so much fun to be got out of life. He began to hum 'Yip-I-addy-I-ay-I-ay.'

'John Samuel!' said his father.

'What?'

'You're not to sing that on a Sunday.'

'Ay? Should I be singing a hymn?'

'You shouldna be singing at all in a cemetery.'

'Then I'm damned if I'll bide in the cemetery!'

John Samuel wheeled off, leaving his father gaping, and as he headed out of the cemetery by the nearest gate he could still see his father's bewildered-looking legs shambling uncertainly behind his wife and daughter. His black gamp was trailing a little; it looked like a dejected tail.

'Och, to hell!' said John Samuel. 'Life's no' a grave-yard.'

He sniffed the fresh, salty air that was blowing in from the gorse and the dunes; it reminded him of hot summer holidays, of warm sand and the smell of rest-harrow, of frothing salt water, of dogs racing and barking, and pierrots double-shuffling on sandy boards while they sang to listeners stretched on turf padded with thyme and crow's-foot. He turned towards the sea; there was just a chance that Mrs Reid and Betsy might be listening to the Sunday band . . . And as he went he whistled:

'And when I told them how beautiful you are . . .
They wouldn't believe me——'

Johnny Ritchie did not reproach his son for deserting him. He trailed off to the evening service with only his daughter as a buffer between himself and his wife, and he felt that his daughter in some way had grown hostile, too. Not that Sarah Annie was unmindful of him; she spoke to him once or twice in a low voice that Mrs Ritchie could not hear, but it required all the dignity of the church building to support him in his new feeling of isolation. Was Annie going to keep this up against him all his life?

He knew her tenacity. And there was a terrible justice in her refusing to speak to him, for that was how he had served his own father . . . When John Samuel asked him in the bedroom: 'What's it all about, anyway? What's mother taken the tit at?' he shrank as if he had been struck, muttering: 'I canna tell you that.' But his conscience forced him to add, before he got into bed: 'She's in the richt o't.'

'What the hell does that matter?' said John Samuel to

himself. Yet as the days lengthened into weeks and months and Mrs Ritchie still maintained her silence towards her husband he began to wonder, uneasily, what it was that gave his mother such strength to hold out. It might be simple obstinacy. But would obstinacy alone make a woman cut off her nose, so to speak, to spite her face? For Mrs Ritchie had not spoken to Johnny Ritchie even on the day that Mary, her sister, came into the house crying that her old father needed more than the half a crown a week that the Ritchies contributed to his keep; her husband, the scaffy, had been sacked from his work and it was Annie Ritchie's duty, the hard, ungrateful besom, to pay up. 'Half a crown's all you'll get,' Mrs Ritchie had said, 'and you should be thankful to get it, for it's just like pouring good money down the sink.' But Johnny Ritchie, anxious for peace, offered Mary five pounds on the spot and promised to make the half-crown five shillings. John Samuel had watched his mother. The effort to restrain her tongue must have been frightful, but she had achieved it; she had cast one glance up at the ceiling and then removed herself from the kitchen. He knew, too, that she never asked Johnny Ritchie for money, even when she required it; Sarah Annie had to watch for things that needed replacing in the house, and had to tell her father privately to leave the extra few shillings in the mug on the dresser. His mother, of course, was a wrong-headed fool, but still . . . It was disconcerting to find that there was something one could believe in so uncompromisingly, whether it was God, or justice, or merely retribution. The whole thing had gone far beyond a childish tiff; it was like the grinding of the mills of God.

But if God was the upper millstone and Mrs Ritchie the nether millstone, Johnny Ritchie was the grain that was being ground exceeding small. He became obsessed with the belief that each coffin he started to make was to be his own, and every time he had to let a lovingly constructed 'kist' leave his workshop to house some luckier person he took it as a fresh sign of God's disfavour, an intimation that he had not yet 'dree'd his weird,' that his redemption was postponed for another term. On these days he would wander up and down the tattie patch, even in pouring rain, before tapping on the kitchen window, for if Mrs Ritchie let him in at the first tap that meant a confirmation of his sentence, and the next coffin would not be his either.

## THIRTY-FOUR

To Mr and Mrs Ritchie, absorbed in their own tense struggle, the news that Britain was at war came as no thunderclap, but rather as an echo; yet it was accompanied by an unexpected vibration, as if a tremor ran through the very foundations of the house, and even in Mrs Ritchie's breast there was a flutter of apprehension. For this war was to be much nearer home than Africa. It was as if an angry devil had come out of the dark undergrowth, in which Mrs Ritchie had once pictured the Boers moving like hairy apes, and at one bound had leaped upon the shoulders of Europe.

But Mrs Ritchie, remembering that although she was in Calderwick she was not of it, and that between Calderwick and the war there rolled the whole of the North Sea, soon recovered her composure. Whatever disaster might overwhelm the wicked, God would see to it that Annie Ritchie's house remained intact.

She turned a deaf ear to her son's excitement and rebuked her daughter's:

'You needna keep running out into the streets as if you had gone gyte. Are you expecting to see the war in the High Street?'

'Oh, mother,' cried Sarah Annie, 'I want to *do* something!'

'You have plenty to do if you're going to college in October. You mind your ain business and the war'll look after itself.'

But would it? Although she was assured that she was safe on her own private line to heaven Mrs Ritchie again felt apprehensive when John Samuel rushed in to say: 'The Government has commandeered all the railways.' It was a

queer mix-up if a woman couldna go where she wanted
to go in a Christian country. It was as bewildering as the
problem that had bothered Mrs Ritchie in her youth, the
problem of reconciling her duty to God with her possible
social humiliation as an old maid; she could not now
reconcile God's private claim on her soul with the claims
of the Government. And when John Samuel said: 'By Jing,
as soon as I'm eighteen I'm going to join up,' she answered
sharply: 'You'll do nothing of the kind.'

Soldiers, she now remembered, were riff-raff—men who
were pledged to stab and shoot into human bodies, disreputable creatures before whom neither man nor woman
was safe when once war licensed them to let themselves
go. The ne'er-do-weels of Calderwick could join up if they
liked, but it was ridiculous of John Samuel to think of it. He
was just a laddie, anyhow; he would be about as much good
at the fighting as his father, and that wasna saying muckle.
The very word 'war' seemed to excite bairns—and not only
bairns—into thinking that now was their chance to burst all
the bonds of decency and respectability.

As if to emphasize the permanence of decency and
respectability Mrs Ritchie set her face like a flint against
any mention of the war. It had nothing to do with her, nor
yet with Johnny Ritchie, silly old fool! who was moving
flags about on a map as if he were fighting the Germans
himself. He and Sarah Annie set up a yammering in the
kitchen about Belgium, but Mrs Ritchie pointed out to
her daughter that women and countries who were raped
had only got what they were asking for. She began to feel
as if she were besieged on all sides by unreason, and the
most sensible thing she heard was Mrs Morton's advice to
lay in a store of provisions since nobody knew what might
happen. Decent people, they agreed, would have to look
out for themselves; the Government was likely to grab all
it could for the soldiers.

And yet Mrs Ritchie was being forced, by almost imperceptible currents, into the main stream of feeling. The very
fact that she listened to Mrs Morton's advice and found it
sensible marked a shift in her position; and on another
day, when she was in the baker's shop at the corner, one

of her neighbours with whom she usually exchanged no courtesies greeted her with: 'Eh, Mrs Ritchie, isna this war a dreadful business? Thae Germans must be a wicked, wicked lot o' folk,' and Mrs Ritchie found it impossible not to agree with the woman. She found, too, that she was no longer plagued by the suspicion that her neighbours were maliciously pulling her to pieces; it was far more likely that they were denouncing the common enemy. And as the wickedness of Calderwick paled before the frightful wickedness of the Germans Mrs Ritchie began to nod and smile to women whom she had cut for years. She even began to read about 'Belgian atrocities' in the newspapers and to listen when they were discussed in the kitchen. These Germans were murderous brutes, a hundred times worse than the Boers had been, treacherous, inhuman baby-killers who defied every law of man and of God. It became clear to Mrs Ritchie that this war was a war against evil. And she was more unrelenting than ever against Johnny Ritchie, who, in his own way, was as bad as the Germans. The struggle in the house now appeared as an offshoot from the greater struggle that was going on in Europe; if Mrs Ritchie were to break her solemn oath and speak to her husband the German standards might well force their way across the sea into Calderwick itself.

Yet a certain bewilderment remained. The war might be a righteous war—a belief which the minister's sermons confirmed, especially after the report spread that angels had defended the British at Mons—and yet Mrs Ritchie still had an equivocal feeling that soldiers were a menace to respectability. The streets of Calderwick began to fill with lads in khaki, and although they had no visible weapons she could not help looking at them askance. Khaki trousers were flagrantly unlike the douce garments in which men could be trusted to behave themselves; but even khaki trousers were less intimidating than the shameless kilts that swung up and down the High Street. To put a laddie into a kilt, showing his bare knees to everybody (and, mind you, it wasn't certain that the creatures had anything on their shanks under the kilts), was to invite him to licentiousness, and Mrs Ritchie was not surprised to hear that the number of illegitimate births was going up. She began to say that it was surely high time all these men were sent to France. It was almost with anxiety that she packed Sarah Annie off to the Training College in Edinburgh, for in these times the only place where a lassie could be secure was in her own home. Sarah Annie, however, had changed surprisingly since sharing her mother's bed; she was growing up into a dutiful daughter, and Mrs Ritchie reflected that Sarah Annie took after her and would know how to keep herself to herself. In any case, no town could be more infested with roving soldiers than Calderwick, for the wide, flat links made a grand camping ground; it was even beginning to be rumoured that the Government was thinking of setting up an aerodrome there.

Soldiers multiplied, women's skirts shortened, prices went up, and Mrs Ritchie still harboured a suspicion that the war was being used as an excuse for licence. She now gossiped in the shops for as long as ten minutes at a time; the threat of German invasion was not so appalling, after all, as the lack of true patriotism at home, the shamelessness of the girls, the extravagance of the workers, the selfishness of profiteers, the immunity of spies and traitors. It was a strong hand the country was needing, and if only every house were as thrifty as Mrs Ritchie's, if every bed were as well defended as hers, there would be less debauchery of man-power and the Germans would have no chance of invading the country. Discipline was what the country was needing, and Mrs Ritchie, cutting down the rations of her household, felt that the swelling casualty lists should be a lesson to folk, and that the memorial services in the churches should bring home to everybody first and foremost the religious solemnity of the war.

Still, had it not been for John Samuel, she might never have overcome her suspicions of the soldiers who were chosen to be God's instruments. John Samuel, going about his business with more work than ever to do, now that his chief had joined up, was beginning to feel as if he were walking about Calderwick under a spot-light. Your country needs *you*, said the recruiting posters; and the spot-light seemed to follow him wherever he went,

showing him up as a civilian, pointing him out as John
Samuel Ritchie who was not yet lost in the anonymity
of uniform. For this uneasy consciousness of himself he
blamed his mother: she was always down on soldiers; she
had forbidden him to join up; she wanted him to live
for ever under a spot-light, never forgetting himself. His
resentment against Mrs Ritchie had deepened since Sarah
Annie's departure; now that the half of the big bed was left
empty it had become a kind of challenge in the household,
like a blank field that challenged invasion, and both John
Samuel and his father were obsessed by that vacant spread
of mattress. John Samuel had looked into the big bedroom
early one morning and seen his mother lying rigidly on the
very edge of the double bed, with the eye of God above her
in its black frame on the wall, and he had felt a curious
disgust, as if she were lying in some obscene ecstasy while
a ray from the eye of God picked her out. Thou God Seest
Me: that was *her* spot-light, he thought; and while she lay
in a rigid trance his father was squirming like a maggot in
another room, but under the same spot-light, the eye of
God. 'I'm a useless stick, laddie,' the old man kept saying,
and instead of sympathizing with him John Samuel despised
him. If he were half a man he would have torn down that text
long ago.

It was time to get away from spot-lights like that text and
the recruiting poster; time to get out into the bright equal
sunshine where everybody stood in the same light. It was
time to escape from the searching ray of God's eye; it was
time to escape from this insistence on being oneself and
saving one's own soul; it was time to lose one's identity.
'By Jing!' said John Samuel to himself, 'if it hadn't been
for the war I would have had to take to drink . . .' It was
time, high time, to join up and go to the war.

But in the first glow of his exhilaration after the deed was
done the first thing John Samuel wanted to do was to go
home and tell his mother. He would shatter the silence that
she spread over the house like a blank field; he would smash
through her fences, for the few words she addressed to him
were like fences, or like gates that opened as grudgingly as
her lips; he would invade the blank field she had reserved for

herself and God. 'Mother!' he shouted. 'Mother!' And then, more defiantly: 'Mrs Ritchie! Where are you?' He pounded on the locked parlour door. Mrs Ritchie opened it.

'What's the meaning of this noise? Have you been drinking, John Samuel?'

'It's no' drink, mother, it's the war! It's the war! I've joined up today. That's what.'

It was grand to tower over one's mother and tell her what was what.

'But—but you're not eighteen yet.'

'I'll be eighteen in two months, and don't you say a word about it. Do you hear? I tell you, I've done it. Now you'll be upsides with Mrs Morton and Mrs Reid and all the others——'

'I doubt that's not the right spirit in which to——'

'Look here, mother, do you think I need my father's black coat-tails to join the army in?'

Mrs Ritchie's voice was Sabbath-like as she replied:

'It's the Lord's battle you'll be fighting, John Samuel, and I wouldna have you forget to ask His blessing on it . . .'

From that day until the day when her son went off to his training-camp Mrs Ritchie maintained her Sabbath expression, even in the baker's shop and in the grocer's shop, where she kept on repeating: 'I suppose you know that my son has joined up . . .' From that day she regarded all soldiers as candidates for a ministry that was even more commendable than the ministry of the Kirk. And at home she spoke to John Samuel with all the meekness, all the wifely decorum, that once had been kept for Johnny Ritchie on Sundays . . . But not even at the station, when John Samuel suddenly kissed her on the cheek, did she say a word to her husband. She had her own duty to do while her son was fighting for the Lord.

## THIRTY-FIVE

They said in Calderwick that Johnny Ritchie pined away terribly after his laddie was sent to the Front. He went about the streets as if he didna want to see folk or to be seen, and when anybody spoke to him it gave him a start. Ay, and even when you were speaking to him he looked no higher than your knees . . . He must have taken it to heart, poor body, that the laddie was awa'; he was gey lost and lonely-like.

None of the gossips knew, however, that after working alone in his wooden shed every evening Johnny Ritchie sat alone in his kitchen until the small hours, overcome by a dejected inertia that hindered him from getting to bed. It was in the cold kitchen that his wife found him one morning, hanging half numb and unconscious over the side of his chair; he died four days later without having recognized even his daughter, Sarah Annie, who had been sent for.

The widow's Christian resignation was much commended. She accepted sympathy; she even went out of her way to seek it, thought her daughter, and that was the kind of thing one would never have expected of her; but she maintained her composure except for a quiver in her voice when she said that of course poor John Samuel had his duty to do in France and couldna be expected to get leave in time for the funeral. She broke down only once, so far as people knew, and that was when a coffin was discovered in the workshop, a grand coffin, lovingly made and finished, which the deceased had evidently designed for himself, since his name was lettered on the lid. Everything but the date! cried the neighbours admiringly, and at that Mrs Ritchie wept. 'Poor Johnny,' she said, 'he was aye a thoughtful creature.'

Mrs Ritchie felt no bitterness against her dead husband. God had taken him to Himself and it was no longer for her or anyone else to judge his shortcomings. Indeed, the fact that Johnny Ritchie was now with God made a great difference to his status; the fear of God somehow included a fear of Johnny Ritchie, and the eye of God was in some sense Johnny Ritchie's eye. Mrs Ritchie had to reassure herself by remembering that if her husband could now see into her heart he would understand that she had been concerned only with his own good and the salvation of his immortal soul; away up there in heaven he would probably be grateful to her for having so firmly done her duty by him. 'Poor Johnny,' she kept on repeating in a tremulous voice, 'poor Johnny . . .'

At the funeral Sarah Annie looked almost sullen beside her mother, and when Mrs Ritchie dropped a bunch of flowers on the coffin and let down her deep crape veil before turning away from the graveside Sarah Annie did not conceal her irritable impatience. What ailed the girl? Had she no decent feeling? And yet one could see she had been crying; her nose was red enough. She was gruff as she hustled her mother into the cab, and altogether made a most unfortunate impression on the mourners, who agreed that the widow, on the other hand, was taking it beautifully, beautifully. It was a great pity the son wasna able to be there . . . Ay, but he would be getting leave . . . Unless, of course . . . On the Somme, was he no'? Ay, this war was a dreadful business.

The unspoken belief that Mrs Ritchie had probably lost both her men-folk gave an extra warmth to everybody's condolences. Was it this that Sarah Annie had resented? Sitting in the cab beside her mother the girl found it extraordinarily difficult to understand her own sullenness. Merely to think of her father made her want to cry; she saw him now as an inoffensive, good-hearted little man who had made coffins all day and sat wistfully by himself all evening in the kitchen when his wife refused to speak to him. It was not unlikely that even his wife regretted his death and desired to show respect to his memory. And yet Sarah Annie felt resentful and outraged by what she termed the mummery of the funeral; she resented Mrs Ritchie's deep crape, her parade of grief, her appropriation—yes, it was nothing less—her appropriation of the corpse and her meek acceptance of condolences; it was an outrage to see her posing with a meek, conscious face as the central figure in an irrelevant stage-show. But why should I mind it? argued Sarah Annie; she has had that same look on her face every Sunday of her life and I never minded it. I thought it was just her way of keeping her end up. Why should I mind it now?

'Poor Johnny,' said Mrs Ritchie from behind her veil. 'It all went off very well. He couldna have conducted it better himself.'

'Oh, mother, what a dreadful thing to say.'

'It's only what your poor father would have said himself, Sarah Annie. He liked to see a well-conducted funeral. I'm sure he'd be pleased that there was such a lot of wreaths.'

'He'll no' likely be caring about wreaths now. And I never thought, mother, that *you* cared about things like that.'

'There's nobody that wouldna want to be kindly remembered. And I'm sure poor Johnny likes to ken that I remember him kindly even if you dinna.'

'Oh, mother, how can you?'

Sarah Annie's eyes smarted with prickling tears and she blew her nose. 'You know fine——' she said, but she could not go on. She was too miserable to speak. And if her mother's reproach was unjust it would not mend matters to hurl counter-reproaches. Johnny Ritchie was dead, and his daughter, from whom the living man had been hidden behind a cloudy abstraction which she called Male Tyranny, now looked across a chasm at her father as she might have looked at a low, gentle hill from which all tumid vapours had been blown away. But there was no bridge across the chasm between them. She was on this side of it, with her mother; and now it seemed to her that the tumid vapour was all about her mother's head. Words, words, words, she said to herself. Sham, sham, sham.

Yet if this swelling drama of heaven and hell, of God and the devil, in which Mrs Ritchie so skilfully magnified herself, were all a sham, what was the reality? Could one never see the truth of any living person? Was it only death that could dispel the vapours? Sarah Annie's head began to ache violently, and she had to help her mother out of the cab before she could find an answer.

At the garden gate Mrs Ritchie paused, like an actress, thought Sarah Annie, making her exit. But she was only waiting for Tom Mitchell, the lawyer, who was coming in the second cab. He stepped out, spats first, and with a gallant bow held the gate open for the ladies. Sarah Annie needs must pass through and follow her mother up to the house. As if this simple action symbolized a destiny for her she felt all at once afraid; she realized that the lawyer was coming in to talk business, and that she had no idea if there would be any money for them to live on. Until now she had assumed that she would be going back to her Training College in Edinburgh; but as she followed her mother into the house she felt as if she were being drawn into a cage.

The familiar smell of waxed linoleum in the lobby increased her perturbation. This house in its prim cleanliness represented her mother, and it was solid and inescapable. As soon as one crossed Mrs Ritchie's threshold the cloudy abstractions that had seemed so unreal out of doors hardened and became almost palpable; Sarah Annie, in spite of her reluctance, felt again the compulsion to be a loyal daughter, to believe that her mother's values were real. It was impossible to face Mrs Ritchie in her own house, on her own ground, and doubt that she knew what was what. It was incredible that a woman who set her chairs at such exact intervals along the parlour wall could be mistaken in her way of living.

And yet in that immaculate and orderly parlour, every corner of which testified to Mrs Ritchie's mastery over chaos, Sarah Annie was now plunged into fresh bewilderment as she heard the lawyer with a word or two demolish her mother's fundamental assumptions. Instead of discovering merely how much of a balance Johnny Ritchie had left in the bank, the widow, after listening to a preamble about heritable and movable property, learned that, the deceased having made no will, the house and the workshop and a third of all furniture and moneys belonged

without reservation to the heir, John Samuel Ritchie. The
house was not hers at all . . . Mrs Ritchie gasped and put
her hand to her throat. The lawyer, consulting his papers,
went on, '. . . a third to yourself, Mrs Ritchie, and a third to
Miss Ritchie, and since the bank balance is well over eight
hundred pounds . . .' Sarah Annie, between stupefaction
and relief, felt almost giddy. There was plenty of money!
Tom Mitchell looked up with a congratulatory smile, which
faded a little when he saw Mrs Ritchie's face. Had the
woman been expecting more money than that? But it was
a fair knock-out to find that old Johnny Ritchie had left
as muckle as eight hundred . . . Maybe that was what was
wrong with her . . . He rose to offer his help.

'The—the house,' said Mrs Ritchie faintly, waving him
off, 'this house, is it no' my house?'

'I have no doubt it'll be your house, Mrs Ritchie, as long
as you care to live in it——'

'Is the house John Samuel's?'

'Of course, of course; he's the heir, you know——'

'Is that the law?'

'That's the law, Mrs Ritchie. If the deceased had made
a will, now——'

'Johnny Ritchie was aye a dovering body. But if I had
kent that he needed to make a will—but it canna be the
law, Mr Mitchell. This house was my house and Johnny's;
what for can it no' be my house now that he's awa'?'

Tom Mitchell took off his pince-nez and stared at the
widow.

'It was your husband's house, Mrs Ritchie, and now it's
your son's; that doesna surely make muckle difference?'

That's like telling mother that her body has never been
her own, thought Sarah Annie. For she's been tied to the
house, and it was only in the house that she was somebody.
It isna fair.

'It was my house as soon as I married Johnny Ritchie,'
insisted the widow, her lips quivering.

'And it was my money that helped to furnish it. And
it's me that's keepit the house in order a' thae years.' She
began to rub her fingers along the arm of the rosewood
chair which she had polished for nineteen years. 'Do you

mean to tell me that I have nae right to this house and the furniture in it?'

'You have a legal right to a third of the furniture, Mrs Ritchie, exactly the same as Miss Ritchie here——'

'Is my very bed no' a' my ain?'

Tom Mitchell, agitating his pince-nez, turned to Sarah Annie:

'You see how it is, don't you, Miss Ritchie? There'll be a tidy sum for you and your mother——'

'But it's a shame!' cried Sarah Annie. 'I'm sure John Samuel doesna want the house. It's mother's house, and she should live in it.'

'Oh, I'm sure you'll be able to arrange matters among yourselves,' agreed the lawyer quickly. He was apprehensive; Mrs Ritchie looked as if she were going to scream. 'The law's not so unfair as you seem to think, for a lady can always depend on her son to support her, can't she? But if your son *should* think of selling the business, Mrs Ritchie, it might be quite a good thing for all of you to let the house go with it . . .'

'I'll never consent to it, never.'

Mrs Ritchie did not scream; she set her lips in a thin, hard line, and became as immobile as the furniture. Her blank, rigid face embarrassed the lawyer in spite of his secret relief, for none of his well-meaning phrases elicited any response. It was Sarah Annie who escorted him to the front door, and as they stood in the lobby she said hurriedly, with a feeling of shame:

'Mr Mitchell, if we need any money can we lift it?'

'Pending the final settlement, Miss Ritchie, I'll arrange any advance you may need. Just you let me know about it. Of course, it would be as well for your brother to come home as soon as possible; he's the heir, you see . . . Poor fellow, he'll be glad to get away from the war for a whilie. Have you heard when he's coming? No? Well, well, he's doing his bit. You and your mother should be proud of him. And until he comes back I'll do my best for you . . . Not at all, not at all . . . The money's there, you know.'

The money's there! The words echoed in Sarah Annie's mind as she shut the door. Her father had gone, but he had

left money behind him; he had slipped out of life as he had
so often slipped out of the house, leaving money behind
him, and without his money the house would have been
as barren as the body of a woman whose husband visited
her bed no more. The house had been Johnny Ritchie's
because he fructified it, and now it must be John Samuel's
rather than his mother's, because he, too, was a man, and
would fructify both a wife and the house. That was how
the law regarded it . . . And what about Sarah Annie and
Mrs Ritchie? In accepting the dead man's money would
they be acting like ghouls? . . . That must be what the law
really thought . . . That was why she had felt ashamed to ask
Tom Mitchell for the money . . . Unmated women, barren
houses . . .

Sarah Annie muffled her face in an old coat of her father's
that was hanging on a peg and burst into tears. If that's the
law's way of it, then it's a disgusting way! she cried to herself.
Father never looked at it like that . . . She caressed the coat
which had so often covered her father's patient back. He
didna make the law. He couldna help it. He wouldna have
wanted the house to be taken from his widow and given to
his son . . . He would have wanted his possessions to be
given like his affections: the fixed centre, the house, to his
wife, and anything else to all of the family alike . . . And
if she and her mother had to take Johnny Ritchie's money
they should take it, as they would have taken his affection,
without any feeling of shame . . . Unmated women, indeed!
The law was wrong-headed; the law was blind; the law took
no count of anything but the crassest physical facts . . .

Sarah Annie's tears dried while she was abusing the law.
Her head still ached but her purpose emerged clearly.
She must stand by her mother, sham or no sham. For
Mrs Ritchie's shams had more sense in them than the
fictions of the law; the swelling clouds with which she
crowned herself at least followed the contour of a spiritual
reality. Although she must have been posing during her
whole life she posed at least as a conscious individual; she
insisted on being not merely a female of the human species,
a breeder of children, a house for men to occupy and own;
she insisted on owning herself. And if in order to assert her

selfhood she laid claim to being in private league with God against the devil, that, thought Sarah Annie, was the fault of her generation . . . Let her do it, thought Sarah Annie; I dinna mind. No, I dinna mind.

She went back to the parlour, where her mother was still sitting immobile in a chair. As soon as the door opened Mrs Ritchie began to speak in a hard, shrill voice: 'Tom Mitchell's havering. Tom Mitchell doesna ken anything about it. If it hadna been for me Johnny Ritchie wouldna have had a penny to bless himself with. It was me that aye had to egg him on. And if I hadna keepit down expenses in the house there would have been neither house nor business by this time. And now Tom Mitchell tells me my very bed is no' my ain, and I've only to wait till my son comes home to turn me into the street.'

'Oh, mother, John Samuel would never do that——'

'The Lord will visit it upon his head if he tries to do it. They're all wrong; they're all wrong, I tell you. I'll never consent to it, never. This house is *mine*!' cried Mrs Ritchie in a hard, unnatural scream. Sarah Annie's heart beat thickly again, as it had done when she followed her mother up to the house, and although her mind counselled patience and understanding her body grew heavy with dejection and indefinable fear.

## THIRTY-SIX

But although she was afraid of she knew not what, Sarah Annie had not imagined one particular difficulty that she now encountered. Mrs Ritchie would not stay inside the house. Every half-hour or so she put on her black shawl and marched down the garden path to the gate, where she gazed up and down the road, looking for someone to talk to. If nobody she knew were in sight she would make for the nearest shop, with the excuse of buying a box of matches or a pennyworth of salt, and there she would tell over and over again her grievances and her injuries. 'Mother, you should have more pride,' protested Sarah Annie; 'I aye thought you had more pride than that.' But no protests could still Mrs Ritchie's restlessness; after wandering round the house, muttering to herself, she would snatch her shawl and be off again.

If only John Samuel could come home! 'It'll be all right when John Samuel comes home . . . It'll be all settled when John Samuel comes home.' This cry, repeated twenty times a day, became at length a fixed conviction in Sarah Annie's mind; all the more as in a few days it began to have a calming effect upon her mother. And on the evening when the long-expected telegram came Mrs Ritchie actually took out her knitting and sat in the parlour with her Sabbath face, the face which challenged the world to find a flaw in its assurance. She even said to her daughter: 'John Samuel's been fighting the Lord's battle.'

It would be all right . . . But when Sarah Annie stood waiting on the station platform next morning, although from old habit her hair was neat under her plain black hat, her black coat and skirt neat, her gloves neat, her whole appearance that of a young lady who has no loose ends, there were worried puckers in her mind. Would she be able to explain the situation to John Samuel before he met his mother? How could she tell him, how could she convey to him, the state his mother was in and the need for letting her have the house? How could she trouble a man who was probably only looking for a respite from trouble and suffering? . . .

'Hullo, Sarah Annie, is that yoursel'?'

Sarah Annie turned round, unpleasantly surprised.

'Oh, it's you, Aunt Mary?'

'Ay, Bob's due on this train. Your Jock's no' coming on it, is he?'

'Yes. We got a telegram last night.'

'Fancy that, now! Baith coming thegither! Weel, there'll be some high jinks the night,' said Aunt Mary Stott, nudging her embarrassed niece with a fat elbow. 'You canna see our kitchen dresser for bottles.'

Aunt Mary had on a brand-new coat with a fur collar. And well she might, thought Sarah Annie, with two daughters in munitions . . . Mrs Reid had been saying the other day: 'This war's fair taking the heart out o' me. And where's all the money coming from?' But Mrs Stott looked as if the war had put new heart into her and as if she knew where some of the money was going to, at any rate.

'I suppose Annie's got nothing but soor dook in the house?' said Aunt Mary, laughing.

'We havena got in any *drink*,' replied Sarah Annie, with a certain stiffness.

'Ay? Then Jock'll just need to come down to Mill Wynd . . . Dod, yonder's the train.'

They could see the smoke of the train winding between fenced-in squares of stubble and turnips, puffing its way towards Calderwick. Sarah Annie's heart began to beat thickly again . . . It'll be all right, she assured herself; in two minutes, in one minute, it'll be all right . . . Nearer and nearer comes the train, across the bridge, past the double home-signals, and the gleaming cylinder of the locomotive hurtles like a gigantic cannon towards the station platform, bringing home two soldiers from the very frontiers of death . . . Passive, like grains of sand blown irrelevantly across a

neat pattern on a linoleum-covered floor, two stray soldiers
are whirled across the fields to Calderwick, blown from the
very frontiers of humanity, where disparate ranks of men
make a shore against the vast sea of death as millions of
grains of sand that do not knit together make a shore
against the formless ocean. Like two grains of sand blown
by the wind the soldiers come back from death into an
incredibly tidy and differentiated world; and as the train
stops with a jolt two shapeless figures, dazed with fatigue
and the revolution of time and space, stagger on to the
platform, their accoutrements clattering, and wait to find
some assurance that they are at home.

Aunt Mary Stott, weeping easy tears, makes it easier for
them to feel a living connection with this forgotten world;
her large soft bosom receives them, her large soft arms
encircle first one and then the other; she kisses them with
wet, soft kisses, crying: 'Oh, my laddies! Oh, Bob! Oh, Jock!
Eh, it's grand to see you again,' and the shapeless figures
take form as Bob Stott and Jock Ritchie, unshaven, and
grinning above all the ironmongery that clanks upon them.
Sarah Annie, preparing to thrust out a timid hand, is more
than ever embarrassed by Aunt Mary Stott's expansiveness,
but when Jock says: 'Come on; kisses all round,' she presents
a cheek to be scrubbed by both of them, even by Bob Stott,
to whom she has hardly ever spoken in her life, although he
is her mother's sister's son.

'See you later,' cries Jock to Bob, as if unwilling to lose
touch with his fellow-stray. 'I ran into Bob yesterday night
in London,' he explains, and Sarah Annie, looking up at
him, wonders if this is really John Samuel, her brother.

'You've an awful lot of things to carry; let me take some
of them.'

'I never thought Calderwick was so small . . . What
a comic toy station!—Hey, do you think I'm going to
carry my kit all the way out to the North Road? Where's
a taxi?'

'We'll maybe get a cab——'

'A cab? Holy Moses! are there still cabs here?'

Is everything unchanged here still? There's the old steeple; it seems to be the only building that has not diminished.

A world in miniature, carrying on an imitation clockwork life . . .

'Let's make for a cab, then. I'm dead-beat. Bob and I had to sleep in the corridor. Here we are. Same old cab, same old horse . . .'

But once in the cab John Samuel's loud brightness was blurred, and the round dark eyes were strained and weary as they looked at Sarah Annie. 'Well,' he said, producing a cigarette, 'how's tricks? Suffragettes still going strong?'

'You're just the same; you havena changed,' cried Sarah Annie. It was a hopeful cry, as from one who looked for permanence, for enduring realities in a diverse, unstable world.

'*You're* just the same,' said John Samuel, but in his mouth it was like a grim condemnation.

'*You're* just the same, anyhow,' repeated John Samuel, looking at her neat black gloves, her neat black shoes, her plain, neat black hat. Gloves! Kid gloves! All black, though; that represented one change, at least.

'So the old man's gone.'

Sarah Annie's eyes filled with tears.

'He'll have plenty to keep him company,' said John Samuel, looking out of the window.

'Oh, John Samuel . . . is it—it must be awful out there at the Front.'

'Well, we don't wear kid gloves in this war,' said John Samuel.

And Sarah Annie, pulling off her kid gloves and twisting them in her hands, felt the tears fill her throat as well as her eyes. This was John Samuel, and for no fault of his own—just because he was a laddie—he had been condemned to crawl through endless wastes of mud choked with dead bodies . . . condemned to live beside death, to watch for death at every moment, to brave death day and night. Sarah Annie did not think of her brother dealing death to others; she saw only in her mind a hail of death-bringing missiles, the point of an enemy bayonet, the thrust of an enemy rifle . . .

'It's a shame!' she cried. 'I dinna see why you should all have to do it. I think the world's gone gyte.'

Why should John Samuel, just because he was born a laddie, have to suffer in a senseless war?

'We're just driven,' she burst out, 'all of us, laddies and lassies——'

'"You in your small corner, and I in mine,"' said John Samuel. 'Well, you can be thankful you're a lassie. This is a sleepy enough corner . . . Look, there's Charlie Burgess still standing in his shop door! What a comic wee place this is! A platoon could bomb it all to pieces.'

'Did you get my letter?'

Sarah Annie forgot everything else in a sudden anxiety about her mother. They were dreadfully near home already and she had not said a word . . . She hadn't reckoned on taking a cab.

'Did I? I dinna mind . . . What letter?'

'Oh, John Samuel, you must have got my letter? About mother, about the house. She's near off her head because the house is yours, and the workshop.'

'All the coffins mine?'

John Samuel threw away the butt of his cigarette and immediately felt for another.

'Tom Mitchell said something to her about you selling the house and the workshop together, and she's scared out of her mind about it. She just canna think of living anywhere but in that house, John Samuel. She's been in it for a lifetime. And I've had an awful job with her all this week, ever since the funeral. She's been at me from morning till night that the house wasna hers and she was to be turned out into the street.'

'So that's what she thinks of me, is it?'

'Of course you wouldna do it . . . You dinna want the house, do you?'

John Samuel laughed.

'I can hardly put it in my haversack, can I?'

'No, but will you tell her that it's hers? Tell her that you'll give it to her. And if you want the house later, mother can come and live with me, when I get a job. I'll look after her . . . But tell her that it's hers now.'

'Give her the house and all the doings, and then I can

go back and get killed, for all she cares. That's about it, isn't it?'

John Samuel's weary eyes now had a hard, questioning look in them that disconcerted and frightened his sister.

'Oh, dinna look at me like that,' she said. 'I canna help it, John Samuel. I canna help the war, and I canna help mother being in that state.'

'What the hell does a house matter?' said John Samuel.

'But it does matter to mother. It matters as if it was a bit of herself.'

'Does she ever think about anything but herself?'

'Oh, John Samuel . . . she's your mother. If it wasna for her you wouldna be here————'

'What the hell do you mean by that?'

Sarah Annie started at the question; it was barked at her in such an unrecognizable voice. John Samuel had leaned forward and was staring at her as if he was fey. The shock braced Sarah Annie, and quite naturally, solicitously, she asked him:

'What's wrong, Jock?'

John Samuel sat up and fished out another cigarette, his hands shaking.

'Nothing,' he said. 'I'm dead-beat, that's all . . . Christ, I could do with a sleep.'

'We're nearly there,' said Sarah Annie, and if she had been anxious at first because the journey seemed so short, she was now anxious because it appeared long. 'You'll soon get into bed and have a good sleep.'

John Samuel smoked in silence and stared out of the window. This was home. He was coming home. This sleepy wee place . . . still going on, still opening and shutting its shops and arguing about possessions; still going to bed at night and rising in the morning to a new day . . . Was there really a war oversea, or was this town an illusion?

'Where's Betsy?' he asked suddenly.

'At Cardonald, in the office of a munition factory.'

'And Davie Reid?'

'Killed three months syne.'

John Samuel did not move.

'And Andy Reid?'

'Missing.'

'You might as well tell me just all that are dead.'

Sarah Annie went over the list.

'And Lizzie Morton's in Serbia,' she finished up. 'That's about everybody.'

'I'm lucky to be here, I suppose.'

John Samuel stretched his legs and yawned.

The cab stopped.

'Well, here we are.'

He clambered out stiffly. This was home. This was the place that had drawn him back . . . there was the house, exactly the same as ever. He stood for a moment looking at it. A small rectangular box of grey stone, with a chimney at each end of the slate roof, and a brown door set exactly in the middle between two sash windows. Like a toy house that hasn't been painted the right colour, thought John Samuel; it should have had a red roof and a green door . . . And a damned toy gate that I can hardly squeeze through . . .

But in the same moment that he tried to belittle the house John Samuel knew that he was afraid of it. His feet weighed like lead as he stumbled up the path and his heart contracted with fear when he saw the lace curtain move at the parlour window.

'Sleep,' he said to himself. 'A good sleep is what I'm needing.'

The door opened, and there, like a clockwork toy figure, stood Mrs Ritchie in a clean white apron, with the Sabbath expression on her face. John Samuel's sense of relief was so great that he could have laughed. That little woman, neat and clean and of miniature size, exactly like the town itself, was his mother, just as he might have remembered her, and he could not understand what he had been afraid of or why he had had such queer ideas about her.

'Hullo, mother! Here we are again!'

'Oh, John Samuel,' said the prim voice he remembered, 'what a great, muckle creature you've turned into. Welcome back. Wipe your feet, now, before you come in.'

'Wipe my feet!' John Samuel began to laugh. 'No French dirt in my house, says she; this is a respectable house.

What do you think of that, Sarah Annie? All right, I'll wipe my feet.'

He began knocking off great gobbets of caked mud. Mrs Ritchie gave a small scream: 'Oh, thae boots'll have to be scrapit. No, no; you'd better just come inbye as you are, dirt and all . . .'

Dirt and all, thought John Samuel, dropping his haversack and his accoutrements in the lobby as if he were shedding the war from himself. He felt foolishly happy and relaxed . . . Dirt and all. This was his home and it accepted him as he was . . . He trudged into the kitchen, an absurdly small kitchen, hardly bigger than a dug-out, but trim and clean and friendly and safe . . . These walls would not open to let in the smother and reek and flying anger of war. Here he could sleep at last.

He sat down naturally in his father's chair and stretched his feet to the fire.

'You'll no' have had any breakfast?'

Mrs Ritchie stood pouring water into the teapot.

John Samuel roused himself with an effort:

'I had some tea at Edinburgh . . .'

'But you'll take some ham and eggs?'

'This is a Sunday breakfast, I see.'

'You've been fighting the Lord's battle, John Samuel. Sit in to the table. But take your boots off first.'

Take off thy shoes from off thy feet, ran in John Samuel's drowsy mind as he undid his puttees. Sarah Annie brought him his old slippers.

'Your poor father's awa',' said Mrs Ritchie, sitting down before the teapot.

'Ay.'

'He would never have wanted me to be turned out of this house,' went on Mrs Ritchie, passing a plateful of fried ham and eggs.

'No.'

'You'll no' be wanting the house?'

'No' the now, anyway.' John Samuel poked at the eggs. He was too sleepy to eat.

'You can have it when I'm awa',' said Mrs Ritchie in a plaintive voice. 'Your father's place'll be aye ready for you here, John Samuel. You'll maybe carry on the business?'

'We'll see about that.'

'What did you say?'

'See about that later.'

'Leave him alone, mother,' put in Sarah Annie. 'He's fair tired out; he's needing to his bed.'

'But he'll have to tell Tom Mitchell. I was only——'

'Leave him alone, mother.'

'You're not to speak to me like that, Sarah Annie.'

'Leave him alone. He'll need the big bed; I'll get it ready. His old bed's ower wee,' persisted Sarah Annie.

'Did anybody say bed?' muttered John Samuel, nodding. He suddenly slipped down in his chair and laid his head on his arms. This was home. Here he could sleep.

Behind his closed eyelids he was in the dark cellar and the door was shut upon him. He was standing on something horrible, slipping into deep mud beneath which lay something more horrible still. And his mother was saying: 'I'll let you out if you're a good boy and do what I tell you. Do you hear me? John Samuel!' He caught at her hand to pull her down beside him; he was slipping, slipping . . . He screamed.

He stared confusedly at his mother, who had been shaking him. Somebody was sobbing: 'Oh dear, oh dear, oh dear . . .' But Mrs Ritchie's face was pale with rage:

'Don't you dare to speak like that to your mother!'

'What the hell's the matter?' he repeated.

'Come to your bed, John Samuel.' That was Sarah Annie. Why was she snivelling?

'Leave him *alone*, mother. Come to your bed . . . It's all ready.'

'I don't know how you can come back with such words on your lips, John Samuel, after the way God has spared you. And your poor father hardly cold in his grave . . .'

'Go to hell!' said John Samuel loudly. 'I want to sleep.'

He lurched beside Sarah Annie and tried to turn into his old room. She pushed him into the big bedroom, where the big bed was turned down: white pillows, white sheets . . .

John Samuel rolled on to the bed, his mother's bed. The

blank field was invaded . . . but the enemy was watching through a periscope. Drunken with slumber he climbed up on the bed-rail and tore Thou God Seest Me from the wall. It fell clattering on the floor, and John Samuel, with a faint, widening ripple of triumph, sank into a dreamless sleep.

## THIRTY-SEVEN

I

John Samuel came on a Friday and he went away to London on the Monday morning. It was a dreadful weekend for Sarah Annie, and she could not forgive her mother for deriving so much satisfaction from what she called 'John Samuel's ongoings.' The more John Samuel put himself in the wrong the better Mrs Ritchie seemed to be pleased; her pleasure revealed itself in the unction with which she called God and the neighbours to witness her son's ingratitude and downright wickedness. Even her hearing had apparently improved now that she had her son's bad language to listen to. John Samuel was indeed ungrateful enough; he empowered the lawyer to sell the workshop and the stock in it, and he spent hours in Mill Wynd, presumably drinking with Mrs Ritchie's disreputable and discarded relations. And when she appealed to his better self, reminding him that he was a soldier on the Lord's side in a righteous war, he swore at her and said that the Lord had nothing to do with the war, for she only kept Him up her sleeve. 'And I'm not an angel,' he shouted, 'I'm your son, and you can bloody well take me as I am.' He was drunk when he said that. It was only when he was drunk that he appeared at his home and forced himself upon his mother, following her from room to room until she had the feeling that she was being subjected to a new kind of assault. On the Saturday night he brought Bob Stott in, as drunk as himself, and Mrs Ritchie was nearly beside herself with rage at this prostitution of her house. 'You can get back to Mill Wynd,' she cried, 'where you belong, the pair of you'; but John Samuel, who had been snickering to himself as he pursued his mother with the ray from a pocket flashlight, suddenly turned hard and ugly. 'This is my house,' he threatened her, 'and I'll get the better of you yet. My number's not up yet.' 'This is *my* house,' said Mrs Ritchie, 'until you turn me out of it——' John Samuel all at once began to snicker again: '*Your* house for the duration of the war, old lady . . . When this bloody war is over,' he sang, 'what a turn-up there will be-e-e.' Then, with another change of mood, he slapped Bob Stott on the shoulder: 'Come along, Bob; we're no' wanted here, my lad; we're no' wanted here. Nothing doing, Bob, for the duration . . .'

That was all the assurance Mrs Ritchie could get about the house, that it was hers 'for the duration.' John Samuel refused to do anything. Legally the house was still his, and his mother could only comfort herself by remembering that the war was not nearly over yet. Meanwhile, she had everybody's sympathy and found it easy to be a martyr in public. 'A real respectable body, Mrs Ritchie,' said the town gossips; 'it's a pity she should have these ongoings to worry her on top of everything else . . . Still, I suppose the laddie has to enjoy himself while he's on leave, poor fellow . . . Ay, the war's responsible for a lot.'

But if John Samuel's easy phrases about the 'duration' appeased Mrs Ritchie they terrified Sarah Annie, who had been trying that morning to talk seriously to her brother. 'I have to go back to the Training College,' she had urged, 'I canna leave mother in this state.' 'Och, she'll be all right,' John Samuel had objected, 'she has plenty to live on and nothing to do . . . She's good at looking after herself.' And then, looking up suddenly, he had said: 'This house is the only hold I have on her . . . Once I give her the house, my number's up.'

'What *do* you mean?'

'I want to come back from the war,' said John Samuel, and refused to explain himself further. All he would say was: 'I'm not taking any chances.' But Sarah Annie was scared, as she had been scared in the cab coming from the station. John Samuel's phrases were like sudden flashes revealing an unimaginable hell of fear and madness. Surely he could not seriously believe that if he gave his mother the house he would be killed as soon as he went back? Surely he could not believe that what had kept him alive in France was some dark emanation of his mother's will? And yet, even now, when he was drunk, everything he said confirmed such an interpretation; for the duration of the war he believed himself at the mercy of his mother, and until it was over he would suspend all action . . .

After all that it was a relief to see him go off on the Monday. His leave was not up, but he and Bob had made up their minds to a spree in London before going back. Sarah Annie thought she knew exactly when John Samuel had made the decision for both of them; it was on Sunday afternoon when he saw his mother and sister starting for the cemetery with flowers. He made a wry face.

'Are you not coming, John Samuel?' said Mrs Ritchie.

'It's hardly time to take my father's place yet,' he retorted. 'Damn this dead-and-alive hole of a town! Is that all you can offer a fellow? A walk to the cemetery!'

'Everybody will be wondering why you're not with us,' said Mrs Ritchie, with cold dignity.

'I canna walk down the street without somebody spotting me, and I'm not going to advertise myself all over the place today. They can wonder and they can go on wondering,' said John Samuel. 'I've had enough of it.'

It must have been then that he had decided to cut and run, thought Sarah Annie. It didn't seem to matter either to Bob Stott or to John Samuel that their families might never see them again; all they wanted was to lose themselves, in drink or in London. She did not betray them to her mother, however, and Mrs Ritchie insisted on coming to the station to see her son off. The Stotts were there in full force, but Mrs Ritchie's small, stiff figure in its black weeds stood like a rock unsubmerged by overflowing Stotts. Whenever John Samuel looked like being washed away from the rock Mrs Ritchie made some remark to him behind her veil, and he had to bend down to listen and reply. So they made quite an effective tableau, thought Sarah Annie scornfully: devoted mother parting from attentive son. And she was not really

surprised when Mrs Ritchie put up her veil and offered her
cheek for a kiss.

'Good-bye, John Samuel.'

'Good-bye, mother. Keep the home fires burning . . .
That's right. Cheerio, Sarah Annie; you're a better sport
than I thought you were. Well, Bob——'

'Are you sure this is the right train, John Samuel?' said
Mrs Ritchie, laying her hand on her son's sleeve to prevent
him from turning to say good-bye to his Aunt Mary.

'Och, what the hell does it matter?' said John Samuel,
breaking loose. He kissed his aunt and got into the train.
'Me and Bob'll land up somewhere!' he shouted from
the window. 'Any old where!' The train moved out. But
Mrs Ritchie was not yet satisfied. 'Excuse me, porter,' she
said, avoiding a farewell to her sister, 'but was that the
London train?'

'Oh ay, that was it, all right. They'll be in London the
nicht,' said the porter.

'Come on, mother,' Sarah Annie tugged at her mother
impatiently. 'What's the use of asking now?' What, indeed?
As John Samuel might have said: there was a war on, and
what did it matter now whether one came to the right
destination or not?

## II

Whatever John Samuel's destination he did not return to
Calderwick again until the war was over. He wrote letters
from time to time, but not to Mrs Ritchie; it was Sarah Annie
who received his infrequent scrawls in her Training College,
and every one of his letters roused in her an apprehension
that was half excitement and half fear. The small, ill-formed
script seemed to hypnotize the girl's imagination so that she
saw involuntarily the landscape of her brother's mind, and
it was an ugly waste, like her own vision of a battlefield,
but in it something savage and cruel, something that was
John Samuel and yet not John Samuel, hit out blindly.
The last of his letters, written from London instead of
from somewhere behind the line in France, was the worst,
perhaps because it had no censorship to evade; without any
preamble it described baldly and with brutal detail various

erotic adventures. 'I'm living as I shall probably have to die, without any sentimental bunk,' the letter concluded. 'You should send this on to my mother, for it's high time she was blown out of her fool's paradise.'

In a postscript scrawled along the side of the sheet there was added: 'I'm not J.S.R. any more, I'm *every soldier*, maybe *every man.*'

Sarah Annie kept that letter under lock and key. But she could not keep it out of her mind, especially whenever she saw a detachment of soldiers marching through the street to entrain for the Front. The tears would come into her eyes, a hysterical lump would rise in her throat; there went Everyman, marching to his death; there went Everyman, having shed his individuality, his spiritual values, become merely a numbered animal whose vitality and courage were doomed to mechanical extinction. 'Oh, why must they be driven?' she asked herself, and the passion with which she asked it frightened her. Beneath Sarah Annie Ritchie there stirred the old instinct of Everywoman, the instinct to save something of these men from annihilation, the instinct that had made some nameless girl in London hungry for the soldier who once had been a boy called John Samuel Ritchie. When death came so close individual differentiation ceased to matter, and Sarah Annie, with tears in her eyes, felt her body yearn towards these anonymous soldiers, as if she could not let them die before they had been accepted by her.

So much, at least, in her brother's letter she could understand. But the foul language! The deliberately brutal words! Every word was a blow aimed at her, or through her at her mother. What would happen when the soldier returned to the fool's paradise? Her mother, meanwhile, seemed to be content, even happy, now that she was alone in the house. But what would happen when John Samuel came home? And was it entirely a fool's paradise? Was there not more in life than the mere flux and reflux of racial instincts? Was there not herself, Sarah Annie Ritchie, as well as Everywoman? And it was not a formless Everyman, it was John Samuel Ritchie himself who hit out so cruelly, with such deliberate desire to wound, from the anonymous waste land in which he was denying his own existence as an individual.

The single, enduring personality of the individual—that, thought Sarah Annie, was what her mother stood for . . . It was some hazy perception of that which made John Samuel believe that his mother was holding grimly on to him and preventing him from being lost in death. Mrs Ritchie was an embodiment of the separate human will that keeps itself from merging in the undifferentiated herd; and there was something to be said for that separateness, thought Sarah Annie, walking back to her lodging . . . What a fool she would have made of herself if she had thrown her arms round the neck of a strange soldier! She was not only Everywoman, she was her mother's daughter. And John Samuel was her mother's son . . . What *would* happen when he came home?

But the letters which Mrs Ritchie received from her daughter—dutiful letters—contained no revelations about John Samuel. Nor did Mrs Ritchie have any apprehensions about his return. A widow, living alone, she was now able to raise high before the whole town the altar on which she made sacrifice; she moved like a priestess, and her black-veiled figure became familiar in the streets as she made her way to church, to prayer-meetings, to committees for the organization of war-work. Her voice was plaintive as she referred to 'my son, who is doing his duty in France'; her slight deafness emphasized her aloofness and added to her pathos; her face, taut with will-power, looked as if it had been carved in ivory. The nice ladies who ran the committees made a pet of her; they said she was a 'character' and terribly good at getting things *done*. Besides, one could not but feel that Britain *must* win the war whenever one looked at Mrs Ritchie . . .

## THIRTY-EIGHT

Strange, strange—the wet boughs, the gleaming twigs; strange the dank wetness of the brown wooden fencing around the new brick municipal houses; yet these brick boxes, alien among the grey stone cottages of Calderwick, were not more strange to John Samuel than the one-time familiar pavements. And strangest of all was the garden path leading up to his own house, for while he walked on it he said to himself in wonder: 'This is *mine*.' How could anything be his?

Even the body that was supposed to be his was strange to him. The left leg that limped, and would for ever limp because some irrelevant pieces of shrapnel had lodged in its sinews, in its kneecap, was not John Samuel's leg; and he would often sit looking at his hands, trying to remember why they had picked up bombs and thrown them into other men's bellies. People told him that his sense of dislocation came from shell-shock, that he would waken up some morning to find that the world had clicked into place again, but it sounded too much as if they were opening a cage-door and chirruping to him to come back. As usual, whenever an idea like that came to him he sought out his mother to tell her about it, and telling her about it amounted to reproaching her for it. She would turn any house into a cage, he shouted. A cage, with seed and water in neat, separate compartments. And then he limped out again to watch the free birds fluttering in the spring rain.

He delighted in the birds, strange though they were. He delighted only in odd things which he never used to notice at all: a ray of sunlight shining on a jar of sweeties in a window; a few blades of grass and fronds of moss growing in a crack between two stones; the far-off chiming of a

coal-bell that dropped round, full, resonant notes into the
sound of street-traffic. These odd sights and sounds were
more himself than the person called John Samuel Ritchie,
who owned a house and money in the bank and was the
son of that hard woman, Mrs Ritchie. 'Tits, laddie, you
should have more backbone in you, and you the son of
your mother,' old Charlie Burgess had had the cheek to
say to him. 'My mother's all backbone,' he had retorted,
'and my father couldna have gotten muckle comfort from
that.' Charlie Burgess had snickered, the creeshy old sinner,
wagging his fat belly under its white apron. What a life—to
stand at the door of a shop all day! Old Charlie should have
been killed in the war, and not Davie Reid.

Whenever the stars came out John Samuel thought of
Davie Reid. It seemed to him now, painfully trying to
remember his past self, that Davie Reid had meant more
to him than he had ever realized. It was just because Davie
Reid had sung, 'Ritchie-bitchie, in a cage'—and how true
that had been!—that he had become a symbol of wild liberty
to the young Ritchie. And later on Davie Reid had done him
the rare service of associating that ideal of liberty with the
infinite stars in the pathless sky. John Samuel could still
recall, as if from another life, how uplifted he had been
when he got the great idea of dodging his mother's God
from star to star through all eternity . . . But now there was
no God to dodge, and Davie Reid was dead; only his bones
remained, only his bones and his teeth . . . When a man
was dead he was deader than dead. Full stop. Finish.

John Samuel prodded his stick into the soft, wet soil,
making full stops. Anything else was sentimental bunk.
And all his feelings for Betsy Reid had just been sentimental
bunk. He had only wanted to kiss her and lie with her and
he had thought it was love. Love! When you threw a bomb
into a man's belly and burst it to pieces you didn't stop to
think about his feelings and his honour and his immortal
soul . . . you just hurled the bomb. And when you went
into a girl's belly you shouldn't stop to think about her
feelings . . . What a sentimental fool he had been! But if
he had grown up a fool it was his mother's fault. Why had
he been doomed to have the wrong kind of woman for a

mother? All backbone, nothing but backbone, exactly as if she were dead—deader even than Davie Reid, for he had once been alive, under the infinite stars, while Mrs Ritchie brought the stars and the sky down upon the world like a coffin-lid . . .

A blade of grass, the flutter of a bird's wing, the memory of a dead man—in these John Samuel recognized himself, but in these only. And not in any sentimental way, either. No, the grass, for all its queerness and greenness, would wither; the bird, for all its wildness, might peck another wild bird to death and itself would die; the man, he knew, was dead for ever. And the rainbows glancing in the scum of the puddles had no meaning; they were just bonny. None of them had any meaning, none of them belonged to any world but this one, and that was why he could delight in them. Even fighting, when you looked at it like that, was natural enough; it was no worse than two sparrows pecking at each other . . . What made it ghastly was the systematic organization of warfare under the banner of Bunk, making chaps fight for Bunk called patriotism or Bunk called God. A man could fight and be reconciled to his enemy and quit fighting; but Bunk could go on fighting for ever and ever, Amen . . . A man could use his fists, or even a bayonet, a bomb, or a rifle, but Bunk used big guns and tanks and poison-gas. A man could kill his enemy and be quit of him, but Bunk preached immortality and kept alive a mob of revengeful ghosts . . . A man could live in this world, looking, tasting, listening, enjoying even the cold and the rain, using his hands, his feet, all his members, but Bunk preached heaven and hell and scared him out of his natural enjoyment . . . And of all the devotees of Bunk, of all the poisonous, deadly, strangling devisers of Bunk, his mother, Mrs Ritchie, was the worst.

Whatever John Samuel's thoughts, they always ended in his mother; she was the spider at the centre of the web. He could not get away from her. That was literally true, for the farther he got away from her in the body the more formidable she became. She had obsessed him like a nightmare when he was over in France, and there had been whole days when he felt that every soldier in the barrage,

French or German or British, was suffering like him from his mother's anger—as if *she* were the earth that spewed out death at them, as if *she* had blasted the trees and darkened the sky and twisted the acres of wire—and he had been sorry for them all, every mother's son, outcast like himself because Mrs Ritchie was a hard woman, an unnatural woman . . . And when he had been buried in the explosion of the shell it was his mother who had buried him, thrust him deep down in a horrible, dark, stifling cellar, where he beat his fists on the door in vain . . . No, the only way to keep these nightmares off was to remain within sight of Mrs Ritchie, to convince oneself daily that she was really only a bony little woman in a black dress, a nasty little woman who believed in the great God Bunk.

If she would only leave him alone! He hadn't been home for a fortnight yet and already she was at him about finding a job, and never a day passed but she reproached him for having sold his father's workshop. 'It's enough to make your poor father turn in his grave,' she kept on saying.

'You go on at me as if I had sold my father's body to the knacker!' he shouted. 'And what if I had, Mrs Ritchie? What if I had? When a man's dead, he's dead.'

'That's a wicked, wicked lie, John Samuel, and may God forgive you on that Day when you have to give account to Him.'

'Bunk! Bunk again! And if it wasna, do you know who should be most afraid of that day? You. Ay, you. You killed my father as surely as if you had run him over.'

John Samuel rushed from the kitchen, but not before he had felt the blast of Mrs Ritchie's hatred that caught him full in the chest. He felt sick. This was what he was doomed to live with. This was his house, and it was a cage. Look at that parlour, for instance. He opened the parlour door and went in. Every chair against the wall, every table with its mathematically exact table-cover . . . He tirled the chairs out of their places, wrecking their neat, inhuman orderliness; he snatched the cover from the big table and left it crumpled on the floor; he took down and smashed the glazed engraving of Moses bringing down the tablets of the Law from Sinai. It was as if he were trying

to force a change of heart upon his mother by turning her
house topsy-turvy, and he did succeed at least in easing his
own sickness. But the sickness became a flat despair. What
was the use of trying? In the afternoon everything would
be put back as it was before, and if Moses were broken
some other illustrated text would hang in his place . . .
Even Thou God Seest Me had been nailed up again over
his mother's bed . . .

Whenever Sarah Annie returned from the Townhead
School, where she was teaching Standard Two, she felt
that the house was vibrating with hatred.

'Leave him alone, mother!' she would say. 'Can you no'
leave him alone? He's no' right better yet; he's no' able for
a job, and there's plenty money——'

'*I'm* all right; it's her that's all wrong,' John Samuel would
break in; and Mrs Ritchie's level voice would persist that
it was a sin to see a young man wasting his life and his
father's substance instead of laying up treasure in heaven.
It wasna the money she was thinking of, for if she needed
money it was only to give it to Christian charities . . . And
there they were at it again.

'All she thinks of is to get money out of a man to glorify
herself with.'

'All you think of, John Samuel, is self-indulgence instead
of doing your duty and taking your father's place.'

'My father's place is in the graveyard. I suppose that's
what you mean?'

'The Lord forgive you, John Samuel,' said Mrs Ritchie,
casting her eyes up.

'Can you no' stop it?' Sarah Annie implored them both.
'I canna stand this, day in, day out. How do you think I
can teach bairns? Can *you* no' stop it, John Samuel?'

'She began it before we were born,' said John Samuel,
thumping the table.

'The Lord liveth from everlasting to everlasting,' countered Mrs Ritchie.

And they were at it all over again.

Sarah Annie tried to reason with her brother one
night after Mrs Ritchie had gone out to the weekly
prayer-meeting.

'She knows I dinna want to go near the kirk; she knows I winna go to a prayer-meeting. What for does she need to bring it up again every single time? She tortures me! It's like letting drop after drop of water fall on the same spot of a man's head,' shouted John Samuel.

'She's only wanting to show you off to the congregation. I've learned a lot about her, and she's play-acting most of the time, showing off before folk. Why should you mind that? Her and me got on well enough before you came back. Could you no' just pretend to give in to her?'

'If I pretend to give in to her I'll have to go on pretending all my life—every day of my life. Think of the dance she led my father . . . and she killed him in the end.' John Samuel laid his head on the table and groaned: 'She wouldna let me die, and now she'll no' let me live. What'll I do? What'll I do?'

'Could you no' leave Calderwick and get a job in Dundee, if you wanted it?'

John Samuel shook his head. Then he looked straight at Sarah Annie: 'If I go away from her, it's worse. I know it's nonsense, but if I'm away from her she's a nightmare to me . . . I canna sleep . . .'

His round eyes were bewildered, as if he were a helpless onlooker at some motiveless quarrel.

'If I canna get the better of her *here*, in my own house, I'm done for. And I have the feeling that the whole world'll be done for if I dinna manage it. It's here or nowhere——'

'But if you *know* that that's all nonsense——'

'I dinna know anything.'

John Samuel started up:

'I dinna know anything. What can I prove? Nothing! Nothing! She has everything on her side. The whole of Calderwick, the whole world is on her side. You ask for bread, living bread, and you get a stone.'

Sarah Annie burst into tears:

'Oh, I wish you had never gone to the war.'

John Samuel said in a curiously dry voice: 'Ay, the war can be blamed for a lot. It's a convenient excuse.'

Yet after that he began to haunt the station, watching the trains go off to Dundee. Once on a time, he remembered, he had climbed into a train with Bob Stott, shouting cheerfully: 'Any old where!' And Bob Stott had been killed. One shall be taken and another left . . . But the trains still went to Dundee and London, or in the other direction—to Aberdeen—with their destinations plainly marked on the carriages. They were as certain of their destinations as his mother was certain that she would arrive in heaven. It was a comfortable thing to believe in sign-posts, even if the sign-posts were wrong . . . And all you had to do was to buy a ticket. You could not travel anywhere without a ticket—a Presbyterian ticket or a Roman ticket or a C. of E. ticket . . . The engines came hurtling up to the platform like projectiles from some huge gun, the doors slammed, and off you were shot—whither? To Dundee, of course, or Edinburgh, to deal in Bunk, to serve Bunk, to write Bunk until Bunk shot you off to the next great war . . .

John Samuel always turned in at the 'White Horse' after visiting the station, and drank himself into forgetfulness. But on the next day he was drawn to the railway again, and on the next, and on the next . . . The trains were so absurdly like his mother. They wouldna stop except at the traditional stations, and they wouldna leave the strait and narrow way. Any poor dog that strayed across the line in front of them would never know what struck it . . . And it was hot air that drove them on.

He stood snickering to himself in the 'White Horse' as he thought of this, and when somebody asked him: 'Where did you get your leg hurt, Jock?' he could not resist answering: 'It was run over by an engine . . . Ay, an engine in Scotland, a damned argumentative engine that got the better of me in the argument.'

'Hoot, you shouldna argue wi' an engine, Jock.'

'Man, I was looking for a wee hole under it to pish into so that I could put its fires oot.'

Ho, ho, ho! roared the bar.

'He's a comic, that Jock Ritchie,' was what they said after he had limped out. 'Did you hear what he said to Charlie Burgess the ither day? . . . Oh ay, he has aye a cheery word——'

'I said till him, I said: "You're no' taking up the

reporting again, are you?" And says he: "I've heard ower
mony reports," says he, "from the arses of ower mony
big guns." . . .'

The only people in Calderwick outside his own family
who suspected that all was not well with Jock Ritchie were
Mrs Reid and her daughter Betsy. Betsy's uneasiness about
him was due in part to a bad conscience, for she had come
back from her munition works at Cardonald engaged to a
member of the firm's directorate, a man who had made
good money out of the war. She could not suppose that
Jock Ritchie would like that . . . Still, it had only been a
bairns' game they had played at; the little silver ring with
the heart on it was too funny for words.

'I have it among my brooches—there it is, mother. I
couldna very well give it back to him now, could I? That
would look as if it had been serious.'

'There's something wrang wi' the laddie,' said Mrs Reid.
'I hope it's no' that. But it's no' very likely. A nice laddie
like Jock Ritchie wouldna break his heart for a limmer like
you, Betsy.'

Yet whenever Jock Ritchie came limping in to have tea
with the Reids, Betsy was not so sure . . . It must be
resentment, she thought, that made him ignore her and
turn to her mother. She sat down at the piano and played
a little piece he always used to ask for, *Träumerei*, it was
called, and it was an easy thing to play, only you had to
put a lot of expression into it. She played it with more
expression than ever, and Jock's air of detachment, she
thought, was just pretence . . . 'Ay,' he said, when she had
finished, 'that used to make me want to kiss you, Betsy.'

Betsy looked at him over her shoulder.

'No, keep it for the munition merchant,' said Jock. 'He
believes in that kind of bunk, I bet. He hasna had to fling
the bombs he made.'

Betsy grew angry:

'He nearly worked himself to death in the war, Jock
Ritchie.'

Jock's eyes remained hard and cold.

'Marking shells is only one-half of the job,' he said, 'and
kissing girls in the moonlight is only one-half of the job.

He's the man for that, no' me. I dinna stop short at kissing nowadays, so you'd better be careful.'

Jealousy! thought Betsy, squirming a little under those hard, appraising eyes.

But Mrs Reid thought: My heart's wae for that laddie. And she said to him, urgently, as she stood at the door with him: 'Is there anything I can do for you, Jock?'

'Nothing,' said John Samuel Ritchie; 'it's ower late in the day, Mrs Reid.' And he limped downstairs without looking back.

'It's ower late in the day . . .' The finality of that remark made her heart heavier, for this was not the Jock Ritchie who used to put things off and put things off, crying: 'No' yet, no' just yet, no' this very minute.' This was a strange, cold creature who could say: 'Now, this very minute, it's ower late to do anything, Mrs Reid.' And he had gone without once looking back . . .

'Not here, the absolute, not here and now!' John Samuel had once cried. 'Let me put it off!' Nothing had seemed final in those days: the sun rose again, bare trees broke into leaf again, a door once shut might open again, and when one's body died the soul might live again from star to star. There had been no final certainty save the certainty of renewal; if there was an absolute it was displaced into a future so remote that he could ignore it. But he had now discovered that there was no future, that death itself was an absolute, a full stop; and every step he took now seemed irrevocable and final, as if with every moment of time some world had died for ever. Only his mother went on and on; in a fixed rigidity, incapable of change or renewal—for there was no renewal—she persisted, like a spear-head of infinite length thrusting through layer after layer of events, and the only immortality in the world was hers, the immortality of Bunk.

Mother earth! said John Samuel, and laughed. The mother earth of the battle-fields; a barren, featureless waste of death. He couldn't face it any longer. 'Now,' said John Samuel.

He limped down to the railway station. The afternoon train for the south was just due. Like his mother, it would be punctual.

## THIRTY-NINE

# I

There was a shuffling of embarrassed feet outside Mrs Ritchie's gate and a buzzing of voices.

'You'd better tell her, Sandy.'

'Mind you, I would have sworn he hadna a care in the world. It fair beats me——'

'Sh-sh. We'd better say it was an accident.'

'It's nae use dovering here. You tell her, Sandy.'

The gate opened and two of the men came slowly up the garden path. Sandy Burgess, the big signalman, advanced first towards the door with much the same deliberate solemnity that he brought to the pulling of his levers in the signal-cabin. Mrs Ritchie heard the gate screech on its hinges and peeped out through the parlour curtains.

Dear me, there was Sandy Burgess and a porter loon from the station, and twa–three mair men standing by the gate . . . What was wrong? Her heart fluttered; had John Samuel been bringing fresh discredit upon her by getting into a drunken row at the station? Was he in the lock-up? . . . Her knees trembled as she went to open the door. I've done my duty by him faithfully, she would say; it's no' my fault . . . I'll take nothing to do with it . . . 'What's a' this?' she quavered, 'what's happened?'

'Mistress Ritchie . . .' began Sandy Burgess, in his measured, booming voice, but Mrs Ritchie was not sure that she heard what he said, for his rumbling tones seemed to be accusing her of something, and she would not be accused; it wasna her fault.

She turned her head from one man to the other, like a tortoise imprisoned in its shell, unable to escape.

'I didna hear you,' she said, and then: 'I canna understand it. I canna understand it.'

'No, nor we canna understand it neither,' said the porter defiantly. 'He was aye that cheery.'

Sandy Burgess nudged him in the ribs: 'Sh-sh, it was an accident.'

'Fell on the line, did he? Right in front of the express? But it was an accident . . .'

Oh ay, it was an accident.

She blinked on the doorstep, looking from one to the other.

'I canna understand it,' her lips repeated mechanically.

'You have the sympathy of the whole town, Mistress Ritchie,' boomed Sandy's voice, and Mrs Ritchie, understanding all at once that these men were sorry for her and that their air of constraint was not an impeachment of her, but an awkward expression of sympathy, swayed against the door-jamb, her eyes filling with tears.

Sandy Burgess was prepared for that.

'Haud up, now,' he said, catching her on his arm, 'I'll gi'e you a hand inbye.'

Mrs Ritchie managed to guide him past the kitchen into the parlour, and subsided on the sofa, repeating in a faint voice: 'Poor John Samuel . . . Poor John Samuel. Oh, dear. Poor John Samuel.'

'Ay, Mistress Ritchie, it's a sad business. A wee nip o' brandy, noo?'

Mrs Ritchie feebly waved the brandy away, and fluttered her handkerchief. Sandy Burgess pocketed the flask again and said: 'Get her a drink o' watter.'

The porter loon ran for the water. He was glad to be doing something, for he had seen Jock Ritchie fling himself down.

Sandy tilted the tumbler and Mrs Ritchie drank, her teeth chattering. Her eyes still turned from one man to the other, but they were now imploring eyes, no longer defensive.

'Sarah Annie!' she gasped.

'Ay,' said Sandy Burgess. 'Send somebody to the school to bring the lassie hame.'

The porter loon dashed out to the gate, but instead of sending somebody he ran round the corner himself towards the school. He couldna get out of his mind the sight of Jock Ritchie.

Sarah Annie did not know it, but as she stood in the doorway, her breath coming in sobs, her eyes staring in her head, her hair falling in dishevelled locks over her cheeks, it was Annie Rattray whom she saw sitting pale and tremulous on the sofa, as once Annie Rattray had sat pale and tremulous on a tussock of grass, disclaiming responsibility for what she had done, years before Sarah Annie was born; Annie Rattray reclining on a submissive element after riding the whirlwind. Something theatrical in the gesture with which her mother was handing back a tumbler to Sandy Burgess made the girl suddenly want to scream.

'Why did you no' leave him alone?' she panted. 'Why did you no' leave him alone, mother?'

It might have been Tina Gove trying to humiliate Annie Rattray before the world. But Annie Rattray had become Mrs Ritchie. All the years she had lived since she was at school now rose up to efface any threatened humiliation; she was the daughter of God, the vehicle of God, the blameless widow of a deacon, the outraged mother of this wicked, wicked girl . . . A cold, fixed intensity gleamed for a moment in Mrs Ritchie's eyes, but she managed to say: 'God forgive you, Sarah Annie,' and then, turning to her audience, she almost whimpered: 'I had to check the poor laddie for the drink he was taking, but that—that . . .' Her teeth chattered again and she looked appealingly from one man to the other.

'Any mother would have done the same,' said Sandy Burgess. 'I doubt the war had a lot to do with it . . .'

The war. Of course. Jock Ritchie *had* been drinking far ower muckle, and it wasna right of the lassie to blame her mother for trying to stop him. The war. Oh ay, the war . . .

'He was young to join up, but he *would* join up,' quavered

Mrs Ritchie. Sarah Annie broke into loud, tearing sobs and crumpled into the nearest chair. Cap in hand Sandy Burgess tiptoed out, the porter loon behind him.

'I was only doing my duty by him,' said Mrs Ritchie, smoothing the antimacassar on the back of the sofa. 'I was only doing my duty by him . . . Poor John Samuel.'

Sarah Annie, through her sobs, repeated: 'You should have left him *alone* . . . Why did you no' leave him *alone*?'

'How could I leave him alone and him so near the Judgment? . . . How can you speak like that now that God has taken the poor laddie to Himself?'

'He just couldna stand being nagged at any longer . . . You should have left him *alone* . . .'

'I hope you dinna ken what you're saying, Sarah Annie. It was an accident.'

'It wasna!' screamed Sarah Annie.

'You're a wicked, wicked girl.' Mrs Ritchie's voice trembled. 'You would blacken your own brother's memory . . .'

## II

In Scotland there is no public inquiry in a case of possible suicide, and the Fiscal respected the determination of Calderwick to regard John Samuel Ritchie's death as an unfortunate accident. It must have been that war-wound of his; the game leg suddenly failed him, poor fellow. The man was as sane as you or me, as cheery as anybody, joking in the 'White Horse' that very morning . . . Did you hear what he said? No? Says he, as he was going out: 'Weel, I'm better off than some, for when I have to put my best foot foremost I ken which one to take.' Ay, poor fellow, he said that . . . And it wasna even as if he was bothered about money. No financial worry at all, I assure you; plenty of money . . .

The Calderwick *Herald* admirably embodied the public sentiment in two columns devoted to John Samuel Ritchie, one of our indomitable War Heroes, who, the *Herald* was proud to recall, had been a member of the staff when he joined up to fight for his country. Two whole columns of first-rate Bunk. Mrs Ritchie cut them out of the paper and laid them inside the big Bible on the parlour table. God had accepted poor John Samuel; for his death, whether an accident or not, might be looked on as an expiation, a sacrifice which God had accepted. Mrs Ritchie knew quite well that God had accepted the sacrifice, for she had accepted it herself. John Samuel was now safe for ever; the good fight had been fought to a finish.

Yet there was still work for Mrs Ritchie to do. It was almost as if the devil, abandoning John Samuel, had entered into his sister, for Sarah Annie kept on flyting at her mother in a most unchristian fashion, even after the production of John Samuel's will had made it clear to everybody that whoever benefited by his death it was not Mrs Ritchie. Prompted by the devil, on the same day that he had empowered Tom Mitchell to sell poor Johnny Ritchie's workshop, John Samuel had signed a will leaving everything he possessed to his sister, Sarah Annie Ritchie. And it was sheer diabolical perversity that made Sarah Annie now refuse to convey to Mrs Ritchie the house and the furniture which she herself had previously admitted ought by right to be her mother's. In vain Mrs Ritchie tried to bring her daughter to a sense of her duty; in vain she appealed to Sarah Annie's better nature and to good Christian principles; the girl remained abusive, sullen, possessed of a devil.

But Mrs Ritchie braced herself for this new struggle. Sarah Annie was a brand to be plucked from the burning. And up in heaven Johnny Ritchie and John Samuel were anxiously watching lest their money should be wasted like good seed on barren ground. The house itself was and had always been by right Mrs Ritchie's, but the money-bags were all that survived of her husband and her son, and it was her duty to see that what they contained was administered as a trust from God and not squandered on private vanities by Sarah Annie. A girl like that had no right to squander anything on herself except what she got from the profession to which she had been wedded . . .

Mrs Ritchie began to spend hours adding up totals on pieces of paper, endeavouring to track down every halfpenny that Johnny Ritchie and John Samuel had left behind them. When Sarah Annie came home from school she was cross-examined about every piece of hair-ribbon, every handkerchief, every sweet she had bought, and detailed lists of expenditure were produced showing that Sarah Annie had to refund so-and-so much out of her salary to make good the unwarrantable sums she had drained away from the capital. Mrs Ritchie had a simple way of securing the refunds: she stopped them out of the housekeeping money and cut down her daughter's rations; there were days on which no dinner at all was provided for the spendthrift. Sarah Annie's obstinacy was heartbreaking, but Mrs Ritchie persisted in her pious task, following her daughter from the kitchen to the parlour, even into her bedroom, to wrestle with her for the good of her soul and the rendering unto God of what was His.

Moreover, Sarah Annie was so flagrantly in the devil's power that Mrs Ritchie could not be sure that her daughter, her own daughter, was not spreading slanders about her in the town . . . Sarah Annie had stopped deaving her mother with insults in the house, and so it was to be suspected that she was gratifying her malice outside. While she was actually teaching in the Townhead School she could perhaps be trusted, but what was she doing on those evenings when she did not come straight home? Mrs Ritchie had her suspicions. That Bet Reid had always been trying to get her knife into her one-time supplanter, and nothing was too mean for that Bet Reid to attempt; Mrs Ritchie was almost certain that Sarah Annie spent those evenings in Mrs Reid's house, hatching vile plots against her mother. Once more her shawled figure could be seen running down to the gate and looking up and down the road, but now it was Sarah Annie she was looking for, her improvident, ungrateful, shameless daughter. The neighbours soon learned that whenever they were accosted at night by Mrs Ritchie it was always the same pathetic question they were asked: 'Have you seen Sarah Annie anywhere?' A general resentment began to rise against the lassie who would leave her widowed mother alone like that evening after evening . . . Encouraged by the voluble sympathy of passers-by Mrs Ritchie began to range farther and farther abroad in her quest for Sarah Annie, until it occurred to her that the best thing to do was to wait outside the school for her daughter at four o'clock daily.

'I'll have a breakdown if this goes on,' said Sarah Annie to herself. 'I canna stand it.' She felt hysterical now whenever four o'clock came, knowing that her mother was waiting outside the building. She could not sleep at night; she could not get up in the morning; she could hardly teach . . . She ought, of course, to escape to some other town where her mother would not follow her, yet it would be almost like a betrayal of John Samuel to run away and leave Mrs Ritchie in possession.

But one morning when Sarah Annie, after a night of weeping, lay sodden with sleep at an hour when she should have been dressing, Mrs Ritchie came in and beat her awake with the hair-brush. 'You'll lose your job next,' she cried, 'and then where will you be? Get up, you lazy, perverse, ungrateful besom; get up!' There was a cold, fixed intensity in Mrs Ritchie's eyes despite the hot fury of her actions, and Sarah Annie whimpered with fear as she tried to shield her face with her hands. That afternoon Miss Ritchie startled her class by fainting over her desk, and startled her colleagues still more in the teachers' room by her hysterical wailing when she came to. The headmaster was sent for, a small, energetic, fiery man, with flying coat-tails, and a large masonic charm on his watchchain which bobbed up and down on his belly as he bustled along the corridor. 'Now, now, now,' he said, 'we'll have no more of this, Miss Ritchie. Can't give way like this, you know. Discipline, you know. Pull yourself together, lassie . . . The supremacy of the head, Miss Ritchie, over the nerves. That's right, that's better . . . This isn't the place for feminine tantrums . . . She'll have to go home. Can you take her class, Miss——'

A cry from Sarah Annie cut him short:

'Not home. I winna go home! Dinna send me home.'

The headmaster whirled round again:

'Hoots, you canna bide here in that state. Home's the best place when you're no' feeling well, Miss Ritchie.'

'You dinna ken my mother,' said Miss Ritchie, that usually so demure young lady, 'she's a *devil*.'

The headmaster looked electrified, but voices on all sides assured him that the epithet was really justified. The women who had helped so often to smuggle Sarah Annie out of school by the boys' door crowded round him and pointed to the ugly bruise on Sarah Annie's cheek. The headmaster's affectations fell off him like a garment, and he emerged a simple and kindly creature, burning with indignation against the she-devil, Mrs Ritchie.

'Is there any friend o' yours in the town that you could go to? If I were you I would go into lodgings, lassie.'

'There's Mrs Reid,' said Sarah Annie . . . Her mother had vowed, not once but often, that nothing would ever induce her to darken Mrs Reid's door. It was the one house in Calderwick where Mrs Ritchie would not follow her. 'There's Mrs Reid,' cried Sarah Annie, and she began quite steadily to rise to her feet.

'It's three o'clock; my mother'll be here at four——'

'I'll interview your mother,' said the headmaster, rubbing his hands together. 'Just you leave her to me.'

Mrs Ritchie, by arrangement, was invited by a senior boy to see the headmaster in his room, and while the goggling classes filed out she advanced and stood beside his desk. A conviction of some unnameable guilt on Sarah Annie's part rose within her; Sarah Annie must have been doing even worse things than neglecting her duties, and the headmaster was now about to call the culprit's mother to account. For a fraction of a second Mrs Ritchie had the unaccountable feeling that the headmaster was going to expel her, and her eyes were supplicating, like a child's, as she lifted them to the point of his chin. The bareness of that chin surprised her, but the surprise adjusted her again to her present self; she was no longer Annie Rattray, waiting to be reprimanded, but Mrs Ritchie, an approved daughter of God, and this man had not even a beard to his chin, sitting cocking up there and looking down at her. The blood that had ebbed to her heart now flushed her pale, long face and invigorated her mind. Who did he think he was, ordering her to come in and see him? Whatever Sarah Annie had done, it wasna her mother's fault . . . Sarah Annie would have to stand alone before God on the Judgment Day if she had had twenty mothers . . . A flicker of anger shot through Mrs Ritchie; she felt like saying: 'This isn't Christian-like behaviour!' Her dark eyes flashed coldly as they met the headmaster's.

'Your daughter's had a breakdown, Mrs Ritchie.'

'Does that mean she's losing her job?'

'It means she needs to lie in bed for a whilie, and she needs to be well looked after. Teaching's a hard job, Mrs Ritchie, an exhausting job, and when you go home after a hard day's work you need peace and comfort. Now, Miss Ritchie has the makings of a very good teacher, and I want to impress on you the need for looking well after her——'

'It's not your business to tell me how to look after my own daughter. I ken what's good for my bairns better than anybody else——'

'Excuse me, from what I hear that's just what you do *not* ken, Mrs Ritchie——'

'I never heard such impertinence——'

'When your daughter comes to school with her face beaten black and blue——'

'It's the first time I ever heard a headmaster objecting to needful discipline——'

'Your daughter's a grown woman——'

My daughter hasna even the sense to get up in time for her classes——'

'You have no authority to——'

'I have the authority of God to care for her immortal soul, and that's more than you have.'

'Woman, you're insensate——'

'Where's my daughter? I've come to take her home, not to listen to you——'

'Your daughter's gone to a friend's house to get out of your clutches, and after that she's going into lodgings, if I have any say in the matter, now that I see——'

'*You* send my daughter into lodgings? You, a married man, send a single woman into lodgings? It's to save my daughter from you and the likes of you that I've come to take her home. What have you done with her?'

'Get out of my school!'

'This is no' your school. You're just a paid servant of

the town, and if you interfere between me and my daughter
I'll see that the town hears of it. Where's my daughter? I'll
not stir from here till I know where you've put away my
daughter.'

Mrs Ritchie mounted the steps of the desk and the
headmaster, clasping his head, turned and ran to the
teachers' room. 'That woman would tempt a man to
murder,' he said. I could hardly keep my hands off her
. . . Go and tell her, somebody, for God's sake, to get out
of the school before I murder her!'

But after standing behind the headmaster's desk for a
minute or two, raised high on the dais above all the
subservient benches, Mrs Ritchie, as if in a trance, walked
slowly out of the schoolroom before any member of the
staff gathered courage to accost her. She knew, none better,
where Sarah Annie was.

The headmaster's desk had been hers, the schoolroom
had been hers, and now she walked through the thronged
playground as if within a magic circle which protected her
from profane encounters. Omnipotent as well as omniscient
. . . hers was the kingdom and the power and the glory.

## III

In the Reids' house Sarah Annie was lying well happed
on a sofa, drinking hot milk. Mrs Reid's indignation still
bubbled up from time to time in ejaculations: 'I never heard
the like! . . . The woman must be clean off her head . . .
She was bad enough when she was a lassie, but nothing
like this . . .'

'Mrs Reid,' said Sarah Annie, setting her cup in the
saucer, 'how is it possible for anybody to grow up into a
woman like my mother?'

'It's just through thinking about nothing but yourself,
Sarah Annie.'

'But lots of folk are selfish, yet I've never met anybody
like my mother.'

'She's waur than anybody else, that's all. Even selfish
folk whiles remember that they're only human, but Annie
Ritchie evens herself with God Almighty.'

The door bell rang a loud, jangling peal. Sarah Annie

started, and dropped her cup from a hand suddenly nerveless:

'That's her! Oh, Mrs Reid, I ken that's her! . . . I never thought she would follow me here . . . What'll I do? What'll I do?'

'Just you leave her to me,' said Bet Reid. She flung the door open, and folded her arms:

'Is that you, Annie Ritchie? Ay, your Sarah Annie's here.'

'I've come to take my daughter home, Mrs Reid.'

'Come in,' said Bet Reid. 'Come in till I tell you what I think of you.'

'I've only come for my daughter.'

Mrs Ritchie advanced into the sitting-room, where Sarah Annie had begun to cower under her rug.

'Come home, Sarah Annie,' she said. 'It's time you were home.'

'Sarah Annie's going to bide here this night. She's not going back with you to be thrashed and bullied and persecuted until she canna call her soul her own.'

Mrs Ritchie looked as if she did not hear a word of Bet Reid's tirade. She looked only at her daughter:

'Are you coming home, Sarah Annie?'

'I'm *not* coming home!' burst out Sarah Annie, in a thick, hoarse voice. 'I've stood more than I can stand from you. You give me no peace. You follow me about from morning till night yattering at me . . . I canna even get enough to eat from you——'

'It's only your immortal soul I'm thinking about, Sarah Annie, and to see that you do your duty. Come home, now.'

'It's only the money that you're thinking about . . . You've never forgiven me for being left that money . . . You're aye yattering at me about the money.'

'I only want the money for Christian charities—it's only for Christian charities . . .'

'Yah!' said young Betsy, who had hitherto stood in the background. She made as if to spit in Mrs Ritchie's face.

'You're an impident limmer like your mother,' said

Mrs Ritchie, 'and it was an ill day for John Samuel when he first took up with you.'

'*You* to mention John Samuel . . .' Sarah Annie nearly choked.

'Nae wonder the poor laddie got down in the mouth,' said Mrs Ritchie. 'But he's safe with his Heavenly Father, and it's you I've come for, Sarah Annie. I'll not stir a foot from this spot until you rise and come home with me.'

Argument, protestation, even threats, left Mrs Ritchie unmoved. She was inside a magic circle; her eyes had a blind inward look and her ears were deaf to the abuse that was heaped upon her.

Sarah Annie suddenly rose up:

'It's not fair on you, Mrs Reid . . . I ken my mother. She'll no' move till Doomsday as long as I'm here. I canna inflict this on you any longer. All right. I'm coming . . . But you're to treat me better, do you hear, or I'll leave the country altogether . . .'

Mrs Ritchie repeated over and over again:

'It's only your good I'm thinking of, Sarah Annie——'

'You canna go with her,' Mrs Reid seized the girl's arm. 'It's no possible. You're no' able to stand it.'

'I ken what I'm going to do,' said Sarah Annie, in a hurried whisper. Mrs Reid's grasp tightened on her arm. 'No, no; not that . . . I'm going to get her out of your house, anyway. I'll give her one more chance and then I'll take the first train south. Anywhere. I dinna care . . . All right, mother. I'm coming.'

## IV

Two days later, on a Sunday afternoon, the Ritchies, mother and daughter, set out for the cemetery, carrying bunches of flowers. Sarah Annie stood aloof in the path while her mother laid the flowers on the close turf that heaved in gentle mounds over the mortal remains of Johnny Ritchie and John Samuel Ritchie. Then Mrs Ritchie knelt down and began to pat the mounds, saying: 'Poor Johnny . . . Poor John Samuel.'

Sarah Annie, as if awaking from a sleep, stared at her mother's black figure kneeling on the green grass. Then she turned and ran for dear life out of the cemetery, even although it was Sunday, even although resentful knots of citizens stared after her; she ran for dear life towards the town . . . There was just time to pack a bag and catch the afternoon train . . .

Mrs Ritchie did not notice that her daughter had gone. She was still patting the mounds, first one and then the other, saying, with tender possessiveness: 'Poor Johnny . . . Poor John Samuel.'

# MRS GRUNDY IN SCOTLAND

## ACKNOWLEDGEMENT

I desire to acknowledge gratefully the help I have received from various collaborators, both voluntary and involuntary. In particular I wish to acknowledge my debt to Mrs Mary Litchfield, who provided much of my information.

I desire also to express my gratitude to the Proprietors of 'Punch' for their gracious permission to quote the extracts from 'Punch' which I have used.

Willa Muir

This book was planned
for the delectation of
LEWIS GRASSIC GIBBON
and can only be dedicated
instead, humbly and sorrowfully,
to his memory

# Contents

## ONE

# Dame Grundy

One could hardly say that a star danced and under it
Mrs Grundy was born, yet she was first heard of on the
boards of the Theatre Royal, Covent Garden. All the other
characters in the play, a comedy in five acts called *Speed
the Plough*, have been long since forgotten, while Dame
Grundy, who did not actually appear on the stage, has
survived for more than a century. And if the playwright,
Thomas Morton, is remembered at all it is because in the
year 1798 by a stroke of sheer genius he created a star
character in Mrs Grundy.

I think that he did it inadvertently. Certainly Mrs
Inchbald, the lady who contributed a flowery preface
to the printed edition of the play, was quite unaware of
Dame Grundy's potential importance, and Mrs Inchbald
was a woman of some experience in the theatre, an actress, a
producer and a successful adapter of plays. 'In this comedy,'
she says, 'there is no one character superior to the rest, nor
any one in particular which makes a forcible impression on
the memory: this proves . . . the fable to be a good one.' Of
course, she was thinking more of the 'serious characters'
than of the subsidiary rustic personages who provided the
comic relief; to the latter she extends merely a vague and
gracious approval on the score that they were 'surely . . .
of pure English growth.' It may be inferred, therefore, that
Dame Ashfield, the farmer's wife, and her bogey, Dame
Grundy, were not taken very seriously by the professionals:
it was the great British public which insisted on singling out
Dame Grundy, on cherishing her and keeping her alive until
she grew into a portentous symbol.

Now what was there in this figure 'of pure English growth'
to justify such attentions? In the play Dame Grundy was

only a farmer's wife of some competence: her butter was 'the crack of the market,' her daughters, the Miss Grundys, thought themselves genteel, and she herself was given to turning up her nose at her less successful neighbours. These are all the facts about Dame Grundy which can be sifted out of the five acts, except that, of course, she went to church, and that Farmer Grundy seemed to be worthy of his notable wife, since he got top prices for his wheat. And yet the woman had immortality conferred upon her, and it was, I repeat, a stroke of sheer genius on the part of Thomas Morton that got her across the footlights into the bosom of every member of the audience. And the genius consisted in this: that the figure presented in the play was not the actual Dame Grundy selling her butter and hectoring her neighbours; it was something more formless, more pervading, more universal; it was the sinister image of Dame Grundy in the consciousness of her neighbour, Dame Ashfield, the bogey that haunted the less successful woman wherever she went. Dame Ashfield could not open her mouth without some reference to her obsession. As her honest husband pointed out: 'I do verily think when thee goest to t'other world the vurst question thee ax'il be if Mrs Grundy's there.' Everything Dame Ashfield did or experienced led unerringly to the one tormenting question: Does this bring me level with Mrs Grundy? Within two minutes after her first appearance on the stage the audience is beginning to sympathize with her husband, Farmer Ashfield, who shouts in exasperation: 'Be quiet, woolye? Allways ding, dinging Dame Grundy into my ears—what will Mrs Grundy zay? What will Mrs Grundy think? Casn't thee be quiet . . .?' Already the bogey of Mrs Grundy has been conjured up. And she remains a bogey; instead of dwindling into a flesh-and-blood farmer's wife on the stage, she hovers like an invisible menace 'off,' a featureless shape, an airy nothing everywhere and nowhere, like some djinn emerging from a magic bottle to darken Dame Ashfield's whole sky. She was never handicapped by being confined within puny human dimensions; from the very beginning she was an immanent presence rather than a person, a creature apprehended by a fear-haunted imagination. And so this looming, visionary figure, embodying the secret fears and resentments of every member of the audience, naturally survived the merely human characters in the play, and continued her own life long after the play itself was dead.

On that first night in the Theatre Royal, I suppose, people laughed heartily every time that Mrs Grundy was mentioned, and did not immediately realize that she was going to invade their own lives. 'Dom Mrs Grundy,' they said with Farmer Ashfield, not observing the little shock of intimacy with which they appreciated his feelings. Yet towards the end of the evening the shadowy outline of Mrs Grundy must have thickened perceptibly; she must have become a composite figure, recognizably drawn from all the inferiority complexes in the house. And the number of inferiority complexes must have corresponded pretty nearly to the number of occupied seats, for there is no human being who has not suffered at some time or other from a sense of inferiority. One could leave the theatre laughing at Mrs Grundy, since the play was a comedy with a happy ending enabling Dame Ashfield to score off her bogey in the long run, but one carried away a sense of having found at last a name to pin on to the vague agitations, the uneasy fears which disquieted one's own bosom at the thought of superior and more successful neighbours. It would become much easier to laugh off envious apprehensions if one could say, Afraid of Mrs Grundy, that's all; or, Only Mrs Grundy again. And so the name of Mrs Grundy passed into common currency. And so Mrs Grundy, from being an imaginary menace in the mind of a farmer's wife, in the minds of a theatre audience, gradually became a convenient symbol to express the sum of social forces that surround and often threaten any individual in the world.

For a long time, however, she continued to be recognizable as an English farmer's wife, a respectable image of success but definitely one of the lower orders. The audiences who patronized the Theatre Royal were largely people of fashion, and although they might appreciate the inwardness of Mrs Grundy as a social bogey they were not likely to forget her plebeian origin. Indeed, to a generation which was anxiously resisting both the power of Napoleon and the subversive revolutionary ideas which had burst out of France, it must have been a comfort to identify such a stoutly respectable figure with the spirit of the lower orders. Mrs Grundy, after all, represented a standard of comfortable achievement; she was a kind of feminine John Bull, downright and sturdy; if she were a symbol of the social consciousness pervading farmers' wives, the upper classes need not fear for their privileges. The feminine backbone of Old England, many must have thought, was represented by Dame Grundy.

This is not mere speculation. The figure of Mrs Grundy herself bears it out. For after Napoleon was settled with, when the muttering discontents of the Radicals were beginning to break into a roar, Mrs Grundy can be found in the pages of *Punch* soundly trouncing upstart disaffection. She is armed with a gamp to trounce the better; she has become less of a rustic and more of an urban figure, a kind of cross between Dame Grundy and Sairey Gamp. This is how she puts John Bright in his place:

MRS GRUNDY TO MR BRIGHT

John Bright, you're no more than a calico feller,
You're all made of cotton, like my umbereller,
You must have been, sartingly, spun with a jenny,
I'd own no sitch son if you'd give me a guinea.
A Hinglishman's birthright, with sitch a poor sperrit,
Is what chaps like you isn't fit to inherit,
If nobody else's heart wasn't no stronger
This wouldn't be no land of freedom no longer.

But Britons won't never give in to invaders
To please you, nor none of your Manchester traders,
Whatever *John Bright* is, *John Bull's* no sitch noddy,
So, therefore, now, let's have no more of your shoddy.

Mrs Grundy here has quitted the shires and come to live in London. But she still has a countrywoman's scorn of factory products; she champions good homespun sentiments against the shoddy produced by the spinning-jennies, and if she has acquired a Cockney accent she has not forgotten her traditions. There is a reassuring continuity in her character, although London has changed her to some extent. I do not think it fanciful to suggest that this change in Mrs Grundy is not arbitrary but reflects a definite social development. If Mrs Grundy's outlines shift and change it is because of the changing stresses in the constitution of society itself. From the figure of Mrs Grundy in this poem, for instance, one can deduce with certainty two aspects of the national life in 1854: first, that the respectable elements in England are drawing together against the threat of Radical disaffection: and second, that the consciousness of the nation is now centred in London, its political focus. The history of Mrs Grundy's development is an interesting reflection of the history of actual social forces.

It is possible to illustrate this suggestion by selecting, again from that excellent authority, Mr Punch, one or two later appearances of Mrs Grundy in England. In June 1866 she is still a feminine John Bull, but this time she is not trouncing upstarts at home; she is shaking her umbrella at Europe.

#### MRS GRUNDY ON FOREIGN AFFAIRS

Ah! drat the nasty foreigners; there's always some
    new bother,
Some fresh to-do or piece of work with one of 'em
    or t'other.
And with the very words for which I haven't
    common patience,
I can't abear to hear about what's called their
    complications.

The French it was at one time, at another 'twas
    the Rooshians,
And now the rumpus is between the Austrians and
    the Prooshians.
Adrabbit them! I can't find words to say how I do
    hate 'em all;
I wish there was some powder, like, or stuff to
    extirpate 'em all!

Can it be that Mrs Grundy has now become a mask for the august features of Britannia herself? Admitted that the

poem sets out to be funny, that the sentiments put in the
mouth of Mrs Grundy are intended as a caricature, yet a
caricature must bear a plausible resemblance to its original.
This is Britannia in all her insularity, still remembering, with
the slow, retentive memory of her kind, the horror she felt
at 'Boney'; and if it is beneath the dignity of a Britannia
to shake her trident at the nasty foreigners, she can at least
assume the *alias* of Mrs Grundy and shake a gamp.

But if Mrs Grundy is now a permissible understudy for
Britannia, the social consciousness of the lower orders must
have widened considerably. Apparently the stress of foreign
complications has evoked a political sense and a feeling of
national solidarity. Mrs Grundy is no longer denouncing
her neighbours in the parish, or in the midlands, she is
denouncing her neighbours in the concert of Europe. She
takes it as a matter of course that she should have her say in
affairs of high policy. The lower orders are accepted already
as a political part of the nation, and the fact that Mrs Grundy
shakes her gamp at Europe is a portent of their inevitable
inclusion among the responsible voters of the country.

After this daring impersonation of Britannia one might
imagine that Mrs Grundy would now rest on her laurels,
that any other rôle would prove an anti-climax. One
must not forget, however, that Queen Victoria was on
the throne, also impersonating Britannia, and that it is
easy to establish a sympathetic communication among
such symbolic figures. Mrs Grundy seems to have realized,
after making her point with the gamp, that she could safely
leave high politics to her more august sisters, for she now
turns her attention to what has been often considered a
peculiarly feminine field, the administration of domestic
morals. Somewhere between the sixties and the eighties
Mrs Grundy becomes aware that she is a Woman, and
that a woman's place in life is to be Womanly. I suspect
that the increasing influence of finance and industry was
what warned Mrs Grundy off politics; she had had her
moment of exalted and defiant patriotic feeling, and now
she was to leave the administration of the country to the
merchants of progress. For Mrs Grundy, alas! can never
initiate anything; she is a valiant guardian of the *status quo*,

a faithful mirror of an existing social consciousness, but her light is always a reflected light.

Looking in Mrs Grundy, then, as in a mirror, one can see that somewhere between the sixties and the eighties the social consciousness of the lower orders becomes aware of new proprieties in conduct; it is made uneasy by art and by literature, which were once the privileges of a leisured class; it defends the respectability of the home against subversive ideas which are no longer merely political. In 1878 Mrs Grundy expresses her fears about the new vogue for classical draperies:

> Dear Mr Punch, *do* just look here. What's this newfangled caper,
> Which, to my 'orror, meets my eye whilst reading of my paper?
> I don't precisely understand the plan they're putting forrid,
> But I've my strong suspicions that it's somethink right down 'orrid.
> Classic! O yes, I know that game, as wants a wigorous stopper.
> Classic's the name for everythink owdacious and improper.
> The Poets and the Artises is always sweet upon it,
> But if they gammon Mrs G., I'll bolt my Sunday bonnet . . .

This is indeed a new element. Poets and artists! Audacious improprieties! This is a new Mrs G., Sunday bonnet and all. I think we might even say that this is a Mrs Grundy verging on the middle class. The standard of life in the lower orders must have been going up, and the standard of respectability arrogates a wider province to itself than before. In 1798 Dame Grundy would not have voiced public disapproval of goings-on in the higher ranks of life, but in 1878 Mrs Grundy has no hesitation in doing so. One can only assume that the 'high life' of 1878 is more conscious of Mrs Grundy's disapproval than it would have been in 1798, that it is more vulnerable because not so remote from her. And if it is not so remote from Mrs Grundy, it

cannot be purely aristocratic. The upper middle class has
come into being, and the lower middle class in the person
of Mrs Grundy voices its envy in disapproval.

That uneasy middle class, neither fish, flesh, fowl nor
good red herring! An aristocratic society, a settled peasant-
ry—these create as well as conserve their traditions; they
are sure of themselves. But an industrial working class rising
into middle-class wealth can only ape its betters and is not
sure of itself. With the growing power of mere money in
England, with the establishment of a middle class, a vast
new field of inferiority complexes begins to sprout; perhaps,
indeed, that is why Mrs Grundy from now on confines
herself to watching over public propriety: she has enough
to do without bothering about high politics.

And in less than twenty years' time, behold Mrs Grundy
well established in the upper middle class, having lost her
vulgar accent and become at last a perfect lady. In February
1891, she ventures to remonstrate with Mr Goschen, who
has reduced her unearned income, and her remonstrance
is extremely ladylike, indeed she says herself:

> Oh! Goschen, Sir, kind gentleman,
> Hear my polite laments.

She associates herself, modestly enough, with the aris-
tocracy:

> Not I alone, the best that breathe,
>     Archbishop, Duke, and Lord,
> Your bust with chaplets rare will wreathe
>     This boon if you'll accord.
> How can we by example shame
>     The mob who mock at rents,
> If we are left to do the same
>     Without our Three per Cents?
>
> Reft of a carriage, life is poor:
>     A well-conducted set
> Needs ready money to procure
>     Their butler and Debrett.
> The country totters, robbed of all
>     Its purest ornaments,

Unless you instantly recall
Our solid Three per Cents.

Incredible, but so it is; this polite effusion is headed:
'Mrs Grundy to Mr Goschen.' Mrs Grundy with a carriage!
Mrs Grundy with a butler! These are indeed changed days.
Mrs Grundy, one would say, has achieved a high measure
of success. But if the head that wears a crown may lie
uneasy, what can we expect of a middle-class Mrs Grundy,
menaced from below by 'the mob who mock at rents' and
threatened from above by Mr Goschen? She is beginning to
think more of her 'securities,' because, poor lady, she needs
security more than ever, and less of impropriety, because she
simply has to be in the fashion, and fashion is allowing such
one-time shocking improprieties as Ibsen's plays, and the
young men of the Naughty Nineties are pirouetting to the
forefront—oh dear, what *is* to become of Mrs Grundy?

I think we need not mourn her plight too much, for she
is, after all, semi-immortal. She can, and does, put a new
face on things. Step by step the amoral power of money
may oust her from her strongholds in the social life of
London, but she can and does retreat to the provinces
whence she sprang. Even although she is threatened there,
she can always find a home in Scotland. She began visiting
Scotland with Queen Victoria, and although the Scots made
her change her style and appearance she is assured of a new
lease of life in the Northern Kingdom.

## TWO

# Mrs Grundy Comes to Scotland

I said that Mrs Grundy began visiting Scotland with Queen Victoria. In the 'forties the Queen first became Scotland-conscious, and with her the upper classes of England. Yet in the 'forties Mrs Grundy was still a lower-class phenomenon, and it is not legitimate to assume off-hand that she travelled in the Queen's train. It might be as well to cast a glance at the condition of Scotland about that time in order to determine how it was possible for Mrs Grundy to cross the border in the wake of Victoria.

For centuries Scotland had been a relatively poor country, a country of awkward cart-tracks and impassable mountains, where it was easier for the individual to throw up lines to Heaven than to extend a network of communication with his fellow-countrymen. Before the Union of the Crowns there was little urban civilization in the northern kingdom, except in Edinburgh, and even there it was an eccentric kind of urbanity, 'a strange medley,' Sir Henry Craik calls it, 'of coarseness and refinement, of rough buffoonery and stately manners,' a town life only two removes from the farmyard and with the farmyard insensibility to the smells of the midden. Throughout the country agriculture was inefficient; crops were poor and at the mercy of bad seasons; in the minds of the farming tenants success or failure depended on the whim of a grim, inscrutable Providence whom it was not chancy to challenge. Whatever happened, be it smallpox or hail-storms, was 'bound to be,' and the wise man resigned himself to make the best of it. On these undrained, unfertilized, sodden or stony 'rigs' the peasant drew no pride from his farming, so he had to draw it from Heaven. In these Edinburgh tenements, dirty, crowded and convivial, the townsman of rank prided himself on his aristocratic lineage, the intellectual on his free metaphysics, the commoner on the tradition that all were equal before God. One and all, however, had their pride. 'God gi'e us a guid conceit o' oorsels' was the pious prayer of all the Lowland Scots. Pride and poverty walked hand in hand. And long after the Union, long after the coming of turnpike roads and better cultivation, right up to the industrial age the old attitude persisted; the Lowland Scot kept his front of God-given conceit before his fellow-Scots and the world. If he had any inferiority complexes—and who has not?—he refused, on principle, to admit them. He was inferior only to his Maker.

This attitude of mind is not favourable to the growth of a social consciousness; a man who can draw his 'conceit' of himself directly from God is not likely to supple himself into agreement with a neighbour or consideration for his wife's feelings. Still less is it favourable to the development of the theatre. When a man is staging himself as the sole protagonist in a drama of Heaven and Hell he will not welcome any objective presentation of his attributes on the boards of a playhouse; he is jealously vigilant over his individuality and he will not be analysed into component parts, he will not identify any part of himself with a stage 'character.' He lives his own drama and he brooks no rivals. Consequently in Scotland before this time a stage figure like Mrs Grundy, the symbol of a social consciousness based on admitted inferiority, had no chance of emerging. There was no native Mrs Grundy—no Mrs MacGrundy. There could not have been such a figure. And where could an English Mrs Grundy hope to find a crack in the armour of these self-sufficient Scots?

Well, there are two answers to that question. In the first place, the self-sufficient attitude of the Scots was a brave and pathetic fiction. That lonely figure stretching from earth to Heaven, gigantically projected by the Scottish imagination, was a racked and distorted image of man; it ignored too much; it was too narrow to be human, and postulated an inhuman tension of the will. In theory the Scot had no feelings of inferiority on any plane lower than Heaven; in theory he refused to recognize Mrs Grundy;

but in fact Mrs Grundy simply retreated to his Heaven and from that altitude came down on him like a boomerang. The social consciousness which might have produced a Mrs MacGrundy, not being allowed to cohere on any plane lower than Heaven, whisked her too up to Heaven, where she led a specious, because unacknowledged, existence concealed behind the veil of that Bride of Christ, the Scottish Kirk. The Scottish Kirk might claim to speak with the tongues of men and of angels, but its voice became more and more unmistakably the voice of Mrs MacGrundy. Mrs Grundy from England had only to ally herself with the Kirk Sessions of Scotland.

The second answer is that the theoretical self-sufficiency of the Scotsman could not survive the growing importance of London as a political and financial focus for Britain, let alone the Empire. That monstrous 'wen,' which was to make England suburban, early began to make Scotland provincial. The increasing wealth which at first fostered the middle classes in London, with their new inferiority complexes, raised a tempest of inferiority complexes in Scotland. It is relatively easy to be proud and poor when everybody of consequence is poor; it is far from easy when money begins to spread itself. And if a man is nourished on the belief that he is one of God's elect, it is easy for him to believe that the higher he climbs on earth the nearer he comes to God. He will follow any chance of material success as a donkey follows a carrot, convinced that Providence is deliberately holding it under his nose.

Now the carrots that were extended to the donkeys in Scotland were all grown in England. They were called 'industrial expansion' and 'improved farming' and 'progress,' but whatever they were called they all meant increased dividends, monetary profit. And the Lowland Scots, by nature logical, followed the logic of capitalism more unswervingly than the English. Believing as they did that the condition of the poor was a divine punishment for individual sin, that 'ilka herring should hang by its ain tail,' they did not disrupt the logic of capitalism by any consideration for the social welfare of their country. Mrs MacGrundy was the only social consciousness they might have had, and at this juncture she was hampered by her ecclesiastical disguise, which excluded her from business life. The callousness of the Lowland Scots to each other in the first scramble for the carrots would seem incredible were it not attested by contemporary records and by our knowledge of the results. 'De'il tak' the hindmost,' they said, and with an energy equal to their callousness doubled and trebled the output of the country, the slum populations, the miles of railway tracks, the tons of coal, the acres of sheep-runs. And then they got a shock: when they showed their statistics to prove that Scotland was a worthy yoke-fellow of her English partner, the illogical English brought up sentimental, irrelevant objections to prove that Scotland was far from being civilized. In effect, the English said: Where is your social consciousness?

The Scots were bewildered, and being bewildered produced some lamentable self-justifications. The 'improvers' in Sutherland, which, one would have thought, was a county remote enough to escape English inquisition, briefed Harriet Beecher Stowe to vindicate their actions in combing the natives out of the heather to make way for sheep. In 1845 that lady assured the world that there were forty-one gigs in the county of Sutherland where not one had existed before 1811, that there had been only two shops in 1812 and no baker at all, whereas 'in 1845 there were eight bakers and forty-six grocers' shops in nearly all of which shoe-blacking was sold to some extent, an unmistakable evidence of advancing civilization.' Shoe-blacking! In 1853, the factor for Her Grace of Sutherland, a certain Mr Loch, was reduced to announcing before the Parliament in London, as 'an instance of the improved habits of the farmers,' that no house was now built for them without a hot bath and water-closets. Shoe-blacking and water-closets! If this is not an appeal to Mrs Grundy, what can it be? The Mother of Parliaments herself was turning a stern eye upon Scotland, but it is doubtful whether shoe-blacking and water-closets would satisfy her. Parliament had more weighty matters to consider, such as the shocking conditions in the working of the Scottish coal-mines. In the words of Sir Henry Craik: 'Down to 1845 a vast system of degraded toil, which crushed the life out of women and young children, was still permitted to stain that civilization which cloaked its hideousness by the boast of expanding wealth. It was only then that the public conscience was aroused, and aroused far more by English example, and by the perseverance of English philanthropists, than by any purely Scottish impulse.' No, the shoe-blacking and the water-closets were offered as sops to Mrs Grundy in England rather than to Parliament. Mrs Grundy had to be assured that Scotland was civilized.

And meanwhile Queen Victoria was becoming devoted to 'her' Scotland. This, of course, roused a certain jealousy in London, but even so there is evidence in the pages of *Punch* that England was genuinely uneasy about the social welfare of Scotland. The jealousy confined itself to jeers at bagpipes and such like barbarous phenomena: the following little note, which appeared in 1858, is simple jealousy, for instance, and nothing else:

#### MUSIC OF SCOTCH WATERFOWL

The Court Circular informs the civilized world that the Queen, the Prince of Wales, and the Princess Alice, attended by some persons of quality, drove the other day to the Falls of the Quoich. What a curious name—Quoich! Is the river, whose Falls we hope Her Majesty found worth seeing, called Quoich because it is remarkable for abounding in, and resounding with, the cries of ducks?

We can easily discount such childish spleen. But there is more than jealousy in the comment, also in the year 1858, that 'Glasgow, believe it or not, wants more water to mix with the intolerable quantity of whiskey wherewith she besots herself.' A few lines farther on, mention is made of 'the contempt with which drunken Glasgow is spoken of by moral and civilized folk.' 'Hech for licentious and drunken Scotland!' says Mr Punch on another occasion. Scotland was regarded in London as existing outside the pale of civilization, the Lowlands and the towns being considered every whit as barbarous in their way as the more primitive Highlands.

Yet in spite of London jealousy the Highlands were succumbing to a peaceful penetration by the upper classes of England. The Scottish lairds were enabled to join in the scramble for English money by the Rutherford Act of 1848, which permitted them finally to disentail their lands and sell them to the highest bidder. The rush for money must have been considerable, for by 1873 the Queen remarked in her Journal: 'So many of the finest, largest estates in the *Highlands* have passed into English hands, chiefly by purchase . . .' The railways brought up loads of English visitors who were called 'the gentry'; some English-speaking residents settled down in Highland country after steamers were launched on Loch Tay; and in parishes where within living memory nothing but Gaelic had been spoken, Gaelic became a 'kitchen language,' and social prestige demanded that English be taught in the schools and even preached from the pulpits. The native sense of inferiority grew apace. A foreign language, foreign manners, foreign standards, bred social confusion and uncertainty in the Highlands. Confusion and uncertainty were already sown in the Lowlands. Scotland was ripe for Mrs Grundy. It was developing a sense of inferiority, a kind of social consciousness. It was beginning to ape its 'betters.'

Yet it is not to be expected that a social ideal can move from one country to another as smoothly as from one class to another in the same country. The uneasy middle classes in England had their models continuously beside them; the uneasy Scots were kept guessing for long intervals of time. But they had to find some cover against the new and bewildering attacks of the English philanthropists, and it was only natural to them that they should look for it in Heaven. And there, although they did not exactly recognize her, they began to divine the existence of Mrs MacGrundy. Mrs MacGrundy was now the sole relict of that deep tribal feeling which once had been capable of fusing the Scots together for days at a time, and it might be possible, they thought, to show the English that although on week-days there was no existing system strong enough to be called a social consciousness, yet on Sundays the Scots were a pious community. To the accusations from England that they were an uncivilized, drunken, licentious rabble of go-getters, they opposed an increasing parade of Sabbath godliness.

The veil covering Mrs MacGrundy grew thinner; she was not yet acknowledged, she did not show her face, but she was pushed forward to save the face of the nation, wearing the sanctimonious mask provided by the Kirk Sessions.

The answer, therefore, to this first attack of the modern commercial world on the pride of the Scots was a monstrously inflated Sabbatarianism.

In the year 1854 the *Caledonian Mercury* reported the following incident:

> While a cab was conveying an infirm lady to church yesterday morning the driver was heartily hissed by a number of passengers in one of the leading thoroughfares of the town.

Mr Punch, commenting on this, remarked: 'An infirm woman on her way to church *hissed*! Oh, Scotch piety, is not thy symbol a goose?' A pertinent comment. For this Sabbatarianism was informed by no exalted religious fervour. Mrs MacGrundy, it is to be feared, had been quietly ruthless during her retirement behind the veil of the Kirk, and we had better not ask what had happened to the Bride of Christ. In the same year Mr Punch published these Rules and Regulations for the Better Observance of the Sabbath in Scotland:

> Any Railway engine heard whistling, to be impounded.
> Any Dog found barking, to be instantly shot.
> Any Fountain found playing in the streets, to be treated as a vagrant under the Police Act.
> Any Hen suspected of laying an egg on the Sabbath, to be unhesitatingly killed and divided amongst the poor . . .

In short, No Nothing in Scotland on a Sunday.

This is hardly an exaggeration. It was a sin, for instance, to be seen walking in the streets of Edinburgh on a Sunday, except on the way to church. The Edinburgh Established Presbytery had 'a communication from the City Mission calling attention to the practice of strolling on the thoroughfares in the city and suburbs on Sundays as a very prevalent form of Sabbath desecration.' One member of the Presbytery 'thought the best plan would be to apply to the civil magistrate.' Another member of

the Presbytery observed that: 'the worst form of Sabbath
desecration was for a father to take his children to such
places as public gardens, where they saw nothing but
what was most demoralizing in its tendency.' Mr Punch
was prompted to remark: 'Walking in the streets on a
Sunday may with special reason be objected to by the
Sabbatarians of Scotland for their own parts. Not all
of them, perhaps, would be able to walk straight . . .
The Sabbatarian spirit of canny Scotland is evidently
Farintosh or Glenlivat.' Pertinent comment again, for
the statistics of drunkenness in the Scottish cities were
alarming. And the number of drunken women taken to
the police stations was greatly increasing, according to the
*Morning Star*. The Free Church Presbytery of Edinburgh,
however, was busy passing a resolution 'to send a deputation
to the authorities of Leith and get them to prevent the sailing
of all wind-bound, or any other, vessels from that port on
Sundays.'

Well, that was a good back-hander for the commercial
interests to get! Apparently the façade of respectability set
up by the Sabbatarian revival was not only to serve as a
cover for national pride, but as a national check to the
cosmopolitan forces of capitalism. In 1866 a compositor
engaged on the *Glasgow Herald* was excommunicated by
the Free Kirk in Glasgow for 'being accustomed to set up
the type of that paper on Sunday evenings.' The unfortunate compositor appealed to the Free Kirk Assembly of
Edinburgh, who merely endorsed the excommunication. In
vain the honest man pleaded that in the strictest households
the Sabbath evening was constantly desecrated by work for
which, unlike his own, there was no necessity. 'So much
the more reason,' thundered one of the reverend gentlemen,
'for the church sending out no uncertain sound in this
matter.' The church was going to impose a discipline on
Sundays, whatever commerce chose to do throughout the
week. Better for a man to lose his job than to break the
Sabbath. The Sabbath was not made for man; he was a
mere afterthought created to observe the Sabbath.

And, indeed, the wage-slaves who had jobs to lose soon
ceased to trouble the church. They were well crushed

beneath the wheels of advancing capitalism and they retaliated by forming Radical associations. The old fervour which had originally made the Scottish Kirk a genuine, though peculiar, expression of Lowland Scottish initiative now passed into the Scottish Socialist movement. Mrs MacGrundy was disembarrassed of these independent and unruly spirits; she reigned undisturbed over the new middle classes who went to church for the sake of respectability.

And in the dullness of conforming respectability these new middle classes of Scotland were bound to assimilate themselves more and more to the respectable bourgeoisie of England. Mrs Grundy and Mrs MacGrundy quietly coalesced. But the Sabbatarian solemnity of Mrs MacGrundy remained, and to some extent remains today on the features of that one-time downright feminine John Bull who shook a gamp at Europe. Mrs Grundy in Scotland is still sanctimonious as well as censorious.

## THREE

# Mrs MacGrundy

## I

One odd thing about capitalism is that while it comes in like a tide uplifting the lower middle and upper middle classes, it presently strands them on the rocks. This effect is first perceptible in the cities and large towns. Mrs Grundy in London, for instance, was suffering from it as early as the 'nineties. The mob from below and Mr Goschen from above were grinding her between the upper millstone of taxation and financial debt and the lower millstone of Socialism. But when the upper middle classes really get into financial difficulties the survivors grow more reckless and tend to desert Mrs Grundy. She has both to retreat and find a new wave of advance if she is not to be abandoned to a lingering death: she finds a new incarnation when the upper middle classes desert the old one, and her outworn garments descend to the lower middle, and from there to the more docile working classes who still have a hope of rising. In Scotland this process repeated itself somewhat later than in England. The middle classes in the 'nineties were still sanctimoniously respectable in Glasgow while their compeers in London were flirting with Ibsen. By this time, however, the Scottish Mrs Grundy had changed her style in the cities, and it is in the small country towns and agricultural districts that she is most recognisable. The more remote the district the more Mrs Grundy approximates to the Sabbatarians of the 'fifties. In the Highland parishes she does not approximate, she *is* the old Mrs MacGrundy, once of the Lowlands and now surviving in various sects of what are well called the 'continuing' Free Churches or Free Presbyterian Churches of Scotland.

The 'continuing' churches are not only the direct heirs

of the 'Sawbbatarianism' derided by Mr Punch, they are 'continuing' churches by virtue of a stubborn tradition derived from the older Lowland Scottish Kirk of the eighteenth century. A consideration of the old Scottish Kirk may help to explain the peculiar tendency of the Scots—a tendency still active—to express their feelings in Sabbatarian ordinances when they find themselves threatened by historical or economic forces. Before studying the contemporary sanctimoniousness of the Scottish Mrs MacGrundy, then, I propose to digress a little and go back to look at the old Presbyterian Kirk of Scotland.

It is the congregations I propose to look at rather than the clergy who ministered to them, for these ministers were the victims as well as the products of the Kirk. It is the emotional fervour of the congregations that is really important. And the first thing to note is that the congregations were as fanatically gloomy and violent under Episcopacy as under Presbyterianism. The Episcopal curates were not more violently 'outed' by the Presbyterians than the Presbyterian interlopers had been resisted by the Episcopal congregations. Feelings were strong and apparently uncontrollable: the unwanted Episcopalian or Presbyterian clergyman was nearly choked and throttled, beaten, stoned and assaulted by an infuriated rabble. In fact, a crowd yelling at the referee in a Glasgow football match today strongly resembles in temper the congregations of the various churches of Scotland at the end of the seventeenth century. If this violent feeling, which existed throughout Scotland independent of creed, was religious, it was religious in a very dark and primitive sense. It was what we should call superstitious: we can suspect that the rabble was directing its fury against a rival witch-doctor rather than a rival Christian clergyman. And when we know at the same time that from 1696 there had been seven 'hungry years' which left the poorer classes of Scotland starving and pestilence-stricken, we can understand the uprush of superstitious feeling. Bad seasons had invariably been regarded as God's judgments on a back-sliding people, and the clergyman in Scotland had always an *aura* of the witch-doctor in times of stress. When a man sees no hope on earth, when he is ignorant of

science and at the mercy of 'acts of God,' his feelings burst
out with terrible intensity and he is ready to storm Heaven
with blind and desperate prayers; he looks for someone who
has the ear of his God, and if his passion is strong enough
he will shout into God's ear himself. In such a temper was
Scottish Presbyterianism born.

The Episcopalians were finally 'outed' and the Scots
raised up a Kirk in which each individual could claim to have
the ear of God. Now, in a church each of whose members
is theoretically independent, the matter of organization is
bound to be difficult. What gives one godly individual
authority over another? The Scots congregations solved
the problem by electing 'ruling elders' who formed the
Kirk Sessions, committees which felt themselves entitled
to control not only the parishes, not only each other,
but also the ministers. A Scottish minister had to have
'natural' authority if he was to hold his own against
his elders; he had either to have a strong character or
to be a more passionate invoker of God than anyone
else in the parish. Graham, in his excellent book *The
Social Life of Scotland in the Eighteenth Century*, says that
the ministers of Scotland were 'a people-ridden clergy.'
They were what their congregations insisted they should
be. And the congregations insisted that they should be
'mighty, importunate wrestlers in prayer,' men who could
play on the emotions and make their hearers weep, men
who soared up to God on a rush of spontaneous, passionate
feeling. They were not allowed to 'mandate,' or prepare,
a prayer beforehand; they were not allowed to read their
sermons; they had to generate an instantaneous emotional
force in which the congregation could find release. An
epitaph in Carluke churchyard commemorates one of these
ministers:

> A faithful holy minister here lies hid,
> One of a thousand, Mr Peter Kid,
> Firm as a stone, but of a heart contrite,
> A wrestling, praying, weeping Israelite.

The ministers who were most followed were of this kind;
they were known as 'affectionate' ministers in opposition to

the 'legal' preachers who argued doctrinal points. In fact,
what a Scottish congregation looked for was excitement,
the kind of excitement which in other countries has usually
given birth to dramatic art. And the Scottish congregation
got more thrills out of the performance than any audience
in a commercial theatre: the spate of bad rhetoric was no
mere rhetoric where every member of the congregation was
personally involved in the drama of Heaven and Hell. Theirs
was a fearful exhilaration.

Yet it remained an emotional debauch; it never took
shape in an objective form; it never allied itself with
intelligence and culture; and when the flood of exalted
feeling ebbed, the unsatisfied lust for excitement found
less reputable outlets. The people loved to meet in the
open for their 'great occasion,' the Communion, and after
'drowning in tears' during the drama of the Sacrament they
might fall to other diversions behind the stone dykes of the
fields. It is a chancy thing to pin one's faith on intensity of
feeling alone. Also, a passion that is repeated too often tends
to be overplayed, and drama degenerates into melodrama.
The abuse of the great open-air festivals hastened their
decay, aided by the progress of agriculture which enclosed
more land and left fewer pleasant patches of comfortable
ground where thousands could sit. The congregations were
confined to the churches, where such mob exhilarations
were more difficult to achieve; but they needed and found
new sources of excitement.

The fearful thrill of contemplating one's own iniquity
easily passes over into a thrill at the iniquity of others.
The hunt for sinners intensified. The church was the scene
where sinners took the stage, to be gloated over on Sundays
by the congregations and rebuked by the ministers. A sinner
might have to stand 'at the pillory' below the pulpit, clad
in sackcloth, for ten, fifteen, even twenty-six Sundays in
succession. What with 'scolds,' 'vaguers' (Sunday stroll-
ers), profane swearers and profligates, the Scottish Kirk
on a Sunday provided marvellous entertainment for the
godly. Scottish religion was like Scottish whisky, a potent
intoxicant.

But once a hunt for sinners is in full cry there is no

knowing where it may stop. The excitement, of course, can be kept going for a while by the feeling that Satan is very near. In the eighteenth century 'trafficking with Satan' was still taken literally. Any old woman might be a witch; any housewife who broke out into 'flyting' was no mere scold but a caller-down of 'terrible imprecations' that were likely to be carried into instant effect by Satan himself. Yet the more one tracks down Satan the wilier he becomes: one has to scrutinize the smallest actions to make sure that he is not lurking behind them. And so the Scottish Kirk found its excitement narrowing down to denunciations and jealous inquisitions. This was where the elders had a chance to exercise their authority. The Keeping of the Sabbath was obviously a question that afforded the widest scope for denunciation; not every member of a congregation can be suspected of lewdness, but every member, including the minister, can be watched for Sabbath-breaking. The eye of a ruling elder, like the eye of God, had a periscopic quality; it could see round corners and over walls, however high.

Under this jealous inquisition the fervour of the congregation began to ebb. It was necessary to walk carefully, and an appearance of piety became more important than spontaneous inspiration. The Kirk Sessions maintained for long in the minds of the populace the civil authority which they once had. Disobedience to the demands of the Kirk Session entailed civil disabilities well into the eighteenth century: the sinner had to 'compeir' or lose his scanty rights of citizenship. He could be fined, he could be refused a 'testification' enabling him to live in the parish, he could be committed to the Sheriff. And as the Kirk Session was almoner, pawnbroker and money-lender to the community before county banks were established, the needy Scot was ill-advised to get into its bad books. Girls murdered their illegitimate children rather than face the ordeal of being pilloried. As late as 1751 the General Assembly, owing to the terrible prevalence of child-murder in country districts, where old customs of courtship persisted, had to order the Act against the concealment of pregnancy to be read from every pulpit. This awful authority of the Kirk Session endured. The Kirk Session tyrannized over the parish;

the ordinary member of the congregation assumed a staid look and kept the Sabbath devoutly.

That is, briefly, the process by which an almost savage exhilaration dwindled into Sabbath Observance. And force of habit is strong; the Scot who feels a need for breaking out nowadays either takes to alcoholic fervour or reverts to the fervour of hunting out sinners. The creed of the Kirk itself remains unchanged, but the creed has never been the determining factor in the strange self-intoxication of the Scots. The ministers have been able to exercise little direction over that. By the time a party of 'Moderates' began to react against the murky excitements of the people and brought a new intelligence and culture into the pulpit, they were suspected by the lower classes, who were already turning into wage-slaves, and resented by the new rich. The lower classes took to whisky, Radicalism and football instead; the business men invaded the Kirk Sessions and helped to co-opt the face-saving Mrs MacGrundy. Every attempt made by the Church of Scotland to widen its sympathies and erect a firm fabric of Christendom, every closing of schism in its ranks, has left behind an intransigent minority of congregations who prefer the old fervour, however perverted, to the new intelligence. And so we return to the Secession Churches, which are strongest in the Highlands, where Episcopal congregations broke the heads of Presbyterian interlopers at the beginning of the eighteenth century. The temper is still much the same, but now it is Presbyterian congregations who resist innovations. Even Free Presbyterians.

The Reverend Mr MacQueen, a minister of the Free Presbyterians, has got himself into great trouble through being present in a house in 1934 while a Christmas party was being given to children. The man who gave the party, the Provost of Dornoch, was 'suspended' from his church for his iniquity in allowing the children to dance, and at Christmas time too. But I cannot do better than quote from the *Scotsman* the efforts of the unfortunate minister to exculpate himself before his brethren in the faith. His visit to the Provost's house in December, he says, 'was purely accidental.' He had gone there 'late in the

afternoon, having no thought of Christmas in his mind.
Provost Murray mentioned to him that the children were
to have a party, and he (Mr MacQueen) at once suggested
that he should go to an hotel for the night. Provost Murray,
however, said there was a bedroom at the back, where he
would neither see nor hear the children. "All I saw of the
children," declared Mr MacQueen, "was at the worship in
the drawing-room when I asked a blessing on the Word of
God."' If he had either seen or heard the children at their
merry-making, I gather, he would have been in a parlous
state of sin. He was goaded into exclaiming, 'Have you a
right to try and search me as doctors would on a dissecting
table?' and his trials are not yet at an end, for that Christmas
party has still to be solemnly considered at the ordinary
meeting of the Synod in May 1936.

Comment seems to be unnecessary. This is Mrs
MacGrundy with a vengeance: born 1850 or so in the
Lowlands and still going strong. Let me introduce now the
Free Church Presbytery of Lewis. Should the Macbrayne
steamer sail from Stornoway at 11 p.m. on Sunday or
4 a.m. on Monday? This question of Sabbath observance
has caused a dispute between the Lewis Free Church Presbytery and the Lewis Church of Scotland Presbytery. The
Free Church adherents contend that the steamer should not
sail on the Sabbath, not even one hour before midnight,
and a ballot is to be taken to test local residents' views.
This might be the Free Church Presbytery of Edinburgh
in the 'fifties, bidding the ships to keep a holy stillness on
the Sabbath in the port of Leith. Mrs MacGrundy is very
much alive today in odd corners of Scotland.

## II

In the less remote rural districts respectability is still
sanctimonious, centring round the Kirk, and rises to its
highest flights on the Sabbath. Families who do not put
in an appearance at church are definitely not respectable.
Although they may keep away from church most of the
year, they can still save their faces by turning up at the two
Communion services; otherwise they are in the position of

the eighteenth-century sinners who were 'fenced' from the Lord's table. The social importance of the Communion services is well shown by the convention which requires the wives and mothers to put on new hats for the occasion. Two new hats a year is the standard; one for each Communion. On Communion Sunday, too, every house near the church must show freshly-laundered curtains. It is, of course, only front window curtains that are insisted on; the houses must show a Sunday face to the world, like their inhabitants. The curtains are a good *motif* to stress, for they typify the whole attitude towards Sunday observance. For instance, you may clean the boots of the family outside the house all through the week, but on Sunday you must keep them indoors and clean them surreptitiously in the back kitchen. To be seen cleaning boots outside on a Sunday would be to disgrace the house and give cause for 'clash,' or censorious gossip. You may go berry-picking or send your children berry-picking on a Sunday, if you take care to hide the 'can' until you are well past the village houses. You may mount a bicycle on a Sunday, but you must let it be inferred that you are off on an errand of mercy or necessity; if you are merely taking a bundle of rhubarb to a friend it must be 'parcelled up' so that it cannot be identified as rhubarb from your garden. If you are rich enough, and progressive enough, to own a vacuum cleaner, you would not dare to use it on a Sunday, because the noise would be audible to your neighbours; you sweep silently on Sundays with the old-fashioned broom. In effect, you can do what you like inside the house on Sundays, but you must conceal any action of yours that might be noticed from outside. If you decide to go motoring for pleasure, instead of going to church, on a Sunday, you must wait decently until after the church service has begun, and even then, if you have a back door, or a convenient street corner near by, you must not park the car brazenly before your front door. I have heard of a Scotsman in Fife today who parks his golf clothes together with his clubs in a locker at the club-house, and when he goes out to play golf on Sunday he dresses himself in his 'blacks' and carries a Bible through the village until he reaches the club-house, where he changes. On the way back he reverses the process.

Concealment is the watchword. You may help a neighbour by 'flitting' some chairs for him in your car on a Sunday, but only under concealment of the dark. And if your wife is pregnant, she *may* appear in the fields or the streets on week-days, but she must on no account display herself in church, unless she is dressed in such a way as to conceal the evidence that she has been indulging in original sin. Once the child is born it may be carried to church, but before it is born its presence is an embarrassment, drawing attention too openly to the human origin of what are, presumably, God's children. Sex is at all times to be concealed, but on Sundays it is anathema.

As sanctimoniousness centres in the church, the approaches to the church and the church itself demand a decent solemnity of behaviour. Especially if the church is on a bye 'kirk-road' the approach to the building shares in the sanctity of the building; once off the high road one must not behave in a 'worldly' manner. A daring youth who lights a cigarette in the bye-road hears it whispered that he 'wasna weel oot o' the Hoose o' God before he was lighting a cigarette.' Mrs MacGrundy also frowns on the habit which frivolous young ladies have of carrying a hand-bag to church. And though a hand-bag, like a pregnancy, may be tolerated in church if it is concealed, no censure is too much for the girl who is caught 'rakin' her pooch' in the kirk. No chance of lip-stick or face powder for the young ladies of the choir in a country kirk! To avoid the necessity for a hand-bag, a handkerchief and a penny for the collection can be stuffed into the palm of one's glove. Sweets, strangely enough, do not come under the ban, but they should not be 'luxury' sweets like soft and squashy chocolates, for these cannot be safely carried in the pocket of a coat or skirt; the traditional church sweets are hard pan-drops, strongly flavoured with peppermint or cloves, sweets which may be considered as aids to digestion either of a meal or a sermon.

Once you have propitiated Mrs MacGrundy by appearing at church, you may permit yourself a certain latitude of behaviour; you may, for instance, if you are bold enough, buy a Sunday paper and conceal it in a paper bag, although not even the boldest would buy a Sunday paper on the way to church. Yet 'vaguing' or strolling for pleasure on the Lord's Day is still faintly reprehensible; a certain apology for it is needed, and you say disarmingly before you go: 'I'm just awa' ootbye to see So-and-so,' or, 'I think I'll tak' a turn up to see how So-and-So's lookin'.' In small country towns in my girlhood the best excuse for 'vaguing' on a Sunday afternoon was to pay a visit to the cemetery, where one strolled up and down the paths, enjoying the fresh air, but with a pious sense of solemnity.

As for the minister in a rural parish, it is still true to say of him what Graham said of the eighteenth-century minister: 'Every word the clergyman said was noted, everything he did was scrutinized.' The Scottish minister is not permitted to shelter his human weaknesses behind the vestments of priesthood: to him is set the almost impossible task of being a good husband and father and at the same time a symbolic figure remote from carnal appetites. In the minds of rustic parishioners there still lingers the primitive feeling which reads into the actions of the minister a magical potency for good or evil, and so there is an element of self-preservation in the jealousy with which his conduct is spied upon. This, of course, is rationalized into the argument that 'a minister maun set an example'; unfortunately, the example which the poor man is expected to set consists both in sanctimonious respectability, the very negation of true religious feeling, and an asceticism which may be religious in a narrow sense but is certainly unfair to his wife and children. Rural parishes, in the Lowlands, at least, of the north-east coast, really never get far away from the problem of whether a minister demeans his office by sleeping with his wife. A hedger, pruning the manse hedge, will report with excitement: 'He's a gey lad, the minister; I saw him walking in the garden taking his wife's arm!' The whole parish is 'hottering to ken' whether the minister frequents his wife's bed or not. 'We ken he maun ha'e been wi' his wife, since there *is* a bairn,' one woman tells another. It is no wonder if humane church heritors build high walls round manse gardens; they are sorely needed. The minister, then, must be ascetic though not celibate, respectable but not 'worldly.' Roughly speaking, 'worldly' is applied to any innovation of recreation or fashion that comes from the towns. In Angus, for instance, the wearing of pyjamas is stigmatized as 'worldly,' and the manse washing-line that displays pyjamas instead of sober night-shirts gives rise to head-shaking. As for the country minister's wife, she is in an anomalous position. Wedded certainly to the man, she is but doubtfully wedded to the minister, and must justify her presence in his bedroom by espousing the affairs of the parish as an unpaid lay Sister. The minister saves the face of the parish before God and Mrs MacGrundy; the minister's wife saves both his face and her own.

Sanctimonious face-saving is what passes for religion in the general life of the rural Lowland community. You can be ill-tempered, cruel, brutal, selfish, unscrupulous, hard, but you are respectable if you observe the sanctimonious formalities. The respectable Scot in country districts today is very like the eighteenth-century Scot who intoned a long grace over the ale to blind a prospective customer to the spavined condition of the horse he was selling. 'Behave yoursels before folk' has taken the place of the Ten Commandments. The lampoons published by the ungodly Mr Punch of London, in 1858, are still true of the Lowland country districts, and one of these is so pertinent that I cannot refrain from quoting part of it:

> Behave yoursels before folk,
> Behave yoursels before folk,
> Sin if ye will, but keep it still,
> An' dinna sin afore folk.
>
> Ye'll tell us ilk statistic sheet
> Proves Scottish purity a cheat,
> But siccan proofs it isna meet
> To gang and blab before folk.
>
> Behave yoursels before folk,
> Behave yoursels before folk,
> When ye're yer lane, do what ye'd fain,
> But oh! be gude before folk.

Behave yoursels before folk! That is a relative, not an absolute standard of virtue, and certainly betrays a social consciousness of a kind. Yet it is a negative social consciousness. The grimness with which these rural Scots repress each other is a measure of how far they distrust themselves.

## III

In the small towns respectability is less immediately dependent on the church. The sanctimoniousness of respectability has a more commercial side: the shopkeeper goes to church not only to prove that he is respectable, but to make sure of getting the custom of his fellow-members. I remember that when I was a girl it was a matter for open reproach if a Free Kirk adherent bought goods from an Auld Kirk shop. You had to support your own congregation. Still, as the self-distrust of the Scots is naturally intensified in the uneasy middle classes, who most of all need an outward and visible 'sign' that their credit in the community is good, it is of interest to note that in a small Scottish town the easiest way of proclaiming that your credit is good is to become an office-bearer in the church. In a large city you may collect 'old masters' to that end or subsidize a political party or give lavish entertainments or become a municipal figure, but in a small town you become a deacon or an elder. And in a small town the minister has a magical prestige, shared, indeed, by lawyers, bankers and doctors, yet containing more irrational elements than the prestige enjoyed by the other professions. The small-town mother still desires to see her son 'wag his pow in a poopit,' or to see her daughter sanctify the married state by wedding a minister.

Yet the ostentatious respectability of the small Scottish town has more of Grundy in it than MacGrundy. You are still careful about the curtains in your front windows, but they have no reference to Communion Sunday. On every day in the week you wash your door-step white, first thing in the morning, and shut the door behind it before 'redding up' the house—or not, as the case may be. You preserve appearances for their own sake, and not to emphasize the holiness of your ways. You shut your shop on Sunday, but if it is a sweet-shop, threatened by unlawful competition from 'heathen' Italians, you may find yourself opening it between church services. Commercial interests are stronger than religious taboos in the small town and have their own sanctity.

It is only to be expected that the nearer one comes to the cities the less obvious does Mrs MacGrundy become. A map showing the concentration of commercial interests in Scotland would give a high coefficient of correlation with a map showing the displacement of MacGrundy by Grundy. Urban standards of respectability in Scotland approximate more and more nearly to similar standards in English provincial large towns. There are visible traces of MacGrundy in Scottish cities, but Sunday trams do run in the streets, although they were started under the pretext of conveying people to church; the sweet-shops and cigarette-shops do open their doors except in the most 'respectable' thoroughfares; church-going for the sake of respectability is still prevalent, but ladies may carry their hand-bags into the House of God and face powder is not taboo. Mrs MacGrundy is only a lingering shade, a kind of racial memory. She once saved the national pride, and she is not yet banished because she might be needed again. Her apologists, of course, insist that if she were to disappear entirely Scotland too would disappear, and we should have instead an English province.

This is a suggestion which I do not wish to refute at this point. For the present I shall only oppose to it another suggestion: that Mrs MacGrundy is a negative, thwarted perversion of what might have been or might yet become a genuine national consciousness. Like Mrs Grundy she can create nothing new; she is merely obstructive and deforming, where she is not a passive reflection of the *status quo*. True, there is nothing to be said for displacing a Mrs MacGrundy in favour of an equally uncreative and more insipid figure like Mrs Grundy, who reflects less and less the genuine provincialism of England and is becoming more and more the creature of a standardized commercial culture which keeps its inferiority complexes chiefly in its purse. But must we, then, keep Mrs MacGrundy?

## FOUR

# A Spot of Detective Work

Let us turn our Mrs MacGrundy round again and take another look at her. Surely, after an intensive study of modern detective fiction, we can extract from the evidence in the last chapter a sufficient number of conclusions to let us define her influence more closely. I am rather partial to the man in Fife who dresses himself in his Sunday blacks and takes a Bible with him when he goes out on the Lord's Day to play golf: let us take him as our text, for he is an honours graduate in Mrs MacGrundy's school. Now, he is obviously sanctimonious; that is to say, he desires to maintain an appearance of piety. An appearance of piety is evidently sufficient for his purpose, and he achieves it by looking as if he were going to the Kirk. In other words, if he strikes an attitude of piety without necessarily being pious, he satisfies Mrs MacGrundy. Mrs MacGrundy, then, trains people to be attitudinarians. Secondly, he is obviously timid. He wants to play golf, but he dare not stride out like a free man with his golf clubs on his back. He is too timid to be a self-sufficient character, to say firmly: 'I want to play golf, Sunday or no Sunday, and my reasons for it have been approved by myself and require no further justification.' And what he fears is not the damnation of his soul to all eternity: he is prepared to shoulder the responsibility for that, since ultimately he does indulge in his game of golf. What he fears is censorious gossip in the town. He does not expect his actions to meet with charitable or understanding interpretation. Mrs MacGrundy trains people to be furtive and suspicious. Out of that arises our third point, that the man is obviously painstaking and persistent in his preparations for playing the part. Think of the trouble he takes! It is no small matter to don a suit of

Sunday blacks, and he adds a Bible, too, under his arm. I should like to think that the Bible marks a lurking sense of humour; but if he has a sense of humour he must keep it to himself. Mrs MacGrundy trains people to be persistent and thorough in their secretive enterprises. She has a searching and observant eye. She would note the absence of the Bible. That is enough to go on with, is it? No, one other point occurs to me. The man could not possibly expect to impose his church-going pretence on his fellow-townsmen unless there were a multiplicity of kirks in the town, making it difficult for them to pin him down. Either he poses as a free-lance, for whom any kirk will do, or he belongs to a large congregation in which his absence passes unremarked. As a detective, I feel that there is a difficulty here. However, it can be referred to our first point: that an appearance of piety is sufficient. Mrs MacGrundy, being searching and observant, cannot possibly be fooled for long into believing that the man really attends a kirk. Nor can he expect her to be so fooled. It follows that we must add something to our first conclusion: Mrs MacGrundy not only trains people to be attitudinarians, she also trains them to accept attitudes, if they are well presented, without reference to what lies behind them. She trains them, in fact, to present and accept impostures with equal solemnity. The biggest *poseur* will get the loudest applause from Mrs MacGrundy.

This is, you will say, an odd picture of Scotland. A nation of timid, suspicious, solemn *poseurs*? Charlatans with a certain outward bravado (remember the Bible and the Sunday blacks), refusing to apply either their intelligence or their sense of humour to the facts of a situation? What has become of that old fervour, that *perfervidum ingenium* of the Scots, which once dashed a wild spume up to the very skies?

Well, speaking as a detective, I find the logic of the argument quite inescapable. That is what Mrs MacGrundy does for people. She has bricked over the ancient fervour, and her bricks are censoriousness and self-distrust. She has clamped the iron lid of Outward Observance upon it, and she sits grimly a-top. Instead of directing the Scottish temper Mrs MacGrundy has thwarted it.

Instead of harmonizing it, she has divided it against itself.

But, you will say, it is only a minority of people in Scotland who follow Mrs MacGrundy today. She is vanishing from the large towns; she is really only a bogey haunting dark corners. And she only 'haunts' on Sundays. The Sunday golfer on whom this case against Mrs MacGrundy has been built up is probably an excellent human being during the week, however ridiculous the figure he cuts on Sundays.

I think I am entitled to recall the fact that less than a century ago Mrs MacGrundy was a very powerful and pervasive bogey, and that her traces are not so easily washed out of the national character. And I cannot admit that one can cut Sunday entirely out of the week, leaving the Scottish character in two quite separate parts. Of course there is a split in the Scottish consciousness; Mrs MacGrundy officially took over the control of Scottish passion, throwing Scottish intelligence behind her, but the split cannot extend to infinity. As a matter of fact, Scottish intelligence has here and there drawn out the ancient fervour, despite Mrs MacGrundy, so there must be an underground communication between the two. For a while the Radical movement in Scotland, developing into Socialism, tapped the ancient reservoir of passion, and individual Scots, escaping from Scotland, have shown both passion and intelligence and thus achieved distinction in a world where a combination of these two is becoming more unusual. The split in Scotland goes deep, but not very deep. Mrs MacGrundy intimidates Scottish intelligence on week-days as well as Sundays, just as Scottish intelligence may intimidate her. She 'haunts' most obviously on Sundays, but if we apply the eye of a detective to the week-days we may catch her at her fell work there too.

I am prepared to stand or fall by the Sunday golfer. Let us put him through the riddle a second time and see what we get. The stage property Bible interests me. Let us assume that the Bible marks a touch of humour, that the man enjoys playing his sanctimonious part in the streets of the town. It is only his front that is solemn; behind him lurks an imp chortling with glee at his success in impersonating a pious church-goer. Well, that makes the man a sniggerer behind the back of authority. He leaves it to other people to determine the standards of public life and sniggers behind their backs like a small boy cheating the police. If he has a wife he will expect her to be his conscience, and he will be apologetically facetious about her in the club-house. He may impersonate the figure of a responsible citizen, but, however likeable he may be, he cannot be called emotionally adult. And if he is not emotionally adult on Sundays, he is not likely to be emotionally adult during the week. If he is a shopkeeper he may cheat you with a twinkle in his eye, but if he can get away with it he will cheat you. Mrs MacGrundy has helped to cheat *him* of his manhood.

Take the alternative case, that he does not snigger, that he feels as solemn as he looks. That means, of course, that he never peeps behind himself and would not thank you for putting Attic salt on his tail. And a man who takes his own attitudes as seriously as that will be not a little pompous and inclined to be resentful of other people. He is saying, in effect: 'I'm as good as you are, although you *are* going to the church. I am also doing my duty in backing up public opinion.' And he will dart suspicious, resentful glances at the people he meets in case they may be laughing at him up their sleeves. Well, if he is not resentful but merely complacent, his intelligence is defective. And if he is resentful, if he has a solemnity behind which flickers a fear that people are belittling him, his social personality is defective. I cannot admit that these failings exist only on Sundays and not through the week. He is fatuously stupid by nature or resentfully priggish by Mrs MacGrundy's upbringing. In either case he is handicapped as a citizen of the world.

But, you will say, we are not all Mrs MacGrundy's bairns. Scotland is not populated entirely by pompous prigs and facetious sniggerers. Quite true. Yet I do not see how you can avoid the conclusion that the pressure of Mrs MacGrundy makes it unnecessarily difficult for a respectable Scot to keep himself out of these categories. And if you do manage to grow up among the middle classes of Scotland without striking solemn or facetious attitudes, you suffer in another way from being surrounded by attitudinarians on the defensive. If you are a kindly person you must suppress your intelligence to keep from hurting their feelings; if you set honesty above kindliness you rouse ill-will and suspicion so easily that social intercourse becomes contentious. The former is a softening, the latter a hardening process, but neither is salutary. Too often the middle-class Scot who is both intelligent and kindly escapes from the dilemma by retiring within himself or within the shelter of a small group of like-minded people, and so ceases to be an effective element in public life.

No, Scotland still suffers as a whole from the deforming influence of Mrs MacGrundy, even although she is a vanishing bogey. I find her rather terrible now that we have looked at her.

## FIVE

# The Victorian Age

How on earth did it happen, you may well ask, that such a specious figure could ever have influenced a nation? To understand that, we must relate Mrs MacGrundy to the complex of historical forces which set the general tone of the Victorian Age. I said, if you remember, that Mrs Grundy came into Scotland with Victoria and quietly coalesced with Mrs MacGrundy. That was, roughly, between the sixties and the eighties, when Mrs Grundy in England was going all 'womanly,' representing an exaggerated domestic and family sentiment. Mrs MacGrundy was never womanly in that sense; she was the heir of the masculine Kirk Sessions, and her main line was Sabbath Observance, the striking of pious attitudes in public. She was designed to reassure the civilized world that Scottish business magnates were not only business men but godly men. At first sight it looks as if there could be little in common between Grundy and MacGrundy, and yet they were but different responses to the same problem, and that problem gave the Victorian Age its peculiar character.

The slow, amorphous, passively resistant social body of old England had digested the Reformation without much apparent *malaise* and recovered even from the fanatical Puritan zeal of the Commonwealth. The soul of the individual, once so tightly hugged in the all-embracing social and religious order of the Middle Ages, had been detached and liberated to follow its own enterprises, but the social body of England remained feudal enough to keep the detached individual from feeling the draught too much. Enterprise went on; certain individuals made discoveries in science; other individuals, pursuing their own ends, founded far-reaching commercial undertakings; but the sleepy body of England drank its beer in the village inn, rode its horses, tipped its hat to the squire, and did not bother. Commerce, still enterprising, planted the English flag in India and America, and the English found themselves acquiring an Empire and a financial policy and a marked belief in progress. They lost the American States, but they pushed into Africa and Australia and dear knows where, and presently the demand of capital for ever-increasing dividends, combined with the striking discoveries of science, plunged the nation into its full career. Science and capitalism were taking giant strides. The advance was spectacular. England woke up to find itself largely industrialized, in the grip of colossal forces which dwarfed mere humanity. The individual soul, now sensible of its detachment and scared by the inhuman look of the machinery to which it was committed, felt the draught acutely. That was the Victorian Age. The atheism of the new forces became a bogey in the public mind, and the controversy staged between religion and science was followed anxiously by the whole nation. There was still a social body, however, and so the individual soul generated a family heat around itself to keep itself warm while it stretched out tentative fingers towards the colossus of Mammon.

That was how Mrs Grundy in England remained a social rather than a religious figure and became so excessively domestic. She reassured herself about God by dabbing little bits of Christianity over herself as ornaments, excrescences of a muddled mind very like the ornaments she dabbed on her furniture or on her houses or her clothing, and she contented herself with sham Gothic buildings to remind her of the Middle Ages. She padded and draped the stark facts around her; she put twiddly bits all over the functional structures of capitalism and then folded her hands complacently. She was strong enough to neutralize even the Victorian Evangelical Movements, which remained sectarian and never rose to the dignity of representing the national consciousness. The North of England might denounce the worldliness of dancing and drinking, but Mrs Grundy drank her beer and went to dances, content to know that the legs of the piano were modestly draped. She had her hypocrisies, of course; she, too, was compromising between God and Mammon by not letting her right hand know what her left hand was doing; but her lies were mainly social lies. Her respectability was family respectability.

Now, the sectarian Evangelicals, who appeared in the Midlands and in the North, where the effects of industrialization were most apparent, strongly resembled Mrs MacGrundy. They also strongly resembled the Chautauqua and camp-meeting movements in the United States. Of all these Mrs MacGrundy was the most triumphant, for she did rise to the dignity of representing a national consciousness. But let us determine, if we can, why the English Evangelicals and the Chautauqua Sunday-school teachers should bear such a marked resemblance to our Mrs MacGrundy. They were characterized by emotional fervour which was narrowed to an almost insane intensity. They were haunted by visions of hell. They fished out texts from all over the Bible and plastered them on tracts and rolled them up in little boxes, from which you drew a 'promise' to comfort you in moments of depression. They drew harrowing pictures of what happened if you entered the Broad instead of the Narrow Way; they denounced gambling, drinking, dancing, the theatre—all the pomps and vanities of this world—and, lastly, they shrieked in horror against Sunday trains. Obviously, they were dominated by fear and clutched frantically at salvation. They were prepared to endure any rigours of discipline if only they could be 'saved.' Saved from what? This looks very like the fear of the detached individual soul in the grip of forces it does not understand. It is to be noted that these revivals broke out most acutely where financial enterprise was least checked. The fear of the individual soul menaced by the capitalist machine? Yet economic 'laws' cannot be stayed by shrieks of salvationism. This was evidently a fear reaching back to primitive, superstitious elements, a fear that paralysed intelligence and trusted to emotional fervour alone. Does it not sound very like what happened to the Scots in the late seventeenth century? I think that the Scots felt the draught earlier, because Scotland, although an old country,

was living on a pathetically narrow economic margin and had
not developed a social consciousness. The stark isolation of
the individual soul unsupported by social forces made itself
bleakly felt in Scotland long before it afflicted industrial
England and those American States which were so new
that they had had no chance of developing a stable social
consciousness. In other words, the Evangelical Movement
in England and the Chautauqua Movement in America
were younger sisters of Mrs MacGrundy, facing a more
complicated although not more terrifying problem than
the Scots had faced earlier. By that time the Scots had
constructed their National Kirk: the old fervour had petered
out into attitudes of piety: the Kirk Sessions were already
serving MacGrundy. Mrs MacGrundy could spring fully
armed, so to speak, from the Kirk Sessions, to command
the nation, whereas her younger sisters remained sectarian
and consequently more ineffective.

The younger sisters produced their attitudinarians too;
they were bound to follow the same course. But the
Pecksniffs in England and in America never quite got away
with it. Mrs Grundy in England merely dabbed on bits of
Christianity, Mrs Grundy in America took to 'culture,'
and the pseudo-religious attitudes of the Pecksniffs were
superseded by other attitudes. But in Scotland they got
away with it all right. Mrs MacGrundy stood up before
the nation claiming to be Christianity itself, and if you did
not want to be branded as an atheist you had to toady to
her. She was a powerful bogey in her hey-day.

So the Victorian compromise between God and Mammon appeared in Scotland as Mrs MacGrundy, who proved
to the world that business men could be godly. She made a
show of obstructing the forces of capitalism on Sundays,
but she drew her income from the enterprise of the business
men during the week. Mrs MacGrundy and the Scottish
capitalist said cannily to each other: 'You claw my back
and I'll claw yours.' Her attitudinarians fraternized with
other attitudinarians—did not Mr Gladstone, that fervent
attitudinarian, sweep through Scotland like a devouring
flame?—but they had a better conscience than any similar
attitudinarian in England.

Let us consider, for instance, one of Mrs MacGrundy's bairns who rose to eminence at that time, Lord Overtoun. He was born in 1843, grew up when Mrs MacGrundy was in her prime, and was raised to the peerage in 1893. Now, he cut a striking figure both as a business man and as a supporter of the Free Church. His chemical works at Shawfield, Rutherglen, were conducted with an industrious rigour that must have excited the admiration of financiers, for he got his men to work twelve hours a day, seven days a week, at less than fourpence an hour, with night-shifts every alternate Friday extending for eighteen consecutive hours without a break. Nasty work, too; tending vitriol tanks and chrome furnaces, where men contracted the dreadful sores known as 'chrome holes.' Sweating made one more liable to these sores, and wives and mothers at home sometimes got chrome holes simply from washing their men's shirts. To minimize the risk of this terrible leprosy Government regulations prescribed respirators and lavatory accommodation, with hot water, soap, nail-brushes and towels. Lord Overtoun's firm, however, was too keen on business to waste money on luxuries for the men. Four enamelled basins and two roller towels for the hundred or so workers in the poisonous 'crystal house'—no soap left lying beside the basins, but a cut of yellow soap weighing four ounces doled out to each man once a fortnight; that was reckoned enough in the way of lavatory accommodation. The sweating furnace-men had to make do with a wooden bucket, a cold water-tap, and bring your own soap and towels if you want them. 'Cloots' of butter muslin were handed out for a while to serve as respirators, but they were checked in daily and served out promiscuously again, so that no man was sure of having his own 'cloot' two days running. The men finally provided their own. If a man got chrome sores on his feet so that he could not stand, he had, of course, to quit; but with sores on the hands he could manage to carry on, and with sores on the belly he could wear a kind of wire cage to keep his clothes from excruciating him. Lord Overtoun's chemical works, you may think, sound rather like hell. But they were a good commercial proposition, even although in 1899 the men struck at last for a minimum of sixpence an hour and an eight-hours' shift, with Saturday afternoons and Sundays off. Lord Overtoun ruled the Scottish market in the chemical trade.

He relaxed from his week-day attitude of devotion to business only to adopt an equally fervent Sunday attitude of devotion to the Free Church and the Young Men's and Young Women's Christian Associations. As a philanthropist he threw a shadow as far as Calcutta, where he endowed the Y.M.C.A. with a magnificent building known as the 'Overtoun Hall,' which had upon its wall a motto: 'Built by Prayer.' He was strong on morality and set his face against gambling. He fined his workmen five shillings a time for bringing in beer, and a shilling for smoking. He disciplined them nobly, docking their meagre pay by a shilling a week so that he might make the grand gesture of handing over £2000 to the funds of the Y.W.C.A. No wonder that when the *Labour Leader* started what it called an 'Overtoun Crusade,' there was dismay among the godly in the West of Scotland. Lord Overtoun was a prince among attitudinarians, and the whole body of respectable opinion backed him up.

Note the rigour with which he disciplined his men. That was the Calvinistic streak in Mrs MacGrundy. If you can persuade yourself that as a successful man you are of God's elect, you may be sincerely persuaded that your workmen are not. And if you are one of God's elect, why, then, as an employer you discipline your godless workmen for their good. Every strike of the working classes in Scotland at that time produced the same evidence of excessive rigour in the imposition of petty fines. The Caledonian Railway strike in 1883, for instance, was provoked chiefly by too long hours and an exacting system of fines.

Well, Mrs MacGrundy had turned God Himself into a respectable figure, and men like Lord Overtoun had every right to believe her when she told them that they were made in His image. Her attitudinarians today are petty by comparison.

However, she is a vanishing bogey nowadays. The Victorian problem is by no means solved, but we are discarding the idea that panic fear is a remedy and we are at least willing to apply objective intelligence to the financial menace, employing, among other resources, political instead of pseudo-religious methods of obstructing the economic system. To be sure, none of Mrs MacGrundy's attitudinarians are doing anything of the kind; these quick-change artists can adapt themselves to any system, but have not the courage or the intelligence to reform anything. Your attitudinarian finds it easier to turn from cant to graft.

## SIX

## *Scotswomen*

Hitherto we have been considering the men of Scotland in relation to Mrs MacGrundy, without paying much attention to the women. Mrs MacGrundy, the heir of the Kirk Sessions, derived her authority mainly from the men, and so I could not avoid putting them in the forefront. I am faintly apologetic about this, since in the mind of the reader Mrs Grundy herself must be associated with women rather than with men. Yet before we examine the effect of Grundy plus MacGrundy on the women of Scotland, it might be as well now to define more closely what these figures stand for.

I wish to make it clear that neither Mrs Grundy nor Mrs MacGrundy represents the whole sum of social forces in the life of a nation. I have said that Mrs Grundy reflects the strains and stresses in the social consciousness of England, but it is a reflection in a distorting mirror. The people who know what they want to do, and promptly set about doing it, contribute the directing energy to the social life of their generation, but they have no credit given them in Mrs Grundy's mirror. Mrs Grundy reflects the composite fears of those individuals who are anxious or uncertain about what they ought to do, the timid who look to their neighbours or to precedent, the people who are unsure of themselves and waiting for a lead. Mrs Grundy reflects what she *thinks* is the established tradition. Pinchbeck is gold to her if it looks like gold. Mrs MacGrundy's mirror is of the same kind, with a slightly different angle of distortion owing to the character of the Scots, who have usually sought religious rather than social sanctions for respectability. Obviously neither Grundy nor MacGrundy could be trusted to recognize genuine creative force in social life or in religion. The Pharisees of Israel, for instance, were early adherents of a convention rather resembling MacGrundy, and we know what they felt about Christianity. Yet the number of individuals who are unsure of themselves and dependent on a convention is generally great enough to make the composite picture of their fears a valuable guide to the history of their age or class, a guide, moreover, which has been usually ignored by the history-books. Today we know a little more about the penetrating effect of what an advanced Victorian critic called 'climates of opinion,' and if we can gather from a study of Grundy or MacGrundy what were the prevailing winds at any time we can both understand better and better excuse the antics of our ancestors, and, perhaps, even forecast our own weather more accurately.

It is to be understood, then, that I do not say that everybody in Scotland who went to church or goes to church is to be considered as one of Mrs MacGrundy's bairns. I do say that there is evidence that Mrs MacGrundy was a preponderant influence, and that her influence is still visible. I do not say that every woman in England between the 'sixties and the 'eighties went all 'womanly' and exaggeratedly domestic, but I do say that the prevailing wind for women at that time blew in that direction.

If we look again at the fears of the Victorian age we can see why the wind should blow in that particular direction. The men were very busy and important on the scaffolding of new constructions, but their souls were shivering. From the chill abstraction of possibly agnostic thought and certainly amoral science, from the cold logic of finance, they returned to their homes in need of warm slippers, large comforting meals at large and permanent-looking family tables, the general assurance of solid domesticity. They also looked for the assurance of stable moral values. The more ambiguous business morality became, the more anxiously they looked for a stage setting of inflexible virtue at home. They needed comfort and the women surrounded them with comfort, a reassuring suggestion that nothing was going to change very much after all.

Note the word 'surrounded.' The women enveloped their

men. They were environments for their families. The men had no occasion to remember that women too might be individuals with a turn for adventurous enterprise. Women, they supposed, existed to feed and foster boys and men. Even girls were 'little women,' learning to foster dolls and younger children, to be good and patient and tactful rather than clever. We have an unfair advantage in considering this mid-Victorian scene; we look back on it along perspectives which make its complacency faintly ridiculous; but we cannot blame the average man of that time for not realizing that his attitude to women was a little fatuous. Nor were the women so meek and downtrodden as appears from a distance. A searching eye might observe that the men, like selfish children, tried rather hard the racial patience of the women who mothered them, but the women, so long as they remained at the centre of home life, had the recognized prestige of mothers. In 1878 Mrs Grundy represented the respectable mothers of the lower middle classes of England. That is to say, the respectable mothers of families were a dominant force in social life.

The homes of England, these brooding maternal hives, were much shrunk at that time compared with the country-houses of earlier ages. Where a woman once had a hundred and one industries to attend to in connection with her establishment, she now bought from shops what she needed, and the vacant spaces in her interests were filled up by intensive maternal activity. Yet by 1870 that brooding intensity had already reached its limit and was beginning to recede. We can guess that from the trend of dress fashions. Loose jackets and crinolines, so suitable for expectant or nursing mothers, had given place to the tight-buttoned bodices and draped skirts of the sex-conscious wife, all bust and bustle. The woman who had bred children while her husband bred money was discovering that money in its turn bred new interests for her. Mrs Grundy in 1878 was beginning to keep a sharp eye on the 'poets and the artises.' Women were actually taking to lawn tennis. In 1882 'rational' dress for women—divided skirts—was openly displayed at an exhibition organized by the National Health Society. In 1883 the Married Women's Property Act became effective.

In 1886 the first woman surgeon appeared. In the 'seventies the New Woman if not yet fully awake must have been stirring. Women, that is to say, were beginning to assert themselves as individuals rather than environments. In a world where money was earned only by individuals it was inevitable that they should begin to press for recognition as individuals. The old balance was becoming heavily overweighted on the side of the individual. The community was served by taxes taken from the pockets of individual men: women were supported by money from the pockets of individual men: but the individual men were inclined to hold that who pays the piper must call the tune, and the power of money was increasing at such a rate that the claims of the community and the claims of the women were in danger of being overshadowed. The shortage of gold which afflicted England between the 'eighties and the 'nineties, with the consequent 'tightness' of money, probably intensified this latent monetary antagonism and helped to make the emergence of the New Woman all the more spectacular. However, in the 'seventies, while these elements were still nascent, we can be fairly certain that Mrs Grundy opposed them. Mrs Grundy would be all for woman-as-environment and strongly against woman-as-individual. Mrs Grundy would stand up for marriage as the only respectable career for a woman. Mrs Grundy would cling to the prestige of the married mother and recoil with horror from the suggestion that women who ignored their family duties should be socially acceptable. If Mrs Grundy had been then asked to 'receive' a divorced woman I do not know what she would have said. Mrs Grundy at that time would have called a business woman an unsexed hussy and a learned woman a freak of Nature. Any woman who left the shelter of the family circle would have been denounced as 'mannish' if not actually outlawed. True, the women who did break out of the family circle made the natural mistake of imitating men, for they saw a world in which men alone were officially recognized as individuals. In spite of their courage the prevailing wind nipped these pioneers. One always suffers in some way from the prevailing wind of one's generation. But Mrs Grundy, by her nature, was bound to be incapable of divining the forces at work beneath this 'mannish' reaction. She merely denounced them. Mrs Grundy is always trying to make firm ropes out of the sands of time, and she cannot help denouncing her recalcitrant material.

At the same time, Mrs Grundy, as a respectable mother concentrating on the erotic emotions and instincts, was extremely sensitive to sexual symbolism. She disseminated a fine fume of sexuality all over her home, and her efforts to conceal it naturally emphasized it. Many innocent objects and actions shocked Mrs Grundy in the 'seventies. The generous baroque curves of the legs on a Victorian grand piano suggested unspeakable seductions, and Mrs Grundy veiled these legs in discreet skirts. Sexual licence peeped at her from behind everything. For many years sex had been the only card she had to play in achieving her social position as a married mother, and now she overplayed it; but women had been too long referred to as 'the sex' for Mrs Grundy to abandon the settled implications of the term. Anything at all that threatened to invalidate the sex-monopoly of matrimony became an object of suspicion, and the objects of suspicion were many. The word 'freedom' suggested to Mrs Grundy only the idea of sexual freedom; she tabooed, therefore, freedom of thought or observation or expression, even freedom of movement. In 1878 the poets and artists patronized by the upper classes were audacious and improper in our Mrs Grundy's eyes. Her idea of art was to lay out family albums on a ball-fringed table-cover: her idea of literature was the *Family Herald*. She had learned to tolerate railway trains, which ran, after all, on rigidly straight lines although they were not obviously bridled like horses, yet the freedom of bicycles on the roads shocked her, and the more dangerous freedom of the New Motor-carriage, which made a first tentative appearance a little later, at about the same time as the New Woman, startled her profoundly. I have no doubt that Mrs Grundy would have prescribed, if it had been in her power, a red flag to be carried in front of the New Woman. She certainly succeeded in maintaining until 1896 the statute which ordained that a man walking with a red flag in his hand should precede a motor vehicle.

And when votes for women were actually mooted in the 'eighties, Mrs Grundy at once jumped to the conclusion that freedom to vote meant freedom to choose one's lovers. She never quite disentangled women's suffrage from what she called Free Love. In short, having identified herself with 'the home,' Mrs Grundy suspected licentiousness in everything outside the home.

This was the Mrs Grundy who brought her code of propriety to Scotland. She represented the respectable middle-class mothers of England. But by the time she had found a footing in Scottish towns she represented rather the respectable grandmothers of England. I think that the effect of this time-lag is still to be perceived in Scotland.

Well, how did the women of Scotland react to this domestic Mrs Grundy from England? One might expect them, if they were themselves home-makers, to feel about Mrs Grundy's code of propriety much as M. Jourdain felt when he discovered that he had been speaking prose all his life without knowing it. But were the women of Scotland in the same position as the women of England?

I think not. The austere Lowland Scottish tradition, which for each individual drew a straight line from earth to heaven terminating in the Day of Judgment, had deeply affected the official status of women. Being women, they could not help mothering their families, but if they sought to influence their children through natural affection they were held to be 'unprincipled and careless.' That is to say, if they exercised their natural faculties of sympathetic understanding, of sensitiveness to emotional needs, they were held to be interfering with the principles of religion. The quick mother-wit that knows when and how to foster a growing personality had no prestige or authority in the eyes of the Kirk. The father-image of mankind sanctioned by the Kirk was as absolute and solitary as its presumable prototype in heaven. None of your environmental nonsense in Scotland. Ilka herring had to hang by its ain tail. Man was an individual reaching to the skies: woman, being more akin to the earth, a lesser individual stopping short of the skies and therefore not to be trusted, even with her own children, unless she obeyed the precepts of the Kirk.

This one-sided view of humanity was, of course, bound up with the lack of a social consciousness. Where all the lines of ideology are vertical, there is not much chance of what one might call horizontal values. In England public life appeared to be just as one-sided, yet there was a body of ancient social traditions which, like 'invisible' exports, were none the less powerful for being unspecified and helped to maintain a balance. England, especially in the south, still had a lively respect for that play of the emotional life which produces both social traditions and social graces. Lowland Scotland had no respect for it, and consequently undervalued women. And where women have no prestige of their own the community has no prestige. It needs only a glance at the whole turbulent and factious course of past Scottish history to see how this state of things divided the nation against itself. Even in the Highlands, where an old tradition of culture bound people to each other and to the soil, the community feeling remained tribal and local. In the Lowlands patches of social consciousness appeared—notably in Edinburgh and Glasgow—but they too remained local. Nor did the Lowland Scots, lacking respect for the emotional life, develop any technique in the management of their feelings: their passionate fervour either flared out violently or was as violently repressed: they were an aggregation of turbulent, ruthless or sentimental individuals rather than a nation joined in one body.

Women, however, even when officially discouraged, remain women. In post-Reformation Scotland, having no social framework to back them up, they carried on their own shoulders the whole burden of keeping the race together. The women of the Lowlands, asking and receiving no credit for being women, developed a strength of character and a vitality on which their contentious and cocksure men depended utterly. All Protestant countries, reacting from the mediaeval Catholic environment, unduly emphasized the individual and decried natural social forces; and in all Protestant countries women, for that reason, developed strength of character; but in Scotland, which, outside the Highlands, was more radically stripped of social elements than any other country, women had less support and showed more individual character than anywhere, I think, in Europe. The Scotsman, in his relation both to his country and to his women, was entirely like a child demanding service from a mother and giving her no credit for waiting on his needs.

Ah, you will say, Scotland, that 'puir auld mither!' Yes, but also 'Caledonia, stern and wild.' A mother with any strength of character is bound to become a formidable personality after a lifetime of coping with selfish children. There were the two types of Lowland Scotswomen; the puir auld mithers and the formidable, possibly wild prototypes of Caledonia. It may be that Scotswomen in their old age took an instinctive revenge on the hard and selfish Scottish tradition; it is also likely that the men who denied them feared them in some corner of their minds; whatever the reason, the Scottish imagination was long haunted by formidable women—especially formidable old women. They lurked in the anonymous ballads. They troubled the Kirk, which was kept busy denouncing them as witches. They obsessed even Sir Walter Scott, that kindest and most tolerant of authors. And we find them in history well up into the eighteenth century—women like Lady Strange, for instance, who boasted: 'My children from the youngest to the eldest loves me and fears me as sinners dread death. My look is law.' I would not venture to say that the race of formidable, outspoken Scotswomen has died out even today. And they bear little resemblance to the kind of Englishwoman who evolved Mrs Grundy.

Lady Strange would have made short work of Mrs Grundy. '*Pretender*, indeed! and be dawm'd to ye!' she said loudly to a wretched man who was disparaging the Stuart king. And the young ladies of her day would have been equally disconcerted by the social taboos of our Grundy. The English Captain Topham, writing from Edinburgh in the seventeen-seventies, said: 'The women who, to do them justice, are much more entertaining than their neighbours in England, discovered a great deal of vivacity and fondness for repartee. The general ease with which they conducted themselves, the innocent freedom of their manners, and the unaffected good nature, all conspired to make one forget

that we were regaling in a cellar.' Nor was a fondness
for vivacious repartee confined to Edinburgh; the kind of
humorous 'flyting' with which young women assailed their
swains was prevalent enough to be nicknamed 'Scottish
courtship.' In a country of individuals these Scotswomen
had to assert themselves as individuals, since as women
they were taken for granted.

There was, of course, another side to it, especially in
the rural districts where life was hard and female labour
incessant. Keats made a journey to Scotland in 1818 and
was painfully impressed by the subdued soberness of the
country girls. He does not reflect that they might have
been stricken with shyness before the Southron; this is
what he says of them: 'A Scotch Girl stands in terrible awe
of the Elders—poor little Susannas.—They will scarcely
laugh—they are greatly to be pitied and the Kirk is
greatly to be damn'd ... These Kirkmen have done
Scotland harm—they have banished puns and laughing
and Kissing ... I would sooner be a wild deer than a Girl
under the dominion of the Kirk.' It must have been a 'puir
auld mither' in her girlhood that Keats encountered. And
though the formidable Scotswoman still exists, the 'puir
auld mither' is distressingly prevalent in Scotland to this
day. The farm labourer's wife is too often regarded as a
mere convenience for her husband and her family; even
the farmer's wife is sometimes in the same position. As for
the middle classes in the towns, for all their fine clothes and
house-proud airs the women are still to a great extent the
unacknowledged servants of their men. I was told a story
by a friend of mine, a Scotsman who revisited Scotland a
year or two ago, which bears out what I say. He had called
on an acquaintance of his, a man in a very respectable
station of life, an 'educated' man, and they were sitting
together talking in the parlour. The fire was getting low.
There was a scuttle of coals beside it. The host sat up in
his chair and yelled reproachfully to his wife, who was
washing up dishes in the kitchen: 'Jean! Can you no' put
a bit of coal on the fire? We're getting cold!' Now, it is all
very well to rationalize this childish attitude by saying that
Scots inherit a deep sense of the difference between men's

work and women's work, and that it is not advisable for one sex to meddle with the work of the other. The Scot who expects women to wait on him hand and foot is the same man who does not voluntarily think of opening a shop-door for a woman laden with parcels. He is the same Lowland Scot who, a few generations ago, monopolized conversation when visitors came into the house, and if his wife put in a word turned on her with: 'Silence, woman!' He is the same Scotsman who thinks that 'intellectual argument' is the only kind of social intercourse, and who assumes tacitly that 'the women' are to be left out of it. He is, in short, the heir of Keats's Kirkmen who had no respect for women's work or influence or functions in the community. The 'puir auld mithers' of Scotland, in their enduring patience, have reared a brood of aggressive, egotistical children who despise them even while they are dependent on them.

The advent of Mrs Grundy, then, did not change the heart of Scotland. The 'formidable' Scotswomen remained individual personalities, adopting as much of Mrs Grundy as suited them; the 'puir auld mithers' may have accepted the taboos of Grundy, but they did not insist on her privileges, and their sons remain as graceless now as they were then. In England Mrs Grundy was the reflection, although the distorted reflection, of a genuine social order: in Scotland she was only the reflection of a reflection.

## SEVEN

## *Grundy* versus *MacGrundy*

To say that on her arrival Mrs Grundy did not change
the heart of Scotland, that she merely nibbled, so to
speak, round the edges of Scotswomen, is not a mere
assumption on my part. She could not obtain admission
to her central domain, the sex-monopoly of marriage, for
a very good reason: the Kirk, and later Mrs MacGrundy,
had already taken awful possession. Why, do you think,
had the Kirk Sessions been kept so busy in their time haling
'fornicators' to the pillory and wringing their hands over the
consequent prevalence of child-murder? It was not because
Scotswomen were naturally more lewd than Englishwomen;
it was because there still lingered all over the country the
memory of an older convention which looked on marriage
with a very different eye from Mrs Grundy, a convention
which would have shocked Mrs Grundy to the marrow. Yet
it was a convention which, for all I know, may once have
been general in Europe and was certainly of respectable
Norse antiquity. According to this tradition, young men
and women only married if a child was born to them, or
expected. Courting couples did not 'walk out' together:
they did their courting in bed. Young men climbed in at
the windows to visit their girls. No stigma was attached
to illegitimate children, no monopoly value was attached
to virginity: children, like other natural increase, were
welcomed as an accession to the potential wealth of the
family. An agricultural convention, obviously. It could
not arise in an industrial civilization with its individual
wage-earners; it could only arise where families lived from
generation to generation on a farm, where an extra mouth or
two made little difference and extra hands were welcomed.
It was the convention prevailing in the Norse sagas; it was

54

still perceptible in the Scottish ballads, where a heroine might admit her lover to her 'bower'; and Scotland at the beginning of the nineteenth century was not yet so remote from its farming origins as quite to forget the old tradition. That was what made the thunders of the Kirk so awful. The poor little Susannas pitied by Keats were probably scared stiff by the conflict between the tradition of country wooing and the tradition of the Kirk. In the towns the emphasis laid on married respectability was all the more severe from the knowledge that such 'on-goings' were prevalent in the country-side only a few miles away. Robert Burns represented the feeling of a large number of his inarticulate country-men in clashing with the Kirk over this question. The Kirk discredited the practice but could not stop it. A kind of dumb, sullen consciousness of the older tradition underlies the life of rural Scotland to this day, and may partly explain the anxiety to parade a sanctimonious respectability. In the Orkneys, which are Norse islands, the convention persists openly even in these post-war years, and Lowland ministers who take the field against it may find themselves silently boycotted.

The Kirk, then, and Mrs MacGrundy had already established a code of sexual propriety more severe and denunciatory than Mrs Grundy's. Mrs Grundy's suspicion that licentiousness lurked round every corner outside the home was not more strong than the fear of Scotswomen that the devil of sex might even assail them within the home. Yet marriage, after the older convention, remained a more or less private affair, celebrated at home rather than in church; sometimes, indeed, arranged with such laxness that 'Scottish marriage' achieved a certain notoriety, in spite of Mrs MacGrundy.

So it was not to be expected that a new code of sexual propriety should find any footing in the rural districts. Nor could Mrs Grundy directly affect the new proletariat in the towns. It is to the middle classes in the towns that we must look for evidence of her influence, especially the lower middle classes moving upwards with the increased advance of 'progress.' Whether they were of the 'formidable' type or the 'puir auld mither' type, the middle-class Scotswomen

received from the middle-class Mrs Grundy at least a
lesson in class-consciousness. She taught them how to
differentiate themselves in externals from their poorer
sisters. Mrs MacGrundy of hallowed tradition served as a
guarantee of general moral respectability, but even the very
poor or the very ignorant could keep the Sabbath devoutly;
to mark the difference between class and class Mrs Grundy
was needed. It was her task to comb the tangled individual
threads of Scottish society into smoothly classified strata.
And first she had to unsnarl the tangles.

The most obstinate tangle of all was the fact that Scotswomen, although they might be performing environmental
functions, always *thought* of themselves as individuals. This
idea, of course, leads to an inward conviction that one
woman is as good as another, whatever her income, and
nothing could be more calculated to upset Mrs Grundy. I do
not know what the new English 'gentry' thought of Lowland
Scottish maidservants, for instance, but I can imagine that
they found the girls disconcerting, with no proper sense
of their 'place' in society. This happens even yet. 'Not
exactly insolent, you know, but—well—very Scotch in her
attitude,' said an Englishwoman once to me, describing a
country housemaid. Quite so. The conditioning of Scots
commoners into upper middle class, lower middle class
and working class could not have proceeded at all smoothly.
Mrs Grundy never knew when some Scotswoman was not
going to jump all her guiding lines and stray into the
wrong division. In fact, to this day the guiding lines are
precarious. The only reliable standard for differentiating
one Scotswoman from another, outside the professional
classes, is a money standard. By this time, however, Mrs
Grundy has learned that, and the first thing she does on
meeting you in Scotland is to inquire, with great pertinacity,
what your income may be.

Involved in that tangle, and making it worse rather than
better, was the official view of women as being individuals,
although lesser individuals than men. The new School
Boards, for instance, would not listen to Mrs Grundy
when she suggested that, surely, girls and boys ought
to be segregated in separate schools. In England it was

as important for girls to be trained in manners as in mensuration; better for them to make a mistake in spelling than a mistake in the social code. But the Scottish School Boards, being composed of canny and logical men, saw no reason for reduplicating schools and were prepared to accord the same education to individuals of either sex. None of your environmental nonsense. The girls who moved in 'county' circles might become Anglified, but the girls in the middle-classes went to the same schools as the boys and studied the same subjects in the same classrooms. Girls attended not only the elementary but also the secondary schools side by side with their brothers. They learned Latin and Mathematics. They did not learn that it was necessary to wear gloves on the way to school. Even in their 'teens they did not learn to observe Mrs Grundy's social conventions. Did they address a schoolfellow as Mr Brown? Not they. Did Brown learn to greet a member of his class as Miss Smith? Not he. As Jean Smith and Willie Brown they hailed each other long after leaving school; the sense of individuality was too strong to permit of the social prefix. It was very distressing for Mrs Grundy. She persisted, of course, in her efforts to change the whole system, and by this time, now that she is threatened elsewhere, she is actually beginning to leave her imprint on the higher levels of Scottish education.

One thing Mrs Grundy was able to achieve: she could not prevent Scottish girls from receiving an 'unwomanly' education, but she could support Mrs MacGrundy in discouraging them from expecting to be treated as full individuals once they quitted school. Your Scottish girl who profited from her education and desired to enter a profession had it made quite clear to her both by Grundy and MacGrundy that she need not expect to rise to the top of it. Mrs MacGrundy argued that no woman could possibly become the 'Head' of anything. Women, these lesser individuals, needed a man to direct them. Mrs Grundy believed that women should defer to men as a way of 'managing' them better. So they combined to agree that in any professional organization, were there even a thousand women to one man, the representative of the male sex must be elevated to authority over the women. In this way the educated Scotswoman could be kept down to some extent, although not nearly so much as Mrs Grundy would have liked.

Another tangle that bothered Mrs Grundy was the difficulty of persuading shopkeepers that there was a social stigma attaching to 'trade.' Even as a lower middle-class figure in England Mrs Grundy in those days knew that she could not rise very far unless she washed her hands of 'trade.' Mr Punch might make jokes about the tailor who had been at Eton, but Mrs Grundy knew that no gentleman soiled his hands with trade of any kind, let alone shopkeeping. In Scotland, to her horror, she discovered that there were city shopkeepers—not even merchants—actual shopkeepers, who could call cousins with the best landed families, in this respect anticipating by many years the later course of social development in England. Mrs Grundy made a wry face, but she had to swallow the fact that *some* shopkeepers enjoyed a social prestige beyond her reach. She had to lower her standards of differentiation, that was all. Instead of deploring the fact that a man was a grocer, she set herself to inquire what class of grocerdom he belonged to; was he in the first social rank of his town, or the second, or the third? And then, her enthusiasm for establishing differences being aroused, she managed to achieve even finer shades of classification, down to the tenth, nay the twentieth rank of grocerdom. In every Scottish town to this day you will find her subtle lines of demarcation between one shopkeeper and another, lines of demarcation which are anything but obvious to the stranger. The 'best' shops are not necessarily the largest, the most enterprising, the handsomest or the most lavishly stocked. There is a conventional hierarchy established long ago by Mrs Grundy, and it remains unquestioned.

These little difficulties being tackled, Mrs Grundy found that her best way of entering the homes of middle-class Scotswomen was to make them house-proud. A house must always stand as a concrete symbol of the woman-as-environment, and although these Scotswomen persisted in thinking of themselves as individuals, Mrs Grundy had hopes of recalling them to a more feminine frame of mind by playing on the symbolism of the house. Here she could really differentiate between the richer Scotswoman and the poorer. The presence or absence of certain furnishings could mark the gradations of class very exactly. A beginning could be made, for instance, with the 'best' room, which Mrs MacGrundy had hitherto kept sacred for the Sabbath or great family occasions like funerals. The Scots had to be gently persuaded that it was no longer a sign of superiority merely to have an extra room unused by the family. It was not easy for Mrs Grundy to overcome the religious scruples of Mrs MacGrundy, who felt that to desecrate the 'best' room was rather like desecrating the Sabbath, but little by little she insinuated her new gospel.

Beside the family Bibles on the table of the best room—and looking not unlike them—appeared the family albums for visitors to inspect; aspidistras and other sober green plants supplied the lack of a conservatory; occasional tables multiplied, and so did the knick-knacks upon them. The middle-class Scotswoman discovered that she could look like a 'lady' as she sat in her parlour, which was almost a drawing-room. That was a great triumph for Mrs Grundy.

Once the 'best' room was conquered, the rest was easy. Now, the most extraordinary objects can be used to mark social superiority. I have seen egg-cups, for instance, used to that end in Durham mining-villages. You pass down the row of houses and in each house you see a pyramid of egg-cups built up in the kitchen window; the bigger the pyramid the higher the social level. In one fishing-village on the East Coast of Scotland the small mats bridging the front lobby used to serve the same purpose; the more mats you wiped your feet on, the greater the social prestige of the house. Where so many possibilities open out, it is not easy to decide which house-furnishings were suggested to Scotswomen by Mrs Grundy and which were the result of national or individual idiosyncrasy. Spare tea-sets displayed in china cupboards were useful, of course, since they suggested inheritance from well-dowered ancestresses; 'silver' tables obviously hinted at wealth; photographs mounted in plush frames spoke of comfortable family connections. I do not know if Mrs Grundy was responsible for these, but I do know that she brought in the piano. Elegant feminine accomplishments are inseparable from the idea of a 'lady,' and Mrs Grundy was trying very hard to become a 'lady' and to take middle-class Scotswomen with her. The piano was installed. Why should the playing of the piano be a peculiarly feminine accomplishment, you may ask? The answer must be found in Mrs Grundy's fine sense of sexual symbolism. When I was very young it was impressed on me that boys played the violin, while girls played the piano. It was 'unladylike' for a girl to play the violin. Therefore the piano. I do not know what would have been said had a girl wanted to play the flute; to imitate the flute by whistling was considered bad enough.

The occasional tables, the piano, the mantelpiece, presented so many surfaces for draping. Mrs Grundy did not like bare facts. Her fingers itched to dispose her twiddly bits of ornamental drapery upon everything that could carry them. She suggested covers and little mats and discreet fringes. Ornamental crochet and bead work and embroidery flourished. The æsthetic poets and artists were still improper, but Mrs Grundy thought that she could do better than they did and keep Art pure by domesticating it. The best room began to look 'æsthetic.' Poker-work, of all things, came into favour; perhaps its name suggested that it was a housewifely occupation. Sprays of flowers or leaves were painted across looking-glasses and cushion-covers. The middle-class Scotswoman began to rise in the social scale as soon as she took to 'fancy-work' instead of plain sewing and knitting. Her new æstheticism wreaked itself on the house. She could take a length of drain-pipe, for instance, cover it with putty and decorate it with shells, then paint or gild the whole to make it into a beautiful umbrella-stand. And she enjoyed doing these things. Her own self-respect was being fortified. Her womanhood was being embellished as well as the home.

In this way Mrs Grundy coaxed middle-class Scotswomen to come more into line with Englishwomen and, incidentally, to swell the increasing volume of trade. Yet these newly embellished homes retained a MacGrundy character. The habit of Sabbath Observance, pervasive as a fog, suggested to Scotswomen a kind of Sabbatarianism in domestic matters. One's best face was for Sunday wear, and the best room, the best china, the best linen, were all reserved for special Sabbath-like occasions. In consequence, the best room or 'parlour,' kept a sober solemnity behind all its twiddly ornaments. One never quite felt that it was for ordinary use. Like a genteel English accent and 'company' manners, it was something set apart from the daily domestic routine. In these lower middle-class flats, opening off common stone stairs, the living-room was usually kitchen and dining-room in one, and intimate friends of the family, 'dropping in' for a gossip, walked straight into it and gave the parlour a miss. There was as yet no starched maid to stop intruders at the door; like the ruling elders of old callers made inquisitorial visits without warning, and the housewife had to show a clean hearth and a clean conscience at all times. So far, Mrs Grundy, although 'ben the hoose,' was not very far ben in the lives of the women. As a social force Mrs Grundy, one might say, was no more than a dickey pretending to be a white shirt.

Mrs Grundy's was a social dickey, Mrs MacGrundy's a religious dickey, and, you might think, there was sufficient resemblance between their functions to make this analysis of their differences unnecessary. Yet the history of Mrs Grundy in Scotland is only made interesting by her ceaseless struggle with Mrs MacGrundy. I have said that the two figures coalesced, but the partnership was an uneasy one. Had there been no struggle, no Mrs MacGrundy, the rise of Mrs Grundy in Scotland would have been exactly parallel, although some ten years later in time, to the rise of Mrs Grundy in England. We should have found in Scotland about 1901 the counterpart of the London Mrs Grundy of 1891, with her butler and her social etiquette and her carriage. As it is, the crossways pull of Mrs MacGrundy actually slowed down the rate of time, so that in Scotland Mrs Grundy was nearer twenty than ten years behind England. And Mrs MacGrundy kept

Mrs Grundy in Scotland from rising to the highest social eminence. Middle-class people in Scotland were shy of taking to butlers, for instance. Mrs MacGrundy's bairns still think that there is something undignified in a man's doing household work.

The pervasive air of stiff solemnity, moreover, was not the only evidence of MacGrundy's power in Mrs Grundy's parlour. There was always a bookcase filled with solid and solemn volumes, including, usually, a set of *Chambers' Encyclopædia*, which was then going into edition after edition. The man of the house, you see, was asserting himself intellectually as well as commercially. He found a grand glow of satisfaction in arguing with his fellow Scots about theology and the Higher Criticism, about science and religion, and he needed encyclopædic facts, the more the better, to enable him to parade his superiority. This was the time when Christian debating societies flourished like Jonah's gourd; in the home, too, argumentative disputation provided social entertainment. But it was not Mrs Grundy who mistook contentious argument for the social graces, and she had little interest in book-learning. Mrs MacGrundy scored off her there.

Mrs MacGrundy also scored for a time in the matter of dress. Scotswomen dressed themselves richly but soberly, as if for the Sabbath. And all classes of urban Scotswomen, except the industrial proletariat, wore good clothes. One woman being as good as another, on Sundays one woman did her best to look as well as another. Mrs MacGrundy's bairns had to sustain the most searching scrutiny from all the rest of Mrs MacGrundy's bairns in the street, and nothing but the best was good enough. On the Sabbath day, to Mrs Grundy's distress, it was well-nigh impossible to distinguish between shop-girls and their master's wife. Even a maid-servant might look as well turned out as her mistress. Mrs Grundy had to tighten up her code to meet this menace: she made it imperative for mistresses to cut their servants in the street. One had to draw the line somewhere. After a while, by the help of English accents and more daring London fashions, Mrs Grundy succeeded in making the class difference more obvious, and wealthy middle-class ladies, no longer in danger of being confounded with their social inferiors, could afford to be gracious in public.

Yet, in thus encouraging expenditure on house furnishings and clothes, Mrs Grundy had the big battalions of commerce more surely behind her than Mrs MacGrundy, who had only saved the face of the business men and was bound to be discarded once they were successful enough to need her no longer. Mrs Grundy increased profits: Mrs MacGrundy demanded subscriptions. There could be no question which would ultimately prevail in a civilization based on salesmanship. In this connection it is worth noting that the ministers of the Disruption in 1843, who founded the Free Church, received overwhelming financial support from the business men, whereas today the Scottish churches seem to spend most of their time bewailing their financial straits. Apparently Big Business is deserting them. Mrs MacGrundy's power has dwindled, is dwindling, and, dare we say? seems fated to vanish. In that case the churches will gain immeasurably more than the cash they are losing.

I need not describe in great detail the gradual displacement of MacGrundy in the urban home. Step by step she was ousted from the parlour. On Sunday evenings the piano began to give out 'classical music' as well as hymns. The *British Weekly* made a tentative appearance as Sunday reading matter, proving to be the thin end of a wedge which broadened into frankly secular, though moral, weeklies like the *People's Friend*. The younger generation began to insist that a fire could surely be lit in the parlour on any evening in the week. And when the children grew up and took to sweethearting they were facetious at Mrs MacGrundy's expense; it gave them a thrill, supported by Mrs Grundy, to break the taboos of the parlour. They actually indulged in parlour tricks and sang sentimental songs straight from the London music-halls.

All this development postulated an expanding economy. A fire lit in the parlour every day costs more money. Attending a concert of classical music instead of a church soirée costs more money. An increasing family costs more money. Mrs Grundy was really a daughter of the horse-leech, crying:

Give! give! Her belief in woman-as-environment needed its complementary belief in man-as-provider. And the world in which she existed was a world that lived by money. The home was a circle into which money had to keep flowing. But the men of Scotland also believed in commercial progress, and, fortunately, the British Empire was still expanding. For a time Mrs Grundy went on prospering.

She could not bear, however, to see good money thrown into the streets or down the drain instead of flowing into the home. Nor could she bear to see her men finding emotional satisfaction outside the home. As we know, she suspected licentiousness everywhere. Yet the sense of power which men began to feel as they earned more and more money tempted them to indulge in private little flings behind Mrs Grundy's back. The sentimental music-hall songs from London were later to reflect the increasing urgency of Mrs Grundy's admonitions to the prodigal fathers. 'Won't you come home, Bill Bailey? Won't you come home?' was to ring out beside harrowing songs describing the awful fate of prostitutes, ditties such as this:

> You made me what I am to-day,
> I hope you're satisfied . . .

And yet, in old England, for all its Grundys, there was a cheerful acceptance of gambling and drinking and prostitution. 'The man who broke the bank at Monte Carlo' was celebrated together with the rowdy topers of the Old Bull and Bush; and if Mrs Grundy protested, she protested in vain. In Scotland she had Mrs MacGrundy whole-heartedly on her side when she denounced gambling and drinking. On these questions the attitudinarians of both creeds were united.

Once upon a time the most godly elder in Scotland could have drunk his whisky with a clear conscience, for something of the old religious idea that a meal is a sacrament still clung to the 'dram.' But, as we have seen, with the spread of the industrial slums violent drunkenness, offering an immediate release from sordid misery, became common. The liquor traffic in a commercial civilization naturally followed the lure of dividends, and public-houses multiplied so much that to this day in most Scottish towns there is a ridiculous excess of public-houses, as of churches, in proportion to the population. The aggregate of the nation's drink bill went on rising. This phenomenon was not purely Scottish; it appeared also in industrial England, and it was in England that the remedy for it was organized. A certain Dicky Turner of Preston had invented the term 'teetotalism,' and now teetotalism with all its Bands of Hope, Blue and Red Ribbons, Good Templars, Rechabites and other temperance associations broke like a flood over the Evangelical districts of England, the United States, and Scotland. Did Mrs MacGrundy attempt to attack the real causes of the 'drink evil'? No, that would have embarrassed her supporters, the business men. And it was not Mrs Grundy's province. Grundy and MacGrundy merely struck attitudes. Every child in every respectable Lowland Scottish family 'signed the pledge' before it was ten and stood up weekly to shout: 'Dare to be a Daniel.' All intoxicating liquor was called 'strong drink,' and that was a term invested with fearful and sinister implications. One could not say 'strong drink' without lowering one's voice, it was so awful. It is unreasonable, of course, to expect that Mrs MacGrundy would show any sense of discrimination. The Kirk Sessions from whom she took her tone had punished with equal gravity sins the most heinous and offences the most trivial, and she was not likely to allow any distinctions between the sipping of brandy after a faint or the drinking of claret with a meal and the swilling of fiery alcohol in a public-house. Mrs Grundy, too, fearing licentiousness, backed up MacGrundy in forbidding any respectable Scotswoman to enter a public-house. For the would-be respectable the drinking of any alcohol, beer or wine or spirits, had to become a furtive indulgence, while the Scottish public-houses, branded as disreputable, remained drinking-dens of incredible sordidness.

Still, Grundy and MacGrundy were both satisfied. Respectable women could save their faces by purchasing their liquor from a licensed grocer. Respectable men could slip furtively round a corner in the street or in the house if they wanted a drink. To this very day you will not find Mrs

MacGrundy's bairns offering or accepting a drink without apologetic facetiousness. Furtive drinking and the Scottish public-house; the attention of young children forcibly directed towards mysteriously thrilling temptations: these were the direct results of all the untempered 'temperance' zeal. It had little effect upon the dividends of the liquor traffic.

Gambling, that other concomitant of a monetary civilization, also evoked edifying attitudes from both Grundy and MacGrundy. Many years ago a contemporary of my mother's was speaking of an old woman who had just died—an old woman who was scarcely a commendable character—and, being humanly anxious to praise the dead, she said in my hearing: 'Well, I must say this for So-and-so, she would not only rise and leave the room if folk were playing cards, she wadna even bide in the same room wi' folk that were playing *dominoes*.' Meanwhile the merchants of progress were piling up fortunes by gambling on the Empire's credit and floating dishonest companies on the stock markets. Mrs Grundy merely envied them their wealth. Mrs MacGrundy waited on them for subscriptions. Probably both ladies had savings invested in the 'Liberator Building Society,' and not until that failed with a resounding crash did they raise any outcry against fraudulent finance. So much for their moral attitudes.

Yet as Mrs Grundy rose in the social scale she left MacGrundy behind her. Cheaper newspapers were bringing all the latest London scandals to the family table—it now took only eight hours to run a train from London to Edinburgh—and Mrs Grundy could not fail to note that the Smart Set in London were patronizing gambling establishments and freely indulging in 'strong drink.' After all, what exasperated her most was the idea of the men going naughtily off by themselves to find amusement. So she relaxed sufficiently to countenance mixed 'whist drives,' and after a little sulking Mrs MacGrundy tentatively permitted raffles at church bazaars. This was taking place in the Lowland districts of Scotland. What was happening meanwhile to the Highlands?

## EIGHT

# MacGrundy in the Highlands

Something had happened to discredit Highland ways in the eyes of Lowland Scots, for the wearing of the plaid shawl, that pleasant garment, was by common consent relegated to the women of the industrial proletariat, who became known in Glasgow as 'shawlies.' Highland reels seem to have shared in the discredit; in 1875, at a tenants' ball in Inveraray, Her Majesty Queen Victoria noted with shocked surprise in her Journal that the band could not play reels . . . and yet came from *Glasgow*! It could not have been Mrs Grundy who objected to Highland culture: she would not have ventured to disagree with her august sovereign, whose fondness for Highland music and Highland tartans was well known. Indeed, Mrs Grundy followed Queen Victoria's lead, and still goes all girlish and Balmoral about the Highlands. No, it was Mrs MacGrundy from the Lowlands who disapproved of Highland ways. Mr James Loch, in justifying the evictions, had already put Mrs MacGrundy's point of view when he averred that the Highlanders were only being rescued from a 'state of degradation.' They were, he said, 'accustomed to a life of irregular exertion with intervals of sloth.' Mrs MacGrundy distrusted irregularity of any kind, and she knew well, too, that 'intervals of sloth' meant sin. The Devil finds some mischief still for idle hands to do. Mrs MacGrundy set herself earnestly to wean the Highlanders from their wicked ways, and succeeded, beyond all expectation, in smashing up the fabric of an ancient and gracious culture.

There is, as it happens, an excellent record of Mrs MacGrundy's achievements in the Highlands and Islands, more eloquent than any words of mine could be. It is contained in the Introduction to Dr Alexander Carmichael's

*Carmina Gadelica,* first published in 1900. The old hymns
and incantations translated in the book were collected,
the author says, over a period of forty-four years. He
wrote the Introduction in 1899, so that the experiences
related in it pretty well cover the period of time we are
now considering. It is to be noted that Dr Carmichael's
opinion of the Highlanders does not coincide with Mr James
Loch's. 'The people of the Outer Isles,' he says, 'like the
people of the Highlands and Islands generally, are simple
and law-abiding, common crime being rare and serious
crime unknown among them. They are good to the poor,
kind to the stranger, and courteous to all. During all the
years that I lived and travelled among them, night and
day, I never met with incivility, never with rudeness,
never with vulgarity, never with aught but courtesy. I
never entered a house without the inmates offering me
food or apologizing for their want of it. I never was
asked for charity in the West, a striking contrast to my
experience in England . . .' Among these people, in the
early 'sixties, Dr Carmichael found a still extant oral
tradition of poems and hymns in Gaelic which were
'generally intoned in a low recitative manner, rising and
falling in slow modulated cadences . . .' He says that
'the music of the hymns had a distinct individuality, in
some respects resembling and in many respects differing
from the old Gregorian chants of the Church. I greatly
regret that I was not able to record this peculiar and
beautiful music, probably the music of the old Celtic
Church. Perhaps no people had a fuller ritual of song
and story, of secular rite and religious ceremony, than the
Highlanders. Mirth and music, song and dance, tale and
poem, pervaded their lives, as electricity pervades the air.
Religion, pagan or Christian, or both combined, permeated
everything—blending and shading into one another like the
iridescent colours of the rainbow.' An inherited culture, in
which Celtic Christianity was blended harmoniously with
more ancient traditions, producing music and poetry and
sculpture—that was what absorbed the Highlanders in their
'intervals of sloth.' Now we shall see what Mrs MacGrundy
did to it.

Between 1876 and 1880 Dr Carmichael had occasion to revisit Lewis. The date is fixed by the fact that he was collecting material for an article in the third volume of *Celtic Scotland*, then being prepared by Dr Forbes Skene; the first volume had appeared in 1876 and the third volume came out in 1880. He went into a house near Ness, where he found the woman of the house at home and her three daughters. They dried his wet stockings, offered him a new pair of the house-man's, and set out a meal for him of 'fried herrings and boiled turbot fresh from the sea, and eggs fresh from the yard. There were fresh butter and salt butter, wheaten scones, barley bannocks, and oat cakes, with excellent tea, and cream.' With an eye on the three comely maidens he asked about their marriage customs, saying: 'I suppose there is much fun and rejoicing at your marriages—music, dancing, singing and merrymaking of all kinds?' I shall not transcribe the whole of the answer he got from the mother, but the matter is so important that I do not apologize for a fairly lengthy excerpt: 'May the Possessor keep you! I see that you are a stranger in Lewis, or you would not ask such a question . . . It is long since we abandoned these foolish ways in Ness, and, indeed, throughout Lewis. In my young days there was hardly a house in Ness in which there was not one or two or three who could play the pipe, or the fiddle, or the trump. And I have heard it said that there were men, and women too, who could play things they called harps and lyres, and bellow-pipes, but I do not know what these things were . . . A blessed change came over the place and the people . . . and the good men and the good ministers who arose did away with the songs and the stories, the music and the dancing, the sports and the games, that were perverting the minds and ruining the souls of the people, leading them to folly and stumbling . . . Oh, the good ministers and the good elders preached against them and went among the people, and besought them to forsake their follies and to return to wisdom. They made the people break and burn their pipes and fiddles. If there was a foolish man here and there who demurred, the good ministers and the good elders themselves broke and burnt their instruments, saying:

> "Better is the small fire that warms on the little
>      day of peace,
> "Than the big fire that burns on the great day of
>      wrath."

'The people have forsaken their follies and their Sabbath-breaking, and there is no pipe, no fiddle here now.' She said all this, Dr Carmichael records, 'in evident satisfaction.' He went on to ask: 'But what have you at your weddings? How do you pass the time?' 'Oh! the carles are on one side of the house talking of their crops and their nowt, and mayhap of the days when they were young and when things were different. And the young men are on the other side of the house talking about boats, and sailing, and militia, and naval reserve . . .'

'And where are the girls?' asked Dr Carmichael, very naturally. 'What are they doing?' 'Oh, they, silly things! are in the back-house [culaist], perhaps trying to croon over some foolish song under their breath . . .' 'But why are the girls in the "culaist"? What do they fear?' 'May the Good Being keep you, good man! They are in the "culaist" for concealment—and the fear of their life and of their death upon them, that they may be heard or seen should the good elder happen to be passing the way.' 'And should he, what then?' 'Oh, the elder will tell the minister, and the good minister will scold them from the pulpit, mentioning the girls by name. But the girls have a blanket on the door and another blanket on the window to deafen the sound and obscure the light.' The girls, we learn in the next paragraph, would be only too glad to have the young men in the 'culaist' with them, for the singing of old songs and the dancing of old dances. But that would make exposure all the more certain, and they would be publicly rebuked. Mrs MacGrundy denounced, 'with no uncertain voice,' the social values of Gaelic culture.

She was helped there by the schoolmasters as well as by the ministers. Dr Carmichael quotes the evidence of 'a young lady' who was not a Gaelic speaker: he does not say whether she was a Lowland Scot or an Englishwoman. This is her story: 'When we came to Islay I was sent to the parish school to obtain a proper grounding in arithmetic. I was charmed with the schoolgirls and their Gaelic songs. But the schoolmaster—an alien like myself—denounced Gaelic speech and Gaelic songs. On getting out of school one evening the girls resumed a song they had been singing the previous evening. I joined willingly, if timidly, my knowledge of Gaelic being small. The schoolmaster heard us, however, and called us back. He punished us till the blood trickled from our fingers, although we were big girls, with the dawn of womanhood upon us. The thought of that scene thrills me with indignation.' Teachers told their pupils that the old men of the community who persisted in telling their 'lying stories' in Gaelic ought to be put on the stool of repentance. The administration of vengeful punishment was then—and still is—an integral element in the scheme of Scottish education, which translated into practice the ideology of the Kirk. Here in the Highlands we can see very clearly how the process worked. No environmental nonsense; no taking one's eyes off the straight and narrow ladder of 'education'; no dalliance with such heathen frivolities as poetry and music—let alone in a 'heathen' language like Gaelic. It is heart-breaking to think of the effect Mrs MacGrundy's preceptors had on an emotional, artistic people such as the Highlanders.

Dr Carmichael gives another example. There was a famous violin player in the island of Eigg. He had a violin which had been made by a pupil of Stradivarius and was famed for its tone. A preacher denounced him, saying: 'Thou art down there behind the door, thou miserable man with thy grey hair, playing thine old fiddle, with the cold hand without and the devil's fire within.' His family pressed the man to save his soul by burning the fiddle. A pedlar came round and offered ten shillings for it, and, in desperation, the old man sold it rather than see it destroyed. He went away weeping for his violin, and crying out: 'It was not at all the thing that was got for it that grieved my heart so sorely, but the parting with it! the parting with it! and that I myself gave the best cow in my father's fold for it when I was young.'

That was what Mrs MacGrundy, the great, grey fiddle-breaker, was doing in the Highlands. The Highland parishes were a grand missionary field for her. Converts are notoriously intemperate and undiscriminating in their zeal, and it is not surprising that the most rigid MacGrundyites are to be found to-day in the Highland parishes. How could people have any spring left in them after the evictions which broke their hearts, and Mrs MacGrundy, who broke their spirits?

## NINE

## *Interlude on Strychnine*

One cannot help thinking that this intemperate zeal of the convert characterized Mrs MacGrundy from the very beginning, even in the Lowlands. The Kirk which produced her had the zealot's temper, that is to say, the temper of the convert. Was it not the zealots of the seventeenth-century Scottish Kirk who had to be adjured, by a fellow-Puritan from England, to remember in God's Name that it was possible they might be mistaken? The godly ministers and elders of the Lewis, in 1880, were only showing the same temper which had characterized the earlier establishment of Presbyterianism in the Lowlands. The advance of MacGrundy in the Lewis must have been in spirit a miniature reproduction of what had already taken place, more than three hundred years earlier, in the Lowlands. We cannot but assume that the Lowland Scots must have possessed at one time a blend of social and religious culture similar to what they were now denouncing so fiercely in the Highlands, and that this savage repression of 'pagan' fiddling, singing, dancing, and story-telling had been directed first against themselves. There is really no other explanation for the intolerance, the savagery of their methods, the narrow cocksureness of their temper. They were foxes who had first lost their own tails before urging other foxes to be docked. They could never have identified social respectability with religion had they not inherited from some source or other a tradition which told them that every action of daily life had a religious significance, that a God or gods inspired every social custom; in short, they must have inherited a ritual culture, which fell into disrepute and was branded as 'superstition.' What that culture might have been we can only guess from the vestiges of it which appear in tales of evil spirits, covens of witches, fairy wells, bushes and trees; it was not originally a Christian culture, and it must have haunted the minds of the Scots right up to the Reformation. I cannot think of another explanation for the savage temper of the Scottish Reformation. The narrow fervour of the early Scottish Kirk could only have arisen in the denial of something that needed passionate repudiation, not simple repudiation. It was not a peaceful change: it looked rather like a violent convulsion.

Mrs MacGrundy's creed, then, was created by men who did not dare to trust themselves or human nature, and had, in consequence, a lively fear of the Devil. All the social elements of culture fell under their ban, and the individual Scot was stripped of everything save his will-power, his logic, and his passionate belief in a vengeful God. With these he constructed a narrow Jacob's ladder which was supposed to bring him to the skies. From rung to rung of that ladder he was flogged upwards by his own determination, by the admonitions of the Kirk, by the stout arms of his schoolmasters. And when the passion ebbed, the habit of determination, the spirit of competition, kept him still climbing on the same narrow ladder, from fact to fact, from one tangible reward to another. Work and pray, ignore frivolities, and you shall climb high, said Mrs MacGrundy.

We can now see Mrs MacGrundy in her true perspective. She represented the rigid hardening of a violent revulsion from earlier cultural values. That explains the odd appearance of her activities in the Highlands today, and also the curious self-distrust of the Scots in general. Mrs MacGrundy, in a sense, was born of the Reformation; in a sense she was carrying out an historical process. But the Reformation was designed not only to detach the individual from his stand-pat social *milieu*: it was designed to encourage individual enterprise in every direction, and especially independent thinking. I contend that Mrs MacGrundy discouraged independent thinking. You dared not look away from her ladder, you dared not pause to think about anything but the next rung. She would have hounded James Watt to church had she known that

he was 'vaguing' on the Sabbath with thoughts of his
steam-engine in his head. She discouraged independent
creative effort of any kind. A Scot who wanted to think
new thoughts had to do it behind Mrs MacGrundy's back.
A Scot who wanted to write poems or make plays or create
music had first to overcome her resistance, for these were
cultural activities that smelt of the Devil. She understood
monetary arguments, the tangible rewards of virtue, and she
did not oppose activities that proved themselves 'profitable'
in a monetary sense: but merely creative activity which
might or might not prove 'profitable' found no approval
in her eyes. Mrs MacGrundy's bairns were not encouraged
to create anything but solid economic propositions. How
deeply she thwarted them becomes strikingly apparent
when we reflect that even in theology, which might be
considered her peculiar province, Scotland contributed
nothing new during all the eighteenth and nineteenth
centuries, until at last one theological scholar—William
Robertson Smith—showed a turn for independent thinking
which cost him his professorial chair. Mrs MacGrundy was
outraged because he exercised his intelligence.

As for literature and the fine arts, the practice of these in
Scotland suffered severely from Mrs MacGrundy's conviction that they were of the devil. Art on the defensive cannot
rise beyond the facetious or the priggishly sentimental. The
vigorous Rabelaisian life of the countryside kept its own
secret vernacular ballads, but it had to creep into print with
deprecating, sickly smiles because of Mrs MacGrundy. I
suppose we should be thankful to the writers of the Kailyaird
School for having got it into print at all, and for persuading
MacGrundy that fiction and drama need not be immoral.
The worst that can be said of Mrs MacGrundy, in short,
is that she discouraged the free play of the mind, the
free play of the emotions, from which all living creative
achievement springs. How Martin Luther would have
loathed her! The best that can be said of her is that
she was a good enough mother to third-rate talents: her
bairns were industrious attitudinarians, painstaking, sober
and determined to 'get on.'

The Reformation was a kind of spiritual strychnine of

which Scotland took an overdose. Instead of acting as a tonic on the individual Scot, it cramped him in a tetanic rigor. And that cramped stiffness was perpetuated in the tradition which I have called Mrs MacGrundy. The only thing to do with a mistake of that magnitude, I should think, is to acknowledge it handsomely and then forget it.

## TEN

# Grundy versus
## the Old Lady of Threadneedle Street

While Mrs MacGrundy was smashing her way through the Highlands, the new individualism was dealing shrewd blows at Mrs Grundy in England. Woman-as-environment was breaking up. Bachelor girls, *divorcées*, business women and suffragettes were all ready to take the stage. There was an evident reaction from the dominance of the Family. In America, where centrifugal forces were less restricted in their advance, divorce was becoming 'rampant' by 1897. In that year Gertrude Atherton issued a book called *Divorce in the United States*, in which she averred that the typical woman of the United States was a 'mental anarchist.' The word 'anarchist' was frightening public opinion rather gruesomely in the 'nineties; you can find a lot of references to dynamiters in the stories of that period. Anarchy was in the air.

By this time, the intellectuals of Scotland were thinking of themselves as British. The problem of social anarchy exercised them too, although Scotland was by no means anarchic. A pessimistic gentleman, writing in the *Scottish Review* for 1898, deplored the fact that British women were nearly as bad as Americans. 'Unhappily,' he says, 'our American sisters are not alone in their electrical and anarchistic spirit . . . Closely allied to this modern loosening of the sanctity of marriage is the steadily growing audacity of the school which openly disseminates its pestilential doctrines of "the free union."' He had caught up with Mrs Grundy's fears of the 'eighties, you see, about twenty years later. Fiction had also caught up on her: the Woman Who Did was becoming familiar. 'The Puritan tradition of family life is dead,' said the Bishop of Lichfield. In spite of the Imperial pomps and vanities of the Diamond Jubilee, various good people were feeling decidedly uneasy about the nation. Ibsen's *Doll's House* appeared now as a portent: Mrs Grundy's daughters had grown up into Ibsen characters, and doors were being freely slammed upon husbands. The New Woman had stalked into the open, and she was horrifying respectable people. Men lamented that she had killed their deference and respect for the sex. She was accused of being brusque, shrill-voiced, hard, self-asserting and aggressive. Things were undeniably changing. Where, oh where, were the kind slipper-warmers of yesteryear?

Apparently there were strains and tensions in the national life for which slipper-warming was no longer an adequate remedy. The uneasiness of the individual now demanded a wider and more stable environment, a more objective environment, than the home. And women were insisting, too, on being treated as individuals, with a right to earn and spend money for their own ends. Even girls were playing 'athletic' games and demanding latchkeys and professional careers. All that Mrs Grundy had feared and endeavoured to prevent was coming true. Her chickens were out of the hen-coop, pecking up grain in what they hoped was a kindly as well as an adventurous world. To the older generation it looked like social anarchy. They saw only that girls and women had become 'mannish.' 'Do we desire a nation of female grenadiers?' inquired our peevish Scot in his pessimistic article. He was overstating his case, for the modern girls showed as yet no desire to march in step, not even as grenadiers.

Of course Mrs Grundy was distressed. She redoubled her efforts to keep young women 'feminine' and to ensure that the sex-monopoly of marriage remained intact. The New Women, with their suggestion of 'free love,' were unfair competitors, and Mrs Grundy kept a jealous eye on them. With all these potential blacklegs in the offing, the home had to be made more attractive than ever. Money had to be spent lavishly on home entertaining. Mrs Grundy became a 'hostess' and trained her 'respectable' daughters to be arch and coy with eligible young men, who were flattered and deferred to and run after. I believe that in her desperation Mrs Grundy would have permitted young men to put their feet on the drawing-room mantelpiece, so long as they came into the drawing-room. The ban on smoking in the drawing-room had to be lifted. Mrs Grundy, at all costs, had to attach the young people to her.

And yet it was not enough. The hands of the clock refused to be put back. The detachment of the individual had to take its course. The children of the new generation were delivering themselves into the new world without Mrs Grundy's help. As a chaperone she was becoming superfluous. What was she to do?

We had better take a look at this new world and see why there was so much turmoil and uneasiness and individual enterprise in it. To begin with, it appeared prosperous, even wealthy. In 1898 shipbuilding and iron and steel were all making record outputs. The Navy had been increased, and one of the most impressive spectacles of the Diamond Jubilee was the Naval Review at Spithead. The Colonies had also been impressively brought into the foreground: we can infer that much money was being invested in them. Betting was on the increase; it had begun to spread from horse-racing to football, and professional bookmakers were raking in money from the working classes. There had been a rush for the new Klondyke gold-fields in 1897. There was a cricketing craze and a bicycling craze, and a crazy floating of companies to exploit the latter. Company-promoting had never been so profitable. Add it all up—the Navy, the Colonies, the Jubilee, Our Noble Selves and our new open-air amusements and our high finance in the City—why, it looked like El Dorado! Why should there be uneasiness? The world was apparently Britain's oyster.

And yet there was uneasiness. Millionaires were multiplying, but so was urban unemployment. The credit market, people thought, depended too much on foreign financial houses. There was distress in various rural areas. Sweating and slums were undeniably prevalent. Money-worship was in the ascendant, but vast fortunes could be lost as quickly as they were made—look at Mr Hooley, who suddenly went bankrupt after a spectacular rise in the cycle boom and brought thousands down with him. Where was all the money coming from? And where did it vanish to? Nobody seemed to know. And the National Debt was increasing all the time. It was a gambling world, a world that went up like a rocket and might, one felt, come down like the stick. The private stockholder was uneasily aware that his private conscience had no control over the economic 'laws' that brought him his income; he did not know how his companies were operated or why his shares went up and down. The guinea-pig director did not know either. Expenditure mounted on all sides, and everybody was a little afraid of it. London, the financial centre of the Empire, was gay, hectic, bustling and indeterminate. The individuals composing the modern world were feeling blindly for a stable environment to which they might attach themselves in safety again. Mrs Grundy was not capable of providing that environment. The country did not know where to find one. And that was why it was uneasy.

Yet in that indeterminate fluorescence new environments for the individual, more abstract environments, were dimly perceptible. Financial interests were amalgamating into rings and trusts. The State was emerging as a social, almost a Socialist agency. In 1897 Parliament passed a Workmen's Compensation Act which for the first time recognized that the welfare of employees should be a direct charge on industry. There was a new cult of public health, and a political campaign against slums and food adulteration and sweating, on the score of national efficiency. Business firms were studying comparative statistics and, on the score of efficiency, assuming a certain social responsibility for their workers. Rudyard Kipling was making the middle classes conscious of the Empire, and the Jubilee had made them still more conscious of the overseas dominions. Finance, industry, business, State, Empire—these vast abstractions were taking definite shape. The State and the Empire seemed the most stable among them. Whatever happened to Mr Hooley, the British Empire would surely go on.

Mrs Grundy, no longer capable of being an environment for the individual and bewildered by all the social anarchy at home, found comfort in contemplating the Empire. She had never believed that women should meddle with politics or business, but surely she could find a function for herself in keeping the Empire together? After all, it was only a wider extension of Home. The Colonials were her 'sons across the seas.' Mrs Grundy's sentimental feelings overflowed, and she bedizened herself with Imperial frippery and bought Mr Kipling's works.

Now she could attach the young people. Now she could offer them patriotic adventure. Now they could leave the home and yet remain home-birds, even at the ends of the earth. At this point, with the might and majesty of the British Empire behind her, I think we might raise Mrs Grundy in the social scale and call her Lady Grundy. Lady Grundy with a Union Jack instead of a gamp. I told you, did I not, that she was a semi-immortal? That was, however, the peak of her achievement. She posed upon it for a good many years, but by this time she is slipping down the slope again.

She was not, of course, Imperial: she was merely sentimental about the Empire. She understood so little of what was happening in the Colonies that the Boer War took her completely by surprise. She has had many shocks since then, poor lady. The Boer War, although it was a 'little' war, shook her badly; she even abandoned her own 'womanly' traditions and scurried out into the street to buy newspapers on the kerb like any man. When Mafeking was relieved her children acclaimed the Empire in a way that terrified her nearly out of her wits. Even Mr Kipling, whom she admired, had rebuked her in a poem called 'Recessional.' She was forced to give up being shocked by infringements of her domestic code at home. True, she made up for it by new activities abroad: she exhorted Britons not only to keep up appearances before their neighbours and their servants, but also before 'the natives.' Yet in extending her mirror over the Empire she made it more vulnerable. Cracks began to appear in it, and the picture it showed was no longer a unity. Her reflection changed disconcertingly from one part of the Empire to another. In India she might still be Lady Grundy, the *mem-sahib*, but in Australia she was stripped of her title, even of her name, and emerged as

Mrs Wowser. Like Rabesqurat, the Mistress of Illusions, she began to multiply her images, in a desperation that went on increasing. For, you see, the Dominions were doing what her own children at home had done: they were detaching themselves as individuals. The Old Lady of Threadneedle Street was proving herself incomparably stronger, both at home and abroad, than Lady Grundy. The Great War cracked the Grundy mirror still more, leaving only one recognizable piece, and even that was taken over by the State and rechristened Dora. Finance and the State were sharing between them all the environmental functions she had hoped to retain. If you want to find Lady Grundy today, you will discover her cowering behind the Throne, hoping against hope to share in the reflected glory of that final family institution.

Where did she stand in Scotland during all this time? It is to be noted that Lady Grundy established England, not Scotland, as the home-centre of the Empire. Yet if England needed to reinforce its uneasiness by a sentimental pride in the Empire, did not Scotland have the same need? Well, I do not think that Scotland was feeling the same uneasiness. Thanks to Mrs MacGrundy, Scotland was busy putting its shoulder to the wheel and had no time to look up and see where the vehicle was going or who was driving it. As long as his own business was doing well the average Scot did not worry about the country as a whole. He still believed that only individual hard work was needed to keep everything going. None of your environmental nonsense in Scotland.

If the standard of wealth had risen in England, it had risen more spectacularly in Scotland, compared with the past. The country which had been poverty-stricken for centuries was now relatively as wealthy as England. If there was distress in rural areas, among the crofters, why, individual effort could tackle it. 'Home' industries were fostered by meekly unofficial committees of ladies; markets were found in London for Harris tweeds. As for the Lowlands, farming had advanced so much that the great farms of the Lothians had the reputation of being the best in Britain. Only a little determination, a little more hard work, Scotsmen felt, and any temporary difficulties were bound to disappear. To the business men of Scotland, the Empire, like Scotland, was only a source of wealth to be exploited. The younger generation, following the spirit of their age, detached themselves more or less painlessly from Mrs MacGrundy and went down to London or to the ends of the earth to make their careers. In England or the Colonies they might adapt themselves to an Imperially sentimental Lady Grundy, but at home in Scotland Lady Grundy never really established her title.

In Scotland she remained a commoner. Her partnership with Mrs MacGrundy kept her down. Mrs MacGrundy might be many things, but she was not a social snob, and she kept Mrs Grundy's snobbery from becoming more than a snobbery of wealth, a snobbery of 'success.' Mrs Grundy did manage to get a footing as a 'lady,' but the Scots ideal of a lady, being a blend of Grundy and MacGrundy, was frequently disconcerted by the behaviour of 'real' ladies from England. And Mrs MacGrundy, that stereotyped figure, had stereotyped Mrs Grundy too. It cannot be said that Mrs Grundy has shown any signs of change or development in Scotland since the late 'nineties; she has merely disintegrated. She did not rise so high as Lady Grundy, she did not begin to disintegrate so soon, but she is now disintegrating more rapidly.

I said that the Old Lady of Threadneedle Street proved herself stronger than Lady Grundy. She has also proved herself stronger than Mrs Grundy in Scotland. To personify an abstraction is to take away some of its terrors, and the Old Lady is a personification which tends to reassure the average citizen that a monetary system need not be inhuman. Behind this reassuring mask, however, the monetary system of our time has stretched its tentacles into every individual life. We are now, in Britain or in the Empire, an aggregation of squirming individuals dangling helplessly from the great central mass of an impersonal monetary system. We can live only if we are able to sell something for which the Old Lady, or one of her international sisters, will give us money. And the Old Lady is not interested in us or our human values: she is interested only in money. Yet, if we have money, we need have no inferiority complexes at all. Before this fact Mrs Grundy's values, based on social inferiority, are vanishing like smoke. She is becoming colourless and bodiless.

How can money values, you may ask, destroy Mrs Grundy? Well, since the Great War, salesmanship has been growing more desperate. The whole fabric of our civilization apparently depends on our buying not only what we need, but what we do not know that we need. And as we can be trusted to buy what we need, provided we have the money, finance has increasingly exerted itself to exploit our inferiority complexes, to persuade us that we lack more, much more, and can be supplied with more, than we should ever have imagined. Advertisement suggests to us that we are unfit to move in society unless we buy so-and-so, that we are personally unhealthy, disagreeable, dirty, inefficient and out of date unless we buy so-and-so. Do people shrink from you—are you sure you haven't halitosis? Do visitors refuse to eat what you offer them—are you sure your plates have been properly cleaned by the proper soap-powder? Are you a failure in your office or your firm—how do you know you are not suffering from night starvation? Despised and rejected at social functions, can you possibly have what is delicately referred to as B.O.? Advertisement, however, trying to look like the representative of a properly functioning environment, not only discourages but encourages you. There is a remedy for your social leprosy, for your inefficiency, for all your drawbacks: buy so-and-so, and you will be all right. Popularity, beauty, fitness, success, all are yours if you only open your purse. The sole contribution you require to make to the social and communal life of your day is the contribution of money.

Well, that means, surely, that one need no longer bother about what Mrs Grundy will say if only one has money. Mrs Grundy has no longer any terrors for us if we can open our purses. There is no need to remain in ignorance of any social code: countless magazines provide us with the necessary instruction. Even if you know that you have no money in your purse, you are crushed by your penniless state, not by a sense of social inferiority. At any moment a scrap of paper may raise you to the level of your class, or beyond it. All you have to do is to get money.

The Old Lady of Threadneedle Street, you see, after polishing Mrs Grundy carefully for a while, has now smashed her up and taken over her functions. Behind its social veneer ours is a monetary consciousness. Yet the lower classes, who have less money to spend, still pay lip-service to Mrs Grundy. That is evident also in these popular mirrors, the magazines. The cheaper the magazine, the more modest and Grundyish the heroines are. And as Scotland, despite Mrs MacGrundy's creed of hard work, is now incomparably poorer than England, the Scottish cheap magazines are more Grundyish than those in England. But it is only a matter of time: these vestiges of Grundy will disappear too. And when we are all dancing to the purse-strings, and the purse-strings are drawn tight, what will our new code be?

I have a real fear that Mrs MacGrundy will stage a come-back. After all, she was born in poverty, and we look like returning to poverty. And if this book will help in preventing Mrs MacGrundy from dominating the scene, if it will help Scotland to make a new consciousness for itself, I shall not have written in vain. What we need, perhaps, is to go back to first human principles. Scotland has always pretended to do that; it has insisted even on reducing the obvious to first principles; but the first principles have usually stopped short at Mrs MacGrundy. I want to get behind Mrs MacGrundy. I want to find out what constitutes a proper environment for the modern individual. I do not desire to fit into, or to look as if I were fitting into, Mrs MacGrundy's tradition. If Scotland were a growing bush, Mrs MacGrundy's bairns would be recognizable as stick insects pretending to be real twigs. A stick insect, clinging for dear life to the bush, its hindquarters rigidly governed and protruding at the correct angle, must cherish in its timid brain an implacable image of rectitude which curiously resembles Mrs MacGrundy. I should myself prefer to be a twig with a growing point, changing with the changing seasons of the world.

But, you will say, why should we have to return to poverty again? Well, there are two million unemployed in

Britain, and Scotland has a startling percentage of these. I can only point to the fact, and ask again: Must we keep Mrs MacGrundy? I can only repeat that Mrs MacGrundy discourages intelligence and freedom, and that we are likely to need all our intelligence, all our passion, all our mother-wit, if we are to adjust ourselves as individual Scots to the right kind of new environment. We need, first and foremost, a revaluation of the function of women in the world: a new understanding of the proper function of an environment and its relation to the individuals it fosters. The one-sidedness of the Scottish Reformation, with its insistence on the claims of the individual, is by this time an anachronism. So is Mrs MacGrundy. She is a feminine symbol which has no real femininity in it.

As for Mrs Grundy, or Lady Grundy, her femininity is that of the 'gold-digger'—an ignorant and partial femininity, based on one-sided assumption, just as surely as Mrs MacGrundy's fake femininity. She is a more accommodating figure, however. She can take on a new face and adapt herself to any new environment. It is Mrs MacGrundy who is to be dreaded, because she may persuade people that she is the national spirit of Scotland.

# WOMEN: AN INQUIRY

TO VIOLET SCHIFF

'Methinks, brother,' replied my father,
'you might, at least, know so much as
the right end of a woman from the wrong.'
*The Life and Opinions of Tristram Shandy*

# Introductory

Men and women are latecomers to this planet, but they have existed for a very long time, judged by human standards. One might reasonably expect the difference between them, if it is an essential difference, to be now capable of formulation. An essential difference would be a difference distinctively human, that is, spiritual as well as physical, and at the same time distinctively sexual.

External differences, such as the presence or absence of beards and other secondary sexual characteristics, do not satisfy the first part of this definition, and are to be disregarded. Many so-called differences in social behaviour are also not essential differences. A valuable book written by the Vaertings[1] has made this clear. In a State where men are dominant, as in most of our civilized States for the past two thousand years, certain attributes are considered to be characteristic of women which are equally characteristic of men in a State where women are dominant, as it is said they were for some time in ancient Egypt. The subordinate sex in each case is excluded from complete development, and is considered to be less intelligent, less courageous, and more domesticated than the dominant sex. In fact, men and women share jointly in what is called human nature, and are alike capable of courage, fear, cruelty, tenderness, intelligence, and stupidity. When exhilarated by power and responsibility they display the more dominating qualities, and in subordinate positions they manifest a 'slave psychology.' Therefore men and women are not to be differentiated

1. *The Dominant Sex*, by Mathilde and Mathias
   Vaerting. Translated by Eden and Cedar Paul.
   (Geo. Allen & Unwin.)

I

as brave or timid, intelligent or stupid, strong or weak, because a classification of this kind is too broadly human and not distinctively sexual.

It is not asserted that secondary physiological differences between the sexes or social differences in behaviour have no significance. Possibly sexual differentiation is so fundamental that it modifies the least reactions of men and women; but to begin an investigation of these would require exhaustive scientific information outside the scope of this essay, which is an attempt to discover if the division of the human race into men and women involves a division of spiritual as well as of sexual functions, so that the creative work of women is different in kind from the creative work of men. From this point of view the differences mentioned are significant as effects rather than causes, and a consideration of them must be dismissed as unfruitful. The aim of this essay, then, is to find a conception of womanhood as something essentially different from manhood. An essential difference would persist through all the variations of behaviour caused by the dominance of either sex: consequently the validity of this inquiry is not impaired by the restriction of its material to the activities of men and women in our present one-sided civilization. The knowledge that it is one-sided, because men have for so long been dominant over women, is valuable in helping to distinguish what is essential from what is accidental. The subordination of women makes it difficult but not impossible to recognize the essential quality of womanhood. In a masculine civilization the creative work of women may be belittled, misinterpreted, or denied: but if it is a reality, its existence will be proved at least by the emotional colour of the denial.

# I

It is therefore legitimate to consider the composite picture of woman presented to us by the beliefs and opinions recorded by men. These opinions are curiously contradictory and at the same time generalized. In spite of the intense interest felt in individual women, generalizations about women are common, whereas generalizations about men are made warily, if at all. Men are fellow-creatures of many different kinds: conclusions are drawn about classes of men, such as kings, statesmen, or warriors, angry men, foolish men, or strangers; but nothing less than a universal attribute of humanity is attached to all men, such as that men are mortal, or subject to Fate, or inconstant. But it is seriously believed by Moslems that women have no souls. Thousands of Christians believe that women are not intelligent. Mystics believe that women are on a lower plane of spiritual development than men. Women have no sense of justice, no sense of honour: women cannot be trusted with political power: women are all the better for a good beating with a stick. These generalizations reflect man as the dominant sex, conscious of his superiority. But one comes at once upon contradictions. Every great man has been inspired by some woman. The hand that rocks the cradle indisputably rules the world. A woman was the first cause of original sin, but a woman was the Mother of God. What does this mean? Half of the picture is tinged with vague contempt, and the other half with vague reverence. Apparently the average man sees woman alternately as an inferior being and as an angel.

One must conclude that he is looking at her through a distorting medium. His conception of her as an inferior being is natural, in a man-made State, and were she really inferior it would stop there. His vague reverence for her remains to prevent this conclusion: it is certainly a compensation for something, a distorted recognition of some half-guessed-at power in women. It looks as if man knows that the inferiority of woman is a fiction, that his domination of her and his refusal to admit her to his own level are not justified. In the background there lurks a fear of reprisals. The distorting medium contains fear as one of its elements.

In men's societies of a primitive or arrested type where the etiquette of conduct betrays its origin, one can see clearly man's fear of woman. Woman possesses some mysterious power which must be averted by elaborate taboos. A woman can ruin a man's chances of success in hunting or fishing by touching his gear. A woman's shadow can blight a religious ceremony. Women are particularly to be feared when they are menstruating or in childbed. The most terrible ghost is that of a woman who dies in childbed. In more developed societies men burn old crones as witches in possession of the evil eye. And even to-day, especially in politics, men find it difficult to rid themselves of the uneasy suspicion that women are dangerous.

This fear proves the artificiality of man's domination. One can be sceptical of any claim to superiority which throws such a shadow. Natural domination, that domination of skill and experience which is expected of a physician in a sick-room, or of a captain on his ship, establishes itself without arrogance and fear, and is exercised within its natural limits in particular directions. The physician does not interfere with navigation; the captain claims no divine right of authority over medical prescriptions. But the domination claimed by men over women has been a kind of magical quality, an absolute and divine right of authority, a mass domination, and, like all other mass dominations, rooted in fear.

But men's fear of women proves only that women are not naturally inferior and subordinate. It does not prove that they are different from men. There remains the other side of the picture, however, with its sentimentalized ideal of women. A reverence for woman as a mother appears clearly: the mother is elevated to a place in heaven and worshipped as the Mother of God, or as the Mother of the Gods. Now motherhood is an undisputed function of women which they do not share with men. At the lowest estimate of their powers all women are potential mothers. Men are born of women, and of women only. It must be an important function, for men have tried to belittle it. The theology of the masculine world branded Eve as the first cause of evil, and explained the pains of child-birth as a just punishment from heaven. Still more significant, however, is the fact that Adam and Eve were created by a masculine God in a garden, and that the theologians could not leave them there. It was necessary to bring them from the plane of abstract art on to the plane of humanity. But only a woman can create human beings, and therefore it was the woman who had to bring them out of the mythical garden into reality—a confession of failure for the theologians, and they wreaked their revenge on Eve. Yet in spite of themselves they were driven to attribute to a woman the decisive action which transformed the figments of a male God into men and women.

But motherhood was smirched with original sin. Later on it was still further belittled. Women were regarded as mere receptacles, passive receptive bodies which created nothing. Men must have felt that motherhood was important, or they would not have tried to explain it away altogether. But the sentimental ideal of woman as the mother still persisted, especially among men, and could not be explained away: so, finally, motherhood was allowed by popular opinion to be a creative function, but of a purely physical nature, and it was further defined as the sole justifiable function of women. Mr Rudyard Kipling expressed this very neatly when he said that blind Nature made man for several ends and woman for only one. In Oriental countries the still more logical conclusion is drawn that women justify their existence only by producing men-children. In a society committed to this point of view childless women are failures in life, and the unmarried woman is a ridiculous nuisance. If social remedies such as polygamy, suttee, infanticide, or euthanasia are not put into practice, the phrase 'superfluous women' comes into existence, and the State is shaken by the problem of what to do with its superfluous women.

## II

Yet if motherhood can be defined, rightly or wrongly, as the sole function of women, it must be a function which in some degree expresses the quality of womanhood as distinct from manhood. Even in this artificially narrowed field of activity one should be able to find some clue to the essential nature of women. It is therefore advisable first of all to compare motherhood and fatherhood.

Fatherhood seems the more casual relationship of the two. It cannot be proved with the same certainty as motherhood. In a masculine State, where the father is the only legal parent, the institution of marriage is necessary to prevent fathers from successfully disclaiming their children. Maternity is not so easily denied, and in a feminine State it could be proved without the aid of a marriage contract. Where the mother is the sole legal parent civil marriage is unnecessary. Hence, as the Vaertings point out, bastardy is unknown in a feminine State. A mother's connection with her child is more obvious and immediate than a father's. A man can be a parent without knowing it: a woman cannot.

Motherhood is also a greater tax on vital energy than fatherhood, even if we take motherhood merely as a physical function. The process of bearing a child culminates in a crisis which exhausts a woman's energy: to such an extent, indeed, that women often die of it. Moreover, it is a process which, once initiated, is not under conscious control, so that the reserve of energy drawn upon is not deliberately assigned to this purpose by its owner. It is not at her free disposal to grant or to withhold; it cannot be exhausted by an act depending on conscious volition. The race in this respect is stronger than the individual.

It may be that here we are on the track of an essential difference between men and women in the distribution of energy. If fatherhood is a more casual relationship and uses up less time and energy than motherhood, it looks as if the specifically sexual life of men does not require such a jealously guarded reserve of energy as that of women. This would be true of all men and all women, for such a fundamental process as the propagation of the human race could not be left to a section of humanity. As far as the race is concerned, all women are potential mothers, and must have the necessary reserve of energy for this function whether they intend to become mothers or not. They cannot waste it even if they would. Thus men have more energy to waste on their own individual purposes than women: that is to say, men have more energy at their conscious disposal.

### III

The implications of this hypothesis must be considered. It is attractive because it establishes an essential difference between men and women which makes them complementary to each other. There can be no question of absolute domination of one sex by the other when the strength of each lies in a different direction. If man's energy is diverted more into conscious life, woman's energy is diverted more into unconscious life, and one is not more important than the other. It is a relative, not an absolute difference; both men and women are human beings, and all that concerns human beings is their joint affair. But it means, as will be seen, a difference in the kind of creative work done by each: they will tackle the same things from a different point of view, and with different results. On this basis men and women would each have an equal right, the right of the creative spirit to do its work without let or hindrance.

Conscious life implies rational thinking. In thinking about things we arrange them in patterns, we give them form and system. But we do not give them content; conscious life modifies or seizes upon things which it does not originate. Growth is a process which is already well advanced before it enters consciousness at all. Our patterns of thought, therefore, can never be final: they must from time to time be broken and re-formed to admit new factors pushed into consciousness. But the existence of thought-patterns makes it easier to recognize the significance of new factors, since a thought, once formulated, can be passed on, and becomes a permanent heritage for the human race, part of the body of knowledge established by the processes of consciousness. These processes are continuously at work extending the body of knowledge, systematizing thought, and endeavouring to systematize life. Consciousness is thus the shaper of form, which is one aspect of life, and its work tends to a permanence beyond the vicissitudes of living. But its vitality depends upon its communion with the unconscious.

Obviously, unconscious life cannot be clearly defined. We can only guess at its nature from the angle at which its processes enter consciousness, from its disruptive action upon our systems of thought, and from what we can remember of its manifestations in dreams. We know that our emotions rise from it like bubbles through water, that it determines our motives and our interests, and that it is not homogeneous by conscious standards. Its interferences with our conscious life are always spontaneous and strongly charged with feeling. We can infer from such interferences that it has purposes. From its manifestations in dreams and trance states we know that it has access to knowledge by other than conscious means. This kind of knowledge, when it makes its way into consciousness, we sometimes recognize by its emotional force and unexpectedness, and call it intuition. But for the most part we serve the purposes of our unconscious without knowing that we do so, and admit its wisdom only through the indirect channels of conscious rationalization.

The processes of the unconscious can, however, be roughly described by contrast with the conscious life. The unconscious is concerned with growth rather than form; it is essentially emotional, spontaneous, and irrational. As far as we know, it is concrete in its thinking and not abstract; it creates living agents and not systems of thought. Thus, while conscious processes supply form and permanence in our world, unconscious processes supply growing vitality and change. The creations of unconscious life are wrought in mortal substances, those of conscious life in enduring patterns which are one step removed from life. Unconscious life creates, for example, human beings: conscious life creates, for example, philosophy. If men are stronger in conscious life, and women in unconscious life, their creative powers must express their strength. Men should excel in translating life into conscious forms, women in fostering the growth of life itself. Men will create systems of philosophy or government, while women are creating individual human beings.

IV

The facts of human life tend to confirm this theory. Starting again from the fundamental relationship of a mother to her child, we can see that owing to the peculiar position of the human race, the physical act of motherhood is only the merest beginning of motherhood as a function. Man, because he is destined for a more complex life than the other animals, is born more helpless than any of them, and takes a longer time to come to maturity. His conscious life constructs itself slowly out of the perceptions of every day, establishing at every point in its development a working relationship with his unconscious life, a relationship which is permanently biassed by the experiences of his first years. He is terribly at the mercy of his mother. She can ruin or strengthen that harmony between the conscious and the unconscious which is a necessary condition of full human development. In short, she must create not only a human body, but a human being, if she is to fulfil her function as a mother. But if it is her business to foster growth in her children, it must be equally her business to foster growth in all the people with whom she is intimate. If she is a specialist in the needs of the growing human spirit, her peculiar knowledge must be of service to men and women of all ages who are still capable of growth. And what is true in this respect of mothers must be true for all women: a special equipment for motherhood does not descend suddenly by the grace of Heaven upon the individual. All girls are potential mothers, and whatever gifts of intuition are necessary for the creative work of motherhood must be accessible to all women. If the full content of motherhood is thus recognized, it must inevitably be recognized as a special application of the creative power of women. Therefore the concept 'superfluous women' can only arise in a society which denies the real functions of motherhood, and which consequently prevents women from free expression and ignores the creative power of womanhood.

Creative power of any kind is, of course, the obverse of an equal power for destruction. No one can put an engine out of action so deftly as the man who designs engines. Woman's power of fostering growth in human life implies, therefore, an equal power of hindering it. We must accept both sides of the hypothesis, and in doing so we find fresh proof that it is true. If the average man sees woman alternately as

an angel and a devil, it is because she exercises both a
creative and a destructive influence upon his inner life. He
would neither fear nor reverence her so intensely if she were
merely an inferior counterpart of himself. Nor would he lay
upon her such peculiar disabilities. These disabilities are not
only of the kind that would suffice to keep an inferior class
in subjection. Inferior classes, whether actually enslaved
or not, are kept in their place by being excluded from
the sources of external power, such as the possession of
wealth, the command of armies, the exercise of political
rights. Certain moral and religious sanctions always rise to
reinforce the law on these points, for the springs of human
conduct lie in the unconscious, and morality and religion
deal directly with the emotions of unconscious life. The
ruling class seeks therefore to impose a morality consonant
with its own interests, and fears a new religion more than
a revolution. But it is always conscious of the expediency
of the conventional morality it imposes on inferiors, and
attaches no ultimate value to it. The model subordinate,
obedient and loyal, is not reverenced or idealized: he is not
regarded by his superiors as a type of perfect manhood,
but only as a perfect subordinate. He may be a bad
man provided that he is a good servant. The position of
women in a men's State does not correspond exactly to
this. True, if we substitute the function of motherhood in
its narrow interpretation for the function of servitude, the
correspondence is exact up to a point. The wife and mother
is excluded from independent access to the sources of external power: and she is expected to be obedient and loyal to her
marriage contract. Moral and religious sanctions are called
in to transform her marriage contract into a vow. The stock
moral virtue required of her is chastity; she must have sexual
relationships only within the pale of marriage. All women,
because they are potential wives, must copy her virtues and
avoid what is forbidden to her. So far this is only another
aspect of the fact that men restrict the function of women to
physical motherhood, and define their own responsibilities
by the institution of marriage. Women are treated exactly
as an inferior class with a definite function, that of
child-bearing. But the correspondence stops here. The

disabilities imposed upon women by conventional morality cut deeper still. The sexually good woman must be not only good but ignorant: whole tracts of human experience are withheld from her knowledge. Moreover, her chastity and her ignorance are translated by men themselves into an abstraction of artificial purity and reverenced as their ideal of womanhood. An ideal of womanhood cherished in men's States, which has for its essential elements ignorance of life and a debased conception of sex, can be regarded with scepticism. It is noteworthy that intellectual ignorance does not have the same prestige, and therefore cannot be so important. Even an 'educated' woman is conventionally more acceptable than a woman who is shocked at nothing. The conventionally pure good woman is shocked at a great many things: that is to say, she does not merely condemn certain phases of conduct, which would be at least a forthright attitude, she is uncomfortable and timid when they are brought to her notice. Now if man's reverence for women is an acknowledgment of her vaguely realized power, at the same time in that very reverence, conventionalized into an ideal, he obviously safeguards himself against her power. Apparently, women can be kept in a subordinate position if ignorance of human conduct is imposed upon them as a necessary condition of social approval. It can be inferred that a fearless attitude towards human life is the first essential quality of a free woman, and that conventional morality is imposed with such emphasis upon women because the creation of moral values is their own peculiar vocation. Men are more concerned to prevent women from having untrammelled judgment and action in affairs of morality than from having access to the possession of wealth. In other words, women are hindered not only from external power, but from the inward power of creating independent moral and religious values. It is precisely this power which is exercised by creative women in their treatment of others, and the conventionalized ideal of the ignorant good woman is the deepest disability laid upon women in a men's State. The conventionally good woman helps to perpetuate the formal traditions created by man, traditions which harden into empty shells unless they are continuously vitalized by the independent judgments of women. She accepts the masculine standpoint that human conduct is to be judged entirely by the values of consciously organized life, which are devised for the preservation of existing systems, and are not necessarily humane. She acquiesces in repression and punishment instead of seeking to understand and cherish. Men praise her for this subserviency and unconsciously despise her.

But in preventing her from aggression upon their forms and traditions men lose more than they gain. She is humbugged out of her womanhood, but she is still a woman, and does not cease to influence their inner life. The systems of society—such as marriage—are preserved, but the individual man suffers. He meets hardness where he looks for tolerance, and condemnation where he needs help. Worse still, for her conventionality is borrowed and therefore unintelligent, he finds himself imprisoned in traditions which he himself would destroy and create anew were it not for the timidity of the conventional women.

Thus in a typical men's State where the creative work of women is ignored, where women are prevented by legal and economic barriers from access to external sources of power and hampered by conventional ignorance of life, they have an insidious influence which evades all the means by which men try to keep it in check. The fabric of the State, the organized systems, remain apparently intact, but the private life of men becomes sour and stale. The more men deny the rights of women in public, the more they are delivered over to the obscure dissatisfactions of their women in private. The conventional women whom men evoke for their own protection have in the end a more fatal, because a thwarted, influence on human life than the fearless women. Among the Hindus, for example, where the social systems of men have been hardened into cast-iron (perhaps because the women have been prevented from free expression), the negative power of women is very great. Women are not merely inferior imitations of men: they create men or destroy them.

The question may be put, If the whole of human experience is the natural concern of women, and if women are indeed endowed with the capacity to understand and foster the growth of the human spirit, how is it possible for women to accept a narrow conventional morality? It is possible because unconscious life is remarkably suggestible, and in a society where womanly traditions are mainly negative the continuous pressure of conventional values is applied to girls almost from childhood. Only rare women with a genius for womanhood can resist the potency of such suggestions.

That it is a woman's destiny to create human beings, whether she fulfils it or not, is amply confirmed by the natural bias of her interests. In spite of convention her interest in human beings is stronger and more spontaneous than her interest in anything else. Almost from the cradle a girl studies the people around her more attentively than a boy does, and is quicker in imitating their tricks of speech and behaviour. A little later she turns naturally to dolls, not because of an absurdly precocious maternal instinct, but because dolls are substitutes for human beings, and her creative fancy can play upon them without restriction. A doll is not necessarily a son or daughter: it is by turns a confidant, a scapegoat, and a talisman. Later still her interest in other people becomes practically a ruling passion: and since she is not merely a potential wife and mother but a potential woman, she is interested not only in possible sweethearts but in everybody. She is inquisitive about human relationships of every kind. She is indifferent to things which have no human interest: she values things for their associations, or the power they give her over other people. The intimacy between an adolescent girl and her bosom friend for the time being is based on a mutual interest in human nature and a common standard of critical values which they apply to each other as well as to the world. They analyse motives, provoke moods, love and hate with such intensity that emotional explosions are inevitable. Their interest is not that of mere spectators at the human comedy: they are ready to play important parts in it; and they test at every point their influence over others.

When fifteen-year-old girls write essays on 'What I should like to be,' the aspirations disclosed are rarely intellectual or material. Nearly every girl wants to be popular, to be an influence for good, to establish a reputation for cheerfulness and kindness, in short, to be successful in handling human beings. When she leaves school the same bias continues. The average girl is more interested in the people around her than in her work, especially if her work has little direct human interest. If her daily work does not consist of personal relations to other people, her efficiency in it depends upon the approval of her employers rather than upon her pride in the work itself. She sees herself as the sunbeam in the office, or as the comforter of her employer's broken life, or as a moral influence—in other words, where no human interest exists in her surroundings she takes pains to invent it. It is this entirely womanly impulse which generates most of the sentiment and scandal among women.

In married life women display the same passionate interest in other people, even though husbands and families absorb a certain amount of it. Neighbours, servants, and children are their dearest topics. No woman is bored when she is discussing other people; and this is true of both educated and uneducated women. The things which primarily concern women as women are human affairs and experiences, material which helps them more capably to scrutinize, to interpret, and to meddle with the people they meet. The result is that they often meddle tediously with other people's lives. Like Hedda Gabler, they must have their fingers in somebody's destiny, destructively if not creatively. Destruction of this kind instead of creation is tragic, but it arises at least from a pre-occupation with humanity, and so, unlike war, it is womanly.

Thus the current of women's interests sets definitely towards actual human beings and concrete situations rather than abstract theories. There are other aspects of womanhood which confirm the hypothesis that women's strength lies in unconscious rather than in conscious life, and which can be briefly enumerated.

The first of these is too obvious to require comment. By general consent of men, women are more irrational and impulsive than men are. Secondly, women have a strong, if inarticulate, affinity with what is called Nature; a fact which is symbolized by the personification of Nature as a woman. Nature in this sense is the sum of that growing life which has not reached the conscious level of humanity. To this growing life, vegetable or animal, women are never indifferent: their reactions to it are strongly emotional, whether sympathetic or antipathetic. When because of some timidity they cannot exercise their creative power on human beings, they readily foster plants or animals instead, and there are women who can do so with the sureness of intuitive knowledge. They are more obviously affected by natural phenomena than men; their sexual life, for example, is governed by the phases of the moon, and it is claimed that their fertility varies with the rainfall and the earth's magnetic currents. Thirdly, they have an immediate sense of the significance of life: they have the same vivid interest in even trivial affairs that one finds in dreams. Women have none of the detachment which is equally prepared to prove that life is significant or that it is meaningless. They assume without proof that life, especially human life, is significant; they are so deeply immersed in life that it is not possible for them to question its value as men do. For this reason they are more tenacious of life than men. Fourthly, they come to maturity earlier than men do, although they live longer on the average. This does not mean that women remain in a state of arrested development as compared with men: the advent of puberty does not put a stop to mental and spiritual development. But it may be interpreted as a sign that the creative work of womanhood requires a less elaborate conscious equipment than that of men. The wisdom of conscious life is a structure slowly built by the individual, and needs a long apprenticeship; it is possible that the wisdom of unconscious life exists independently of the individual and waits only for admission. Incidentally, the fact that women have a reasonable expectation of living for twenty-five years after they have ceased to bear children is another proof—if proof be needed—that maternity is not merely a physical function: women go on living as long as their children need them. Lastly, although their creative work consists in the handling of individuals, and although

they are finely aware of their own individual reactions,
women rarely achieve a conscious individuality. They are so
largely unconscious of themselves that they need emotional
support for their personalities: it is their danger that they
tend to live in a state of perpetual reference to other people;
and when they express themselves as individuals, they do so
spontaneously and not deliberately. Thus women as a body
show a timidity which easily relapses into conservatism, and
can only be overcome by urgent necessity. Conservatism
becomes the spiritual death of women, as of men: but
in women it springs from a timidity of intellect, from
a weakness in conscious life; in men from a timidity of
emotion, from a fear of the unconscious. This difference
between men and women is illustrated in dress, for example.
As the consciously organized life of men develops, their
clothing expresses less of the emotion, the temperament, the
spontaneity of unconscious life: it becomes a uniform,
symbolic of their status as rational members of an organized
society. They are sure of themselves and of their traditions,
consequently fashion is a convention which sits as easily
upon them as other conventions, and changes as slowly.
It is a reasonable law, deliberately accepted for the sake
of convenience and orderliness. Women, on the other
hand, are not afraid of temperament and colour in dress;
they express in their clothing the spontaneous, vivid, and
irrational qualities of unconscious life. But because they
are unsure of themselves as members of a public body,
they need the assurance of 'being in the fashion' to give
them the necessary confidence for wearing even the most
daring creations. Fashion among women is thus not a law
accepted for convenience; it is a kind of emotional support,
and it fluctuates as often and as widely as emotions.

## V

In this weakness of women's conscious life we have the key
to men's domination over them. It is the domination of
the more articulate over the less articulate consciousness.
Man is the intellectual organizer of life. He arranges life
in patterns, or, as has been already suggested, translates it

into conscious forms, and he is therefore more interested in the nature of his patterns than in the material out of which he composes them. He begins, where woman ends, with the individual human being and individual experiences; his aim is to lift these into a world of enduring and proved forms. The Platonic idea, for example, is a purely masculine conception. It is possible that man's world of ultimate abstractions is another aspect of the world from which woman works towards the individual, and that his consciously constructed philosophy, if it were perfected, would coincide with the content of her intuitive wisdom. Thus a circle would be completed in which woman seeks to express the infinite in terms of the individual life, while man seeks to express the individual in terms of the infinite. The difference between them remains, however, not merely a difference in aim but a difference in equipment. Woman is the gateway through which the wisdom of the unconscious comes to be translated by man into conscious form. Her wisdom, derived from unfathomable sources, must be expended upon life incarnate and narrowed into the practical details of everyday circumstance. Her intelligence is fettered, as it were, to actual life, and is best stimulated by concrete situations. Man, on the other hand, moves away from human life: his intelligence ranges freely in a world of speculation and can create perfectly abstract universes of knowledge. His work consequently takes visible shape beneath his hand: it can be tested; it can be destroyed and shaped again; it can achieve completion. The work of woman has none of these attributes: she has no objective proof of success; in the last resort she must depend upon her subjective valuations. Thus the more organized and objective certainties of men impose themselves easily upon women. Men can prove their theories even when they are wrong; women cannot prove their intuitions even when they are right. In his world, that of organized form, man dominates woman naturally.

But woman should dominate man in her own field, the creation of free and harmonious individuals; for the potential progress of humanity may be determined by man, but its actual progress is determined by woman. In a society which recognizes the domination of men and denies that of women, the creative work of both is hampered. The danger for men lies in that very quality of detachment which gives their work its value. Left to themselves they become more and more detached, substituting for the fluctuations of life a stable and systematic perfection of theory which is rigidly imposed upon individual members of society. Religion becomes a creed, morality a code of law, government a party machine: even art, which is of all their activities the most accessible to the vitality of unconscious life, is intellectualized and engenders theories of æsthetics instead of works of art. Human beings become mere pegs on which to hang the theories, economic units, and man, the heir of all the ages, is in danger of being crushed under the weight of his own machines. The financial machine in our own day is an excellent example of masculine activity pushed to extremes: it has been successfully detached from human values so that it exists for the production of money and not for the production of goods and services to humanity. The mere individual has ceased to be of any importance, and even the inventions or discoveries of his intelligence are valued only in terms of money. It is a curious paradox that men who, as individuals, are surer of themselves than women, and who command their conscious energies more freely, should inevitably create systems to which the individual is subordinated. A system of this kind is not necessarily an evil, but when it makes no allowance for women's values, for their sense of the significance of human life and the individual human being, it moves to its extreme logical conclusion and becomes inhuman.

This over-emphasis of masculine activities was conceivably necessary at a point in history when civilization was in its infancy and the need for organization was greater than the need for individual freedom. Perhaps at such a point the domination of men over women began. But the discrepancy between human and institutional values is now so great that even men feel it acutely; it has disquieted women for some time and is forcing them into the open. It looks as if during the next few generations the really creative New Woman will emerge, for conventional morality is no longer so powerful among women, and they are gradually deserting the blind alleys into which they rushed in their first efforts at self-assertion.

It does not follow that women by themselves can save humanity. Men must face their own problems, and women are naturally ill-equipped to create new forms of society. But it is the business of women to create the creators of social forms, and they cannot escape a certain responsibility for the present tension in our organized life. Absolute domination by either sex is no longer necessary; the modern world needs the creative work of both. Woman by herself loses a sense of proportion, just as man by himself loses touch with reality. Man's intellectual conclusions must be checked by woman's intuitive knowledge of the human spirit, and woman's spontaneous wisdom must be helped by man's intellectual vision. Both are creative although they depend upon each other: there is no room on either side for false pride or humility.

## VI

It is now advisable to consider attentively the statement that creative women need new and independent moral values since conventional morality expresses a man's standpoint rather than a woman's. If the latter part of this statement can be proved, that conventional morality is necessarily masculine, then the first part must inevitably be accepted.

It has already been postulated that women derive their greatest strength from unconscious life and are concerned with growth. Their energies and interests turn spontaneously towards the living human beings upon whom their influence is exerted. This influence, because it is largely unconscious, is not rational but emotional; when it is directed positively towards other people it is best described as love. Creative love is the fundamental attribute of womanhood, as perhaps creative thought is of manhood. Its aim is to foster harmony and strength in the individual.

Woman thus sees humanity as a collection of individuals

of whom no two are identical, growing separately like trees in a common direction, expressing in visible forms, each of which is significant, a common unseen life. If one may use a rough symbolism, women see humanity in vertical lines, while men see it in horizontal strata. The perfection of each individual is women's business, and the combination of individuals into social systems is man's business. These two aspects of life are necessarily continuous and inseparable: the difference between them here, as throughout, is one of emphasis. Women emphasize the wholeness of the individual in himself; men, the relation of the individual to his neighbours. It follows that women cannot disregard or eliminate anything which manifests itself in the life of the individual. Man resembles a tree only by analogy; he cannot be lopped of his branches; he can achieve strength and harmony only by carrying everything with him. Nothing is accidental or superfluous in his behaviour; virtues and vices are alike significant. From this point of view whatever prevents the harmony of the complete individual is bad; but it cannot be cut off, it must be fused into the whole, if possible. Woman therefore cannot shirk any issue or turn from the investigation of any human impulse, whatever its nature. She believes in the significance and continuity of all that life which passes into human consciousness, and to her goodness and badness are relative terms, depending on the nature of the immediate problem. Thus she cannot believe in original sin, although she recognizes mistakes. Man, on the other hand, believes in the significance of his systems which cut across life horizontally, and he desires to fit the individual into his patterns. Whatever disrupts his patterns is bad and must be cut off. This condition naturally is uniform in its operation, and therefore badness is a constant quantity, something definite which can be written down in a code of prohibitions. Nonconformity with the law is original sin, and arouses his indignation. But as there are many systems, each system has its own code of offences and penalties, and each casts out its own offenders. The Church excommunicates them, the State imprisons them, Society boycotts them, professional bodies expel them; they are dishonoured and ignored, thrust out of the system whose stability they threaten. We penetrate to the very heart of the difference between men and women when we observe that the outcast, whose individuality is formally denied by his fellows, remains none the less an individual to the women who love him. Obviously a morality which satisfies the one point of view does not satisfy the other.

The morality honoured by men is thus a morality designed to preserve the systems which men create. Because it upholds the values of consciously organized life it distrusts the impulses of unconscious life, which it calls original sin, or personifies as a devil. Less civilized and more impulsive races are easily suspected of being direct agents of the devil, as are also the adherents of rival or opposing systems. Women, because they are natural supporters of spontaneous action, are particularly to be distrusted, and masculine morality, as we have seen, imposes a still more stringent code on women than on men. So it happened that Eve, a creative woman vindicating the importance of individual moral values and of an individual conscience that should make each man the equal of God, was necessarily abhorrent to an organized theology. So in the United States it happens that the earnest business man regards negroes and Socialists as public dangers; and in exactly the same way in Scotland the earnest Calvinist believes that Roman Catholics are damned. The follower of a systematic morality has always a black list. Each system produces its own code of offences for nonconformity, and its moral standards are therefore valid only for itself: they are not necessarily religious or universal.

In such a morality the individual is considered only as one who conforms or does not conform to the code required, never as an individual in himself. Further, because it distrusts the spontaneity of unconscious impulses, systematic morality believes that all individuals are bad in their hearts, that they are good only when they are afraid to be bad, and that penalties for badness must be sufficiently grievous to frighten them. Thus systematic morality depends upon fear of punishment. The kind of punishment imposed has only an arbitrary relation to the nature of the offence committed, and no relation at all to the psychological problems in which the offender is involved: it is designed merely to make him suffer, and, if he persists in offending, to remove him. The public school imposes its two hundred or its four hundred 'lines' or so many strokes with the birch, or resorts to expulsion; the State fines varying sums, or imprisons for varying periods, or resorts to capital punishment; the business firm reprimands, or fines, or resorts to dismissal. In each case the system and the code which supports it are more important than the life of the individual. Morality of this kind, when it is perfectly developed, is quite impersonal; its abstract impersonality is revered by men as an ideal, which they call Justice.

This systematic morality with its impersonal judgments, its definite codes, its uniformly graded punishments, and its unquestioning repudiation of the offender is a logical pendant to the systems which men create. It is precisely what is usually called conventional morality, and it is essentially masculine in its attitude to the individual. Women, if they are to create free and harmonious individuals, cannot sacrifice an individual to a code; they cannot agree that goodness is only the fear of punishment; they cannot believe in the efficacy of external punishment, and they cannot permit the offender to be cut off. To the creative woman an offender is a question which she must try to answer. Her morality must be psychological rather than punitive, personal rather than impersonal, and fundamentally religious. It is clear that many actions which systematic morality considers bad must appear good to the creative woman, and inversely what she considers good must often be condemned by systematic morality.

Women must therefore create their own independent moral values. It may be objected that if each woman creates her own morality the result will be confusion. This objection, however, arises out of a misapprehension. It is not the business of women to condemn or to punish, or to exact conformity with any definite code of conduct: it is their business to understand the processes at work in the human soul and to help each individual to the fullest and most harmonious expression of his powers. There will always be enough men in the world to secure the existence of systematic morality; any confusion produced by the action of women will be only the rich confusion of life itself. Besides, creative love is not mere sympathy or even affection; if women cannot sacrifice an individual to a code they are equally unable to sacrifice their intuitions about the human race to an individual. Creative love demands a high discipline from those who would exercise it.

## VII

The first condition that is required from women is that they shall know themselves. A woman who is ignorant of her own weaknesses cannot help others, for she is incapable of correcting distortions caused by her own fear or anger. The conventional woman hangs conventional ideas between herself and her own nature, thus negating her deepest instincts. She despises and represses part of her own humanity; consequently she has a repressive instead of a fostering effect on other people. Women must therefore be frankly sincere with themselves if they are to be creative, and must make allowances for their own faults in dealing with others. One can only mete out to others the measure one has already meted to oneself.

But though the instrument is imperfect the possibilities are great. The second condition for the exercise of creative love is a boundless faith in the capacity of the human soul for growth. This is where women cannot let the doctrine of original sin stand between them and the individuals with whom they have to deal. The gospel for women is contained in the words, 'the kingdom of Heaven is within you,' qualified by the knowledge that Heaven is not a static condition of bliss but a vital harmony of body and spirit. Such a belief demands the fullest scientific knowledge of what promotes or hinders health of body and of mind; and it is the business of the creative woman to get all the information she can.

Religion and morality for women thus resolve themselves into a belief that human life is significant, serving a destiny greater than itself, and the interpretation of that belief into terms of conduct. Because each individual is a unique

problem the details of this conduct can never be codified;
therefore the morality of women is ultimately spontaneous
and individual, depending for guidance upon their creative
energies, expressed through love.

The whole world needs creative women, and seems to be
unaware of its need. Women themselves do not know how
necessary they are. The result is that many waste themselves
in trying to be men, and many are content to justify their
existence by simple drudgery. There still remain many who
feel that a woman should be more to her husband than the
keeper of his house, and some of these reserve themselves
for men with obvious disabilities, because they think that
the average man has no real need of them. But, although
the desire is unformulated, nearly all women desire to have
a creative influence on their husbands. If it were not so,
the 'best-sellers' which circulate among women would not
resemble each other so strikingly in one respect: the hero is
always at odds with the world and is rescued from a gloomy
fate by the great love of the heroine. If he is a reputed villain
so much the better; the field of action for the heroine is all
the clearer. Only a courageous woman looking for really
difficult work would marry an ordinary man instead of a
villain with a heart of gold.

Women's creative work is implicitly recognized in many
beliefs and customs. The difference between the morality
of men and women, for example, is finely illustrated among
the Syrian Arabs, where a prisoner on his way to execution is
absolved from his sentence if he can lay hold of a woman's
skirts. It is felt, though not understood, by those men of our
own country who complain that women have no sense of
justice. It is exploited by commercial firms who establish
women welfare workers to humanize their business systems,
within limits. And the tradition that woman's place is the
home is possibly not entirely determined by the subordinate
position of women, but may arise from a sound intuition
about the nature of women and their functions. The home
is a strategic centre for the creation of human beings.
Moreover, a home does not imply a husband: marriage
is a desirable but not a necessary condition for women's
creative work. Nor is it bounded by the four walls of a

house; whatever affects the people within the home is a woman's proper business.

## VIII

This raises the question of public life for women. There is certainly room for creative womanhood in the public life of the State. The modern State is a highly organized system of government resting upon other systems, such as those of finance, law, and industry; but these complicated organizations ramify downwards until they touch the lives of all the individuals who compose the nation. The point at which they do so is a fitting point for the public activities of women. Women have already begun to mediate between the system of law and the individuals upon whom punishment by imprisonment is imposed; they have called attention to the impossibility of reforming offenders in a prison which ignores individuality and the psychology of the individual. It is true that such mediation is at present usually subject to the veto of the controlling system, and is therefore limited; a disability which is likely to hamper women until the value of women's work is recognized as equal to that of men. But the obscure dissatisfactions of our time, caused by the discrepancy between institutional and human values are, on the one hand, compelling women to penetrate into public life, and, on the other hand, threatening the stability of all institutions. If women are true to themselves their full co-operation with men is inevitable.

This means that women must carry their womanhood with them into all occupations, otherwise the advantage of their entry into public affairs will be entirely lost. Besides, a woman who tries to do a man's work in a man's way pays too high a price for the effort. A man can be formal and abstract without losing his human qualities or ceasing to be creative, since his energies are distributed in that way, but a woman cannot. She must expend more energy than he does to achieve the same formal outlook; she must abandon the creative love for the individual which is essential for womanhood; and, because she has killed herself spiritually, a formal woman is twice as formal as any man, and her work is necessarily barren. Most women are instinctively aware of this danger and protect themselves from the hardening of traditional routine by simple indifference to their work and an escape into marriage as soon as possible. But this is merely an evasion of the problem which women must solve in the next generation or two, the problem of leavening the organized systems of society with human values so that mechanical routine is reduced to a minimum. Meanwhile, women are obviously in their proper place in any occupation which deals directly with human beings.

## IX

The differences that have been indicated between the sexes in this essay do not form a hard-and-fast dividing line. Men are not all intellect and consciousness, nor are women all intuition and unconsciousness. It would be juster to say that some men are more intellectual than any woman, and some women more intuitive than any man: but even this statement does not adequately cover the case. The different determination of energy which hinders women from supreme intellectual detachment, and men from supreme human understanding, is subtly operative between these two extremes throughout the intervening space where men and women have a common field of action. It should therefore be traceable in their respective contributions to art.

It is perhaps unwise though interesting to attempt the drawing of distinctions between men's art and women's: so much depends upon one's idea of the nature of art. But it may be possible without becoming entangled in controversy to suggest tentatively some differences, and it seems worth while to see how far the argument will carry us.

From the point of view of this inquiry a work of art ranks as a supremely conscious creation. It has perfection of form and it is permanent: *ars longa, vita brevis*. But it is also directly and vitally connected with the forces of unconscious life; it depends upon, or rather it is characterized by an intensity of emotion which it transmits as if by magic to other people than its creator. Its form can be judged dispassionately, but not its content. It is detached from human life, and is at the same time a revelation of it in a way which is more immediate and more moving than a mere explanation. Thus, although it is as deliberate a product of conscious processes as a mathematical theory or a philosophical idea, or an economic system, it is more intimately linked to unconscious life than any of these; it is perhaps closer to unconscious life than any other kind of conscious creation. For this reason, because it belongs to both worlds, the esteem in which it is held varies according to the values of the people among whom it is practised. And in certain cases the place assigned to art seems to confirm the general theory of this essay, that women create unconscious more than conscious life, and that men associate the values of unconscious life with women. For in communities which are too rigidly organized, because entirely devoted to some system, and which therefore distrust the personal values of unconscious life, communities such as those of the business men here or in the United States, art is distrusted, the artist is considered to be effeminate, and the appreciation and culture of art are left half contemptuously, half respectfully to the women. On the other hand, in communities where the framework of conscious life has not hardened and unconscious values are not depreciated, the formal perfection of art arouses men's admiration, and the artist is looked upon as the best type of manhood. The artist must thus possess both masculine and feminine qualities; that is to say, he has immediate access to the intuitions of unconscious life, as a woman has, and he creates conscious form, as a man does.

It has been already admitted that the difference between men and women is only a relative difference, that men have unconscious and women conscious powers; the fact that art belongs to both worlds therefore allows both men and women to be artists, while at the same time it makes more difficult than ever the attempt to draw a distinction between men's art and women's. There are, however, one or two possibilities which suggest themselves. In the first place, if the energy of women is more absorbed by unconscious life than that of men, it can play less freely in the world of conscious form and is therefore less able to achieve that perfect fusion of form and content on a grand scale which is supreme art. Certainly the greatest artists of historical times have been men, and there is no reason to think that the domination of men is even partly responsible for the lack of great women artists. But if women are handicapped in those arts, such as literature, painting, and the composition of music, where the finished product takes a permanent form detached from the human personality of the artist, they should have an advantage in arts like dancing, singing, and acting, where the actual personality is the medium of expression. And as a matter of fact in arts of this kind women have attained supreme rank. It seems permissible to say that the nearer they are to concrete human life, the more freely and naturally they can create.

Again, it may be suggested that the tendency to elaborate form at the expense of content is a danger to which men are more susceptible in art than women. Women's greater vitality and comparative weakness in conscious life expose them rather to the opposite fault, a failure to achieve a strictness of form perfectly adequate to the intensity of the emotion expressed. This weakness would be more likely to occur in the rendering of a sustained than of a transient emotion or mood; consequently one would expect perfection of form from women artists in works of small compass and natural spontaneity, such as lyric poems, rather than in an epic or a long descriptive poem. The more elastic the form, the more shapeless it is, the more women are able to use it for sustained work. In literature, at least, this seems to be true. The loose bulk of the novel makes it attractive to women as a medium of expression; and any long works of the first rank written by women are to be found in this form.

Further, since it is women's business to create individuals rather than systems of society, one would expect the art of women to be concerned largely with actual individual experience and concrete situations. In one sense, of course, all art must do this; but individual experience can be transmuted into symbols and so generalized, or projected into future worlds, and that is precisely what women are unlikely to do. No woman has ever written a great myth or a Utopia.

Finally, if women are essentially creators of human life, we may surmise that they are more interested in the relation of art to life than in art for art's sake. But this supposition must be made with many qualifications. It is not suggested that in the act of creating or appreciating a work of art women pause to ask, 'Of what use is this to life?' If the emotion that they experience is authentic and vivid they will accept its significance simply, as they accept the significance of any vivid experience. But it is suggested that if they reflect upon art at all, this is precisely the question, formulated or not, which will decide their attitude to it. In estimating a work of art women are more likely to be influenced by its content than by its form, and they are capable of drawing practical conclusions from it which would hardly occur to men.

Among the different kinds of art, those which express themselves in a medium closely related to the normal activities of daily life seem to be the most favourable for women. There are more great women artists in literature than in sculpture or painting, and more in these than in music. Literature is expressed through language, which is a medium in constant use between individuals; a paint brush in our civilization is a less usual means of expression, and the making of music still less usual. One might also hazard a guess that in literature the vocabulary of women contains fewer unusual words than that of men. For the difference between spoken and written language is roughly analogous to the difference between women and men; a correspondence which may influence the style of women both as speakers and writers and their preferences as readers.

## X

It may be affirmed, then, that women are more directly linked to concrete life than men, and that they naturally incline to utilitarian standards in judging the importance of things. Men create ideas, and women make use of them: women create human beings, and men make use of them: both men and women seize what they need for the service of their own purposes. Is this difference discernible in the intellectual work of educated women, in the subjects they deliberately choose for research, and in the contributions they make to knowledge? This question, and many others, remain to be answered; and, with them, the fundamental question whether the education of women, and especially their 'higher education,' is planned to secure the development of an enlightened womanhood, as distinct from manhood. The present inquiry pretends to be nothing more than a stimulus to the further investigation of essential differences between men and women; but it is clear that if there is any truth in our conclusions, an honest re-statement of women's aims is necessary. The conception of womanhood which has been adumbrated here, if it is accepted, demands so many adjustments in the attitude of women towards themselves, towards morality, religion, sex, and education that it is impossible within the limits of this essay to give even a hint of them.

# 'WOMEN IN SCOTLAND'

# Women in Scotland
## from Left Review 1936

Scotland, taken by and large, is, I suppose, a Socialist country. Yet it is difficult to speak of women's movements in Scotland, since most Scottish working-class women—and men, too—are dominated by the belief that outside the home men should have all 'the say'. In Scotland, again taking it by and large, woman's place is still considered to be the actual home. A Scotswoman at a mixed public meeting or on a mixed committee feels that it is not her 'place' to let her voice be heard, and she will not risk speaking up unless she has something very urgent to say. In consequence, the ordinary women of Scotland, petty bourgeois and proletarian alike, in the rural districts and in the industrial towns, are untrained in public life, almost unrepresented, relatively unorganized and largely inarticulate outside the home. Even in purely feminine movements, such as the Women's Rural Institutes and Women's Citizen Associations, the ordinary working women let themselves be run by their 'county'. In other organizations they let themselves be run by their own menfolk, or by the Kirk, except when it comes to staging a bazaar or a social function. Ordinary Scotswomen, politically speaking, are as difficult to tempt into the open as the occupants of a Hindu zenana. The ratio of men to women contributors in this Scottish number of the *Left Review* is a fair reflection of what happens in Scottish public life.

Inside the home, of course, the tables are apt to be turned. A Scotswoman who is too timid to utter a word in public may tongue-lash her family in private with great efficiency. Inside the home she may have plenty of 'say', since her husband and her children are entirely dependent on her services. A Scotswoman at home can be a formidable figure; she is essentially a mother rather than a wife and comrade; she provides meals, darned socks and other comforts to the whole family, and from her point of view a husband is often enough only a more exacting child among the other children. It would be a mistake to assume that the 'missis' is a cypher merely because she keeps silent or goes off to wash the dishes whenever the menfolk argue about politics or religion. Her authority is rather a different kind of authority from her husband's; his is the concentrated authority of an individual, hers is the more diffuse, pervasive, atmospheric authority of an environment. And like other atmospheric conditions it can cause profound electrical disturbances.

This is an old pattern of domestic life. The mother as environment for her family is, so to speak, the basic diagram of womanhood. It is a pattern that survives from a world immeasurably older than our monetary civilization in which we are caught up today, and you would recognize it, with local variations, in many parts of the world at different stages of history. It sounds a reasonable enough partnership: the man, as an individual, emerging from the home circle to dominate the alien world outside; the woman, as an environment, dominating the home circle. But it remains a reasonable partnership only when there is a fair balance between the prestige and rights of the partners, and the progress of our economic system has destroyed that balance. Today, at the present stage of capitalistic development, the circle of environmental authority within which a mother stands has both shrunk in area and dwindled in relative importance. Artificially created environments such as the State, the Big Business Monopoly, the factory, have encroached upon it and are steadily encroaching upon it.

These rival environments have economic status, while a mother has none. They interfere with and determine the education, the scale of nutrition, the medical treatment, the employment, the leisure recreations and personal loyalties of a woman's children. Unlike other mothers, the human mother cannot go out nowadays and forage independently for her youngsters' needs; she is hedged in by the bars of our monetary civilization as if she were in a zoo; she must 'make do' with what she happens to get. That greater environment, the State, also has to 'make do', in theory, with what it can get from individual tax-payers, but it possesses compulsive powers and can control the amount of its levies. A mother has similar responsibilities on a smaller scale but no comparable rights. In theory, the father of the family is the conduit-pipe through which money flows into the house; in theory, the mother gets all she needs and administers it to the family, remaining outside the competitive economic market, preserving among the money values of the world an intact island of simple human values. It is a pretty theory. It has survived for so long simply because a woman nursing her own babies does not behave like a Milk Marketing Board. But in fact, in the world of today, the non-economic environmental services of women are horribly exploited. The monetary system by this time has encroached upon every corner of the home, and the simple human nucleus that makes a mother's world has shrunk almost to a pin-point. Her elemental needs, food, clothing and shelter for her children, are all prescribed by outside economic agencies over which she has no control.

The husband, of course, is equally a victim of economic circumstances, but his place is not considered to be exclusively the home; he has a certain economic status, he is in direct communication with the outside world, he is active politically and can make his voice heard in public. That is what makes the position of working-class women in Scotland so ambiguous today; they are confined to the home, and the home is shrinking visibly around them. They are still living by a tradition which modern economic life is hammering to pieces.

And the results? A startlingly high maternal mortality rate, a high infant death-rate, a general increase of unfitness, a rapid fall of the population. These are all signs showing not only the effects of economic depression but the profound, if inarticulate, discouragement of the women.

What is to be done about it? You can, of course, assume that in a new state of society private home environments will vanish completely. A mother would then rank as an individual, as a paid breeding-machine; she could park her children in State crèches, schools and institutes, and exercise her maternal gifts in administering the food, clothing and housing of a nation rather than a family. This system might possibly produce more hygienic human beings than come out of the industrial slums where over-driven mothers are trying to cope with family life on the Means Test, but nobody really believes it is humanly possible. The alternative policy is to create a right balance between the home environment and the outside world. That means a fifty-fifty partnership between men and their wives. It means that a mother should become also a political comrade, with an economic status of her own and a 'say' in public affairs. I suggest that Scotsmen accustom themselves to this idea, and do their utmost to enlarge the environmental circle within which their women are cramped. With a right balance between environment and individual, the family can be a solid basis for national life. A nation made up of such families would survive the disappearance of any State. Moreover, such a national ideal would appeal to the discouraged women of Scotland. Scotland as a nation has been for so long a 'puir auld mither' that Scottish mothers are likely to have a fellow-feeling for her. And if this fellow-feeling is not to be exploited by monopoly capital behind a barrage of Nationalist slogans, it must be used now as a means of enlightening Scotswomen. For they need to be shown where they stand, and I suspect that they are waiting for a lead.

Scotsmen, co-opt your women!

# CANONGATE CLASSICS

Books listed in alphabetical order by author.

Most Canongate Classics are available at good bookshops.
If you experience difficulty in obtaining the title you want,
please contact us at 14 High Street, Edinburgh EH1 1TE.